DAISYC

Elizabeth Elgin is the bestselling author of *All the Sweet Promises*, *Whisper on the Wind*, *I'll Bring You Buttercups*, *Where Bluebells Chime* and *One Summer at Deer's Leap*. She served in the WRNS during the Second World War and met her husband on board a submarine depot ship. A keen gardener, she has two daughters and five grandsons and lives in a village in the Vale of York.

ELIZABETH ELGIN

Daisychain Summer

HarperCollins*Publishers*

HarperCollins*Publishers*
77–85 Fulham Palace Road,
Hammersmith, London W6 8JB

The HarperCollins website address is:
www.harpercollins.co.uk

This paperback edition 1995
1

Published simultaneously in hardback in Great Britain
by HarperCollins*Publishers*

ISBN 978-0-00-783316-0

Set in Linotron Sabon by
Rowland Phototypesetting Ltd,
Bury St Edmunds, Suffolk

Printed and bound in Great Britain by
Clays Ltd, St Ives plc

To my grandsons
James, Simon, Matthew, Martin and Tom

The Pendenys Place Suttons　　　　**The Rowangarth Suttons**

Albert Elliot — Mary Anne Pendennis　　　　Sir Gilbert Sutton — Mary Whitecliffe

Nathan

Clementina — Edward
1863–　　　1859–

John — Helen Stormont
1858–1910　　1860–

Anne Lavinia
1857–1920

Nathan — Julia
1888–　　1893–

Andrew
MacMalcolm
1887–1918

Robert
1886–1916

Giles
1888–1918

Alice
Hawthorn
1896–

Tom
Dwerryhouse
1891–

Elliot — Anna
1887–　Petrovska
　　　1901–

Albert — Amelia
1889–　Newton
　　　1884–

Sebastian
(Bas)
1918–

Kathryn
(Kitty)
1920–

Tatiana
1922–

Andrew
(Drew)
1918–

Daisy
1920–

1

1920

She should have told him long before this. When she held their firstborn in her arms she had said it would be, yet that baby was four weeks old now, and still he did not know. Nor had he asked. It was as if he had pushed that part of her life behind him; locked it in a small, secret corner of his mind, never to be spoken of again.

'Whatever it was,' Tom had said, 'is in the past. It's you I want, Alice. Just you.' And in that moment she had known that one day she would tell him the truth of it, explain how it had been so he might understand – and forgive.

'Very well, if you choose not to know. But since you are taking me on trust, I'll make you a promise, Tom. The day I hold our firstborn in my arms, then you shall know – every last word of it . . .'

Yet was this really the right day on which to tell him? Why not yesterday, or tomorrow? Why today, the first anniversary of their wedding?

She dropped to her knees beside the cot. She spent so much time just gazing at her daughter, trying to believe the wonder of her birth, the ease of it and the joy. And Tom, eyes moist, holding her close, telling her how happy he was.

'She's so beautiful, so perfect.' The tiny fingers had twined around his own and claimed his heart. 'I thought newborn bairns were – well . . .'

'Ordinary?' she smiled. 'They are. Every one of them. Pink and puckered, or looking as if they've been in a fist fight. But there's one exception – your own. They are always born beautiful, and perfect.'

'I love you,' he'd said, huskily, and she knew that when the midwife came to shoo him from the room he would go to his hut, and weep. Tom was like that. Hard on the outside and given to sudden anger, yet soft and gentle inside.

'And might a man be told his daughter's name?' Alice should choose, he'd always said, if they had a little lass.

'Daisy Julia Dwerryhouse,' she announced promptly.

'Daisy Dwerryhouse.' He liked the name, truth known. 'And Julia for – ?'

'For my best friend – her godmother.'

'You've asked her?'

'No, but she'll come. She didn't get to our wedding. I want her here, for the christening.'

That had been when the midwife bustled in, bearing a cup of sweetened gruel, announcing that the new mother needed to sleep and that he could come up, later, and see them again.

Alice lifted the sleeping child, kissing her as she laid her in her pram, raising the hood against the bright August sunlight. She had wanted to buy the magnificent perambulator long before Daisy was born, but no! she had been told. Didn't she know it was bad luck to have the pram in the house before the babe – the first babe, that was?

So Alice had chosen a model in shiny black, with large wheels and the body suspended on leather straps and paid a deposit on it, explaining that it wasn't convenient, yet, to have it delivered, and so flushed with excitement had she been that the awfulness of it only struck her on the way home.

Five guineas, the pram would cost, to be paid for with her own money; her private money Tom didn't know about – money Giles had given to her. Sir Giles Sutton, Julia's brother, who died not of war wounds, but because of them;

a stretcher bearer and the bravest of the brave. Giles, whose name reminded her that today she must tell Tom what she should have told him before they were married, yet had bitten back the words because she hadn't wanted her secret to lie between them on their wedding night.

She gazed at her child, a small smile lifting the corners of her mouth. Beautiful, her little one, with eyes blue as Tom's and a newly-grown haze of hair that promised she would be as fair as he was. And did you ever see such a mouth; pink as a rosebud, puckering into little sucking movements as she slept.

Reluctantly, Alice turned away. She had a man to feed and a cake to ice for the christening, Sunday week. It might have been nice, she thought, taking the cake from its tin, sniffing its richness, if the christening could have been tomorrow; the date on which they were married. But she wanted Julia to stand godmother and a christening on a wedding anniversary might seem they were flaunting their happiness in the face of a woman whose husband had not come back from the war.

Julia did not travel south for their wedding. Alice had forbidden it. *I love you dearly*, she wrote, *but my joy would be your sadness. Come instead when our babe is christened – if the good Lord grants us one quickly –*

Hastily, she rewrapped the cake, glad that food rationing was over. Eighteen months after the Armistice the very last commodity was de-rationed. Sugar, it had been, and many the housewife who spent the whole day baking cakes the likes of which had not been seen for five years. And with sugar on sale to all again, they could really put the war behind them – or try to, though with some the scars were slow to heal.

She glanced through the window, smiling. The man who stood beside the pram never passed the gamekeeper's cottage without stopping. Tom's employer had been besotted by Daisy before she was a week old. 'She is exquisite,' he'd

3

said as Daisy Dwerryhouse fixed him with her eyes, and since then Mr Hillier called often to peer into the pram and smile his pleasure. Once, he had held her, then passed her quickly back, shaking his head sadly.

'Foolish of me not to marry and have children of my own, Mrs Dwerryhouse. Too busy making my way in the world,' he'd whispered shakily, making for the door.

Ralph Hillier. So rich that folk hereabouts said his pocket was bottomless. Poor, lonely man. Alice welcomed him with a smile.

'Good morning, sir.' She bobbed a curtsey. Not being servile, but mindful of her position and Mr Hillier's position and to put their strange friendship onto its proper footing. To remind herself, too, that he owned the house in which they lived and paid her husband's weekly wage. 'She's asleep – again.'

'No matter. The vicar tells me she is to be christened next Sunday. Would you think me presumptuous if I gave her a small gift?'

'Why, not at all! Thank you for your kind thought.'

'Hmm.' He liked his gamekeeper's wife. There was a dignity about her he couldn't fathom; that, and her way of speaking that lifted her above her class. 'Daisy Julia, isn't it to be?' he asked, seeing in his mind's eye the name and date inscribed on the silver christening mug he had already ordered from a Bond Street jeweller.

He left, smiling almost shyly, raising his hat, thanking her, and she stood at the door until he reached the garden gate, nodding her head deferentially.

Poor soul. Alone in that great house. Pity he couldn't marry some war widow with children of her own; heaven only knew there were plenty of them around, Alice frowned.

She looked at the watch pinned to her apron; the one she had looked at so often when nursing, in France. Tom would be home soon for his dinner; would arrive promptly at noon because that had been the time of their wedding. They were given no choice. There was to be a service of thanksgiving in the church at two, followed by sports for the children and a splendid tea for all, the vicar had said. She and Tom had chosen to marry, though they hadn't known it at the time, on the day the entire British Empire was to celebrate the victory of the Great War – and another reason, she had conceded, for not asking Julia to be there.

Alice raked the fire, then pulled out the damper to redden the coals, placing the vegetables on the hob to simmer. Last year, just about this time, she had been brushing her hair, twisting it into a knot, tilting her rose-trimmed hat this way and that before she was satisfied enough with its angle to secure it with a hatpin. A bride in waiting, ready to walk to the church, yet one year on she was a wife and mother, fervently grateful for something she thought she had lost for ever. Blessings she had in plenty – and a secret, still to be told. It hung over her like a confession unwilling to be made, because the penance might be more than she could accept.

Tom came home one minute before noon, dipping into his gamebag, telling her to close her eyes. She knew what he had brought her, had hoped he would remember.

'Just to let you know I haven't forgotten,' he smiled, giving her the flowers, tilting her chin to lay his lips gently against hers.

He had brought her buttercups, the flower so special between them. He had picked one and held it beneath her chin, so long ago. Seven years, if you counted.

'You're my girl, aren't you, Alice – my buttercup girl,' he'd whispered, kissing her for the first time.

'Alice?' His voice invaded her thoughts. 'You were miles away, lass.'

'No, love – *years* away.' She felt her cheeks pinking. 'I was remembering when you first gave me buttercups. And

5

I know I shouldn't be thinking back – not today, especially – but there's something I want to tell you, Tom; something I promised more than a year ago.'

'To love, honour and obey?' he teased.

'No. Something else I promised and I've made up my mind to tell you, today.'

'And what if I don't want to know?'

'You *must* know, Tom. For both our sakes. What I did – it wasn't what you thought . . .'

'How do you – *did* you – know what I thought?'

'Because I saw betrayal in your eyes, and it wasn't like that.'

'I still don't want to know, Alice.'

'And I still want to tell you. When I held our firstborn, I said it would be.'

'Sweetheart.' He reached for her, holding her tightly. 'This has been the best year of my life – don't spoil it?'

'But you've got to know about the child, Tom – how it really was.'

'You call him *the child*, always. He's Drew, Miss Julia's son, now. He's a Sutton.'

'Yes.' Oh, he was a Sutton, all right! 'But Tom, will you let me tell you? Not meaning to hurt you, but won't you hear me out? I love you so much, you see, that I can't bear to have this thing hanging over us.'

'All right, then. We'll talk about it tonight – there'll be no pleasing you, until we do. When Daisy is in her cot, we'll talk about it.' He nodded towards the mantel clock, smiling. 'And round about now, a year ago, you were saying, *I will* – so what have you to say to me?'

'I love you, Tom Dwerryhouse; so much that it's like a pain inside me, sometimes. I love you so much that I've got to tell you.'

'And I love you so much, wife darling, that I'll listen – but later. So does a man get a kiss, and his dinner, then?'

*   *   *

They sat either side of the fire, Tom with a mug of ale, Alice twisting the stem of a wedding present glass, gazing down at the last of the Christmas sherry.

'Happy anniversary, lass. Thank you for Daisy and for the twelve-month past. It's been good, but I don't have to tell you that, do I?'

'I know it. But will you love me as much when I've told you?'

'Dammit, woman!' He hit his knee with his hand. 'Can't you let sleeping dogs lie?'

'You said that tonight you'd listen . . .'

She rose to kneel at his feet, her hand on his knees, remembering the quickness of his temper, the highs and lows of his emotions. 'It has always bothered me, Tom, that you thought I married so soon after your death – after they *told* me you'd been killed, I mean.'

'Aye – and I'll admit it bothered me, an' all. When the war ended – when I got back to England – I came to Rowangarth, looking for you. I thought you'd have waited. Even though you thought me dead, I'd never have imagined that so soon after, you'd take another man to your –'

'To my bed?' she interrupted, sharply. 'Make a child with him?'

'Since you put it that way – yes.' He winced at the directness of her words. 'But Alice love, must we rake up the past? It's you and me, now, and Daisy. That war is over, and best forgotten and all the misery it caused.'

'I was in France, too, don't forget. I saw the degradation of men treated no better than animals. But it can't be forgotten until what it did to you and me is brought into the open, Tom.'

'You're set on me knowing, aren't you? Even if you hurt me?'

'You won't be hurt – angry, more like. Reuben knew about it, and Julia. And Nathan Sutton, an' all. They'll bear out my story.'

'Seems the world and his wife knew; everyone but Tom Dwerryhouse. When you walked in on me that day at Reuben's house – why didn't you tell me, then?'

'When I'd just seen a ghost? When you were standing there, back from the dead? And you didn't help any, Tom. You turned away from me as if I were beneath contempt – tipped your cap to me and called me milady. You knew how to hurt!'

'I'd come looking for you. I couldn't go to Rowangarth; I was dead – or so the Army had told my folks.'

'I understand that, and that you were a deserter. You had to be careful, or they could have had you shot.'

'Not any more. The war was over, by then. They'd have put me in prison, though – still could . . .'

'There'll be an amnesty for you, soon – for all deserters. The newspapers say so.'

'Happen. But we are talking about *now*, and about you and me. I went to Reuben's house. I thought he'd get word to you that I was back. I couldn't wait to see you, touch you . . .'

'And instead he told you I was married and had a child; that I was Lady Sutton, newly widowed.'

'Something like that. It was as if he'd slammed a fist into my face. You wedded and bedded and though your being a widow made you your own woman again, I knew you'd never leave your son and come away with me, even if you still loved me – and it seemed you didn't.'

'But I *did* leave my son. I left him with Julia and her ladyship because Rowangarth was where he belonged – his inheritance. And I followed you here, Tom, wanting to tell you the truth of it, even then.

'You've said I never use my son's name – always call him *the child* – and you are right. I had little to do with him – I was ill after he was born. I wanted to die. I tried to. I'd been nursing Giles, you see. He died in the 'flu epidemic.'

'Died of it – like my mother did.'

'Just as she did, Tom.' She rose to her feet, backing away from him, returning to her chair, standing behind it as if to shelter from the fury she feared would come.

'I had a difficult confinement, Tom. When my pains started, we couldn't get the doctor. He was working all the hours God sent – half of Holdenby was down with that 'flu. Julia was with me from start to finish. She'd just delivered the child when Doctor James arrived.

'There was only time to tell Giles he'd had a son before he died. Her ladyship was sitting beside his bed. She said, afterwards, that he'd gripped her hand, as if he understood.'

She stopped, taking in a shuddering breath, tilting her chin defiantly, wondering, now that she had started the awful business, where it would end.

'Go on,' Tom urged.

'I had a fever. Doctor James said I'd taken influenza from Giles. I was so ill they kept the baby away from me – didn't want him to get it. Julia was in a bad way. She'd just come back from France. Andrew had been killed only days before the Armistice and it was as if she wasn't with us; as if she were sleep-walking, all the time. I thought she'd die of a broken heart.

'But the baby saved her sanity. She had to look after him, you see – find milk for him, make sure he lived. By the time I was well enough to get out of bed he was six weeks old – and Julia's. They'd bonded, each to the other. The child was the son she would never conceive and I was content to leave it that way.'

'It didn't bother you that some other woman had your bairn?' He shook his head in bewilderment. 'It was like giving him away.'

'Yes, it was. But I didn't want him – didn't want to touch him, even. When I was well enough to think for myself, I was even glad there'd been no milk in my breasts for him.'

'Alice!' He slammed down his mug, spilling ale over the hearthstone. 'How could you – your own son? There must have been some affection for Giles Sutton? You must have felt something for him, or how could you have got that child?'

'I had great affection for Giles – always. I worked at Rowangarth for his mother, remember, and when he was brought to our hospital wounded and more dead than alive, I asked Sister if I could stay with him. He was in another world – on morphine. They used to give them morphine, Tom, to let them die peacefully – those who were lucky enough to be got to a hospital, that was.'

Her eyes filled with tears and she was back again in France with the stench and the horror and the hopelessness of it all. Then she pulled her sleeve across her face, sniffing loudly, facing him defiantly.

'Yes, I felt affection for Giles Sutton, I'll not deny it, and pity, too. And I think I could have cared for the child, if it had been gently got. But that bairn wasn't the result of love or affection, Tom. When Giles was brought to our hospital, I was already four weeks pregnant. And before you pass judgement,' she hastened, 'before you say what I can see in your eyes – let me tell you just one thing. The child – Drew Sutton – was got the night I'd been told you were dead. Your sister wrote to tell me. Julia was in Paris, on leave with Andrew. I had no one to turn to, so I ran out of the nurses' quarters, half out of my mind.'

'And someone . . . ?' His face was chalk white, his lips so tight with distaste he had difficulty speaking.

'Yes. *Someone.* He smelled of drink; his eyes were wild. He didn't know what he was doing – I'll swear it.'

'He *must* have!'

'Don't, Tom? Let me tell it the way it was?' she whispered dry-mouthed. 'We nurses were quartered in what had been the schoolhouse of a convent. There was a shed at the back where the nuns once kept their cows. He dragged me in there. I didn't have a chance and anyway, I think I wanted him to kill me. You were dead, and I wanted to be dead, too.'

She walked across the room to stare out of the window, taking in gulps of air, holding them, letting them go in little steadying puffs. Then, hugging herself, she turned to face him again.

'I fainted. I must have done, because when I could think clearly again, he'd gone. But it had happened — there was no telling myself it hadn't — and I got myself back to the schoolhouse. It was dark, by then, and when I got upstairs, Julia was back.

'She was waiting there, with Nurse Love. I'd thrown your sister's letter down, and they'd read it. They were kind to me. Julia held me — then it all came out. Not just about you being reported killed, but about *him*, and what he'd done to me. Julia took my uniform off — it was all dirty and torn — and got me into a bath. Nurse Love wanted to tell Sister, have the Military Police arrest him, but Julia said not to.

'She was livid, though. You know what she could be like, when she had a temper on her? She said to wait a bit — that with luck no harm had been done. She was only thinking of me. She knew I'd been through it before, you see.'

'But she was wrong. Harm *was* done, it seems, and you passed that child off as Giles Sutton's. How could you, Alice?'

'Because Giles didn't die, did he, though it might have been better if he had — with hindsight, that is. He survived to become only half a man. He told Julia one night that he would never father a child, though I think I'd known it, all along. I'd helped dress his wounds, you see. There were no niceties in those wards, in France. And she told him that life was cruel, because I was carrying a child I didn't want.'

She looked into his eyes, hoping to find understanding there, or pity, even, but there was none.

'Anyway, Nathan had been coming in every day, to see Giles,' she rushed on. 'He was stationed only a couple of miles away – an army chaplain, you'll remember – and Giles told him about me and the terrible mess I was in; said it was on his mind to ask me to marry him – say the child was his. The baby would be the one her ladyship had always wanted, and if it was a son, so much the better.'

'So you were glad to wed him, Alice – let him claim the child as his?'

'Not glad. Grateful, more like. And I didn't say yes, right away. I had this feeling inside me that I was going to hear from you or about you. I couldn't accept you were dead, you see. I thought that one day you'd come back.

'Julia stood by me. She'd wanted me to go to Aunt Sutton to have the baby and maybe get it adopted into a good home. Then Giles came up with a better idea – to marry me.'

'And the rest we know, Alice. I suppose it was Nathan who married you and him?'

'In the convent chapel,' she nodded, eyes on her hands. 'Just Julia and Nurse Love as witnesses. I'd not have done it, but Geordie Marshall came to see me. He was passing through Celverte – where we were nursing – and he brought me your Testament, and letters I'd written to you. Said that you'd been sent on special duties and that he'd heard that twelve of you in an army transport had all been killed by a shell. No chance you were alive, he said, but at least it had been quick and clean. I was grateful for that. I'd not have wanted you to die like some I'd nursed . . .'

'And you got away with it? Didn't you feel one bit of shame, lying to her ladyship – deceiving her?'

'No.' She shook her head vehemently. 'It wasn't me told the lies. I just went along with them. And they were white lies. Sir Robert had been killed – you knew that already –

and with Giles not being able to have children, the title would have been lost to Rowangarth – passed to the Pendenys Suttons and you know how that would have grieved her ladyship.'

'So what did you all cook up, between you?' He looked at her as if she were a stranger; a lying, deceiving woman and not the girl he married a twelve-month ago; not the mother of his Daisy.

'We cooked nothing up. So Nathan Sutton and Julia knew about it – that didn't make them criminals. And the child would be born in wedlock, which made him the rightful Rowangarth heir – what harm did we do? Her ladyship was overjoyed, looking forward to it being born . . .'

'And you? Did you feel grand, being a lady of title in the house where once you'd started off a housemaid?'

'No, Tom. That part of it took a lot of getting used to. And I'll admit I was always aware of the deceit. But it was Giles told his mother the child was his. He didn't mention about it being a rape child. Said he'd come across me all distressed, because I'd just heard that you'd been killed – told her he'd held me and soothed me and well – it had happened between us, just the once. An act of comfort.'

She drew a deep, shuddering breath, covering her face with her hands as if she were afraid to look at him; see the hurt and disbelief in his eyes.

'Tom, love – don't you think it was better for the poor, dear woman to think her grandchild had been conceived that way? And it explained away the fact that he was born eight months after we were married. When a boy was born, that night Giles died, it helped her, a little, to accept it.

'I had the child named Andrew Robert Giles for all the Rowangarth men the war had taken. Julia was pleased about it because he's Sir Andrew, now – he's got her husband's name. Little Drew – there, I've said it again. It's as if telling you has driven all the hurt out of me and I can really think of him as Giles's son. Do you forgive me, Tom?'

'For what?' Still he sat there, making no move to take her in his arms, kiss her, tell her he understood. 'It wasn't your fault some drunken soldier got you pregnant, though that nurse was right – he should have been found, and arrested. But what worries me is that yon little Drew has already inherited a title and stands to gain a whole lot more, when he comes of age. Can that be right? If Giles Sutton had died childless – and in all honesty, he did – then the title should have passed to the Pendenys Suttons – to Mr Edward, Giles's uncle. That's how it should have been.'

'You mean that some drunken soldier's hedge child has landed on his feet, did he but know it?'

'Don't, Alice? Don't use such talk. It isn't like my lass.'

'But am I your lass, now?' she demanded, head defiantly high. 'Oh, I wish you could see your face, Tom Dwerryhouse. You look all holier-than-thou, even though an army chaplain – a priest – connived at the deception, as you want to call it. Don't you think we did it for a reason – or do you think we set out to cheat the other Suttons – those at Pendenys Place – out of what is rightly theirs?'

'To my way of thinking,' he said deliberately and quietly, 'that's exactly what you all did.'

'Passing off a bastard as a Sutton, you mean?' she flung, face white with outrage.

'Alice – what's got into you?' He took a step towards her as if he knew he had pushed her too far and was willing, now it was too late, to make amends. 'I told you before we were wed I didn't want to know about that little Drew at Rowangarth, nor why you could bring yourself to leave him there, and come to me. You know I was willing to put it all behind us and start afresh, here.

'And we've been happy, Alice, till now. Why must you

rake over what's past? What's done is done, and if Giles Sutton died happy, and the son of his marriage –'

'*My* son, Tom!'

'All right – *your* son! If the bairn is acceptable as a Sutton, then who am I to gainsay it, wrong though it might be in law.'

'Dear, sweet heaven, you can be so stubborn!' She stood, hands on hips, cheeks blazing red. 'I wanted to tell you. I thought you'd understand, aye, and happen sympathize, an' all. But everything is either black or white to you, isn't it? You don't allow for the shades of grey, in between.

'And I wasn't going to tell you all, because I thought there'd be no need to. There was one thing I didn't want you to know; but since you see fit to set yourself up as judge and jury and find us all guilty, then best you should know that young Drew *is* a Sutton! He's taking what would, in the course of time, have passed to his father – to Elliot Sutton!

'There, Tom! You have it all, now – every last sordid bit of it. The drunk who tumbled me on the floor of a cowshed was the man you so hate, so think on before you pass judgement on me!'

She stood, tears streaking her cheeks, shaking with anger and dismay at what she had said. And she looked into the face of the man she loved and saw hatred in his eyes.

'*Elliot Sutton!*' he spat through clamped jaws. 'So he had his way with you, in the end?'

'Aye. He tried it in Brattocks Wood, didn't he, when I was a bit of a lass. But I had Morgan with me then, and Reuben within calling distance. And I had a young man who thrashed him for what he'd tried to do. But no one was there to help me that night in Celverte, Tom; neither the dog nor Reuben, nor you! You were dead, remember?'

'Thrashed him? I should have killed him!' He drove his fist hard into the palm of his hand. 'That first time he tried,

I should have beaten the life out of him. And I would, if I'd thought I could've got away with it.'

His face slablike, he rose to his feet, walking across the room and out of the house and she knew better than to try to stop him. To leave in a rage with a flinging open and a banging shut of doors would have seemed more normal. Things done in temper, in the shock of the moment, she could understand, and forgive. But to walk calmly out with never a word, closing doors gently and quietly behind him, sent apprehension coursing through her.

It was then she was grateful for the discipline of her nursing years and she closed her eyes, breathing deeply, resisting the urge to take his beer mug and hurl it against the wall.

She straightened her shoulders and tilted her chin. She would *not* weep on her wedding anniversary; not for anything would she!

'I'm sorry,' she whispered to the empty room. 'So sorry, Tom . . .'

He did not return until it was dark; long after she had lit the lamps and given Daisy her evening feed.

She sat beside the hearth, rocking the chair back and forth, worrying, waiting, and he came as quietly and suddenly as he left, his face pale, still, yet with contrition in his eyes.

'I'm sorry, lass,' he said, his voice rough with remorse. 'It was none of it your fault. You did what you had to do – what was best for all concerned. It was just that it was too much to take – *him*, having touched you.'

'Where have you been?' She rose slowly to her feet, wanting him to take her in his arms and not stand in the doorway, putting the length of the room between them.

'Walking. Just walking. I must have covered the entire boundary of the estate. And I was thinking, Alice; thinking

16

how much I hate that man. I was even hoping to meet him around the next corner, because I wanted to kill him; beat the life out of him . . .'

'It was all my fault.' Tears trembled on Alice's whispered words. 'I could think of nothing else but to tell you. I didn't want you to think wrong of me for seeming to forget you so soon after I'd heard you'd been killed; didn't want you to think I could love any man but you, much less get a child with him. And I didn't want you to think I was so unfeeling that I could desert a child to come to you. I knew all the time I ought to have loved him, but I couldn't, even though he was born Sutton fair, and not dark, like – like *him*. I couldn't have borne it if Drew had fathered himself.'

'So the little lad is fair?'

'He is, thanks be. To my way of thinking, he looked like his grandfather – his *real* grandfather, Mr Edward Sutton – but Julia could only see Andrew in him, because that was what she wanted to see, and Lady Helen swore he'd come in Sir John's likeness. But no one could say, or even think, that he looked like Elliot Sutton. It was the one good thing in all the sad and sorry mess.'

'Then I'm glad about that. No child deserves to be saddled with such a father.'

'His father was *Giles* Sutton and never for a minute forget it, Tom. Am I forgiven?'

He smiled, unspeaking, and opened wide his arms as he'd done when they were courting, and she ran to him as though she were seventeen again, clasping her arms around his waist, resting her head on his chest.

'I love you, Tom – let's never speak of it again?'

'Not ever, bonny lass. But I'll never forgive that man for what he did. I swore, out there, that if I could ever do him harm, I would – *will* – if ever I get the chance. I killed finer Germans than him . . .'

'Then it's a good thing you're never likely to set eyes on him again. Y'know, Tom, I used, in my dreamings, to think of you and me living in Brattocks Wood in Keeper's Cottage, and Julia and Andrew not far away and Reuben nicely settled in his almshouse. I'd think of it when things got bad, in France.

'But Julia's husband was killed and I thought I'd lost you, yet it was meant to be, my darling. Fate landed you and me here, miles and miles away, and I'm glad. Up there, I'd be scared half out of my mind that you and him would meet.'

'Happen you are right.' He unclasped her clinging arms, standing a little away from her, cupping her face in his hands.

'I love you, my Alice. I never stopped loving you, even when I thought I'd lost you. The past is over and done with, I promise it is.'

'Happy anniversary, Tom.'

Yet even as they kissed passionately, kissed as if there was to be no tomorrow, she knew he would never completely forget; that his hatred for Elliot Sutton would fester inside him and that if ever he could do him harm, he would.

Without so much as the batting of an eyelid.

2

Helen, Lady Sutton closed the door behind her, then let go a gasp of annoyance.

'The fool! The smug, unfeeling fool! I am so *angry*!'

'Oh, dear.' Julia MacMalcolm kissed her mother's flushed cheek. 'Why don't you sit down and tell me what happened at the meeting to make you so very cross.'

'That vicar! I don't know how I kept hold of my temper!'

'Don't let him upset you. He's only a locum. He'll be gone when Luke Parkin is fit again.'

'But Luke won't get well and we all know it, Julia. Six months, at the most,' she whispered bitterly.

All the men she could once rely on, lean upon – all dead. her husband, her sons, her son-in-law; bluff, brusque Judge Mounteagle and soon, Luke Parkin. That ugly war – how *dare* they call it the Great War – had taken so many young men and now the older ones, weakened by four years of too much responsibility and too little consideration and overburdened with the worry of it, were themselves falling victims to its aftermath.

'Sssh. Just tell me?'

'We-e-ll, it was the usual parish meeting – or should have been. I knew they'd be talking about the war memorial; I was happy about that.' She had promised any piece of land the parish saw fit to choose so the war dead of Holdenby should be remembered. 'But to suggest a German field gun should stand beside it!'

'A *what*!' Julia flushed scarlet. 'Whose damn-fool idea was that?'

'Our temporary vicar's! He said that any city or town – Holdenby, even – could claim a German gun as spoils of war and wouldn't it be a splendid thought to have one here and site it beside the war memorial? So I said that upon further consideration, I wasn't at all sure that I could offer that piece of land – leastways, not if an enemy gun was to stand on it. Indeed, I said, if anyone was thoughtless enough to bring one here, I would hope to see the wretched thing rolled down the hill and into the river! *That's* what I said!'

'And then you swep' out! Good for you, mother! How could he even think such a thing?'

'How indeed, when not one household in Holdenby came through that war without loss. The last thing they want to see is a German gun. Julia – did we *really* win? It makes me wonder when I see heroes with no work to go to; men with a leg or an arm missing, begging on street corners. Half our youth never to come home again and oh, I'm sorry! I didn't mean to remind you.'

'You didn't, because I don't need reminding. And I'm glad you put him in his place. *If* Luke retires, I hope that vicar doesn't get ideas about getting the living for himself. When the time comes for a new parish priest, I think it should be Nathan. I'd like to have him here. He'll be back from the African mission, soon – and who better?'

'I agree, and since Rowangarth will have some say in the matter, perhaps we can help him. Nathan saw service as an army chaplain – he'd be a popular choice, hereabouts. But this is not the time to talk of such things. We must hope for a miracle for Luke. And meantime –'

'No German field gun,' Julia supplied.

'Not on any piece of Rowangarth land!' And since Rowangarth owned every square yard of Holdenby village and much, much more besides, it seemed that Helen Sutton would have her way.

'I shall miss you when you go to Hampshire for the christening.' Deftly, she changed the subject.

'You're sure you'll be all right, mother? Drew can be rather a handful, now.'

'Of course I can manage. I've been looking forward to having him all to myself. And isn't it wonderful that Alice has a little girl of her own?'

Dear Alice. She at least was happy. It was to her, Helen acknowledged, they owed the beautiful boy who would one day inherit Rowangarth. So sad that Giles never lived to see his son.

'I reared the three of you with no trouble at all. One small boy won't put me out in the slightest.'

'But we three had a nanny – and a nursery maid!'

'So you did, but nannies are going out of fashion and there'll be Miss Clitherow to help me – if I need help.'

'Yes, and Cook and Tilda and Mary' – all of whom spoiled Drew dreadfully.

'A growing child cannot have too much love and affection. Children are treated differently, now,' Helen smiled, calm again, for just to think of her grandson gave her such feelings of love and gratitude that any anger was short-lived.

'I'd thought to leave a day earlier – stay the night with Aunt Sutton, whilst she's at Montpelier Mews.'

'A good idea.' Her sister-in-law, Helen frowned, spent so little time in England, now. 'How long since anyone saw her?'

'Oh, *ages*.' Since not long after Andrew was killed, Julia recalled. 'She couldn't wait to get back to France, once the war was over. We can have a nice long chat – catch up with the news, then I'll go on to Hampshire. It will mean being away for five days – you're sure you can manage?'

'Of course.' She loved him dearly, the grandson who was walking sturdily, now, and had cut most of his teeth with scarcely a disturbed night. Drew, who made her young again. 'Think of it, Julia. He'll be two, at Christmas.'

'Mm.' The months had rushed past. Soon, there would be the second anniversary of Andrew's death to be lived through and that of Giles who died the day his son – Alice's son – was born.

'Julia?' Her mother's voice came to her softly through her rememberings.

'Sorry. Just thinking . . .'

'Aah.' Her daughter was often just thinking. Sometimes she was far away, eyes troubled; other times there would be a small smile on her lips and she would be a girl again, impatient to come of age, marry her young doctor. There hadn't been a war, then, nor even thoughts of one. Her elder son, Helen pondered, had been in India and Giles with his nose in a book, always, and nothing more to worry her than the next dinner party she would give. Lovely, gentle times. Days of roaring fires and hot muffins for winter tea and sun-warmed summer days and the scent of flowers at dusk and the certainty that nothing need change.

But then the war had come and nothing could be the same again. Only Rowangarth endured.

'And talking about Alice – and we must talk about it, sooner or later – do you think you might mention it to her – and Tom, of course – whilst you are there?'

'That people should be told she was married again, you mean?'

'Well, it *is* all of eighteen months since she left Rowangarth; people will want to know what is happening.'

'But it isn't anything to do with *people* – not really, mother, though I agree with you. I'll have a word with her. After all, she's done nothing wrong. She had every right to remarry.'

'I accept that – and Tom *was* her first love.'

'Her *only* love.' Her once and for ever love. 'None of us ever pretended she cared in the same way for Giles – those of us who knew the real truth of it – about their marrying, so soon after Tom was killed, I mean . . .'

22

The *real* truth of it? Not even her mother knew that, nor ever could. There were things never to be told – even to Drew.

'I know, my dear. I have always accepted the circumstances of Drew's conceiving and been grateful to Alice for leaving him with us. I'd longed so for a grandson, you know; for a boy, for Rowangarth.'

'And you got him,' Julia smiled. 'And what's more, you can't wait to have him all to yourself, can you?' Best drop the subject of Drew's getting. For his sake alone, it must remain a closed book. 'Do you suppose he'll miss me?'

'I'll do my best to see that he doesn't. And you deserve a break, Julia. Just think how much news there'll be to catch up on; it seems such a long time since Alice left us. And I'm sure she'll let you share her little girl, if your maternal instincts get the better of you.'

Her maternal instincts, Julia brooded. Drew had been hers from the moment of his birth. She it had been who fought for him when Alice lay desperately ill and unable to feed him. That fatherless babe had given her something to live for after Andrew's killing. She was Drew's mother, now.

'You must take a lock of his hair, for Alice,' Helen smiled. One of his fair, baby curls, now cut off. Drew had remained in his long baby clothes until he walked, though Julia hadn't entirely agreed with keeping little boys in nursery frocks, she acknowledged, and allowing their hair to grow untrimmed so that many were hard put to know if the child was a girl or a boy. But it had been the custom when her sons were toddlers and she had wished it for Drew, though now he was a real little boy, her hair cut short and wearing his first breeches. 'Well – if you think it won't upset her too much. That child is the image of his father when he was little, you know.'

'Take one of his curls? No – she won't be upset.'

Not in the way you mean, mother. Alice won't go all

emotional and want to take him from us when she sees a lock of his hair. She never wanted him, couldn't love him — but you didn't know that, dearest. And never say Drew is the image of his father, because he isn't — and please God he never will be.

Only she and Nathan knew, and perhaps Tom, now. And Giles had known; had married Alice knowing she carried another man's child, then claimed it to be born a Sutton — a *Rowangarth* Sutton, and Rowangarth's heir. Little Drew. Two years old, at Christmas.

'Alice says I'm to take tweeds and tough shoes.' Julia, too, was adept at subject-changing. 'They live right out in the country — it's quite a walk, I believe, into the village to post a letter. And it's Reuben's birthday in September,' just three days after Andrew's, 'so she wants me to bring his present back with me.'

'Dear old Reuben. He misses Alice for all there's a letter from her every week. That's why people should know Alice and Tom are married, now. Reuben isn't getting any younger. There might come a day when Alice is needed here.'

'But she can return to Rowangarth any time she likes. She's done nothing wrong!'

'Of course she hasn't — but there's Tom . . .'

'A deserter, who could be put in prison for it, if people knew? Is that what you mean? But who is going to tell on him? Not you, mother; not me! I agree with what he did and so would Giles, if he were alive. Tom was a soldier who was pushed too far! He was reported killed in action — the authorities think him dead — so all we need say is that he wasn't killed at all but taken prisoner and the Red Cross was never told about it. He wouldn't be the first man to come back from the dead! I see no reason why the pair of them shouldn't walk through Holdenby, heads high!'

'Julia, child — hush your anger! You'll never be rid of

that Whitecliffe temper! Small wonder the old lady was so taken with you. And I agree with you about Tom Dwerryhouse; there is nothing I would like more than to see them both back here, even though it can't ever be.'

'And why not, pray?'

'We-e-ell, if they were to come back to Keeper's Cottage – and we all thought that when Reuben retired, Tom would live there, with Alice – *if* they came back, just what would their position be? Alice is Drew's mother; Drew – Sir Andrew – will one day inherit, so he would be Tom's employer . . .'

'Mother, how you do run on!' Julia laughed. 'I don't think Tom and Alice will ever come back here. From what I read in her letters, she's well suited in Hampshire. But I would like her to be able to visit us, from time to time. Tom would understand her need to see Reuben. And remember, she is still Drew's legal guardian.'

'Exactly – and that's one reason I want it to be known she isn't Alice Sutton any longer. I would like her to come home to Rowangarth whenever she has a mind to. She was my son's wife, albeit for less than a year, and I cared – *care* – for her, deeply. And she'll never take Drew away from us, I know it.'

'She won't. Not ever. I know it too, dearest. So what are we worrying about? I'll have a talk with Alice and Tom – see what they think. We'll be able to work something out and had you thought, there might soon be a pardon for deserters, so Tom wouldn't have anything to be afraid of and never, ever, anything to be ashamed of. He fought in the trenches which is more than Elliot ever did!'

'Julia! Why ever must you bring *him* into it? And why, since we are talking about your cousin –'

'My nasty, over-indulged, *awful* cousin!'

'Talking about Elliot,' Helen went on, calmly, 'why do you always get so prickly when his name is mentioned and make excuses not to meet him?'

'Because I detest him, mother. No, I *hate* him. I dislike his womanizing and his arrogance and I won't ever forgive his mother for arranging two safe postings for him when he joined the Army. She *bought* them, for him!'

'You mustn't say that of your Aunt Clemmy!'

'Not even when it's true?' Julia jumped to her feet and stood, arms akimbo, at the window, staring out across the lawns and the wild garden to Brattocks Wood. 'And I hate him because he's alive – because he hardly got his boots dirty in that war, yet Robert and Giles and Andrew will only be names, soon, on a war memorial!'

And she hated him, too, for what he had done to Alice, and the fact that they could never be sure that one day he might not say, 'Giles's son? Are you *sure* . . . ?' That was the reason she hated him so much, though she could never speak of it. Giles was Drew's father as far as her mother was concerned, and if she ever learned the truth of their deception, her heart would break.

'Oh, darling – forgive me?' Julia hurried to her mother's side, falling to her knees, laying her head on her lap as she had done since childhood. 'And try to understand my bitterness?'

'I do.' Helen dropped a kiss on her daughter's head. 'I know what it is like to lose the man you love, always remember that, will you, when you think the world is against you.

'And go upstairs, why don't you, and take a peep at Drew, then come with me for a walk around the garden, before the light goes. This is such a beautiful evening. Let's walk quietly, and count our blessings?'

'Let's. I won't be a minute.' Blessing-counting. It always worked for her mother, Julia thought sadly as she opened the nursery door. Why, then, did it do nothing for her? Why could she never accept Andrew's death nor cease to want him until her body throbbed and ached from it? And why, no matter what her common sense told her to the

26

contrary, did she still fear the harm Elliot Sutton could do?

'Alice – I do so long to see you,' she whispered as she tucked in the cot blankets. 'You can't know how I have missed you; how much I would give to have you back here.'

But Alice would never return to Rowangarth.

Clementina Sutton began her scheming the moment she learned about the people next door, in Cheyne Walk. She had been anxious, during the war, about the house standing empty next to hers, worrying that the Army would commandeer it as a billet for soldiers or, worse, that it would be filled with refugees, *foreign* refugees, thus lowering the area in general and the value of her own property in particular.

She had bought the London house for mixed reasons, though mainly to use for entertaining during the social season when mothers, desperate for good marriages for their daughters, paraded them at dances and parties, at race meetings and concerts like hawkers setting out their stalls.

It was at one of these events she had hoped her eldest son Elliot would meet a suitable young lady and if she came with a title, it wouldn't matter how poor she was; Clemmy Sutton had money enough to support her. Nor would it matter if she were plain as a pikestaff, so long as she came from a line of good breeders and had the stamina to produce two sons at least. And if that were not all, the favoured young lady would have the ability – and the sense, if she knew what was good for her – to turn a blind eye to her husband's excursions into infidelity for it was certain that no one woman, no matter how beautiful and bedworthy, would satisfy her Elliot. Clementina had come to expect it and even to forgive him for it, because it wasn't his fault he was born so handsome and so attractive to the opposite sex.

Mind, it had to be acknowledged that Elliot always seemed to attract the worst kind of woman; sometimes married ones but most often women that she, his mother, would refuse to touch with the end of a long stick. Ladies of easy virtue. *Whores*! Why did they attract him so when he could have had all the pleasuring he wanted free, and in his own bed, if only he'd had the sense to marry!

Of course, with the coming of the war, young women had been quick to throw off their chaperons with alacrity and delight; had raised their hemlines, spoken to young men to whom they had not been introduced and smoked and drank cocktails in public. And they had taken to uniforms with high delight, driving ambulances, being lady typists in the Women's Army Corps – even nursing as her niece Julia had done; gone to France an' all to do it, risking life and limb for her stupidity.

Well, now that was over, and young women would be falling over themselves to get their hooks into a husband and husbands not so easy to catch, either. Stood to reason, didn't it, with many millions of men killed and thank God her own three sons had come through it unscathed, though Nathan had ended up in the thick of it with the soldiers in the trenches and him not caring one jot for his mother's feelings.

But now she could forget the war and its inconveniences, for she had embarked on the task of seeing her eldest son safely wed – and before another year ran, if she had anything to do with it!

'I think,' she said to her husband, 'that I might have acted a little hastily, putting up that fence . . .'

'Fence?' Edward Sutton lowered the evening paper he was reading.

'At Cheyne Walk.'

'Aah. To keep out the gypsies next door?'

'Not gypsies, Edward.' She squirmed at her own foolishness. 'There was a man – a giant of a fellow . . .' He had lived in the basement area, emerging from it from time to time to yell at dogs or glower at any passer-by who was foolish enough to linger outside. A thick black beard he'd had and terrified Molly more and more with every sighting. 'I got it wrong; *Molly* got it wrong. The dark fellow was a Cossack it would seem, and Cossacks were loyal to a man to their Czar. I should have known better than to listen to her, but what can one expect from a woman of her class?'

'Or for three shillings and sixpence a week,' he added, raising his newspaper again.

'She gets a pint of milk a day *and* old clothes! And all she does is caretake an empty house . . .'

'So am I to take it that the fence will be removed – or at least lowered a couple of feet? Are the new tenants next door all at once acceptable?'

'I don't know. One hears such stories. That is why I shall go to London and see for myself; see if they are *socially* acceptable, that is.' She might even leave her card, though card-leaving did not have the same social power it once had. Standards had been lowered since the war ended, she sighed. Things would never be the same. The working man had fought a war and thought he was as good as his master, now! 'Shall you come with me?'

'I think not.' Edward Sutton disliked London. Even this house he lived in – Clemmy's great, ornate, completely vulgar house – was to be preferred to noisy, smoky, overcrowded London. 'I'm sure you can manage without me.'

'Of course.' She hadn't for a moment imagined he would want to leave Pendenys. 'But if you don't come, I shall need someone with me. I shall take a couple of servants.'

'Take whom you wish, Clemmy.'

She usually did. She considered it cheaper to buy train tickets for them than pay out good money to keep permanent servants there – apart from what they ate and stole in her absence.

'Yes.' She intended to. After all, it was she who paid their wages, not her husband.

'When will you go?'

'Tomorrow, Edward, I think. I shall take a cook, a housemaid and a footman.' Sufficient to impress the people next door if they were what she supposed them to be. She would have taken her butler, pompous and arrogant though she thought him, had she imagined for a moment he would agree to go with her. But the Cheyne Walk house was far beneath the man's dignity. For one thing, its cellars were completely empty of wine and for another, it did not provide him with his own sitting-room and a man in his position, he stressed, whenever London threatened, was entitled to his privacy. A snob, Clementina brooded, who looked down his nose at her; at Mrs Clementina Sutton whose hand fed him. She only put up with him because as butlers went he knew what he was about and she got his expertise cheaply on account of his liking for red wine. They understood each other, she and that butler!

'I said I would take –'

'Yes, my dear. Do as you wish. Take Elliot, too.' Elliot had been on his best behaviour these few weeks past. Soon, his instincts would surface and better they surfaced in London – and under the eye of his mother!

'You can't bear to be alone in the house with him, can you?' she countered tartly. 'Can't speak a civil word to your own son . . .'

'Clemmy – let us not quarrel over Elliot?' he sighed. 'Leave him here at Pendenys, if that's what you wish.'

She did not reply. Her mind was back at Cheyne Walk and the people next door. Refugees, of course, but *what* refugees! Not destitute, if what she had heard was to be believed, and real aristocrats, possessed of a title! A daughter, too, and unmarried; strictly chaperoned by the fierce Cossack whenever she ventured out.

She purred inside her, just to think of it. To have what

she had been searching for landed next door to her was past belief. Such luck – even if they were Russians. She wouldn't mind betting they'd got out of St Petersburg with a small fortune sewn into their corsets and the benefit of a London bank account set up long before the shooting of the Czar. Oh, my word, but it was worth looking into. Well worth looking into!

Tom Dwerryhouse checked his pocket watch with the station clock and found they agreed. He was in time. He had sent the pony along at a brisk pace, determined that Julia MacMalcolm should not arrive before him and take the station taxi.

He needed time alone with her to explain the way it had been; thank her for what she had done for him. But mostly he wanted to tell her that he knew about young Drew and that Rowangarth's secret was safe with him. It was why he had taken time off work and harnessed up the pony and trap provided by his employer for the use of the estate workers – them being so cut off from civilization. The pony and cart could be used by any employee at any time, provided due notice was given to the groom who looked after Ralph Hillier's hunters.

He had, Tom considered, done very well for himself, all things taken into account. A decent employer, a good house, now that Alice had licked it into shape; a suit of clothes every second year and boots and leggings, an' all. And by far the most important, he had Alice and Daisy.

Why, then, should Miss Julia's coming disturb him? Not entirely on account of her being gentry and him being working class nor because he was an army deserter, either, though he wasn't proud of it nor ever quite free of the fear that one day the Army would arrive to cart him off.

He set his jaw tightly, shaking such thoughts from his head because they were not the cause of his misgivings. The truth of it, he was bound to admit, was that she was coming from Rowangarth; from the place where he and Alice met and where they had expected to end their days. Keeper's Cottage on the Rowangarth estate had a woodman in it now because these days there was no need of a gamekeeper there; not until young Drew — Sir Andrew — was old enough to handle a shotgun, that was.

Yet that was still not all and if he were honest, he would admit it. Miss Julia would be bringing the north country with her and Tom Dwerryhouse was a son of the north and no matter how well suited he was with the way his life had turned out nor how contented Alice was with her new little bairn and her own hearth, one thing could never be denied. Northern roots did not easily transplant into southern soil. He was surprised Mr Hillier had seen fit to do it, him being a northerner, an' all. But maybe it was all right for the likes of someone who owned another house in Westmorland and who could take off whenever the fancy took him. Windrush Hall, on the edges of the New Forest, was where it was convenient for Ralph Hillier to live, being close to a port and near enough to London where most of his business deals took place. But whenever his early years tugged on the thread of memory, he need only order his motor to be driven round to the front entrance and he could be away and back to his roots.

It was different for Tom Dwerryhouse who could never return to Rowangarth. For one thing, most folk thereabouts thought him dead, killed in the last year of the war; and to go back there would be to carry hate inside him for a man he might meet at any time. Elliot Sutton lived only a cock-stride from Rowangarth and for Alice's sake — and for young Sir Andrew's, too — it were best the two of them should never meet.

A signal fell with a clatter. A porter pushing a trolley and the stationmaster with top hat and green furled flag appeared on the platform. The train, no more than a noiseless speck down the track, would arrive on time. Julia was coming, and bringing their past with her.

She got down from a third-class compartment, lifting a gloved hand to bring the porter hurrying from the far end of the train and the first-class carriage that usually put a sixpenny tip his way.

She had not changed. Everything about her proclaimed her status; her understated air of command, her well-labelled leather suitcases, the way she held her head, even. She was still a Sutton. Not even what she had endured in the war could wipe out her breeding. She saw him, and smiled, and he walked towards her, removing his cap.

'Tom!' She held out her hand, her voice low with emotion. 'It is so good to see you. How long is it?'

'More'n five years, Miss Julia, and it's right grand to see you, an' all.'

They walked unspeaking beside the porter, waiting as he lifted her luggage into the cart.

'Step up carefully, Miss Julia.' Tom offered his hand, settling her comfortably, laying a rug over her knees. Then he jerked the reins, calling, 'Hup!' and clicking his tongue.

They were well out of the station environs before he said, 'I want to say I'm sorry about what happened to the doctor, Miss Julia. And I'd like to thank you for being so decent about giving me a reference. It got me the job, though I'd have understood if you'd have wanted no truck with a deserter, after all you'd been through.'

'Alice gave you the reference, Tom . . .'

'Aye, but written in your hand, Miss, and it was you signed Alice's name to it. I'm grateful.'

'Then don't be. Any man who had the guts to desert that war has my understanding. And Tom, there's one thing I'd like to say to you. You must not call me Miss Julia. Not only am I Mrs MacMalcolm, now, but I am also a guest in your house. Alice calls me Julia – I would like you to do it, as well.'

'But it wouldn't be right! I used to work for her ladyship and you are still her daughter.'

'Those days are long gone and besides, Alice is my friend. I still look on her as my sister and it would please me if you would treat me as she treats me.'

'It'll be a mite strange . . .'

'Alice found it strange, too, but it didn't take her long.'

'I can but try,' he smiled, touched and embarrassed both at the same time. 'Though how you can show such kindness to someone who ran away –'

'But I understood and my mother understood, too. Alice told us how it was. It was a terrible thing to have to shoot a man – a *boy* – in cold blood. That you threw down your rifle afterwards and risked the death sentence for what amounted to an act of mutiny, was a brave thing to do.'

'No, it wasn't.' He shook his head vigorously. 'I was beside myself with disgust; all twelve in that firing party were. One man stood there shaking as if he was going to throw a fit and another was sick. I just stormed up to that officer and told him I wouldn't do a thing like that again, and they were all of them in such a state that I got away with it. But I wasn't acting the hero. It's this temper of mine . . .'

'I can understand. I've got one, too. My mother calls it my Whitecliffe temper,' she laughed. 'Act first then think afterwards. You and me both, Tom.'

'Aye. I was thinking on the way here about Rowangarth and that no matter how much I miss the old days, it's as well I'm here. If Alice and me lived there, then I'd always be on the lookout for *him*.' His eyes sought hers, asking understanding.

'Elliot Sutton, you mean?' Her gaze met and held his. 'So you know?'

'I know. Alice told me. It bothered her, you see. Told me it all.'

34

'I see. And do you agree, now, that we did what we had to do? Giles needed a son and had just been told he would never father one – his injuries, you see – and Alice was demented with worry about your death and the pregnancy she didn't want – a child she could never accept, or bring herself to love.'

'And her ladyship . . . ?'

'She believes what Giles told her; that Drew is Giles's son, conceived in a single act of compassion. She accepts it. She even thinks that Drew was meant to be.'

'I've come to accept it, too.' Tom slowed down the pony at the crossroads, turning to the right. 'Almost there. And I'm grateful to Sir Giles. He was a decent man, and a brave one, too. Geordie and me would go out into No Man's Land at night with the stretcher bearers, picking up the wounded. We'd hide ourselves and keep watch; try to give them some protection if they were seen by the German gunners. It took a brave man to be a stretcher bearer, like Sir Giles was. Brave fools, we called them – and the orderlies and doctors who went under the barbed wire with them.' He slid his eyes to where she sat and saw her sudden sadness. 'I'm sorry, Miss. We must try not to look back . . .'

'Oh, but you are so wrong, Tom! We must *always* look back. We must remember, so it won't happen again to Drew and Daisy. But we must always remind ourselves that the pain of remembering will grow less – or so I'm always being told.' She lifted her head, and smiled. 'I'm so looking forward to being with you both. I've missed Alice so. And as for seeing my god-daughter – oh, this will be such a wonderful holiday for me!'

Alice stood at the gate, waiting impatiently for the sound of the pony and cart. Beside her, in her shiny black perambulator, her baby girl slept.

The house was clean and shining; a joint of beef roasted

in the fire oven. Vegetables stood ready for cooking; an apple pie cooled on the slate slab in the pantry.

Flowers from the garden were newly arranged in her best vases; Julia's bedroom was as perfect as ever it could be. She hoped Julia would not find it inconvenient, there not being a bathroom at Keeper's Cottage, but no one hereabouts had one. Water, except at Windrush, came out of wells or pumps or rain butts.

And why was Daisy asleep? Why couldn't she be awake to fix Julia with brilliant blue eyes? She didn't smile, yet, but she recognized voices and turned towards familiar sounds. She knew the minute Tom gave his warbling whistle. Tom loved her so much . . .

Impatiently, she walked to the turn in the lane, standing still, listening; walking back to the gate, again, sure the wheel must have fallen off the cart.

Then she heard a faraway sound and held her breath, making out the steady clopping of hooves, the round grinding of wheels. Her cheeks reddened; she felt a sudden tensing of her hands.

Then Tom was pulling on the reins, smiling, calling, 'Well, here she is, now!'

Slowly, carefully, Julia got down, then stood, not moving nor speaking, as if she didn't believe any of it. Then as one they ran, arms wide, clasping each other tightly, saying not a word, standing close, cheek upon cheek.

'Oh, my word!' Alice was the first to find her voice. 'Let me look at you. My dear, dear Julia — I've missed you!'

'And I you.' Julia's eyes pricked with tears and she blinked rapidly, smiling through them. 'Sixteen months! It's been so long. And do let me see her!'

'Asleep, as usual,' Alice sniffed, pulling back the pram cover. 'Don't know what I did to deserve such a placid babe.'

Daisy Dwerryhouse lay on her pretty pink pillow, face

flushed from sleep, half-moons of incredibly long eyelashes resting on her cheeks.

'But she is *beautiful*! She is *incredible*!'

'If you don't mind, I'll leave the pair of you to it.' Tom deposited suitcases on the doorstep. 'Best take the pony back. Supper at half-past six, will it be?' He didn't even try to conceal his pride.

'There or thereabouts,' Alice nodded. 'Let's go inside, Julia? You must be fair gasping for a cup of tea. The kettle's on the hob and the tray set and oh, my dear, it's so good to be together again!'

'It is,' Julia whispered throatily. 'So very good . . .'

When Tom had excused himself after supper and Daisy had been fed and settled in Julia's arms in the fireside rocker, Alice set about restoring order in the kitchen.

'You must be tired, love,' she murmured.

'Not if you aren't.' Julia cupped the little head protectively in her hand, smiling softly. 'She smells of breast milk and baby soap. She has a mouth like a little rosebud. You should have called her Rose . . .'

'No. Her mother is a buttercup girl and daisies go best with buttercups. Now – tell me about Aunt Sutton? How was she, when you called?'

'She insists she came back to London to see her bank manager, but she let it slip that she also visited her doctor – then went to great pains to hide it. Said she might as well let him have a look at her, whilst she was over, but she was altogether too casual about it. It's my belief she came especially to see him and when I said as much she told me it was all stuff and nonsense and that she had no intention of taking the pills he'd given her. A fussy old woman, she called him.

'She'll be back in the Camargue, now, and I've got a peculiar feeling about it all. I wonder if I should try phoning her doctor – get to the bottom of it.'

'He wouldn't tell you – you know he wouldn't.'

'No, and nor would Aunt Sutton. All she said was, "Fiddle-de-dee!" If only Andrew was here . . .'

Alice remained silent, then, drying her hands, she walked to where Julia sat, standing behind her chair, hands on her shoulders. For a moment she stood there, then said softly, 'Is she asleep? Why don't you take her upstairs to her cot? I don't have to tell you how to do it, now do I?'

Julia was quite composed by the time she came downstairs and Alice was setting out cups and saucers.

'Kettle's just on the boil,' she smiled, removing her apron. 'Now we can have that chat. Tom won't be back, yet.'

'Does he always work this late?'

'Bless you no – leastways, not these days. Windrush was very run down when Mr Hillier bought it. The Army were in it right through the war – the place had gone to rack and ruin. Game covers overgrown and hardly a pheasant in them. Tom's had to start from scratch. There was no shooting last back end, though he's hopeful there'll be good sport come October. He'll need another keeper, by then. Mr Hillier is keen to have his business friends from London for a few shoots, so Tom wants it all to be in good order.

'Said he was going to make up the hour he took off, this afternoon, but really it's only to let you and me have a good gossip.'

'And you're happy, Alice? No regrets – about leaving Rowangarth, I mean, and starting afresh here?'

'No regrets –'cept that I miss you and Reuben and her ladyship. We're so out of the way, here, and I only see people on shopping day – apart from the district nurse. She calls once a week but we shan't be seeing so much of her, once Daisy gets to be six weeks old. I write to Reuben, though it isn't often he writes back . . .'

'I see him often. He's fine, Alice, and tells me what you

have written, though often you've already given me the same news. But I'm sure he'd like to see Daisy.'

'I'd like him to. If he decided to visit us, either Tom or me would go to London and meet him. Wish I could persuade him to come.'

'Or you and Daisy could come to Holdenby to see *him*?'

'Oh, my goodness!' Alice set down the tea tray with such force that the cups and saucers rattled. 'You know I couldn't! When I left Rowangarth the excuse was that I'd had a bad time getting over Drew's birth and I was going to Aunt Sutton for a change and a rest. But that was ages ago! What are they going to say if I turn up with a baby in my arms?'

'Well, you won't shock Reuben nor mother, because they knew you were really going to Tom and they know about Daisy, so who else is there? Everyone else at Rowangarth is your friend. Oh, I tell them from time to time that you are fine and they know that you and I write to each other – but I'm sure they often thought about you and wondered when you'd be back. So why don't you let me tell them that you have married again? You had every right to.'

'But married to *Tom*?'

'A deserter, you mean? But who knows about that? Mother, Reuben, and me – and we aren't going to tell. And the Army thinks he was killed, so where's the bother? You know the way we feel about it – we're on Tom's side.'

'Yes, an' I'm grateful. But what do I say – that I'm Alice Dwerryhouse, now, and that Tom was never killed? Are folks going to accept that?'

'Of course – if you tell them he was a prisoner and the authorities were never told about it by the Germans. It happened often, in the war – men turning up like that. Everyone who knew you both would be glad.'

'Aye,' Alice frowned. 'I think they'd believe it – especially as Jinny Dobb knows about Tom, already.'

'Old Jin knows! How on earth . . . ?'

'She saw him the day he came back to Reuben's cottage, when he came looking for me. Reuben had to tell him I'd wed Giles, and had a bairn . . .'

'I know. I'm not likely to forget that day. But you're sure Jin saw him?'

'Certain. She told me she had and wanted to know why I wasn't going with him.'

'Yet she never said a word about it to anyone – not to my knowledge, at least.'

'She promised she wouldn't. But when I left Rowangarth, Jin must have suspected I wasn't going away for the good of my health.'

'Well – there you are, then,' Julia smiled. 'It would be a five-minute wonder. They'd all be so busy ooh-ing and aah-ing over Daisy that they'd pay no heed to what you and Tom had been doing.'

'I don't know . . .' Alice frowned, biting her lip, cupping her blazing cheeks in her hands. 'I'd have to talk to Tom about it. I mustn't do anything to risk him being caught and happen he'd not be so keen to have me visit – well, you know what I mean?'

'Elliot Sutton? Well, you'd just have to promise to keep out of Brattocks Wood. And anyway, you'd have no need to go there. Reuben lives in the village, now.'

'But I think I'd want to go there – just once, for old time's sake. It was where Tom and me did our courting, remember. I used to take Morgan out and hope like mad I'd bump into Tom.'

'And you'd want to tell the rooks what had been happening, wouldn't you,' Julia teased. 'Then I'd have to come with you, that's all. Have you any rooks here, to talk to?'

'Some over in the far wood – but I haven't made their acquaintance, just yet. And happen I've grown up a bit, since I used to tell my secrets to the Rowangarth rooks.'

'They'd be glad to see you, for all that,' Julia urged.

'Maybe. But what about her ladyship? Would she be

glad? And if I did come – and I'm not saying I will, mind – where would I stay? There isn't room for me and Daisy in Reuben's little house.'

'But mother would love to see you again – and as for sleeping, what's wrong with Rowangarth? It was your home, wasn't it? You would stay with us.'

'What would they all say, though – Miss Clitherow and Cook and Mary and Tilda?'

'Alice – you know staff don't usually make comments about mother's house guests, even though I know they would all say, "Welcome back, Alice!"'

'There's Tom . . .' She was wavering, she knew it; knew, too, that she desperately wanted to see Reuben just once more – see Rowangarth, too.

'Tom was a prisoner of war. I shall tell them that and mother will confirm it. And anyway, Tom wouldn't be coming with you – not on your first visit. Are you afraid Will Stubbs would poke and pry and ask his business?'

'Will!' Alice gasped, remembering the inquisitive coachman, bursting into laughter. 'Is he still a terrible busybody?'

'As bad as ever, though he's careful to keep his own affairs a secret – or so he thinks,' Julia grinned. 'We all happen to know that he's setting his cap at Mary.'

'Mary Strong? Her ladyship's parlourmaid?'

'The very same Mary. And Alice – don't revert to your old ways entirely? You were once married to my brother – you were Lady Alice Sutton. Mother thinks of you still as hers. If you should come home to Rowangarth, don't call her milady or refer to her as her ladyship? You used to call her dearest, as Giles did – remember?'

Nodding, Alice closed her eyes. She remembered so much and almost all of it security and kindness and the sweet sense of belonging. All at once, Rowangarth called her.

'I couldn't leave Tom,' she gasped.

'Not if he'd want you to pay Reuben a visit? Tom was

fond of him – and Reuben isn't getting any younger.'

'You think I don't know it? He'll be seventy-five, come September. I'd hoped you would take his birthday present back with you – give it to him on his birthday. I've got tobacco and mints and knitted him two pairs of good thick socks.'

'I'll take them, gladly, and see he gets them, too. But mightn't it be nice to be able to tell him on his birthday that one day soon you'll be bringing Daisy to see him? At least don't dismiss it entirely?'

'Don't, Julia! I want so much to visit, and you know I can't! There'd always be Elliot Sutton at the back of my mind – not just meeting him, though that would be bad enough. What if he saw me – and blurted it all out? What then?'

'Elliot won't say anything – not now. If he'd been going to make trouble, he'd have made it when he realized he'd been cheated out of hopes of the title. He can't know – not for certain – that Drew is his. Hateful though he is, I'd give him credit for keeping his mouth shut.

'And you wouldn't be staying long – a week, at the most? Surely for so short a time we could make sure you and he didn't meet?'

'*We*? You and your mother, you mean? But she doesn't know that Elliot Sutton is Drew's father – had you forgotten?'

'No. But I'm trying to. From the day he was born I always thought of Drew as Giles's son – just as mother does. You must do the same, Alice. Elliot Sutton is a womanizer and a lecher but he isn't so stupid that he'd stand on the top of Holdenby Pike and shout it out to the three Ridings, now is he?'

'N-no . . .'

'There you are, then! We stand together, you and I – just as we did when we were nursing. We each took care of the other, in the old days – we can do it again. We'd wither cousin Elliot at a glance. And remember, Alice – I hate him as much as you do.'

'You can't. You don't know what it's like to – to'

'To be raped by him? No, I don't. But he's alive and my husband was killed in that war, so I hate him more than you do – and never forget it!'

'I believe you do,' Alice said, wonderingly. She hadn't thought, not for a moment, that anyone could hate him as much as she. 'You really do . . .'

'Oh, yes. And you and Daisy would be safe with me. And bring Morgan with you, if you'd feel better. Morgan hates him, too . . .'

'Oh, I couldn't come. It wouldn't be right to leave Tom on his own. I want to come, Julia – you know I do – but how could I?'

Yet even as she said it, she knew it was only a matter of time. One day, and soon, she would return to Rowangarth. Nothing was more certain.

3

'I tell you it *was* Alice,' Mary Strong insisted. 'That's where Miss Julia has been! Miss Julia and her ladyship were talking on the telephone and it was Alice Hawthorn they were talking about! Her ladyship said, "Where are you ringing from, Julia?" and then she said, "Good. That's handy to know if ever we need to get in touch with Alice."'

'Alice *Sutton*, don't you mean, and have you forgotten, Mary, that parlourmaids don't listen to private telephone conversations?' Cook corrected, her mouth a round of disapproval. 'And then what did she say?'

'*Then* . . .' Mary pushed her cup across the table to be refilled, taking another piece of cinnamon toast without so much as a by-your-leave, '. . . *then* her ladyship said, "And how are Daisy, and Morgan? We mustn't forget dear old Morgan."'

'Alice took Morgan with her, didn't she,' Tilda frowned, 'when she left for Aunt Sutton's, I mean. And why has she stayed away so long without so much as a word? Surely she's better, now. And who is Daisy?'

'Don't know anything about any Daisy,' Mary shrugged. 'But I happen to know that Alice keeps in touch with Miss Julia. I've said so all along, haven't I? I know her writing on the envelopes.'

'Aye, and as for us not hearing a word,' Tilda defended, 'we did make it pretty plain when Alice came back from France *Lady* Sutton that things had changed, now didn't we?'

'Things *had* to change,' Cook murmured. 'Alice wasn't

44

below stairs any more – Miss Clitherow made sure we knew that, right from the start. And we still aren't any the wiser, are we?'

'Curiouser, though.' A pity, Mary thought, she'd had to move on in mid-conversation, so to speak, but there was a limit to the time it took any one person to walk across the hall. 'Wonder if Miss Julia will tell us about it? After all, Alice is supposed to be with Miss Sutton and that's where Miss Julia was supposed to be going. The very last thing her ladyship said to her when she left was, "Give my dearest love to Anne Lavinia, don't forget. Tell her we don't see half enough of her." I heard her!'

'A lot of *supposing*, for all that,' Cook murmured, half to herself.

'Yes, but Miss Sutton spends most of her time in France,' Tilda insisted. There could be no doubting it when her ladyship always gave her the stamps from the envelopes for her little brother who collected them. 'So why do Alice's letters have a Southampton postmark on them?'

'Hmmm.' Cook thought long and hard, then ventured, 'Happen letters from France get brought over to Southampton on ships and the Post Office there –'

'Happen my foot!' Mary interrupted, forgetting herself completely. 'I see *all* the letters that come into this house and Miss Sutton's have a Marseilles or a Nice postmark on them so why, will you tell me, don't Alice's?'

'That's *enough*!' Cook snapped, aware the conversation had gone too far. 'What Upstairs does and where their letters come from is none of our business and we'd all do well to remember it if we want to keep our positions in these hard times. And not one word of what's been said in my kitchen is to go beyond these four walls – do I make myself clear?' She fixed Mary with one of her gimlet glances. 'We're all getting as bad as Will Stubbs,' she added as a final reminder.

'There'll be none hear anything from me!' Mary

countered archly. 'Never a word passes my lips when I'm in Will's company. I hope I know my place here and have always given satisfaction, Mrs Shaw!'

'That you have, Mary; that you have – so don't spoil it!'

Whereupon her ladyship's cook rose from her chair, indicating that morning break was over. 'Now let's all of us be about our business. If we're intended to know, we'll be told when Miss Julia gets home, Tuesday. If not, then we keeps our eyes down and our mouths shut tight!'

All the same, she pondered, there were things that didn't add up, postmarks on letters apart. Just why had Alice stayed away so long? And who was Daisy?

Clementina Sutton was in a tizzy of delight. Not only had the first visiting card she left at the house in Cheyne Walk been accepted by a servant dressed in black from top to toe, but the next day – the very next day, mark you – a card had been delivered by the black-bearded Cossack which indicated, if Russian etiquette ran parallel with English, that Clementina was now free to call. Hadn't the Countess added the time – 10.30 – in small, neat letters in the bottom, left-hand corner, and tomorrow's date?

The *Countess*. Just to think of it made Clementina glow. Merely to look at the deckle-edged card bearing what could only be the family crest embossed in gold and the name Olga Maria, Countess Petrovska beneath it, gave her immense pleasure.

She knew little of the family next door, save that they had fled St Petersburg where the Russian revolution started, though now those Bolsheviks were calling the city Petrograd, if you please! Mind, the Bolsheviks appeared to have gained the upper hand, so were entitled to call it what they wished. The last of the British troops sent to help restore the Czar to his throne had long ago left and heaven help anyone who had the misfortune to fall foul of the men

– and women – who waved their triumphant red banners. Shot, like as not, just as the Czar and his family had been.

But it couldn't happen here, Clementina insisted nervously, even though men were joining trade unions as never before and threats of strikes were always present. But they wouldn't strike. For every man who withdrew his labour there were ten only too grateful to take his place. She dismissed the British working man from her mind, thinking instead of tomorrow's call. Investigating the pedigree of refugee Russians and whether the daughter of the house was in the market for a husband might prove interesting. It could turn out to be an extremely enlightening talk.

Talk? But what if the family next door spoke no English; used French as their international language as diplomats did? She would not only feel a fool, but be shown to be one! Then she comforted herself with the thought that any foreigner of any consequence spoke English and if the Russians did not, then they were not worth wasting her time on – which would be a pity, because the daughter of a countess was exactly what she had set her heart upon, for Elliot.

She sighed deeply, then began to search her wardrobe for something suitable to wear, regretting having brought so few clothes with her. And this town house, though small, she resolved, must be brought into full working order and before so very much longer, too. Elliot had dillied and dallied far too long. Now he would be given to understand that he had a twelve-month in which to get himself wed – or else!

She closed the wardrobe door firmly. Nothing there; nothing half good enough in which to call upon a countess. Best take a stroll through the Burlington Arcade and along Bond Street – buy new . . .

Julia felt a warm glow of homecoming the moment the station taxi entered the carriage drive that swept up to the steps of the old house. For more than three hundred years Rowangarth had stood there, blessing Suttons on their way; welcoming them back.

'I've missed you both!' She kissed her mother's cheek, then swept the small, pyjama-clad boy into her arms, closing her eyes, hugging him to her, amazed he should feel so solid, so robust against Daisy's newborn fragility. 'It's good to be back, though it was such a joy being with Alice again. I wanted to bring her home with me.'

'Come inside, do. It feels quite cold out here.' Helen Sutton shivered. 'I promised Drew he should stay up to welcome you, though he's been fighting sleep this past half-hour.'

'Then I shall take you upstairs at once, my darling, and tuck you in,' Julia smiled, kissing him again. 'Have you had your supper?'

'Mm. Mummy not go away again?'

'No, Drew. Next time, you shall come with me. We'll go for a lovely long ride on a puffing train – now what do you say to that?'

He regarded her solemnly through large grey eyes – Andrew's eyes – stuck a thumb in his mouth, then laid his head on her shoulder. Almost before she had tucked the bedclothes around him, he was asleep.

'Now, give me all the news,' Helen smiled as they sat at dinner. 'How was Anne Lavinia?'

'She seemed fine. I gave her your love, as you asked.' Best not spoil tonight with vague suspicions about her health. 'She'll be back in France, by now. I think it was business brought her home. Figgis has retired now, remember. There's no one in the house, so maybe she thought she'd better check up on things – pick up bills. And she popped in on her doctor. Nothing wrong. Just a quick check-up,' Julia hastened, feeling better for having mentioned it, albeit briefly. 'It was good to see Alice again. She and Tom are very happy – and as for little Daisy! Five weeks old and a beauty already. I could have stolen her to be Drew's sister!'

'She *is* Drew's sister,' Helen reminded, fork poised. 'Had you forgotten?'

'No.' Nor was she likely to. 'The christening was lovely. Quiet, but lovely. Alice sent you a piece of cake, by the way.'

'And Morgan – I almost forgot the old softie. Is he all right?'

'Morgan's fine. I'm glad Alice took him with her. He's never looked so fit – thinner, because he gets a lot more exercise.'

'And no titbits from Cook,' Helen supplied.

'Absolutely not. His coat shines, now. He shares brick kennels with Tom's two labradors, though he's really Alice's dog. When Tom is at work, she lets Morgan out and he sits beside Daisy's pram, on guard.'

'Good. Giles would have been pleased . . .' Helen paused, reluctant to ask the question uppermost in her mind. 'About Alice – did you feel – I mean . . .'

'Did I ask her about well – what we talked about – and yes, I did. I put it to her, then left it at that; didn't want her to feel I was pressurizing her to come home. Where Tom is – that's really her home, now. But I don't want to lose her. The war took so much from me and she is one of the people I have left who understands. She was with me the day I met Andrew . . .' Her eyes took on a remembering look, then she tilted her chin, and smiled. 'When I left, Tom drove me to the station. He told me they'd talked about it – about Alice visiting us, I mean; said there was no reason at all why she shouldn't stay with us. And he agreed with me that people should know that he and Alice are married.'

'Then what are we to tell them?' Helen frowned. 'That he wasn't killed, but taken prisoner . . . ?'

'Exactly that. Alice and I will tell the same story, be sure of it. No one shall ever know what really happened. We wouldn't be so foolish as to say anything that would get him arrested, now would we?'

'Then everything would seem to have worked out very well.' Helen smiled tremulously. 'And if we ever need to get in touch with Alice – about Drew, I mean – I believe there is a number we can use?'

'In the village – it's called West Welby, by the way. You can ring up from the Post Office, there. They've got a tiny switchboard at the back of the office, and if you give them one-and-sixpence for every trunk call, they'll put you through with no trouble at all. Just one snag. They use an extension phone, so it isn't very private. People waiting at the counter for stamps and postal orders can have a good old listen.'

'But they could get a message to Alice?'

'Of course they could. Alice sews for the postmistress; I believe they are quite friendly. But you seem obsessed with getting in touch with Alice. What has put the idea into your head?'

'I don't know. Just don't want to lose touch, I suppose. And she *is* Drew's mother, you know. In law –'

'Dearest! Alice left Drew in our keeping and she knows we would do anything we had to for him. And I'm sure that if a real emergency arose, we could always ring Windrush – that's where Tom's employer lives. Mr Hillier seems a decent man and he's devoted to Daisy. Never passes the house without taking a peep at her if she's outside, in her pram. He gave her a beautiful christening mug . . .'

'So everything would seem to be all right?'

'More than all right. They are all very happy and one day soon Alice *will* visit us. I shall tell Reuben when I give him Alice's birthday present that before so very much longer he'll be seeing her. And would it be all right if she and Daisy stayed here?'

'It would be perfect. And it would be good for Drew to

get his nose pushed out a little. He gets far too much attention, that young man,' she said fondly, complacently. 'And he can get to know his sister.'

'His *half*-sister,' Julia cautioned. 'But he isn't old enough, yet, to be told the truth of it. We'll have to be very careful when we do tell him; say the right things and not have him imagine his mother abandoned him.'

'You are the only mother he's ever known, Julia; he even calls you Mummy. But I agree we must break it to him carefully – when the time comes.'

She stopped, abruptly, as Mary brought in a joint of mutton.

'What were you saying about Aunt Clemmy being in London?' Julia hastened, filling the void.

'I was – er – saying, dear, that she went down there two days ago, though why,' Helen sighed, 'I haven't the slightest idea. She did tell me, though, that Nathan should be on his way home from Africa by now. So good to see him again . . .'

'Will you carve, milady, or shall I?' Clearly, Mary realized, there were to be no snippets to carry back to the kitchen.

'You do it, Mary – then I'm sure we can look after ourselves quite nicely,' Helen smiled.

No news at all, Mary brooded, as she closed the dining-room door behind her, because everyone already knew that the Reverend Nathan was expected home at any time and it was the best-known secret hereabouts that Mrs Clementina spent more time in her London house, nowadays, than ever she spent at Pendenys Place. And anyway, who was interested in the Pendenys Suttons? Even that Mr Elliot seemed to be behaving himself these days, she shrugged. Not so much as a whisper of scandal from that quarter. There were times, she was forced to admit, when life around Holdenby could be very dull indeed . . .

* * *

Tom rocked back and forth, humming softly. This was his special time; the time he took Daisy after her evening feed, laying her over his shoulder, cradling her tiny body with his hand, loving her nearness, the softness of her and her sweet baby smell.

'Is she asleep, yet?' Alice whispered. 'Shall I put the kettle on?'

'Leave it for a while. Sit yourself down, lass.'

Gladly, she did as he asked her, pulling off her shoes, wriggling her toes, contentment pulsing through her like a steady, warm heartbeat.

She looked at her husband through half-closed eyes, seeing the small smile of pleasure that tilted the corners of his mouth. This last half-hour of the day always belonged to Tom and Daisy; their together time, when he would rock her to sleep.

She smiled, wondering what pleased him so — apart from his daughter, that was. Closing her eyes, she set her chair rocking.

My, but they'd had a grand time, the three of them, Tom thought. These past four days had done Alice a power of good. He had never before realized how close the two women had grown. Sisters? They were that, all right. And how proud he'd felt at the christening. It was, Julia had said as he'd driven her to the station to catch the early morning train, quite the nicest she had ever been to.

'I did so enjoy it. Daisy was very good,' she smiled. 'Well, apart from that cry of utter rage when she felt the water on her head. Did you know, Tom, that Daisy is my only godchild? No one has ever asked me before.'

'It was kindly of you to accept, though Alice wouldn't have taken no for an answer. The day the bairn was born she said she wanted you to stand for her. And it was good of you,' he murmured, 'to give her such a lovely present.'

'It belonged to Grandmother Whitecliffe. I know it isn't usual to give a brooch at a christening, but I thought sapphires would suit her eyes — if they stay so beautifully blue, that is.'

'Alice was overcome. There are twenty-one stones in it. She counted.'

'Very small stones, Tom. I really chose it because it was in the shape of a daisy, though daisy petals aren't blue and the pearl in the middle should have been yellow.'

'Alice says she won't be allowed to wear it till she's old enough to take good care of it.'

'She's my only god-daughter — take good care of *her*.'

'You know I will. And here we are . . .' He slowed the pony to a walk, guiding it carefully into the station yard, tying the reins to the fence before helping her down.

'It's been grand, having you with us. Come and visit again — bring the little lad.'

'I will. As soon as Alice can accept him, I promise I will. And thank you for making me so welcome. When things get bad, I shall know where to run, now . . .'

'It still hurts, then?' There was understanding in his eyes, and compassion.

'Like the very devil, Tom. Sometimes I want to beat my fists against the wall, and scream. It's a good thing I've got Drew to keep me sane.' The train let off a hiss of steam, then clanked to a stop. Smiling bravely, she turned to him, holding out her hand in goodbye. 'Don't wave me off, Tom? Just give me a hand with my cases, then go?'

'If that's what you want . . .'

'It is. I like to be met, but partings dismay me.'

'Right, then!' He lifted her cases high onto the luggage rack, then stepping down he gathered her to him, holding her tightly. 'Thanks for all you did for Alice when she was in need of a friend. If there's ever anything we can do for you, we'll do it — no questions asked.' He cupped her face in his hands, laying his lips gently to her forehead. 'You're a lovely lady, Julia MacMalcolm. Come and see us again, soon? Don't wait for the next christening?'

'I won't – be sure of it. Now off you go – please? No goodbyes . . .'

He thought a lot about Julia and her ladyship on his way home and about the little lad up there at Rowangarth. And he thought about what he and Alice had talked about, last night in bed. It had been her decision entirely, yet he had agreed with it, even though he told her to sleep on it, then sleep on it again before she wrote to Lady Helen. But when Alice's mind was made up there was nothing would change it. She would think on, like he said, yet still she would write that letter to Rowangarth, and now that she had accepted the way things were, it was best for all concerned she should do it.

He felt a sudden pricking of tears and coughed sternly, blowing his nose loudly. And it hadn't really been tears he had felt – more like a tingling of happiness – nay, *gratitude* – that his world should be so damn-near perfect, because how many men had everything they could wish for on the face of this earth? How many?

Tom Dwerryhouse was not a praying man, but he had lifted his eyes to the early morning sky and whispered, 'Thanks'; whispered it so quietly that only God could hear him. Then he shook his head, feeling foolish at his daftness, and slapped the reins down hard and called, 'Hup!' to the pony.

But how many men were lucky as Tom Dwerryhouse? Certainly not Giles Sutton nor his brother Robert, nor Andrew MacMalcolm. They had nothing but a hero's death; no Alice, no nestling girl child to rock to sleep. And Julia had so little. Only young Drew, and her memories. Happen this morning he should not have kissed her good-bye, but he'd done it on an impulse, seeing the naked sadness in her eyes, the aloneness. It had been a kiss of compassion, of comfort, and she had not taken it amiss. That brief closeness between them had prompted him to whisper,

'No goodbyes, but don't look so lost, Julia lass. Alice

shall come and visit, I promise you. All I ask is that she won't meet up with young Sutton. I couldn't abide it if he was to upset her again. If I ever thought there was the smallest chance of that, I wouldn't want her to go.'

'He won't upset her, be sure of that! You know how I detest him,' Julia had said, tight-mouthed. 'Alice and Daisy will be safe, at Rowangarth.'

'Detest? Aye, that's how I feel about him an' all. That one's a creature only a mother could love – and there must be times when even she loses patience with him.'

'Don't worry, Tom. Always remember that I don't want them to meet, either. It's every bit as important to me he should never suspect that Drew is his.'

'But mightn't he suspect already?' Tom frowned.

'He might, but suspicion is one thing; proof is quite another. It's his word against Rowangarth's, don't forget. Even his brother Nathan is on our side. Elliot wouldn't dare!'

'Happen you are right. And why are we spoiling the last of your holiday talking about *him*,' he'd laughed, making light of it, and she had stepped onto the train, taking the window seat, smiling. She was still smiling, chin high, when he turned for a last look at her. She would be home, now, at Rowangarth, poor lass; back to her lonely bed with no one to kiss her, make love with her, tell her everything would be all right.

'*Damn* that war!' he gasped.

'Tom?' Alice was at his side in an instant, eyes anxious. 'What is it, love? What was it you just said?'

'Dreaming,' he mumbled, cursing his carelessness. 'Must have nodded off. Aye – happen I was dreaming . . .'

'About the war! It's been over two years, almost, yet still it's always there, at the backs of our minds. Don't think anyone who was in France will rightly forget . . .'

'No. It's got a lot to answer for. But let's get this bairn up to her cot? She's fast asleep.'

Carefully, he got to his feet, cupping the little head

protectively in his hand. Then half-way up the stairs he turned abruptly.

'Alice, I do love you – but you know it, don't you?'

'I know it,' she said softly, and there was no need for reassurance, because her eyes said it for her. *I love you. I shall always love you . . .*

'Off you go,' she said softly. 'Put her in her cot. I'll set the kettle on. We'll have a sup of tea, then I've got a letter to write . . .'

'There, now.' Alice lay down her pen and corked the ink bottle. 'That's over and done with. I'll post it in the morning when I go to the village. Just one thing more, Tom . . .'

'Whatever else?' he smiled indulgently. 'Can't it wait until morning?'

'That it can't! I'm in the mood for setting things to rights. I've written to Rowangarth – now there's one thing more I must tell you.

'You mind you said that Daisy did well at her christening – had so many lovely things given to her that the West Welby lads'd be courting her for her dowry – or something daft like that . . . ?'

'A joke, love, though I've given the matter a deal of thought,' he said gravely, though his eyes were bright with teasing, 'and there's none in that village half good enough for our Daisy! But what's brought all this on?'

'Like I said – setting things to rights, because happen you should know that you might be more right than you realize – about the bairn, I mean . . .'

'Alice?' He moved towards her, but she got to her feet, taking up a position behind her chair. And she always did that, he frowned, when something bothered her. 'Tell me, sweetheart?'

'Our Daisy *does* have a dowry,' she whispered, eyes on the chairback. 'First thing I did after she was born was to open a bank account in her name.'

'And what's wrong with that, bonny lass? Nice to think she'll have a bit of brass to draw on if ever she should need it. I've set my heart on her getting a scholarship to the Grammar School – there'll be fancy uniform to buy, and –'

'Tom! Stop your dreaming! There's years and years before we need think about that. She's hardly six weeks old, yet! And if you're set on educating her,' she added reluctantly, 'she can always be paid for.'

'And just how, might I ask? It costs good money every term at that school if a child hasn't the brains to get a free place, though happen we'd manage.' Rabbits to sell, he calculated. Rabbits were vermin and all a keeper caught, it was accepted, were his own. And rabbit skins and mole skins fetched a fair price and –

'Will you *listen*, Tom? It would be nothing to do with managing. Daisy has enough money of her own!'

There now, she'd said it and please God that Dwerry-house temper wouldn't flash sudden and sharp.

'Her own? Tell me, Alice?'

His voice was soft, ordinary almost. They weren't going to have words if only because it was Daisy they were talking about. She drew in a breath of relief.

'When I was married to – when I was at Rowangarth and I thought of you as dead . . .'

'When you were Lady Sutton, wed to Sir Giles,' he supplied. 'Lovey, we've had all this out. It happened. You did what you had to. Don't talk about it as if it's something to be ashamed of. Just tell me about Daisy's bank book.'

'All right, then. Giles made me an allowance – I didn't touch it, hardly. It didn't seem right. Any road, when I came to you there was most of it left . . .'

'And all we've got in this house – it was that money paid for it,' he gasped.

'No. You know that after you and me were wed, I sent to Rowangarth for my things – my *own* things – all the bedding and linen I'd collected, the rest of my clothes, the chest of drawers Reuben gave us . . .'

'Aye. And instead of them being delivered by the railway, they came in a carrier's motor, and all manner of things, beside!'

'Yes. Another bed, a washstand and jug and bowl, and rugs and kitchen chairs and –'

'It was good of Julia to send them and wrong of me to think otherwise.'

'Furniture Rowangarth had no need of, and kindly given. And the rest of our home came out of my own savings, Tom, I promise you. I didn't use a penny of Giles's money. All I ever took from it was money for Daisy's pram – and whilst I'm about it, that pram cost *five guineas*. Our little one was to have the finest coach-built perambulator I could lay hands on, I vowed. And besides, it'll come in nicely for the rest of our bairns. Good things always last,' she added with defiant practicality.

'That great posh pram will outlast six more, then!' he laughed. 'We're going to have to be busy if we're to get our value out of it.'

'Sweetheart – you aren't angry? You don't think I should have told you before this?'

'I'm not angry.' He loved her too much. They were too happy, the three of them, that he'd be a fool ever to lose his temper again. 'But might a man be told how wealthy a daughter he's got?'

'Aye. I reckon I owe you that.' Alice opened the dresser drawer, slid her fingers beneath the lining paper and took out the bank book. 'See for yourself . . .'

'Heck!' His eyes widened; he let go a gasp of disbelief. 'That's enough to buy this house we're living in and then some!'

'That's just about it. And not a penny of it can be touched till she's seven and can sign her own name to get at it. But I don't want her to know about it, Tom; don't want her thinking she can have all the toys she wants, nor any bicycle she thinks fit to choose. Daisy Dwerryhouse cuts her coat according to *our* cloth; I've made up my mind about that. So not one word, mind . . .'

'Not a word! But think on, eh – our Daisy rich!'

'Rich my foot! She's got something put by, that's all. Rich is – well, it's like Mr Hillier is and the Pendenys Suttons.' She stopped, abruptly. 'Sorry, Tom. We don't talk about them, do we? Only about Nathan . . .'

'Only about the Reverend, who's the best of the bunch of them. But tell me what's in yon' letter to her ladyship?' He nodded towards the envelope on the mantelpiece, waiting to be stamped and posted. 'Or am I not to know?'

'I think you know already, but I'll tell you all about it when I get her reply – which will be soon, I shouldn't wonder. Now give the fire a stir, will you, and hurry that kettle up. And Tom – I do so love you. We aren't too happy, are we?' she whispered, all at once afraid.

'No, sweetheart. I've always been of the opinion that we get what we deserve in this life and what we've got, you and me, we paid for – in advance. So stop your worriting and make your man that sup of tea!'

Almost without thinking, his hand strayed to his pocket and the rabbit's foot he kept there; his lucky rabbit's foot. Reuben had given it to him the day before he'd left Rowangarth to join the Army; given one to Davie and Will Stubbs an' all, and all three of them came through that war. He had great faith in that old rabbit's foot, he thought, curling his fingers around its silky softness. It had taken care of him in the war and now it would take care of Alice and the bairn – and their happiness. Stood to reason, didn't it? And Alice *should* go home to Rowangarth just as soon as maybe – let old Reuben see Daisy – be blowed if she shouldn't!

He smiled his contentment, pushing the kettle deeper into the coals.

Too happy? Of course they weren't!

4

'I think you should read this letter. It's from Alice, and it's about Drew.'

'It's nothing –' Helen Sutton's head jerked sharply upwards, eyes questioning.

'It's nothing wrong,' Julia smiled comfortingly. 'Read it.'

'My spectacles.' Still a little alarmed, Helen reached into the pockets of her cardigan. 'I must have left them upstairs. Read it for me?'

'Only if you drink your coffee, and relax. It isn't anything awful. Listen . . .'

My dear Julia,

It was lovely our being together after such a long time. Those few days were so good and just like it used to be. We must not let it go so long again. Seeing you made me realize how much I have missed Rowangarth.

I have thought about it a lot – talked to Tom about it, too, and he agrees that I must visit Reuben, though before I do I hope you will tell them all about the way it is now – about Tom not being killed and our getting married – prepare them beforehand.

There is something else, too, more important. We talked about it after you left. Drew is rightfully a Sutton. Rowangarth will belong to him one day and he belongs to Rowangarth. He is yours, and I think the time has come for me to give him up completely. Not meaning that I must never see him again, but I want you to adopt him, and even though you look upon him as your son, my dearest friend, I would wish her ladyship to do it so he may keep his Sutton name.

I accept that legally Drew is mine, but things change. I am no longer Lady Sutton and Drew must be brought up by his own kind. Will you think seriously about it?

'There's more, of course, but that's the bare bones of it. Just think – Drew, ours. I think Alice could well be right . . .'

'Adopt him? Oh!' Helen let go her indrawn breath in a startled gasp. 'I would like to – I think I always wanted to, truth known – but I never dared ask for fear of losing him.'

'But Alice would never have taken him away from us. Just as she says in the letter, Drew is a Sutton and belongs here. I think we should think seriously about it – make an appointment with Carvers.

'Alice means it kindly. She doesn't want rid of Drew; she just wants what is best for him and for us. Shall I ring them up now – ask when's best for us to see them? Do you want me to come with you?'

'Don't fuss me, child! This is a serious matter. We must look at it from all angles.'

'But what is there to look at?' Julia buttered and jammed a slice of toast, cutting it into small slices, arranging it on Drew's plate. 'All you would be doing is assuming responsibility for Giles's son until he comes of age. Legally signed and sealed – that's all it would amount to. For the rest, there would be no change. Alice left Drew in our care. He has been ours, I suppose, from the day he was born.'

'You are right – and I *do* want Drew. It was a surprise to me, that's all, yet you seem not one bit put out, Julia. Did you talk about it with Alice when you were there?'

'Not a word. All we talked about was that perhaps she

would visit Rowangarth – and now she'll have to, won't she? There'll be papers to be signed, though there shouldn't be a lot of legal fuss, especially if we are all in agreement. Which Carver do you want to see – old, middle, or young?'

'I feel I should see the old gentleman. I wouldn't like to upset him.' Carver, Carver and Carver – father, son and lately, grandson, had dealt with Rowangarth's affairs since before ever she and John were married, Helen pondered. 'I have heard, though, that the young Mr Carver is very astute and wide-awake.'

'Well, middle-Carver is more the financial side of the partnership, so I'll tell their clerk you would like to see the old man but would take it kindly if you could meet the grandson, too. You haven't met him, have you?'

'Not yet.' Helen shook her head. Giles had always taken care of legal matters after John died – when Robert had returned to India, that was.

'Then you'll get two for the price of one, that way. I'll ring them now.' She wiped strawberry jam from Drew's chin. 'When do you want to go? Friday? That would give us plenty of time to have a good long talk about it.' And still come to the same conclusion. Of course her mother must adopt Drew. She pushed back her chair noisily and made for the telephone.

'That's it, then. Eleven on Friday will suit them nicely,' Julia beamed, returning to the table again. 'And Drew and I will come with you.'

'Julia, dear, you mustn't rush things so.' Helen had not yet recovered from the suddenness of it. 'We must think very carefully . . .'

'Of course we will – and there's no one more careful than Carver-the-old. But you know that what Alice suggests makes good sense – and there's the other matter,' she rushed on. 'Alice wants it made known that she and Tom are married and I think it's something we should do at once, don't you?'

'Yes, I do, though it will be like letting her go, sort of. I care so much for her. Having her was such a comfort. And when she had Drew – oh, it would have been such a good day, had Giles not died.'

'But he left us Drew. And he was very ill – you know he was, dearest – and often in pain from his wounds. Don't let's be too sad?'

'You are right. This is a good day and we will start it by giving Miss Clitherow Alice's news.'

'I agree. Best she should be the first to know. But let's both tell her? Then I'll go to the kitchen and tell them exactly the same story – and let them know how glad about it we both are.'

'Tell the same story? Don't you think that sounds as if we are being a little underhanded?'

'Telling lies about Tom having been a prisoner of war and Alice leaving Rowangarth to be with Aunt Sutton, you mean, when all the time she was with Tom in Hampshire? Yes, it is underhanded, but sometimes you have to stretch the truth a little.'

'Yes, of course,' Helen sighed, comforted. 'But first you must tell Reuben. He's known about Alice and Tom all along – it's only right we should put him in the picture. And don't you think Miss Clitherow should be the one to tell staff about it?'

'No, I don't.' Julia's reply allowed for no compromise. 'It's such lovely news that I want to be the one to tell them. Besides, Miss Clitherow might tell it *her* way. She never quite approved of Alice becoming Lady Sutton.'

'But she *did*, Julia! She was extremely correct about it and insisted that Alice was given the respect due to her.'

'She overdid it. Alice didn't know where she stood. All right – so she had been your sewing-maid, then came back from France mistress of this house, though she never once exerted her authority. She was still Alice, and staff should not have been barred, entirely, from showing her kindness. And it was Miss Clitherow at the bottom of it!'

'Did Alice complain? I never once thought she wasn't happy.'

'She was happy as she could be. But she and Giles didn't live a normal married life – we both know it – yet for all that, she nursed him and cared fondly for him – and she gave Rowangarth a son.

'But *I* want to tell staff about Alice and Tom. When Miss Clitherow has been told I shall go downstairs at once and take Drew with me if he isn't asleep. I'll have tea with them – like I used to.'

She called back staff teatime, with bread and jam and cake and sometimes, on special days, cherry scones. So long ago. So much water under so many bridges. So much heartache.

'I remember. Cook spoiled you, just as she spoils Drew. You were always her favourite. And you are right. I'll leave it to you to tell staff.'

'Fine! I'll put Drew in his pushchair and walk to the village. I intended calling on Reuben, anyway, to tell him about the christening and take his piece of cake. Now I'll be able to tell him that Alice plans to visit. He'll be so pleased.'

'But not a word about the adoption, mind!'

'Of course not.' Not until they had seen the Carvers, old and young, and the legalities were set in motion. 'Do you know, dearest, for all I was glad to be home again, I still had a sad feeling, leaving Alice. But now I'm so glad. Drew will be ours completely and Alice and Daisy will soon be coming to stay.' She lifted the small boy from his high chair, throwing him into the air so he laughed with delight and demanded more. 'Come on, young Sutton – let's get you cleaned up. There isn't a child anywhere who can get himself so sticky at breakfast! You've even got jam in your ear! Say 'bye to grandmother!'

Child on hip, she slammed out of the room, almost like the Julia of old, Helen thought. *Almost . . .*

Clementina Sutton, feeling quite splendid in a rose-red calf-length silk costume and toning bell-shaped hat, brought the knocker down three times, then took a deep breath.

It was all most exciting. She had never before met a Russian, much less been received by a countess who had one thing above all in her favour. She, Clementina, did not have the cut crystal voice of a true aristocrat – she knew it. Even her expensive schooling had not entirely removed her Yorkshire accent. No! She had never had that, exactly; more undertones of northness, perhaps. Yet she still had to pause, she admitted, before saying *butter*, *government*, and *good luck*. It was the way with northern vowels. They could give one away, no matter how very rich one might be. But the countess, being foreign, would have no ear for English dialects. It would be quite relaxing to sip tea from a samovar and not have to watch every word she said.

The door was opened by the same black-clad servant, who took the offered card, indicating with a graceful movement of her hand that the caller was to sit. Then she walked down the hall to announce the visitor. And she didn't walk, Clementina pondered; rather she placed one foot before the other with the haughty, considered precision of a ballet dancer so that her long, full skirt swirled as she moved. Far more pleasing, Clementina thought nastily, than the pompous plodding of the flat feet of Pendenys' butler.

'*Plis?*' Again the delicate movement of the hand, the indication she was to be followed.

A middle-aged woman, also dressed in black – even her beads and eardrops were of jet – rose to her feet, her hand extended.

'Olga Maria Petrovska,' she said softly, inclining her head.

'Clementina Sutton of Pendenys,' came the prompt reply. 'It is kind of you to receive me.'

'Please to sit down. Tea will be brought – or coffee?'

'Tea is most satisfactory. You will realize that I live next door to you – when in London, of course.' She spoke carefully, slowly, shaping her mouth like a mill girl in her eagerness to be understood.

'Ah, yes. Karl – he is our coachman and houseman – keeps me informed of what happens in the world outside. I am little interested in it at the moment. I am in mourning. I rarely receive visitors.'

'I am sorry. Might I ask for whom?' The woman's English was good – very good – for a foreigner. 'That dreadful war – will we ever forget it?'

'The war – yes. But for me my *bête noire* is the uprising, the Bolsheviks. My husband and elder son were killed by the rabble; Igor is still in Russia – though I would beg you not to speak of it outside this house. *They* have their spies everywhere. And I mourn for my country, also.'

'But they will be defeated and punished, those terrible people. You will go home to Russia . . .'

'No. Perhaps Igor and Anna, but not me.'

'Your children?' Clementina was enjoying herself immensely.

'Igor is my younger boy; Anna my only daughter. Basil, our firstborn, died at his father's side, defending our home. Igor tries to – to find things we left behind us,' she hesitated, 'but please not to talk of it until he is safely back?'

'Not a word,' Clementina breathed. 'I have sons of my own. You have my sympathy and understanding . . .'

The door opened without sound and the servant in black placed a tray on the table at the countess's side. Then, dropping a deep, graceful curtsey, she left on feet that seemed scarcely to touch the floor.

'Please – something we have done wrongly?' The countess challenged her caller's inquisitive, roaming eyes.

'N-no. Foolish of me, but I had expected a samovar. And your furniture . . .' she faltered.

'You expected us to be very Russian? You thought to see oriental carpets, silk hangings and rare paintings? And it surprises you that I use so English a teapot?'

'I didn't know what to expect,' Clementina said with complete candour. 'I had thought that –'

'That you would have wealthy people living next to you? Then you are much to be disappointed. Our homes – the winter town house and the one in the country we used each summer, are gone. We could not bring them with us, nor our estates and possessions. To arrive here with our lives was itself a miracle, thanks be to Our Blessed Lady.' She crossed herself and nodded to the – what was it? Clementina frowned. Some sort of religious picture?

'A holy icon,' supplied the countess. 'Once, it hung over my bed. Always, in summer, we left Petersburg for the country – so much cooler. And when we heard of the trouble in the city, we stayed there, even though winter was near – Anna and I, that was . . .

'My husband and our sons returned to Petersburg at once – the mobs were looting, we were told. They got out what valuables they could from the town house and left them with me in the country – until the revolutionaries were defeated and it was safe for us to go back. But they were not defeated. We dare not return to Petersburg.' She passed a cup with hands that shook.

'And then?' Clementina breathed.

'Igor stayed behind to take care of Anna and me. My husband and elder son returned to St Petersburg to do what they could. Basil and Igor were in the army during the war, at the Military Academy. They were too young to be sent to the Eastern Front – Basil might have lived, had he been there.'

'And your younger son? Why did you not insist he left Russia with you?'

67

'Because he is a man – or almost a man – and his Czar needed him. Besides, there were - *things* – still to be found; hidden things. Anna and I brought what items of value we could with us – and Our Blessed Lady. It was She got us to safety. I pray to Her each night for Igor's life – that he may soon find us here. This house – he knows of it . . .' She stopped, abruptly, breathing deeply, lifting her shoulders, ashamed she had let down her guard before a complete stranger. 'Do you think it will rain today?'

'That is very English of you,' Clementina smiled. 'And might I say how well you speak our language? I thought –'

'That I would speak only Russian? I have French, also. Our children had an English governess and spoke only English in the schoolroom. But I am so angry with those Bolsheviks that I took a vow that only English should be spoken – except on saints' days – until there is a Romanov on the throne once more.'

'Dear lady – forgive me – but the Czar is dead; his heir, too.'

'I fear so. But there are Romanovs still alive; the Grand Duke Michael – the Czar's brother – what has happened to him we do not know. We only know that our Czar, God rest him, was murdered.' She bowed her head and crossed herself piously. 'But I speak too much which I ask will not be repeated by you. For the sake of my son, I ask it.'

Once, in the Imperial days, she doubted she would have received any woman without first checking her pedigree most thoroughly. Indeed, in St Petersburg, their circle of acceptable friends had been select and small. Now, even though she was as nothing in a strange country, she should not let her standards drop. It was just, she sighed inside her, that she was lonely and homesick for Russia and afraid, still, that those who had in even the smallest way served the Czar would be hunted down no matter where they might be.

'Not a word shall pass my lips,' Clementina breathed, eyes wide, heart bumping.

'So, Mrs Clementina Sutton of Pendenys – now you shall tell me about *your* children . . .'

The countess had, Clementina was to think later, deftly changed the subject and not one more word about her refugee neighbours had she gleaned. Yet the countess had indicated that though in mourning she would return the call, Clementina thought with satisfaction, and meantime she had deduced that the lady was a widow; that her elder son had been killed and that her younger son was somewhere in Russia, still – St Petersburg, perhaps? – looking for *things*, though what he sought was still a mystery. Nor had she met Anna.

Anna, had her parents' title been English, would have been *Lady* Anna, she frowned. In England, of course, a countess would be the wife of an earl and she was as sure as she could be that Russian aristocracy sported no earls. Maybe though, the husband had been a count? She shook her head. It was all very confusing – and there was something else that might well put a different complexion on things. Anna Petrovsky could already be promised!

She removed her costume and placed it carefully on a hanger. It had been a mistake, she admitted; a very expensive mistake and entirely the wrong colour in which to impress someone who must surely detest anything red.

When the countess returned her call she would be more careful and dress more suitably. And when that happened, surely Anna – *Lady* Anna – would accompany her mother? She did so want to meet her; decide whether she was wasting her time in patronizing the family next door. It might well be, she was forced to admit, that she would have to cast her net wider in her quest for a wife for Elliot, though she hoped not. After all, it was not essential her son's wife should have money; what she must have, though, was breeding. Breeding such as Helen had. No amount of money would buy it – a fact of life she had learned the painful way – and no amount of poverty could disguise it. But only let the girl next door be in the market for a wealthy husband, she pleaded silently, and the search was over – and Elliot's womanizing too, did he but know it!

'Well now, Miss Julia, and what have you come to tell us?'

Cook placed two cushions on the kitchen chair, then perched Drew on top of them. Ever since this morning, when Miss Julia had begged afternoon tea in the kitchen in exchange for some very, *very* good news, Cook had been on tenterhooks.

'Like I promised – good news; cherry scone news.' Julia drew her chair up to the table. 'And no, Mrs Shaw, Drew may not have all those cakes'. Deftly she removed an iced bun from his plate, returning it to the tin, 'even though I know you made them especially for him.'

Eyes bright, she waited until cups had been filled and passed round and Mrs Shaw had nodded that tea might begin before she said, 'It's about Alice.'

'She's well again? Her ladyship is coming home?' Tilda gasped.

'Yes – and *no*. She is very well, but she is no longer *her ladyship* and she won't be coming to Rowangarth just yet. She has her very own home, now. That is where I have been – acting godmother to her little baby. Alice has married again . . .'

'Oh, my word!' Cook dropped her knife with a clatter, gazing stunned around the table. At Mary, who'd suspected, hadn't she, where Miss Julia had been; at Tilda's bright pink cheeks and at Jinny Dobb, whom Julia had said should be asked. There was no pleased surprise on Jin's face, Cook thought. Jin, the sly old thing, merely looked – *sly*. Her face was without emotion – if you could

70

ignore the I-know-something-you-don't-know look in her pale blue eyes, that was. '*Married*?'

'A year last July, Mrs Shaw.'

'So when she left . . . ?' At last, Mary found her voice.

'When she left us she wasn't going to Aunt Sutton. I'm sorry if you were deceived, but Alice felt that people she knew and cared for might not take too kindly to her leaving her little boy behind.'

'But she *did* leave him behind, for all that!' Tilda Tewk had a way of putting things that was rarely the embodiment of tact.

'Yes, but not for the reason you might think. Alice had a choice – and she made it!'

Julia took a deep breath. This was not as easy as she had thought. Miss Clitherow had taken the news calmly; below stairs, it would seem, they had not the same control of their curiosity – nor their emotions.

'You mean, she had the choice between this little lad, here, and – and . . .'

'And should we be talking like this in front of him?' Mary whispered, sliding her eyes to the small boy.

'It's all right. He doesn't understand. The cherry on his bun is of far more interest to him, at the moment,' Julia smiled. 'And Alice wasn't an uncaring mother. She put Drew's interests first; best he should grow up with his inheritance, she felt, and mother and I agreed with her.'

'But where did she go, if it wasn't to Miss Sutton?' Tilda demanded. 'Was it to *him* – the man she's married to?'

'To *him*,' Julia said softly. 'We wanted her to, once we knew he was not –'

'Dead?' For the first time, Jinny Dobb spoke. 'That Tom Dwerryhouse hadn't been killed, after all?'

'That Tom was alive,' Julia nodded. 'The Army thought him dead, but he'd been taken prisoner.' The lie slipped out easily.

'And them Germans had locked him up and never told no one about it?' Cook choked.

'It happened a lot.' All at once Julia felt relief that the news was to be accepted with no more than a modicum of surprise. 'When it happened, things were in a turmoil at the Front. The Germans and Austrians were getting the better of us and things were in a bad way. No news of any kind was getting through. But how did you guess, Jin? Did you see it in the bottom of your teacup?'

'Something like that, Miss.' Slowly, she smiled.

'But *married* . . .' Cook took her apron corners, ballooning it out, ready to weep into it as she always did, when overcome.

'And a mother,' Tilda gasped, her romantic heart thumping deliciously. 'What did she have, Miss Julia?'

'A little girl. Daisy Julia Dwerryhouse. She's very beautiful. I took my camera with me. As soon as the reel has been developed, you shall see Alice and Daisy – and Tom.'

'Then she's had two beautiful bairns,' Cook pronounced, taking another bun from the tin, placing it defiantly on Drew's plate. 'And this lovely little lad here has a sister!'

'A half-sister. Alice asked especially that I should tell you all about her remarriage. I hope you'll all be happy for her. Mother and I are. We are hoping she will come and stay with us as soon as Daisy can make the journey.'

There, now! She had done it! Not only had she broken the news about Tom, but she had also let it be known that the Suttons – the Rowangarth Suttons, that was – were delighted about it. How the Pendenys Suttons would react to the news remained to be seen. To Nathan, it would come as no shock at all; to Elliot, it might have entirely different repercussions.

Determinedly, she pushed Pendenys to the back of her mind. Drew was *Giles's* son; was even Sutton-fair, even though Elliot was dark as a gypsy.

'Where is she, Miss?' Tilda's voice broke into her broodings. 'I want to write – tell her how pleased I am.'

'Alice would like that. I know she misses you all. She's in Hampshire, but I'll write down her address for you. And might I have another scone, Mrs Shaw? There is no one can bake cherry specials like you!'

Cook obliged, beaming, spreading the butter thickly. 'But oh, my word; Alice Hawthorn wed and to her Tom, and a little babbie an' all!'

'It's like a story in a love book, isn't it?' Tilda breathed. 'One with a happy ending . . .' Tilda, who read every love story ever published, was an authority on happy endings. 'I'll write to Alice tonight.'

'Us all will,' Cook nodded. 'And send a present for her little lass.'

'Good. Well, best be off!' Julia made to lift Drew into her arms, but Cook was quick to ask,

'Leave him with us, Miss Julia? He does so enjoy playing with my button box. Just like Sir Giles did . . .'

'Very well. But make sure he doesn't put buttons in his mouth, and don't dare,' Julia gazed pointedly at the cake tin, 'give him another iced bun – not even if he says prettyplease for it!'

'And I'd best be getting back to the bothy.' Jin rose to her feet. 'Thank you kindly for having me, Mrs Shaw,' she murmured, following Julia out.

'You knew, Jin Dobb.' Julia closed the kitchen door behind her. 'Alice told me you knew about Tom right from the start, yet you never breathed a word – not even to me. How ever did you manage to do it?'

'Easy, Miss Julia. For one thing, I promised Alice I'd never tell I'd seen him, and for another – well, scrubbing woman in the bothy I may be, but it was nice, all them months, knowing summat that lot in the kitchen didn't know! And Miss – it was a sin and a shame there couldn't have been another come back from the dead . . .'

'It wasn't to be, Jin. And I've got Drew.' She took a long, unsteady breath. 'Alice left me the child . . .'

'That she did. And take heart, Miss. I saw happiness in Alice's hand and there's happiness to come for you, an' all. I know it.'

'How can you know, Jinny Dobb?' Julia's words were harsh with bitterness. 'You've never read my hand.'

'No more have I. But it's all around you, like a glow. No one can see it but Jin, and Jin Dobb isn't often wrong!'

'It isn't possible. I couldn't. Not again!' She didn't want to be happy with any man but Andrew.

'Not love again? With respect, Miss, there's first love and there's last love and love of all shapes and sizes in between, so don't shut your heart to it, when you chance on it . . .'

'But I *won't* chance on it, so don't ever say such a thing again!'

'I won't.' She'd said what she had to say – now let it rest.

But Miss Julia *would* encounter love – when her heart was good and ready, that was; oh my word, *yes*! What she would make of it might be altogether another thing, but love again she would. One day . . .

5

Clementina Sutton had fretted and fumed alternately for the remainder of the week. How much longer she could remain in the London house waiting for the countess to return her call, she did not know. And when was she to meet Anna Petrovska? Clearly, something must be done, yet etiquette decreed she could not call again at the house next door. Correct behaviour demanded that she must now await a return visit and as yet the silly woman hadn't even left her calling card!

How long before she must return to Pendenys? How long dare she leave Elliot alone, virtually, with no one to pull on the reins when he became bored and restless and decided to take himself off in search of pleasure!

His father didn't care. Edward disliked his eldest son with undisguised feeling and avoided the poor boy like the plague. Trouble was, she brooded, Pendenys Place was so vast that avoidance came easily. So many rooms, inner doors, outer doors, unexpected staircases. People could go for days without meeting, if they were set on it.

It was then she had jumped moodily to her feet, lifted the lace curtain that covered the window and saw, oh, thanks be! a young woman in the garden next door who could only be Anna Petrovska.

At once she felt relief she'd had the good sense to have the fence removed; the fence she caused to be built – with good reason, mind! – when it seemed certain the people next door might be European refugees, common soldiers or gypsies.

In less than a minute she was standing at the garden wall, smiling a welcome over it, whispering, 'Good morning, my dear – you must be Anna. I have heard so much about you.'

'Good morning, ma'am. Are you the lady who called on Mama – Mrs Sutton of Pendenys? I am so pleased to meet you.'

She extended a delicate hand. 'Aleksandrina Anastasia Petrovska,' she smiled. 'Anna . . .'

'You have a very beautiful name.' Genteelly Clementina touched her fingertips.

'Ah, yes, but *so* long. I decided when I was a little girl that my birth-name was too awful to have to print out, so I insisted I became Anna. Vassily and Igor had short names – it was most unfair!'

The corners of her mouth lifted in an enchanting smile to show white, even teeth. She was, Clementina was bound to admit, not only aristocratic but beautiful and if Elliot didn't think so, she would box his ears!

'You have the same name as the poor little Grand Duchess,' she murmured for want of something better to say.

'Ah – the dear Anastasia, God rest her.' Exactly as her mother had done, she crossed herself, head bowed. 'She and I share the same natal day – birthday. I was called in her honour. We were, Mama assures me, born only two hours apart.'

'Are you Roman?' Clementina had to ask it, even though it was as wrong to enquire about a person's religion as it was to ask the extent of their bank balance. 'A Catholic?' Well – all that crossing themselves . . .

'I am Orthodox – *Russian* Orthodox . . .'

'And is that Christian?' Clementina sensed difficulties.

'Yes, of course!' She laughed with delight. 'We are as devoutly Christian as the English, only we worship a little differently.'

'Aaah.' Clementina's relief was heartfelt. 'You mentioned *Vassily* and Igor. I thought –'

'Vassily *is* Basil. I forget we speak only English, now, by command of Mama, though today they talk away in our own tongue – twenty to the dozen, is it you say?'

'Then today is a saint's day?'

'No. Far, far better. Last evening my brother returned safely to England and we all laughed and cried and hugged and kissed. Mama is so *happy*.'

'He's back? Then be sure to tell the countess how very glad I am.'

'I think you may tell her yourself. She intends to call on you tomorrow or the next day, she said, and give you her good news. You will not spoil it for her? You will be suitably surprised – yes?'

'Not one word will I breathe,' she beamed, happy beyond words. 'And when she calls, might I hope you will be with her?'

'I shall visit, I thank you. Now, you see, I am permitted to take off my black clothes, though Mama still wears her mourning – for Vassily and Papa, of course . . .'

'I shall look forward to your coming. Is your brother well? Were things bad for him, in St Petersburg – oh, your mother told me about it, never fear,' she hastened to add.

'He came back safely – and successfully – though doubtless you will hear of it, soon. But Igor is safe, now, and we will try to start living again!'

'Of course you will! And you, my dear – you'll be getting married?' Clementina hesitated. 'When the countess is out of mourning, that is . . .'

'I fear not.' All at once, the dark eyes were sad. 'My marriage money, now, is much diminished – and besides, no one has spoken for me though Mama says I am old enough.'

'And how old would that be?'

'Nineteen – soon . . .'

'Then you must hope. You are very beautiful and that will more than compensate for your dowry. The solution is simple. You must insist upon a wealthy husband! Forgive me, I beg you, for saying so on such a short acquaintance.' A husband like Elliot, perhaps? All at once, Clementina decided that no other but Anna Petrovska would do. She was the answer to all her prayers. The girl had beauty and breeding and was not so well-heeled, it would seem, that she could afford to be over choosy. And she, Clementina, had the brass. She had a money tree grown tall and thick from a seed planted by Mary Anne Pendennis! 'And I do so hope I may have the pleasure of receiving you, very soon.'

Clementina knew when to end a conversation. She smiled a goodbye, stumbling in her eagerness to get to the telephone and call Pendenys Place.

'Edward!' she gasped when finally her husband lifted the phone. 'Tomorrow! I won't be home! I must stay here a few more days!'

'What is it, Clemmy? You sound quite upset. Has something happened?'

'Happened? *Everything* has happened! Oh, I do believe things are working out, at last!'

'Are you all right?' *Working out?* What bee had she got in her bonnet, now?

'I am perfectly all right! Will you tell Elliot to telephone me back – *at once*!'

'I'm afraid he's in York – a visit to his tailor.'

'*Damn*! Well, the very minute he gets back, tell him to get himself down here! Train or motor – I don't care which. But I want him at Cheyne Walk by ten in the morning – and no prevaricating!'

'But what if he has other plans?'

'Then he'd best cancel them. And if he starts making excuses, just say, "*Allowance*" to him! Now don't forget, Edward. Ten o'clock tomorrow! Perhaps it's best he should get the overnight train. Either way, I want him here!'

Edward Sutton was given time to ask no more; the click

of the receiver put paid to that. But no matter, he shrugged. He would telephone again tonight when hopefully his wife was calmer.

He reached for the bell-pull. Best order his son's packing to be done, for Elliot would do as his mother ordered. Any mention of his allowance usually carried the veiled threat of cancellation and commanded instant obedience. It was the only thing, Edward considered with relish, that could bring his wayward firstborn to heel — apart from a good thrashing, that was, and no one yet had dared to give him that. Only the gamekeeper, and that hadn't been half hard enough, he thought with regret.

He turned his thoughts to his wife. What in heaven's name was she up to, now?

Tom Dwerryhouse walked the game covers, his dogs at his heels. He had schooled them from brash, bouncy pups to obedient retrievers. They were a fine pair; would work well when the shooting began in October. Until then, it pleased him to see the covers so well stocked with game. This year, Mr Hillier would have the shooting he so looked forward to.

He was a decent employer, Tom conceded, understanding that the keeper had yet to be born who could conjure up instant sport when an estate had been left to neglect over the war years and everything that ran or flew taken by the soldiers to eke out their rations.

He'd had to start from scratch, yet now he had good reason to be satisfied with the young birds in his rearing field. Plump and fine-feathered, they would be turned out before so very much longer to join last year's rearings.

He squared his shoulders, lifted his chin with pride. Before so very much longer, Windrush shoots would be the talk of the county — he would see to that — and it made him wonder if now wouldn't be the best time to bring up the matter of an assistant. Soon, the night patrols must start. With the coming of earlier darkness the poachers would be out. Not, Tom accepted, that the one-for-the-pot man was all that much of a nuisance. That kind of poacher took one or two birds only, easily hidden beneath his coat, his need to feed his family far outweighing the risk of being caught and brought before the Magistrates.

It was the organized gangs from the towns a keeper feared; those who took birds by the score. That, Tom said, was greed and not need and the time was not far distant when he would have to talk to Mr Hillier about taking on another man.

He grinned, suddenly, remembering Daisy and the smile she had given him that morning. Her very first smile, and for him! Not wind, Alice assured him solemnly, and before so very much longer they would hear her first chuckle, she had promised.

He was a lucky man. The country was plagued with the Irish troubles, with unemployment and the workhouses full of decent men, tramping the roads begging, almost, for a job; any job. And where were the homes for heroes those fighting men had been promised, once the war was over? What wouldn't so many of them give for a house such as his? He shivered. Someone had just trailed an icicle the length of his backbone – or was it that someone had just walked over his grave?

It was neither. It was a feeling of sudden alertness; the scent of danger primitive man must have known. It had served Tom well on those forays into No Man's Land and he had obeyed it without question. He spun round, aiming his shotgun at the bush.

'Come out. Come out slow . . .' he hissed.

There was a rustling and a voice said, 'All right, mister.' Two hands appeared in a gesture of surrender, then a face; white, thin, full of fear.

'Out here . . .' Tom took a few steps backward. The man straightened himself.

'Don't shoot, sir?'

'I won't. It isn't loaded.' Tom lowered his gun. He didn't need to threaten. He could take the man with one hand behind his back. Skin and bone, he was. 'After game, were you? This is private land!'

'Not birds, sir. Had a couple of snares down, for a rabbit . . .'

'Got bairns, have you?' Poor devil. A square meal – one like Alice cooked – would send his stomach into cramps, by the look of him.

'One little lad. At home, with the wife.'

'And where is home?'

'Near Camborne – Cornwall. She's with her mother. Had to leave her there. No work, see.'

'So you're tramping – looking for a job?'

'That's it. But who'll employ a man with a badly foot? I was a keeper myself before the war, but who wants a lame keeper? You should know the walking that's got to be done.'

Tom knew – especially now. He'd been wondering about another keeper, he thought wryly, and one had popped out of the bushes in front of him, though one who'd be little use to anybody!

'I know,' he said. 'And what's to do with you, then?'

'Wounded in the war. My foot. Two toes gone. Makes it awkward, when it comes to walking.'

'Then how come you're damn-near starving? What about your pension? The Army gives pensions to badly wounded men.'

'Pension? You don't get one of them when it was your own doing – or so they said!'

'And did you? Did you shoot yourself?' It hadn't been uncommon. Driven to desperation, some soldiers had put a round into their own foot; an easy way out of the Army – a ticket to civvy street.

'Did I hell! We went over the top, one night. I tripped

and my rifle went off. Did you ever know what it was like, out there in No Man's Land?'

'I knew,' Tom said grimly. 'I was a marksman.'

'And so was I. Like I told you, I was a keeper, and I know how to shoot, mister. If I'd had a go at my own foot I'd have made a tidier job of it than that!' He stuck out his right boot. The front of it had been hacked away to accommodate the distortion of flesh and bone. 'So they wouldn't give me a pension. Told me I was lucky I wasn't being put on a charge with a firing squad at the end of it.

'My wife goes out scrubbing. She goes without so the boy can eat. If I had a loaded gun now, it wouldn't be my foot I'd aim it at!'

'That's enough!' Tom rapped. 'You're alive, man! Think back to how it was, and be grateful. There's many a one who'd be glad to be as hungry and alive as you!'

'Aye. Then more's the pity I wasn't one of them,' he said without self-pity. 'I'd be a hero, now, with a tidy grave-stone to show for it – and my Polly with a widow's pension.'

'Sit you down, man. You don't have to make excuses to me. How bad is that foot? In pain, are you?'

'Sometimes. It's my balance, though. I have to walk on my heel. Bairns make fun of me and you don't get any help – not a penny parish relief – when your discharge papers say you shot yourself in the foot. A coward, that makes me, and I'll swear on my son's life it was an accident.'

'How old is he?' Tom was still remembering Daisy's smile.

'Just gone three, though I haven't seen him for six months. Don't know how it is with him and Polly – no fixed address, as they say, for them to write to. But you believe me, don't you, sir?'

'I believe you.' He did – and besides, what right did a deserter have to stand in judgement on any man? 'But you're a long way from your wife and child – how come you ended up here? You'll not find work in these parts, either.'

'Maybe not. But I was billeted here, in the war, for six months. All of the summer of 'fifteen. A grand time it was, and the war something that was happening to the other poor sods – not to me.

'The Army took over Windrush Hall as a billet. Polly was in service, then, 'bout two miles away. That was when I met her. When I knew I was going to the Front we got married and she went back home, to Cornwall. Her father was badly. She helped her mother to nurse him, though he died . . .

'But that time around these parts were the best months of my life. I knew this estate and the big house, too, like the back of my own hand. Can't blame me, I suppose, for making my way back.'

'No, though the army left a right old mess behind them when they moved out. Windrush had gone to rack and ruin and as for these woods – nothing but a wilderness and not a game bird in them. I came here about eighteen months ago; been trying to lick things into shape, ever since. Reckon we'll have some decent sport, though, come October.'

'Aye, sir. And you'll not turn me over to the constable? I'll be off your land as soon as maybe if you'll turn a blind eye to the snares.'

'Did you catch anything?'

'A rabbit. It's in the bush, yonder. I'd aimed to light a fire, tonight – cook it. That was one thing you learned in the army. You were never stuck fast to find a way to cook a rabbit.'

'Nor a chicken,' Tom grinned. 'But look over there.' He pointed to the church tower. 'Over to the right – that clump of oaks. There's a hut, beside them. You can kip there.'

It was a keeper's hut, usually to be found near the rearing field but moved away, now the chicks were grown, to the edge of the estate. On small, iron wheels with a tin roof, it was snug and dry with a stove inside it and a kettle and pan. A fine place for a keeper to shelter in on cold, wet nights when a poacher might be forgiven for thinking the weather was on his side.

'I know it – remember it from way back.'

'Then you'll know there's a little iron stove in there. Find yourself some dry wood, and light a fire. You can cook your rabbit on it. There's matches on the ledge over the door, and water in the beck, nearby.'

'How will I get in?' he demanded, eagerly.

'About twenty yards from the door you'll see some stones. The key is under the big one . . .'

'I'll find it – and I'll not take liberties. I'll leave it tidy.'

'You better had! And there's no hurry, for a couple of nights. If anyone finds you there, tell them Dwerryhouse said it's all right.'

'I will, and thank you, sir. God bless you, and yours.'

'Aaar. Be off with you,' Tom grated, embarrassed. 'And here – catch!' he called to the limping man, throwing his packet of sandwiches. 'Have these. You need them more than I do. And by the way – got a name, have you?'

'Purvis, sir. Dickon Purvis . . .'

Tom turned abruptly, striding angrily away. It should not have been like this – a decent man begging, his wife and bairn miles away. And when he'd see them again, only God knew. Nothing but skin and bone, poor devil. He'd never see another winter through, in his condition. What would become of his wife, then? And what about the little lad; what if it had been Tom Dwerryhouse with a badly foot and Alice and Daisy miles away and living on charity and Alice taking in sewing, like as not, to help ends meet?

'Come on!' he snapped at his dogs, though they had never left his heels all morning. 'Home!'

He took a deep, steadying breath. Alice would cut him more sandwiches and besides, he needed to see her, tell her about the man. Alice would listen, understand his anger, and happen Daisy would smile for him again.

And that lot had better not start another war! They'd never get him into a uniform again, if they did; not if they begged him on bended knees and offered him a cushy billet for the duration.

Then he stopped his rantings, and thought on. *They* would never get him. How could you call a man to the colours who'd been killed at a place called Epernay; wiped out with eleven others on a March morning, more than two years ago?

'Alice!' he called, breaking into a run. He needed to touch her, hold her, pour out his bitterness. At his garden gate, he paused. The big black, shiny pram stood there, with Morgan asleep beside it, head on paws. It would be all right. Alice would know what to say to ease his conscience.

She heard the snapping of the sneck as he opened the gate and came, smiling, to stand on the doorstep.

'Hullo, love,' she said softly and all at once his world was sane and safe again.

'Put the kettle on, lass, and make us a sandwich, eh?'

'But I cut you some, this morning. Didn't you think on to take them?'

'I did, love, only – oh, come on inside, and I'll tell you . . .'

'Well, now.' Julia checked that the compartment door was properly closed, then settled Drew beside the window. 'That wasn't as awful as you thought, now was it?'

'I wasn't entirely looking forward to it,' Helen admitted, 'but Mr Carver was very understanding, and the young one seems efficient enough, though he asked a lot of questions.'

'Officious, more like.' Julia had not liked Carver-the-young. His manner had been patronizing; he didn't like doing business with women, and it showed.

'Neither could see any difficulty. We might not even have to go to court, if everything works out as it should. And I suppose it's only right they should want to meet Alice and have a talk with her. After all, we might be domineering in-laws, bullying her into giving up her son.'

'Gracious, mother – they know we aren't like that! It will all go through smoothly.'

'I hope so. And do keep hold of Drew. He mustn't stand on the seat.'

'Sit down, you little horror!' Julia ordered. 'But you've got to admit he was very good at the solicitors,' she defended. 'We'll have a good run on the lawn before bed-time – tire him out,' she smiled.

'Play cricket,' he demanded, then turned his attention again to the window and the fields and animals slipping past it.

'He's a good little soul,' Julia smiled, fondly. 'He ought to have someone his own age to play with.'

'A sister, you mean? But he has one, and when Alice visits they'll have the time of their young lives.'

'But Alice will be with us quite soon – especially now that the Carvers want to see her. Daisy will hardly be big enough to have a rough and tumble with Drew.'

'Perhaps not just yet – but Alice will come to see us often, I hope. And when they are both old enough to understand, we shall tell them they are –' She left the sentence in mid-air.'

'We'll have to be careful,' Julia frowned. 'But the sooner they know, the better. It would be awful if they were never told, then fell in love.'

'Julia!' Helen laughed. 'That kind of thing only happens in storybooks – not in real life. And even if you and I were determined they should never know, there would be some busybody think it their duty to tell them.'

It was Helen's turn, now, to reassure her daughter. And soon, Drew would be theirs entirely and Alice would visit often. She had loved Alice deeply; would ever be grateful for Drew – for the little boy who laughed with delight as the engine driver let go three important hoots at the approaches to Holdenby station.

'He does so love trains. I suppose he'll want to drive an engine, when he grows up.'

'Most small boys do, mother. But Drew will grow up to care for Rowangarth and those who work for it – and Shillong, too. And to make a happy marriage, I hope, and have sons.'

'He isn't two, yet.' Helen put out a protective arm as the train began its slowing in a series of small jerks. 'And at nearly two, hardly anything is more important than a ride on a train. This has been a good day, hasn't it?' She looked for her handbag, gathered the parcels from the seat beside her. 'And there is Will, in the yard.'

Will, thought Julia; waiting with the carriage and pair. They really ought to have a motor. It was so unlike her mother to forbid one to her. Everyone had motors, these days. Why must Julia MacMalcolm not be permitted to drive?

'Come on, young Sutton!' She scooped Drew into her arms. 'Say goodbye to the train.' And why shouldn't she drive? Why, just because Pa had been killed in a driving accident, should motors be taboo at Rowangarth? 'And come and say hullo to the horses.'

Their homecoming was robbed of its usual pleasure. Immediately she saw the expression on the face of the housekeeper who waited at the top of the stone steps, Julia knew that something was wrong.

'Milady – this came, two hours ago. I took the liberty of ringing the solicitors, but they said you had left and didn't know which train you'd be coming back on.'

Julia held out her hand for the small, yellow envelope that could still send fear tearing through her, even though the war was long over. Tight-lipped, she ripped open the telegram.

'It's signed *Bossart*. That's the name of the farmer Aunt Sutton stays with. *Mlle Sutton injured. Please come with haste*. What's happened, mother?'

'Injured. A motor!'

'No. She rarely drove, in France. Doesn't like the wrong side of the road. Probably an accident horse-riding.'

'Then the best way to find out is to go at once. I can get the overnight train to London. With luck, I could be with her by tomorrow evening.' Helen frowned. Her fear was real, her distress obvious.

'Mother – first have a cup of tea, then we'll talk,' Julia soothed. 'Take a deep breath. It might not be as bad as it sounds. Perhaps Monsieur Bossart was being over-cautious.'

'I shall go tonight, for all that!'

'Then I shall come with you. Do you think we could take Drew?'

'Certainly not! You must stay here. Anne Lavinia would want you to.'

'Then let me at least see you safely onto the boat train?'

'Julia! I am not quite in my dotage. I'll manage. And let us hope you are right. Monsieur Bossart might be over-reacting. I can get the last train from Holdenby and still be in good time for the York sleeper to King's Cross. When we have had our tea, I want you to ring up York; make a reservation for me. I shall manage well enough but oh, poor Anne Lavinia.'

Aunt Sutton, to most. Her husband's sister, Helen thought sadly. Forthright, outspoken, unmarried. A woman who cared more for horses than for most human beings. Julia had always been her favourite; Julia, so like her aunt in many ways.

Poor, poor Aunt. Julia stirred her tea thoughtfully. She had visited her doctor when in London, but this appeared to be an accident, not an illness. She wished there was some way she could be with her.

'Mother – why don't I go to France, instead? You could take care of Drew, then.'

'No. I shall go.' Her voice was firm. 'John would wish it to be me who is with her – if it is serious, that is. And like you say, I think I shall find her not as ill as Monsieur implies. She'll be all right. She's a very strong-minded lady. Whatever it is, she'll pull through!'

'If that's what you want. I'll phone Reservations, then I'll ring Pendenys. They ought to be told, and mother – why doesn't Uncle Edward go with you? After all, he's her brother and more nearly related than you.'

'I agree. So stupid to forget such a thing. By all means he must come. But don't suggest it when you ring, Julia. If he feels he should be with me, he'll say so at once. Be tactful.

'And now I must ask Miss Clitherow to give me a hand with my case. Don't want to pack too much – travel as light as possible . . .'

God – let everything be all right? Julia lifted her eyes to the ceiling. *She's such an old love . . .* Picking up the phone, she asked the operator for York station.

6

'It's Mr Edward, milady,' Mary announced. 'With the motor.'

'At last!' Already, Helen was gathering up her cape and travelling bag, eager to be away. 'Now be sure to take good care of Drew, and yourself . . .'

'I'll be sure,' Julia soothed, following her mother to the door at which Edward Sutton waited. 'Don't worry about a thing. Just have a safe journey and give my best love to Aunt Sutton, when you get there.'

She was relieved her uncle was going to France – had offered to go at once, without being asked. Now she would worry less, even though her mother was capable of making the journey alone – a considerable achievement, come to think of it, when not so very long ago a lady wouldn't even have visited the shops alone.

'My dear!' Raising his hat, Edward Sutton kissed his sister-in-law's cheek. 'Tell me – are we going to arrive to a ticking-off, when we get there, for panicking? Shall we find it's nothing more than a broken arm?'

'No, uncle,' Julia said softly, firmly. 'I think Monsieur sent the telegram without aunt knowing. Had her injuries been slight she wouldn't have allowed it, be sure of that. You know what a tough lady she is!'

'Then the sooner we are there, the better!'

'Oh!' Helen's eyes lit, surprised, on the young man in the back of the car. 'Is Elliot coming, too?'

'Elliot is summoned to London,' Edward smiled wryly,

'though for the life of me I don't know why. Doubtless Clemmy has her reasons.'

'Doubtless.' Helen's relief showed in her expression, her voice. 'And I'm so grateful you'll be with me, Edward. The journey there I could have coped with; what I might find when I get there is altogether different. Have you told Clemmy?'

'I have. Sadly, she is not able to go with us. A previous engagement, I believe, though she would come at once should Anne Lavinia's condition warrant it.'

'Of course,' Julia murmured. And please God Aunt Sutton was sitting up and taking nourishment, when they arrived. 'Let me take your bag, mother, and get you settled in the motor. You'll be in York in good time for the sleeper. Good evening, Elliot,' she murmured, opening the door. 'I thought – just for a moment – that you too were going to France.'

'Sadly, Julia, I am needed at Cheyne Walk and one's own Mama –' he shrugged, his cousin's vinegar-tipped words washing over him.

'One's own Mama must be obeyed,' Julia nodded, eyes mocking. 'I do hope you find Aunt Clemmy in good spirits,' she added obliquely, stepping aside as the chauffeur closed the door. 'Take care, dearest,' she smiled. 'And try not to worry too much?'

She stood until the car was lost round the sweeping bend of the drive then turned sadly, shivering in spite of the warmth of the evening, wishing she were going with them.

Dearest Aunt Sutton, get well soon. I love you very, very much, you grumpy old love . . .

Walking quickly up the steps she bolted the door behind her, taking the stairs two at a time, eager to be with Drew, draw comfort from the love she felt for him. Drew, the natural son of Elliot who had lolled, bored, in the softly-cushioned car. Could he know that the child he had fathered so brutally lay asleep upstairs – a fine, Sutton-fair boy who would one day be master of Rowangarth?

Yet if Elliot knew — or even suspected — why had he kept a still tongue? Was he ashamed of what he had done, that early spring evening in France, or would he, one day in a future so distant that they would have all completely forgotten about it, claim Drew as his own?

She lifted her chin, setting her mouth tightly. He would not, could not claim Drew. Drew belonged to Rowangarth and there was nothing Elliot Sutton could do about it!

Gently, she touched the sleep-flushed cheek. Drew was hers, the child she and Andrew had never made together, and she would go to any lengths to keep him.

'Goodnight, little one,' she whispered — and why, oh *why*, should even the sight of her cousin evoke such revulsion inside her, make her wish, passionately, that he too had been killed. 'Any lengths at all, Drew, I promise you . . .'

Tom gave his best boots a final rub, then clasped on his leggings. To be summoned to Windrush at all was unusual; to be sent for in such haste at nine o'clock at night made him wonder what the blazes Mr Hillier was about.

But doubtless it was about a new gun his employer was eager to buy or some such matter that could well have waited until morning, truth known.

'Won't be long, love,' he smiled, kissing Alice's cheek. 'I'll be back to rock Daisy off, once you've fed her . . .'

'Come on in, Dwerryhouse and sit you down!' Ralph Hillier called as the footman closed the door behind him.

'Sir?' Tom frowned, unused to being invited to sit in his employer's presence.

'Sit down, man,' he ordered irritably. 'I'll not keep you. Just wanted a word about things in general — and maybe get to know what's going on in the hut at Six Oaks. I saw a light in it. Didn't go to investigate — that's your job. Was it you, in there? Didn't know you'd started night patrols, yet.'

'With respect, sir, if I'd been on the lookout for poachers, I'd not have lit the lamp in the hut,' Tom laughed. 'Don't go letting them know I'm around!'

'So you weren't out after poachers?'

'No, Mr Hillier, though if there were any about, I hope they saw that light – worry 'em a bit! Fact is, there's a roadster in the hut – a decent man to my way of thinking,' he hastened. 'Down on his luck and tramping in search of work – if tramp you can call it, with one foot injured bad.'

'War wounded, was he?' Ralph Hillier had not fought in the war; his lame leg had seen to that.

'Aye, though without a pension to help keep him. Seems the brasshats decided he'd done it deliberate and didn't deserve one.'

'And had he?'

'He said not, and I believed him. The man was once a keeper. If he'd wanted to work his ticket home, he'd have done a neater job on his foot, to my way of thinking.'

'So you said he could sleep in the hut?'

'Only for a couple of nights – cook the rabbit he'd taken. Thin as a rake – nothing of him – and a wife and bairn back home in Cornwall. I hope I did right.'

'You did, though you might have thought to mention it, first. Skin and bone, you said?' Ralph Hillier had a guilty conscience about the war. Not only had he not fought in it, he had made a lot of money from it, buying and selling army supplies. 'Hungry, was he?'

'Half starved, from the looks of him. I gave him my sandwiches to tide him over till he got the rabbit in the pot.'

'A job,' Ralph Hillier frowned, rising impatiently, standing back to the fire. 'There's no one going to employ a man that's lame, now is there?'

'There isn't, sir – unless it's a gentleman with a bit of compassion in him, like.'

'Now what kind of job could I give him, Dwerryhouse? Cleaning shoes? Running errands? Dammit – that wasn't the right thing to say, was it?'

'Yon' Purvis won't run anywhere again.'

'Purvis? You got his name, then?'

'I did. He was on my beat – it's my business to get it.'

'It is. And you'd say he was all right?'

'I don't know about him being all right, sir, but I believed what he told me about his wife and bairn and about the army cheating him out of a pension. But I'll move him on in the morning, if that's what you want.'

'I don't want it, and you know it!' Ralph Hillier snapped. 'If the man is genuine then it's my duty to do something for him. If I gave him a couple of pounds to help him on his way, d'you think he'd spend it in the nearest ale house?'

'That I can't say, though if you've got a pair of boots you've no need of, I think they'd serve him better. The ones he's wearing aren't a lot of use.'

'I see.' He gazed long into the fire before he said, 'And if you were me, Dwerryhouse, what would you want to do for him?'

'I'd want to set him and his family up in Willow End Cottage and give him a job as dog boy.'

There now, he'd said it. He looked down at the toes of his boots.

'You would, eh? But then, you're a crafty devil, aren't you, Dwerryhouse. In need of another keeper, aren't we? Is that what you're getting at?'

'No, sir. If I'm to speak truthfully, I can manage this estate nicely on my own – well, near as dammit. I could do with a hand, though – especially at rearing time. I'm not one for buying fancy feed for chicks; like to make my own. Someone to see to the dogs and mix the feed – help generally with the rearing – would suit me nicely. And him once being a keeper, he could school your dogs – keep 'em in form.'

'Ha! And how's that little girl of yours, eh?'

'She's grand, thank you kindly. Smiled, this morning, for the first time.'

'I see. And is that usual?'

'Alice says it is. Next thing, she'll be chuckling, I'm told,' Tom grinned, eager to talk about Daisy yet sad his suggestion had fallen on barren ground. 'I was doing a blackbird for her – you know, that *tock-tocking* they give out when they've been alarmed. It must have tickled her fancy.'

'A blackbird?' *Tock-tocking*, whatever that was? 'Willow End Cottage, did you say? But it's in a bad state, or so I'm told.'

'Don't you believe it, Mr Hillier. Nothing that a good scrub out and a lick of paint won't put right – and fires lit, regular, so it won't go damp.'

'Hmm.' Again the gazing into the fire. 'All right, then. I'll hold you responsible for his good behaviour since he'll come without references. He can have Willow End. Ten shillings a week as dog boy, all the fallen wood he can gather, and the usual rabbits. One month's trial, after which he can send for his family. Is that all right?'

'I'd say, sir, it's a fine and kindly gesture and he'll thank you for it. And Alice'll be glad, having another woman living within earshot, an' all – especially when I'm out nights watching the woods.'

'Right, then. You'd better tell him in the morning. And don't forget to let them know in the estate office!' Abruptly, he picked up his newspaper, the interview over. 'And not a penny more'n half a sovereign, remember!'

'Right you are, sir. I'll see myself out – and I reckon Purvis will do all right for Windrush.'

A bit of a come-down, Tom pondered, from keeper to dog boy, but ten shillings a week, a roof over his head and firewood and rabbits was more than a lot of men had, these days. And with luck there'd be a pair of boots thrown in, an' all!

Not a bad bloke, Mr Hillier — for an employer, that was. A bit abrupt in his speaking, but he'd pulled himself up from nothing, talk had it, and didn't have the easy way with words that real gentry were born with, Tom allowed.

He wished his father were alive, could tell him what had happened between him and Ralph Hillier. 'The job of keeper is yours, Dwerryhouse,' Mr Hillier had said. 'I owe your father a favour from a long way back, though you might not know it. If your references are all right, you can start at once.'

That had been two years ago, though what the favour, nor when, Tom had never discovered. Sufficient that a deserter should get a job so easily, he'd thought gratefully and left it at that.

He made quickly for home, and wondering what odds to offer that tomorrow didn't find Mr Hillier gazing into Daisy's pram, doing his best to make a sound like a blackbird alarmed, he grinned.

A secret man, his employer, and not given to outward emotions, yet a man with a kind heart beneath his waistcoat, and a man who remembered favours owed . . .

At King's Cross station, Elliot Sutton wished his aunt and father goodbye, then took a taxi to Cheyne Walk.

'I hope you'll find Aunt Sutton much improved.' He raised his hat, smiling charmingly at his aunt.

'I'll keep in touch with your mother,' Edward said briefly as his son drove away.

'Perhaps you should have looked in on Clemmy,' Helen frowned. 'Put her in the picture . . .'

'At seven in the morning?' Edward demanded. 'No, I'll leave it to Elliot to tell her, though he knows no more than I. And what's going on there and why Clemmy needs Elliot so urgently is beyond me. She has her reasons, I suppose, and I shall be told when the time is right.

'Now let's get ourselves onto the Dover train. We should have a smooth crossing. I'll send a telegram to Monsieur Bossart from Calais – let him know we're on our way.'

'You are a good man, Edward. I really shall be glad of your company and the sooner I see for myself that Anne Lavinia is all right, the better.'

'But you know I'm fond of her – she's my sister, after all. It's my duty to go to her, apart from the fact that I want to. So stop fretting, Helen. We should be there by early evening and till then, leave all the worrying to me.'

'I will indeed.' He was so like John; so good, so considerate. He didn't deserve Clemmy nor Elliot; a pity he'd had to follow the only road open to most second sons and marry where money lay. Clementina, the only child of a wealthy ironmaster, had proved to be his salvation, if salvation it could be called, and now Clemmy was richer than ever, her foundries having profited from the war. Sad that Edward could not have been as happy as she and John; a pity his firstborn had been so indulged by his mother.

'What are you worrying about now?' Edward cut in to her thoughts. 'You were frowning.'

'Oh, just – just hoping Clemmy won't worry too much,' she hastened, blushing.

'Clemmy will not worry at all. My wife is receiving a countess this morning and cannot possibly spare the time to worry about anything else. That Elliot's presence is needed there makes me think she has started her matchmaking again. She wants him married, you know.'

'Just like every mother,' Helen defended loyally. 'Now things seem to be getting back to normal after the war, I think Clemmy has every right to expect grandchildren.'

'She has one in America already, don't forget.'

'I mean an heir, for Pendenys. We have Drew – it's only

97

natural Clemmy should want to see things settled, too. Let's hope Elliot soon finds himself a wife.'

'You are too charitable, Helen. All I can hope is that the young lady, whoever she might be, comes with plenty of backbone. She'll need it, married to my son,' he murmured as a taxi drew up beside them. 'But let's see to Anne Lavinia first and leave Elliot's future in Clemmy's most capable hands.'

If anyone could get the better of his eldest son, it was his wife. Clemmy had the money; she it was who called the tune. And sooner or later, Elliot would dance to it.

'So, you've got yourself here at last! What kept you?'

'Mama!' Elliot bent to kiss his mother but she jerked her head away. 'I didn't think to – to –'

'To find me up so early? I'm up because there's a lot to do and only three servants to do it! The countess and Lady Anna are calling this morning, so shape yourself! I want you bathed and shaved and your linen changed as soon as maybe! Breakfast is in five minutes; the hairdresser is calling at nine. And a word to the wise, Elliot! The girl next door has taken my fancy, so behave yourself!'

'Mother, dear – you aren't playing Cupid again? You know, I really am capable of –'

'You are capable of *nothing*, boy! I've warned you and warned you. I want you settled down. I want grand-children!'

'But you have one already, in Kentucky.' He shifted uneasily, an eye on the staircase, and escape. His mother was in one of her or-else moods. Do as I say, *or else*! His allowance, that's what it would be. She had only stopped it once, but what an uncomfortable month it had been.

'The one in America doesn't count. I want a grandson from you, Elliot, and born in wedlock, an' all. Your Aunt Helen has one. Giles did his duty. Rowangarth has an heir.'

'Ah, yes – the sewing-maid . . .'

'*An heir*, Elliot, no matter by who! That grandchild of Helen's kept the title from Pendenys. Your father would have had it, but for him! Helen always lands on her feet!'

'As did the sewing-maid — or was it on her back?'

'That will *do*!' Clementina's cheeks blazed bright red. 'I'm not going to argue the toss with you. You've sown your wild oats from Leeds to Paris and back! Now either you find yourself a wife, *or else*!'

Or else no allowance; bills unpaid and no money for a wager, either! And this morning, he was forced to admit, his mother looked as if she meant it.

'Mother, dear — can we not go in to breakfast?' Did they have to talk about it in the hall in full hearing of below stairs, who would be shivering with delight at every syllable of it? 'Can't we have our chat over a cup of coffee? I understand perfectly your wish to see me married.' And I know how damn-awful it is to be without money and that you know that I know it, too.

He opened the dining-room door, jabbing the bell-push as he walked past it, pulling out his mother's chair.

'Married? You do? And you are willing to be nice to Lady Anna and the countess — just to please me? It's all I ask and you know you can charm the birds from the trees when you set your mind to it.'

'I will be nice to them.' The worst was over. She had had her say; now she would change to the surely-you-can-do-this-one-little-thing-for-me approach which was better than the dramatic '. . . and-in-my-own-house-too!' — followed by a fit of sobbing vapours. 'I promise you I'll be especially nice to your countess.'

'And to Lady Anna?'

'Her too, mother. And now can we eat like civilized people? Breakfast on the sleeper was untouchable. Oh, and father says he'll keep in touch about Aunt Sutton and that you are not to worry.'

'Ha! Can't see why he should go tearing off to France

at the drop of a hat! And why does Helen have to be poking her nose in? She's no more related to your aunt than I am! We are both sisters-in-law, so why was that telegram sent to her in the first place?'

'Why indeed?' Elliot comforted, glad they were on a different tack. 'But you can't be expected to drop everything, mother. You have a full social calendar . . .'

'Yes, I have.' She held out her coffee cup to be filled. 'And it's probably nothing worse than a cut finger! They are soft, those Suttons – not like my side; not like your Grandfather Elliot and the Pendennises . . .'

She stopped, horrified. This morning, when she was at home to a countess, the last person she must think about was her Cornish ancestress Mary Anne Pendennis!

She gazed across the table at her son; at the only Sutton who was Pendennis dark. All the rest were fair and grey-eyed; all but Elliot whom she loved all the more because of it.

'You are a great comfort to me,' she whispered. 'Only settle down with a respectable girl and you shall have anything you could ever want. That is *my* promise to *you*, so think on, Elliot . . .'

7

The Countess Petrovska arrived punctually, accompanied by her daughter and the servant in black. The servant pressed the bell-push, curtseyed deeply, then returned to the house next door, hands demurely clasped, eyes on her boots.

Clementina Sutton's door was opened at once by the footman who had waited there for five minutes, flexing his white-gloved hands. Fuss, fuss, fuss. You'd have thought the Queen and Princess Mary were visiting, not some women the Ruskies had flung out!

The footman bowed; Clementina appeared in the sitting-room doorway.

'My dear countess.' She offered a hand, fingers limp. 'And Lady Anna.'

Anna Petrovska smiled prettily, then bobbed the smallest of curtseys in deference to an elder.

'Countess — may I present Elliot, my son?'

Elliot bowed low over the offered hand, raised it almost to his lips, his eyes all the time on those of the countess. Then he turned his gaze to Anna, nodding, smiling, claiming her attention for a fleeting, intimate second.

He did it so beautifully, Clementina thought with pride. Money, that's what! Money paid for education and grand tours. It didn't buy breeding, but most other things came within its giving. So vast a sum spent on Elliot's upbringing had returned a good dividend. If only he had been born fair like all the other Suttons he would be perfect, she sighed.

'Please?' she gestured with a hand. 'I have rung for tea and coffee. Do sit down.'

Elliot hovered attentively, moving side tables a fraction nearer, offering a footstool, his eyes appraising Anna.

She was tall and slender. Her brown hair was thick and simply dressed. Remove the combs either side of her face and it would cascade almost to her waist.

Elliot Sutton liked long hair; deplored the newest short cuts women were taking to. Tresses and breasts were fast disappearing and both excited him.

Anna Petrovska had high, rounded breasts he could cup in each hand. Her eyes were demurely downcast, her lashes thick and long on her cheek.

She was undoubtedly a virgin. He liked taking virgins but this one he would first have to marry.

Now the servant in black – the one he had watched this morning from his bedroom window – was altogether another thing. Virginal, too, but servants were available. He had observed her closely, pegging sheets to dry; had never before seen so menial a task so gracefully performed. The servant's breasts were rounded and high, too; her waist was handspan small and her ankles, when glimpsed, had excited him.

He wondered if she spoke any English, but a kiss was a kiss in any language. Mind, he had promised his best behaviour, and there was the rub. If he was to impress the countess as his mother had so firmly demanded, perhaps it were best to place the servant out of bounds for the time being.

'My mother tells me,' he smiled at Anna, 'that you speak the most beautiful English almost all the time.'

'Except two days ago, when Igor came home,' she dimpled. 'Then we forget and we laugh and cry in Russian. Did you know, Mr Sutton, that it is possible even to weep, in Russian?'

'Your son is home, countess?' Clementina knew it already, but she wanted the entire story.

'He is, thanks be. And the boy did well.' Her eyes misted briefly, then she lifted her chin. 'Ah, you tell them, Anna. It still pains me to speak of it!'

'Igor was hurt?'

'No. All the time he was in Russia he was in danger, but never hurt,' Anna spoke slowly, softly. 'My mother is distressed about our houses – our homes. Igor was much put out, you see, to find so many people living in the Petersburg house. *Eighteen* –'

'All those people? They just walked in without a by-your-leave; took your house?' Clementina was genuinely shocked.

'They did. But not people – *families*! Mama was desolate when Igor told her. Our rooms shared out, two to a family. Igor had great difficulty getting in there – finding what we had left hidden . . .'

'Such a beautiful house.' The countess had recovered her composure. 'On the Embankment near the Admiralty – close to St Isaac's Cathedral, you know,' she confided as if her new-found acquaintance knew St Petersburg as intimately as she.

'Near the river?' Clementina faltered, grasping at the word embankment.

'Ah, yes. The Neva . . .' Briefly Anna's eyes showed sadness. 'Such a river. It freezes over in winter, then in the spring the ice begins to break. Such a noise it makes – to let us know winter has gone.'

'You will return, one day,' Clementina comforted, 'to take back what is rightfully yours.'

She made a mental picture of Pendenys Place, that monument to her late father's riches; saw it packed to overflowing with people from the mean streets of Leeds and her butler, her pompous, plodding butler, pouring her best wines down his greedy throat.

'Tell me, dear lady, about your country house? Surely not there, too . . . ?'

She handed a cup to Elliot who placed it on the table at the countess's side.

'Peasants there, too. Families farming our estate as if it were their own. Igor had to work there, merely to find something we had hidden in a barn . . .

'There is much still there – I pray it will never be found – but my son returned with the important things – the title deeds to both properties, and our land. We had taken them from our vaults as a precaution and put them in safer places. One day, perhaps, Igor will be able to go back there and claim what is ours – *his*.'

'I would like to meet Igor. He did well. You must be very proud of him.'

'You shall, and I am, madam. He was also able to find the English sovereigns – gold, you know – and the American silver dollars. They were more than sufficient to buy him out of trouble and pay for his journey back to England. But he had to dress like a peasant and work and act like a peasant to do it.'

'Oh, dear.' Genuine dismay showed on Clementina's face. 'But so very brave,' she gushed.

'So brave. He has proved himself a man, and worthy to inherit his father's title – such as it is worth, now.'

'Igor,' whispered Anna, 'was also able to obtain the keys to safe deposits we have here in England. My father had left them with a trusted servant. And most important –'

'The Petrovsky diamonds,' the countess exulted. 'Without those we should have been lost, but now we shall not starve. And Anna's marriage dowry is secure.'

'So Lady Anna may now be – courted . . . ?' Clementina breathed.

'She is young; not yet nineteen. I would like to see her betrothed, though, by the time she is twenty. There is time,' she said comfortably, 'and we cannot yet be sure of which of our own young men have escaped the revolution. Many are scattered in Europe, now. But we can wait. Petrovskys do not put up their womenfolk as the English aristocracy does. Had we remained in St Petersburg, of course, Anna's marriage would already be a *fait accompli*. As it is –' she shrugged, expressively. '– we must wait a little . . .'

'I see.' Clementina was clearly disappointed. Lady Anna was not going to fall like a ripe plum into her eager hands. 'She will marry a fellow countryman, perhaps?'

'Not of necessity. So many of our young men died at the Eastern Front and later, fighting the Bolsheviks. Once, only a Russian husband would have been considered, and from Petersburg, too. But now –' Again the eloquent lifting of her shoulders.

'Oh, I do so understand.' In spite of the setback to her plans, Clementina put on a brave face. 'It is a parent's privilege to want only the best for their children. I have two sons yet unmarried, but like you, there is no hurry.'

He had, Elliot thought, as his eyes smiled secretly into Anna Petrovska's, to give full credit to his mother. Not by the flickering of an eyelid had she betrayed the frustration of her hopes. And since the girl seemed not to be in the marriage market, then the way was open, surely, for a liaison with the servant in black?

He stood at the door when they left, smiling with something akin to relief, bowing low, behaving himself to the very end.

'And that,' said his mother as the front door closed, 'was a wasted morning. I had great hopes of the girl next door – she is attractive, you must admit, Elliot.'

'Extremely attractive – but only for a fellow aristocrat, it would seem.'

'Oh, yes! That Igor found the loot they'd hidden. Keys to safe deposits – they probably knew that uprising was coming for years – got their money and jewels out before the war started, I shouldn't wonder. When the uprising came it was already safe. It's called hedging their bets and now they've got their hands on the family jewels, too, they're going to be a mite pernickety!

'Well, you're going to have to try just that little bit harder, Elliot, because I've set my heart on Anna Petrovska – or someone like her!'

'Did you have to say all those things, Mama?' Anna tearfully demanded when they were safely out of earshot. 'You know my dowry will not get me a Russian aristocrat and I wish you hadn't said I am not yet wanting a husband. Soon I shall be nineteen, then twenty, and too old! And I did so like Mr Elliot Sutton!'

'Then that is good, because Mrs Clementina is married into an old family and has a great deal of money – that, at least, I have discovered. And always, rich people in England want a title or two in the family. They are name-droppers, the English *nouveaux riches*, and the lady next door runs true to form. Indeed, she is too eager, too obvious. Does her son please you, Aleksandrina Petrovska?'

'I find him pleasant – and handsome.' Anna blushed deeply.

'Then you shall have him, daughter. Your mother will see to it that he doesn't escape. Only we must not appear too interested – give me time to consider what else is on the market.'

'But I am not on the market. I am drawn to Mr Sutton. He has such beautiful dark eyes.'

'He has the eyes of a gypsy, though what he looks like doesn't matter. What you must consider, child, is his inheritance, and when I have established what I believe to be true, then you may rely upon me to do what is best for you – as your dear papa would have wished, God rest him.'

In that moment, though she could not know it, Clementina Sutton's hopes for her son became fact, for Anna Petrovska had fallen deeply in love.

* * *

And that, Catchpole thought sadly as he firmed down the last of the six young rowan trees he had just planted, was his final job for her ladyship. Now, with the rowan trees safe in the earth, he could hand Rowangarth's lawns, flowerbeds, rearing houses and forcing frames to his son, a situation which pleased him enormously. For one thing, he would be able to keep a watching eye on his offspring, warning him of the likes and dislikes of trees and shrubs grown with loving care over the years, and for another, Rowangarth's walled garden, the most peaceful place on the face of God's earth to Percy Catchpole's way of thinking, would still be his to wander in when the mood was on him.

'There you are then, son. Alus – *alus* – make sure of the continuity. Rowan trees have grown here since that old house over yonder was built, and while they thrive, the Sutton line won't die out . . .'

Suttons had lived at Rowangarth since James Stuart succeeded to the Tudor throne and rowan trees planted at each aspect of the house had ensured its freedom from all things evil and especially from witches. Once, in every generation, new rowans were planted as an insurance.

'It very nearly did, though – die out, I mean.' That little lad had saved it in the nick of time. 'Both sons lost to the war – even Miss Julia's husband.'

They still called her Miss Julia, but then, she had been married for so short a time. Three years she had been a wife and her man in France, except for a few days together. So few days, you could count them on the fingers of two hands, Cook once told him.

'Nearly,' Catchpole nodded. 'There are things, though, that must survive.' Like the creamy flowers in the steamy orchid house; milady's orchids they were called. Once, no one could wear them, save herself. She had carried them in her wedding bouquet and Sir John had said thereafter that no one else but she should have them. 'There's yon' special orchids – her ladyship's own. But you know all about them, lad. Alus watch them and let me know if those plants ever show signs of distress . . .'

'I will, dad.' Young Catchpole had served his time at Pendenys Place and been glad to see the back of it, truth known. The Pendenys Suttons weren't real gentry – apart from Mr Edward who'd been born at Rowangarth. That Mrs Clementina paid starvation wages, now, on account of there being so few jobs and too many wanting them, was a known fact. That woman would be an ironmaster's daughter till the day she died. 'You can leave it all to me – though be sure there'll be a lot I shall ask you.'

'Aar.' Mollified, he made for the kitchen garden and the seat set against the south-facing wall where he had smoked many a contented pipe. 'Just one last look around, then it's yours, lad. You'm working for decent folk, now, and never you forget it.'

Mary Strong looked at her wristwatch, tutting that Will Stubbs was late again. She had been able to buy that watch and many more things besides, from the money she had saved in the war. Good money she had earned in the munitions factory in Leeds. Fifty shillings a week – sometimes more – though every penny of it deserved on account of the peculiar yellow colour they'd all gone, because of the stuff they'd filled the shell cases with. But she was a *canary* no longer, and back at Rowangarth, taking up her position as parlourmaid again as if that war had never been, though heaven only knew it had!

Gone, now, were Rowangarth's great days; the luncheon parties and dinners and shooting weekends in the autumn and winter. Just her ladyship left and Miss Julia and that little lad Drew – Sir Andrew – to care for. Tilda, once a kitchenmaid and promoted to housemaid, and Cook and herself; that was all the house staff that was needed, now. And Miss Clitherow, of course; straight-backed as ever, ruling her diminished empire as if Sir John were about to roar up the drive in his latest motor, and Master Robert and Master Giles roaming the fields with young Nathan, from Pendenys. And Miss Julia a tomboy from the minute she'd learned to walk, Cook said.

Mary sniffed and dabbed an escaping tear. Things would never be the same; the war had seen to that – taken all the straight and decent young men and sent back men old before their time and unwilling ever again to speak of France. And they had been the lucky ones . . .

'There you are,' she snapped as her young man appeared from behind the stable block, face red with running. 'I swear you do it on purpose, Will Stubbs! One night you'll come here to find me gone!'

'Sorry, lass. Young lad from the GPO got himself lost round the back of the house – a telegram for Miss Julia. Had to sort him out.' Telegrams were always delivered to the front door, parcels to the back.

'A telegram?' Mary forgot her pique. 'From France, was it?'

'Now how would I know? I didn't ask and if I had, he wouldn't have told me. So say you're sorry for being narky and give us a kiss, like a good lass.'

Julia MacMalcolm had learned to dread the small, yellow envelopes since the day, almost, she had fallen in love. They had rarely brought happiness; rather disappointments and death in their terse, cruel words. That day in France they had been laughing with disbelief and weeping tears of pure joy; even dear, straight-laced Sister Carbolic had joined in their unbelieving happiness. The war was over! No more broken young bodies, blinding, killing. Their harsh hospital ward had shone with a million sunbeams, that November day. *Over*! Soon, she and Andrew would be together and nothing and no one would part them again.

Then the telegram came in its small, yellow envelope.

Andrew dead, six days before the Armistice. She didn't just dread telegrams. She hated them.

'Probably good news, from France,' Miss Clitherow had smiled, though her eyes were anxious.

'Of course.' It would have been kinder, could her mother have phoned. One day, people said, it would be as easy to telephone from France as it was to ring up the grocer – but until then . . .

She slit open the envelope. She should have known, she supposed. And hadn't she expected it?

Aunt Sutton passed peacefully away. Returning immediately. It was signed *Sutton.*

'*No!*' Julia handed over the telegram. 'Read it . . .'

'I'm sorry. So very sorry. What can I do – say – to help?'

'Nothing, Miss Clitherow.' From which Sutton had the telegram come? Which – or both? – was returning immediately, and when? What was she to do?

'What will happen, Miss Clitherow? Surely they'll bring her home to Rowangarth?' Tears spilled from her eyes and she shook her head in bewilderment. 'And did they get there in time, I wonder.'

'The telegram was sent a little after noon; see – the time on it . . .'

'Then they would be there, with her?'

'Be sure they would, Miss Julia. Now let me ring for tea for you and then, perhaps, it might be wise to telephone Pendenys.'

'No. Uncle Edward is in France, remember, and Aunt Clemmy and Elliot are in London. We'll have to wait – stay by the phone; they'll ring, once they get to Dover. And no tea, thanks.' She strode to the dining room, pouring a measure of brandy, drinking it at a gulp, pulling in her breath as it hit her throat.

Rowangarth was plagued. First Pa, then the war and now Aunt Sutton – accidentally, and before her time.

She slammed down the glass, running, stumbling up the

stairs to the little room where Drew lay asleep. Drew was all right. She drew in a shuddering breath. What was there to do, now, but wait? *Andrew, I need you so . . .*

She closed the door quietly, trying to ignore the ringing of the doorbell. Let Tilda cope with it. She wanted no more bad news, no intrusions into her sudden grief. She wanted to weep, to cry out her sorrow – but in whose arms?

She walked slowly, reluctantly, down the stairs, then ran into the welcoming, waiting arms she had so longed for.

'Nathan! How I need you!' Her cousin, thinner than ever, his skin bronzed by the African sun.

'Tears, Julia? What is it, old love?'

'Oh, my dear! You just home and to such sadness.' She hugged the young priest to her, giddy with relief. 'But you are always around, somehow, when I need you. Come inside, won't you?' She pushed the crumpled telegram into his hands, then placed a hand over her mouth. 'Sorry. Brandy. I needed it . . .'

'Always around? But I came because when I got home they told me Pa was in France and Elliot and mother in London. Thought I'd come here, and find out what's going on.'

'Read it, Nathan.'

'I'm sorry.' He reached out, gathering her to him again. 'I know how deeply you cared for Aunt. Is that why Pa is in France?'

'Yes, and mother, too. Injured, the telegram said. They went at once.'

'All right, love. Let it come.' He had taken it calmly, but a priest must soon learn to cope with grief. 'Then tell me, uh?'

'There's nothing to tell. Monsieur Bossart sent the telegram; Mother and Uncle Edward would get there late last night. I was waiting – for *good* news.'

'You're cold, shaking. Come and sit down. I'll put a match to the fire.'

'Don't go, Nathan? Stay with me? I can't cope with this. Stay at Rowangarth, tonight?'

'Of course I will. Not a lot of use being at home, come to think of it; no one there. I'll just nip back to Pendenys and pick up a few odds and ends. Won't be long. We'll have a pot of tea when I get back. Chin up, Julia?'

Gently he kissed her forehead. Always there when she needed him? And he always would be, just as he would always love her, though please God she would never know.

'Only be a few minutes,' he smiled. 'And then I hope to meet my godson. He's well?'

'Drew's fine – *wonderful* – walking and talking. But hurry back, Nathan – please?'

8

Exactly on time the train from King's Cross to Edinburgh pulled into York station and Julia wished she could have brought Drew to see the thundering green monster that hauled it. But her mother was returning from France and it was not a day for watching trains.

'Dearest!' Julia saw her at once; saw sorrow in her face, the sorrow they all felt.

'Oh, my dear! Awful. So awful.'

'Hush, now.' Julia took her hand, holding it tightly. 'The Holdenby train is already in. Let's get ourselves settled.'

With luck they would find an empty compartment and her mother could pour out the heartbreak she had carried with her from the bedside of a dying woman.

'I spent last night in London,' Helen offered when they were seated on the train that would take them to the tiny, one-line station. 'I wanted to get back, but –' It had been her instinct to make like a small, bewildered animal for the safeness that was Rowangarth, but there had been things to do. 'I went to see Anne Lavinia's solicitors, you see – and her doctor. Only when I told him she had died, would he tell me.'

'I know Aunt had seen him last time she was in London, but she made nothing of it.'

'Well, it *wasn't* nothing. She had a serious heart condition; she shouldn't have been riding that great strong horse. Probably that was why she took a tumble. She didn't regain consciousness – died not long after we got there.'

'She went the way she'd have wanted to.' Julia's mouth

was tight with hurt. 'Will it be in France?' She couldn't say the word; not burial.

'No. We want to bring her home. She was born at Rowangarth and your Uncle Edward and I want her in the Sutton plot. She'll be near your Pa. When all the French formalities have been seen to, Edward will come home with – with her.'

'When?' The train began to move. Julia looked out to see the Minster towers, blinking her eyes against tears.

'A week today, I think it will be. I'll have to see the vicar. Sad that it couldn't be Luke to do it.'

Luke Parkin had a kindly way at burials; gentle-voiced, so those who stood at Holdenby gravesides drew comfort from his compassion. Poor Luke.

'Mother – I don't want *that* vicar!' Not the locum; Luke Parkin's stand-in, Julia called him derisively. 'Nathan is home – why can't he read the service? There's nothing in canon law, surely, that says he can't?'

'Oh, but I'd like that. Your aunt would have, too. I phoned Cheyne Walk, by the way. Clemmy and Elliot will come back to Pendenys, of course, when I can give them a date.'

'Of course.' Julia didn't want Elliot at the funeral; not standing there, imitating sorrow. And why should he be alive and Andrew dead? 'Try not to be upset, mother. You know how Aunt Sutton loved horses . . .'

'Yes, I do. Her solicitor holds her Will, by the way. He wants to see you, Julia.'

'Yes – but not yet.' That she was her aunt's sole bene-ficiary had not slipped her mind, though now it seemed less important than on the day she had learned of it. Just a few days after their wedding, it had been. She and Andrew hadn't had a honeymoon – not the usual one, because of the war – but 53A, Little Britain had been an enchanted place. Andrew's cheap lodgings near St Bartholomew's church had seen their first, fierce loving. She still paid the rent on those rooms; couldn't bear to let them go. Now, she had two London addresses and decisions would have to be made.

'Try to make it soon, dear. He said things had best be settled quickly. He's putting her death in *The Times* obituary – save me the trouble, he said.'

'He'll charge for it, you know.'

'Doubtless he will but oh!' Helen covered her face with her hands. 'It seems that life is slipping away from me. Everyone I love, leaving me one by one.'

'But there's me, and Drew. We won't leave you.' Julia smiled as the train hooted three times as it always did when it neared the bend, half a mile from Holdenby station. 'And we are almost home, now.' Soon they would be back within the shelter of Rowangarth's dear, safe walls and things would not seem so bad. 'Chin up, dearest.'

Alice waited in the village shop that was also a Post Office and telephone exchange, glancing up at the clock almost every minute, wondering what could be so important. Julia's last letter had told her of Aunt Sutton's death. Dear Aunt Sutton; such a fine lady. Indestructible, somehow. Alice had never linked her with death.

> . . . I know how much you cared for her and I have ordered flowers for you, Alice. I will write a card, with your name on it. But there is something, more important, and I need you with me.
>
> Is it possible Tom will allow you to come to London? I'll telephone, and explain. Can you be at your Post Office at eleven, on Wednesday morning . . .

So now she waited, one eye on the clock, glancing all the while through the window at Daisy's pram.

Julia had always been dramatic, always spoke before she thought. Marriage and widowhood hadn't changed her.

To her, everything was larger than life; her lows abysmally low; her highs acted out on a pretty pink cloud.

Alice had passed the letter to Tom who said of course she must go. Daisy would be no trouble, her being on breast milk and sleeping most of the time, though he'd heard London water was dirty, and best boiled – especially if a baby was to drink it.

'It seems that Julia needs you urgent and a few days away will make a change from the quiet, here,' he'd smiled. 'Though by the time you get back, there'll be someone in Willow End . . .'

'It's here, Mrs Dwerryhouse,' called the postmistress from the switchboard at the back of the shop. 'Just lift the phone, my dear. You're through, caller,' she said most professionally, then went to stand at the counter to let it be known she wasn't listening in. And anyway, she'd be content with Alice's half of the conversation.

'Julia? What's the matter? You've got me worried.'

'Sorry, love. Didn't mean to. But I'm coming to London. It's Aunt's funeral on Friday and I plan to travel down on Saturday. I'm her executor, you see – me and her solicitor. I'm seeing him on Monday. But could you come down, some time after that – I'd meet you at the station. Daisy will be all right. I'll get hold of a pram and cot, for her. We'll stay at Aunt Sutton's. There'll be plenty of room – but *please* come?'

'Julia! Calm down! What's so awful about seeing a solicitor that you want me there? What's really the bother?'

'Little Britain, if you must know. I've made up my mind to go there!'

'To Andrew's place? But you haven't been there since he –'

'No. Not since he died. You understand, Alice, so I want you with me. I'm not brave enough to go alone. Please tell Tom, so he'll understand. I'm sure he'd let you come if –'

'Oh, whisht! He's already said it'll be all right. I'll travel on Sunday, though. Tom has most Sundays off, so he can see me and Daisy onto the train. There'll be a couple of cases – nappies, and such like. But I'll come, Julia. When I know the train times, I'll write you. I'll send the letter to Aunt Sutton's – and yes, I *do* know the address! I've stayed there before, remember?'

'I know you have. That's why I need you with me. Bless you for coming – and say thank you to Tom, for me.'

'Goodness, mother, I didn't know a small boy needed so much paraphernalia!' Julia put her head round the sitting-room door. 'Be with you in a tick. Almost finished packing, then we'll have a sherry. I think I've earned one!'

'You could always leave him with me . . .'

'Thanks, dearest, but no. He's got to meet Daisy.' And more important, Alice.

The door closed with a bang. Her daughter had never learned, Helen thought, the smallest smile lifting the corners of her mouth, to enter and leave a room in a lady-like manner. Only she could hurtle into a room, setting it into chaos at once, or leave with a door-slamming that set ornaments dancing.

Thank you, God, for Julia and Drew, she had whispered inside her as she stood at her sister-in-law's grave. Had it not been for Nathan's kindness, she must surely have broken down and sobbed, and that would never have done. So she had listened instead to the gentle, sincere voice reading the burial service – so like Luke Parkin's, the poor dear man – and thought about anything save that Anne Lavinia was leaving them.

Another Sutton gone; one more from the good days, she had thought with pain; days that would never come back.

Things were changing. Now, young people danced all the time; an act of defiance, almost, to convince themselves that the fighting was over and never, ever, would they go to war again. So they laughed too loudly, some of them, and smoked too much and danced foxtrots and two-steps and lately, a dance called a Tango.

And young women cut their hair defiantly short and wore tight brassieres to flatten their breasts as if it were important they should look more like willowy boys than girls. Now, picture houses flourished, with two different films each week, even though there had never been such unemployment with mills and factories going bankrupt every day of the week.

Seaside outings seemed to have become essential and charabancs set out every Sunday morning as if everyone was frantic to live a little before people who should know better started another war.

I think, when the living is vacant, that Nathan should be our next parish priest. Helen directed her thoughts to the flower-covered coffin. *It would be splendid to have Nathan with us. He'd be such a good influence on Drew; Drew needs a man, Anne Lavinia – even you, who had little time for men in your life, must agree. Maybe, even, Nathan could give Drew his lessons. I don't want to send him away to school.* Not as they had sent Robert and Giles away. So many precious young years gone, but they hadn't known, she and John, that neither of their sons had so few years left to live.

I shall miss you, dear Anne Lavinia, but I will never forget you. Not John's sister. Two of them gone, now. Only Edward left, of the three of them.

She looked over to where Edward and Clementina stood. Clemmy was heavily veiled; always went too far, when it came to a public show of grief. Jaws clenched, Edward stared ahead. Remembering, was he; thinking back to the way it had been at Rowangarth, when they were all little?

Ashes to ashes, dust to dust. Helen had stooped, taking a handful of Holdenby earth.

Goodbye, Anne Lavinia Sutton . . .

*   *   *

Once the train had come to a standstill, Alice laid Daisy on the seat, reaching for her cases, placing them one by one on the station platform. Then she scooped up her daughter.

'We're here in London and oh, it's such a place you'd never believe it, Daisy Dwerryhouse!'

Carefully she stepped down, and then she saw them. Julia did not move nor take Alice into her arms, kiss her, say how glad she was to see her. Instead, her eyes spoke for her.

I'm sorry, they said. *I know it shouldn't have been this way, but try to understand?*

A small boy held her hand. He was sturdy and he was fair. His hair was carefully parted and looked as if it had recently been combed. He hopped from one foot to the other, excited by the noise and bustle.

'I had to bring him,' Julia whispered. 'I promised I would, next time I went on a train. And you've got to come to terms with the way it was.' She held out her arms for Daisy. 'Let me have her – show her to him?'

Bemused, Alice did as she asked, running her tongue round lips gone suddenly dry.

'Drew, darling,' Julia said softly, 'this is my dearest friend, Mrs Dwerryhouse and this –' she bent low so the small boy might see the child she held, '– is baby Daisy. Say hullo.'

'Hullo, baby,' he repeated obediently, then gazing up, he held out a small, gloved hand and whispered, 'Hullo, lady.'

Alice looked down at her son; at the child of rape she had wanted never to love, and saw only a small boy, not yet two years old; saw Julia's son.

'Hullo, Drew,' she said softly, bending down, cupping the small face in her hands. 'You are so like Giles, except that you have Andrew's eyes . . .'

The child pursed his mouth, frowning. Giles and Andrew were words he did not know and Mrs Dwerryhouse was a word too difficult to say. So instead he smiled brightly, pointing to the engine that still hissed steam and puffed coal smoke.

'Puffing train,' he said.

'*Nice* puffing train,' Alice nodded, kissing Julia warmly. 'It's all right, love. You've done well. He's grown into a fine little boy.'

'Let's get a taxi.' Julia closed her eyes briefly, relieved that the meeting of mother and son had gone better than she had dared hope, holding up a hand to call a porter. 'Soon be at Montepelier Mews. Sparrow knew where to lay hands on a pram and cot.'

'Sparrow? I'd forgotten . . .'

'But she's been looking after Andrew's place for me – you knew that. I sent her the key to Aunt's house – asked her to light fires, air the beds. She's there, now.' Emily Smith, who had cleaned for Andrew and devotedly washed and ironed his shirts. His cockney sparrow, he'd called her. 'I send her wages each month – surely you remember? She still talks about Andrew as if he'll soon walk through the door, back from Bart's, and asking how her rheumatics are. It's as if she wiped the war from her mind. Bless you for coming, Alice. It's going to make going back to Little Britain so much easier.'

'Do you have to go back?' Come to think of it, did she have to keep up the lease on Andrew's lodgings, act like Sparrow who tried not to admit he would never come home?

'Yes, I do, but I'll tell you about it when we get to Aunt's house.'

'Yours now, don't forget.'

'Not quite. Almost, though. Still a few things to be seen to before it's legally mine. And I haven't been in Hyde Park, yet. I was waiting for you . . .'

'Then we'll take the children there, tomorrow,' Alice said firmly. What was Julia up to? Why the urgency of this visit? She offered her hand to Drew. 'Come along, Drew. Take lady's hand.'

Her eyes smiled into Julia's. *It's all right*, they said. *At least my problem is solved – now let's get you sorted out, Julia MacMalcolm!*

Aunt Sutton's little mews house behind Montpelier Place had changed little, Alice thought, since she had stayed there that enchanted May, seven years ago. Then, she had been maid and chaperon to Julia Sutton, her employer's daughter, and never had she had such a time! It had been in nearby Hyde Park that Julia and Andrew met and –

'Sparrow! Here they are! Here are Mrs Dwerryhouse and Daisy.'

Alice shook her head, blinking away the past, smiling at the small, thin woman who bobbed a curtsey then said, 'Oh, the little love,' to Daisy, who was, for once, wide awake and gazing about her with blue-eyed alertness.

'Hullo. Am I to call you Sparrow, too?' Alice hesitated.

'Bless your life, mum, everybody else does! It was the doctor gave me the name and if it's good enough for him, then who's to say different? The kettle's on the boil, Mrs MacMalcolm. You'll both be wanting a drink of tea?'

Alice looked around her, remembering. The house was still pretty and white; white windows and doors, outside; white-painted woodwork inside, with white-painted furniture in a style popular at the turn of the century and Anne Lavinia Sutton had not thought to change. The house was full of greenery, then. Pots of ferns and trailing plants everywhere, though now there were none to be seen. Died from neglect, she supposed. 'The plants?' she ventured.

'Mm. I shall have to buy more. I want it to be just as it was when Aunt lived here. Sparrow will see to them. She's coming to live in, caretake the place – did I tell you?'

'You didn't – but it's time for Daisy to be fed. Can I go upstairs?'

'That you can, mum,' Sparrow smiled. 'The cot is made up and a warmer in it. And there's a comfy chair for you to sit in. Anything you want, just call out. Sparrow's here to take care of you all.'

'She's so pleased to be moving in here,' Julia murmured as she watched Daisy feeding contentedly. 'She's a widow; her son was killed in the war, too. She's only got the pound I send her each month for keeping an eye on 53A, and a few shillings a week pension. Hadn't much to live on, when her rent had been paid. She'll be a lot better off, when she lives here. Paradise, she says it will be.'

'And will she still look after Andrew's lodgings?'

'No. I – I'm going to let the place go. The lease expires at the end of the year. I won't renew it.'

'I see. I think you'll be doing the right thing, though it's going to hurt, isn't it?'

'It'll hurt like hell – as if I'm betraying him. That's why I want you with me. I'm not brave enough to do it alone. You were with me the night Andrew and I met. You are a part of us. I want you to be there when I say goodbye.'

'And I will be, though it won't be goodbye, Julia. Just an acceptance that he's gone. It won't be easy. I didn't want to let Tom go. And where is Drew?' she demanded, eager to talk about other things.

'Drew's fine. He's in the kitchen with Sparrow. He always finds someone to fuss over him. At Rowangarth he's got Cook wrapped round his little finger – now it's Sparrow. They've both got one thing in common – a cake tin filled with iced cherry buns.' Julia was smiling again. 'You do like him, Alice? Seeing him didn't upset you, like it used to – bring it all back?'

'No. I'm Alice Dwerryhouse, now. Drew is your little boy. And nothing that happened was his fault; I accept that, now. How is the adoption going?' she murmured.

'We-e-ll – I've been going to tell you about that. After a lot of thought – mostly by Carver-the-young – I think it won't be so much an adoption as a change of legal guardian. Young Carver says it's all that's necessary and won't be half so much fuss. Things are a bit behind, because of Aunt Sutton, but we'll keep you *au fait* with everything. You aren't going to change your mind?'

'You know I won't. Drew belongs at Rowangarth – it's as simple as that. And one day, when they are older, we'll tell them, won't we?'

'You and me both, Alice. One day . . .'

They took the motor bus to Newgate Street, walked up King Edward Street, then they were there, in Little Britain; in the street where Andrew's lodgings stood beside a shop that sold stationery and newspapers, a few yards from the gates of St Bartholomew's church.

53A, Little Britain. Julia looked at the windows, clean and shining, and the curtains; exactly the same curtains as when he had lived there.

'It isn't much of a street, is it?' Alice had need to break the bleak, brooding silence.

'No, but it was near the hospital and it was all he could afford. He was saving hard, you know, to buy his own practice. I told him I'd have money when I was twenty-one, but it made no difference, the stubborn man . . .'

'I remember the day you first came here. Oh, but you had me worried, Julia. There was I, supposed to be looking after you, see you came to no harm, and there you were, insisting on going out alone – and to a man's lodgings, an' all!'

'Things change, Alice. The war changed them,' she smiled, sadly. 'I remember how agitated you were when I told you I was going to call on Andrew. It wasn't right, you said. And what if his wife answered the door . . . ?'

'Yet you came back safe and sound and in love. I could see it in your eyes.'

'I told you it would be all right; said I wouldn't do anything unladylike. Word of a Sutton, I said. I was shaking, though. It was such a relief when it was he who opened the door. And I remember exactly what he said.'

'Tell me?'

'He opened the door. I couldn't speak, I was so ashamed at what I'd done. After all, I was running after him, wasn't I? Then he smiled. He smiled and he said, "My dear – I hoped you would come." And that was it, Alice. I knew there'd be no going back for either of us.'

'And there wasn't. Now unlock the door, love . . .'

The passage was dark and gloomy because all the doors leading off it had been closed. Julia stood still, listening, then tilting her chin she walked on, opening the kitchen door, standing again, waiting.

The room was clean, the table top scrubbed to whiteness. The cooking range was black and shining, a fire laid ready for a match.

'When we were married – next morning – I couldn't light that fire,' Julia murmured. 'I'd never cleaned out a grate nor laid a fire in my life. I was so angry, I wanted to weep. So we boiled a kettle on the gas ring and ate bread and jam for our breakfast.'

'And I'll bet he didn't care.'

'He didn't. We just left everything and went to Aunt Sutton's. She hadn't come to our wedding, you'll remember, so I wanted her to meet Andrew.

'She gave us an oil painting of Rowangarth – a very old one – for a present, then announced, calm as you like, that she'd just made a new Will and I was to get everything.'

'She liked Andrew, didn't she?' There was nothing for it, Alice knew, but to go along with Julia's heartache – let her get it out of her the best way she knew how.

'Mm. She said he had a look of Pa. Mother thought so, too. Mother adored him, right from the start.'

'We all did. He was a fine man.' Alice opened the parlour door and the same air of loneliness met them.

'We never sat in this room. Not ever,' Julia said, half to herself. 'We were only here three days and when we weren't out walking in London we were – well, we went to bed. Do you think that was awful?'

'Of course I don't, silly!'

'His surgery.' Julia turned her back on the parlour, gazing at the door opposite and the small brass plate bearing her husband's name. *Andrew MacMalcolm MD.*

Alice opened the door wide, then stood aside.

The desk was highly polished, everything on it arranged by Sparrow with care and precision. Medical books and journals stood tidily on a shelf; a sheet was draped over a skeleton, covering it completely. Sparrow had not liked that skeleton.

'I have all his instruments, at Rowangarth. I went to the field hospital after he was killed, took all his things away with me.'

'Yes. You told me that day you came home to Rowangarth. I'd almost gone my full time, with Drew.' Julia had come back from the war a sad, pale-faced wraith. There had been no comforting her, so desolate was she. It had taken the birth of a baby to wrench Julia MacMalcolm back to life. Drew had been her salvation.

'I'm not going upstairs today, Alice – I couldn't. Tomorrow, maybe. But I want to take the bed back to Rowangarth, and I want –' She lifted her chin, her eyes daring Alice to defy her. 'I want to take everything in his surgery back, too.'

'No reason why you shouldn't.' What was going through that tormented mind, now?

'No, Alice – you don't understand. The room next to the sewing-room at Rowangarth. Do you remember it?'

'Not particularly, 'cept it was full of old furniture and bits and pieces nobody wanted. No one used it.'

'Yes – but think! The window and the fireplace – the door, even . . .'

Alice shook her head, unspeaking.

'*Think*. Almost the same black iron fireplace with a window on the wall to the left of it. And the door opposite it. Just like this room. I could hang Andrew's curtains at the window. All his things, Alice – arranged just as they are here. I'd have his surgery at Rowangarth, don't you see?'

'No! Not his surgery! You'd be creating a shrine – hadn't you thought?'

'Yes, I'd thought. I thought about it even before we came here. It's the only way I can do it, Alice – give up these lodgings, I mean. Don't you see? I'm not being maudlin nor mawkish. I still love him every bit as much as the first day I came here. I'm going to do it, you know!'

'Then if you're set on it – what can I say?' Alice took her friend's hand, leading her to the door. 'Let's go, now? Before I go home, we'll see to it, together.' She closed the front door, locking it behind them. 'And I know what today is. It's his birthday, isn't it – the last day of August. He'd have been thirty-three . . .'

'Yes. That's why I wanted to come here, today. And bless you for remembering, love.'

'Did you think I'd forget those times – any of them?' She linked her arm in Julia's. 'Now let's get back. Between them, I'll bet those two bairns are driving poor Sparrow mad.'

'You're a dear person, Alice. I couldn't have gone there without you. You're still my sister, aren't you?'

'Still your sister,' Alice smiled. 'Come on. Let's get ourselves to the bus stop!'

'Talking of buses,' Julia murmured. 'Or talking of the nuisance of having to wait for buses when you've got a car, I mean –'

'No!' Shocked, Alice stood stock still. 'You don't intend buying one? What would your mother say? You know you can't keep a car at Rowangarth, so why think of getting one?'

'But I already have one. Aunt Sutton's. It's in her garage at the end of the Mews. She drove it all the time in London, remember. I shall drive it up to Holdenby.'

'Not with Drew beside you, you can't! It wouldn't be safe – not even if you tied him to the seat!'

'Not yet. And certainly not with Drew to distract me. But that car is mine now, and I intend using it, Alice!'

'There'll be trouble, Julia.'

'There will.' Her chin tilted defiantly. 'But Will Stubbs learned about motors in the army – he could look after it for me.'

'You've been determined all along, haven't you, to get your own motor?'

'Yes. And if Andrew had gone into general practice, he'd have needed one, so what could mother have done about that, will you tell me?'

'In your own home, it would have been different. But it isn't right you should take Miss Sutton's motor back to Rowangarth; not against her ladyship's wishes. Don't do it, Julia. It'll be nothing but trouble, I know it. Your mother is set against motors and you should try to understand her feelings.'

'And this is 1920, and I'll be twenty-seven, soon. I endured almost three years in France. I saw things that will stay to haunt me for the rest of my life. So now that I have my own motor, I *shall* drive it and there is nothing either mother or you can do about it!'

So Alice, who knew Julia almost as well as she knew herself, said, 'All right! Subject closed. But don't say I didn't warn you!'

'Elliot and I,' said Clementina Sutton firmly, 'will be going to London, shortly.'

'But you've just come back.' Edward laid aside his news-paper. 'Have you mentioned it to Elliot?'

'I've *told* him. We'd have still been there, if it hadn't been for Anne Lavinia.'

'Yes. Sad her funeral had to interrupt your stay! But why go back there so soon? Is something happening that I don't know about, Clemmy?'

'Happening? But that's just it – *nothing* is happening! And can I, just for once, have your attention, Edward, because this is important. It is time Elliot was wed!' she announced dramatically.

'I agree with you entirely. But who would have him?' The question slipped out without thought.

'*Have him*? His own father asks who'd have him! Why, there's half the aristocracy would have him, truth known! There's those with no brass and daughters they want off their hands, for a start. Plenty of that sort about. And there's young girls as'll never get a husband, what with the shortage of young men, these days.'

'Clemmy – *please*? So many families lost sons to the war. I beg you not to be so – so direct.'

'But it's a fact of life that it's a buyer's market when it comes to brides, so –'

'So you intend to *buy* a wife for Elliot? And have you anyone in mind?'

'I have, and you know it, Edward Sutton. There's a girl next door, at Cheyne Walk. A refugee, but well connected – well, in Russia, that was . . .'

'I see. And talking about Russia, there was a small piece in the paper – the Czar's brother Michael has been officially declared dead, now. Seems he was shot about the same time as the Czar – at a place called Perm. There's a son, it seems, who might still be alive.'

'So there's still a Romanov? The countess will be pleased.'

'Don't think the son will count, m'dear. Born out of wedlock.'

'Hm!' There'd be weeping and wailing again in the house

next door in Cheyne Walk, Clementina thought grimly. Weeping in Russian, hadn't Lady Anna said, and crossing themselves like Papists. A peculiar lot, really. It was a sad fact, Clemmy admitted, that she still might have to cast her net wider if those Petrovskys weren't on the breadline as she'd thought they would be. But go to London again she would, if only to sort it out, one way or the other. 'She's a lovely-looking girl,' she said absently, 'and well-bred enough for Elliot.'

'Then I'm pleased.' Anyone, Edward reflected, was good enough for his eldest son. It was a sad and deplorable fact. There wasn't a father worth his salt around these parts who would want his daughter married to Elliot – his past record had seen to that. 'And when will you leave?'

'Tomorrow. You'll be all right on your own.' It was more a statement than a question.

'Of course, my dear. And there is Nathan to keep me company, don't forget.' He opened his newspaper again, regretting that Nathan had not been their firstborn. But even if he had, Clemmy would have ruined him, just as she had spoiled and ruined Elliot. 'We'll have plenty to talk about. Just enjoy yourself, in London . . .'

And stay as long as you like – the pair of you!

'Well – home tomorrow, Alice; both of us. Have you had a good time?'

They were walking in Hyde Park; Julia pushing Daisy's pram, Drew with his hand in Alice's.

'It's been lovely.'

No. Nor all of it had been lovely, Alice thought sadly. Some of it had been awful, especially after the removal van left 53A, Andrew's furniture inside it and Julia standing there, her face ashen, unwilling to lock the front door for the last time. She had not spoken a word, all the way back to Aunt Sutton's house. Her face had been harsh with grief, just as it was that morning she had arrived at Rowangarth, wet and cold and half out of her mind with misery, just three weeks after the end of the war.

'What is he like, your aunt's solicitor?' It was all Alice could think of to say.

'He's nice. Far nicer than young Carver, and he doesn't dislike women – or if he does, he's careful not to let it show. We'll soon get things settled. Aunt made a watertight Will, so he's only waiting for something from France before it's all wrapped up.'

'And can you afford to keep the place going?' Alice demanded, ever practical.

'No trouble at all. Aunt left quite a bit of money. Carefully invested, there'll be income enough to take care of expenses. Mind, if I were to put it on the market, that house would fetch a pretty penny, or so Mark Townsend says.'

'That's his name?'

'Mm. He wants me to make a Will. I've never made one you know and I ought to if only for Drew's sake. Once Carvers have settled Drew's business, then I'll go back to London and get one drawn up, and witnessed.'

'Can't Rowangarth's solicitors do it? You said that the young Carver had his wits about him.'

'I know. But I don't like Carver-the-young. Oh, he's scrupulously honest, but there's something about him I don't like. His eyes are shifty, Alice. He never looks me in the eyes when he's talking to me. Andrew did. Always.'

'Andrew was different, and very special.'

They had come to the place, now; to where it had started all those years ago, near the Marble Arch gate. Emily Davison selling suffragette news-sheets for a penny and young women appearing out of nowhere it had seemed, eager to buy from her. And the police appearing out of nowhere, too, and that awful fight. Alice Hawthorn giving the big policeman an almighty shove from behind and him falling on top of Julia, knocking her unconscious.

That was when it happened. Julia had opened her eyes and fallen immediately in love with the young doctor who bent over her.

'Give me the pram. Drew and Daisy and me will walk back, slowly. You stay here, for a while?'

Call him back to you, Julia. Say goodbye then tell yourself he has gone. Remembering the good times will be easier if only you can accept that he isn't ever coming back.

'We'll wait for you at the bandstand. Take your time, love . . .'

9

'Tired, Alice love?'

'Mm. But happy.' It had been a long day and that last mile seemed so long in her eagerness to see Keeper's Cottage again. 'Being with Julia was grand. She's got herself sorted out – as much as she ever will, that is. She's had all the furniture from Andrew's surgery packed up and sent to Rowangarth, would you believe? Intends setting it out in one of the spare rooms – just as he had it. I didn't agree, but who am I to deny her a bit of comfort – me, who's so lucky. Oh, Tom, this little house is good to come to home to. So quiet, after London. No one here, but you and me.'

'And Daisy. And there's Willow End now, don't forget. Seems that Purvis is going to suit. Mr Hillier said I was to tell him to send for his wife, so we'll have a neighbour before so very much longer.'

'How soon?' It would be good to have someone near. 'I'll do a bake for her so she'll have something in the house to tide her over. And I'll put down extra bread and –'

'Stop your fussing, lass! When her and the lad arrive is going to depend on when her cousin is coming this way with an empty lorry. Seems he makes a trip twice a month to Southampton docks. Purvis says they haven't got much in the way of furniture, but it'll be a help, them getting moved here for nowt.'

'Poor things. Ten shillings isn't much of a wage.'

'Happen not, but it's riches to that man down the lane. And a house and firewood, remember. He's been living frugal since he moved in; sends most of his wage to his Polly. But for all that, he's come on a pace since I came across him in the woods.

'Having to beg strips a man of his dignity, Alice. To have a roof and a job makes a lot of difference to a man's pride – and a man that hasn't had a fair crack of the whip for a long time. His little lad is called Keth, by the way.'

'*Keth*?'

'Said his wife wanted something a bit different.'

'Then I hope Mrs Purvis isn't going to be different in her ways; not hoity-toity.'

'Don't think so. By what I've gleaned, she's a decent woman who'll be glad to be with her man again. Now give that little lass to me and I'll get her to sleep. I've missed her.' Missed them both more than he'd ever have thought. Each day had seemed endless. He'd been glad, truth known, just to see the lampglow from Willow End windows at night. 'Think Mr Hillier has missed our Daisy, an' all. Bet he'll be at the garden gate tomorrow, trying to get a smile out of her.'

'She smiled a lot while we were away, especially at Drew. He hardly left her side. Said he wanted to take her back with him.'

'I'm glad you've come to accept him, Alice. Nothing of what happened was the lad's fault. And you'll be going to Rowangarth before long, to get that legal business seen to. He'll see her again, then.'

'No sooner back home than I'm talking about going away again. I'm sorry, Tom. It has to be done, though it won't be yet, a while. Before the bad weather sets in, I'd like it to be – and I do want to see Reuben again.'

'And you shall, sweetheart.' Tom settled his daughter on his shoulder, setting the chair rocking. 'I don't begrudge you going. Rowangarth was good to us both and I'm not likely to forget it. And lass – have you anything more to tell me?'

'Aye,' she said softly, gentling his cheek with her finger-tips. 'I love you, Tom Dwerryhouse.'

And tonight she would sleep in his arms again . . .

'*Well*!' said Clementina Sutton, brandishing the letter. 'He's obviously read it, yet not so much as a word about this did your father utter, last night when I rang him. I asked him if there was any news and he said no, there wasn't. *Ooooh*!'

'What's happened now?' Elliot disliked dramatics at breakfast.

'You may well ask!' She handed over the letter. 'Read it! From Kentucky – from Amelia! Go on. Read it out loud!'

'*All* of it?'

'The second page. Half-way down. I don't believe it!'

Obediently, reluctantly, Elliot did as she commanded. Then his eyebrows flew upwards.

'*Another* baby? That's twice in – how long is it? How old is that boy of theirs?'

'Sebastian is about two and a half. And you're missing the point. My youngest son a father twice over in three years yet you, heir to all I've got, can't even get yourself down the aisle. Now do as you're bid, and read that letter! *Out loud*!

'Er . . .

and you'll all be glad to know that Albert and I expect a brother or sister for Bas in six weeks. We didn't announce it before this – things just might have gone wrong – but now I am safely seven months pregnant I feel I can uncross my fingers and give out our news. We are both delighted. We had intended visiting Pendenys Place as soon as it was safe to travel again, but decided against it for obvious reasons. However, when the babe is old enough we shall book passages and let you see your grandchildren at long last. It might be nice, Albert thinks, to have the new babe baptized in Yorkshire England by his Uncle Nathan, but it is early days, yet . . .

'Congratulations, Mama. You don't look old enough to be a grandmother twice over,' he smiled, knowing what was to come. 'I'd never have thought Amelia and Albert would have had children. Why did Albert imply she was too old?'

'Albert *didn't* say she was old, now that I think back on it. A *little* older, he said, which could be two or three years at the most. You should know. You stayed with them in Kentucky. You're the only one who has met Albert's wife. But it was you who put it around he'd wed a woman old enough to be his mother. Well, your trouble-making has come back to make a fool of you, my lad, because I'm not best pleased, I can tell you!'

'But Aunt Helen was delighted when she became a grandmother.'

'Your Aunt Helen –' She stopped, button-mouthed. *Looks years younger than me*, she had been going to say. 'Helen needed a boy for Rowangarth – and so the title shouldn't pass to us, at Pendenys,' she added, vinegar-voiced. 'And she got one, just in the nick of time. I'd bet it was more relief than delight! So relieved, she overlooked the fact that it had taken a servant to get that child for her!'

'Mama, dear – I know how much you want me married and now that the war is over, I agree entirely with you.' She was getting red spots high on her cheeks – a sure sign that a tirade of abuse was imminent. 'Find me a suitable wife and I'll go down on bended knee to her – I promise you.'

'You couldn't find one for yourself, I suppose? Too much trouble, is it? Albert got himself wed without help from anyone and so did your cousin Giles, so what's so special about you, my lad? Lose interest in a woman, do you, once you've had her in your bed?'

'Mother, I beg you!' Elliot dropped his knife with a clatter. 'You can be so – so *direct*!' And so common, when she was crossed. He'd been with prostitutes more refined than she. But it was all because of Mary Anne Pendennis. A woman who'd followed the herring boats from port to port, gutting fish, his great-grandmother had been. A fishwife. And when the season was over, she'd taken in washing which made her a washerwoman, too! And beneath his mother's ladylike exterior lurked a Cornish washerwoman who could curse like a fishwife when angered and not all her riches would ever breed it out of her. It was all a question of pedigree and there was no avoiding the fact that somewhere in his ancestry, a mongrel bitch had got over the wall!

'You'll get more'n *direct* if you don't shape yourself and get me a grandson; and get me one in wedlock, an' all! I want no more hedge children – do I make myself plain? I'm taking tea with the countess at the Ritz, tomorrow; intend getting to the bottom of it even if I have to ask her outright if her daughter is in the market for a husband. And if I get the answer I hope I'll get, then you'll start paying attention to Anna Petrovska – *or else*!'

'Or else what, Mama?' It was the nearest to defiance he was capable of.

'Or else you'll see how nasty I can be, son! On the other hand,' she lowered her voice to a soft coo, 'only give me a couple of grandsons and I'll turn my back on your goings-on, I swear I will. Now do you get the message – because if you aren't for me then you're against me – it's as simple as that. Think on, Elliot . . .'

Only two days after her return from London and before she could do the baking she had intended, Alice watched a large, green-painted lorry drive up Beck Lane and come to a stop outside Willow End Cottage. They had come, and Tom not even thinking to tell her!

Clucking with annoyance, she set the kettle to boil. At least she could make them a pot of tea though it would have been more neighbourly to have been able to offer something more substantial. She was slicing the currant loaf when the knock came at the back door.

'Hullo! Anyone at home?'

The woman who stood there was young, her thick, dark brown hair pulled into a severe knot in her neck. Her face was pale but her smile was wide and open.

'You'll pardon the intrusion.' She stepped into the kitchen, 'but in case you think we're tinkers and breaking in – well – I'm Polly Purvis. Come to live at Willow End, only my Dickon don't know we're arriving. Only knew myself, late last night when Sidney told me if I wanted a lift to Hampshire I'd better shift myself! Sidney's my cousin. He had an extra trip on if I was interested, he said, which was better'n waiting a fortnight to get here.'

'Goodness – what a rush . . .' So overwhelmed was she it was all Alice could think of to say.

'No rush at all, m'dear. Took no more'n half an hour to get our bits and pieces loaded. Most of what I started out with all sold, see? Had to be. But things'll be better, now. I shall like this place, I know it. You'll be Mrs Dwerryhouse?' She held out her hand, still smiling. 'And it's your husband I have to thank for all this – and thank him I will, when I've got things seen to! But best be off. Sidney can't wait. Got to be at the docks in less'n an hour . . .'

In a flurry of long black skirts she was gone, striding down the lane at almost a run.

'Well!' said Alice to the kettle on the hob. 'And what do you make of that!'

Friendly, though, and a countrywoman – that was plain

enough, for who but a countrywoman knocked on back doors then walked in, unasked?

Work-roughened hands she'd had. Alice had felt their sharpness against her own. Sleeves rolled up to the elbow; a long, flower-patterned pinafore tied at her waist. And such a smile! Dark, though. A bit of gypsy in her, somewhere. Maybe, like Jinny Dobb, she could read tea leaves, look into the future. But of one thing Alice was certain. Her new neighbour would not be difficult, as she had feared. Rather the opposite, she thought as she stirred the coals to hasten the kettle. Her new neighbour seemed outgoing and uncomplicated and one who wouldn't be opposed to a gossip over a cup of tea! She wished she had been better prepared; been able to do the bake she had intended offering in welcome. Now, she sighed, a pot of tea and a plate of currant bread would have to suffice.

The green lorry parped its horn as it passed her house. The new tenant at Willow End had spoken nothing but the truth; there had indeed been little to unload.

Alice walked carefully up the lane, teapot in one hand, plate in the other. The small boy sitting on the doorstep sucking his thumb got to his feet as she approached.

'Hullo,' she smiled. 'It's Keth, isn't it?'

The boy nodded, dark eyes gazing up into her own.

'And I'm Mrs Dwerryhouse. I live at Keeper's, down the lane.'

He was too thin, but there were a lot of too-thin children about, these days. Fatherless bairns, most of them, with mothers hard put to it to feed them on the pension the Army allowed.

'Well, if it isn't Mrs Dwerryhouse and carrying a pot of tea! Come you in, and welcome. You'm my first caller. Sit you down, m'dear!'

'I'm sorry. Can't stay. I've left my little one in her pram. I'd intended baking you a pie. As it is . . .' She placed the plate on the table, gazing around her.

The floor was bare. A table stood in the middle of the room with three chairs around it. Arranged beside the fire, already burning brightly, stood two rocking chairs and an upturned box with a cushion on it.

'A cup of tea would go down a treat – and is that curranty bread home-baked?'

'It is, though I've been away and my cake tins are empty.'

'Away, is it? Well, now that I've got here, it'll take more'n wild horses to drag me from this house. Beautiful, it is – and Dickon and me never setting eyes on each other for nigh on six months. When he finds us here and smells his dinner cooking, he'll be bowled over!'

'You've brought meat with you, Mrs Purvis?'

'No, but first thing I set eyes on was a rabbit hanging in the pantry. I'll soon get the skin off it and get it into the pot. I've brought potatoes and onions with me. It'll be such a surprise for him!'

'A lovely surprise, but I'll leave you to it. I'm going to the village. Is there anything I can get you when I'm there?'

'Thank you, but no. I've brought adequate with me, though it's kindly of you to ask. And tomorrow, when I've got myself straight, I hope I might return the compliment and entertain you to tea.'

Brought adequate? Alice frowned as she walked the lane that wound into West Welby, yet both of them thin as rakes, just like Dickon Purvis. But she would find a way to help them; do it without hurting their fierce pride. She, who had so much, whose little one was chubby-cheeked and whose husband walked straight-backed and true, would help the unfortunates who seemed to have so little. Not only was it her duty, but it would be in thanks for her blazing happiness. And she would favour especially the thumb-sucking Keth. A few mugs of milk, a few slices of dripping toast would work wonders for that pinched little face!

She raised her eyes to the clear September sky.

I'm so happy and I thank You with all my heart. And may it please You to let me keep it, God?

'Psst! Lady Anna!' Glancing at the house next door in case the formidable Cossack should appear, Elliot Sutton stood at the back garden wall hidden, he hoped, by a large flowering shrub. 'Good afternoon to you.'

'Why – Mr Sutton!' She pretended surprise. She had known he'd been watching her from an upstairs window and it did not disturb her to hear him call her name. 'Should we be talking like this?'

'I see no reason why not. We are neighbours; we have been introduced and anyway, it is more fun this way – secretly.'

'Yes, it is. And since our mothers are at this very moment discussing our future, then I think it perfectly correct for you and me to talk. After all, there is the thickness of the wall between us!' she smiled, impishly.

'Our future? I wouldn't say that, exactly!'

'You wouldn't, Mr Sutton? Then I have a half-crown in my pocket that says you are wrong.'

'I accept your wager!' He threw back his head and laughed. Not only was Anna Petrovska disturbingly direct, but free from maternal supervision there was the makings of fun in her. 'Though I'd rather you made it a kiss!'

'Then a kiss it shall be.' Her eyelashes dropped coquettishly. 'And you shall pay it tonight, at this very place at – nine o'clock, say?'

'How about ten? It'll be darker!' He said it in all seriousness, his eyes challenging hers. 'Though if the hairy Cossack sees us –'

'Karl? Don't worry about him. He wouldn't tell Mama. He and I are the best of friends.'

'What is he, in your household? A butler – a caretaker?'

'Neither. He is – Karl,' she shrugged. 'We are grateful to him. He helped us escape from the Bolsheviks. We owe him a great deal, though who he is we have never quite discovered. Sufficient that he is a Czarist. When we got to England we kept him with us – a debt of honour, you see.'

Elliot Sutton did not see. In his eyes, the man was a hanger-on, though since Anna Petrovska seemed so attached to him he had the good sense not to say it.

'Debt of honour – yes, of course. And here he comes, now, to protect *your* honour, my dear!'

Karl bore down on them, gesturing, calling out in Russian, ignoring Elliot completely.

'My mother is home – yours too. I must go.' Then she smiled, her eyes teasing. 'Until ten,' she whispered.

'So you've made a start?' Clementina remarked as Elliot entered the room. 'I saw you out there – wouldn't be surprised if the countess didn't see you, an' all!'

'Don't worry. The faithful Karl came to warn Anna. But might one be informed of one's fate?'

'*One's* fate? Talk straight, lad! If you want to know if the countess is willing for you and Lady Anna to meet, then the answer is yes. And don't thank me,' she rushed on. 'I'm only the mother who's got your interests at heart which is more than you deserve what with your carrying-on and your wilful ways and –' She stopped to draw breath. 'And from now on, you'll mind yourself with women – and you know what I mean! That girl next door is a virgin. And don't look so shocked. Virgins still exist, though I reckon it's all of ten years since you chanced on one!'

'Mother – *please*?' She really should take more care. The family – and himself in particular – were well used to her directness, but one day she would forget herself in polite company and he shuddered, just to think of it. 'And I do thank you for all you have done for me. I appreciate it more than you know. But do you think she should be addressed as *Lady* Anna?'

'Her mother's a countess, so surely her daughter has right to a courtesy title.'

'But her father, I believe, was a count. Does that entitle Anna to –'

'It entitles *me* to call her what I want, and as far as I'm concerned, the daughter of a countess is entitled to the courtesy. And them that don't like it can lump it! Anna Petrovska is aristocracy!'

'*Russian* aristocracy. Is it the same as ours?'

'Their Czar was our king's cousin; that's good enough for me! Now then – when do you aim to shift yourself and get this thing settled?'

'I intend, dearest mother, to meet Anna at ten o'clock tonight. We made a wager this afternoon, and it would seem I have lost it. I must honour my debt.'

'Sneaking out in the dark? You'll do no such thing!'

'Try to stop me!' He planted a kiss on his mother's cheek, pinching her bottom as he did so.

'Impudent young puppy! Mind your manners!' She made to cuff his ear, but he sidestepped her.

Impudent, yes – but hers, she thought fondly as he waltzed nonchalantly out of the room. Elliot had the devil in him but she would always love him best. People misunderstood him because he was handsomer than most men – and richer than most, an' all. Or would be, one day.

'Now mind what I've told you,' she called to his blithely retreating back. 'Watch your step, son – *or else* . . .'

Of course he would watch his step, Elliot Sutton promised the mirror image he so often gazed upon. Didn't he always – or almost always? And hadn't his mother as good as promised that as soon as he was married and had provided a couple of sons for Pendenys, he could please himself what he did?

He frowned, wondering what it would be like, getting sons with Anna Petrovska. A virgin, his mother said; an *aristocratic* virgin. Yet there had been a challenge in her eyes, a promise. She might make him a tolerable wife in spite of her careful upbringing. He must now, he admitted sadly, forget about the servant in black, next door. Too near to home. Best he should concentrate on establishing himself with Anna – with *Lady* Anna. All things considered, he'd had a good run for his money. He must watch himself for a while; be on his best behaviour until he had done his duty by Pendenys and earned his reward for doing it.

He sighed, pleasurably. Anna Petrovska, he supposed, would do very nicely; better, indeed, than some of the mare-faced daughters of English aristocrats with their lumpy, childbearing hips. It pleased him to think that the Almighty had created women in man's image, but had had the good sense to create them sufficiently different to make them interesting and pleasurable – and infinitely accommodating. It was his unshakable belief, his gospel.

He hoped the girl next door would not put on the required show of modesty and refuse him twice before she accepted him. And more to the point he hoped she would be there, tonight. She had very kissable lips. And very exciting breasts. It mightn't be half bad, married to her.

He began to think of expensive motors and a bank account credited with an amount equal to his mother's approval. Aleksandrina Anastasia Petrovska. Would she – or wouldn't she? More to the point, when she did, would she prove fertile? His own virility, he knew without doubt had already been established. There was nothing wrong with the breeding prowess of Sutton males. Even his cousin Giles had surprised him, getting the servant pregnant. A sly one, that sewing maid; pretending modesty, fighting for her honour. Like a wildcat she had clawed him, that first try in Brattocks Wood. If it hadn't been for the damned dog things might have been different, like the second time. At a place called Celverte, hadn't it been? Very vague, that second time. He'd been well in his cups that night. Pity he couldn't remember more about it.

Yet think – could he have had anything to do with that

child Julia hawked about with her? Could he, had Giles lived, have challenged him?

But the child Drew was everything a Sutton should be; was fair, as Giles was. He supposed he should give credit for that begetting to Giles who, after all, was dead whilst he, Elliot Sutton, was gloriously alive – and that was all that mattered.

But it was a thought, for all that!

'Take her will you, Tom?' Alice withdrew her nipple from her daughter's lips. 'Asleep, already. Put her over your shoulder, just in case there's any wind to come up. Don't want her waking, soon as she's put down.'

'What is it, love?' Tom gathered his daughter to him. 'Got a bad head?'

'No.' She rarely got headaches. 'Just that – oh, it's nothing!'

'Then why've you hardly said a word since I came in, tonight? Summat's bothering you.' He knew her too well to accept denial.

'It's something or nothing. I suppose. When I went to Willow End –'

'To see if she'd got herself settled . . . ?'

'Settled – yes. She put the kettle on and we had a chat. And then she said – oh, I'm daft, even to think it, but –'

'But best you tell me, for all that.'

'Well, like I said, I thought I'd push Daisy down the lane – give Keth the sweeties I'd bought for him in the village – just trying to be friendly. Polly Purvis is a worker, I'll say that for her. She had a stew cooking and the windows cleaned and bread rising on the hearth, when I got there.'

'She was in service in these parts, I believe, when she met Dickon. But you knew that.'

'I did, Tom, though Polly reminded me of it. Said she'd soon get the family on its feet again, now they were together and money coming in regular. Said she had contacts around these parts from way back and would be looking for work, to help out.'

'But what about that little lad?'

'She isn't going out to work. She intends taking in washing, if there's nothing to stop her doing it. I said I was sure Mr Hillier wouldn't mind, if she hung it out of sight at the back.'

'Nor will he. But it isn't the washing that's bothering you, is it, Alice?'

'No. It's more something she said. "We'll manage all right," she said. "And once Keth goes to school, I'll be able to go out mornings, scrubbing." And had you thought, Tom, that she'll even have to dig that garden of theirs; Dickon can't use a spade with one foot near useless, now can he?'

'Come to think of it, he can't – though there'll be plenty who'll give a hand. But go on?'

'Well – I wished her luck, told her I was sure there'd be work. And then she said it. Said she looked like Mary Anne and that any woman in their family who'd ever looked like Mary Anne inherited her luck, too.'

'Mary Anne *who*?' All at once, Tom was uneasy.

'Mary Anne *Pendennis*, that's who! I couldn't believe it at first, so I said – casual as I could – that Pendennis is an uncommon name but she said no, it isn't. Not around Cornwall, it seems.'

'But there'll be a fair few Mary Anne Pendennises in Cornwall.'

'So there will, I grant you. But how many by that name married a northerner – a foundry worker, by name of Albert Elliot? Polly had all the family history off pat.'

'Too much of a coincidence.' Now Tom knew the reason for his unease.

'Is it? Think on this, then. Didn't Mrs Clementina call her house Pendenys Place, and name her first son Elliot – her maiden name? And Nathan and Albert she called for her father and grandfather. Coincidence, Tom? And Polly Purvis was Polly Pendennis, before she married Dickon. She's actually related to Clementina Sutton. Polly's grandfather was a Pendennis. She told me he had two sisters; one of them called Sarah Jane – the other –'

'Don't tell me! The other was Mary Anne! But what luck did that great-grandmother of Elliot Sutton's ever have? Took in washing, didn't she, and worked as a herring woman. You think that's *lucky*?'

'Look, Tom – Polly said it. *Mary Anne's luck*, because Mary Anne's husband ended up with his own foundry and their son got even richer.'

'All right, then. Polly Purvis – Pendennis – is cousin twice removed to that Elliot? Can't hold that against the woman!'

'No, but there's her son – that little Keth. He's dark, too. I don't think I want him to come to my house.'

'Dark, like his many-times removed cousin, Elliot Sutton, you mean? So you're going to hold it against the bairn? You, who said you'd make a fuss of the little lad; feed him up a bit? Yet now it seems he's got bad blood?'

'I didn't say that, Tom!'

'Bad blood,' Tom urged, his temper rising quick, Alice acknowledged, as it always did when he got himself bonny and mad. 'And that little lad isn't going to be allowed near our Daisy because he's Elliot Sutton's distant kin? Oh, Alice, I thought better of you. And it isn't even proven, either!'

'It is, Tom. As far as I'm concerned, it is.'

'Then you'll tell Polly Purvis; tell her about Elliot who is dark because it threw back from a great-grandmother he never knew? But being *dark* is nothing to do with it; being *wicked* is more to the point and being spoiled and indulged by his mother and made to think he can do no wrong. He's what that foolish Mrs Clementina made him and the washerwoman four generations back has nowt to do with his womanizing nor his wickedness!'

'I never thought to hear you defending one of Mary Anne's, Tom!'

'But Elliot Sutton *isn't* one of hers! He's got her Cornish darkness, that's all. Mary Anne Pendennis was a woman who worked hard to help her man start his first foundry, and was a decent woman, if all Reuben told me is true. I'll not have you thinking such nonsense, Alice! I thought you had more sense about you. I thought –'

'Whisht, Tom! Stop your shouting or you'll wake the bairn. Here – give her to me and I'll put her to bed. I won't have you frightening her!'

'And I, lass, won't have you getting yourself into a tizzy because Polly Purvis seems to be related to that Elliot, and so distantly related as makes no matter,' he insisted, his voice gentle again. 'And I'm sorry I made a noise. It's something I'll have to check, this temper of mine.'

'Very well, and I'll try not to let myself worry over it. And I'll not take it out on that little Keth, either.' Her lips moved into the smallest of smiles. 'And when he comes to see Daisy, I'll give him some toast, well drippinged, and sugared bread, an' all. Does that please you?'

'It does.'

'Then will you take that little lass up to her cot, or are you going to sit there, nursing her all night?'

'I'll take her up now – if you'll forget all you've heard this day about Mary Anne Pendennis and not chew it over with Polly Purvis and make more of it than it deserves. Any road, who wants to be saddled with kin like *him*? Do the young woman a favour, and forget it? And remember, that Cornish great-grandmother is nothing to do with you, nor me, nor Daisy!'

'Nor is she. And I won't talk about it again – I promise . . .'

She watched her man cradling their child, supporting her

with a work-roughened hand, and tears sprang to her eyes, just to see the way he loved her.

And he was right – or almost so. That long-ago Mary Anne had nothing to do with her nor Tom nor Daisy. But what of Drew, her firstborn; almost the same age as Keth, and Keth's cousin, though many times removed.

Yet Keth was dark – Mary Anne Pendennis dark – and Drew was Sutton fair and she, Alice Dwerryhouse, was a happy, contented woman who would be kind to the little boy who lived at Willow End, if only because he had the misfortune to look like a man whose very name she detested. And would never say again, if she could avoid it.

10

He saw her from his window as she turned the corner by the church, and hurried to his front door. When she opened the gate to his tiny front garden, he was standing on the doorstep, arms wide.

'Lass!' He folded her to him, awkwardly patting her back.

'Reuben! Let me look at you,' she smiled tremulously. 'So long . . .'

'Too long, Alice. But come you in. I'd heard tell you'd be arriving today. I've been watching out for you.'

'News still travels fast, in Holdenby.' She closed the almshouse door behind her. 'I hope you've got the kettle on.'

He had. He nodded to the tray, set ready with cups, then asked, 'And where's that little Daisy, then?'

'Fast asleep in her cot, with Julia watching over her. I'll bring her to see you, in the morning – Drew, too.'

'Aye. I like to see the boy. Her ladyship brings him, sometimes, when she visits us pensioners. He's growing into a fine lad – a Rowangarth Sutton if ever I saw one.' He looked at her, meaningfully.

'He is, thanks be. And I'm coming to accept that nothing of what happened was his fault,' Alice said softly. 'All at once I saw him not as –' She stopped, cheeks flushing. 'I saw him as Julia's son. He said, "Hullo, lady," when we met. That was when I began to see things differently. And tomorrow, Lady Helen will be his legal guardian. It's why I am here – to sign the papers.'

She could talk to Reuben and not watch every word she said. Reuben knew about Drew's getting: knew everything.

'And how's Tom? Seems he got himself a good employer. Gentry, is the man?'

'N-no. I wouldn't say Mr Hillier is *gentry*, exactly. But he's a gentleman and so taken with Daisy.' Best they should talk about Daisy. 'Makes a real fuss of her. And Tom's well, and a fond father. There's nothing too good for his little girl. It'll be the start of his first real season at Windrush Hall, come October. Since we went there, he's been busy rearing birds, and stocking up. There was only rough shooting and vermin shoots for Mr Hillier, but this year the game birds are thick in the covers. There'll be good sport.'

'You'll be wanting to be back before it all starts, lass. It'll be Tom's busy time.'

'I know,' she smiled guiltily. 'I've got to stop this gallivanting about. I've been away from home twice, this summer.'

'Home? Is *home* down there now, Alice?' Reuben lifted the kettle, pouring splashing, steaming water into the teapot.

'Home's where Tom is though we'll always be northerners, him and me. It felt as if I'd never been away when I got into York and saw the Minster.'

'You travelled up with Miss Julia, didn't you?' Reuben stirred the pot, noisily. 'What was her doing in London this time?'

'Legal business – about Aunt Sutton's estate. I met up with her in London. I was glad of her company. It's a long journey, with a baby.'

'So you're happy, lass? It turned out all right for you?'

'I'm happy, Reuben.' She picked up the teapot. 'But I worry about you and I miss you. I wish you'd come and live with Tom and me. We've got three bedrooms.'

'An' you'll need them all when you have more babbies!'

Thanks, lass, but I manage well enough, here. This little house is easy to keep warm; at Keeper's, I rattled about like a pea in a tin can. And there's Percy for company. Percy Catchpole's retired – didst know?'

'I did, but I'd still rather you were near me.'

'And I'd rather you were here, Alice; you and Tom living beside Brattocks Wood, like we alus thought it would be. I looked forward to seeing you and him wed, and bairns around you.'

'But that can't ever be, Reuben. Rowangarth has no need of a keeper, now.' She took his hand, holding it to her cheek. 'Even if Giles had lived, he'd not have wanted birds reared to be shot out of the sky. He was against any killing. And come to think of it, if Giles had lived me and Tom wouldn't have been married.' She sipped her tea, frowning. 'There won't be any keeper here, for a while. Drew won't be handling a gun for another ten years.'

'You're right – but even old men have dreams. You can't blame me for wanting you up here, even though it would have its drawbacks – if you see what I'm getting at?'

'You mean I wouldn't have felt easy living near Pendenys? You are right – and as for Tom being here, when him and Elliot Sutton could meet and cross swords – oh, no! I'd always be on edge. Tom has a temper on him when he's roused; best we're well away from Rowangarth.'

'So Tom's still bitter about young Sutton?' He held a match to his pipe, puffing thoughtfully, avoiding her eyes.

'He is, Reuben. When he found out who Drew's real father was, I never saw him so mad. He went white and quiet and walked out of the house; didn't come back for hours. He said he'd shot better Germans. Tom can hold a grudge for ever. Some things he'll never forgive and one of them's Elliot Sutton.

'So you see, that's another reason we couldn't come home to Rowangarth – not if something happened to make it possible. If Elliot and me chanced to meet, it might stir something up; something about Drew, I mean. While I'm out of sight I'm out of his mind.'

'But Elliot Sutton is bound to have seen young Drew from time to time.'

'I accept that, Reuben, but Julia is very protective of the boy. As far as she's concerned, Drew is her brother's child. Julia isn't afraid of Elliot as I am, though she hates him every bit as much as me, because he got through that war without ever getting his boots mucky, whilst Andrew was killed. She'll never forgive him for that as long as she lives. But forget him. Tell me, what's been happening in Holdenby.'

'Not a lot, 'cept that the Reverend Parkin was buried, last week. Another of her ladyship's friends gone, though it's thought hereabouts that Mr Nathan is looking for a living and Holdenby vicarage might suit him nicely. And talking about those Pendenys Suttons, talk has it that yon' Elliot is courting serious.' Without meeting Alice's gaze, he refilled his teacup.

'Talk by way of Will Stubbs, I shouldn't wonder.'

'Will had it from Pendenys' groom, so there'll be a grain of truth in it. Some foreigner, I believe. Seems no one at Pendenys had seen hide nor hair of him these last weeks. Busy chasing the lass around London, I shouldn't wonder. But while he's down there he's out of your way, now isn't he? No chance of you bumping into him whilst you're here.' He patted her hand reassuringly.

'I'll be able to walk in Brattocks Wood, then?' All at once, she felt less uneasy.

'Don't see why not. I'd mention it, though, to the woodman; tell him who you are. Suppose you'll be wanting to have a word with they old rooks?' he winked.

'You remembered, Reuben! But good news or bad it's best told to the rooks.'

'Surely no bad news?'

'None at all. I'd just be catching up with things, and oh, Reuben,' she sighed, 'it's so good to be back. I didn't realize how much I've missed you and Rowangarth and – and *everything*.' And even though he didn't hold with such goings-on, she cupped his face in her hands and gently kissed his cheek. 'But me and Tom are happy, and there's a home for you in Hampshire, so think on. And I'd best not stay too long – not tonight.'

Wouldn't be polite, for one thing, and for another, Daisy Dwerryhouse would soon be clamouring for her evening feed and there was no one but she could give it her.

'You'll come again tomorrow, lass?'

'I'll come, Reuben – and Daisy and Drew. I promise.'

The air held a hint of chill as she walked back to Rowangarth and dusk came suddenly as it always did, in late September.

Dear Reuben, Alice thought dreamily as Daisy fed gently at her breast. He hadn't changed in the almost two years since she left. He was snug in the little almshouse with his dogs for company and Percy not far down the road when he needed to talk about the old days; times when there had been two coachmen at Rowangarth and three gardeners – and three apprentices living in the bothy: Robert and Giles away at school and Miss Julia a tomboy who would one day grow up to beauty.

They had been good days, and her ladyship so fair and beautiful that just to look at her made you think of fairy-tales and happy-ever-afters. Alice called back the golden days. Fourteen, she had been, with all memory of Aunt Bella behind her and Rowangarth her first real home.

Yet still she had not been prepared for the feeling of homecoming that this afternoon had reached out to gather her close. To turn the sweep of the drive and see the old house, unchanged and unchanging, made her want to weep with joy.

And then the scent and sound and feel of the house. The slightly musty, slightly smoky smell that came from old books and wide chimney flues; beech logs snapping in stone hearths, flames flickering on old wood and old, uneven walls. Dear, safe Rowangarth that would one day belong to Drew. She had been so happy, so in love in that precious summer of 'fourteen. And then war had come.

She laid Daisy against her shoulder, patting her back, rocking her gently as Tom always did. Tom would be missing his little girl tonight. Happen he'd have taken the dogs to walk the game covers and let it be known the keeper was not sleeping, or maybe he'd have called on Polly and Dickon; shared a sup of tea with them. They would do all right in Willow End. Dickon had a settled look about him, now, and young Keth had stopped sucking his thumb and smiled more often.

Yet nothing could change the fact that Keth Purvis was dark – Mary Anne Pendennis dark – because from way back he was related to her. Did that mean, she frowned, he would grow up in the image of Elliot Sutton, with the same gypsy looks; grow up to remind her?

Not that the boy could help the way he was. Nature could be capricious. Drew, who should have been dark, had been born Sutton fair. During the long weeks of his coming it was the thing she most dreaded; that the rape child she carried would be born to father himself and make a nonsense of the fact that Giles had claimed him.

Yet Drew had been lucky and because of that luck she should be grateful to the Fates who had decreed it and not harbour suspicions about the young boy at Willow End.

'Asleep?' The voice from the doorway broke into her thoughts.

'No, Julia. Just thinking – about Keth Purvis, if you must know.'

'The child you say looks like Elliot Sutton? Surely you don't hold that against him?'

'Not really. Keth's a nice little boy.' Of course he was. Keth would be company for Daisy; would walk with her the mile to school and back, four summers from now.

But why did he have to remind her, every time she saw him, of a March evening and a stable in a French village called Celverte? The twenty-sixth day of March. The day they told her that Tom had been killed; the night Elliot lurched down the path towards her. The last day, come to think of it, that Julia was ever to see Andrew. A black day.

'A nice little boy,' she repeated, firmly. A little lad who came to her door for dripping toast. An ordinary, dark-haired child, for goodness sake, and shame on Alice Dwerryhouse for thinking otherwise! 'And would you mind, Julia, if I slipped down to the kitchen for a chat? If I remember rightly, Mrs Shaw always puts the kettle on, just about this time.'

A chat with Cook and Mary and Tilda, just like it used to be, before she climbed into bed and listened to the night sounds she remembered so well; to creaking boards and rattling window frames and outside, in Brattocks, the cries of hunting owls.

'I'll come with you. Bet you anything,' Julia smiled, 'that Cook has made cherry scones.' Mrs Shaw always made cherry scones on special days. 'And I do so wish you were staying, Alice. For ever, I mean. I wish you were in the sewing-room again and you and I sharing secrets like we used to. And Andrew with me, still, and Tom waiting for Reuben to retire so he could leave the bothy and live with you in Keeper's Cottage.'

'I know, love. But those days won't ever come back.'

'No.' Julia's lips tightened, then she shaped them into a smile and lifted her chin. 'I'll put Daisy in her cot for you, then take a peep at Drew. You go on down; tell Cook I won't be a minute, there's a dear girl.'

Alice was right, she thought as she quietly opened the door of Drew's bedroom. Those days were gone. For ever.

Elliot Sutton studied his newly-shaven face, his freshly oiled hair, the red carnation in the buttonhole of his evening coat. Tonight, he was going to the theatre with

Anna. The countess had agreed they could be together unchaperoned, which was tantamount, he supposed, to the announcing of their engagement even though he had not formally asked her to marry him. Anna would accept him for all that, because her mother approved and her brother Igor, too, though he had scowled a lot when asked for his permission to call upon Anna; demanded to know if Elliot's intentions were gentlemanly and honourable. How very quaint! What would brother Igor have said, he smirked, had he been told the entire truth; that Elliot Sutton was *not* a gentleman and had the greatest difficulty behaving like one. And his feelings for the young lady were not in the least honourable! She attracted him; and since it was required of him to provide heirs for Pendenys and to re-establish himself in his mother's esteem, he was prepared to go through the motions of courtship and marriage to achieve that end.

Yet Anna was undeniably beautiful. That night they met in the garden, at ten, had been quite delightful. She had made a wager with him which she expected him to pay in full; half a crown, though he'd insisted on a kiss, instead. She kept him waiting, of course. Virgin or not, Anna Petrovska knew all the rules of the game.

'Mr Sutton?' She came out of the darkness without a sound.

'You are lucky. I was about to go inside.'

'About to,' she whispered, 'but you did not. And you lost your wager, though I have decided to accept neither the money nor the kiss. I was joking.'

'Then why did you come,' he demanded petulantly.

'To tell you I had been joking, of course! So thank you, but sadly I cannot stay.'

'Oh, but you can!' He grasped her wrist, over the wall, holding it tightly. 'You may wish to call our bet off, but I don't. One thing you have yet to learn about living in England is that a gentleman always honours his debts – his gambling debts, especially. So I shall pay that kiss – there's nothing else for it.'

Still holding her firmly, he swung his legs over the wall to stand beside her. Then pulling her to him, he tilted her chin and laid his lips gently on hers; on lips full and soft and slightly parted; lips he found pleasing.

'If I let go of your hand, will you run away, Anna?'

'No,' she whispered huskily.

'Good girl.' He gathered her to him, holding her close, one arm around her shoulders, the other on her small, rounded buttocks. 'You know my mother and your mother would like us to marry,' he whispered, kissing her again. Their marriage was what the wager had been about.

'I know no such thing!' she gasped. 'And it is neither right nor proper of you to say such a thing!'

'Then why is such a proper young lady allowing me to hold her and kiss her and –'

'I must go!' All at once, the game had gone too far. This Englishman was not only attractive, he was a danger to a lady's good name! 'Call on me tomorrow – in the morning.'

'You shall not go, Anna Petrovska – not until I say you may. Now tell me, dearest girl, will you marry me?'

'Mr Sutton!' She struggled to free herself. 'Let me go. *At once*!'

'I take it you have refused me?' His voice was indulgent and teasing.

'I have! You are acting very badly and if you don't let me go I shall call for Karl!'

'And Karl will not hear you because you will *not* call for him!' He kissed her again, roughly and with passion and felt her body tremble then relax against his. 'Now tell me that you find me attractive and would like to marry me and sleep in my bed and – and everything that goes with it. Say, "I will marry you, Elliot Sutton, and be your willing lover and let you teach me things I never dreamed of . . ."'

'No! I will *not* marry you!'

'Splendid! You have refused me twice.' Every young lady refused her suitor twice – it was expected and allowed. 'And that makes it simpler for when I ask you again. *When* I ask you, you will say yes, Anna, because your mother wants it and my mother wants it!'

His hand on her buttocks tightened and he pulled her closer so she might know the need she had aroused in him. Then he cupped a breast in his hand, fondling it until she cried out.

'I shall say yes!' She lifted her mouth to his, knowing that all the things she had been told about men were not only true but quite delightful.

'Then goodnight, Anna Petrovska. I shall call at half-past ten tomorrow. We will walk beside the river, I think, and I shall tell you about myself and about Pendenys Place, where you will live with me. And better far than all that, I shall tell you how rich I will become when I marry you, and how enjoyable it will be to make children together!'

He had heard her small moan of pleasure, gratified it had all been so easy. But they were all the same, those so-called aristocrats – no better than servants when it came to parting with their virginity. They would get children with no trouble at all and then he would claim his reward from a grateful, doting mother. He winked at his mirror image, answering the knock on his door with a sharp, 'Come!'

'Madam's compliments, Mr Elliot.' The servant curt-seyed deeply. 'I'm to tell you that the car is at the door.'

He threw on his silk-lined cloak, well pleased with the way he looked. Tonight, he would ask Anna to marry him and she would accept. He would marry her because his mother wished it and the countess wished it and, though she had kept her eyes steadfastly, modestly downcast in his presence ever since that night in the garden, he knew that Anna Petrovska wished it, too.

So what choice did a man have but to make the best of it and hope the girl was as fertile as she was beautiful. Because she *was* beautiful. Properly dressed and bejewelled, she would make heads turn. He could have done a lot worse for himself, come to think of it. A whole lot worse!

Alice walked the path in Brattocks Wood; past Keeper's Cottage where now a woodman lived; past the spot where Tom had first kissed her and held a buttercup to her chin. The wood seemed larger and lighter, but perhaps that was because the woodman had cleared thickets that would once have been left as game covers. He had cut down spindly trees, too, and placed a log seat beneath the ages-old oak. The tall trees at the far edge of Brattocks had not changed, though; rooks still nested in the elms.

'Rooks! It's Alice Dwerryhouse – Hawthorn as was and for a little while a Sutton, an' all. I was her ladyship's sewing-maid, if you remember.'

She told them all; about being married to Tom and about Daisy and living in a gamekeeper's cottage so near to the New Forest that she could see deer and wild ponies all the time.

'Drew Sutton isn't my little boy, any longer. This afternoon, her ladyship became his guardian – legal, like. It was the way I wanted it; the way it should be.

'On Friday, I'll be going back to Tom, and heaven only knows when I'll be here again; could be a year. Could be longer. So I'd like you to know that I'm grateful for all my blessings and to tell you that I hope – all the time – for Julia to be happy again. Not for her to forget Andrew or even to stop loving him, you'll understand, but for her to find someone to love in a different way. I wouldn't feel so guilty, then, about Tom and Daisy and me being so happy.

'That's about all, I think . . .' She remained, eyes closed, her fingers spread wide on the rough bark of the trunk. It was the way you told it to the rooks. You didn't *tell* them, exactly. You just connected yourself to their tree and sent them your thoughts. Tom laughed at her for doing it but

Tom didn't understand. No man did. '. . . so I'll say goodbye, and thank you.'

There were no buttercups, now, in the fields that edged the wood; only a few foxgloves and a second flowering of honeysuckle and thistle heads, fluffy with seed. Tomorrow would be Michaelmas Day and then it would be October, and the guns would be out. Tom and Dickon would be busy, then, until January with Mr Hillier inviting his friends to Windrush for a weekend's shooting. And happen they'd see less of Mr Hillier, after that, beside Daisy's pram.

She hurried to the fence and the stile she had climbed over so many times in her other life. There was no sign of life at Keeper's Cottage; no movement, however slight, of the white lace curtains at the windows. She and Tom would have lived in that house if there hadn't been a war; if Sir Robert hadn't been killed and Giles hadn't died of an illness any healthy man would have thrown off.

She climbed the stile and hurried across the wild garden, glancing to her left and the avenue of linden trees, their leaves yellowing, now; storing memories of Rowangarth to take back with her.

She found Julia in the kitchen garden, pushing Daisy along the box-edged paths, Drew at her side, and called to them and waved her hand.

'There you all are! Are we going to see Reuben, before it gets dark? Shall Lady sit Drew on the pram, and take him, too?'

'You've got it all sorted out, then?' Julia raised a cynical eyebrow. 'Told it to the rooks, have you?'

'That I have. And they heard me, an' all!' Oh please they'd heard her and especially how desperate she was for Julia to be happy. 'But don't ask me what I told them, because I won't tell you!'

She took a deep breath, then let it go in little sighs of contentment. She hoped the rooks didn't think she was too happy and that she wasn't grateful for it. But perhaps it would soon be Julia's turn? She hoped so, even though her common sense told her it could never be. Julia Mac-Malcolm had loved too well, and no one could ever take Andrew's place.

'By the way – I meant to tell you this morning, only with going to Carvers I completely forgot. I had a letter from Mark Townsend, Alice. Aunt Sutton's solicitor – remember? I'd mentioned to him, you see, that you were going to have to go back to Hampshire alone – and cases and a baby to get across London.

'So he said he'd see what he could do. There'll be a Miss Edith Jones meeting you at King's Cross. She's one of his lady clerks and she'll give you a hand to Waterloo. So there you are – that's fixed!'

'But how nice of him. I was a bit worried, I'll admit it, though I'd have taken a taxi and be blowed to the expense. He's a thoughtful man . . .'

'Yes, he is. And much, much nicer than Carver-the-young. I like him very much.'

But there was no softness in her eyes as she said it; no blush on her cheeks. No matter how kind or nice or considerate the man, he was not Andrew MacMalcolm. It was as simple and sad as that.

Alice opened the high, iron gate, closing it again after them. Then taking Drew's hand she whispered, 'Do you suppose Reuben will have sweeties in his tin for Drew? Shall Lady ask him?'

Drew. Julia's son; her ladyship's ward and heir to all they could see. Little Sir Andrew Robert Giles Sutton, not yet quite two years old and to whom nothing was more important than sweeties in the tin on an old man's mantel-shelf. And please God his generation should never know war, because if it did, then all the killing and suffering and sacrifice would have been in vain.

She should, she thought, have mentioned something so important to the rooks . . .

11

Alice lay safe in Tom's arms, listening to his deep, even breathing and the soft sounds of contentment from the cot beside their bed. She was home, because home was where Tom was and it seemed wrong that she should be so happy whilst Julia ached for a love that was gone. Since locking the door on Andrew's lodgings for the last time, Julia had at least come to terms with her widowhood; that her man was gone for all time. But acceptance was a cold bedfellow when Julia was a young and passionate woman. It was a waste that all her emotions should be centred on one small boy; wrong for Julia and wrong for Drew, Alice frowned.

Her thoughts wandered to Rowangarth and her green years; to Brattocks Wood and the gamekeeper's cottage. Strange that someone else should be living in Reuben's house; that nothing had changed yet everything was different. Cook was still there and Mary and Tilda, and the straight-laced, straight-backed Miss Clitherow. And the rooks, keepers of her secrets, still nested in the tall elms. Rowangarth still pulled at her heart, reminded her of the way it had been. She missed it more than ever she realized; missed Reuben and her ladyship and oh, just *everything*. Yet now she was home she was contented; grateful she and Tom were together, trying not to remember Julia's sadness at their parting.

'I don't want you to go, Alice. These last few days have been almost like old times.'

Drew had loved Daisy, been gentle with her. It was sad that a little boy should be brought up by two women when he ought to have had a mother and a father and a sister of his own to love. It wasn't natural and neither was the life Julia was living. Julia was a young woman and needed the love of a man, though she would never acknowledge the fact.

'How is Julia?' They had talked about it, earlier that night. 'Is she learning to accept things, now?'

'She tries, Tom. But Andrew was her great love, her life. The man hasn't been born, yet, who'd measure up to him.'

'Then happen it might help if she were to change her yardstick or find someone who is Andrew's opposite. Reuben once said he thought her and Nathan Sutton might have made a go of it.'

Alice sighed impatiently into the darkness. Julia had always thought of Nathan as a brother; as more Giles's twin than a cousin. He and Julia knew each other too well ever to become lovers.

Tom muttered in his sleep and turned on his side away from her, leaving her free to move without awakening him. She stretched her body, wriggled her toes, wondered when sleep would come, remembered the butterfly.

Keth Purvis had been waiting beside the gate when she and Daisy got home. He had been there every day, Tom said; demanding to know how much longer they would be away.

'Open it.' Shyly, Keth had given her the matchbox he carried. 'It's for Daisy. A present.'

'A butterfly,' Alice smiled. A beautiful, gaudy Red Admiral.

'I didn't kill it. It was dead when I found it . . .'

'Thank you, Keth. Daisy will love it – when she's old enough. Shall we put it somewhere safe, till then?'

Alice had cut him a slice of bread, then; buttering it, sprinkling it with sugar, and he had taken a large bite, closing his eyes ecstatically.

'I'm glad you've come home, missis,' he'd whispered.

Keth was a good little boy; he *was*. She had been wrong ever to think of him in Elliot Sutton's image. It wasn't the bairn's fault he'd taken on Mary Anne's likeness and he *wasn't* going to grow up selfish and wicked like that one at Pendenys.

She sighed impatiently, wondering if Julia too was lying awake, thinking of Andrew, wanting him.

Please God, send someone for Julia to love — not as she loved Andrew because that wouldn't be possible. But isn't there some way You can help her find a little happiness and not have her stay unloved for the rest of her life?

Julia MacMalcolm was not lying awake in her bed. She sat, instead, in the unlit conservatory, thinking about Mark Townsend.

Shortly after Alice left, his call had come. About her Will, he'd said, and when would she be in London again?

'Not just yet. But there's no hurry, Mr Townsend. Perhaps you could send me a copy, to look at? I'd thought to come to London about Christmas time — bring Drew to see the shop windows and the decorations . . .'

'Not before then? There's another matter, you see — your aunt's car. I took the liberty of looking at it, yesterday — Sparrow gave me the garage key — and I'm not at all sure you should drive it, Mrs MacMalcolm. It's very old. Miss Sutton bought it years before the war and it's going to need money spending on it — apart from the fact that it's been standing idle for almost two years.'

'Then what do you suggest?' she frowned.

'Perhaps I should have a mechanic give it a thorough check. Maybe, in the long run, it would be cheaper to buy a new motor.'

'But Aunt's car . . .' It would seem like a betrayal, almost, to get rid of it.

'That motor is long past its best, in my opinion. There's a new little Austin just on the market; perfect for a lady.

About a hundred pounds and a splendid job. I took a look at one in the showrooms near Marble Arch.'

Marble Arch! They had met near there, she and Andrew. She didn't want to talk about car showrooms near Marble Arch; about anything near Marble Arch.

'I don't know. I'd have to think more about it.' It wasn't going to be easy, having a motor at Rowangarth. 'And Mr Townsend – would you not mention motors on the phone, in future? I am alone, now, but my mother isn't happy about cars and I wouldn't want her to hear me discussing them – not yet, at least. My father was killed in a road accident, you see, and she won't entertain keeping one here. Perhaps some other time . . . ?'

'I'm sorry – forgive me? Perhaps when you do decide to come to town we'll talk about it then. And when you come, could you give me a little notice? Perhaps then I could book pantomime seats – for Drew, I mean, if you think he's old enough.'

'That might be nice,' she had said, though for the life of her she couldn't think why. Could she, maybe, have been at a loss for words? Excuses were hard to find when the invitation had most likely been kindly meant. And it would mean nothing more to him than Aunt Sutton's solicitor taking out Aunt Sutton's niece and her child. A business courtesy, that was all. So it would not seem quite so graceless, would it, if she were to tell him – nearer the time, that was – that lately Drew was restless cutting the last of his teeth and might it not be better if they were to forget the pantomime, this year? Some other time, maybe?

Yet in all truth, the real reason lay with Andrew and the fact that she had no inclination to find pleasure in the company of any man – even for Drew's sake. It should be she and Andrew, she thought bitterly, taking Drew to his first Christmas panto, with the baby of their own coupling asleep at Montpelier Mews, watched over by Sparrow.

Why had it happened? Just six days before the war

ended. She had been so sure Andrew would come back to her, which only proved that nothing in life was certain — except that she would love him always and that no other man would do. She shivered, all at once cold. Best get to bed.

I want you, my darling. I need you to touch me, kiss me, make love to me. I'm a woman, Andrew; a flesh-and-blood woman and I shall never forgive the war for taking you from me. Why did you make me love you so much? How am I to endure a lifetime without you?

She picked her way carefully across the dark conservatory, jaws clenched, head high. She would endure it because she must. The war had not taken her memories. At least she had those; enough to see her through two lifetimes. She walked quietly up the stairs, hugging herself tightly.

Please, God, help me not to want him so much? Show me, please, how I'm to live without him? Help me to count my blessings? Blessings like Alice, who listened, and Drew who loved her, made it possible to live out each day. *But God, why did he have to die? And why is Alice so far away?* She wanted her back at Rowangarth. Only Alice understood.

Tomorrow, everyone would know. In the morning, it would be in all the newspapers of any consequence.

Olga Maria, Countess Petrovska, formerly of St Petersburg, is pleased to announce the engagement of her daughter Aleksandrina Anastasia to Elliot Edward Sutton of Pendenys Place, Holdenby, York.

Of course it had been she, Clemmy, who had had the bother of it all, borne the cost of it, even though the announcement of an engagement should appear to come from the girl's family. But it would be splendid to read it in the morning papers, to breakfast leisurely, then receive the callers and telephone calls she knew would come; tell them about Lady Anna and how beautiful and well-connected she was – or had been – before they had been forced to flee St Petersburg. And she would not call that city Petrograd, even though that was now what it was called – what the Bolsheviks *decreed* it should be called. Those Bolsheviks had a lot to answer for; not only for the havoc they had caused in Russia but for the trouble they were trying to stir up in every civilized country in Europe. Encouraging working men to join trade unions and to demand better jobs and working conditions, as if jobs grew on trees and there weren't millions on the dole or parish relief!

A man with a job was lucky, these days, and never let him forget it! And as for the miners, refusing point blank to take a cut in their pay! It defied words and it was all too much. What was more, she would not waste time thinking about the ungrateful wretches when there were far more important thoughts with which to fill her mind.

At last, Elliot had proposed! Soon – perhaps at Easter – he and Anna would be married. Little more than a year would see the first of her grandsons safely in the nursery at Pendenys Place. Anna Petrovska knew where her duty lay. Young ladies of her station in life were well-schooled in such matters. Find a husband – a *rich* one – and give him sons; thereafter, duty done, enjoy life to the full. Be discreet, of course. Take care not to break the eleventh commandment – Thou shall not get caught breaking any of the aforementioned ten!

Elliot knew all about the two most important; those concerning adultery and not coveting his neighbour's wife, and Elliot must be careful from now on, if he knew what was good for him!

The Yorkshire Pullman hurtled north. From her seat in the dining car, Clementina watched lights shining in the distance. She would soon arrive at York to be met by car and driver.

She lifted a finger, summoning the steward, accepting

another cup of coffee, asking for the bill. Tonight, her tip would be generous to match her relief. Elliot down the aisle at last, his philandering over – or over as made no matter. He would make the odd slip from time to time, of course. It was natural in one so handsome, so attractive to ladies. They would never leave him alone, so he would be forgiven for the odd excursion into infidelity. And Anna, if she knew which side her bread was buttered on – aye, and jammed, too – would turn a blind eye to it as most wives did. Anna Petrovska was no fool, in spite of her air of wide-eyed virginal innocence!

Clementina smiled at the chauffeur who held open the car door for her, causing him much embarrassment. She smiled again at her butler, who stopped in his plod-footed perambulations across the hall, his mouth wide with amazement.

She took the stairs quickly and, guided by the aroma of her husband's after-dinner pipe, threw open the door triumphantly.

'There you are, Edward!' She bent over his chair so he might kiss her cheek then tugged on the bell-pull before sinking into a low, leather chair. 'Such news! The announcement will be in tomorrow's papers so he can't go back on it without making a fool of himself! Tell me you are pleased!'

'I did, my dear, when you rang me this morning. I am still pleased.' And not a little relieved. He'd be even more relieved when the knot was tied. 'When is it to be, and where? The Minster?'

'I think not, Edward. Holdenby will be better.' Clemmy Sutton preferred to be a big fish in a small pond. 'And I'd thought Easter might be a nice time.' June would have been better, though, but June was all of nine months away; too long for Elliot to behave himself! 'The countess wants it in London, would you believe? Insists on an Orthodox priest, the awkward woman.'

'So what have you decided, Clemmy?' Edward Sutton paused as the door opened and his wife ordered a tray of tea from the footman who stood there.

'Decided? She can have her ceremony, I suppose. Nothing to stop them being married twice. All the better for it, I suppose.' A quiet ceremony in London in the Russian manner if they must, then a proper marriage in a proper English church by a proper priest; by her second son, if all went to plan. Such an event it would be! Lilies for an Easter wedding. Easter brides always carried Madonna lilies.

Pendenys would glitter. There couldn't be a better setting than Pendenys Place. Marquees on the lawns – at least three – and a ball, afterwards, for the carefully chosen few; after the bride and groom had left for a honeymoon in Venice, that was.

'When did it all happen?' It was best, Edward knew, to show interest. Elliot was his son and heaven only knew he'd wished him married and out of harm's way more times than he cared to admit. But only when vows and rings had been exchanged would he believe it. Elliot had come dangerously close to wedlock in the past, to be saved only by his mother's chequebook.

'Happen? When did he propose, do you mean? It was at the theatre, two nights ago. Venice, I think . . .'

'Where?'

'Venice for the honeymoon! They were at Drury Lane when he asked her. Her mother seemed pleased, though her brother scowled a lot.' Igor scowled all the time. 'I think they must travel by Orient Express and Golden Arrow.'

Then on to Florence and Rome, and if Anna were not expecting by then, maybe to Lisbon and Madrid and home by way of Gibraltar. But the better-class brides were usually pregnant long before the honeymoon was over!

She would have such fun, Clemmy sighed, planning

the wedding and the honeymoon; refurbishing rooms at Pendenys for their use – for live at Pendenys the newlyweds must! Room for three families, here. Her father had built wisely. A pity he was not alive to witness his grandson's triumph.

She hoped her second son would shift himself and secure the living at Holdenby. It would be quite delightful to have him marry them. Nathan spoke so beautifully; his voice was so sincere. Or should she, perhaps, have the Bishop? Or the Archbishop of York?

Pure joy shivered through her. She had not been so happy for a long time. And just wait until morning when Helen would open the papers! It would make her think, and no mistake. Bound to, when her elder son had been set on marrying a woman of another race; her younger son had married a servant and her daughter – the living, breathing image of Anne Lavinia – had married the son of a coal miner! And such a hurried, hole-and-corner wedding that had been that she was sure, at the time, that Julia must have been three months gone!

But no matter. She, the daughter of an ironmaster, would show the lot of them! Who needed blue blood? It was brass that mattered and Pendenys had the brass! She would show the North Riding aristocracy how a wedding should be; show them all that she could spend money as well as make it!

But how to celebrate the engagement? A splendid dinner in London? Perhaps, though, now that it was almost October, a shooting party at Pendenys. She hoped the Petrovskys would understand how it was done; know how to conduct themselves at an *English* country weekend.

'Madam.' A white-gloved footman set down a silver tray.

'Oh, take it away!' She waved an impatient hand. 'I'm much too busy to sit drinking tea!'

And it *wouldn't* wait until morning! She must ring

Helen; tell her the good news and make her green with envy. She would ring her *now*!

Julia gazed around her. The curtains fitted perfectly; the iron fireplace with its kettle hob was an exact replica of the one in Andrew's surgery at 53A, Little Britain. Even the skeleton seemed at home, though she must always keep the door locked. Anyone entering without warning, could be frightened into hysteria by the grinning, gap-toothed skull.

She moved the stethoscope a little to the right of the blotter then straightened pencils and pens on the inkstand. The room was uncannily perfect. Andrew would never be lost to her, now. She could open the door of this room any time she wanted; believe herself a wife again and her man no farther away than St Bartholomew's hospital.

She closed and locked the door, placing the key on the ledge above it. Now, whilst Andrew was so near to her she could almost believe her foolish daydreams, she would open her wardrobe, gaze at the blue dress she had worn in Hyde Park and at Harrogate; worn to her wedding and again for Andrew's leave. Four days of complete happiness and nights so passionate that even now she had to close her eyes, just to live them over again.

They had said goodbye at the Gare du Nord on the twenty-sixth day of March, their hopes high now Andrew had exchanged the trenches for the comparative safety of a field hospital. Their last goodbye, had she but known it. That day, too, had brought sorrow to Alice. Tom killed, and Elliot Sutton –

Quickly she checked her thoughts. She could not, would not, think of her cousin whose engagement had this very morning become official. She slid the hangers along the rail, stopping at the hobble-skirted costume.

Had she really worn it and had she, to Alice's shock and dismay, pulled that too tight skirt high above her knees and kicked out like a hoyden at the policeman? And had she, not long after, opened her eyes to look upon a young doctor and instantly and for ever fallen in love? Did it really happen? Seven years ago – did it?

She closed the wardrobe door on her remembering. Her mother and Drew were visiting at Pendenys. Soon they would be home for Drew's mid-morning sleep. He still needed it, even though he was almost two. And she would steel herself, she knew, to listen to her mother's account of it all, even though she had no wish to hear about engagements and weddings and honeymoons.

She wanted Andrew; wanted Alice with her to remind her that Andrew *had* happened – that those so-few nights they spent together might never lose their brilliance.

Julia was glad she had visited the red-brick house at the turning of a beech-lined lane in the New Forest. Now, she could recall at will the village shop and Daisy's pram at the back door, with Morgan asleep beside it.

'I miss you, Alice,' she whispered to Julia-in-the-mirror. 'I want you back here with me, living for Andrew's letters and phone calls and you taking Morgan to Brattocks in the hope of seeing Tom. And Giles in the library, still; Robert growing tea in India and war an obscene word.'

Yet now Andrew and Giles and Robert were gone and Alice was far away.

'And she isn't,' Julia whispered to the wide-eyed woman whose lips trembled on the edge of tears, 'ever coming back. She and Tom will never live in Reuben's cottage.'

Best accept it. Alice would never return to Brattocks Wood.

'You understand, both of you?' Cook demanded. 'Miss Clitherow's orders. No one to go into that room.'

As if they would, Tilda thought. Morbid, that's what; moving all the doctor's things from his surgery and putting them next door to the sewing-room. And worse than morbid if you thought about that skeleton. Not that she'd seen it, but a skeleton was a skeleton; a dead body that ought to have been buried, decent. You couldn't blame Miss Julia, though. So in love they'd been.

Tilda Tewk understood. She too had loved; kept his photograph on the kitchen mantel all through the war. And like Miss Julia, the parting of the ways had come. Tilda made the supreme sacrifice; ended their romance and said goodbye to him with her heart. For his own good. The Prince of Wales must marry a princess; put duty before love. Her beautiful, boyish David could no more marry a kitchenmaid than an ordinary mortal could take wing and fly off to the moon.

'Course I understand. That surgery is all Miss Julia has left of the doctor. Private, it should be, between her and him.'

Understand? Then young Tilda had the better of her, Cook frowned. Unnatural, that's what, especially as nothing could bring back the dead and Miss Julia should acknowledge it and not accept being alone for the rest of her life.

'All right, then. As long as it's understood.' Cook looked at the kitchen clock. 'Time for elevenses. Get the kettle on, lass.'

No matter what, life must go on.

Anna Petrovska, her mother and Elliot, together with the servant in black, Karl the Cossack and the three Pendenys servants, travelled north by railway to be met at the station by Clemmy and three motors.

The Petrovskys and the Suttons rode in the largest car; their five servants in the second-largest with their luggage in the smallest one, following at a discreet distance because the chauffeur-handyman who drove it was not possessed of the fine, bottle-green livery worn by the regular drivers.

It was most upsetting, Clementina brooded, that Anna's

brother had not been able to accept her invitation to the lavish weekend to celebrate her son's engagement; had declined it, be the truth known. Confined to his bed – or so the countess said – by a particularly painful bout of stomach gripes, brought on by eating foreign food in an English restaurant in Soho.

Stomach gripes? He simply had not wanted to come! That young man would be out of his bed the minute the train left King's Cross station.

But wait! Only wait until the Petrovsky money ran out, because they couldn't live for ever on pride and house deeds, no matter how splendid the houses! The magnificent mansion in St Petersburg and the vast country estate belonged to the peasant Bolsheviks now, and serve that young man right! How dare he look down his nose at Clementina Sutton.

'We shall soon be there, now,' she smiled, grateful it was still light enough for them to see the magnificence of Pendenys Place enhanced by a setting October sun. *Then* let them try to patronize her Elliot!

But she would show them all how things were done. Her son's wedding would be the highlight of her life, would open doors hitherto closed to the daughter of an iron-master! And if Elliot so much as looked at another woman between now and the wedding, may heaven help him!

12

Clementina picked up her hairbrush, brandishing it belligerently. She could not believe it; not after all she had done to make her son's engagement Holdenby's best-remembered event since the Armistice. She had spared neither money nor effort; had driven her servants to the point of despair and so upset her husband that on one occasion he had taken himself off to the top of Holdenby Pike. And now the countess had completely spoiled it all!

They had been sitting in the great hall after the last dancer had left and the orchestra departed, Clementina wallowing in the glory of a shooting weekend that had gone magnificently, with pheasants all but throwing themselves at the guns; two dinner parties the likes of which St Petersburg could scarce have matched; and the ball – oh, *such* an affair!

'Well now, Countess.' Clementina had nodded to the footman to refill brandy glasses. 'I think the weekend went rather well?'

'Indeed.' Olga Petrovska eyed the gently swirling liquid in her glass.

'And an Easter wedding – are we agreed?' She glanced at Anna whose flushed cheeks and overbright eyes confirmed that Easter could not come soon enough.

'It will depend,' the countess retorted flatly.

'*Depend*?' Clementina sat bolt upright. 'On what?'

'On how soon the young ones can find a home.'

'A *home*?' But they will live here, at Pendenys Place!'

Of course they would! Where better than this house with

rooms to spare and servants to wait on them and no worries about food bills nor wine bills!

'I fear not, Mrs Sutton. My Anna must have her own home, be mistress of her own establishment. In Russia, she would not even consider a young man who did not have the means to provide this.'

'Not have the means?' Clementina's jaw sagged. 'But my son's expectations are – *phenomenal*!'

'Expectations, dear lady, do not buy establishments – merely castles in the air.'

It had been so awful, so degrading. How dare the woman imply that Elliot could not afford a wife! Didn't she realize he was no mean catch? Didn't she know that young men – *rich* young men – were thin on the ground, a fact that refugees with little to commend them but a title would do well to dwell upon!

Furiously she brushed her hair, dismissing the maid helping her prepare for bed. Tonight, Clementina wanted no one to see her tears, for tears there would be. Anna was so perfect, was all she could have hoped for in a wife for Elliot. Anna, it was plain to see, was completely besotted. They made such a handsome couple; would have beautiful children – if ever they got as far as the church, that was!

'*Aaaagh*!' Clementina's emotions spilled over and she flung the brush across the room to hit the wall and fall with a clatter. 'Drat the woman!'

How could she prevaricate so; be so damn patronizing! She would be glad when tomorrow came and the old biddy took herself back to Cheyne Walk.

'*Ooooh* . . .' Her shoulders began to shake, her head drooped. Anger gave way to tears and she laid her head on her arm and sobbed out her misery. Even penniless foreigners got the better of her, looked down on her. It was too much to bear! She jumped at the closing of the door, dabbing her eyes guiltily, sucking gulps of air.

'Whatever is wrong, Clemmy? I could hear you at the

end of the passage.' Edward placed a comforting hand on that of his wife. 'Has it all been too much for you?'

'No, of course not!' Her despair was all at once gone and she was angry again. 'It's *her*! Who does she think she is? Pendenys isn't good enough for her Anna! You heard her, didn't you? Her daughter couldn't possibly marry a man who hadn't the means to –'

'Hush, now. Calm yourself, Clemmy. You want Elliot to marry Anna, don't you?'

'You know I do!'

'Then buy them a house. You know you can afford it.'

'But I want them to live here,' she wailed, 'with me.'

'Nevertheless, I think the countess is right,' Edward said softly, 'though she was wrong to imply that Elliot could not support a wife,' he added by way of mitigation.

'Yes, she *was* wrong, Edward – I suppose it's because she's foreign, you see.'

'But a countess,' he reminded her.

'I know.' She turned to him, bewildered. 'Do you *really* think . . . ?'

'I really do. Their own home,' he insisted. 'That way, Elliot will the sooner settle down.'

'Settle down? I hope you aren't implying that –'

'After the war, I meant. Young men are still unsettled by it.'

'Ah, yes.' That war, and Elliot being sent to France. Once, she would have given all she owned in exchange for the certain knowledge that her eldest son would return safely. So why was she worrying about a house? And think of the pleasure it would give her to furnish it with nothing but the best, as Elliot deserved. A house not too far away, mind! 'They *shall* have a place of their own!'

'You are quite right.' His relief was heartfelt. 'And in the morning, why not suggest that Anna be allowed to remain here with us? You'd like to have her stay a few days more, now wouldn't you?'

'Y-yes.' Yes, of course she would. Better by far the girl stay behind at Pendenys, away from her scheming mother. 'But I don't want that maid of hers. She – she *floats*.' And she was far too attractive to be given the run of the place, even though she spoke not one word of English. 'And the countess must take the Cossack back with her, an' all – he's frightening the servants!' Tomorrow, at breakfast, she would beg the countess not to insist that Anna return to London with her, although it would dent her pride to have to capitulate so completely. 'I'll ask her, in the morning.'

'And she will agree, I'm sure of it. Now why don't I ring for some milk – help you sleep?'

'Mm. Hot milk, I think, and a little honey . . .'

Tomorrow, she sighed, was another day. Tomorrow, it would all come right. It must!

'I declare, Helen,' Clementina sighed as she took tea at Rowangarth, 'that I am sick of the very sight of houses. Either too big or too small.' Or too far away from Pendenys, though she would never have admitted it. 'We shall never find one in time for Easter!'

'Did you know,' Helen offered, 'that Denniston House is on the market?'

'*That* place! Yes, I knew. As a matter of fact I have the keys with me. But we shall not even consider it. They couldn't live there. The place is a slum!'

'What is a slum?' Anna frowned.

'A slum is a house not fit to be lived in,' Julia supplied, offering more tea.

'And is it – not fit to be lived in?'

'Not really.' Julia smiled affectionately. Denniston House was merely neglected; had stood empty since the last wounded soldier left it, two years ago.

'But Mrs Clementina said it is also gloomy and full of ghosts. Did someone die there, tragically?'

'No ghosts, Anna.' Just memories of a young wife,

desperate to get to France; her and Alice bicycling to Denniston each day – and Sister Carbrooke and Staff Nurse Love, and the wounded soldiers.

'Then please forgive me, Ma'am,' Anna turned bewildered eyes to her fiancé's mother, 'but why do you not wish us to live there?'

'Because it was once a hospital – in the war, my dear. Goodness only knows how many germs they left behind them.'

'Then people *did* die there and there *are* ghosts?'

'No one died whilst I worked there,' Julia defended. 'Why don't we go and see it, you and I, Anna? You said you have the keys with you, Aunt, and it isn't far from here. You'll look after Drew, mother? Oh, and can you ride a bicycle by the way?'

'*Bicycle?*' Clementina gasped. 'If you *must* go, take the car. It's waiting, outside . . .'

Now they stood, gazing at the old house, Julia calling back the past, Anna wanting desperately to prove Elliot's mother wrong.

'Sometimes I despair, Julia. I would have been happy to live at Pendenys Place, but Mama insists no house, no wedding and now it is November, then it will be Christmas and Easter – and still nowhere to live. No house we have looked at seems to satisfy,' she sighed. 'Some are too big and some are too small. This one seems the first that is neither.'

'It certainly isn't a slum.' Julia fitted the key in the lock. 'Needs money spending on it, though, but it's more roomy than you'd think.' She gazed around her, dry-mouthed, heart thumping, letting the silence wash over her. 'And it does have electricity. It was put in by the military when they took it over as a hospital.' She let go her indrawn breath, willing herself to be calm. Aunt Clemmy had been right, in part. There were ghosts here; memory ghosts from a time when she and Alice had been young and lived defiantly from day to day and letter to letter. And where had the carbolicky smell gone and why had she come back here, opening old wounds?

'This was once Ruth Love's ward.' She pushed open the double doors to their right.

'But it's quite big. It would make a lovely drawing room!' Anna walked the length of the room, pushing open the creaking glass doors at the far end, stepping into a conservatory in need, now, of putty and paint.

'It would.' No noise here, now; no laughter. No wounded soldiers caring little about their broken bodies because they were safe in Blighty, the squalor of the trenches forgotten for as long as it took them to get well enough to be sent back there. Where were they all, now?

The room opposite had been Matron's office, she recalled, though now through the open door they could see the rows of empty shelves that told them it had once been a library.

'This,' Julia opened a door at the end of a small passage, 'is the butler's pantry.' They had used it, though, for sterilizing instruments and preparing trays of dressings, ready for the medical officer's rounds.

'Does the house have cellars,' Anna demanded.

'Three. And a kitchen and scullery and a staff sitting room.' And so many memories, Anna Petrovska. Memories of ambulance convoys and paper sacks for flea-ridden, blood-soaked uniforms. And the nurses' sitting room over the stables, where just sometimes there had been time to listen to gramophone music. 'There are seven bedrooms, if I remember rightly, and two bathrooms.' And attics, where the live-in nurses had slept.

'If you were me, would you live in this house, Julia?'

'I'd live anywhere, with Andrew.'

'I'm sorry. Forgive me – I didn't think. Elliot was lucky to have come back from that war.'

'Yes. He was.' Julia set her lips tightly. All at once there were too many memories and she wanted to go home, to Rowangarth. 'You could always come back again and look at it; bring Elliot with you. I'll have to get back – Drew, you know . . .'

'Ah, yes. He's a beautiful little boy. He calls you Mummy, yet he is not yours, Mrs Clementina says.'

'He's my brother's child. My brother is dead and his widow remarried. She left Drew with us. She is still my very dear friend,' she added hastily. 'I miss her. Once, she too nursed here.'

Once, in another life, when they had loved and hoped. She laid her hands to cheeks that burned. 'Do you want to go upstairs?'

'Yes, I do, but I would like Elliot to see it with me. What do you think, Julia?'

'Would I live here, you mean? Yes, I would. It needs cleaning and decorating and carpets laid, of course. And the kitchens could do with a couple of decent cookers and new cupboards. But Denniston House isn't too big that it's unfriendly nor too small to be a nuisance for space. It could easily be made into a home.'

'Mrs Clementina doesn't like it, I know it. And Elliot, if I asked him, would say he didn't like it, also. But *I* like it!' Anna tilted her chin. 'And there are no ghosts here. I would feel it, if they were.'

'Anna – don't say you like the place just because you want nothing to delay your wedding,' Julia cautioned. 'The very next house you look at might be ideal.'

'*This* house is ideal,' came the firm retort. 'It is just right for us and if Mrs Clementina doesn't like it, then perhaps –' she smiled impishly, 'she won't visit too much! Now – shall we go upstairs?'

'N-no. You go.' All at once, Julia felt the need to be alone. 'I'll take a look at my old ward – remember Ruth Love and all the soldiers we nursed . . .'

And remember a young girl, Anna, one week a wife; remember that no task was too menial nor too heartbreaking. All that young probationer wanted was to pass her exams, then volunteer for France. She had been impatient that a sea separated her from her love; would have gone to hell and back again, just to be near him – to see him, even. One distant glimpse of him would have been worth all the fetching and carrying and bedmaking and swollen, throbbing feet. Andrew, who had been straight and tall and good to look at. Major Andrew MacMalcolm, waiting for her at the Gare du Nord station, so handsome in his uniform she had wanted to cry out her need of him for the whole of Paris to hear.

Andrew's hands, his healing hands, had touched her intimately; his mouth had covered hers possessively; his lips trailed every part of her wanting, aching body. And the woman she had become wanted him now. Every wild and wanton pulse beat out for him still, yet no man who lived and breathed would ever be able to satisfy her need nor give her that feeling of ecstasy when they had lain close after each exquisite coupling.

Eyes closed, she hugged herself tightly. Andrew was never coming home. Andrew's beloved body lay in a grave in another country. Two years, almost, since that telegram was delivered to a hospital ward in Celverte. She had been demented with anger and disbelief and then desolation took her and she had gone home to Rowangarth and Alice's waiting arms; to Alice, who understood.

Now, she was an incomplete creature; only half a woman giving all that was left of her affection to one small boy. She was dried up, unloved. No man would ever take her again. Three years being a wife; only ten nights of them spent in Andrew's arms.

So be it. She had loved and been loved and now she must learn to live with the aloneness.

'Wait for me!' She clattered up the stairs on angry, urgent

feet. 'Changed my mind!' Too many memories, Anna Petrovska. I can't face them alone . . .

That night, at Rowangarth, Julia thought about Anna's defiant chin and her wish to live in Denniston House in spite of Aunt Clemmy's scathing comments about it. All at once, the ghosts left her and she smiled. With Anna and the countess to contend with, Aunt Clemmy would not have things all her own way! Perhaps Anna Petrovska was exactly the wife that Elliot needed.

Then her sudden smile faded. What little she knew of Anna she liked, and she was far better than her cousin deserved. Julia hoped he would not hurt her too much . . .

Tom Dwerryhouse was a contented man. His first three shoots at Windrush had gone well; so well that he had money in his pocket to prove it. Pleased by the abundance of game birds, guests had tipped generously and not only himself but Dickon, too. This Christmas, the folk at Willow End would not go without.

The thought pleased him and he smiled into the leaping flames of the fire. He had so much; Alice in his arms in a candlelit bedroom and Daisy, fair as a lily and eyes so blue you couldn't help but notice them.

She smiled a lot, now, and laughed a lot, too. She had him twined around her little finger — aye, and Mr Hillier an' all. Mr Hillier called her his little flower and she smiled and blinked her eyes at him, scarce six months old and already a little flirt! Yet truth known, Tom admitted with scrupulous fairness, it wasn't right that the man who owned Windrush Hall and paid his wages every week should single out Daisy Dwerryhouse for such attention when there were eight more children on the estate that he never so much as looked at. It was something, he considered, that might well be taken amiss by other employees, yet who was a gamekeeper to say his employer nay? And happen he'd soon tire of the bairn. Mr Hillier was known for his fads and fancies; was rich enough to indulge them, whatever the next one might be. He had spared no expense, entertaining his shooting guests from London lavishly.

'Well done, Dwerryhouse,' he'd said, when the last of them had left. 'There'll be something extra in your pay, this week.'

'I reckon it'll run to a goose, this Christmas,' he murmured, 'and happen we'll ask Willow End for supper, on Boxing Night. Think you'd better be looking out for something for young Keth's stocking.' Tom smiled, wanting to share his good fortune.

'Hm.' Alice counted the stitches on her needle. She was knitting a jumper for Drew for Christmas; one in bright red, with enough wool over, happen, to make a matching hat with a big, bright pompom on the top of it. Drew, Julia's son.

'I said –'

'Sssssh.' She had a stitch too many on her needle and it was throwing the pattern wrong.

'Sorry.' Tom stretched out his legs, offering his slipper soles to the fire. Something was bothering Alice. She'd been quiet all day, hardly speaking, answering him with a yes or a no, most times. 'You all right, bonny lass?' He had to ask her. 'What's upsetting you?'

'Nothing.' She bit on her lip, then laid her knitting on her lap, gazing up with troubled eyes. 'No – something *is* the matter, Tom. It's the fifth, you see – of November.'

'Bonfire night?' There was to be sparklers for the estate children and potatoes baked in the embers of the fire – Mr Hillier's orders. And gingerbread men, from Windrush kitchen.

'Not bonfire night, Tom. It's Julia. Had you forgotten?'

Dammit, but he had! When folk would be laughing and joking around bonfires and having the time of their life, there'd be Julia remembering that this day, two years gone, a land mine had snuffed out her man's life as if it had been of no more consequence than a candle flame.

'I'm sorry, Alice.'

'You weren't to know . . .' Just six days before that war ended; when Julia had been entitled to hope that her man had come safely through it all.

'No.' He'd been safe out of the fighting, then; hadn't heard the war was over, even, 'til next day. Safe, he'd been, with Henri and Louise and Chantal – pretending he was a French soldier who'd been shell-shocked and could neither speak nor hear. Tom Dwerryhouse – deserter.

'She'll go through hell again, Tom. She loved him so.' And as if it wasn't enough, that lot at Pendenys would be rubbing salt in, talking about the wedding that was to come and Mrs Clementina making such a fuss as if her Elliot was the first man ever to get married. Married! The only thrill for that one on his wedding night would be clean sheets! 'I've tried to put a letter together, but words can be cold things, sometimes.'

'Then why don't you ring her up, have a chat with her – let her know you understand? I'll give you the money to pay for it. Push the bairn down to the Post Office, early on. You'll be the one Julia wants most to hear from; give the lass a bit of comfort, why don't you?'

'Telephone?' Eagerly she snatched at the idea. 'Think it won't upset her, too much?'

'Reckon she'd be more upset if you didn't. You're sisters, in a way, and that's what sisters are for. Have a nice long talk with her.'

'You're a good man.' Alice laid aside her needles and wool, then knelt at his feet, her head on his knees. 'I understand, you see. You were once dead, so I know how she'll be feeling. It'll be like she's got a great, cold stone inside her, just where her heart ought to be.'

'I love you, Alice Hawthorn.' He ran his fingers through

her hair. 'We have so much, you and me. There's times I think I've been too lucky.'

'We get what we deserve, Tom . . .'

'And Julia – did she get what she deserved?' He shook his head, sadly. 'And what of me, Alice – a deserter?'

'There's none blames you for that – not knowing the circumstances. Let's hope there's a heaven and that poor young lad that was shot knows how you felt about it.'

'Aye.' The feeling of revulsion was back, yet not so long ago he'd been feeling pleased with himself and planning what he'd be eating for Christmas dinner.

He dug deep into his waistcoat pocket, bringing out two florins. 'Have a talk to her; let her know you understand, and lass – give her my love, remember? Tell her I'm thinking about her, an' all . . .'

Since the boy from the Post Office at Creesby delivered the cable from America, the matter of Elliot Sutton's marriage had become even more urgent.

'There's nothing else for it,' Clementina had mourned. 'I shall have to buy that house if ever the boy is to be wed!'

She had not wanted it to be Denniston House; had wanted her son and his wife to live at Pendenys. Denniston was a come-down; after Pendenys, any house was a come-down. Elliot was used only to the best and even refurbished to the highest of standards, that house could never take the place of the one in which he had been born.

Already, she had set gardeners to work at Denniston, pruning shrubs, cutting back the undergrowth of years, weeding overgrown paths, opening up the kitchen garden. Servants swept and scrubbed there, now, from morning to night. Soon, painters and decorators would move in and maybe, just maybe, they might soon talk about the wedding again – if the newly refurbished house met with the approval of the countess, that was!

Elliot had taken the full force of his mother's annoyance,

that day of the cablegram. She had rampaged through the house, nose twitching, for the stink of the cigarettes he smoked. She found him in his bedroom pomading his hair and his smile of greeting when she entered almost made her falter in her resolve. But she had seen that smile many times before and this time his charm wouldn't work on her. There were things to be said and say them she would!

'Take a look at that!' she hissed. 'Go on, lad – read it!' The piece of paper she pressed into his hand was brief.

Daughter born 1st November. Mother and baby well. Letter follows.

'Brother Albert has indeed excelled himself.'

'Yes, he has, and you'd do well to think on about it if you know what's good for you! Your brother got himself a wife and has given me two grandchildren with no trouble at all yet you, who have been denied nothing and will inherit all this,' she waved a wild, encompassing hand, 'can't even get himself down the aisle!' She paused to gather breath, her heart thumping. 'With no trouble at all, I say, and as things stand now, that boy Sebastian could inherit every stick and stone and penny-piece I possess! I want you married, Elliot – do you hear me?'

'Mother dear, we *will* be married, I promise you. Anna and I have decided to go to London tomorrow and tell her mother of the progress that has been made. By the time she visits us at Christmas, Denniston House will be much improved. She will approve of it, I know she will. And Anna,' he added softly, laying a soothing arm across his mother's heaving shoulders, 'wants to be married every bit as much as you – as *I* – want us to be. She will persuade her mother, be sure of it. I guarantee all will be well.'

'London? Why London, all of a sudden, and where will you stay?' The intuitive tingling at the back of her nose was back again. 'There are no servants at Cheyne Walk, now; who's to look after you?' And keep an eye on him and see he didn't take up with his womanizing and card-playing. 'Just who, will you tell me?'

'I can fend for myself with Molly's help. I'm a grown man. I went through a war, remember . . .'

'Molly?' The basement woman; the caretaker. 'She'll not be a lot of use to you. You must take a footman at least.'

One she knew could be relied upon to inform her at once if Elliot got tempted back into his old ways. Until the wedding, at least, her son must behave himself. Nothing must go wrong. She, Clementina, had not yet got the measure of the countess and as for that son of hers, that Igor . . .

'If it will please you.'

'If *what* will please me?'

'That you feel it right and proper there should be someone in the house apart from myself and the caretaker. Send as many servants as you wish down there, though they'd be better employed working on Denniston House.'

'Hmm.' What Elliot said made sense, she frowned. And surely, with Anna – and Anna's mother – next door, the boy would be hard put to it to *find* trouble, let alone land himself in it.

'I'm not so sure,' she wavered. 'Perhaps just a footman . . .' The ginger-haired one with eyes that missed nothing. 'He could see to your clothes and your breakfasts, I suppose.'

'And I could eat at the club – or next door, with the countess.'

'Y-yes, I suppose you could. But Elliot –' Her eyes narrowed and a forefinger jabbed. 'Just mind what you're about in London and no hanky panky, either, with that young lass. She's real taken up with you – I don't want her walking down the aisle three months gone. Just behave yourself, remember!'

'*Mother!*' was all Elliot could say, because in all truth she had read his intentions most uncannily.

'I've told you — think on,' she said softly. 'Anna is a lady and you'll treat her like one. We aren't out of the woods, yet.' And nor would they be until her eldest son was safely down the aisle. Only then could Clementina Sutton breathe freely again.

Friday was the morning on which Alice did her weekly shopping in the village. Any other day she would have welcomed a chat with the butcher, the grocer and, sometimes, in the shop that sold knitting wool and sewing cottons. But this Friday was the fifth day of November. This day, two years gone, Andrew had been killed.

She manoeuvred the pram through the Post Office doorway, then asked at the counter for the call to Rowangarth.

'Holdenby 102? That'll be long-distance,' the Postmistress said. 'I'll have to get through to Trunks, first. Might take a minute — no hurry, is there?'

There was no hurry. It was a call she was unwilling to make, yet make it she must.

A picture of Rowangarth invaded her mind as she stood there; the black oak chest on which the telephone stood; the pad and pencil and flowers, always, beside it. This time of year those flowers would be chrysanthemums; big, mop-head blooms from the greenhouse, arranged in a pewter jug. And Mary would answer the ringing in her best voice, then hover, as much as she was able, so some small part of the conversation might be heard and carried below stairs. Dear, unchanging Rowangarth. Home. Calling her back . . .

It was not Mary who answered the phone.

'Rowangarth. Julia MacMalcolm,' said the voice.

'It's me — Alice . . .'

'Alice! Oh, thank God!' There was a fleeting silence, then a whispered, 'Bless you for ringing. I needed someone to understand. So far, no one has said anything and I want so much to talk about him.'

'Then who better than me?' Tears tingled in her eyes and she closed them tightly. 'Bad, is it?'

'It's bad. Y'know, I awoke this morning – sharply, sort of – and I thought, "This is it. This is the day." Then I lay there, in the dark – waiting. But nothing happened, Alice. I wanted to hear his voice, but I didn't. I suppose, though, it could have been the time – early in the morning, I mean – when it happened. They never told me the time.'

'No, pet, they wouldn't.'

'Do you know that once, oh, *ages* before we even thought there'd be a war – when we could talk about death because it wasn't going to happen to us –' Julia rushed on, 'Andrew said that if ever we were parted, some part of him would go to the top of Holdenby Pike and he'd find me there, he knew it.'

'Then maybe he's up there now, waiting. Why don't you go there?' She would go anyway, Alice thought despairingly. 'You used to go there together a lot . . .'

'Yes. We did. I love him so much, Alice. I need him so. It's like an ache, always inside me. Is it ever going to get better, do you think?'

'Do you want it to, lovey?'

'No. I don't want to let him go, just yet. I know where he's buried, now. They wrote to tell me. I'll go to him, one day – say goodbye – but not for a little while. Think I might go to the top of the Pike, though. Better than sitting in his surgery, all day. I'd planned to do that . . .'

'The Pike, Julia.' Alone up there, she could weep and rage and cry the grief out of her. 'And why don't you go to Brattocks?'

'The rooks? Tell it to the rooks?'

'It might help.'

'It won't. It *can't*. Not even the rooks can bring Andrew back.'

'No, but they do understand.' Daisy had awakened and was waving her fists to command attention. 'Daisy sends

190

you her love – and Tom and me, too. I'm not good at saying things, but if it gets so you can't bear it today, just remember I'll be thinking about you.' And oh, why couldn't she be with Julia, today; hold her close, be there with a shoulder to cry on?

'I know, dearest friend. I don't think I could have borne it if you hadn't phoned. You understand better than anyone – better than mother, even. I miss you so much, Alice. I want you back here, at Rowangarth. We'll meet soon, won't we?'

'Soon, Julia. Take care . . .'

Gently, she hung up the receiver and, making no attempt to hide her grief, walked to the counter.

'That'll be three and sixpence exactly,' the Postmistress said. 'You all right, Mrs Dwerryhouse?'

'I will be, in a minute. That was my friend. Her husband was killed – just two years ago. One more week, and it would have been all right – he'd have come home.'

'Dratted old war. But you and me were lucky, weren't we – having our men back safely, I mean.'

'Yes,' Alice whispered. So very lucky and oh, Julia, forgive me my happiness?

For just a little while Julia stood, staring at the telephone, sending her love and gratitude to Alice. Then resolutely she lifted her chin, walking up the stairs, thinking, 'What if . . .'

What if she opened the sewing-room door and Alice were there, really there; opened it like once she used to because there had been a letter from Andrew, telling her he loved her.

But Alice was miles and miles away and happy, with Tom, so it wasn't any use telling the rooks about her loneliness nor pleading with them that Alice should come back to Rowangarth. Miracles didn't happen – not for Julia MacMalcolm.

Swallowing hard on the ache in her throat she walked resolutely past the sewing-room, then reached on tiptoe, searching with her fingers for the key she had hidden on the lintel. Carefully, she unlocked the door of Andrew's surgery then, closing it quietly behind her, she leaned against it as if to keep out anyone who might try to intrude upon her grief. Hugging herself tightly, she closed her eyes.

Darling, where are you? Why did you leave me? Why wasn't my love strong enough to keep you from harm?

Mouth clenched tightly, she crossed the room, trailing her fingertips across the desktop, pulling out his chair, sitting on it to lean chin on hand, gazing at the pencil he had used, his pen, his inkstand.

I want you, my love. I need to hear your voice, softly, feel your mouth on mine. I need you to touch me — every part of me. I need you to make me want you. I'm a woman and I have a woman's needs. We loved so fiercely, so well. Why didn't we make a child?

She slammed the palms of her hands hard down on the desktop, jumping to her feet to stare out of the window as if perhaps she might see him there. But she saw only the wraith of a wife distraught, walking trancelike across the frozen grass and Alice, clumsy with her unborn child, running arms wide to meet her.

That had been the first day of the rest of her life. All else before it was only a dream. Andrew was dead.

13

1921

Clementina Sutton was happy, for despite all the setbacks and in spite of Countess Petrovska's downright cussedness, the calling of the banns had been arranged and a wedding date agreed. And as if that were not enough, her youngest son and his family were at that very moment making for Southampton on the liner *Aquitania*. Life, all at once, had taken a turn for the better.

'Two pageboys to carry the train, Helen? Are they old enough, do you think?' Clementina murmured, accepting a second cup of coffee. 'Young Sebastian is almost three and able to behave himself, but I'm a little dubious about your boy, Julia. He's not likely to wet himself in the middle of the service?'

'No, Aunt, he is not,' Julia pronounced firmly, 'though whether he'll agree to wear a fancy suit is quite another matter!'

These days, Aunt Clemmy seemed never to be away from Rowangarth and her endless chatter about the wedding was becoming an annoyance.

'Agree?' Clementina sniffed. 'Surely he'll do as he is told!' So like the boy to throw a tantrum and upset all her carefully considered plans. But what could one expect from a child with a servant for a mother?

'I'm sure Drew can be persuaded, Aunt; it's the outfit, though, he might not like wearing.' Gainsborough's *Blue Boy*, Clementina had decided, to be copied in the minutest detail.

'I have chosen the material for the suits,' she rushed on,

'and the shop is to have paper patterns especially made to match the boy in the painting. When Albert arrives, Sebastian and Drew must be measured at once.' Lilies in the church; small boys in satin and the sun shining through the stained glass of the east window, she daydreamed. An eye-opener for the nobility of the North Riding who looked down aristocratic noses at new money! 'But I must leave you, my dears. There's the nursery to be opened up for Albert's two, though whether Amelia is bringing a nanny with her she didn't think to tell me. So inconsiderate.' So much to do; so little time! 'I'll telephone you tomorrow when I've been in touch with Cunard about times – docking, you know. They're on the *Aquitania*, did I tell you?' She took her leave in a flurry of delight.

'If Aunt Clemmy were a dog, she'd be wondering which of her tails to wag,' Julia observed. 'I'll be glad when that wedding is over! Seven weeks, still, to Easter. How are we to survive it?'

'With fortitude,' Helen smiled, 'and when we feel like exploding we must try to remember how relieved Clemmy must be feeling, seeing Elliot settled at last. And I shall enjoy meeting Albert again. How long is it since we saw him – eight years, almost? Amelia seems a dear person. Do try to be pleased about it, Julia, if only for Anna's sake. You like Anna, don't you . . . ?'

'Very much, though what she sees in *him*, heaven only knows!' And she would try to be less bitter about it, even though she could never forgive Elliot for avoiding the fighting, nor for that March evening in Celverte.

'I am glad,' Helen sighed, 'that Anna is to wear a traditional gown.'

So many brides, now, insisted on the new, short style and it wasn't right, really it wasn't. A bride should wear a long, romantic dress; Anna's was to have a train flowing out from the waist, with masses of tulle veiling, frothed into her tiara; the Petrovsky tiara, Clemmy was at pains to stress. The one Igor smuggled out of Russia, she constantly reminded. She hoped they wouldn't have to sell it, meantime, though what they did with it after the wedding Clementina couldn't care less. But she wanted it on show, truth known, for the ceremony; let people see that the bride came from a tiara-owning family!

'Hope the weather is fine and bright for them,' Helen murmured, dreamily. She did so enjoy a wedding. 'Clemmy is to have marquees on the lawns, though if it rains on the day, there'll be room enough inside Pendenys.'

'Mother, it *won't* rain; the heavens wouldn't dare do anything to upset Aunt's day of triumph.'

'Julia, it is Anna's day, remember, and my dear – don't be too upset?'

'I won't be – leastways, I won't let it show. And I'm trying, dearest, to accept things. It's only that ours was such a lovely wedding – just family, and me in the blue dress Andrew liked so much . . .'

Her voice faltered to a halt. It was useless trying to delude herself. She missed Andrew, still; needed him as desperately as ever.

'And orchids in your hair – you wore them for Pa,' Helen said softly. 'So nice to think that Nathan will be marrying Elliot and Anna. By Easter, he'll be properly inducted into the parish – and living in the vicarage, too.'

'So he will. It'll seem strange, him not being at Pendenys, I mean.'

Once, he had always been there in Julia's life; he and Giles inseparable. And Robert safe in India, too, with everyone wondering about the mysterious woman who was keeping him from Rowangarth. Cecilia, now a nun in a teaching order near Shillong, and loveless, like herself.

'Darling – don't look so sad,' Helen whispered. 'It does become bearable, I promise you.'

'Maybe so, but Aunt Clemmy acting so damn smug doesn't help. And I'm trying to come to terms with Andrew being gone – it's just that I don't want to be reminded all the time how happy we were.'

'I know, I do know. And February is the dreariest month. Why not get away for a few days, you and Drew – might buck you up no end.'

'Go to London – to Montpelier Mews?'

'There, or to Hampshire. Why not go to Alice?'

'Could we, do you think?' Her daughter's sudden eagerness told Helen that a holiday could do nothing but good.

'It would make a change. Drew loves Daisy and didn't Dwerryhouse say you'd be welcome any time at all? When Clemmy gets the pattern and material for the pageboy suits, Alice could make Drew's outfit and you could look after Daisy whilst she is sewing. And it's so much warmer down there, didn't you say? Drew could perhaps get outdoors to play.'

'And there's a little boy living down the lane, too. Drew could have a playmate his own age. Mother – could we?'

'I think you should. Write to Alice; arrange for her to be at the Post Office, so you can ring her.'

'Why didn't I think of it? We could stay a couple of nights in London. Sparrow could take care of Drew whilst I dash round the shops – get something to wear at the wedding. It's a great idea. I'll write now!'

The liner *Aquitania* steamed slowly into Southampton Water in the wake of the pilot boat. From the ship's rails, Albert Sutton saw only a grey land mass, mist-shrouded, and hoped it was not an omen. Truth known, he had missed England at times even though now he was thoroughly contented with his life.

'Sir?' The steward at his side coughed deferentially. 'Mrs Sutton's compliments, and will you return to the cabin?'

'Anything wrong?' He dipped into his pocket, pulling out a coin.

'A cable arrived – madam seemed not to be upset by it.'

'My dear, how kind! It's from your folks.' Amelia offered the cablegram as Albert closed the door behind him. 'Read it, Bertie.'

Welcome home. At the dockside to meet you. Fondest good wishes.

Albert shaped his lips into a smile. At least Mama was trying, though her displeasure on hearing of his marriage had been made all too clear at the time. Now, of course, her adored Elliot was being married and she wanted all her sons at Pendenys in a show of happy families.

He recalled his early dislike of his eldest brother; one who could do no wrong and would inherit the lion's share of their mother's wealth. Not that it mattered, now. Amelia too was rich, and generous with her money. An unashamed Anglophile, she had singled him out and he had not resisted. Younger sons with no expectations fended for themselves and married if not for money, at least where money abounded.

Theirs had been a convenient marriage – neither denied it – but tolerance had turned to affection and with the birth of their second child there were times when Albert truly cared for his American wife. With each pregnancy she had blossomed into an attractive woman whose looks belied her years. Albert Sutton was, he was bound to admit it, almost happy. Until now.

The cable, received in the ship's wireless office, bore a Southampton office of origin which probably meant that his mother would be at the dockside, unpredictable as ever. For a fleeting moment, he wished he had not allowed himself to be persuaded into this visit. He had thought of a score of reasons to remain in Kentucky – mares in foal was only one, but Amelia had excitedly overruled them all.

'It's about time I met your family – and that they meet Bas and Kitty.' She relished the thought of an English christening for her daughter by an English priest who was also the baby's uncle. Amelia intended engaging an English nanny for her children; one genteelly spoken, yet firmly kind. The visit to her husband's roots, to the country house he called a great, cold barn of a place, was eagerly awaited and with a society wedding thrown in – an *aristocratic* society wedding – Amelia's excitement spilled over. She had long since ceased to condemn a country she once declared had arrogantly grabbed half the world. In her desperate years she had married an Englishman who had given her status and children; now she wished to be a part of his heritage. She was impatient to step ashore and was delighted, on answering a knock on their stateroom door, to find his father standing there, undisguised pleasure lifting his face.

'Albert! Welcome home! It's been too long.'

'Come in, sir! We hadn't expected being met!' They clasped hands. 'Meet my family. Amelia, my dear, this is my father.'

'At last!' Smiling, she held out her hand, then kissed Edward's cheek warmly. 'I am so glad to know you, father – might I call you that?'

'You might, and must.' Edward dropped to his knees. 'And this is Sebastian, my American grandson,' he smiled.

'How do you do, sir.' Gravely the small boy held out a hand. 'Will you call me Bas? Everyone does, 'cept when I'm naughty. Would you like to see my sister? She's really Kathryn, but we call her Kitty. She isn't a lot of fun, right now, but mother says she will improve, with keeping.'

He led Edward by the hand to the Moses basket in which the small baby lay swaddled, ready for the journey north.

'My grandchildren are a delight. Bas is a fine boy and I'm sure Kitty will be a darling child – when she improves,' Edward smiled, eyes bright with teasing. 'Now – have you gone through the formalities? Have the Customs men been on board?'

'Everything has been seen to, except these.' Amelia

waved a hand to the luggage piled high on the floor.

'Then that is easily taken care of. The car is at the dock-side and the estate truck. If the stewards will give our driver a hand to load them, they can follow on behind us. How many pieces are there?'

'Eighteen,' Albert supplied. 'I must say you've got everything well organized, father.'

'I have been known,' Edward smiled, 'to get it right, occasionally. And might I formally welcome you to our family – to the Place Suttons, Amelia? You are prettier – if an elderly gentleman might be granted the liberty – *far* prettier than Albert described you. I thank you most warmly for my grandchildren. Clemmy will be waiting, impatiently. It was she who sent the flowers.' He nodded to the large bunch of red roses atop the pile of cases. 'She begs pressure of work and apologizes for not being here to greet you,' he added gravely.

A smile flickered briefly on his daughter-in-law's lips, then slowly, deliberately, she winked a violet-blue eye. In that second, a bond was formed between them and long before they had left the *Aquitania* Edward Sutton, did he but know it, had found an ally for life.

Alice opened the shed door, sending it rocking back on its hinges in her excitement.

'Well, now.' Tom looked up from the traps he was cleaning and oiling. 'Good news, was it, that telephone call?'

'She's coming to stay, Tom – her and Drew. Going to Montpelier Mews first, then coming on here! Got some sewing for me to do, though if you ask me she's fed up with all the Pendenys wedding talk.'

'Stands to reason,' Tom acknowledged. 'Can't be a lot of fun for the lass and her still grieving for her man.'

'I know, love.' There were times Alice felt guilty for being so happy. 'She loved him so much. Right from the start, she was smitten. Went looking for his lodgings without a shred of pride.'

'Pride, Alice? What has pride to do with loving? But we'll make her welcome. She's a grand lass.'

'She's that all right, and a real lady, an' all. Don't know where I'd have been without her when . . .'

'When you fell for Drew, you mean? Yet with hindsight that bairn was meant to be. He saved Julia's sanity – was the grandson her ladyship was desperate to have. You're not still bitter about what happened?'

'Not any more. I'm getting fond of the little lad. I've come to think of him as Julia's and it isn't him I should feel anger against. None of it was his fault. Truth known, I can't wait for Friday, to see how he's grown, and I can't stand here chattering, either! There's their room to be got ready and baking to be done. Your dinner'll be on the table in half an hour, so think on, and don't be wandering off, Tom Dwerryhouse!'

She was gone in a flutter of excitement, cheeks flushed, eyes bright. She missed Julia, Tom frowned. Miss Julia was the first human being Alice had ever been close to; the sister she had never had. Once, not all that long ago, Julia had been a good friend to them both, he acknowledged soberly. Would she could find happiness again . . .

Elliot Sutton was not in the best of good moods. The family was gathering at Pendenys Place. Nathan visited daily from his vicarage in Holdenby; Albert and his Amelia had arrived from Kentucky and now Countess Petrovska had joined them though Anna's brother remained in London, pleading a meeting with White Russians who were intent upon setting up a minor court around a minor Romanov.

The talk, Elliot thought peevishly, was of nothing but the wedding, Nathan's forthcoming induction into the living of All Souls and the christening of the child Kitty who, whenever he went near her, began to cry angrily as if she knew how much he disliked babies and small boys, Elliot brooded as he made his way to Rowangarth. Babies made mewling noises he found irritating and small American nephews were an annoyance, too, when they came in the shape of a three-year-old with a too-frank gaze and an inquisitive mind.

He would be glad when Easter had come and gone; when the wedding – *both* weddings – were over and done with and his life returned to normal.

'Elliot,' his mother had purred. 'You'll take this parcel to Rowangarth, won't you?'

'Do I have to, Mama?' He resented being treated like a messenger boy.

'You do. The servants are far too busy. It's the pattern,' she explained in response to his questioning eyebrows, 'for the wedding suit for Julia's boy, and the material. Julia is waiting to pack it. She's going away – London, I believe, and then to stay with the sewing-maid.'

'And is there any message?'

'No. She knows all about it. Now shape yourself, boy, or is it too much that for once I ask you to do something for me,' she demanded, archly. 'And please don't scowl. If you drank too much last night you have only yourself to blame for it!'

'So you monitor every glass I pour, now?'

'While you are living under my roof – yes! Last night you had more than was good for you. Thank heaven the countess seemed not to notice. Now be off with you! Ask your Aunt Helen to excuse me for neglecting her, lately. She'll understand, though . . .'

Understand that his mother's life seemed so happy and full that she could think of little else save how happy and fulfilled she was. And as for the countess's bombshell last evening at dinner – he wouldn't have been surprised had his mother risen from her chair and kissed the arrogant cheek soundly!

Shrugging, he glanced at his watch, realizing that with luck Aunt Helen might ask him to stay to tea. And not a bad idea, at that. Rowangarth would seem a haven of tranquillity after the turmoil Pendenys had become. Even with Julia's undisguised stare of dislike to contend with, Rowangarth would be bliss.

He kicked moodily at a tussock of frosted grass, then made for Brattocks Wood. Be damned if he wouldn't beg dinner, too. He wouldn't be missed, if he did. His mother would remain on her pretty pink cloud, scattering benevolence to all and sundry because she had done exactly as she'd all along intended; acquired a real title for Pendenys. It happened without warning, almost. Amelia had been the cause of it.

'And what do we call you, my dear?' Amelia's remark had been addressed to Anna. 'I mean – is it Lady Anna or Lady Petrovska – or what? And when you are married, will it be Mrs Sutton or Lady Sutton? Do please forgive me, but in America we –'

'You will call her neither,' the countess had interrupted harshly. 'You call her countess – both now, and after!'

'C-*countess*?' His mother had gone so deathly pale Elliot had thought she would swoon. 'Anna is . . . ?'

'She is the daughter of a count; therefore she is a countess. It is her right by courtesy and by birth to assume the title for the whole of her life. How you do it in England I do not know, but Anna is Russian-born and that is the way we do – *did* – it in Russia.'

'In Russia,' Clemmy echoed hoarsely.

'And in my neck of the woods,' Amelia had smiled cheerfully, 'she'd be plain Mrs S. on account we waved goodbye to our aristocrats around the time of the Boston Tea Party!'

Elliot climbed the fence that separated parkland from woodland, thinking back with near embarrassment to his mother's simpering delight. Had the countess given her the missing Romanov jewels, she could not have been more overcome. There were times when Mary Anne Pendennis would have been ashamed of her granddaughter's preoccupation with blue blood. Whatever else, Mary Anne had had her pride!

He smiled sourly. Here he was in Brattocks Wood yet not so very long ago it had been forbidden to him – on account of the sewing-maid, of course. Until he apologized for his bad behaviour towards her, Giles had insisted, he must not set foot on Rowangarth land again – that, or be escorted off it by the keeper!

A pert little thing, the sewing-maid, with an air of innocence about her. And Giles had fallen for it, had married her, in the end. He wondered if cousin Giles ever suspected that he hadn't been the first with the brown-eyed Alice; wondered if she had ever thought fit to mention that night at Celverte and what happened in the cowshed.

Or had it happened? Had she given him the slip again like that first time here in Brattocks?

The cowshed encounter had all been a little hazy – because of the wine, of course. He remembered seeing her in her nurse's uniform – that much was clear – and he remembered the straw-stuffed palliasses.

But it was all of three years ago and anyway, Giles had beaten him to it – that much was obvious. The boy was a Garth Sutton, if ever there was one. Crafty old Giles!

'Julia! What the heck . . . ?' He looked up to see his cousin blocking his path and so taken aback was he that he stopped in his tracks.

'What am I doing here, Elliot?' she finished, tight-mouthed. 'I am walking in my own woods – or in my nephew's woods, if we are to be precise. What brings you to Rowangarth, might I ask?'

'You might, and if you were half decent about it, I might tell you.'

'Please yourself.' Julia held out her hand for the parcel he carried. 'If it's material and a pattern, then go no farther.'

'You're going south, I believe; *she's* to sew it up for you.'

'*She* being Mrs Dwerryhouse, Elliot? Yes, Alice has offered to make Drew's pageboy suit.' Julia tilted her chin, meeting his eyes, silently challenging him. 'And please remember she is my nephew's mother.'

'I'm not likely to forget it. Strange company you Garth Suttons are attracted to. Now me – I've landed myself a countess, would you believe? Anna thinks highly of you, Julia, though God knows why. Still, I'm sure you wish me well.'

'*Wish you well*!' All at once she saw him for what he was – arrogant and spoiled; womanizer and rapist. A coward, too, who had allowed his mother to manipulate him into safe postings when other men accepted the horror of the trenches without protest. 'Wish you well, Elliot? God – if you only knew how many times I've wished you in *hell*!'

White-hot hatred had replaced the agitated thumping of her heart and she grasped the parcel. Then turning abruptly, she made for the stile.

'Strange company I said,' he shouted after her. 'Your brothers, and you, too! All of you drawn to the gutter, weren't you? You talk about your nephew as if he were really something! But he's only half a gentleman, Julia – though you wouldn't recognize a gentleman if you fell over one!'

His head thumped almost unbearably and yes, he *had* taken too much brandy, last night. But did she have to be so damned superior; did her eyes have to mock him so? He shouldn't have said what he did, but she was so damned aristocratic; hadn't had a great-grandmother who'd gutted fish and taken in washing! All from the top drawer, Julia's lot! He saw the jerking of her shoulders, the stiffening of her back; saw her turn, then walk back along the path towards him.

'What was that, Elliot – the remark about Drew? Say it

again, will you?' She spoke quietly, each word a hiss of venom. 'Tell me – *what* is Drew? Only half a gentleman? Then what the hell does that make *you*!'

She longed to fling the truth of Drew's getting in his face, but she dare not. She bit hard on her lip and sent hate sparking out of her eyes.

'You should watch your lip!' he countered. 'You can be too outspoken, Julia. That tongue of yours'll get you into trouble one day. And yes, if you want to hear it I'll say it again for you. Your precious Drew *is* only half a gentleman. What else can you call him with a servant for a mother?'

'His mother, Elliot, is my dearest friend and his father was my brother, who was so badly wounded in the trenches that he never got over it.'

Her voice was so even and quiet that had he been possessed of half an iota of sense he'd have cut and left. But Julia irritated him, so he formed his lips into a sneer.

'Your brother was a conchie, and you know it! He was a coward who didn't volunteer until someone sent him three white feathers! Serve him right they made a stretcher bearer of him!'

Red lights flashed in front of Julia's eyes and she closed them tightly, shaking her head so she might think clearly, realize the full implication of his words. Three white feathers, the badge of a coward.

'And I thought it was a woman's trick,' she gasped, 'but all along it was you sent Giles those white feathers!'

The red lights were gone and with them her anger. Now she thought rationally again, knew exactly what she was about. Slowly, with relish almost, she lifted her hand, then brought it down with all the strength she could muster, slamming it into his face with such force that he staggered backwards and fell sprawling to the ground.

'You – you *bastard*,' she spat. 'Get off this land! Get off it, or I'll kill you!'

He got to his feet, knowing he was no match for the force of her hatred, running towards the fence, climbing it clumsily. Then he turned.

'Bitch!' he flung. 'You're mad. Mad as a hatter!'

She stood unmoving, watching him go, glad she had hit him, wishing she had pulled her fingernails down his face and marked his prettiness.

Her right hand tingled. She had hurt him. Long before he reached Pendenys the imprint of her hand would be there on his cheek for all to see. How would he explain it away? What would he say to Anna, to the countess, should they ask him?

She smiled derisively, then turned for home. If she hurried she would be in time for tea, glad beyond measure that in four days more she would be at Windrush, with Alice.

'It is so good,' Julia said softly, 'to be here.' They sat either side of the parlour fire, the room softly lit by lamplight, fireglow patterns shifting on the beige-washed walls. 'If I hadn't got away I'd have gone out of my mind – Elliot said I'm mad, did you know? Nothing but fuss, over the wedding. I'm trying, really I am, but things aren't easy at the moment.'

'No, love,' Alice soothed. 'Best get things off your chest, whilst you're here. You'll feel a lot better for it. But tell me first – how is Reuben?'

'He's well – sends his love, and I'm to tell you he's keeping warm indoors, this cold weather.'

'And Jinny Dobb and Mrs Shaw, and the rest?'

'All fine. Jin's back in the bothy, looking after the apprentices, and Mary and Will Stubbs are walking out, but no sign of a ring, yet. Miss Clitherow is unchanging and I think Tilda's affair with HRH is over, by the way.'

'Poor Tilda; such a romantic.' Alice was glad of the smile that briefly lifted the face of her friend. 'And Nathan in the vicarage, now? I think Giles and me must've been his very first marrying.'

'You were. So long ago, yet only three years. Another life . . .'

'You said that Nathan is to give Drew his lessons,' Alice prompted as the familiar, faraway look was back in Julia's eyes.

'Nathan thinks he'll be ready for half-days when he's four. Mother feels a man's influence will be good for him – he's in a household of women, after all. We don't want him to go to boarding school. I think that if mother had known she would have Robert and Giles for so short a time, she wouldn't have given away their young years.'

'Julia! You mustn't think like that – neither of you. Drew won't ever go to war, be sure of that; nor Daisy. That was the war to end all wars, remember? No government in its right mind would let it happen again. And it won't be all that long before *all* women get the vote and can see to it that it doesn't! I'm sorry to mention that wedding, but won't Nathan be marrying Anna and Elliot? Twice wed, didn't you say?'

'Twice. My dear cousin will be well and truly married. The first time, privately. The countess insists on it. According to the rites of their own church, then the *real* ceremony, as Aunt Clemmy calls it, will be at Holdenby, a couple of days later.

'Countess Petrovska is giving them all a bad time but the other day, it seems, she announced that Anna is really a countess – or would be, if they were still living in Russia. I believe Aunt Clemmy was so delighted that she could hardly get a word out. The old countess is a terrible snob. When Amelia complimented her on her excellent English, she said that in Russia the aristocrats spoke English or French all the time. Said that only the peasants spoke Russian. She's so damned stuck up you wouldn't believe she was Anna's mother. Anna is a dear girl . . .'

Alice laid aside her knitting, dropping to her knees beside the fire, poking out the ashes, building it up with beech logs. The sight of Julia had shocked her. There was tension in her face that was never there before and now she made little nervous movements with her hands all the time. It would be a good thing when that wedding was over; when Easter had come and gone and spring brought everything alive again. Life always seemed better for sunshine.

'How is mother-in-law?'

'Alice – you called her mother-in-law! She'd like to have heard that.'

'A slip. But she was the nearest I ever had to a mother for just a little while.'

'Then I wish you would always call her mother-in-law. You are still Drew's mother, remember; once, you were Lady Sutton. The war took so much away from mother; you were one of its few blessings.'

'I still think of her as mother-in-law, especially since Tom's Mam is dead. She died in that same 'flu epidemic that took Giles. Remember – Giles always called your mother Dearest? But I'm Alice Dwerryhouse now, not Lady Sutton. I'm a servant again – or the wife of one.'

'You will always be my sister. I don't know how I'd have borne things if it hadn't been for you. As soon as mother suggested visiting,' Julia smiled, 'I couldn't get here soon enough. And you don't mind making Drew's wedding suit, do you? He only agreed to wear it when I told him we were going to see Lady to get it made.'

'You know I don't mind. You can take care of Daisy whilst I'm sewing. Put the pair of them in the pram – one either end – and push them out. It'll do you good, my girl! Now I'll just set the kettle to boil. Tom'll be back from his night rounds, soon, and he'll want a sup of tea. And you haven't told me about Mr Albert's wife. Is she really as old as they say?'

'Not a bit of it,' Julia murmured as Alice pulled out the

dampers on the kitchen fire and laid a tray with cups and saucers and sliced and buttered a currant teacake, ready for when Tom's whistle told her he was home. 'Amelia is the nicest person, and she's not so old she can't produce two lovely children. Nathan is going to christen the baby. She's to be called Kathryn Norma Clementina – the two last names for her grandmothers.'

'And is Amelia pretty?'

'Incredibly. Her eyes are the most beautiful shade of violet. Motherhood becomes her. She intends taking an English nanny back to Kentucky. At the moment, the children are in the old nursery at Pendenys, with one of Pendenys housemaids looking after them.

'Bas is a dear little boy; very good-mannered and not a bit spoiled. Amelia is really taken with the Sutton family history. Rowangarth especially intrigues her. She remarked on how amazing it was that one family could live in a house for over three hundred years and Aunt Clemmy said there were Suttons in the North Riding when there was nothing in the United States but buffalo and Red Indians; that Suttons were old-established even before the English colonized America and most certainly long before *that dreadful slavery* was abolished.

'It didn't go down very well with Amelia, I can tell you. Kentucky, where they live, was a slave state, once. Aunt Clemmy can be so direct, at times. It's most embarrassing.'

'But it isn't Mrs Clementina and the wedding that's making you so edgy, is it?' Alice took up her knitting again. 'Something is upsetting you. Want to talk about it, lovey?'

'No – oh, it's nothing!' Julia jumped to her feet. 'Think I'll have a peep at the children.'

'They're all right. I've just been, so sit yourself down,' Alice ordered. 'What is it, Julia? I haven't seen you like this for a long time. Is Drew too much for you?'

'No.' The reply was swift and decisive. 'Drew is the one

thing that keeps me sane. But if you must know, it was whilst I was in London . . .'

'Ah. How is Sparrow?' Alice did not lift her eyes from the needles in her hands.

'She's well. The house is dry and warm; her rheumatism isn't so painful, now. She was so glad to see us – took Drew over completely.'

'And did you do any wedding shopping?'

'I looked, but there was nothing I liked.'

'Then why don't I make up something for you?' Alice smiled.

'Thanks, but it's all right. I've got a nearly-new costume at home and I can borrow one of mother's hats. I went to lunch with Mark Townsend,' she finished in a rush, her cheeks all at once red.

'The solicitor?'

'Yes. And last night we went to the theatre. Don't know what came over me. Didn't know how to say no, I suppose.'

'Did you enjoy it?' Alice demanded, matter-of-factly.

'That's the trouble – I did. But I shouldn't have gone out with him.'

'Stuff and nonsense, Julia! If a solicitor can't take out a client once in a while, it's a poor lookout. Surely you aren't feeling guilty about it?'

'But I am.' Julia gazed, eyes troubled, into the fire. 'I really wanted to see that show, but all the time I kept saying sorry, inside me, to Andrew. And supposing someone had seen us? What if he's married, I mean . . .'

'Do you think he might be?'

'I don't know. I'd never thought about it, one way or the other, till we were on our way to the theatre in a cab.'

'Then that proves it – just how unimportant Mark Townsend is, I mean. But you mentioned that Elliot said you were mad. Why?' Alice demanded, firmly dismissing the matter of Mark Townsend.

'Oh – just the mood I was in, I suppose. It was before we left for London – in Brattocks – I hit him.'

'You did *what*?'

'I clouted him. Hard. My hand was stinging for ages afterwards. He was so shocked he fell over!'

'Then good for you, Julia MacMalcolm!' Alice threw back her head and laughed out loud. 'But what did he do to get you so upset?'

'Just being his usual obnoxious self. He was boasting about what a good match he was making: implying that I hadn't, I suppose.'

She told it, mouth taut; pouring out her hatred yet remembering to leave unsaid things that might hurt Alice. Her words were harsh, touched with angry tears.

'So you see,' she finished, 'it was he sent those white feathers to Giles. Only you and I and Giles knew about them, so it must have been Elliot. There was nothing else for it. I slammed my hand into that face as hard as I could.

'I was wild with rage, yet I walked away so calmly you wouldn't have believed it. But I could have killed him, Alice. I wanted to. I've thought a lot about it, since. I think, sometimes, that maybe I'm unbalanced – going out of my mind.'

She covered her face with hands that shook and then the tears came, hot and salt-tasting on her lips; tears held back too long.

'There now, lovey.' Alice reached out, cradling her close, making little hushing sounds, patting her gently. 'Mad, indeed! That man would make a plaster saint doubt its sanity. You did right to hit him. I'm only sorry I wasn't there to see it. Just imagine – you giving him a fourpenny one and me, hanging from a tree branch, whooping and cheering like mad!' She dipped into her pocket, offering a handkerchief. 'Now dry your eyes, there's a love. That's Morgan barking. Tom's back, and locking up the dogs. We'll have that drink, then it's straight up to bed for you. You're worn out.

'And tomorrow, young Keth will be down to say hullo to Drew, and they can play music on Daisy's gramophone. Did I tell you, Mr Hillier bought her one, for Christmas? He spoils her something awful.'

'Sorry about that.' Julia drew in a shuddering breath. 'I needed that weep, though, and to tell someone what was bothering me. You don't think I'm mad?'

'Not you,' Alice smiled gently. 'You're a Sutton, and madness doesn't run in the Rowangarth line. So let's have a smile from you? And as for Elliot Sutton – well, that one's going to get his come-uppance afore so very much longer, and when it happens, I hope I'm there to see it,' she added, defiantly.

'Swinging from a branch, cheering?' Julia forced a small smile.

'Cheering like the very devil. What are sisters for? And it'll all be the same, as they say, a hundred years from now. This old world'll still be turning and you and me, our troubles long forgotten – so what are we worrying about?'

'A hundred years?' Julia gave back the handkerchief, calm and composed, now; head high. 'D'you know, at this very moment I'd give a lot just to know what will be happening to my world *five* years from now!'

'Then isn't it a good thing we'll neither of us know till it happens, unless,' Alice frowned, 'we could catch Jin Dobb when the 'fluence is on her. Happen she could tell us?'

'Jin? Oh, no. I think,' said Julia gravely, 'that all things considered, we'd best just wait and see . . .'

14

1926

Cook rocked gently in her chair, nodding to the rhythm of a waltz, played on a piano. What it was called she had no idea, but they would tell her, when it came to an end. They had such beautiful voices, those gentlemen who made announcements over the wireless. Who could have thought, she marvelled, that music played in London could fill Rowangarth's faraway northern kitchen.

Miss Julia had explained it – or tried to – but it was still as much a mystery to Mrs Shaw as the opening of leaf buds in their season, the arrival of swallows from who knew where and the waxing and waning of moons. Sufficient to the elderly cook that Lady Helen had given that wireless set to below-stairs staff two Christmases gone, and life at once had taken on a special magic. Now, the habit of a lifetime had been broken. Since the arrival of the wireless, Cook had ceased to read the daily papers so religiously. Not that she had ever believed all they gave out. Bad news had seemed worse in stark black and white with headlines screaming to be read, yet now good news – what little there had been these last five years – sounded far better for being read in a charming, cultured voice.

Mind, there had been some good news to remember. Ireland – or the better part of it – had been given back to the Irish; the Free State, they called it, now. And Lady Astor, arguing in Parliament for votes for *all* women. A woman in Parliament at last; who would have thought it possible in the days before the war? But for all that, Mrs Shaw was not altogether sure that younger women deserved to be entrusted with the vote they clamoured for. Flappers, most of them — well named, an' all — with their feminine parts squeezed tightly into bust bodices so they looked flat-chested as a lad — and hair cut short to match it. The young men no better, either, with their gaudy pullovers and trousers so baggy they flapped in the wind like long, full skirts. But Lady Helen said it was the war years coming out in them; the relief it was all over — a tilting at a faceless authority who could no longer send them to die in stinking trenches. They would outgrow it, her ladyship said, and please the Lord they would, Cook sighed, for nothing would do now but that the young should enjoy themselves, going hiking and biking and spending every free night in picture houses or dance-halls — them as could afford it, that was! Dance, dance, dance! Even Tilda was at it; her who wouldn't have said boo to a goose was away to Creesby on her nights off, eyebrows plucked, skirts too short by half and lips coloured an alarming red though Miss Clitherow forbade lip rouge on duty.

'And that brings us to the end of a selection of piano music,' came the smooth voice of the announcer. 'In a few moments it will be time for the news bulletin, after which music for dancing will be played until closedown.'

Cook reached out to switch off the set. She was tired, would give the News a miss, tonight. And best she should leave the kitchen to Tilda and Mary who would push back the chairs and two-step or waltz to the music until eleven o'clock, when the wireless closed down for the night.

She measured milk into a saucepan, remembering still; smiling indulgently at Tilda's latest heart-throb. Rudolph Valentino, indeed! His arrival on the picture house screens had set female hearts bumping with his dark, brooding eyes and a haughtiness to match them. There were women who were known to see his latest film five times over, and swooned at every watching, or so it was said. And no wonder, when he carried a young woman into his tent in the desert, and her bewitched by the black, blazing eyes. Heaven only knew what had gone on behind that closed flap. Giving young lasses ideas, he was; lasses who would remain unwed the whole of their lives. Stood to sense, didn't it, there being not enough men to go round, now.

Yet on the good side, there had been the Empire Exhibition in London to prove that, in spite of that war, Britain was still great, and the wedding of Prince Albert to the bonny Elizabeth of Glamis had made the entire Empire happy. Twice she had refused him, or so talk had it, and quite right, an' all! A man, even a prince, was required to propose three times before being accepted. There had been pictures of that wedding on the newsreels at Creesby picture house, with people going especially to watch it. Such a loving couple. They were the Duke and Duchess of York, now. *York*, she thought with pride. The little duchess carried Yorkshire's name and was greatly loved in the Ridings.

Cook measured an exact teaspoonful of cocoa into her cup, blending it thoughtfully into a paste. There had, she was forced to admit, been more sadness these last few years, than joy. Unemployment had reached terrible levels with men who had survived the war being denied the homes fit for heroes they'd been promised. From the degradation of the trenches to the degradation of begging — or selling bootlaces on street corners to make that begging legal.

The death of Queen Alexandra had been a great sorrow, too. A dear, gentle lady; beautiful and charming — a pity about her being deaf. Sister to the Empress Feodorovna of Russia. Born a princess, Alexandra had never once lost her dignity, even though she'd known all about her husband's carryings-on. She had even allowed that Mrs Keppel to the King's bedside as he lay dying though she, Cook decided, would have given her the length of her tongue and ordered her out of the palace! An era had died with Queen

Alexandra, Cook sighed. With her passing, the gracious times they had known at the turning of the century were finally gone; times when all had known their proper station in life, be it high or low. Now, flappers showed shameless knees, smoked cigarettes from long, fancy holders and were not unknown to allow young men privileges that should, by rights, have been saved for the wedding night.

'There's milk in the pan,' she said to Tilda and Mary who had arrived in meticulous time for the dance music. 'See that Miss Clitherow gets her hot drink, will you, and don't forget to leave the fire safe when you go to bed.'

End of an era, that's what, and the mood of the miners getting uglier by the day. She must remember when she said her prayers tonight to especially thank God that Lady Helen was the kindest, fairest lady to work for and who gave her servants good food and respect. And a wireless set.

She grasped the banister as she climbed the back stairs to her room, pausing on the first-floor landing to draw breath. Either the staircase was getting steeper, or Mabel Shaw was getting older. The latter, she supposed, for there was nothing so certain in this uncertain world as growing old. Unless it was death, of course.

She shook such morbidity from her mind and defiantly climbed the remaining stairs to her bedroom in the eaves. Growing old, indeed!

Already the sycamores had broken leaf and the buds on the hawthorn hedges were showing bright green. The sky was April blue, the sun shone brightly with a warmth that promised the arrival of spring.

'There's a lot of water for this time of year.' Ralph Hillier frowned as he and his gamekeeper gazed at the swollen river.

'That late snowfall,' Tom offered. 'Dratted nuisance.' A nuisance to keepers whose wild pheasants had begun to nest; a bother to fruit growers with trees in blossom and to everyone, when the risk of snow in April was rare in the south, though at Rowangarth it had been less of a phenomenon. 'Nature, sir – reminding us never to take things for granted.'

'Much damage?'

'No. We were lucky. Most of the sitting hens survived it.' Tom Dwerryhouse was a good keeper, marking each nest he found on a plan of the estate, visiting them regularly, making sure the hens were sitting close and that vixens with cubs to feed were not allowed to take too many. 'A hundred and forty-eight nests, this year, and only six of them deserted.' Best ever, in spite of the snow.

'Here, Beth! Heel!' He whistled to the labrador bitch who ran back and forth with delight, snuffling and sniffing the scents of an earth awakened from winter. 'She's still a bit wild, but she'll be all right for the guns, come October. She behaves better with Dickon . . .'

Dickon Purvis had had the rearing of Ralph Hillier's newest retriever; had chosen her as the best in the litter and taken her under his supervision the moment she was weaned. For Dickon, Beth was wholly obedient; today, out with comparative strangers, she took liberties, leaving them without permission, tilting at authority like a naughty child.

'She's a beauty.' Ralph Hillier bent to fondle the large, intelligent head. 'Purvis will be trying her with the gun, soon?'

'Aye, but she'll be all right.' Bethan of Winchester – her real, pedigree name – was fearless as she was beautiful. 'Dickon's reared you a good little bitch.' Tom gave credit where it was due.

'How is Purvis doing?'

'No complaints. Him and Polly look like being fixtures at Willow End and their lad is doing well at school. Dickon is walking the better for a decent pair of boots.' Credit again where it was due. Footwear was an accepted part of a keeper's wages; Dickon Purvis, though only a dog boy, had received the same, and specially lasted by a shoemaker in Southampton to accommodate a deformed foot.

'So he'll be getting ideas; wanting a keeper's job now he's better on his feet?'

'No, sir. Purvis knows where he's well off. That foot'll never be right – gives him gyp in bad weather. He could teach me a thing or two, though, when it comes to training gun dogs, but where would a lame keeper find work when there's able-bodied men fighting at factory gates for a day's work?'

'You're right,' Ralph Hillier frowned. 'Things are bad. She's going too near the river!' He nodded anxiously to where the young, inquisitive bitch regarded a small branch that circled and spun on the swirling water. 'She'll be all right?'

'Right as rain. Dickon says she's a strong swimmer. Leave her. If she goes in, she'll get out. You don't want a retriever that's feared of water, do you? And sir – talking about jobs. You don't think the miners'll come out on strike, do you, all things considered, I mean?' Tom stood respectfully as his employer made himself comfortable on the trunk of a fallen tree.

'Sit yourself down, man.' He indicated a place beside him, his eyes still following the labrador. 'Come out?' he murmured. 'I hope they don't, but they'd have my sympathy, if they did.'

'You, sir?' Tom's head jerked up in surprise. Wealthy Mr Hillier who had bottomless pockets, siding with the coal miners?

'*Me*! What would you do, Tom Dwerryhouse, if I cut your wages, then asked you to work more hours?'

'I reckon,' Tom answered cautiously, 'that I'd be on the lookout for another job. But you wouldn't do that?'

'No, I wouldn't. You suit me well. But there's little work

for the colliers; half of them with their dole money run out and forced onto parish relief. And digging coal is a swine of a job – dangerous, too.'

'You don't have to tell me about the pits, sir. My dad was a collier till the coal dust got to him. That's why I went into keeping.'

'Yes. A good man, your father. He's the reason I'm sitting here today.'

'You knew him?' Tom gasped. 'You knew my dad?'

'I owe him my life,' the elder man said tersely, turning to observe the effects of his words.

'I wondered . . .' Tom shook his head. 'Up north, I mean, meeting you – you giving me a job when I came out of the Army.'

'You were curious – yet you never asked?'

'I didn't, Mr Hillier. You don't look a gift horse in the mouth.'

'But it still bothered you? What I was doing in your village – me, a man with a chauffeur-driven car?'

'It did. And a job for the giving, an' all.'

'But I wasn't there looking for a gamekeeper. My estate agent hired and fired, not me.'

'But you still took me on – provided my references were good, you said . . .'

'I did.' Ralph Hillier took in a long, deep breath. 'I was there to pay off an old debt,' he murmured, staring at the river. 'I owed your father, Dwerryhouse, but I was too late. I found that both your parents had died.'

'An' I was too late, an' all – about Mam, I mean. When I got back from the war she'd died in the 'flu epidemic.' He gazed at his boots, remembering. 'But what did you owe my father?'

'My life, that's what. And don't look so gormless.' He spread out his hands, palms down. 'Take a good look. Whose do they remind you of?'

'My dad's.' Tom saw for the first time the prick-sized

219

blue-black marks. 'Though yours hardly show. Dad's hands were pitted bad.'

'Coal marks. Miner's hands.'

'*You*, Mr Hillier?'

'Below ground, at Torvey Main, where your dad worked. Remember the accident, there?'

'No. I was a young bairn. But he told me about it. He was hurt. Never went down again – what with that and the coal dust on his chest.'

'Nor did I. I was a Workhouse child, Dwerryhouse; no folk of my own – well, none that owned me. I left school when I was twelve and was sent down the pit to work. I was a can lad, then later I helped load the bogies.

'I was working beside your father one day and we heard a rumbling. Nothing much, but we stopped what we were doing and stood still. Then it came – a cracking sound, and your father grabbed my arm. "Roof! Run!" he yelled. But we weren't sharp enough. It came down and we caught it, me worst of all.

'Your father got free, then pulled me out. My leg was crushed and he carried me half a mile to safety. Those behind us further down the seam weren't so lucky. Never brought out. Still down there, for all I know . . .'

There was a long, awkward silence, then Tom said, 'That roof fall was the beginning of the end for dad. He never rightly recovered – and they paid him nothing.'

'I never knew. I was taken to hospital. They kept me on the charity ward till I was fit as made no matter. Petted me, the nurses did – fed me well. The Workhouse Master saw to it that I got compensation. Fifty pounds, would you believe? Don't know if they expected a cut of it, but I didn't give them the chance. Just pocketed it, and left. Got myself lodgings, then started trading – buying and selling – anything and everything, as long as I made a penny profit on it.

'Took a market stall and folk pitied me – a lad so young,

hurt down the pit. I played on that pity. By the time I was sixteen I had my own horse and cart; a coal round during the week and a market stall on Saturdays. By the time the war came, I'd already bought a half-share in a small engineering works. We were tooled-up, ready to go onto war production long before the fighting started. From then on, everything I touched turned to money – and the rest you know.'

'Aye. You paid what you thought was a debt to my father by giving me a job and –' he smiled briefly, 'by making a fuss of our Daisy.'

'I fuss Daisy because I'm fond of her. Maybe I think of her as the daughter I never had or perhaps I'd have liked my girl to be like her if ever I'd married, and fathered one. She's a little charmer.

'But I've levelled with you, Dwerryhouse – now will you tell me one thing? Tell me why you never talk about that war? You've only mentioned it in passing, and then only when you were after me for a job for Purvis. And why, when there's a service in the church on Remembrance Sunday, aren't you there, wearing your medals like most other men?'

'Now see here!' Tom was on his feet, face blazing red, his mouth traplike. 'I *did* join the Army, though I'd think twice and thrice afore I did it again. And I did fight in the trenches on the Somme and other hell holes and spent my fair share of time out in No Man's Land, sniping.

'But I was taken prisoner, and no one told. My mother was given to understand I'd been killed – aye, and Alice, an' all. And if I don't choose to wear any medals, then that's my business and no one else's! And they don't give medals to dead men – because that's what I am as far as the Army's concerned. Dead, and forgotten!' he flung, shaking with temper and doing nothing to disguise it. 'And with your permission, sir, I'll be getting back. I'll take Beth with me, leave her with Purvis, though I'm of the opinion she should be with me at Keeper's, now, in the kennels.'

He whistled to the bitch and she came at once. Then he turned abruptly on his heel and made for home.

'*Dwerryhouse*!' Tom sensed the command in the voice and common sense cooled the anger in him. He stopped, then slowly turned, walking back to the tree trunk.

'I beg your pardon, sir.' He brought a forefinger to the brim of his cap. 'I had no right to walk away without permission.'

'Stop it, man! And don't tip your cap to me ever again. I don't hold with it, and you know it! Just don't get so uppity when I mention the war, that's all.'

'I'm sorry. It won't happen again. Only you'll not find many ex-soldiers want to talk about it. We were fools – cannon fodder, and of no value. Can you blame me for being bitter?'

'No, I can't – especially when a badly leg kept me out of it. But what's been said between us today is *not* to be repeated. I don't often talk about my private life and I don't want it blabbed all over Windrush. It was just the talk of the miners going on strike, maybe, brought things back.

'And you're right about Beth. Tell Purvis she'll be with you, from now on. Tell him he's done a good job on her, mind.'

'Then with respect, Mr Hillier, don't you think it would sound better, coming from you? A word of praise means a lot to Dickon.'

'Very well, I'll do that and I'll ask him to find me another good pup, and start training it up. That please you, Dwerryhouse?'

'It does, sir. Thank you.'

'Then we'll get back. Tomorrow, if you'll bring your plan of the wild nests, I'd like to take a look at a few of them. Meet me at Windrush at about ten – that all right with you?'

They walked back in near silence, Ralph Hillier musing that his keeper was a chip off the old block. His father, he remembered, had been given to flares of temper. And by his side, Tom made a silent vow to count to ten before flying off the handle – and especially about the war. What would have happened, he thought, if he'd told the truth, said, 'Medals? They don't give medals to deserters. It wasn't all that long ago they shot them!'

He closed his eyes briefly and shook memories out of his head; memories of a cold dawn and a boy being led, stumbling, to his execution. That morning in Epernay would stay with him for the rest of his days. Memories of murder.

All at once he wanted nothing more than to be with Alice and Daisy; Daisy home from school, with Keth leaving her safely at the gate after the long walk home. He had so much to be thankful for; so many blessings, though his quick temper wasn't one of them.

'See you tomorrow, Mr Hillier.' He paused at the gate of Keeper's Cottage. 'Sharp at ten, I'll be there.'

Clementina Sutton's Rolls Royce came to a stop beside the front steps of Denniston House; the house in which her son and his wife lived; where Anna had been in labour for almost twenty-four hours.

She alighted slowly, gazing around her. She had been opposed to the purchase of Denniston House as a home for her son. It had stood neglected for two years after the Army moved out, taking with them their black iron bedsteads and the stench of disinfectant and suppurating wounds.

Now, though, it was exactly what she had intended it should become; the home of a gentleman, though heaven only knew the money she spent on it with furnishings and fittings of the very best and the gardens and surrounding woodland brought under control after years of neglect.

Now, an immaculate drive swept through spring-green grounds with drifts of white narcissi growing beneath pink blossoming trees and lawns looking as though they had been clipped with nail scissors.

She glanced briefly at the small car parked not far away and the bicycle propped against a tree trunk. Doctor James was here, thank goodness, and the midwife. Surely Anna would be delivered, soon? Certainly she had been too long in labour – for a second child, that was. At least, Clementina sighed, Anna was a good breeder. She and Elliot had spent their honeymoon in Venice and Florence, travelling there by Orient Express and Golden Arrow, and Anna pregnant by the time they got back. She must, Clementina frowned, have conceived on the train! How ever was it possible to get pregnant on a *train*? But peaky-looking she had been when they returned, six weeks after the wedding, giving birth ten months later to a girl.

They had called her Tatiana for one of the Russian grand duchesses and a pretty little child, she was bound to admit, though she had longed for Elliot's firstborn to be a son; an heir for Pendenys.

Yet to give Anna her due, Clementina conceded, she was soon pregnant again, only to miscarry at four months which was a mystery indeed, since Tatiana had caused not one iota of trouble.

'Where is Mr Elliot?' she demanded of the footman who answered the door. 'No! Don't bother!' Her son was in the library. She had only to follow her nose to find him there. Drat those foul-smelling foreign cigarettes! The stink of them clung to the upholstery and curtains; surely now that Elliot was a married man a pipe would have been more in keeping?

'There you are!' She flung open the door unannounced. 'Why wasn't I sent for sooner? This thing has gone on far too long. What can Richard James be thinking about?'

'I fear it has nothing to do with the doctor, Mama.' Elliot stubbed out his cigarette, then reached for another. 'I have tried to see Anna, only to be ordered out by that Wagnerian midwife. And in my own house, mark you! I had planned to be out tonight. Anna wasn't due for at least two weeks.'

'Due? A baby comes when it is good and ready,' Clementina snorted. 'Nature knows when the time is right and there's nothing any of us can do about it. What has been done to help the girl, might I ask?'

'How would I know,' Elliot shrugged. 'No one gives a thought to the father, worrying on his own.'

'And tippling more brandy than is good for him!' She replaced the stopper firmly, then placed the decanter out of reach of her son's hand. 'Now get yourself upstairs and wash your mouth out. You reek of the stuff! I'll ring for coffee, then we can decide what's to be done.'

Anna had miscarried her second pregnancy and her third; nothing must go wrong with her fourth attempt to produce the urgently needed son, Clementina frowned anxiously. Pushing the bell with an impatient finger, she was pleased to find it was answered almost at once.

'Bring coffee for two, then be kind enough to go to Countess Anna's room and tell Doctor James that Mrs Sutton would like to see her daughter-in-law.'

'Yes'm. At once, ma'am.' The housemaid bobbed a curtsey, in such a tizzy that she wasn't at all sure which order to carry out first. But Mrs Clementina was well known for upsetting staff the minute she set foot in the place. Not like the little countess who was a lady through and through. And it wasn't a housemaid's place to go knocking on the door of a sickroom, no matter who told her to!

'Cook says the coffee will be up at once, ma'am,' said the terrified housemaid a minute later, 'and Doctor James says – says – well, I'm to tell you he'll be down, soon . . .'

Down, soon? A red-faced doctor had roared something that sounded very much like 'interfering old hen', then slammed the door on her! She bobbed another curtsey then hurried away, determined not to become involved in what was obviously turning into a melodrama.

'Down soon, will he?' Clementina's hand shook as she spooned sugar into cups of black coffee. 'Something's wrong, mark my words. I said mark my words if it –'

'Yes, I heard you – mother dear . . .'

'This is going to be another girl. Had a girl with no trouble at all, then lost the next two, didn't she?' Clementina demanded, red-faced. 'Boys, I shouldn't wonder. Some women can't carry boys. Slip them, half-way. Two boys, she lost. I'd take wagers on another girl!'

'Mother! I don't care if it's a piebald monkey!' Pregnancies were beginning to bore Elliot. 'All I want is for it to be born!'

'All *you* want! And what do you think that girl upstairs wants?' Clementina had been delivered of three sons in as many years and her entire sympathies were with Anna – or would be if the girl was about to produce the grandson she so desperately wanted. 'You men are all alike! Stupid, the lot of you!'

'But necessary, in the scheme of things.' Complacently, he refilled his cup. 'You can't entirely dispense with our services.'

'*Services*!' Clementina winced. Her son could be so direct, uncouth almost, at times. 'Watch your mouth, young man. I want none of your London whorehouse talk here!' Oh, Mary Anne Pendennis! You surface at the most inappropriate times!

'Then calm yourself, mother. We are all on edge. There'll be news, soon.'

News came sooner than either expected when the door was opened without ceremony by a doctor who was clearly at a loss for words.

'What is it, then? Tell us, man. God, but you took your time!' Elliot snapped.

'Please, Richard?' Clementina asked with more calm than she felt.

'It was a boy. Sadly, he was stillborn.'

'A boy!' Clementina was on her feet in an instant, shaking with anger and disappointment. 'You fool! You let my grandson die?'

'The child was already dead when I got here twelve hours ago, Clementina. Go down on your knees and give thanks that I was able to save the mother! And in case either of you is interested, Anna is very poorly. She had a difficult labour and has lost a lot of blood. She will need a great deal of care during the weeks ahead, and most certainly,' he looked directly at Elliot, 'she must not, in my considered opinion, conceive another child for at least a year! And where is the monthly nurse? Why is she not here?'

'Because I – because my son and I – considered a monthly nurse unnecessary,' Clementina retorted, archly.

'Why? When I had expressly advised that after two aborted pregnancies, a monthly nurse was a necessity?' The doctor snapped. 'Two weeks before the expected birth she was to come, I said, and stay for two weeks after! Well – it's too late, now, though I hope you'll both consider the fact that had that nurse been here as I suggested, so terrible a tragedy might never have happened!'

'I'll go to her,' Elliot muttered. 'She'll want to see me.'

'No!' The doctor's arm shot out, making a barrier in the doorway through which Elliot could not pass. 'For one thing, I forbid it just yet, and for another, Anna doesn't want to see you. She doesn't want to see anyone – not even her mother.'

'Her *mother*!'

'Countess Petrovska is on her way. She left London, I understand, almost as soon as she learned her daughter was in labour. She could be here at any moment.'

'Oh, *no*!' Clementina's voice rose to a wail of torment. Her grandson, her much wanted, *needed*, grandson stillborn and now the Russian harpy was on her way north like an avenging Amazon! 'I must go. I can't bear it! I can't!' She gathered up her handbag and furs and hurried to the door.

Outside, the chauffeur threw down his cigarette and covered it with the sole of his shoe.

'Where to, ma'am?' Clearly, all was not well.

'To Rowangarth.' She was shaking with angry, unshed tears. She could not go home to Pendenys; tell Edward that his grandson had not lived. And what would happen to it? What did they do with stillborn babies?

But Helen would know. She would tell her sister-in-law all about it. Helen would know what was to be done. She couldn't wait to hear Helen's soft voice, feel the gentle arms around her. In Helen's comforting presence, she could sob out her misery. Helen would listen, and understand. 'Take me to Rowangarth, and be sharp about it!'

The world had gone mad. Completely and indisputably mad!

15

Alice frowned, folding the letter carefully, returning it to the envelope. She had known the day must come, yet still she foolishly hoped that Drew would never ask.

> ... Yesterday, when Drew came home from his lessons with Nathan [the letter had read], he asked me why my name is MacMalcolm and his is Sutton. Said he thought we should both have the same name.
>
> I told him he was called Sutton because one day all of Rowangarth would be his. It had to be Sutton, I said, because Suttons have lived at Rowangarth for hundreds of years and people had got used to them being there. Thankfully, Mary brought the tea in then, and he turned his attention to the chocolate cake.
>
> I was shaken, though. I told Nathan and he said Drew should be told as soon as possible. How we tell him, of course, must be up to you and me, Alice, but Nathan was adamant we must both be there when Drew learns who his real mother is.

Nathan was right, Alice acknowledged. The sooner Drew was told, the better – but how was she to travel north or Julia come to Hampshire with all the talk of a general strike? The miners had a grievance and most people sympathized with them. The mood of the trade unions was ugly. If pit owners did not withdraw their threat of a cut in miners' pay, the country could be brought to a standstill.

No shop workers, no tram nor train nor bus drivers would report for work; no food would be delivered and firemen would ignore calls for help. No petrol in the pumps; no bread in the shops. Of course a general strike might not be called, though everyone she had spoken to thought it would.

. . . What are we to do, Alice? Can you be at the Post Office on Friday at ten, so we can talk about it? Shall Drew and I risk the journey south, knowing it could be some time before we could get back home?

Alice ran her tongue round suddenly-dry lips. What they both dreaded had happened: Drew was growing up and asking questions; must be told the truth. Or almost the truth. Never would he know that Giles was not his father. It could cause him pain enough to learn Julia was not his mother; that his real mother had left him to marry again and have another child – a daughter she had not deserted.

And that, Alice fretted, taking out her frustration on the bread dough she was kneading, led to another matter. Why was Daisy their only child, still? Drew was got with only one coupling and Daisy had been quickly conceived. Why, then, had she and Tom not had more children? Was Tom content with one little girl? Surely every man wanted a son?

She gathered up the dough, slamming it down on the floured board. Questions, questions, questions; Tom away at the far end of the estate all day, sandwiches in his game-bag just when she needed him most, and Julia not telephoning until tomorrow.

Mind, people hereabouts must realize Tom was not her first husband. *Alice Hawthorn Sutton, widow of this parish* she had been at the reading of the banns in West Welby church. But when the war ended widows were plentiful, and none in the village had remarked on it. No one asked questions about those four awful years if they could avoid it.

Yet no one at Windrush knew of the child of her first

marrying. Drew belonged to Rowangarth and it to him. Drew called her Lady; the name which had been hers from the minute his baby tongue baulked at Dwerryhouse. She could never be Mother, or Aunt Alice. Drew would always, she hoped, call her Lady – even when he knew.

She looked up at the mantel clock. Time for their morning cup of tea. Today, it was Polly's turn to come to Keeper's Cottage. They had established the ten o'clock pattern of visiting the first day Daisy left for school, her hand in Keth's. It had helped break the sudden loneliness.

Carefully, Alice shaped the dough into a round, laying it in a bowl, setting it to rise beside the fire. Then she rinsed the flour from her hands, set a tray with teacups and plates, cut two slices of raisin cake. She did it carefully and methodically as though she were a nurse again, laying out instruments from the sterilizer, pushing her own worries always to the back of her mind, intent only on the task in hand.

Nursing had taught her much; had dinned a discipline into her that please God would never leave her. Tom would be home for his tea at half-past five; until then she must not, would not fret over Julia's letter. She even smiled as she heard footsteps on the path outside.

'Come in, Polly,' she called. 'Kettle's just coming to the boil . . .'

Elliot Sutton entered his wife's room without knocking, then stood at the foot of the bed, unspeaking.

'You may stay five minutes.' The monthly nurse fixed him with an uncompromising stare.

Petulantly, he glared back. This one was worse than the midwife. This one, hastily summoned by Doctor James, had a mouth like a trap and a gaze that would stop a runaway horse.

'The countess is far from well. In no way must she be upset. Please to remember that, father.'

'And please to remember,' Elliot spat, 'that whilst in my

house and in my employ you will address me as sir. Not Mr Sutton, not father, but *sir*. Is that understood, nurse?'

'Perfectly, sir.' She paused in the doorway. 'And you and all members of your household will address me at all times as Sister Brown, or ma'am. Five minutes only, if you please!' The door closed quietly.

'How *dare* she?'

'Elliot – please?' Anna's eyes filled with tears. 'Don't make it worse? I've said I'm sorry, but I won't take all the blame.'

'And nor will I. Having babies is a woman's work. You gave me a dead son! Three babies lost! You can't blame me for that. I want a son. Pendenys needs one. What's to be done?'

'I don't know. God knows I have tried.'

'You were stupid, Anna.' He moved across the room to stare out of the window, unwilling to meet her eyes. 'You made a fuss over nothing. You got yourself upset and started in labour before your time and all because –'

'Because I caught you! I saw you going into her room; heard you making love! Can you wonder I was upset?'

'You threw a tantrum that would have done credit to a servant!'

'Like the servant you were seducing, you mean? How long has it being going on, Elliot?'

'Don't blame me; blame that fool Richard James. Separate rooms you and I, he said . . .'

'But I'd already miscarried two children. He was only thinking about the babe!'

'He certainly wasn't thinking about *my* needs!'

'*Your* needs? Sweet heaven! Couldn't you have kept yourself decent – done without a woman for just a few months? And if you couldn't, did it have to be in *my* house with one of *my* servants? But I don't want to talk about it. I want you to leave, now. I don't feel well and there's nothing more to say. Nothing can bring the little one back. It was my loss as well as yours!'

'But there *is* something to say, and say it I will, Anna.' Eyes narrow with anger he returned to stand beside the bed. 'Now look at me! One more chance I'll give you, and that's all!'

'No! Not yet? Doctor James said there must not be another pregnancy for a year, at least. Surely he told you?'

'*Told* me? The matter is between you and me and no one else. It has nothing to do with Doctor James!'

'If I have another pregnancy so soon after, it could prove dangerous – don't you care for my wellbeing? Oh, I was a fool, I'll admit that, now. I thought you cared for me. We've been married five years, yet there has never been happiness between us, nor love. Only moments of animal need. Our children were not conceived in love.'

'Children? I have one child – a *girl* – and I need a son. Either you give me one as soon as possible or I'll find a wife who can!'

'Find a . . . ?' Her eyes widened with shock, her face drained of colour. 'But you already have a wife.'

'So I have. And her refusal to provide an heir is grounds for divorce, to my way of thinking.'

'I have *not* refused! I ask only that you listen to the doctor – give me a little time?' She was weeping again; great, jerking sobs. 'Just leave me alone until I am stronger – it's all I ask.'

'If you refuse me your bed after your lying-in is over, I shall divorce you!'

'Oh, but you will *not*!' Her cheeks blazed red again, and she straightened her shoulders to face him, chin tilted. 'For one thing, I have proof of your adultery. If this marriage is to end, it is I who will end it! But we were married in the Russian church and my religion allows no divorce.'

'We were married in the English church.'

'No,' she cried savagely. 'The first service with an

Orthodox priest was the real one; the one that married us. There will be no divorce unless I want one – and I don't!'

'What is going on, here?' The nurse stood in the doorway, her face stern. 'Such a commotion! I heard it from the end of the passage!'

'With your ear at the keyhole, more like!'

'Sir – my patient is upset. I think you should leave.' Her eyes sparked anger as she opened the door wider.

'No. *You* will leave – *now*! You're fired, in fact! Get out of my house!' Elliot yelled.

'I am sorry. Doctor James engaged me and only he can dismiss me. I am asking you again, sir, to leave this room!'

'And I am refusing! I don't take orders from menials in my own house!'

'Very well.' Calmly she walked across the room, jamming a forefinger on the bell-push, holding it there defiantly.

In no time at all, a housemaid answered the summons. 'Yes'm?' she asked, fearfully.

'You will please arrange to have Doctor James telephoned at once. He is to be told that the countess is not at all well and Sister Brown suggests that all haste would be beneficial. Is that understood?'

'Yes'm. At once'm.' She turned to leave.

'No!' Elliot rapped. 'There will be no need. I am leaving.'

'Miss?' Saucer-eyed, the housemaid stood her ground.

'Very well. Doctor James need not be called – for the moment. You may go.' She turned her attention to Elliot, flaying him with a look of contempt before slamming the door in his face. 'Now, mother,' she said softly, 'dry those tears, then I'll wash that poor, pretty face and give you something to help you sleep.'

'I'm sorry, truly I am.' Anna dabbed her eyes. 'I should not have shouted so. I'm ashamed. Did you really hear me at the end of the passage?'

'No, of course not. Your husband was right – or almost

so,' the nurse chuckled. 'I was outside the door, though not quite with my ear to it. Now, I'll tie back your hair with a ribbon and get you settled down.'

'Don't leave me?' Anna pleaded.

'Don't worry. I'm going nowhere until my four weeks is up.' Tactfully, she made no further comment, though when the doctor made his afternoon call, she thought grimly, she would suggest that her bed be moved into the adjoining dressing room. She didn't trust that husband; not one iota, did she! 'Now open wide,' she commanded, offering a spoon. 'Drink it down and you'll be asleep in no time. And I won't leave you, never fear.'

She sat beside the bed, the small, frail hand in her own, until Anna's eyelids drooped and her breathing became more gentle. Then, pressing the bell-push beside her, she walked softly to the door, closing it behind her.

'Yes'm?' The same wide-eyed servant bobbed a curtsey.

'Sister's compliments to the housekeeper, and could she spare me a minute – as soon as possible?'

The housekeeper moved on urgent feet, sensing that the drama reported by a terrified housemaid was not yet over; pleased to co-operate with the dragon lady who by all accounts had got the better of the master.

'Thank you for coming,' the nurse smiled. 'Mrs Martin, isn't it? I will be most grateful if you could inform anyone who might enquire – at the door, or on the telephone – that the countess will not be receiving callers at the bedside for a week, at least.'

'And what am I to tell them, if they ask how she is?'

'Say she is as well as can be expected, in the circumstances, and thank them for their kindness. But a *week*, remember!'

'A week, Sister. But what about –'

'No callers, unless Doctor James says otherwise. And no callers includes the countess's mother, Mr Sutton's mother and all others else. If there is any trouble, send for me at

235

once and I will deal with it. I'm sorry to put you to such stress, but you and I –' she lowered her voice, conspiratorially, 'we understand, don't we?'

'We do, indeed.' The housekeeper's cheeks flushed with triumph. 'And will you be so kind, when it is convenient, to tell the mistress that myself and all the staff wish her a speedy recovery. She is very dear to us.'

Sister Brown nodded her approval, then quietly re-entered the room, standing beside the sleeping woman, lifting her wrist, counting her pulsebeat. Poor pretty little thing. How could that husband upset her so? She had heard enough, outside the door, to make her anxious and the sooner the doctor called the better. There were things he must be told, and tell them she would! Men – *pah*!

'From Julia.' Only when they had eaten and Daisy was asleep in bed did Alice pass the letter to Tom. 'Read it.'

'Well –'twas only to be expected,' he murmured, eventually. 'Drew's a bright lad. I'm surprised he didn't ask afore now.'

'Me, too. I knew it'd have to be faced one day, though I'll not worry about it any more than I have to, till Julia phones, tomorrow.'

'You think they'll come down here?'

'It would be best if they did, though I ought to see Reuben before so very much longer. He's almost eighty, remember. It's that strike, though, that's got me worried. Do you think it'll happen, Tom – and how long is it going to last?'

'If I knew that, lass, I'd be running the government, not keeping for a living. But if there is a strike and she can't get back home, then she'll have to stay with us till it's over. It'll be good for the girl to have a bit of a change. Can't be much of a life for her, all on her own. It'll be good for Drew, an' all. He can get to know his sister a bit better –

and our Daisy can get used to the fact that she's got a brother. Daisy's affected, too, remember.'

'I know, love. But Drew is her *half*-brother. She's yet to have a brother – or a sister – of her own. Tom –' She paused until she had her husband's full attention. 'What I'm trying to say is – well, you aren't being *careful*, are you? Daisy's touching six – surely we can afford another bairn? There's times when I'm on my own that I'd like another babe.'

'Well, I haven't been careful, as you call it, for a long time – since before Daisy went to school. Didn't you tell me you wanted to get your value out of that pram? And didn't you have a talk about babies to the district nurse?'

'I did. She told me not to worry. Said worrying could stop a woman conceiving.'

'There you are, then. Folk have to take what the good Lord sends, Alice, when it comes to babies. You and me are doing all the right things, so stop your worrying and happen soon you'll be taking the dust sheets off that pram.'

'Tom – I do so love you.' She went to kneel at his feet, her head on his knees. 'And I promise you I'll take what is sent to us, be it one child or many. But I often think back, and tell myself there won't be any more children for us. Remember when you left to join the Army and Jinny Dobb told my fortune? Maybe it'll be like she said. She told me there would be three men who would shape my life, and she was right. She told me a lot that came true; said I'd have two children, an' all. *Two*, Tom. Drew, and Daisy.'

'And Jin Dobb is a daft old biddy with her signs and prophecies and her tea leaves. Take no notice, love. It's up to us to prove her wrong. So stop your worrying, till morning. Just be at the Post Office at ten, and you'll find that Julia's got it all worked out. They'll be coming to Windrush, be sure of it, and you know you enjoy her being here.'

'I do. I miss her something awful, at times. I miss Reuben, too. But it's grand, down here. Mr Hillier is a good man to work for – even if he spoils Daisy something terrible. I'll settle for what Fate sends, be it babies or a cottage in the New Forest. Julia would give all she's got to be in my shoes.'

'I reckon that lass'd give all she had just to see her man for a few minutes, and say goodbye to him, decent like. And Alice – I love you, too. Always remember that I loved you from the day we met, and I'll never change . . .'

Alice was at the Post Office far too early and she found herself with nothing better to do than watch the church clock moving slowly towards ten, all the time thinking and wondering and worrying. Because it *was* a worry. As Tom had said last night, Daisy was involved, too, and who was to know how she would accept it because, like Drew, she could not be told the whole of it. Daisy loved her Dada as he loved her. He walked tall in her life and Daisy might not like what she was soon to be told.

Alice clucked at the slow-moving finger of the clock. She wanted Julia to telephone *now*: tell her everything would be all right – that they would work it out together as they had done since the day they set out on the great adventure to London.

But that was almost thirteen years ago and so much had happened since then. Sufficient that she and Julia were still close, still sisters, and that somehow between them they would tell a small boy and girl that they were brother and sister. And please God, neither would feel deceived or betrayed.

Two minutes more. Thankfully, she rose to her feet.

'Alice? It's me.' The call came through two minutes after ten o'clock. 'We're coming to you on Monday, if that's all right. Staying Saturday and Sunday night with Sparrow.

We'll be arriving about eleven. Can Tom meet us with the pony and trap?'

'No need. We have a taxi here, now. I'll book it to meet you at eleven. Can't wait for Monday, except that –'

'Except that it might not be easy telling Drew, you mean? But I think we should talk about it, first – best not to rush things.

'I'm a bit worried about the strike, though. If it happens, you might be stuck with us for ages, eating you out of house and home!'

'You'll not find me complaining – nor Tom. And Daisy's so pleased you're both coming.'

'I'm pleased, too. I've got to get away, Alice. It's all sadness and upset, here. Anna had her baby two days ago. A son – stillborn. She's rather poorly, still. Richard James won't allow visitors and Aunt Clemmy is a pain, weeping and wailing and demanding to know what she's ever done to deserve such punishment. *She*! Never a word of sympathy for Anna. I sent flowers and a letter, but I'm not allowed to visit. It's all so awful. I can't wait to get to Windrush.'

'Even though things might be a bit awkward?'

'Even though. We'll have to make sure Drew isn't hurt.'

'Yes – and Daisy, too,' Alice warned, mindful she could be heard by anyone coming in to buy stamps, considering every word she said.

'Hell! I hadn't thought about Daisy.' Julia was at once contrite. 'But we'll be gentle with them both, won't we?'

'Aye – but it's going to need the wisdom of Solomon – and then some.'

'It'll be all right. We just mustn't blunder in – must play it by ear. We'll manage.'

'We usually do.' All at once, Alice was grateful for Julia's confidence. 'See you Monday, and take care – both of you.'

It would be all right, Alice insisted as she walked home to Windrush, asking herself why she was worrying so when there were many with burdens far heavier to bear. Anna Sutton for one, who had just lost a child – as if being married to that man wasn't tribulation enough.

'We'll think of something,' she said out loud, and in that instant the sun came out from behind a cloud to give her comfort. Manage they would. They had been through worse together, and survived it.

'You'll be all right?' Sister Brown paused in the doorway of Anna's room. 'I won't be gone long. If you want anything at all, get out of bed and press the bell-push.'

It was a fine kettle of fish, she fretted silently, that her patient was apprehensive about being left alone, due entirely, of course, to her arrogant bully of a husband. How could so gentle a lady have married such a man?

'And you'll go to the public telephone and ring my brother-in-law; ask him to come as soon as possible?'

'I shall do that, never fear, and when I get back I'll come up at once.'

'I'm grateful, nurse. And will you do one thing more for me? I would like to see my little girl. Why is she being kept from me?'

'I'm not at all sure. I understand that when your labour started she and her nanny were sent to Pendenys Place.'

'Sent away? On whose orders?' Anna's cheeks flushed crimson.

'I believe the order came from Mr Sutton's mother.'

'Then I want Tatiana back with me! I am not so ill that I can't see my own daughter. Will you please ask Mrs Martin to have a car sent to Pendenys at once, to collect her?'

'There now,' the nurse soothed. 'I'll see to it. You mustn't get yourself upset.'

'Believe me, I shall be all right – as long as you are not away too long.'

'I'll be as quick as I can.'

The door closed with a finality that brought back Anna Sutton's fear of being alone with her husband – especially now.

Why had it happened? She should, she knew, have been angry with Natasha, ordered her from the room. But she had not, because in all truth, her anger should be directed at her husband.

Since it happened, Anna had felt afraid and alone, not knowing where to turn for advice. Not to her mother – not yet, at least – and certainly not to her mother-in-law. She had thought, briefly, of asking Julia to visit, but Julia had sent flowers and a letter, saying she was going away.

There remained but one person, Anna pondered, to whom she could pour out her unhappiness; who would treat what she had to say with confidence. Nathan Sutton was the only soul she could trust with her devastating news.

She bit hard on her lip to stop an escaping sob. She was finished with tears! Since this morning, she knew she must fight back, or be lost.

She had not expected Natasha to come to her room. She must have been waiting until Sister Brown left for the housekeeper's room in which she took her meals. Scarcely had the nurse left when the door opened quietly to admit the black-gowned servant.

'Little countess, I beg you to forgive me – and to hear what I have to tell you. I am ashamed and I don't know what is to become of me,' she gasped, falling to her knees at the bedside, speaking softly, urgently, in her mother tongue. 'I beg your understanding. I did not betray your goodness to me. I am a stranger in a strange country. Please to listen? It was not my wish to hurt you so.'

'Hush, Natasha. You should not be here. You must go!' Anna gasped.

'No! You will hear me; you *must*. He gave me no choice. He forced himself on me. Help me, little countess? I am sick with shame.'

It had been her instinct, Anna brooded, to dismiss her from the room, but she had not. The desperation in the servant's eyes had said more than her anguished pleading, so she had taken the agitated hands in her own and said softly that she forgave her.

'Now, Natasha, will you go before the nurse comes back? My mother is coming to see me this afternoon. I shall tell her that you are not happy working here for me – ask that when she returns to London she will take you with her. Believe me, it is best you should leave Denniston House.'

But Natasha had remained on her knees for there had been more to tell and of such enormity that all Anna could do was to send for the priest who was her husband's brother – lay bare her soul to him.

She closed her eyes, pretending sleep. She was so miserable she wanted to die.

16

'Can I come in?' Nathan Sutton tapped gently on the door of Anna's bedroom, smiling as he entered; a smile not only of greeting but to hide the shock he felt on seeing her so small, so fragile in the huge bed. Her eyes, deeply brown and beautiful, only served to accentuate the harsh, blue-black rings beneath them, the paleness of her face.

'Nathan, my dear.' She held out a hand. 'It is kind of you to come. I have need to talk to someone and there is only you. Is the door closed?'

'Firmly.' He took her hand in his own. 'Your baby – I am so very sorry.' It had to be said, and anyway, she would want to know.

'Is he – did they . . . ?'

'I said your goodbye to him.' Gravely, Nathan interpreted her question.

'I am glad. They took him away and told me nothing. I couldn't bring myself to ask.'

Her voice trailed away, her eyes filled with tears and he longed to gather her frailness to him. Instead, he took a handkerchief from his pocket and offered it, angry she had been treated so.

'Do you want me to tell you?' His voice was gentle.

'Yes, please.' She wiped her eyes, taking a deep, calming breath. 'Perhaps they are still angry with me; it is part of my punishment – not being told, I mean. They wanted a boy for Pendenys and I could only give them a stillborn child.'

'Anna – your little one is in heaven; that is all that must concern you, now.'

'You are sure? With Our Lady?' Eagerly, she grasped his words to her.

'I am sure. I prayed for him. There was just myself and the Verger there. He was laid with all the other Suttons; he isn't alone. I said the baptism service over him, too. Every baby has the right to be baptized.'

'Then he *is* with Our Lady!' The pale cheeks flushed briefly pink. 'Thank you with all my heart for your compassion, Nathan. Now I shall try not to grieve so, for him. Is it too much to ask that perhaps you –?'

'Gave him a name? I called him Nicholas. I was sure you would approve. I'd have called him for your father, but I didn't know his name.'

'He was Peter, but Nicholas is a good name – our Czar's name, God rest him.' She crossed herself reverently and for the first time Nathan perceived the depth of her faith.

'So you are a little happier, now? And when you are well enough and feel you would like to see his grave and perhaps take him flowers, will you first tell me, and I will be there with you – and Elliot, of course . . .'

'Elliot will not be there. He was not there when you – you –' She stopped, distressed.

'When I gave the little one back to God, to care for?'

'Yes. He should have been there, shown compassion for his son, but all he did that day was to blame me – threaten divorce.'

'Anna!' He had thought she worried for her baby; wanted to be told he had been decently laid to rest – yet divorce? 'What are you trying to say? And should you be saying it to me, your husband's brother?'

'Perhaps not.' She stirred restlessly, her hand making a vague, dismissive gesture. 'The doctor has refused me visitors and for that I am grateful. I don't want to see the accusation in their eyes, be reminded that three times I have failed them.'

'*Failed*? But you have done your best – more than your best. No blame attaches to you, Anna.'

'But it *does*. You say I should not be talking to you, but today you are not my brother-in-law. You are a priest, and as such I sent for you so urgently. Can you hear my confession? In your church, is it possible?'

'It is perfectly possible, Anna, if you wish it. As a priest I am bound by a vow of secrecy, though I cannot give you a penance nor grant absolution.'

'But you can listen, and perhaps understand?'

'I can – and what you tell me will be sacrosanct, even though it clearly concerns a serious family matter. You spoke about divorce?' he prompted.

'I didn't speak about it. Elliot did,' she whispered, lying back against the heavily embroidered pillows. She looked, Nathan thought, like a doll in a lace-edged box; a pale, pretty doll with its long dark hair tied back with a ribbon, dressed in a pretty pink, lace-edged bed jacket. Poor, lonely doll.

'Tell me, Anna?'

'It is all such a muddle. Where am I to begin?' she hesitated.

'At the beginning,' he smiled. 'I am a good listener. Divorce, you mentioned?'

'No. Elliot mentioned – *threatened* – it, when he came to see me, afterwards. I had hoped for a little kindness. Not his understanding, of course, because every man wants a son and clearly I had failed him again. But there were no words of sympathy, no kiss of comfort, and when I told him that Doctor James said I must not fall pregnant for at least a year, Elliot said it was none of his business. When my lying-in is over – in less than two weeks – he says he will – will . . .' She stopped, fighting tears.

'Will expect to come to your bed again,' Nathan supplied, lips tight with distaste.

'Yes. And I can't face another pregnancy just yet; I simply cannot. It could prove dangerous. The doctor was insistent, but if I refuse Elliot, he will divorce me. It is grounds enough, he says. What am I to do? I'm so afraid.'

'But Anna, you wouldn't be refusing – merely postponing, and on medical advice, too. No lawyer would touch such a petition, and my mother would not want the scandal of a divorce in the family. I think you have nothing to fear, in that direction. My brother will see sense.'

'He will have to. My religion does not allow divorce. It would cut me off from my church, and that I will not allow. Besides, I don't want a divorce.'

'You still care for Elliot? Then that is the soundest of foundations,' Nathan urged, 'on which to rebuild your marriage.'

'No, I do *not* care for him. Oh, I was besotted by him. I wanted to marry him. He was handsome and exciting. Every time we met and touched I was – how do the English say it? – in a dither. But our honeymoon was nothing more than a prolonged mating.' She dropped her eyes to her hands. 'I am sorry, that is the only way I can describe it. I had thought – hoped – we would make a child of love, but I was wrong.

'I would wish with all my heart to be free of our marriage, but we made our vows in *two* churches and there can be no changing it. I am well able to conceive. Tatiana was a healthy baby born and is a delight. That I slipped two babies was a sorrow to me, but our son came so near to his full time. He was whole, Nathan? Did you see him?' she whispered.

'I saw him. He was beautiful. Doctor James said he could think of no reason –'

'No reason he should be born dead, and before his time? Then I must tell you!'

She fidgeted with her sheets, straightening them,

246

smoothing them to give herself time to realize the enormity of what she was about to say.

'There is more, Anna?'

'Much more. First, I want to tell you why I went into early labour. I wasn't due for two or three more weeks – and it was my fault. I killed my son before he was born.'

'Anna! How could you have done? Be careful what you say. You mustn't even allow such thoughts.'

'But I did! I flew into a rage. Such a temper I was in. I screamed and lost all control. I beat Elliot with my fists until I collapsed, exhausted. I was out of my mind. I wept all night and next day my pains began.'

'But what upset you so?'

'It was Natasha – you know her? She came with us to England when we left Russia. When Elliot and I were married she came to Denniston House to work, though she is not of the peasant class. Her mother was Mama's dressmaker and Natasha was sent to our summer house to deliver a box of sewing.

'St Petersburg was too hot, so we always moved to the country, in summer – quite near the Czar's summer palace at Tsarskoye Selo, but the year of the uprising we had not returned to the town house, even though the snows threatened – the trouble in St Petersburg, you see . . .

'When Natasha came with the sewing, she told us of the unrest there, and the looting and rioting, and Papa said that Igor must escort her back to her parents. It was the least we could do. She was a gentle young woman, and very beautiful. Something – *awful* – could have happened to her.

'But Igor brought her back to the summer house. Her home was deserted when they got there – her parents and sister gone. We could do nothing but keep her with us and when we knew we must leave, she begged to come to England with us.

'Along the way, Karl offered us his protection. Karl was

a Cossack, and loyal to the Romanovs. My mother felt duty bound to give them both shelter and employment.' She turned her face from him and he knew she was weeping.

'Anna,' he whispered. 'If it upsets you —'

'No. I asked you to come, and I must tell you. There'll be no peace for me, until I do.' She mopped her eyes with the corner of the sheet then smiled briefly, bravely. 'Natasha is so lovely. She has the grace of a ballet dancer. She walks proudly, and men are attracted to her. Even so, I didn't think that Elliot would notice her. He would joke about her, call her the servant in black; but never did I think —' she faltered.

'Go on,' Nathan prompted, though he already knew what she would say. 'Tell me?'

'When I got pregnant again, Doctor James said Elliot must not come to my room — you know what he meant? He was afraid I would miscarry again. To lose two babies before their time is not good; this time, he said, every possible care must be taken — and that included Elliot leaving me alone.'

'And he did?'

'Oh, yes. No blame attaches to him on that score. But one night I couldn't sleep. I was getting big and clumsy and I couldn't rest easily, no matter which way I lay. So I got out of bed. I meant to go downstairs and read a book I had left there — but I saw Elliot. He was walking carefully; it was obvious he didn't want to attract attention. He didn't see me, so I followed him — to Natasha's bedroom!

'And don't ask me if I'm sure, because I heard them. I stood, listening. They were making love, Nathan, and I don't know how I stopped myself banging on the door, throwing it open, confronting them. But I walked away, shaking and trembling so much I could hardly stand.

'When Elliot came to my room later to say goodnight to me, I told him I knew what he'd done. I asked him how long it had been going on and he said he would do what he wanted in his own home – especially as he got no comfort from his wife.'

'And that was when you lost control, Anna? But you were provoked. You mustn't blame yourself.'

'I must, Nathan. I do. I was reared always to keep a hold on my feelings; never to raise my voice, never to do anything unladylike. Yet I flew at Elliot like a wild thing. I kicked and thumped and screamed. I think the whole house must have heard it. I was out of control. I hated Elliot so much it frightened me. I wanted to kill him, but instead I killed my child.

'The shock must have done it. It was why I had such a difficult labour. The poor little thing was already dead inside me. He couldn't help himself to be born.'

'Anna dear, hush.' He reached for her, cradling her in his arms, making small soothing sounds, insisting she was in no way to blame. 'It was my brother's fault. In his own home, such a thing was unforgivable. Please don't cry? It's over and done with, now. Next time – if there is a next time – all will go well, I know it. And be sure about one thing. Elliot can't divorce you, Anna. Rather, it is the other way round, although it would be his word against yours.'

'Proof, you mean? I already have that.'

'Of course you have – and Elliot would be the last to deny it in the normal course of events. But if you threatened *him* with divorce, then you would have to have a witness – and you haven't got that!'

'Oh, but I have. Natasha, you see. She came to my room this morning. When nurse went for her breakfast, Natasha slipped in. She knelt, weeping, begging my forgiveness, saying Elliot had forced himself on her.'

'So she would bear out your story – if you insisted? I think it best, though, that she leaves Denniston House – for her own sake, I mean.

'I have already decided that, Nathan. Tonight, my mother is coming to see me. She arrived from London last evening and is staying at Pendenys. I will ask her to take Natasha back to London, when she returns. She must. Natasha is pregnant.'

'She is *what*!' Nathan jumped to his feet, walking to the window, staring out, seeing nothing. 'Is she sure? Is it Elliot's child?'

'She is sure. She says it can only belong to my husband, and I believe her.'

'And does Elliot know?' Nathan began to pace the floor, his body stiff with anger. 'What has he to say for himself? More to the point, what is he going to do for the poor girl?'

'He doesn't know and he mustn't know. Natasha begged that he isn't told. She fears what he will do, if he finds out. It is best, that way. And if he knew he would taunt me with it. Your brother knows how to hurt. Oh, I would like nothing better than to return to London with Mama and Natasha. Elliot dare not harm me, there. I would have Igor's protection. I could stay at Cheyne Walk until I was well enough to return to my – to my husband's bed.

'But I dare not even think about going. Elliot would say I was deserting him; he would use it against me. What am I to do, Nathan? I'm in such a turmoil I can hardly think. I should be angry with Natasha, but I feel nothing but pity for her – a stranger in a strange country. How she must long for her mother, now.'

'And what is to happen to her, to her baby? Who will support her? God! I am so angry!' Nathan drove a clenched fist into the flat of his hand. 'If my brother were to walk into this room now, I would give him the thrashing of his life!'

'No, Nathan! Remember I have just spoken to a priest. I am sorry, but you cannot, must not, do anything about it. It is what I want. Mama and I will help Natasha. It may be we can find somewhere for her to go until the baby is born. After that, we will have to think again. Perhaps she will want to keep it; perhaps she will not. It is too far ahead for us to decide.

'All I ask is that you pray for her, and if there is any mercy left in you, Nathan, will you pray for me, too? Will you beg forgiveness for what I did to my son?'

'I will, my dear Anna. It is the very least I can do. In some way, you see, I am responsible. My calling demands that I be my brother's keeper, though how I am to hold my tongue let alone my temper, I don't know.

'But I accept that what you have told me must not be spoken of again, and I will try to think what is to be done for the best, for you all. You know I will help in any way I can?'

'You have already helped more than you know. Come and see me again, if you can spare the time.'

'I will find the time. And when I come, I shall expect to find you much better. Perhaps to have Tatiana home will help, though if it distresses you to tell her about the baby, let me do it for you?'

'I never told her — and she is too innocent to have noticed any change in me. I shall tell her I have back-ache and that I must rest for a while. She will accept it.'

'Then I will go.' He took her hands in his, kissing her cheek. 'Try not to worry too much . . .'

Nathan Sutton had reason to be glad he had not driven to Denniston House in his motor; rather that on a fresh April day he had chosen to walk there. Now, he could walk back to his vicarage, slamming his heels down in anger with every step he took; walk the shame and disgust out of him.

Quickly he descended the stairs, nodding his thanks to the housemaid who handed him his hat and gloves, wanting nothing more than to be out of the house in case he should come face to face with his brother.

He strode down the drive, head down, hands in pockets, crunching his feet into the gravel, wondering what was to become of Anna in her unhappiness and of Natasha, whom his brother called the servant in black.

He was glad that Julia had gone south else he might have been tempted to trust her with Anna's confidences. Julia would have understood. She, more than anyone – except perhaps Alice – knew the full extent of Elliot's wickedness. Dear, proud, lonely Julia who must never know how much he loved and wanted her.

'Damn you, Elliot!' he spat.

Drew Sutton waited at the front gate of Keeper's Cottage, impatient for Daisy to come home from school, eager to tell her that Lady was making a tea party for them and that Keth was invited, too.

Drew liked Daisy and Keth; liked having someone to play with. Rowangarth was quite the nicest place to be and his lessons with Uncle Nathan were fun, most of the time, but at Windrush there were young ones to roam with and Lady baked cherry buns and Uncle Tom let him help feed the dogs and lifted him high to peep into birds' nests. Uncle Tom made everything come right again; made him feel less sad that his father had died because of that war. Yet grandmother had said that many small boys and girls had no father – only heroes to be proud of.

He pushed the war out of his mind because to think of it would spoil his holiday and staying at Daisy's house was almost as nice as Christmas.

Best of all, though, about coming to Windrush was the big, fat double bed he shared with his mother, snuggling close to her when he awoke, smelling her sweetness.

At Rowangarth he had his own room and his own bed, but at Keeper's it was fun, sharing with mother.

He stopped his thoughts, stilling the swinging gate, tilting his head the better to hear the distant footsteps. Then he ran towards them calling, 'Daisy! Keth! We're here!' laughing as Daisy threw herself on him and hugged him tightly. He grinned at Keth who understood about girls and that Daisy was like that.

'Hullo, Keth,' he smiled, disentangling Daisy's arms, picking up her discarded satchel. 'Lady is making us a party and she says you are to come, too. Sherbet and red jelly and gingerbread men. We're to ask your mother first, though.'

They linked arms, glad to see each other, all at once finding they had nothing to say though it didn't matter because they were together again.

'Keth got caned at school today,' Daisy broke the silence dramatically. 'Bang! Wallop! All over him!'

'One stroke on my hand,' Keth sighed, raising his eyes protestingly skywards. 'For looking out of the window and not paying attention. She always – always . . .

'Exaggerates?' Drew offered.

'Yes. She's always doing it.'

'Girls do,' Drew sympathized, recalling Tatiana's tantrums.

'Stop saying things about me or you won't come to tea,' Daisy cried. 'I'll eat all the gingerbread men and give the jelly to the dogs!'

Then she ran ahead of them, giggling, because she was happy about the party and Aunt Julia coming to stay and because she loved Drew very much; almost as much as she loved Keth.

But mostly she was happy because when Aunt Julia visited Mam was extra happy and talked a lot and laughed a lot and made red jelly and gingerbread men with curranty eyes.

'Ten more minutes and then what time will it be?' Tom demanded of his daughter.

'Half-past, Dada.'

'And half-past seven is bedtime!'

'Oh, not tonight? Not when Drew is here! Please, Dada, can't we stay up – just this once?' She fixed him with

253

wide blue eyes, smiling appealingly. 'Can't we finish our pictures? We're nearly done.'

Aunt Julia had brought wax crayons and colouring books. Aunt Julia brought lovely presents on account, Daisy had long ago decided, of her being very rich and living at Rowangarth which was very big and creaky and lovely to have holidays in.

Eyebrow raised, Tom glanced across at Alice who smiled and said just this once – if they weren't too long finishing and didn't prolong it. Daisy wasn't quite sure what prolonging it meant, though Mam was always telling her she was good at it. She smiled across at Drew, who smiled back and said, 'We'd better write our names on our books or we'll get them mixed up.'

'Oh, all right,' Daisy sighed. 'Though my name is longer than yours. It takes ages to write it. It was awful when I was learning it at school. It's the longest name in our class. Wish I was called Daisy Sutton,' she grumbled.

'Well, you can't be. You have to have the name you were born with,' Drew explained patiently. 'I must be called Sutton because people who live at Rowangarth are always called Sutton.' He stopped then, frowning. 'Mother is Mrs MacMalcolm, though. Sometimes I think I would like to be called MacMalcolm, like she is. Drew – Andrew Mac-Malcolm. That would be a longer name to write, Daisy,' he smiled comfortingly. 'Almost as long as yours.'

Julia's head jerked up at the sound of the dear familiar name; her eyes met Alice's, warily. Tom rose to his feet.

'Think I'd better see to the dogs,' he murmured, giving the sleeping Morgan a prod with the toe of his boot. 'Come on, old lad – dogs can't sleep indoors. And happen I'll check the coops,' he added, 'since I reckon you've got something to talk about.'

Alice raised her eyes to his and because he loved her so, because he understood every smallest thing about her, he answered her unspoken question without hesitation.

'Aye, bonny lass — *all* of it,' he said softly, closing the door behind him.

All. Alice closed her eyes. Not just about Drew being called Sutton, but because once she, too, had had that name and borne a Sutton child.

'Drew, darling.' Julia cleared her throat noisily and for a moment Alice thought the telling would pass; wanted it to pass. 'Drew — do you remember that not so very long ago you asked why you and I had different names?'

'Yes, but I've forgotten what you said.' He stared down, concentration creasing his forehead, at the daffodil he was colouring.

'That, I think, is because Mary brought in tea — and there was chocolate cake.' She tried to smile, but her lips were all at once too stiff.

'I like chocolate cake.' Drew laid down his crayon, selecting another of light blue. Chocolate cake was more important than what a boy was called. He began to fill in the outline of a periwinkle and Daisy, too, resumed her crayoning. She wasn't interested in names; only if they were long ones or short.

'Daisy, love.' Alice's voice sounded strange. It caused her daughter to lift her head at once. 'I think you'd better listen, too. What Aunt Julia — what we are *both* going to tell you — concerns you, as well.'

Without comment, Daisy closed her book, then made a fist with her hand on the table top, resting her chin on it. She knew she must listen. Mam's face was serious; exactly like when she had said *No*, to a bicycle. Not until she was eight . . .

'Drew — you do know that I love you very much and that Lady loves you very much? Lady is my sort-of sister, you see, and —'

'That's because I haven't got a father, isn't it? I get two lots of love from you and Lady.'

'Partly so,' Julia nodded. 'But there is more to it —

something very important and it's time you should know. Come and sit on my knee, sweetheart?'

'Do I have to?' Sharing a bed was one thing; sitting on your mother's knee in public – especially when you'll be eight at Christmas – shouldn't be expected.

'Not if you don't want to. Perhaps you're getting a bit old for cuddles,' she said softly. 'I suppose, really, that you're old enough to know why I am called Mrs Mac-Malcolm and your name is Drew Sutton.'

'You said important. Very important, is it?'

'More like *serious*. You know that your father was a very brave soldier and that he died, not long after the war was over?'

'Yes. On the day I was born. Grandmother told me that. Did my mother die, too?'

'Drew! You *have* been thinking, wondering . . .'

'No, not really. It was just something I sort of – *felt*. Really, I didn't want to know, because I wanted *you* to be my mother. And no one seems to mind that you are . . .'

'You *want* to belong to me, darling?' Julia's eyes pricked with small, sweet tears. 'I think that's the nicest thing you'll ever say to me.'

'Is it?' he demanded, mystified, anxious to get back to his colouring book. Then he frowned. 'I know my father's name – what was my mother called?'

'Alice.' Julia's reply was little more than a whisper.

'But that's Mam's name, too!' Clearly, Daisy was delighted.

'*My* name,' Alice stressed softly. 'But did you know, Drew, that once I was called Alice Sutton?'

Drew shook his head, unspeaking, realizing all at once how important their talk had become.

'Drew – you do know how much Lady loves you? Well, it's a special kind of loving.' Julia's voice was firm, now, though it had lost none of its compassion. 'And she loves you because that night your father died, she had you. You are her son. Lady and Giles were once married. In France, it was, when she and I were nurses there.'

'*Lady*?' Drew's eyes grew wider, his lower lip trembled. Then noisily he pushed back his chair to stand beside Julia, as if in need of her protection. 'It was Lady had me, then gave me to you? Why didn't you want me?' he demanded of Alice. 'Was I a horrid baby? Did I cry a lot and keep you awake at night?'

'No. That wasn't the reason,' Alice whispered. 'You did cry a lot, though, when you were first born, but I didn't hear you . . .'

'Lady was very, very poorly after you came, Drew, and you cried because you were hungry.' Julia took the small, pale face between gentle hands, forcing their eyes to meet. 'Lady had influenza, and you hadn't to go near her. You were such a precious little baby, you see. Your father had died and your Uncle Robert; we wanted you to grow up well and strong, or there would have been no one to care for Rowangarth.'

'Inherit it? Isn't that the word? When I'm twenty-one, Uncle Nathan said. I knew about that, but I don't understand. I really belong to Lady, don't I?' There were tears, now, in his eyes, and Julia gathered him to her, resting her cheek on his head.

'No, Drew. You belong to Rowangarth, just as one day Rowangarth will belong to you. Lady married Uncle Tom, then, and came to Windrush to live with him. It was best you stayed with grandmother and me. Lady knew it, too, and she knew I was sad and lonely because my Andrew had been killed and I had no one to love. No one but you, Drew. You were so important to me and to grandmother, too.'

'And is that why I'm called Andrew? Did you call me that because –'

'No, Drew.' Alice ran her tongue round lips gone dry. 'It was I who called you Andrew. I chose your names. You

257

are called for three brave, good men; names to be proud of. And I hope you'll forgive me for leaving you. Uncle Tom was my first sweetheart, you see. The Army told me he'd been killed, at Epernay, and I married Sir Giles and we had you.

'But Tom wasn't dead. It had all been a terrible muddle. A long time after the war was over, he came back to England and asked me to marry him. He said you were welcome to come and live with us. Tom wanted you, Drew, but you are Sir Andrew Sutton. Your place is at Rowangarth, not in a gamekeeper's cottage. A Sutton has lived at Rowangarth for more than three hundred years.'

Drew sniffed loudly, pulling his sleeve across his eyes. 'I'm not crying – not really – but it's all very sad, isn't it? I don't think I like wars.' He turned large, grey eyes on Julia and her heart contracted with sudden pain, because they were Andrew's eyes. 'Why were they fighting, mother?'

'Only God knows, child,' Julia sighed. 'If I ask myself why it happened until the day I die, I'll never know. Someone got killed in a place called Sarajevo. People – countries – took sides over it. And a little country called Belgium wanted to stay out of the fighting so the British went to help them. That was how it seemed, at the time.

'But I think, really, that every so often, men just want to fight each other. Men, especially the old men who let it happen, can be very stupid. There won't be a war ever again, though. Our war was so awful that no one will allow another to happen.'

'I don't think I'd like to fight in a war,' Drew faltered. 'You have to kill people, don't you?'

'You do, child.' Alice found her tongue. 'And your mother and me know all about that, because we were in that war, too, nursing soldiers who'd been wounded. And Major MacMalcolm, who was a very fine doctor, was there, too. He didn't like killing and neither did your father.

He went to war, but to save life, not take it. Your father was a very brave gentleman, Drew.'

'So do you understand,' Julia whispered, 'that no one wanted to deceive you. We just thought it best to wait until you were older before we told you that –'

'That I have two mothers? Well, I suppose if I can't have a father, two mothers is very nice.'

'But you aren't hurt – upset?' Alice pressed, remembering how once she had not wanted to see him, touch him, even; how Julia had faced her on King's Cross station with the child she refused to own.

And she had gazed down at a small boy who had tried to say Mrs Dwerryhouse, and couldn't. Lady, he'd called her. She accepted him, then, because he'd become Julia's child; found herself free to like him. She could even, she'd admitted, begin to forget Drew's getting in a cowshed, in Celverte.

'No. I think I'm upset about the war. Do you mind, Lady, if we don't talk about it any more?'

'But do you understand,' Alice persisted, 'that it was right of me to leave you at Rowangarth?' Suddenly, she must have his forgiveness.

'Yes,' Drew frowned, 'but could you take me away, if you wanted to?'

'I wouldn't want to, Drew. Rowangarth is where you are happiest. But even if I said I wanted you back, I couldn't have you because Lady Helen – your grandmother Sutton – is your legal guardian now, and she will never let you go. I shall always be your other mother, though, and I hope you will still call me Lady. Is that all right?'

'Yes. I think it's very nice, really.' He returned to his seat at the table, picking up the bright blue crayon.

'Do you, Drew Sutton?' Daisy's arm swept the width of the table, sending books and crayons flying; Daisy, who had been shocked into silence. 'Well, I *don't*! Nobody cares about me! Nobody asks me if it's all right!' She rounded on Alice with fury in her eyes, her body rigid with anger. 'How *could* you marry anyone else? How *could* you love anybody but Dada? I hate you! I hate you all!'

'Daisy! How dare you speak like that? You must never hate anyone!' Dear, sweet heaven, but they'd forgotten Daisy's feelings. 'Come to me, little lass?' Alice coaxed. 'Let me tell you, so you'll understand?'

But her child was gone, flinging across the room, banging doors behind her, sobbing as though her heart would never be whole again.

'Go after her,' Julia urged. 'She's upset and it'll be getting dark, soon. We never gave a thought to Daisy.'

'Aye, though she'll want no truck with me, yet a while.' Alice threw a shawl round her shoulders. 'It's Tom she wants; she'll be looking for him.' She let go a shuddering, despairing sigh and Drew was quick to notice.

'Don't cry, Lady?' he said softly. 'I'll pick up the crayons. Daisy didn't mean it. I don't think she likes sharing you with me, but she'll like it a bit more, when she gets used to it.'

'You're a good boy, Drew.' Gently, she kissed his cheek. 'I'm off, now, though I'm sure she'll be with Tom.'

'Can you tell me something else?' Drew frowned when he and Julia were alone. 'If Daisy and me have one mother between us — a sort of —?'

'A *natural* mother?' Julia prompted.

'Yes. Then does it mean she's my sister? I'd like it, if she was.'

'You and Daisy are *half* related.' Julia forced a smile. 'She is your half-sister, though she'll be glad, when she's thought about it, to have a big brother.'

'Hmm.' He rose from his knees to stand once more beside Julia's chair. 'I suppose I *am* quite grown up, now.'

'You are indeed, Drew — but what is all this leading to?'

'Well — you know we don't kiss or cuddle now — not when there are people around, that is. And often I call you Mummy.'

'Yes, though I'm sure private cuddles are allowed, and kisses, too.'

'I know — secret ones. But I think I'm too old to call you Mummy. Mummy is a word for small boys.'

'I see.' Loving him desperately, she struggled against the smile on her lips. 'What shall you call me, then, now you are growing into a big fellow?'

'Daisy says *Mam*, but it doesn't suit you, and *mother* is very nice, but I'd like something special.'

'Then why,' Julia said softly, 'don't you use the name your father used? Giles called your grandmother Sutton *dearest* and sometimes I call her that, too. It's a very sweet and loving name.'

'Dearest?' He smiled at Julia; smiled as Andrew had done, gently, and with love in his grey — or had they been green? — eyes. 'Would you like that?'

'I would like it very much,' Julia whispered huskily, knowing that if she lived to be a hundred, she would never love her son more. 'And I think I'd best boil a kettle. They'll be in need of a drink, when they get back. And what about you, Drew? It's time for bed, young sir. Would a cup of cocoa and a jam sandwich suit?'

'Please,' Drew grinned.

'Then upstairs and undress yourself. Fold your clothes neatly.'

'I'll do that — and dearest.' He hesitated in the doorway. 'I'm not sad or sorry about what you've told me tonight — 'cept for one thing. I wish I'd known my father.'

'My brother Giles — *your father* — was a dear, good man and if he'd lived to see you grow into a big boy, he'd have been very proud of you. Now off with you, and get into your pyjamas. Supper will be ready, when you come down.'

It would seem, Julia thought as she set the kettle to boil, that her son was indeed growing up, yet please God he would never know who his father was; his *real* father. And she would do anything, she vowed fiercely, to keep it from

261

him. She would swear before God Almighty, if she had to, that Drew belonged to Giles.

She glanced up at the mantel clock. She hoped they would soon be back — and that Daisy wouldn't be too upset.

Oh, *damn* Elliot Sutton! Would they ever be free of his evil?

Alice ran quickly towards the rearing field, calling Daisy's name. Stubborn, that child was and quick-tempered, like Tom. She was spoiled, too, by her Dada and by Mr Hillier and too pretty for her own good. She had only to flutter her eyelashes to twist either man around her little finger.

'Daisy!' she called again, angry with herself for not considering her daughter's feelings more; dismayed by Daisy's show of temper. Drew hadn't flown into a rage when he'd been told and Daisy must learn to bite on her tongue, an' all.

But Drew was placid and gentle as the man who had claimed him as his own; given him his name. Drew could have, should have, been Giles Sutton's son.

She saw Daisy ahead of her, making for the rearing field, calling Tom's name as she ran; saw too the light in the keeper's hut.

She stopped, leaning against a tree, taking in deep gulps of air. She would go no farther. Daisy would be all right. Tom would comfort her, say all the right things. They were close, the two of them; so close that had she not loved Tom so much she could have been given to jealousy.

She turned, walking the woodland path back to her home, breathing in the scents of April, glad that Julia would be there to understand, when she got back; Julia, her sister.

Daisy ran sobbing, a pain stabbing into her side. She knew where to find her father, her adored Dada. On an April night he ought to be at the rearing field, closing up the coops of pheasant chicks, making them safe against foxes. Oh, *please* he'd be there and not at Willow End or even walking the game covers? Tonight he *must* be at the rearing field.

The coops were all closed for the night, bricks securing their night-boards, but she saw a light in the hut; the keeper's hut they had moved on its small iron wheels from Six Oaks, where it always wintered. Dada was there, checking the bins where chick food was kept or counting his snares, perhaps, or maybe just sitting, thinking, as he sometimes did. Thinking miles away, Mam said.

Mam. She hated Mam; would never forgive what she had done! She threw herself against the door, calling for her father, flinging herself into his arms, sobbing pitifully.

'Well now, if it isn't my best girl.' He took his handkerchief, drying her tears, smiling gently. 'You didn't like it, then, what they told you?'

'You knew, Dada? All the time, you knew? Aren't you angry, too? How could she do such a thing? How could Mam love anyone else?'

'Ah, but you see – it isn't as bad as all that when you take a deep breath and think about it, little lass.' He sat down on an upturned box, taking her on his knee. 'Was that war to blame, see? They told your Mam and my Mam an' all, that I'd been killed – me, and eleven others – blown to smithereens in an army truck.

'But that shell didn't get me, though those Germans did; took me prisoner and told no one about it. Not for six months after the war was over and done with did I get back home. A whole year I'd been reported dead, Daisy. You couldn't blame Mam for giving up hope and marrying Sir Giles. And a good job she did, or there'd have been no more Garth Suttons at the old house – and no Drew.'

He closed his eyes, begging the Almighty not to strike him dumb for all the lies his tongue was telling. But could

263

he, in all honesty, tell her the truth of it? Daisy Dwerry-house's Dada a deserter; one they could still send to prison if ever they found out. And could he tell a little lass about Drew's savage getting?

'She didn't wait for long.' Daisy had stopped weeping, now, save for an occasional shuddering sob. 'Only a year.'

'Dead meant dead, in those days. Mam had no reason to think she'd ever see me again.'

'But she *did* see you again, Dada! Didn't you hate her when you found she was married?'

'It was a shock, lass, I'll admit it. But she was a widow by then and free to marry me. And marry me she did. She gave up a fine house aye, and a title an' all, to live here with me. Can't you try to understand the way it was, Daisy?'

Understand, when both she and Drew could only ever know half the truth of it?

'I suppose I do, Dada, but I wish it had never happened – her marrying another man, I mean.'

'Marrying your Aunt Julia's brother? But he was a good man, Daisy, and I'd be the first to say so. He refused to kill, but he went to war for all that, to help the wounded. He was braver than I was, I'll tell you that for nowt!'

'But how could she forget you, Dada? If Mam died, would you get married again – *would you*?'

'Would you like it, if I did?'

'No, I *wouldn't* like it! I'd run away with the gypsies!'

'There now – doesn't that tell me that you still love your Mam? Deep down, doesn't it? And I reckon those old gypsies wouldn't want you, Daisy Dwerryhouse. You're too fair, too pink and pretty for them. Gypsies are dark folk.'

'Like Keth?'

'Something like Keth. Now – are you going to listen to your Dada? Are you going to believe me when I tell you that not for one minute did Mam forget me or stop loving me. It was just that she loved Giles Sutton different, like.

'You're only a little lass now, but one day you'll know what love is like between a man and a woman. And when you find the man you want to marry, I hope you'll love him as much as I love your Mam – and as much as she loves me.'

'You're sure? Promise me that you and Mam love each other more'n anyone else in the world?'

'I promise, sweetheart, hand on my heart. And I promise that one day you'll love some young man every bit as much as you love me and Mam – only you'll love him *differently*. And when it happens to you, Daisy, will you remember tonight, and that your dad was right?'

'If you say so . . .'

'I do say so – oh my word, yes!'

'Dada.' She took a deep, shuddering breath. 'I was awful, wasn't I? I told Mam I hated her.'

'Then we'd better get back to Keeper's Cottage, my girl, 'cos you're going to have to say you're sorry and beg your Mam's pardon. And you're going to have to say sorry to Aunt Julia, too, and to your brother, for such behaviour.'

'Drew's my *brother*?' Her eyes opened wide.

'Of course he is – on account of you both having the same mother; your half-brother, to be exactly right. And you know all about mothering and fathering, lass. You're a country bairn and you know how baby creatures are made, so don't let's be having any awkward questions.

'Now – think I'll blow out this lamp and lock up, then we'll walk home real quiet by the back way. There's a herd of deer over by Six Oaks; if we keep down wind of them you'll see their little fawns – lovely little creatures. You'd like that, wouldn't you?'

'Yes, please. And I *am* sorry and I'll say sorry to Drew and Aunt Julia and especially to Mam.'

'There's my girl.' He took her hand in his, loving her, wondering what he would do to any man who used her as Elliot Sutton had used Alice. Strangle him with his bare hands, like as not; just as he wanted, still wanted, to kill Elliot Sutton.

'Quietly now,' he breathed. 'Don't want to frighten those deer . . .'

'Is she all right?'

'Fast asleep.' Alice drew back the bedclothes, snuggling into Tom's arms. 'Daisy'll get over it. We'll just have to be extra careful, for a while. But Tom – had you thought – it isn't something she'll be able to keep to herself; having a brother, I mean. What's the village going to think, when they find out? How are they going to feel about a mother who could leave her own son? What shall I tell them?'

'You'll tell them nothing, love, because it's none of their business. Folk understand that widows remarry – and heaven only knows, that war left plenty of widows behind it.'

'But what about Polly? What is she going to think about me being a lady – a *real* lady, I mean.'

'If I know Polly Purvis, she'll laugh her head off about it and pull your leg something awful. Polly hasn't had a good deal from life, with Dickon lamed and the Army refusing him a pension, yet she's happy. Polly will understand, be sure of it. And any right-minded woman down in the village will see the sense in not taking a boy away from his inheritance.'

'But if they don't, Tom?'

'Then they aren't worth bothering about! Now give us a kiss, then blow that candle out and let's get some sleep. The worst is over and lass – I love you.'

Tom lay unmoving, listening to his wife's even breathing, wondering if she were really asleep, loving her fiercely, protectively. Tonight, she had suffered, had risked Drew's condemnation and felt the full force of Daisy's anger. And what had been said tonight must have brought other things back to her; the worst night of her life she always called it – the night she had learned of his death; the night Elliot Sutton took her in rape and left her pregnant with Drew.

This year, for the first time, that date in March had passed without comment. She was forgetting, he had thought, thankfully. The wounds were healing. Yet tonight, for all he knew, that wound had been opened again and all the hurt and shame laid bare. Oh, yes, he could kill Elliot Sutton just as easily as he could kill any man who harmed Daisy; could do it as cold-bloodedly as Geordie Marshall had squeezed the trigger of his rifle when they were out sniping in No Man's Land.

And why was he thinking about that damned war again? Would it never leave him, never leave any of them who had been lucky enough to live through it? Why wasn't he thinking about more important things; that Drew and Daisy were brother and sister, now? And why did no one seem to realize that Drew had another half-sister at Denniston House? Anna Sutton's child. Just as Drew and Daisy had one mother, so Drew and Tatiana had one father.

It was a muddle, a nasty mess. Was Julia aware of it or had she pushed it to the back of her mind, only to be faced should it become necessary? He sighed deeply and Alice stirred in his arms.

'You asleep, Tom?'

'No.'

'Me, neither.' She turned to face him, pressing close, lifting her mouth to his. 'Kiss me, sweetheart?'

17

'I think,' Julia said two days later, 'that Drew and I should go home.'

'The strike, you mean?' Alice was anxious about it, too. 'By what the papers say, it seems there'll be no avoiding it.'

'Well, you can't blame the miners.' The miners had Julia's sympathy; hadn't Andrew's father dug coal? 'If we leave tomorrow by the afternoon train, I could stay overnight at Montpelier Mews. Perhaps Mark Townsend will know better how serious things are.' She shrugged apologetically. 'I'm sorry, Alice. I arrive here, throw everybody's life into chaos, almost, then announce that I'm leaving. And I ought to stay a little longer, make sure Drew and Daisy are over the worst.'

'They are. I'm sure of it, though it'll take a while for Daisy to accept my being married before,' Alice smiled sadly. 'And Drew must be uneasy about things – wondering who he really belongs to.

'But you must tell him, always, that I shall never take him away from you. Once he's sure of that, he'll be all right.'

'And you agree we should go?'

'I do, Julia. Best you both get safely home, though I'd like you to stay. Why don't you go to the Post Office – ring up Mark Townsend? He'll know better what's going on. He seems a decent man. You've always listened to him, in the past.'

'Ring him? But I know what he'll say. He'll tell me to

go to London – then he'll ask me out for a meal, or something. He seems to take it for granted that I'll go out with him, when I'm in London. Yet I can't say I don't enjoy his company. I get so lonely, Alice. I need, sometimes, to be flattered, treated like a woman. Then I feel guilty because I know there can't be anyone for me but Andrew – not ever.'

'I can't see why you should feel guilty.' Alice sensed her friend's need to talk. 'And I don't see why you can't go out with a man without feeling you've committed mortal sin. I know how you feel, though. When I married Giles I felt I was betraying Tom.'

'But you *had* to marry Giles; it's different for me.'

'I know that,' Alice sighed. 'But there has to be something more to life than shutting yourself off from all feeling, living only for Drew. You might as well do what Cecilia did, and go into a convent!'

'You're right, I suppose. It's just the awful feeling of guilt if ever I go near another man. I worry, Alice. I know how marvellous it is to be loved, you see. Really loved. I ache all over for Andrew, sometimes. It's more than seven years, but I still rage inside me that I can't have him. There – I've said it! I need to be made love to.'

'But only by Andrew.' Alice reached out for Julia, hugging her warmly. 'Yet there's got to be more to life than caring for Drew and Rowangarth. And think on, will you? One day Drew is going to fall in love and then where will you be?'

'A bitter, interfering mother-in-law,' Julia laughed derisively. 'Oh, Alice! Wouldn't it have been wonderful if Drew and Daisy could have married?'

'Heaven help us, they're bairns, still! Goodness only knows, though, who they'll choose when the time comes. But yes – it would have been nice if they'd been able to fall in love. We'd have had the best of both worlds, you and me.

'But they can't fall in love, and Julia — neither could Drew ever marry Tatiana, and what's worse, if ever he wanted to you couldn't tell him why — not without breaking his heart.'

'So you've thought about that, too?' Julia's face was all at once grave.

'The minute Anna Sutton had her I realized it, though I kept it to myself. No use looking for trouble — and anyway, it'll likely never happen.'

'But if it did, I suppose I could always tell him they were first cousins and it wasn't advisable, couldn't I?'

'Julia — cousins *can* marry. And much notice he'd take, if he grows up like you, that is! You'd have fought the world to marry Andrew!'

'I would. But I needn't have worried.' Julia's eyes took on a yearning, remembering look. 'Mother liked Andrew right away. Mainly, I think, because he was so direct and honest, but partly because he had eyes like Pa's — grey eyes that sometimes seemed green. She told me, afterwards; said he'd looked at her with Pa's eyes. "It was as if your Pa was telling me he liked him, too," she said.'

'You don't have to tell *me*,' Alice grinned. Andrew had been in Harrogate and Julia had sneaked out to meet him. 'You burst into the sewing-room in a state of panic. "Andrew has asked me to marry him and he's calling here tomorrow morning!" you said. "Without an appointment!"'

'But whilst we're talking about — well, *things* — there's no reason at all why you shouldn't sometimes go out with Mark Townsend, so stop your worrying.'

'Even though I have a feeling he's attracted to me?'

'Even though! And anyway, that's his problem, not yours!'

'Oh, Alice love — how I needed to talk to you. And how I wish,' Julia said earnestly, 'you weren't so far away. I miss you so much and I know it's selfish of me, but I'd give almost anything to have you back at Rowangarth.'

'Happen so. But it would take a small miracle for that to happen and Tom and me have already had our fair share of those.'

'I know – but I can hope. And meantime, I think we can take it that Drew and I will be leaving tomorrow. Think we'll walk to the village and check on train times to London – order the taxi, too.'

'Fine. And if Mark Townsend is reading things into a situation that doesn't exist, that's his lookout. So get yourself off to the village. I'm short of an ounce of wool, so you can get it for me whilst you're there. And be back sharp at half-past twelve for your dinner!'

'Alice! You sounded just like Hawthorn when she told Andrew and me to be back by half-past three for tea – *or else*!'

'Well – I was supposed to be in London to chaperon you and there was I, letting you out in public with that young doctor!' Funny, really, when you thought about the way it had once been.

'And I shall never cease to be grateful that you did. Dearest Alice – don't ever leave me? Never stop being my sister?'

'I won't, love. I know I'm a long way from Rowangarth now, but if ever you need me, I'll be there, I promise.'

Poor, lonely Julia, with the ghost of Andrew's love for ever by her side. No other man could measure up to him and no matter how attracted he was nor how patient, Mark Townsend would never have her, of that Alice was sure.

Olga, Countess Petrovska, had not been best pleased with what greeted her on her arrival at Holdenby and by evening her mood had changed from one of suspicion to downright displeasure.

On stepping from the train she had been met not by her daughter's conveyance but by Mrs Sutton's motor and taken not to her daughter's bedside as she wished, but to Pendenys Place. And as if that were not enough, she was then told she might not visit her daughter.

'Countess, you must realize that no one, not even myself,' Clementina soothed, 'has been allowed into the sickroom. The doctor is most insistent. Only Elliot, of course, though now Anna is insisting that she sees Tatiana.'

'And she will see her mother, too,' the countess bristled, 'or I shall want to know why! I am told she went into early labour and that the baby did not live, yet now I may not see her? The doctor must respect my rights as a mother. In Russia, he dare not have forbade me!'

'But this is not Russia and in England we take the advice of our physicians. And if you were to go to Denniston House, you would not get past the monthly nurse there. She's a dragon. I know. I have tried myself to see Anna, only to be turned away. "Doctor's orders," is all she says!'

'Then I shall see that doctor at once and he shall give another order – that Countess Petrovska is allowed to see her Anna at all times. I have not journeyed from London only to have doors slammed in my face! You will please to order your driver to take me to the doctor without delay!'

'But that may not be convenient. The doctor is a busy man. He might be taking surgery or even sick-visiting. Stay here for a while, and rest. Let me ring for tea and then we will telephone for an appointment.'

Clementina was becoming agitated. The countess had an autocratic manner and if she offended Richard James there was no knowing what blunt answer she might receive.

'I do not care for your English tea,' Olga Petrovska sniffed, allowing herself to be guided to a chair. 'I will take coffee. And why are my bags being taken upstairs? Surely there is a bed for me in my daughter's house?'

'Of course, of course.' Clementina pressed the bell-push.

'I thought it better, though, if you were to stay here. There is more room at Pendenys and more servants to look after you. You will be comfortable here.' And less able, she had long ago decided, to interfere in a clearly explosive situation, with Elliot at odds with the world in general and the monthly nurse in particular and Anna demanding that Tatiana be returned to Denniston House without delay. One would think the child had been kidnapped, the fuss that was being made! And no one, save Helen, giving one jot of sympathy to Clementina Sutton who had been deprived, again, of the grandson she so desperately needed! 'You and I, countess, must support each other in our loss. That our grandson did not live has devastated me.'

'I would rather support my daughter,' the countess snapped. 'It is she who carried and delivered the child. It is *her* loss and I intend to comfort her as only a mother can. So I will take my coffee, then you personally will telephone for an appointment for me — *today*! And if one is not given, I shall go to my daughter's house and not two dragon nurses shall deny me access to Anna!'

'I'll do it now,' Clementina murmured, all at once at a loss for words. And besides, she had not the stomach for a fight. The countess in full high dudgeon was not to be gainsaid. The countess imagined she was still in Russia, giving orders to peasants! Small wonder they'd had a revolution there! And when she did see Richard James, the whole wriggling can of maggots would be upended and heaven only knew what sordid facts would come to light.

Because trouble was brewing at Denniston House. All was not right, there. She, Clementina, could sense it and the countess seemed hell bent on blundering in and making things worse! Where it would end was any fool's guess, and for two pins she would walk out of this house where she was no longer appreciated, throw herself on Helen's understanding and let them all get on with it, Elliot

273

included, she thought vindictively as she picked up the telephone. Elliot *especially*!

'I shall not cancel our passages,' Amelia Sutton said sadly, laying aside the cable from England. She had reserved a stateroom on the liner *Mauretania* for the end of May: in nice time, she had calculated, for the family christening of Albert's expected nephew or niece, and the fact that the poor babe had not lived was no reason for putting off the trip. For one thing, she liked England and her Sutton relations – well, *most* of them – and for another – and far more important – Anna would need all the comfort and understanding she could get.

She, Amelia, was thoroughly contented with her life. She had a devoted husband and two healthy children, something she had never hoped to achieve at one dismal period of her life. It behoved her, therefore, to support and sustain the poor, pretty Anna in any way she could.

'I said I fully intend to go to Pendenys as planned,' she repeated. 'It's our duty to stick together as a family in times of distress. To lose a child must be the most awful thing – don't you agree, Bertie dear?'

'Oh, I do, Amelia. I agree entirely.' And amazingly, he did. He was very fond of his children and for once felt sympathy for his brother. 'Poor Elliot. He'd set his heart on a son.'

'Poor Elliot my great-aunt Fanny!' Amelia snapped. 'It's that little Russian girl I'm sorry for.' She had never taken to Bertie's brother. Elliot had visited with them here in Kentucky before the war and his arrogance and boredom and condescending manner to all things American earned him her dislike. She'd have bet her last dollar he was a womanizer into the bargain, and had been relieved, she recalled, to see the back end of him. 'It's Anna I feel for. She'll be grieving for that baby. Thank heaven for little Tatiana; at least it proves she's able to bear a healthy child.'

But three pregnancies and three disappointments just made you wonder what was going on, over there. 'Something's very wrong with that marriage, Bertie. Mark my words if it isn't!'

'You could well be right, but Amelia – don't interfere?'

'Y'know darn well I wouldn't – not in husband and wife business. But if ever it came to taking sides, I'd be right behind Anna, so be warned!'

'I know my dear; I know.' Affectionately, he kissed her cheek, fighting a smile. Amelia would take sides with the devil himself against Elliot. She didn't like him; she never had. And come to think of it, he thought soberly, he wasn't all that fond of his eldest brother, either. Elliot had been spoiled, even in the nursery, and Elliot would get what he wanted no matter who suffered. And Elliot would never change.

'So! At last I am seeing my daughter!' Countess Petrovska sat straight-backed at the bedside, her mouth ever traplike, though kindness showed in her eyes. 'What a place is this Yorkshire, when a mother must ask permission to sick-visit her child!

'Well, now that I am here, I shall stay until you are well enough to travel. When you are, you will come with me to London. You will return to your mother's house. I have decided.'

'No, Mama! I can't! Elliot would say I was deserting him! It's all such a muddle – you don't understand . . .'

'Oh, but I do! I have visited your doctor and he told me everything – *everything*, Anna. For one thing, you are not to have another pregnancy for a year!'

'Yes, and I agree with him. I'm so tired. I seem always to be carrying, or miscarrying. I'd like a little time to get really well, only Elliot doesn't agree.'

'Then for once, Elliot will listen to medical advice. And if that fails, then he will listen to *me*! You and Tatiana will come to London. There is to be no argument!'

'But there *is*, Mama, much as I would like it. Elliot says if I refuse him his – his *rights*, then it is grounds for divorce. He will divorce me, and find a wife who will give him a son. He says so!'

'And you believe him? Oh, Aleksandrina Anastasia Petrovska, what an idiot you are! Of course he won't – *can't* – divorce you.'

'No. Maybe not – not now, that is. But there is so much you don't know, Mama.'

'It does not surprise me. When I walked into this room and saw you I knew you were not only grieving for your baby. You look ill, my Anna, and afraid. I am your mother; I sense these things and you must share your worries with me.'

'I have already spoken to Nathan.'

'Your brother-in-law? The priest who married you? Ah, yes, he seems a good man. And what did you speak to him about?'

'It was a confession . . .'

'Even so, you must tell me.'

'Very well. I told him it was on my conscience that I had been to blame for the little one's death.' The words rushed out in a whisper.

'And were you, Anna Petrovska?'

'Partly so . . .'

'Then I think you had better tell it, Anna. Everything.'

'You won't like it, Mama.' She leaned back against her pillows, eyes closed.

'If it concerns your husband – and I have the feeling that it does – then I am quite sure I won't like it! Nevertheless, I am waiting for you to tell me, then we shall decide what is to be done.'

'But promise you won't rant and rage? And promise, when you know, to stay here with Tatiana and me for a little while, at least?' Any moment now, she would weep and Mama did not like tears. She took a slow, calming breath.

'I shall stay. For one thing, it seems I am needed here and for another, I think I will be stranded in this place for some time if this great striking happens. It will close everything down, I am told. This country gets more like Russia with every day that passes! There will be a revolution here, too, if the King is not careful!'

'The King doesn't rule as our Czar did, Mama. Don't worry. We shall be safe enough here — *if* it happens. That at least I'm sure about.'

'Then I must know what it is you are *not* sure about. I am your mother; I will listen. It is what mothers are for.'

And so wearily, tearfully, Anna told her . . .

'A penny for them?' Mark Townsend reached out across the candlelit table, laying his hand on Julia's.

'They aren't for sale.' She did not draw her hand away. 'They concern you, partly.'

She felt relaxed. Tomorrow it was likely that she and Drew would return to Rowangarth. There would be time to get home, Mark said, before it happened. *If* it happened. On the surface, all seemed normal, and though news broadcasts over the wireless were understated, the newspapers were less guarded in their opinions. Some sided with the miners, some did not; but whatever their views, some show of protest seemed inevitable. Miners had fought for their country, Mark had said; others worked impossible hours in the pits to feed the wartime factories with coal. Either way, he considered, the mine owners had no right to increase a collier's working day and at the same time cut his pay. Julia had warmed to him for that. It was exactly what Andrew would have said.

Andrew. Always, no matter what, her thoughts returned to Andrew, yet now there was Mark who could always get tickets for whichever theatre took her fancy and who took her to supper, afterwards, and made her feel a woman, again.

'So tell me, Julia?' He broke into her broodings with such suddenness that she said,

'I was thinking about you, Mark. You were Aunt's solicitor, now you are mine. You are always there with good advice when I need it — and with comfort, often. Yet I know nothing about you; nothing at all.'

'You know all there is to know; that I shall always look after your interests with great care — and that I am very fond of you.'

'I'd realized that,' Julia said with her usual directness, 'and I realize you know how desperately I resent Andrew's death, still. But I know little about you, save that you live near Montpelier Mews and that —'

'That Sparrow glowers at me whenever I arrive to take you out,' he laughed.

'Sparrow was devoted to Andrew, but I was trying to ask, I suppose, why it seems there is no woman in your life. Forgive me, but you did insist that I tell you.'

'I did — and there was a woman in my life, once. In the war, it was, and I'll admit she still colours my thinking. When I think I'm out of the woods, something happens to —'

'I'm sorry, truly I am! I shouldn't have asked. It was wrong of me!' Julia gasped, all at once angry with herself.

'No — it's all right. It really is.'

'But it *isn't* all right! Oh, Mark — will I ever learn? Here am I, touching thirty-three, and still I jump in without thinking. Utterly tactless.'

'Straightforward, I'd say,' he smiled, 'and truthful and honest. And a very lovely lady whose company I find delightful. There now — does that satisfy you?'

'It does. And I do understand, truly I do. The war did a lot of cruel things to people who loved each other and —'

'More champagne?' He lifted the bottle from the cooler.

'And are you satisfied, now, that you and I can enjoy each other's company without fear of – *complications*, shall we say?'

'We can, Mark. And bless you for understanding and for being so tactful about everything,' she smiled. 'And I didn't mean to be nosey or even to warn you off. Oh, dammit! Yes, I *was* trying to tell you that I'm in love with Andrew, still, and I never thought –'

'Julia,' he smiled. 'It *is* all right! So let's make a pact? When we are together, there'll be no mention of what happened to either of us; that for just a little while, we'll neither of us fret about what happened in the past? And meantime, I think we should talk about getting you both back safely to Rowangarth before the trouble starts – because there *will* be trouble. Lord knows how long it's going to last, but I'm afraid there'll be no avoiding it.'

'Then will you look in on Sparrow, occasionally, to see that she's all right – especially if the telephones are affected and I can't get through to her?'

'I'll make sure Sparrow doesn't come to any harm, I promise you. So finish your drink, my dear Julia, before it gets warm and flat – then I'll take you home.'

On the first day of May the Trades Union Congress declared their support for the coal miners, angrily condemning the commission which recommended they should accept a cut in their hourly rate.

Not a penny off the pay! Not a minute on the day! became the battlecry.

The following day the striking miners were joined by gas and electricity workers; building sites closed. That day, Julia sent a telegram to Alice, telling her they had reached Rowangarth. Letter follows, it ended, though if ever that letter reached her could well be a matter of luck.

'It's bad, isn't it?' Alice whispered, placing the small yellow envelope behind the mantel clock. They were waiting for the evening news bulletin; the wireless at least gave out the truth impartially. Soon, Tom said, there might be no newspapers. Even if printers didn't join the strike, it was only a matter of time before the transport unions came out in support so there'd be little point in newspapers if there was no way to get them to the newsagents. Best stick to the wireless, Tom said, all at once grateful that electricity had not reached Keeper's Cottage and that they had lamp oil and candles to last for a month.

'Surely the government will make sure that the broadcasting people don't go on strike.' Stood to sense, didn't it. 'At least they'll be able to tell people what to do if things get out of hand.' The new-fangled wireless sets were at last proving their worth.

'And will they,' Alice whispered, 'get out of hand?'

'Lord knows. But there'll be nobody at Windrush going on strike, even though the boss said that anyone wanting to withdraw his labour is free to do so. But nobody'll bother. Mr Hillier sides with the miners, and that's good enough for us.

'You know we're having a collection for them? We asked if it was all right and Mr Hillier said that however much we gathered together, he'd ten-times it, and see that it got to the people who need it most!'

'So things should be safe enough, here at Windrush?' Alice pleaded, desperate for comfort.

'Safer than most. We're out of the way, here. You could drive past the lane end and never know this estate exists. We might get a bit short of food, though . . .'

'But we've got potatoes and onions and carrots in the shed, and I bought in extra flour and lard and a few tins – as many as I could afford. But Polly,' Alice frowned, 'lives from hand to mouth. There'll be little in her store cupboard.'

'They won't go hungry at Willow End. What we've got, we'll share.'

'*If* it happens, Tom . . .' Still, Alice grasped at straws.

'It'll happen. It's Them against Us; the rich against the working man. Like it was in the war, I reckon – those men in London giving their orders and not giving a damn what became of the men in the trenches . . .'

'But in the war we helped each other, Tom. Julia is gentry, yet she rolled up her sleeves like a good 'un!'

'Miss Julia's different. But there's going to be a confrontation, only this time *They* are going to have to take notice.'

'Tom Dwerryhouse, you're a Bolshevik! If most folk thought like you there'd be a revolution here, like in Russia!'

'And happen there could be and never forget it, lass! Any road, I'm for the miners. My dad dug coal till a roof fall lamed him.'

'And so did Andrew's father. Julia is on our side, even though she belongs to *Them*.'

'Like I said, Julia's different. Now hush your worrying and turn up the volume. I want to hear what the wireless has to say about it.'

Alice closed her eyes. She didn't want to hear that her lovely, contented world was threatened. It was the war come back again, only this time it could be Briton fighting Briton, just as it had been in Russia, nearly ten years ago.

The disembodied voice announced in clear, unemotional tones that from midnight, railwaymen, dockers and drivers, printers and engineers were to support the miners. Trains, buses, food deliveries and newspapers would all be disrupted; gas and electricity supplies affected.

Alice reached for Tom's hand. Now she was very afraid; soon, the country would be in turmoil. Tomorrow, when May was but three days run, most workers, though they could ill afford it, would side with the miners. The country would come to a chaotic standstill.

All at once she could stand no more of the carefully

modulated voice. Quietly she left the room, her whole body shaking, to stand at Daisy's bedside.

Little lass – forgive us our foolishness? This was the England Robert and Giles and Andrew had died for; aye, and Jinny Dobb's nephews and millions of young, straight men. This was the country that was to have been a fit place for a hero to return to. *But don't worry, Daisy. Dada will take care of us . . .*

On the next day, the General Strike was complete. May, the most beautiful and hopeful of months, when winter was gone, when green leaves unfurled and bluebells grew thickly and buttercups glowed golden in the meadows, saw Britain at war again – with itself.

Volunteers who had no time for trades unions banded together to keep essential services open. They tried to deliver milk, letters, food to the shops. Some donned steel helmets, legacies from the trenches, and drove buses for those who wished to go to work or those, fearful for their jobs in a country where unemployment loomed large, who thought it politic to make the effort to get there. In cities and towns, fighting broke out between strikers and strike-breakers with the police, truncheons flailing, keeping order as best they could. The government, alarmed at the threat of anarchy, called an emergency Cabinet meeting.

'There's one good thing about this awful mess,' said Cook, who'd declared there would be no striking in Rowangarth kitchen since Lady Helen was the best of employers, 'there are no dratted newspapers!'

During the war years papers had been dreaded, though read from end to end as a painful, patriotic duty.

'Maybe not,' Tilda countered darkly, 'but bad news travels fast, for all that. There were some tramcar drivers in Leeds wouldn't join the strike and crowds pelted them with lumps of coal!'

'And who told you that?' Mrs Shaw demanded sharply.

'It was Will,' Mary defended. Will Stubbs still had a liking for other people's business and an ability to be uncannily accurate into the bargain. 'There was a train held up at a level crossing near York. There were strike-breakers driving it – trying to get milk through. People threw stones at it!'

'Never!' Cook could not accept that folk hereabouts could be capable of such violence. In cities, happen, where living conditions were far from ideal, but not in Holdenby; oh, surely not?

'Will says,' Mary persisted, 'that a few of the mills are trying to work, but their stocks of coal are almost gone.'

'Well, I'm going to Creesby tonight,' Tilda announced defiantly. 'At least the picture house is open.'

Strikers had turned a blind eye to the cinemas. They were places in which entire communities could gather; in which the great majority who did not own a wireless set could watch the newsreels and cheer on their fellow strikers. Or loudly boo those whose conscience demanded they should side with the employers; consciences, or fast-emptying pockets, that was.

'You'll do no such thing, Tilda Tewk! Lord only knows what might happen to you on the way there, and it'll be a six-mile ride back – and no street lamps! This house'll be locked and bolted at sunset, Miss Clitherow's orders, so you'll find yourself shut out in the cold, all night!'

'Like them poor miners are locked out at the colliery gates,' Tilda sniffed.

'They'm not locked out! They chose to strike,' Cook argued hotly, 'though I reckon I'd starve afore I'd go down one of them deep, dark holes!'

'What do they mean by anarchy?' Tilda, robbed of her evening in the cosy darkness, demanded petulantly. 'This news-sheet says there'll be anarchy, if folk don't support the government.'

News-sheets, hastily printed by non-striking newspapers, warned of anarchy – or even worse – if men and women did not recover their lost senses and return to work, for worse than anarchy was the threat of empty bellies and hungry bairns!

'Anarchy,' Mary supplied, 'is another word for revolution. Like they had in Russia.'

Will had said so. Will pedalled off on his bicycle to Creesby on his free nights, sniffing out gossip instead of courting her like he ought to! Mary Strong was already heartily sick of the strike.

'Revolution?' Cook whispered. Revolution in England? The King and Queen and all the royalty taken out and shot and the gentry fleeing to France, their homes taken over by workers? It didn't bear thinking about!

She sat herself firmly in the fireside rocker, pulled her apron over her face and wept, just as she had done in the war when things had got beyond bearing.

Mary and Tilda exchanged glances, tiptoed to the back door, then made for their bicycles, determined to prove for themselves the truth of Will's claims. Loyal to her ladyship they might be, but anarchy bore an exciting ring and they wanted to experience it for themselves.

'We'll be locked out,' said Tilda, dramatically.

'Don't care.' Mary knew, anyway, where to find the broken catch on a downstairs window.

'Miss Clitherow'll go on something awful.'

'Let her!' Mary had spent the war years in a munitions factory in Leeds and had a fair bit of brass tucked away in the bank. Mary was not so intimidated by her betters.

'But what if her ladyship rings?'

'Then let old Clitherow answer it. Me and you are on strike an' all for a couple of hours, Tilda. And Cook's in such a tizzy she'll never notice we're gone.'

Cook dried her eyes on her apron, set the kettle to boil, then turned on the wireless set. The government, said the announcer, had declared a state of emergency and tomorrow, on the fourth day of the strike, the Attorney General would announce his deliberations on its legality.

A state of emergency, and the law coming into it, an' all. It was altogether too much. Cook ignored the boiling kettle and retreated once more into the folds of her pinafore.

Revolution, that's what, and in England!

Five days from its commencement, the Attorney General pronounced the strike to be illegal and that workers could be sued for their part in it. One by one, the unions abandoned the miners. For just eight days, open rebellion had blazed furiously, then died in ignominy. It had not been so much the threat of a court appearance that sent men back to work, but the sobering thought of a wife demanding a pay packet that was not forthcoming. You couldn't feed hungry bairns, they said, on hot air. Only the miners stubbornly continued to strike. Let them, reasoned the mine owners. Empty heads would lead, in the end, to empty bellies.

Yet the man in the street took heed never to forget the injustice of it. The war he had fought for king and country had taught him to think for himself – and to remember. Many, previously opposed to trades unions, flocked to join them if only as an act of defiance, even though only last year they had thrown out Ramsay MacDonald's Labour government.

'Is it going to be all right now?' Alice demanded of Tom when the country shook its head and wondered what it had all been about.

'As right as it'll ever be,' he comforted, though men would still fight each other for a day's work and queue at factory gates for jobs that didn't exist. 'There are times, love, that I'm not ashamed I walked out of that war – do you know that?'

'Aye, Tom. The older and wiser I get, the surer I am you did the right thing. Giles Sutton hated that war. He vowed he wouldn't kill and he stuck it out – 'til someone sent him three white feathers. It was then he went as a stretcher bearer.'

'I remember. Brave fools we called them. They'd crawl through the barbed wire at night into No Man's Land, trying to get the wounded back and –' He stopped, blocking out the horror of it as he blocked it out almost every day of his life.

'Do you know who sent Giles those feathers, Tom? It was *him* . . .'

'Elliot Sutton?'

'Him. He let it slip, to Julia. She went for him like a wild thing. Punched her fist into his face. Told me that, if she could, she'd have killed him.'

'Good for her! And I know you sometimes hanker for Rowangarth, Alice.' He gathered her to him, laying his cheek on her hair. 'And I know you miss Julia, and Reuben. But we're better off, here; away from trouble – away from *him*.'

'I know. Times when the longing comes over me, I remember the night they said you were dead and I tell myself how lucky I am. But Tom – I'd like to see Reuben. He's getting old. Now that things are settling down, can Daisy and me go up there, maybe soon?'

'That you can, love.' He could deny her nothing, he loved her so much. 'I reckon I can give you the train fare, an' all.'

'Thanks, but I've got it.' She always kept it, safely hidden beneath her handkerchiefs, as an insurance. 'I've a couple of pounds; it's always there – just in case.' In case Reuben should need her . . .

'Then write and tell him you'll be coming as soon as maybe, and tell Julia you'll be needing a bed, at Rowangarth.'

'You're a good man, Tom.' She reached up gently to kiss him, understanding why he, her husband, could never go with her to Rowangarth. For one thing, Tom could not rightly stay in a house that had once been hers for the short time she had been married to Giles; been Lady Alice Sutton. But deep inside her, she understood his real reluctance to return there. Denniston House was but a cock-stride from Rowangarth, and Tom's hatred of the man who now lived there would never diminish. Tom had a temper that could flare white hot at only the mention of Elliot Sutton's name. Much as Julia longed for it and the small miracle that could take them all back to the gamekeeper's cottage at the edge of Brattocks Wood, it could never be – could it?

18

Amelia Sutton had declared her intention not to let the trouble in England interfere with their visit and now, as they waited at the river mouth for the pilot boat that would guide them up the Mersey, she felt a sense of homecoming, even though she was as American as Thanksgiving Day. She loved the amazing greenness of an English springtime and besides, Albert's Yorkshire abounded in race courses and to attend race meetings delighted her. Horses – family apart – were her life. The British appreciated good horseflesh, so they passed muster with Amelia Sutton. It would be sad, though, to see Anna's unhappiness, but Bas and Kitty had been warned not to talk about the baby and to be especially kind to their Aunt Anna. And there would be other babies, Amelia reasoned. Elliot's wife was young enough to give him half a dozen sons, if that was what he wanted. Elliot. She dismissed him from her mind and told her children they might go on deck to watch the liner come alongside.

'We shall soon be at Grandmother Sutton's,' she told them, eager to show off the children it had once been doubtful she would ever bear. Sebastian, brown-haired, brown-eyed and serious though given at times to be led into mischief by his sister; Kathryn, hair Mary Anne black, her eyes the blue of a summer sky. Fearless on horseback, she out-rode and out-jumped her brother.

Amelia smiled contentment. Bertie, Bas and Kitty. She loved them with all her grateful heart. Her mother-in-law's bossiness did not deter her; Amelia Sutton's own wealth guaranteed that. 'Soon be at Pendenys . . .'

'That place gives me the creeps,' Bas brooded. 'So many rooms and passages and staircases. I still get lost in it.'

'It's spooky,' Kitty laughed. 'It's got ghosts in dark corners and footsteps behind you, always, and the eyes in the portraits follow you when you walk past. I just love it. I could live there for ever and ever!'

'Out!' ordered Albert. 'Do as Nanny Eva tells you and don't lean over the rail!'

'Y'know, Bertie, mother-in-law was real put out that I filched the maid she loaned me to look after the children. She's made a great nanny.' English nannies were popular in America and it was with great glee that Amelia had lured housemaid Eva Roberts back to Kentucky, when Kitty had been a newborn babe. One in the eye for Her Mightiness, she had gloated. She wondered, serious again, how the little Russian countess was making out with the formidable Clementina.

'We must be especially kind to Anna,' she murmured. 'The poor girl must have a lot to put up with. D'you reckon she'd appreciate a visit to Kentucky? It would surely do her good.'

'We could ask, dear.' Anywhere, Albert supposed, must be preferable to Pendenys. He understood his son's dislike of the place; had always liked better the shabby cosiness of Rowangarth. 'And you must make sure the children don't mention the baby to Tatiana. Seems she was never told it was coming.'

'They know.' Amelia was more concerned that on their last visit her children had called Elliot's daughter Tatty Anna because she was still wearing diapers. 'I'm more concerned that they've gotten the child into knickers. Well – nearly three and still in diapers, last time we were here.' Nanny Eva had seen to it, she recalled smugly, that Kitty had been dry as a bone at two and a half.

'Nappies. They're called *nappies* in England,' Albert corrected absently. 'And we can't criticize what Russian mothers do. Let's play it by ear, when we get there?'

Four weeks would soon pass, he supposed. Left to him, they wouldn't visit half so often. Had it not been for Amelia's insistence on family togetherness, he'd be content never to leave Kentucky. And the annual visits did, he supposed, serve to remind him how miserable had been his lot as a younger son and how very right he had been to marry Amelia. 'Think I'll go up on deck – see what the youngsters are getting up to.'

He kissed his wife's cheek with genuine affection and so aware was he of his extreme good fortune that when his daughter said, 'Hi, daddy. We've just been talking about Tatty. D'you figure she'll be old enough to play with us, this visit?' he didn't have the heart to correct her.

'Oh, at four and a bit I think she will be.' He smoothed Kitty's wind-whipped curls. 'And if she isn't, there's always Drew.' Young Andrew. The baby born in the nick of time to take the title Mama so desperately wanted for Elliot. Albert liked young Drew Sutton. 'Look – there's England.' He pointed to the tall buildings emerging from the blur of the skyline. 'Soon be on dry land again.'

'I'm going away for a week or so, Dwerryhouse – up north,' Ralph Hillier announced suddenly as he and his gamekeeper walked the game covers. 'There's no need to shout it all over the place, though you'll know where I'm off to.'

'I've a fair idea, sir.' The estate workers at Windrush had not joined in the General Strike but shown their sympathy for the miners by collecting fifteen pounds for them. It was an amazing sum by any comparison and Ralph Hillier had swelled it by a massive one hundred and fifty pounds. 'You'll be taking all that money with you?'

'To the miners at Torvey Main, where I once worked. Will I be coming across any of your family, Dwerryhouse?'

'I doubt it. Dad made sure Jack and me never went down

the pit.' His elder sister was married to a farmer and his younger one doing very nicely in bespoke tailoring. 'But I appreciate what you are doing. There'll be a few hollow bellies around Torvey afore the miners give in. Some say they'll stick it out for months. It's the bairns I worry about.'

'Do you think I hadn't thought about them, too.' Absently, Ralph Hillier bent to fondle the head of the labrador bitch at his heels. 'Apart from the money there'll be a van load of food going up there, too. I'll leave it at the Miners' Institute; they'll see it gets into the right hands.' He picked up a stick, throwing it. 'Fetch, Beth.' He smiled as the young bitch carried back the stick in a gentle mouth. 'That's a fine gun dog I've got. I was looking at that spaniel of yours, Dwerryhouse. He's slowing down a bit.'

'Morgan! Aye – it's to be expected. Not quite sure how old he is; fifteen, happen. He's Alice's dog, though he's more attached to Daisy. Alice brought him with her when she came here to wed me. When will you be going to Torvey, sir?'

'Tomorrow, all being well.'

'Alice plans to go north next week – her and Daisy. She wants to see Reuben. He's getting old, like Morgan.'

'You'll miss them.'

'Aye, but Reuben is her only blood kin. He was good to her when she was a bairn. She's fond of him. And I don't begrudge the visit. It's like going home, for Alice. She was sewing-maid, once, at Rowangarth.' It was all he was prepared to say about the matter; about anything that concerned Alice's past, no matter what talk might be circulating in the village. 'You'll give my regards to anyone who might remember me, sir – when you get to Torvey . . . ?'

Igor Petrovsky arrived at Denniston House uninvited and unannounced. It was a surprise to everyone save his mother, who had graphically related Anna's situation in a lengthy phone call to Cheyne Walk.

'Please to have my car garaged,' he instructed the footman who answered the door. 'Where is Mr Sutton?'

'Sir – might I have your name?'

'There is no need to announce me. Where is he?'

tely, the servant pointed to the library. Igor nodded his thanks, then walked swiftly to the double doors, flinging them open, closing them firmly behind him. The footman hesitated, then tiptoed to stand with an ear to the doors.

'Why, Igor! Come in, old fellow. Nice to see you!' That was the master, putting on the charm.

'I wish I was able to say the same but I cannot. I do not find it in the least *nice* to see you. Indeed, I am angry that my mother insisted this visit is necessary.'

The listening servant walked softly away. He could wait. They would hear the outcome of it before so very much longer for Denniston House had one advantage, from a servant's point of view. Sound carried well.

He hurried to the kitchens, there to warn all staff to be alert to the ringing of bells, for a ringing of bells there would be, he smiled, wondering if Russians still fought duels.

Duels. Count Petrovsky slapping the master's face with a glove, provoking a fight like it happened in the films. More was the pity that duelling wasn't allowed here any longer. It would have been a grand sight seeing Elliot Sutton led out to pistols at dawn.

The thought pleased him and he smiled again. Not pistols, but trouble, for all that. Trouble for the master, if he wasn't mistaken!

'Tea, you lot!' Julia called. 'In the conservatory!'

They ran towards her, calling, laughing. Bas, Kitty, Drew and Tatiana. Tatiana with her nanny, of course. And tomorrow there would be Daisy. Alice and Daisy coming to Rowangarth. Tomorrow, at four, they'd be arriving. She would take Drew to meet them, at York. Dear, dear Alice . . .

'What's for tea, Aunt Julia? I'm starving.' Kitty, so fleet of foot, ahead of the rest. 'Is it cherry scones?'

Cook's special-day scones – ever since Julia could remember, and today was special, because the children were together again. Drew's cousins, the young-generation Suttons. Five, there would be, when Daisy arrived. Daisy was counted a Sutton, too. Five beautiful children who always opted to play at Rowangarth and never at Pendenys or Denniston House.

'I'll see to them, Mrs MacMalcolm.' Nanny, carrying Tatiana, murmured, red-faced from running.

'Sure you can cope – they're an unruly lot,' Julia grinned.

'I'll manage, ma'am.' Children were no trouble at all, when they were eating. Compared to some grown-ups she could mention, children were little angels.

'I'll leave you to it, then. If they get out of hand yell for me. I'll be in the library.' Though why the library, she really couldn't think. Usually, if not in the conservatory, afternoon tea was taken in the small parlour.

'Sit down, dear,' Helen murmured as her daughter pushed open the door. 'Are the children all right?'

'Right as rain. Denniston nanny is in charge. Why the library?'

'Why indeed? A whim, I suppose. This was Giles's room, really, and I thought if I told you in here that Giles would be a part of it, too.'

'Told me? Dearest, you're not ill?' Richard James had visited yesterday. 'Did Doc James –'

'Richard merely reminded me that in a few more weeks he and Effie are retiring to Scotland. And I shall miss them so, Julia. All my friends gone – or going.'

Judge Mounteagle dead and his wife in Kenya, now, with her eldest son; Luke Parkin – dear Luke – dead, and his wife in a home for clergy widows, in Bath; Edwin and Tessa almost always in France and Martin and Letty Lane in Italy. A minor post in a consulate there, but gratefully accepted. Two more years before she saw Martin and Letty again. So lonely, now. Just she, Julia and Drew. And memories.

'But that was all?' Julia insisted. 'He didn't give you a check-up, or anything?'

'He didn't need to. I am well, Julia, but growing old. I'm sixty-five, next birthday – had you thought?'

'I hadn't.' Her mother was still beautiful. She could never be old. 'But why, suddenly, all this serious talk – because there *is* something; I can see it in your eyes.'

'Not serious, exactly. Pour, will you, before the tea spoils? I was going to keep it, but then I realized that Alice will be coming tomorrow and I wouldn't be able to get a word in edgewise. Best I tell you now.'

'Tell me *what*?'

'It's called taking stock for my old age, I suppose. And this isn't a sudden decision. I've talked it over with the Carvers; all three of them. They fully agree with me. They're seeing to it – selling the tea garden, I mean . . .'

'*Selling* it? Letting Shillong go?' She couldn't be. The Rowangarth Suttons had always grown tea. Julia's cup hit the saucer with a clatter; tea slopped over. 'Dearest, you *can't*!'

'I can. I have – well, almost. Young Carver advised me to take the offer.'

'*Him*!' She might have known, Julia brooded. Shifty-eyed. She had never liked young Carver. 'What offer?'

'Lyons made one, almost six months ago; an offer too good not to consider. Sutton Premier is very fine tea. They were anxious to have the garden.'

'But *can* you sell it?'

'Without asking you – is that what you're trying to say?'

'Well – *yes*. And tea has always kept Rowangarth going. You know as well as I do that Rowangarth estate is only just ticking over, holding its own.'

'And what we get for the garden, properly invested, will leave us financially sound.'

'Young Carver said so, I suppose!'

'No. Carver the elder. When it comes to investing capital, there's none to touch him. Your father always said so.'

'But how can you – face me with a *fait accompli*, I mean. Out of the blue . . .'

'Not out of the blue. I've thought long and carefully about it. And I *shall* sell, Julia. Your Uncle Edward agrees.'

'So you've told *him*?'

'Like you, Uncle Edward holds shares. He will sell his, he has assured me. You had none, but you inherited your Aunt Sutton's. Your Pa left his shares to me, as did Robert. Giles's will go to Drew, and I am Drew's legal guardian. So there'll only be you, Julia, with ten per cent, holding out.'

'In short, I'm outvoted?'

'Yes.' It was a simple, final confirmation. 'You would be all right for money, dear.'

'But I don't want any more money! I have Aunt Sutton's money and her house. And I have what Pa left me and Grandmother Whitecliffe's jewellery must be worth quite a bit. I have the army widow's pension, too. I don't *need* money, mother.'

'I shall sell,' Helen said quietly. 'Please let's not fall out over this – not you and I? I am doing the right thing, I know it. Think about it, won't you?'

'But we've always had the tea garden.'

'Yes. And one condition of the sale is that two chests of tea will still be sent each year to Rowangarth, just as they always have been. And I'm glad Alice is coming tomorrow. She is still Drew's mother; she'll have to be told.'

'You don't ever want to let Alice go, do you?'

'Not if I'm honest. She was Giles's wife; my daughter, for just a little while. And she gave us Drew. I wish she were still here – she and Dwerryhouse.'

'And Daisy.'

'Daisy, too. I shall never stop hoping they'll come back to us. But you do understand – about selling the tea garden? It really is for the best. All Drew's time, when he grows up, will be spent looking after Rowangarth. We can't go on for ever, being absent owners. It's well-managed, now, but I'm facing old age, Julia. I want things cut and dried. I'm tackling all my problems and worries and trying to leave everything straight and sound for Drew, that's all.'

'You're right, of course. When I draw breath and think about it, I shall know you have done the best thing for us all. But dearest – don't talk about getting old? Not you?'

'Very well. Not for a little while, at least. And do you think we could ring for more tea – there's something else, you see . . .'

'Dearest – not more problems?'

'Not a problem – more a worry faced.' Helen rose and walked to the far window. 'Come here. Look . . .' She drew aside the lace curtain, pointing down into the stableyard. 'What do you think to it? It's a thank you to my daughter for – well, for being my daughter, I suppose. And an atonement . . .'

'*Mother*!'

From below, yellow duster poised, Will Stubbs tipped his cap, grinning. Will liked motors, had learned a lot about them during his war years.

The little car beside which he stood was square and black and shiny. Its radiator was brass-banded, its running-boards rubber-covered. At the back end was a folding luggage rack.

'It's for you, Julia. They call it a baby Austin, I believe. Stubbs said it'll do forty miles an hour, but there isn't the need to go that quickly, is there? Oh – and the windscreen is made of special safety glass.' She looked anxiously over her shoulder, her eyes searching for Julia's. 'Stubbs says it's a little beauty – a woman's car.'

'But dearest.' The car outline blurred and Julia blinked tears from her eyes. 'You hate motors. No motors at Rowangarth – not ever, you said.' Not since Pa had killed himself in one.

'I'm afraid cars are here to stay,' Helen murmured. 'And this one *is* a baby.' So small and sweet a motor, surely, would be safe enough? 'I've been selfish, Julia. I had no right to forbid you your own car. I had a word with Pa – he told me it was all right.'

'Darling!' Julia held her mother close. 'How I wish I could talk to Andrew as easily as you can talk to Pa.'

'You could, child, if only you'd be still; if only you could stop hating the war, hating the world for parting you from him. Accept it, as I learned to do and then perhaps one day, when your mind is quiet you'll hear him, with your heart. It's time for you to take stock, Julia, as I am doing.'

'But I've made a Will – it's with Mark Townsend.'

'I'm not talking about possessions.' Helen shook her head impatiently. 'I'm talking about memories. It's almost eight years, and you haven't been to France, yet, to Andrew's grave. That can't be right, dear.'

'Perhaps not. But if I go and see his name on a gravestone – then it'll be final, don't you see? We never said goodbye, he and I – don't make me do it, mother?'

'I won't. Really, it isn't any of my business – but I wish you'd go. You owe it to Andrew and you owe it to yourself. But let's go and see this little motor and perhaps you can give it a try on the estate roads, get the feel of it.' She pulled Julia's arm into her own. 'Stubbs is longing to explain it all to you.'

'And shall you learn to drive it, mother?'

'Not I! I shall stick to my pony and cart, but when you're better at it, I might let you drive me into the village. Oh, hurry, *do*!'

* * *

Count Igor Petrovsky stood, back to the fireplace, glaring across the room at Elliot Sutton.

'We have to talk, you and I. Aleksandrina Petrovska is my sister and my responsibility, therefore. My mother is not happy about the way it is, here. I think you should explain yourself to me.'

'And Anna *Sutton* is my wife, and wholly *my* responsibility and I would remind you of that. Nor do I give a damn about what your mother thinks. Who asked her to interfere, anyway?'

'No one asked her, but I am here and you *will* listen. My sister is not well and we think she would get better the sooner if she returned with us to London.'

'Away from me, you mean?'

'Exactly.'

'But I need my wife here, at Denniston. I have a right to her company.' His cheeks had flushed a dull red; his mouth curled down at the corners.

'Her company? What you really mean, Sutton, is that you have a right to her *bed*? But you have forfeited that right! Oh, I grant you it is Anna's duty to be with you, and I know she will return when she is fully well again.

'But when she does come back, then Karl will come with her. He will be her personal servant and a member of your household staff. He will care for her as he did in London – before she married you – and if you make her unhappy, then I shall know about it.'

'You're mad. *Mad*! You're all the same, you Ruskies. Couldn't stand it in the trenches, could you? Walked out, the lot of you – left it to us to sort out your mess and guard your Front!'

'And how would you know that, *Mister* Sutton? You were nowhere near any Front – east or west. You never fired a shot! But we are not here to talk about how you managed to keep your boots clean for four years; I have come to tell you that my mother intends to stay at

Denniston House with Anna until she is strong enough to travel. There is to be no argument!'

'And my wife? Does she go along with your wild scheme? Does she want to desert me? Didn't you know that in England desertion and the refusal of conjugal rights are grounds for divorce?'

'And do you know that in my family there is no divorce? So you will forget your threats. I do not intend to give you *carte blanche* to kill my sister with yet another pregnancy. You are an animal!'

'And you!' White now with anger, Elliot pointed a shaking finger to the door. 'You will get out of this house or I'll have you thrown out! Is that clear?'

'No. Suddenly, I am not understanding your English so well. But is *this* clear?' With two great strides he had crossed the distance between them. Grasping Elliot by his jacket lapels he raised him off the floor, holding him so that his feet dangled as if they belonged to a rag doll. Then, laughing, he flung him back into his chair again. 'There now – did you understand; understand that I am young and fit and that I would like nothing more than to thrash you as you deserve?

'And you will *not* divorce my sister. Rather, it is she who will divorce you. She has grounds, I would say – her husband's adultery. So watch your step, Sutton. I dislike you intensely. You are a suddenly-rich peasant as far as I am concerned, who has yet to learn to conduct himself as a gentleman.'

He walked slowly, provocatively to the door, smiling softly as though he wanted his sister's husband to be the one to strike the first blow. In the doorway, he paused.

'I shall be staying here at Denniston House, with or without your invitation. There are things to be discussed – Natasha Yurovska, for one. She too will return to London.'

'The servant? What is she to you?' Elliot sneered, all at once brave with the distance of the room between them.

'She is nothing to me, save that we brought her with us into exile and, like my sister, I consider her to be my responsibility. She is not my mistress – so be warned. You have me to deal with now, and I am not a defenceless woman!'

The door closed quietly. Elliot Sutton reached for the silver box on the desktop, taking out a cigarette, lighting it with shaking fingers, inhaling deeply.

So they knew about Natasha, but if they tried to use it against him, then it would be his word against hers that he'd ever slept with her. Oh, Anna knew he'd been to the servant's bedroom but there were ways to keep her silent. Tatiana, for one. And as for Natasha Yurovska – who would take the word of an inarticulate servant against that of a gentleman?

He slammed a clenched fist hard down on the desktop. Damn them all! Damn his mother for insisting he marry the mawkish Anna and damn Anna for being a mare who couldn't breed!

No one understood him; no one at all. The Garth Suttons despised him; even his own father disliked him. Be damned, then, if he wouldn't go to someone who appreciated him; someone to whom he could pour out his misery and receive sympathy in return. And all for half a sovereign! There were whores in Leeds who would listen all night for half that amount!

Savagely he tugged on the bell-pull.

'Have my car brought round to the front door,' he ordered the footman who answered the summons. 'And I shall not, after all, be dining at home.'

To hell with the lot of them! He was off in search of comfort and understanding. And who could blame a man for that when his entire family conspired to keep him from his wife's bed?

He paused to fill his cigarette case, then, smiling, made for the back stairs.

19

For all it was nearly June, Reuben Pickering's kitchen fire burned brightly. It was his only means of cooking and the elderly felt the cold, Alice supposed, even in summer.

'Tell me,' she smiled as she set the kettle to boil, 'just how old you really are.'

'Seventy-nine, next, though keep it to yourself. I've been swearing to seventy, since Armistice day,' he winked.

'Then tell me, whilst we're on the subject, how old do you reckon Morgan is?'

'Ar – let's see. He'm no more than fourteen. Was only a pup, when young Giles found him. Did I ever tell you how we got him?'

Alice shook her head, though Reuben had told her often.

''Twas not so long after you came to Rowangarth – from your Aunt Bella's, I brought you. You'll remember Bella?'

Alice did; remembered her grudging acceptance of her orphaned niece. Twelve loveless years there had been, but mostly she remembered being hungry.

Then Reuben had taken her to work at Rowangarth and to happiness, because three years later, when she was walking Morgan in Brattocks Wood, she met Tom.

'Aunt Bella – yes. But tell me about Morgan?'

'Well, one day Giles brought this spaniel to Keeper's. In a bad way, it was. He'd found it at the side of the road, hurt bad. He wrapped it in his jacket, brought it to me. The poor thing had been abandoned; been beaten, an' all.

'Poor little beggar'd be better out of its misery, I told

him, but he'd have none of it. Sent for the vet, then between us we got the creature on its feet again. The veterinary was called Morgan, if I remember rightly. Reckon that's how the daft animal got its name.'

'Giles couldn't bear suffering – not ever. That's why he died, helping other people. And Reuben – Daisy knows about Giles and me . . .'

'Best she's been told,' he nodded comfortably. 'How did she take it?'

'Badly, at first, though now she likes having a brother. She's playing with the Sutton brood, at Rowangarth. She and Drew are coming to see you, later. She's got a present for you; wants to give it to you herself. Knitted you a kettle-holder, so mind you admire it!'

'I've made sure,' Reuben chuckled, 'there are sweeties in the tin. Drew visits with her ladyship and always has his sweeties. Her's proud of that boy, Alice. Alus has him with her when she visits Rowangarth pensioners. There's a silver lining to every black cloud, and that little lad's a silver lining if ever I saw one.

'But playing at Rowangarth? Young Catchpole won't like 'em running wild over his gardens. Five of them, eh; five young Suttons growing up. Sad about that little lad at Denniston. You could even feel sorry for Mrs Clementina; she was real cut up about losing that grandson, talk had it. But in a strange way it's Fate, I suppose.'

'Karma, I believe it's called. As you sow, so shall you reap . . .'

'Ah, well, I alus said as that one's sins would find him out, and I'm right. They're catching up with him, mark my words. Terrible trouble at Denniston, I've heard. A right old set-to between Elliot and Countess Anna's brother. Came to blows, I heard, though I saw Elliot not long after and his face looked all right to me. Not like when your Tom walloped him,' he chuckled.

'I don't know anything about that.' Alice filled the teapot

from the boiling kettle. 'But I heard — and you're not to repeat this to a soul, Reuben — that Anna Sutton is going to London to her mother's house before so very much longer. Seems she's got to get her strength back. Julia said Nathan is taking her to the churchyard, now that she's on her feet again, to see the little one's grave. And I heard,' — Mary had had it from Will Stubbs and sworn it was gospel truth — 'that Elliot Sutton isn't best pleased since he hasn't been invited to London.'

'Serve him right. He's a bad 'un and he'll come to a bad end. That wife of his is a lady; not like him. But breeding outs, Alice, and the Russian lass is twice too good for that one. But forget him. You'm home, girl, and there's better things to talk about. What's news, from Rowangarth?'

'We-e-ll . . .' Alice spooned sugar into Reuben's mug. 'Lady Helen has bought Julia a motor. I'll bet it took a bit of doing, after the way Sir John was killed.'

'Killed himself, more like,' Reuben brooded, 'trying to speed at sixty miles an hour. 'T'isn't natural, going that fast. He could've burst his ear drums.'

'He did worse than that. Poor Lady Helen. Just before dinner, they came to tell her. Mary waiting to serve and Cook getting bad-tempered, keeping things hot. Not long after I'd gone to work at Rowangarth.' She clutched her mug, staring into the fire, remembering. Then she smiled.

'And Lady Helen's had a good offer for the tea garden and is going to sell, but you'll know about that; it's no secret. But it's as if she's putting her affairs in order, Reuben. I hope she hasn't had a premonition.'

'Not her! Her ladyship's good for a score more years, yet. Do you ever wish you could turn the clock back, lass — do things differently?'

'No, Reuben. I wouldn't change anything. Mind, it was a tragedy at the time; I was half out of my mind with worry when I fell for Drew. But it was all meant to be. I wish you'd come to Windrush, though; live with Tom and me.'

'Nay, lass. The young and the old don't mix. Just keep writing me letters and come home to Rowangarth whenever you can, and I'll be content.'

Home to Rowangarth, Alice brooded. But home, didn't they say, was where the heart was and her heart, all of it, was Tom's. Home was at Windrush, now.

Anna Sutton shivered in spite of the warmth of the day. Clutching her wrap around her she sank into a chair, staring through the windows into the moist greenness of the conservatory, thinking about the tiny grave. He was real to her now, the son she had never seen. He was Nicholas, the son she had caused to be born before his time, and she had vowed, as she laid white flowers over him, that she would make retribution. When she was well enough, she would return to Denniston House and Elliot's bed. It would be loathsome, but it would be her penance and she would submit to what was expected of any wife. But only when she had found the courage to submit to it. Staring at the bare earth, her hand in Julia's, she made her decision. She had thought to refuse to go back to London with her mother, ignore the doctor's advice; remain with Elliot and let happen what may. Yet the sight of the little mound of earth had stirred such feelings inside her that the need to make her husband suffer as she had suffered could no longer be denied.

'Will you look after the grave, Julia?' she asked softly, sadly. 'I would like someone to come and see him whilst I am away.'

'You're going, then? You've made up your mind?'

'I shall stay at Cheyne Walk for as long as I think necessary.' She tilted her chin defiantly. 'Alone.'

'You won't regret it,' Nathan smiled. 'The summer is

ahead of us – getting well again is all that matters. Julia and I will bring flowers.'

'And you'll pray for Nicholas?'

'I will.' Nathan had taken the frail, cold hand in his own. 'And for you, too, Anna . . .'

'So she's going?' Elliot Sutton spat. 'That mother and brother of hers – they've put her up to it. Well, I'll be glad to see the back of the bitch!'

'Elliot! Do *not* talk like that! An ailing wife is no use to you. She'll miscarry the next baby as well, and then where will you be?' Clementina sighed.

'I'll get rid of her! There's got to be grounds for divorce. Surely Carvers can find a way?'

'The Carvers do not accept divorce petitions. Old Carver wouldn't entertain one. They've been solicitors to both Sutton houses for a long time and I can assure you that –'

'An annulment, then? An annulment would be respectable.'

'It wouldn't. It can't be. Anna hasn't give you grounds for one.' Clementina waved a dismissive hand.

'She's clearing off – leaving the marital home. Isn't that grounds enough?'

'Leaving your bed – isn't that what you mean? Oh, there are times when you disgust me, Elliot. You're like a lusty young tup; you all but paw the ground when there's a female in sight!'

'Mother! You can be so *crude* . . .'

'No. Just plain-speaking, and what's more, you'll listen to what I have to say! Oh, I know about that Natasha. You've been in her bed, haven't you? There's not much I don't get to hear about, in the end. She's going back to London, too. Shouldn't wonder if the countess doesn't know about what you've been up to an' all – is taking her out of harm's way. Is no woman safe from you? I don't know where you get it from!'

'Well, it can't be from the angelic Suttons so it's got to be from Mary Anne!'

'Aye, and maybe it's because you've been spoiled, denied nothing. Well, I'm done with it. You'll say goodbye to Anna in a civilized manner and you'll wish her well – tell her you'll miss her.'

'Oh, I'll do that, all right. I'm a good actor. But it's her last chance. I let you push me into marrying her; you were determined to have her! Breeding, you said; just what the Place Suttons needed. Aristocracy, you insisted. God, mother! If you wed me to half the daughters in Debrett's it wouldn't change what we are! Tradesmen, that's what; foundry owners!'

Clementina's face blanched, her eyes narrowed into slits. She drew in a breath and held it till she was near to exploding.

'Get out!' she gasped. 'Get out of my sight before I take my hand to you! *Out* . . .'

'Tcha!' He shrugged, then turned on his heel. At the slamming shut of the door, Clementina threw herself on the sofa, pummelling its softness with wild, angry fists.

'God help me,' she wailed. 'What am I to do with him?'

She wished she had the courage to take a whip to him; lash him and thrash him until her anger was spent and her body drained of all feeling. Why was life so cruel to her?

'It would seem,' said Countess Petrovska to her son, 'that those Bolsheviks have found the Czar's treasure.' She folded the newspaper and dropped it to the floor beside her.

'Oh?' He laid down his knife and fork. 'As far as most think, the Czar moved his capital into European banks when the war started. It's highly unlikely that –'

'I'm not talking about gold nor share certificates. It's the Romanov jewels. The paper says they've been found. Those Bolshevik pigs will be happy, now. I'd heard the Czar had hidden them well, but it seems not well enough! The article in the paper said the Czar had sent trainloads of his personal things to Siberia and they've been discovered by the Reds. Imagine, Igor? Those exquisite pieces in Bolshevik hands. Pearls before swine. It doesn't bear thinking about!'

'No.' He had problems enough without fretting over something he was powerless to do anything about – his sister's husband, for one. Today, soon, they were leaving for London, though he wasn't at all sure that Elliot Sutton would accept Anna's departure without protest; wouldn't make a last-minute appeal to her not to leave him. And his sister might well be swayed; might still have some semblance of feeling for him. Or the man might use Tatiana as a pawn; insist the child stay behind, at Denniston House.

'They'll sell them, you know! They were desperate for money, those Bolsheviks, but now they will auction those precious things abroad and buy tractors and machinery and guns. We shall never be rid of them, now. I shall never see Russia again. You, perhaps, and Anna, but they will lay me in foreign soil. Ah, but it doesn't bear thinking about,' the countess moaned.

'Then don't think about it! Think of Anna and what is to become of her!'

'But we know what is to happen. Anna is returning to my house, to be cared for – to get well.'

'And after that? She will return to her husband like a mare to the stallion.'

'Igor! Watch what you say to your mother! You are not with your drinking friends, now! Your sister knows her duty, though the sooner she produces a son the sooner she can slam her bedroom door in that man's face!'

'But that hasn't happened yet, nor will it for some time. Have you finished eating, mother? Isn't it time to see to your cases, get ready for the journey?'

'There are servants to do that. Does your mother's company so upset you that you are sending her out of the room?' she bristled, bright-cheeked.

'No – but when Elliot Sutton comes in, can you leave us alone together? There are things I must say to him and I'd rather we were alone.'

'Very well.' She spooned apricot conserve onto her plate. 'And might an old woman ask what the so-private business is about?'

'You may not, though when we have Anna safely in London, I will tell you.'

'Is it something serious – important?'

'Important? Not really – but serious, yes; serious for Sutton, that is. You *will* leave us, mother?'

'If I must.' She bit into her toast. 'I shall expect you to tell me, though.'

'I said I would – but later.'

'Very well.' She pushed back her chair. 'Your helpless mother knows when she isn't wanted!'

'Ha!' Igor grinned. 'Helpless . . . ?' He dabbed his mouth, then rose to his feet to gaze from the window. He was, truth known, looking forward to the interview and turned as the door opened.

'Ah, Sutton,' he murmured. 'Might we have words, you and I?'

'We're to say goodbye to Tatty.' Drew offered his hand to Daisy at the stile. 'Mother says she's going to London, today. It's a pity. She won't have anyone to play with, in London.'

'She'll have her nanny,' Daisy retorted. She did not like Tatiana Sutton. She was petted and spoiled and her nanny always there to spoil everyone's fun.

'Nannies don't count,' Drew sighed. 'And Tatty's only four.'

'When *I* was four,' Daisy countered airily, 'I was in school. And I walked there, every day. I didn't have a nanny to pick me up and carry me when I got tired!'

'You had Keth.'

'I know. I miss Keth. I wish he was here. I like Keth better than you! I like Bas better than you, an' all, and you can go on your own to Denniston to say goodbye to Tatty Anna. I'd rather you did,' she said pettishly.

'But why, Daisy? I thought you liked her.'

'Oh, I do, I suppose. But if you must know, I don't want to go to Denniston House.'

'But you said you liked Aunt Anna, too. I know she likes you.'

'Of course I like her. But I don't like *him*. I don't like Mr Sutton. He glares at me as if I've no right to be there.'

'Well, you're my sister, so you have every right. Do come, Daiz? Be kind to little Tatty?'

'We-e-ll – Tatty hasn't got a brother, I suppose.' It made her sad to think about that poor dead little baby. 'All right, then. I'll come.'

She smiled brilliantly and all at once Drew was glad she was his sister. Daisy was so very, very pretty . . .

'Words?' Elliot Sutton hovered at the serving table, lifting silver lids, peering into warming dishes. 'I suppose so.'

'It's about my sister.'

'Oh?' Elliot filled a coffee cup, spooned kedgeree onto his plate, then seated himself at the table. 'And what is the matter with her now?'

Breakfast at Denniston House was an informal meal, with tea and coffee keeping warm on hotplates and dishes of eggs, bacon, kidneys or kedgeree for the taking. No servant was in attendance unless summoned; talk could be intimate or private, even, with no one there to listen and report back to the servants' hall.

'Matter? Nothing that rest and quiet and a little kindness won't take care of.'

'I could forbid it, you know.' Elliot poured cream into his coffee. 'I'd wager that even now if I snapped my fingers she would stay with me. What you all seem to forget, Petrovsky, is that Anna is *my* wife, *my* responsibility and is answerable only to me.'

'But you will not snap your fingers,' Igor said softly, 'because, with or without your permission, I intend to take my sister back to London. You are a very stupid man, but not so stupid, surely, that you would ignore the advice of a physician.'

'Richard James is an old fool. He's retiring soon, and not before time. He wasn't all that brilliant, was he, when it came to saving my son? That baby shouldn't have died. It was your sister's fault. She threw a fit, and killed it!'

'And what provoked that fit of anger? Was it you, perhaps, getting found out? Hell, man, if you had to go off the rails, did it have to be on your own doorstep?'

'Don't presume to tell me what I may or may not do in my own home!' Elliot Sutton's fork clattered to the table. 'You are a guest in my house. Watch your tongue or you and your mother will be returning to London alone! A man has his rights, remember?'

'Anna will *not* remain here. And she will not come back to you until medical opinion deems it right that she should.'

'Even though I could divorce her? I could use desertion and refusal of my rights as a husband. Had you thought of that, Petrovsky?'

'I had but only briefly. You will not consider divorce, though if you do, Anna will counter-petition on the grounds of your adultery.'

'She'd have to prove it first. The servant won't tell, even supposing I did bed her – and I'm not admitting I did. It would be my word against that of a menial who can hardly speak a word of English. Anna doesn't have a leg to stand on and if you persist in your arrogance, I shall send for my wife this instant and forbid her to leave this house! What have you to say to that!'

'Not a word,' Igor shrugged derisively. 'You will not

send for Anna because I say you shall not. Instead, you will listen to what I have to say.

'Anna will come to London. That is final. And Natasha Yurovska will go with us. From now on the servant, as you call her, is my responsibility and I shall decide what is to become of her. And when Anna does return to this house, Karl will come with her. He will report to me anything untoward that may go on here and if I order him to do so, he will flog you within an inch of your life – and laugh as he does it. Now is that quite clear?'

'You're mad!' Elliot jumped to his feet, slamming his fist on the table top. 'I will not have that monster in my house! How dare you tell me who I employ? You go too far!'

'But I have not gone far enough! I had thought to spare Anna the embarrassment of your being told, but I can see you are too stupid to let well alone.

'Natasha Yurovska is pregnant. It is your child and I have decided she will go away to have it. You will never find her and when it is born it will be given up for adoption, because she does not want to keep it – indeed, she has no financial means of supporting it, even if she did.

'I hope she has a boy to grow up into a son any man could be proud to have fathered, but you will never know where he is or who has him. That will be your punishment – especially if you never have a son by Anna.

'So if there is one iota of sense left in your head, I'd be very careful about what you do and how you behave in the future, Sutton, or I will ruin you – is that understood?'

'Natasha *pregnant*?' The words came out in a whispered gasp. 'I don't believe it! It can't be mine!'

'It's yours, that much is certain. And Anna knows about it – has known for some time – so if I were you I'd take care. Never forget that I am waiting to throw your reputation into the nearest midden and I, too, shall laugh as I do it.

'By the way, your mother doesn't know that Natasha is

pregnant, though I am only looking for an excuse to tell her – so be warned!'

'I don't believe you; not one word of it!' His face had paled; nervously, he paced the floor. 'But you are all the same, you refugees. You come to this country with hardly a penny to your name and start laying down the law as though you've every right to – and in my own home, too!'

'The fact that it is also my sister's home gives me that right, especially when I think she has been badly treated. Well, it's your turn now to suffer and suffer you will unless you mend your ways, Mister Elliot Sutton. You are not dealing with a frail woman; now you have me to reckon with and I do not like you. Always remember that I do not like you and remember it especially when you think of taking out your anger on my sister.' He walked to the door, opening it slowly, turning to face the man he disliked to the point of hatred. 'We are taking the noon train to London and shall be leaving in about an hour. It will give you time to say goodbye to Anna and Tatiana – do not upset either of them. And stay away from Natasha Yurovska – is that understood?'

Alice walked slowly through Brattocks Wood, indulging her memories, making for the tall trees where the rooks nested.

She had not made friends with the Windrush rooks, had never stood, hands on the tree trunk, to send her secrets whispering upwards. But the Rowangarth rooks understood. She had told them her fears and joys since she had come here, a young girl of scarce fourteen years and there was so much to tell them.

She stopped to let the indescribably happy feeling flow through her. This was the spot – the very spot – where she and Tom had met. She had been walking Morgan – Giles's badly-behaved spaniel – heard the roar of anger.

'Drat you, dog, you great daft animal! There'll not be a

game bird left in this wood!' Tom, walking towards her with Morgan in tow. 'Does this creature belong to you?'

'No, but he's with me.' The new under-keeper had been very angry. 'He belongs to Mr Giles and he isn't a creature. He's called Morgan . . .'

That had been the start of their loving and she had run to tell the rooks about it; told them about going to London to chaperon Miss Julia and later about the pearl ring Tom had given her, before he went to war.

Those old rooks knew all her secrets, all her heartaches. Now, she must tell them how happy she was and how bonny a lass Daisy was growing into, but oh, if they could just think on about it, could they remember that, happy as she was, deep inside her heart Rowangarth was still her home.

She reined in her thoughts. Alice Dwerryhouse was just about as happy as any woman could be. She and Tom and Daisy and Reuben, and Julia, too, for a sister, so did it matter where she lived?

It doesn't matter, not really. She sent her thoughts winging to the topmost branches of the elm trees. *I have so much and Windrush is a happy place to be – but think on, will you?*

'*Think on, you old, black, secret-keeping birds, that I love Rowangarth till it hurts yet I know, too, that Tom and me have had our miracle.* And any road, it was Julia's turn, now, for a bit of happiness.

Elliot Sutton tossed yet another brandy down his throat, neither tasting nor feeling it. His mood was ugly. He had been bettered by Igor Petrovsky; brought to account, humbled, and no one did that to the heir to Pendenys!

He had said goodbye to Anna; kissed her reluctantly-offered cheek. Tatiana was already in the car, happy to be away. She sat beside the countess, eager to board the train that would take them to London.

'Goodbye, my dear.' The words had been hard to say, the smile on his face false. 'Get well soon. I shall miss you.'

'Goodbye,' Anna had whispered. That had been all. She had lowered her eyes and he hadn't known whether they were tinged with sorrow or relief.

With the luggage in the second, smaller car, sat Natasha Yurovska, eyes on the tightly-clasped fingers on her lap. She still wore her black; it was how he would remember her. Because he would think of her, often; wonder when her time came if she would have a boy. And he would be angry, as even now he was angry, to think of Elliot Sutton's child being given to anyone who might have the charity to offer it a home.

His son might end up a labourer. It was too much to bear because he'd had a son; a stillborn son who had been perfect in every way, they had told him. Anna couldn't give him a living heir. Maybe, she never would.

He held up his hand as the first car drew away. *Go, and take your bitch of a mother with you!* He didn't care if he never saw Anna Petrovska again. God! he hoped he never would! Long before the cars were out of sight he turned, running up the steps, slamming the door behind him.

'I will not be in for lunch nor dinner,' he told a passing housemaid. 'If anyone wants to know, tell them I'm in Scotland.'

Creesby, that's where! He would lunch at the Coach and Horses, then drive to Leeds. There was amusement to be found there and anyway, he couldn't go to London; couldn't stay at his mother's Cheyne Walk house — not when *she* would be next door.

The longing for a woman — any woman — stabbed through his loins. He'd had enough of behaving himself. He would do the rounds of the music halls — there were still a couple left, in Leeds — eye up what was on offer. He didn't need Anna. She could stay in London for as long as she pleased; for ever, if that was what she wanted.

He slammed shut his bedroom door. If only that child had lived!

The Coach and Horses at Creesby had known better days. Once, before the coming of the railways, it had been a staging-post, a hostelry where coach horses were changed, where passengers stretched their cramped legs and took refreshment; where often they stayed the night before taking to the road again to London or to Edinburgh.

Now, the inn maintained a shabby dignity; its bedrooms still boasted good beds though their quilts were faded and worn and its dining room served meals on better than average plates, served vegetables in bruised silver dishes. But mostly, now, it was noted for its discreetness; where not too many questions were asked if the same young gentleman booked a room with a different wife each week.

Elliot Sutton had once been a regular visitor, though since his marriage the landlord had seen neither hide nor hair of him. It came as a pleasing surprise, therefore, when that same young gentleman strolled into the best parlour, smiled all round and ordered a large brandy as though he'd never been away.

'Afternoon, Mr Sutton. This is a rare pleasure!'

'Nice to see you again, Jed.' He didn't particularly like Jed Bates, though best keep on the right side of the man. Anna was in London until only God knew when and the bedrooms at the Coach and Horses, if he remembered rightly, had thick walls and stout bolts on the doors. 'I'll take a plate of your beef, and a little Stilton to follow. Anything decent in your cellar?'

'Got a lovely drop of burgundy, Mr Sutton. Right up your street.'

Elliot was mollified. Here, he was appreciated, treated with due respect. He would empty his plate, empty the bottle, then drive to Leeds there to find a woman – one who, with luck, would sell him her favours for the night.

He might, come to think of it, drive her back to the Coach and Horses.

He smiled, swirled the brandy round the glass, then took a slow, appreciative sip. And he damned to Anna Petrovska!

Julia sat at the open window of the sewing-room, smoking a cigarette, smiling as she watched the children who played below and at Jin Dobb who shook her duster at them, telling them to be off, the noisy young beggars.

'They're so lovely, Alice. I wish they were all mine. Andrew and I would have had at least four of our own, by now.'

'Well, you've got Drew,' Alice snipped off the cotton, 'and Bas and Kitty and Daisy visit as often as they can, so you'll have to be content with that. Can't expect any more of your own unless you get wed and we all know you won't.'

Alice held up the dress she was sewing for Julia. Dresses were so simple, these days; she could cut out and sew one up, almost, in an afternoon. Almost sleeveless, most certainly shapeless, with a waistline dropped to where no natural waistline should be and a skirt so short and skimpy that unless fashions changed, shops that sold yardage would be going out of business.

'This rose colour suits you.' She shook out the dress, then held it critically for inspection. 'But there's nothing to it. Needs something to lift it, sort of.'

'Mm.' Julia stubbed out her cigarette, then lit another.

'If I remember, rightly, there's a piece of gold lace in the drawer. A narrow panel of that from the neckline to the waist would look a treat. You could wear it with your gold kid slippers – and Julia! You smoke too much!'

'Anything you say, love.' She had no interest in clothes and but for the fact that her mother was giving a dinner party for Richard James's retirement, she wouldn't be bothering with a new dinner dress at all.

'I do say. And can you put Daisy to bed, tonight, at the same time as Drew? I've promised to go to Reuben's, this evening; bake him a few loaves and make him a decent supper. All right?'

'You know it is, though I'll be bored to tears. I'll bet you anything you like that Aunt Clemmy'll be over, weeping and wailing about Anna going off to London and worrying about her Elliot being deserted by his wife. Don't know how Anna puts up with her; not with her *and* Elliot.'

'Well, Anna won't have to put up with anything for a while.' Alice smoothed out the piece of lace. 'When do you think she'll come back to Denniston House?'

'Never, if she has any sense. She took her maid Natasha with her, so she plans on a fairly long stay. It's Tatiana I'm sorry for, poor lonely little soul. By rights, there should have been four in Denniston nursery.'

By rights. If every woman had her rights, Julia Mac-Malcolm would have a husband and the delight of filling her own nursery to capacity. Two Sutton-fair sons she had planned for and two girls with their father's red hair.

'Do you suppose,' Alice interrupted her daydreaming, 'you could give me five minutes of your time to see how this looks on you? You were miles away.'

'I know. Thinking about children — four of them — if you must know.'

'Well, they're all right and having the time of their lives, so stop your worrying.'

'Yes.' Julia closed her eyes tightly against sudden pricking tears. 'All right. Of course they are . . .'

Elliot Sutton left his hat and gloves at the cloakroom, then strolled into the bar area to the rear of the back stalls. The old Palace had hardly changed since he'd picked up his first woman here. Seventeen he'd been and she'd cost him all of five shillings, on account, she said, that he was new to it and something of a bother. Becky, if he remembered rightly; cheeks red with rouge and hair black as his own. They said you always remembered the first one. He wondered where Becky was now, twenty years on.

He ordered a large whisky, then sat at one of the tables. The women were not so free with their favours these days; not so willing to please. Many of them had found protectors and taken to the streets, though a few still frequented the Palace. He could wait.

' 'Scuse me, sir – mind if I wipe your table?' A barmaid took a cloth across the cracked marble top, then set down a clean ashtray.

She moved on, then, but not before she had struck a chord in his mind; the voice, was it? He hadn't bothered looking at her face. He waited for her to turn, and then he knew. Just before the war, hadn't it been; before the Brattocks Wood affair with the sewing-maid? All that time ago – more than ten years – and still he remembered her.

She had been beautiful – she still was – and eager for him. He recalled her round, high breasts, the nipples that showed beneath the bodice of her dress; remembered her smile and eyes that invited.

There had been trouble, of course. It had cost his mother plenty, she had screamed at him. The last time, she spat, she would pay for his indiscretions. And why, his mother had demanded, couldn't he take himself off to London or Leeds, even? Did it have to be in Creesby, so near to home? And did it have to be the daughter of a pork butcher?

He picked up his glass then walked to the bar counter. She was busy arranging bottles and he coughed so that she turned to face him.

'Can I help you, sir?' she smiled. 'Another of the same?'

For a moment he did not speak, but smiled teasingly, intimately into her eyes. And then he said, 'Hullo, Maudie. Remember me?'

20

'There now.' Alice snapped off the cotton. 'There's all your shirt buttons seen to and your socks darned. Before we leave, I'll do you another baking of bread and pop a cake in the oven for you.'

'You'll have a sup of tea afore you go back to Rowangarth?' Reuben had already set the kettle to boil. 'Tell me, lass – how does it feel eating your meals with her ladyship? You'm not gentry any longer, yet you stay as Miss Julia's guest. How do they take it, below stairs?'

'It's all right, now. When I was Lady Sutton they didn't like it – told me I wasn't one of them, any more. But now I'm married to Tom it's as if I'm back in my rightful place and they treat me like I'm Alice again – 'cept when they serve my meals. Mind, Miss Clitherow doesn't quite know what to make of me.'

'That's because you'm young Drew's mother; you're still entitled to respect. You get the best of both worlds, Alice Hawthorn, when you come home to Rowangarth.'

He still sometimes used her maiden name. Was it because he was getting forgetful or was it because he wanted the old days to come back again? She worried about him she admitted as she took cups from the dresser. He was the father she had never known; he held her secrets – all of them.

'You'll come again tomorrow?' he asked.

'You know I will. You're my reason for being here.'

'Ah. Then I'll show you tomorrow where my tin box is hidden. There's one or two valuables in it, and my bank book. You'll have to know, Alice, so that when anything happens to me it'll be all straightforward.

'Reuben – *don't*! I won't have you talking like that!'

'It comes to us all, lass. I've written out my Will. It's done proper. Jinny Dobb and Percy have witnessed it. It's in the box, with the other things. You're to have all I've got, Alice; all that's here and the money in my bank book. 'Cept my pocket watch, that is. Tom's to have that, and my guns.'

'Don't! Please don't, Reuben? Oh, I'm grateful to you, but it's you I'd rather have, not what you leave behind you. But what has brought all this on? You're feeling all right, aren't you – no aches or twinges, or anything?'

'I'm grand, only it's right I put my affairs in order so the right people get what I leave behind me. I'd not want your Aunt Bella to get her hands on it. Us haven't heard from her for years, but she'd be on that doorstep like a black crow, the minute she heard I'd gone.'

'Well, you're not going anywhere yet, Reuben Pickering,' Alice scolded. 'I want you to see Daisy grow up. I want you to live to be a hundred.'

'Then I'll do my best to oblige,' he chuckled. 'Nice to know I'm wanted.'

'I want you to come and live at Windrush. Tom wants it, too. Remember that if things get too much for you, you've only to write me a letter.' She reached for his hand across the table top, laying it to her cheek. 'Promise?'

'You'm a good girl, Alice.' The old, pale eyes misted briefly. 'But I'll stay here, a while. Let's face it – where would old Percy and Jin Dobb be without me? I'll bear your offer in mind, though . . .'

Her cheeks went white, then flushed bright red and he could see she was making an effort to cope with the shock of seeing him again.

'Remember you? You know I do,' she whispered. She

let go her indrawn breath with a little huffing sigh, then raised her eyes to meet his. 'Mr Elliot Sutton – after all these years!'

'But what are you doing here, Maudie?'

'Serving ale – trying to make an honest penny.'

'You're not married?' He gazed pointedly at her left hand.

'No. Never found a young man that suited me, and after the war there wasn't a lot of choice, was there? Most of the men I'd known didn't come back.'

'You haven't changed, you know.' He dropped his voice to an intimate whisper. 'You're still the Maudie I remember. I recognized you at once.' His eyes lingered on her breasts and her still-tiny waist; her eyes were provocative and inviting as ever. 'Have you ever thought about me – about *us?*'

'Often,' she whispered. 'I wasn't likely to forget you, now was I?'

He flushed with pleasure. Here was a real woman; one who could teach Anna a thing or two about pleasing a man.

'And do you still live in Creesby, Maudie?'

'Nah. Parents both gone; my brother's taken over the shop. I live with my Auntie Madge, now, in Leeds.'

'I missed you – you know that. We had some good times together, didn't we?'

'That we did, Mr Sutton.' She smiled almost sadly.

'Elliot – please? After all, we were once very – *close.*'

'So we were,' she whispered. 'But there's customers waiting to be served.'

'Come back quickly?' he murmured.

He watched her, eyes narrowed, the tip of his tongue tracing the outline of his lips, and when she returned he pushed his glass over the counter, asking for another of the same. 'And one for yourself,' he smiled. 'Do you still drink sherry?'

'Not often. I'm more what you would call an ale lady, now.' She gazed straight into his eyes. 'You learn to cut your coat according to what cloth you've got, you see. But since you're buying, Mr Sutton, I'll take a sherry with you.'

'I've got to see you again,' he whispered throatily. 'You can't know what a delight it is to meet up with you after so long. Will you come out with me, for a meal?'

'Can't,' she said flatly. 'Got to work, haven't I?'

'But you get a night off, surely?'

'Aye, on Wednesdays, when we aren't so busy.'

'Then next Wednesday – say you will? Where can I pick you up?'

'We-e-ll – as a matter of fact,' she dropped her eyes to the counter. 'I'd thought to go to Creesby, see my brother at the shop, next week. How about if we were to meet at the Coach and Horses – outside, of course, so's not to cause you embarrassment.'

'You were never an embarrassment, and you know it. You'll meet me inside, and we'll have a meal. Shouldn't wonder if I don't stay the night there.' He raised a quizzing eyebrow.

'Will you, now? I heard it said the landlord there isn't all that particular who he lets his rooms to, these days.' She turned away, momentarily, so he couldn't know if she were teasing or accusing. 'If you know what I mean?' She turned to meet his eyes and he knew she was neither teasing nor accusing.

'You mean you'll – you'll . . . ?' His face flushed with triumph. He hadn't thought she would be so easy.

'Like I said, Mr Sutton – *Elliot*,' she whispered, 'I never forgot you. Hardly a day went past that I didn't think of you.'

'So next Wednesday . . . ?'

'Next Wednesday,' she nodded. 'Meet me in the snug, at the Coach, at seven. Now off you go. You've had enough. Any more an' you'll not be able to find your way home. By the way, what are you going to tell your wife?'

'You know, then, that I'm married?'

'Like I said – I've thought about you often, heard things, over the years.'

'I shall tell my wife nothing. Besides, she's in London,' he admitted, sulkily, 'with her damned old mother, so serve her right, eh?'

'Serve her right,' Maudie repeated gravely. 'After all, we usually get what we deserve, don't we – sooner or later? Now, off you go. Seven o'clock, on Wednesday . . .'

Daisy, Drew, Kitty and Bas sat in the long grass in the wild garden, chewing reflectively on liquorice sticks.

'I miss Tatty,' Drew murmured. 'Poor little thing – all alone in London. Bet she'll miss us, too.'

'And will you miss me,' Daisy tilted a provocative eyebrow, 'when Mam and me go home on Wednesday?'

'You know we will. I wish you could stay for always, Daiz.'

'Me, too.' Bas, the eldest of the Sutton brood, echoed earnestly. He liked Daisy. She was good fun – better than most girls he knew. Daisy was pretty – very pretty; could take a dare, too. And unlike his sister, she wasn't bossy – except sometimes, when her temper flashed. Daisy's temper sure was something to see, he acknowledged – unless you were on the receiving end of it, of course.

'I know something,' Kitty announced. 'I don't think I should tell, though.'

'Why not?'

'Because it's – well – it's *grown-up* talk. I heard it.'

'Okay, then. If you feel you can't . . .' Bas knew how to treat his sister. Show her indifference and she wanted to be centre stage.

'We-e-ll – since Tatty isn't here, I suppose I just might, though really I shouldn't.'

'Oh, c'mon, Sis. You know you're just bustin' to.'

'Do tell?' Daisy coaxed, blue eyes wide.

'All right, then. It's about Aunt Anna and Uncle Elliot.' She looked about her, furtively. Kitty was a performer, an actress. Hadn't her mother always said she would end up on Broadway? 'There's trouble in the camp,' she whispered. 'Leastways, that's what Nanny Eva said to Mrs Martin. Countess Anna was being made to go to London by her brother – the Russian, you know – and Himself in a right old state about it. Those were Mrs Martin's *exact* words!'

'So what's new? We all know she's gone to London,' Bas sighed.

'Yes, but there's more to it than meets the eye – that's what they said.'

'Well, I know *all* about it.' Drew too looked around him furtively. 'I know because my mother told me. Aunt Anna is going to London to get over being sad about the baby. Tatty didn't know she'd had a little brother – they never told her they were having another baby. She thought her mother was in bed because her back hurt and Tatty thinks they have gone to London for a holiday and so Aunt Anna can see a doctor who knows about bad backs.'

'Yes, but that isn't the truth, is it?' Kitty hissed. 'Mrs Martin said Uncle Elliot was a right so-and-so; said she didn't blame Aunt Anna for walking out on him, so there!'

'Walking out on him means she's leaving him, doesn't it,' Daisy frowned. 'It means she's run away from him. My Mam wouldn't leave our Dada. They love each other,' she sighed.

'Mm. Guess Dad and Mom do, too,' Bas murmured. 'It sure must be awful if your folks don't get on.'

'Then isn't she coming back?' Drew demanded, wide-eyed. 'I hope she does. I'd miss Tatty.'

'Mrs Martin said she'd beg from door to door before she'd have any more truck with *that* swine. I think she meant Uncle Elliot.'

'What does *having truck* mean?' Another peculiar English phrase, Bas frowned.

'I don't know,' Kitty breathed, 'but it sounds rude, doesn't it?'

'My mother hates Tatty's father,' Daisy offered. 'I heard her tell Keth's Mam that he never got his boots dirty in the war. And Mam knows what she's talking about, because she was in that war.'

'Why does she hate him, Daiz?'

'I think it's because Dada hates him.'

'Seems like everyone hates Uncle Elliot,' Bas grinned, 'except Grandmother Sutton. But I think you're making it all up, Sis. How come you heard all those things Nanny Eva and Mrs Martin said? And how come they let you?'

'I was in the toy cupboard in the nursery. I heard Nanny ask Mrs Martin over to take tea with her, so I hid in there so I could listen to what grown-ups talk about when there are no little ears about. And don't you dare tell on me, Bas, or I'll be in trouble with Mom!'

'I wouldn't dream of repeating such rubbish, because it just isn't true.'

'It is, so! You believe me, don't you, Drew? You believe that Uncle Elliot is a right so-and-so?'

'Yes, I do, Kitty.' He really did, because he knew his mother hated Uncle Elliot, too. Not that he'd hidden in a toy cupboard, or anything. It was just something he knew without ever being told. 'But don't let's talk about him?'

'Okay by me,' Kitty shrugged airily. Then, as if reluctant to relinquish the limelight, she added, 'Anyway, he'll soon be dead.'

'*Dead*!'

'Sure. The way he hits the bottle, Mrs Martin said, he'll never see forty.'

'But forty's old, anyway!'

'Yes, it is,' Daisy nodded, comforted. 'Come on – let's all go and see Uncle Reuben. He's got a stick of

Scarborough rock he said we could have, next time we called.'

'What are we waiting for?' Minty pink rock, Bas reasoned, was to be preferred to Uncle Elliot, any day. And Mrs Martin spoke nothing but the truth. Uncle Elliot *was* a right so-and-so . . .

Elliot Sutton looked at his wristwatch as Maudie pushed open the door of the snug at the Coach and Horses a little before time. He rose to his feet, smiling, indicating a chair, pulling it out.

'Sherry?'

'Please.' She smiled up into his eyes.

'For you my dear – anything. And by the way, the landlord suggested we eat upstairs, save any – er – embarrassment. To yourself, of course,' he added, smiling. 'I've booked a room.'

'Good.' Her smile was provocative, just like the Maudie of old. He pulled his tongue round his lips in anticipation of what was to come. A meal, wine, then bed. He'd never actually slept with Maudie; their couplings had been furtive, snatched whenever the opportunity arose. Now there would be time to indulge his fantasies. The lights turned low, a slow undressing, the bed soft and suggestive – and Maudie's eager thighs. He remembered them well. And she had been cheap, if he remembered rightly. There had never been payment – before, or after.

'Tell me what you've been doing, Elliot, since –'

'Since last we made love?' he murmured. 'Well, there was the war, of course, but we won't talk about that.'

'Saw service, did you?'

'Mm.' Eyes down, he gazed modestly into his glass. 'London – hush-hush stuff – then Paris, then the Somme.' Celverte, surely, allowed him to talk about the Somme – the area, if not the battles. 'But tell me about you?' His eyes sought hers, earnestly.

'Well, after we – we parted, I stayed at home for a while, then I went to Leeds to that big munitions factory. Made good money, there.'

'And then?'

'Then Mam and Dad died in the 'flu epidemic. Awful, it was – both of them, within a week. So my brother took over the shop and I went back to Leeds, to Auntie Madge. Been working in one bar or another ever since.'

'Then you are wasting your talents, Maudie. You deserve better.'

'You, for instance?' She stared at him brazenly.

'Me for sure,' he smiled. 'Oh my dear, you can't know how it's been for me. I wanted a son so desperately and I had one, stillborn. It broke my heart, almost. And now my wife has taken herself off to London – left me, she says, till she feels like returning. You wouldn't have left me, would you, Maudie? If you'd been my wife you'd have given me a son, wouldn't you?'

'I would, an' all. A fine, strapping lad and tall and dark, just like you.'

'Dearest girl – we won't lose each other again, will we? We'll be lovers like we used to be, only better. It *will* be better, won't it?' he pleaded, eyes moist with self-pity.

'Whatever you say.' She dropped her eyes to fidget with her fingers. 'I only want you to have what you deserve.'

'And a man like me deserves love, doesn't he? I'm a passionate man, Maudie.'

'Oh, I know that. Who better than I?'

'Then let's go upstairs, now?' He grasped her hand, holding it to his cheek. 'I'll tell them not to serve the meal for half an hour. I slipped the landlord a couple of quid,' he said softly, placing the room key on the table top. 'He understands. A small gratuity helps him to forget faces.'

'No. Not just yet,' she smiled. 'Let a girl get her breath – and finish her drink. We haven't seen each other in years; what's a few minutes more?'

'Don't tease, Maudie?' He fixed her with begging eyes then leaned closer, lowering his voice. 'If it's – er – a question of money . . . ?'

'No!' Her reply was sharp. 'Money would put me in the whore class, Elliot, and I've never been that!'

'Sorry, my dear. I just thought –'

'Then *don't* think! Besides, I don't like being rushed. Think I'd like another sherry – help me decide.'

'Decide what?'

'Like whether or not I'm going upstairs with you; decide if I want to eat your food, even . . .'

'But we agreed, didn't we, that we'd –'

'We agreed nothing! *You* presumed. You thought Maudie was waiting there like a plum for the picking, ready to jump into your bed when you snapped your fingers! Well I'm sorry, Mr Elliot Sutton. Not tonight. Not any night, as far as I'm concerned.'

'What the hell . . . ?' He gazed at her, stupefied. 'Now see here, old girl, enough is enough. Stop playing games!'

'But I'm *not* playing games. I'm very, very serious. I suppose you could even say that this is the day of reckoning!'

'Maudie! What have I ever done to you to deserve this?' His eyes were round with pleading, his voice softly persuasive. 'We were lovers, remember?'

'Oh, I remember, all right! We were fine together, till your mother walked into dad's shop.'

'My mother? She *wouldn't*!'

'She would. She did. Fifty quid – that was all I got. She told me to leave you alone, called me a trollop – even when I begged her to believe the baby was yours.'

'*Baby*?' He could hardly say the word. All at once he was living a bad dream. But soon, surely, Maudie would burst out laughing, tell him she'd been pulling his leg? He grasped her wrist across the table. 'What baby? Tell me!'

'Ours. Yours and mine. I was three months gone and I

never told you. I wrote to your mother instead, asking her to help me. Oh, I knew the likes of you would never marry the likes of me, but I expected you to behave like a gentleman and support your own child. But your mother didn't want anything to do with it, so I went to Auntie Madge and it was born there.

'She was a brick, my aunt; looked after the little thing so I could go to work. Then when the war came, I earned good money – took care of the three of us. We managed without Sutton charity.'

'So where is it, now?' His face had paled, taken on a haggard look.

'In Creesby, with my brother – the one who took over dad's shop. His wife and him can't have children and they wanted someone of their own to leave the shop to – a boy to help run the business, see? So they adopted him, legal. It was best they should. A lad needs a father.'

'A *boy*? No, Maudie – you're making it up! I told you I was desperate for a son, but that's cruel!'

'Cruel, Elliot? More like rough justice, I'd say.' Her voice was soft, too soft, then she smiled sadly. 'But you do have a son. One day his name will be over the shop door, so you'll have a son in trade. I called him Edward – your dad would've liked that, I thought. He's twelve, now; a boy to be proud of.'

'I don't believe you!' Now his cheeks had flushed an angry red, his hands gripped the table as if he were fighting for control of his emotions. 'Your brat could've been anybody's. You weren't particular who you went with!'

'No, I suppose I wasn't because I went with you – but *only* with you. Here.' She dipped into the pocket of her coat, pulling out a photograph. 'That's him. He fathers himself. Tall and dark, like you, and twice as handsome. Oh, he's yours, all right!'

He looked at the photograph and knew at once that he

had a son; a boy he couldn't own! Dark and black-eyed, like himself. Not Sutton fair, but one of Mary Anne's. A Pendennis.

Damn you, Anna! he screamed silently inside him. And damn his mother for making him marry her. He looked up to see Maudie pulling on her gloves.

'Goodbye, Elliot,' she smiled. 'I've enjoyed our talk. You can keep the photograph.'

She walked away from him, straight-backed. At the bar counter she paused, nodding in the direction of the table she had just left.

'I'd take him a brandy, if I were you – a stiff one. He needs it,' she said to the landlord.

She was smiling as the public house doors swung shut behind her. She was still smiling as she knocked on the back door of her brother's shop.

Elliot Sutton gulped down the brandy the barman placed on the table, then ordered another. He didn't know whether to get raging drunk or to slink into a corner and weep; weep because he had never felt so miserable in the whole of his life. Natasha Yurovska pregnant by him, perhaps carrying a son, though he would never know, and now Edward; the heir he wanted, destined to become a pork butcher.

Yet by Anna, only a girl, miscarried babies and a dead child. Fate was cruel to him because it was jealous of him; envied him his looks, his lifestyle, his expectations. And because of Fate he knew he would give no son to Pendenys – and on a son his mother's favours depended.

No child of his for Pendenys, and Nathan so taken up with goodness that he'd likely never get around to fathering one. So it would be Albert and Albert's all-American boy who would have Pendenys, in the end. It was too much to think about, let alone to bear. He felt like going to London, *now*, dragging Anna into his bed, showing her where her duty lay. But there was Igor to contend with and the black-bearded Cossack and besides, he was too drunk. Tonight, drink was all that was left to him. Tomorrow, he would think things out, plan what he would do, but tonight he would drink until things became bearable then go home to Pendenys where his mother at least would understand how he felt; understand about Anna, that was. She didn't know about Natasha – not all of it – and best not remind her about Maudie; best not tell her she had sold her grandson for fifty pounds.

She should have insisted he marry Maudie, he brooded. Maudie would have given him any number of sons, by now; wouldn't have run home to her mother because she didn't feel well.

'Hey!' He raised a finger. 'Bring me another!'

Get drunk, that's what! It was the only way to ease the hurt Maudie had inflicted on him. Another couple, and he wouldn't give a damn.

'Don't you think, sir, that perhaps you've had enough?' the barman murmured. 'Maybe it would be as well if you –'

'And maybe it would be as well if you did as you were told and brought me another brandy!'

He pushed back his chair, walking carefully to the bar, then, picking up the glass, emptied it without once taking it from his lips. Then he slammed a fistful of coins on the counter and walked towards the door.

Home to Pendenys, that's where. And he hadn't had too much. He knew what he was about. Elliot Sutton could hold his drink as well as any gentleman.

The evening air hit his face like ice-cold water and he leaned against the wall to steady himself. Then he walked to his car, opening the door, picking up the starting handle.

It was, he thought, gazing down at the small hole, like trying to insert a latchkey in the dark. It wasn't easy, drunk or sober. He went down on his knees, cursing quietly. Damn the thing. Couldn't get it in. Never start the car, at this rate . . .

'Now then, squire – want a hand?'

Elliot gazed up, saw the work-soiled overalls, the toe-capped boots. Carefully he got to his feet.

'Wouldn't mind, old man. Know how to crank up a car?' He handed him the starting handle, then fished in his pocket, bringing out a coin. 'Get it going, there's a good fellow.'

'Granted soon as asked, young sir.' The man inserted the handle, then swung it with ease. The car engine kicked, started, then settled down to a measured throb.

Elliot got into the car, slamming the door. Then he released the brake, blowing the horn loudly, defiantly. Damn them all! He didn't care! He was Elliot Sutton of Pendenys; why should he?

'What's this, then? You come into money?' the landlord asked as the man dropped a shilling on the counter.

'Nah. Pull us a pint, and have one yourself. Easy come, easy go, eh? All I did was start up a car.'

'Mister Sutton's, you mean?'

'Don't know who he was. Only know he wasn't capable of getting his motor started. Shouldn't be driving. He'll knock someone over and lame them if he isn't careful.'

Young Sutton, had it been? The man had heard about him and his rich mother. An arrogant little bastard, by all accounts. Still, he'd parted with a shilling and a shilling paid for three pints of best ale. Live and let live.

Elliot Sutton let go his indrawn breath, his clenched hands relaxed on the wheel. He'd made it home. Nothing at all wrong with him. God! but he was tired; would sleep like a baby the moment his head touched the pillow. He steered into the carriage drive, Pendenys ahead of him. It was almost dark; neither one thing nor the other, this shifting half-light. Not far to go, now. He accelerated, sending the car hurtling forward.

He didn't see it there until it was almost too late; laid in the middle of the drive – a young ram, sound asleep. He parped loudly on his horn, startling the creature, sending it scrambling to its feet to face the glare of headlights, stupefied.

'Bloody animal!' He steered to the left. The ram, panicked by the blaring horn, jumped high in the air. He felt the bump, slammed on his brakes. Damn it. He hoped it hadn't scratched the paintwork.

The steering wheel refused to respond to his hands; the car spun into a skid. He reached for the brake, pulling on it with all his strength, closing his eyes as he went out of control. He didn't see the oak tree; he only heard the sickening, tearing sound as he crashed into it; felt pain slam through his body.

Out! Get out! Open the door! Handle jammed – bloody thing jammed! *Got to get out!*

There was a roar that filled his head and a bright red light that hurt his eyes. God! He was on fire!

'No!' he screamed. '*No . . .*'

The cowman going in for early milking found the motor, saw the mangled body of the ram a few feet away. Wide-eyed with shock he ran back towards the gate-lodge. They had a telephone at the lodge, connected to Pendenys, could ring from there – tell them . . .

'Mr Elliot's car, I think. Burned out,' he choked. 'Can't be sure, though, it's in such a mess. Ring them, will you?' He wanted nothing to do with it; didn't want to be the one to have to tell the bad news. He could have sworn there was someone inside that car, slumped over the wheel. 'Ring Pendenys?' he pleaded.

Was it Mr Elliot, in there? It didn't bear thinking about.

The mistress would go out of her mind. Eyes averted, he walked quickly away.

God! What a way to die!

'Met the postman at the bottom of the lane.' Tom laid the letter on the kitchen table. 'Said I'd save his legs. It's from Julia.'

'I'll read it when I've finished dishing up, though what she can have to say to me I don't know,' Alice smiled. 'It isn't five minutes since I saw her.'

'So tell me?' Tom demanded when she had slit open the envelope. 'Left something behind at Rowangarth, did you?'

'No. Oh, dear Lord! Here – read it for yourself. She's wanting me to ring her.'

'Alice?' Her cheeks had flushed bright red, her eyes were wide and moist with tears. 'Reuben? Not Reuben?'

'Read it, Tom!'

'"... and I have to tell you" – good grief!' His eyes met hers. 'I don't believe it!'

'Read it, I said! Read it out loud, so I'll know!'

'All right – *and I have to tell you that Elliot is dead. He crashed his car. Can you ring me – reverse the charges? I can't believe it. I just can't.*'

'Oh, Tom.' She rose to her feet. 'Hold me, love?' She wrapped her arms around his waist, laying her head against his chest. 'I feel, oh . . .'

He pulled her closer as he felt the shaking of her body, resting his cheek on her head, making little hushing sounds. And then she began to weep, as terrible a sound as he'd ever heard; sobs that seemed to tear her in two.

'There now, lass. Don't get yourself upset – not over him.'

'Upset?' She pushed him from her, gazing into his face with wild eyes. 'Not *upset*, Tom. Shock, happen, though it's a relief, really. He'll never be able to hurt Drew, now, don't you see? And I wasn't crying from pity. I was crying because I'm ashamed – of myself, my thoughts.

'When I read that letter, you see, it was as if there was a singing inside me and all I could think of was that I wanted to go back there, dance on his grave!' She pulled her sleeve across her eyes, then took a deep, steadying gulp of air. 'I'm sorry, though, for his mother. She loved him, didn't she? I think she was the only person in the world who did – but she loved him, for all that.'

She would remember Mrs Clementina when she said her prayers, tonight; Mr Edward, too. It was the least she could do.

'And you'll ring Julia, like she wants?'

'I'll go to the village, later on, then walk back with Daisy and Keth, after school. Daisy'll have to be told. Now get on with your dinner.' Her face was wooden, her voice little more than a whisper.

'I can't eat it, Alice. All at once I'm not hungry.'

'Me, neither. Give it to the dogs . . .'

Alice waited beside the public telephone, heard the post-mistress ask, 'Is that Holdenby 102? Will you accept a charge call from Mrs Dwerryhouse?'

She turned from the little switchboard, nodding to Alice to pick up the receiver.

'Julia? *When* . . . ?'

'Oh, love – I've been waiting for you to ring. It was some time on Wednesday night; late, they think. Are you all right?'

'I am, now. It was a long time before it sank in, though. What happened?'

'We don't know – not for sure – but a sheep ran out, they seem to think. It was near to home; they'd got sheep grazing on Pendenys parkland. One of the men from Pendenys Home Farm found the car. They told Uncle Edward first. Aunt Clemmy was still asleep. Amelia was there, thank goodness; she waited until Doc James got there before she would let them tell Aunt Clemmy. Then she phoned us.

'Mother's been at Pendenys on and off, ever since. Poor love – she's badly shocked; brought it all back, Pa being killed the same way, I mean. I think she's wishing she hadn't bought me a car, now. I believe it was awful, at Pendenys. Aunt Clemmy fainted when they told her.'

'And Anna?'

'She's on her way back. Coming by train. Amelia will be at York, now, meeting her. Amelia's been a brick. I'm glad she's there. Mother looked washed out when she came home, last night. Aunt Clemmy's under sedation, most of the time. They don't think she'll make it to the funeral and mother thinks it's best if she doesn't.'

'When is it?' Alice needed to know the exact time; needed to ask God, silently and secretly, to forgive him for all the misery he had caused.

'Saturday, at noon. I'll be there, but not the children. Miss Clitherow will look after them at Rowangarth – and Tatiana's nanny . . .' There was a silence, then she said, 'I hated Elliot. I've got to say it, even though it was a dreadful way to die. I still can't grasp the fact that he's gone – I just can't.'

'I know how you feel. I carried on something awful when I read your letter. I was glad Tom was there. I said I wanted to dance on his grave, though I'm sorry, now, that I said that.'

'Don't be, Alice. I'm not sorry, either – only for Aunt and Uncle and Anna. I know Anna loved him once, but it's anybody's guess, how she's going to take it.'

'I know. If he'd been my husband . . .' Alice left the sentence unfinished.

'I told Drew – gently as I could. He looked bewildered, as if he couldn't quite understand what dying meant. I thought he was going to cry, then he said, "Poor little

Tatty. We'll have to be extra kind to her, now." Just what Giles would have said. He's so like Giles that you'd think he was –'

'He *is* Giles's,' Alice said softly. 'You've got a lovely son, Julia.'

'I know. You and me both, Alice. Bless you for phoning, love – and for understanding . . .'

'Oh, I understand, all right – and Julia, take care, when you're driving?'

21

Clementina Sutton stood at the stone-mullioned landing window, staring trancelike into the courtyard below. She wore an unfashionably long black dress which fitted her tightly because she had last worn it long ago on the deaths of her Rowangarth nephews and, briefly, for Julia's husband. But this day she cared little for her appearance when uppermost in her mind was the certainty that nothing in the world would make her attend her son's funeral. She could not face it, would have thrown herself weeping to her knees at the graveside had Edward insisted she be there.

'I shall stand at the window – watch him go.' No one would be allowed to see her torment because no one – not even Helen – could understand the enormity of it. She did not have the self-discipline to conduct herself as Helen would on such occasions; hadn't the breeding, truth known, nor Helen's courage. The funeral, she had insisted, must be private with none there save family, and Nathan to conduct the service, commit his brother to the earth.

Why was this such a beautiful day, the sky so brilliantly blue? How dare birds sing? She had wanted to be alone with Elliot, see him one last time, say her own private goodbye, but they had refused her, begging her gently to remember him as he was.

'Four cars,' she murmured. 'Who are they?'

'Edward and Anna are in the first one, and Albert and Amelia following; then the Petrovskys.'

'And?' Clementina fretted.

'Your butler and my housekeeper – and Mrs Martin,

from Denniston. I thought staffs should be represented.'

'Yes.' It should have been a big funeral – weren't they Suttons, after all – yet it was best, this way. 'Where are the children?'

'Better they shouldn't be there, Clemmy. Such sadness is not for little ones . . .'

'No.' Clementina gazed fixedly at the scene below; four black cars – she refused to look at the flower-laden hearse – four groups of people, black-clad, and Pendenys servants and Denniston House servants standing on the steps, stiff as black statues, staring ahead, unmoving. 'Do you understand how I am suffering, Helen?'

'I do.' She reached for Clementina's cold, white hand. 'Only too well. But you will be brave, my dear. Elliot would want it.'

'Where is Julia?' She did not want to talk about being brave.

'At Rowangarth, with the children and the nannies. She wanted to be with the children . . .'

'Ah, yes.' Clementina fingered her jet beads with nervous fingers. She needed to weep, but tears were denied her. There was to be no comfort. Her reason for living was being taken away from the home he had been born in; leaving behind the inheritance she had so jealously amassed in his name. How dare death take the son she had schemed for and cheated for? How could life be so cruel?

Helen, too, gazed down to where her brother-in-law stood.

'You'll stay with Clemmy?' Edward had asked her. 'She's so upset, Helen. There are times I fear for the state of her mind. God knows where it will all end.' He had given her the bottle. 'Look – could you try to get her to take a couple of these tablets? I daren't leave them lying about – don't know what she might do. Not deliberately,' he hastened, 'but they are heavy sedatives and she might just – accidentally, you know . . .'

'I'll be very careful, Edward. Two, you said?'

'If you could persuade her — when we've left for the church, that is. It's awful to see her, though, when she's taken them. It's as if she's in another world, like a bewildered child that doesn't know what's going on. Yet without them her grief is terrible to see. I can't grieve for Elliot, Helen. There's this awful feeling inside me, but it's numbness, nothing else.'

'The grief will come, Edward; I promise it will.' She held out a hand for the tablets. 'I'll do what I can,' she had said.

Clementina stared, unblinking. They were getting into the cars, now. Soon, they would take her son away, take him from her. They would drive him to Holdenby where men in black wearing crepe-trimmed top hats would be waiting to walk, snail's pace, through the village in front of the hearse. She saw it all in her mind, her heart. Slowly, then, to the church gates where Nathan would be waiting. And he would walk in front of Elliot, chanting meaningless prayers; Nathan her heir, now, who had no wife, no son to give to Pendenys.

'Helen,' she moaned. 'Help me!'

'There now, there . . .' Helen drew her close. 'Be brave. Say goodbye. Let him go with your love, Clemmy. If it is any comfort, remember that I know what it is like to lose a child.'

'No! Not just a child; not just a son. *Elliot*. He was my life, my whole life. Oh, he could be a naughty boy but I love — *loved* — him so. There is nothing left for me, now.' Her voice rose, harsh and tormented. 'It would have been better if I had been in that car beside him!'

'No, Clemmy! You must never say that again! You must be brave. Edward needs you; he needs comfort, and Anna and Nathan and Albert. They grieve for Elliot, too. Be strong, for their sakes.'

'I can't be strong. I try, Helen, but I don't want to go

on living without Elliot. He was the one I loved, you see.'

'Then think about Anna? She loved him, too. Anna is too young to bear such sadness on her own. Help her, Clemmy – for Elliot's sake, be kind to Anna and Tatiana?'

'Why should I be? You say she loved him, yet she didn't give him the thing he wanted most of all. She gave him a dead son, Helen, and for that I'll never forgive her!'

'Ssssh. You don't mean it; you know you don't. You are tired, Clemmy. Come now – try to sleep? I'll stay with you, hold your hand.'

'But I can't sleep! Whenever I close my eyes it's all I see – the car in flames and that stupid sheep. He swerved to avoid it, hit the tree, you know. I'll have that tree cut down!'

'My dear, don't torment yourself. Remember that Elliot loved you dearly.'

'No! It's all my fault!'

'*Nobody's* fault. Just a terrible accident.'

'*Listen*, will you? I was angry with Elliot. I said things I shouldn't have. I said he was no better than a young tup – only the other day I said it! And it was a tup – a young ram – that ran out and killed him! What am I to do?'

'You are to take your tablets. I insist that you do, Clemmy. They will help you – let you sleep,' Helen murmured, guiding the stumbling figure across the landing, pushing open a bedroom door. 'There now – lie down.' She eased off Clementina's shoes, then shook two tablets from the bottle, offering them, eyes pleading.

'I wish they were poison, Helen. I could sleep, then, and never wake up.'

'You mustn't talk like that! Please take them – for me?'

Reluctantly, truculently, Clementina placed the tablets on her tongue, then swallowed them obediently.

'Poison,' she murmured, sipping the water Helen had poured. 'And just see if I don't have that tree cut down!

It's *my* tree; this house is mine and everything in it and all of it for Elliot. He had everything to live for.'

'Hush, now.' Helen took the trembling hand into her own, holding it tightly. 'Lie down. Try to sleep?'

'I don't want to sleep. I want to stay awake, be with him right to the end . . .'

'But Edward is with him, and his brothers, and Anna. Please try to rest?'

'I want a cigarette, Helen.'

'But you don't smoke. It would make you cough. Besides, I don't know where –'

'There are cigarettes in the box on Elliot's dressing table. Bring me one – please?'

'Very well.' Frowning, Helen slid the bottle into her pocket. Clemmy hadn't liked the cigarettes Elliot smoked, said the smell of them nauseated her.

Reluctantly she crossed the landing, shivering without reason, all at once reluctant to enter Elliot's room. For a few seconds she stood, staring at the ornate carving on the heavy door, the brightly polished brass fittings. Then fearfully, almost, she turned the knob.

Alice glanced at the mantel clock. Ten minutes past noon. Soon, he would be gone for ever. Soon, when Nathan murmured, *Ashes to ashes, dust to dust*, she would know that never again need she fear Elliot Sutton. Never again would she walk in Brattocks Wood, follow a sudden turn in the path and see him there.

Once, she had done that and he had barred her way, taking her wrist, demanding she tell him her name.

That had been awful, but nothing so awful, so evil, as the night in Celverte. That night, she didn't have the strength to fight him; that night she had learned Tom was dead and she wanted to die, too, on that cowshed floor. But Elliot Sutton had not killed her; only taken her savagely. Yet now he was gone and she need never again fear he would stumble on the truth of Drew's fathering. The deceit had died with him.

She ran up the stairs, opening the door of the alcove cupboard, easing back the linoleum that covered the floor, prizing up the piece of board that revealed the opening below.

The small cash box lay there. In it she kept her precious things; Daisy's sapphire christening brooch, the pearl engagement ring, her marriage lines, Daisy's birth certificate. But most precious of all was the buttercup spray she had pressed in her Bible. Tom had given it to her. His buttercup girl he'd called her, and from their first kiss came the certainty that she would love him till the day she died.

Carefully she opened the envelope in which it lay; carefully she took it out. It was brittle, now, and brown. Tom had taken it with him when he left for France, laid it in the little Testament that was his mother's parting gift.

She had never thought to see her buttercups again, for Tom was dead, she thought, and who, when they laid his body in the hastily-dug grave, could care about a spray of buttercups? But they had come back to her and now they were her talisman; while she had them she knew nothing could harm her nor Tom nor Daisy.

She smiled tenderly, tearfully, returning the envelope to the box, hiding it away again. Elliot Sutton was dead. She knew she should pray for him, but could not. She eased the linoleum back and then, before she rose to her feet, she closed her eyes and bowed her head.

'Dear Lord,' she whispered. 'Thank you with all my heart for my happiness – and let me keep it, please?'

Ashes to ashes . . .

Anna Sutton stared down into the deep, dark grave and the ornate coffin being lowered into it. It was almost over. She had concentrated hard on the words of the service in church, and though they were strange to her she had been glad of Nathan's gentleness in the saying of them.

In Russia, the giving back of the dead was different. There, the coffin was not closed until the moment of interment, but she supposed they had not been able to do that for Elliot. It wouldn't have been kind.

She thought of that handsome face; of eyes that teased and laughed but that mostly mocked; called back the darkness of him and the tallness, remembered the first time he had touched her in the twilight of the little garden at Cheyne Walk. That night she had wanted him with an intensity that shocked and shamed her. Such feelings were strange and new to her and from then on her days had been spent thinking of him and her nights in dreaming of tomorrow, when she might see him again.

And then she remembered her wedding night and when it was over she had found the truth too late. Elliot did not love her. She had lain at his side, staring into the darkness, certain that what took place in that hotel bed was not an act of love. Elliot had taken her. It had been necessary to get the son Pendenys needed so much. She had merely been another woman in his bed – like Natasha Yurovska.

Next day they boarded the Orient Express and had mated – it was the only word to describe it – from London to Venice and from there to Florence. And when they returned to Denniston House she was already pregnant – with a girl, had she but known it.

She began to shake and Edward saw it and reached for the black-gloved hand, holding it tightly so she might feel the comfort of his sympathy for her.

Sympathy for Anna, he brooded, not for himself nor Clemmy and not for Elliot. He felt nothing inside him but a coldness, a numbness. Grief would come, Helen had promised him, but he did not want to grieve for his firstborn, for the son who had not been Sutton fair. He had wondered, sometimes, if Elliot were his, then chided himself for his thoughts. Elliot had been no changeling. He, so

344

warmly welcomed, had been beautiful from the minute of his birth; a beauty he quickly learned to use for his own ends. Elliot could charm the birds from the trees with a smile; could crook a finger and have any woman he wanted.

How many women had he seduced? How many children had he fathered – hedge children, Clemmy would have called them. Somewhere, was there perhaps a son? Edward Sutton hoped not. It would be too cruel to think about.

He glanced across to the tiny mound that covered his grandson's grave. Soon, when the earth settled, they would place a white marble cross there. There would only be his initials carved into it, for he had not lived. Nicholas, his grandson. Now there was only Bas who disliked Pendenys almost as much as he did.

I'm sorry. Edward's sombre thoughts spanned the distance between father and son. *I cannot to my shame mourn you, Elliot, but I pray with all my heart that God may yet accept your soul . . .*

He glanced at Anna, his lips moving in the smallest of smiles. 'Be brave,' he whispered.

She pressed the hand that held hers in reply. She would be brave. Soon it would all be over. She had held her head high, worn her black, received condolences from those who called. She was Aleksandrina Anastasia Petrovska. She did not weep in public.

She lifted her eyes. Someone was looking at her, she could feel it. Across the grave she met Amelia's eyes and inclined her head in the smallest of bows. And Amelia returned her courtesy, then concentrated on the prayer book in her hand.

Poor little Anna, she brooded. But at least she was free of him, now. Had she loved him, Amelia demanded silently, right up to the end?

She recalled a bride, love shining brightly in her eyes. My, but that had been some wedding! Must've cost Bertie's mother a pile and every dime of it well-spent, if the satisfied smile on Clementina's face was anything to go by. Amelia hoped they would deal kindly with Anna and the child. Talk had it the Petrovskys had little but aristocratic pride on which to live.

Life was strange. She and Bertie had come to England to celebrate the birth of a child – a boy, they had hoped – and instead had stood witness to two deaths.

Instinctively she reached for her husband's hand. Dear Bertie. She had not the right to be this happy with her life – not at a graveside. She snapped shut her prayer book and forced her eyes to the coffin.

Dear Christ in heaven, forgive him his sins and teach him better ways? And I thank You most humbly for Bertie and Bas and Kitty. Amen.

A sweep of white caught Anna's eye and she turned to see Nathan standing beside her.

'My dear – there is nothing more we can do for him, now. Come with me, to Pendenys? Mother will want to know about it – and Aunt Helen. Let's tell her that all went well, shall we?' He turned to Edward Sutton. 'Are you all right, father?'

'Thank you, yes. And thank you for what you have done. It couldn't have been easy for you. Your mother will be glad to see you.'

He nodded to Countess Petrovska before replacing his hat, wondering what lay behind the slablike mask that was her face, what thoughts were forming in her mind.

Would she insist that Anna and Tatiana return to London with her? Would Anna want to go or would she want to stay at Denniston House? It was hers now, he supposed. He wondered how generously Clemmy would deal with Anna, would support her and the child who had been born a girl. Poor little Tatiana. Had she been a boy, the sun, the moon and the stars would have been hers for the asking.

He walked behind Nathan and Anna to the waiting cars, glad it was all over; glad until he realized that this day was the beginning of a life to be spent in Elliot's shadow; a life regulated by Clemmy's moods. It had never been easy, he sighed; now, it would be almost impossible to bear unless, of course, Clemmy turned to Nathan to fill her lonely days – find him a wife as she had found one for Elliot.

Poor, poor Nathan . . .

June came to Rowangarth in a blaze of beauty. Wild roses and honeysuckle trailed the hedgerows and elderflowers hung in sweet-smelling clusters along the lanes. In Brattocks Wood, the first foxgloves flowered and the cow pasture was golden with buttercups.

Helen raised her hand as Julia and Drew crossed the lawn. Drew. Eight, at Christmas. So precious; so like Giles.

'Hullo, darling.' Helen offered her cheek for his kiss. 'How did it go, today?'

'Ooooh . . .' The contents of the tray Mary carried towards them were of more interest. They always waited tea for him. It was one of the nice things about the end of lessons at the vicarage. 'Uncle Nathan says I must learn French, grandmother.'

'But you already speak it quite well.'

'Yes, but now I've got to learn to read it and spell it and oh, French verbs are going to be *awful*.'

'All part of growing up,' Julia smiled. 'And here comes tea. Hope it's curranty bread and cherry buns. And did you know, Drew, that Mrs Shaw is making a party for you, tomorrow, to say goodbye to Bas and Kitty? I think you should phone Pendenys, and invite them over.'

'And Tatty? Can she come, too? I know we must be kind to her, but do I have to ask her nanny? And I wish Kitty and Bas didn't have to go back to America,' Drew pouted.

'There'll still be Tatiana, dear.'

'But she might go back to London – and she's a *girl*.'

'So is Kitty,' Julia reasoned.

'Kitty is different. She doesn't always have her nanny with her and she can climb trees and –' And she could spit further than any of them, though best not mention that. 'Kitty likes Pendenys, but Bas says it's haunted and he never wants to live there. Do you know that one day, Bas might have to come and live at Pendenys for ever? He says it's an awful thought.'

'When will you ever learn, Drew Sutton, that no one *has* to do anything?' Julia frowned.

'But it's true! Bas heard the grown-ups talking. If Uncle Nathan doesn't get married soon, there'll be nothing for it but for Bas to inherit and that's going to be one heck of a nuisance. Well, that's what he said – and it's all because Uncle Elliot died.'

'Children who listen to what grown-ups say can often get it wrong,' Julia warned. 'And you're not to talk about Uncle Elliot – leastways not when Aunt Clemmy is there. It makes her sad.'

'She's acting like a drama queen, Kitty says. And Bas says he'll be glad to go home it's been so awful at Pendenys since it happened. Bas would like it if they never came again, but they might come over for Christmas – help Aunt Clemmy to be happy again.'

'Child! Stop your prattling! Drink up your milk, then be off and phone Pendenys and Denniston. Four o'clock tomorrow, tell them. And hurry,' Helen ordered. 'There are things I want to tell your mother – privately.'

'Nice or nasty?' Drew took another cherry bun.

'Neither. Just ordinary things – about the estate.'

'What about the estate?' Julia demanded when they were alone.

'Nothing that need worry you. First, though, we have an appointment with Carvers. Since – well, the accident – everything has got a bit behind. The papers are ready for the share transfer of the tea garden. We're to go there at two, tomorrow. And there's another thing. Williams told me several days ago, but it slipped my mind.'

'*Williams*? Oh – the woodman. Anything wrong?'

They heard so little from the woodman and his wife who came, after the war, to live in Keeper's Cottage. They seemed, Julia frowned, to keep themselves to themselves, and though she hadn't exactly avoided them, to see Keeper's Cottage with someone else living in it – someone who wasn't Alice and Daisy and Tom – didn't exactly please her.

'Williams gave notice, a week ago. In all the upset, I forgot.'

'So when are they leaving?'

'Seems there's no hurry. It was just a warning, so to speak. He'll work out his month and then maybe more – till they find a place of their own, that is. I told him I was willing for them to stay on.'

'But has he come into money, or something?'

'He has, Julia; quite a lot. Five thousand pounds, in fact.'

'Heavens! A relative in Australia, was it?'

'No.' Helen smiled mischievously. 'A benefactor in the Irish Free State, though you're not to breathe a word to anyone. I told him I would respect his confidence. It was the Irish Sweepstake. Isn't it splendid? I've always been aware of these lotteries but never have I heard of anyone winning anything. Well, Williams *has* won – or to be more precise, his brother has.'

'But it's supposed to be illegal; they aren't allowed to sell tickets in England. And I thought you didn't approve of gambling, mother.'

'The Sweepstake isn't gambling; it's for the hospitals in Ireland. They could do with one like it here. And as for being illegal – everyone knows they sell tickets here. Williams' brother drew a horse though he thought it didn't have a hope of getting round the Grand National course, much less winning. So he offered Williams a share in the ticket; hedging his bet, I suppose you could say. Anyway, the horse – I forget its name – was placed, so there was ten thousand pounds to share between them. Now promise you won't say a word, Julia?'

'Promise. But what will they do with all that money?'

'They plan to go back to Wales – buy a cottage. They should get a decent place for five hundred pounds. The remainder he intends to put in the bank – it should make quite a bit of interest for them. Mrs Williams is going to work for her sister who has a cake shop and tearoom. They'll be quite comfortably off. Williams' wife has always missed her family, I believe.'

'So Keeper's Cottage will be empty?'

'I suppose so – but probably not until Michaelmas. They've got to go to Dublin, I believe, to get the money, but it's all cut and dried. It's nice, isn't it, when work is so hard to find and people are going hungry, to hear of someone having some luck.'

'Nice.' Alice and Tom should be coming back to Keeper's, Julia frowned, but Rowangarth didn't need a gamekeeper and Tom had a good job at Windrush; better than a woodman's. 'Oh, dammit, mother – why did you have to tell me that!' she demanded. 'You know how much I ache to have Alice home again!'

'I know, dear. But we couldn't even think of offering the job to Dwerryhouse. It would mean a cut in his wages and there would be Alice to think about.'

'Alice would come like a shot – I know she would.'

'But Dwerryhouse is well settled and has a good employer, and Alice only lives a day's train ride away.'

'I know, dearest, and I'm being selfish. It's just that I miss her so – and you'd like her back, I know you would.'

'Ah, yes. She cared for Giles when he was so ill after the Army sent him home. And she is Drew's mother. How can I help but want her home? But I want what is best for her

350

and I think you shouldn't tell her about Williams. She might fret to come back, and Tom could well want to stay at Windrush. We mustn't do anything to cause friction between them. Let's agree not to say anything until Keeper's Cottage is empty?'

'All right.' Julia's mouth set stubbornly. 'But Drew should soon be taught to handle a shotgun properly and who better to do it than Tom?'

'Not for a couple more years at least, Julia. Please leave it? If the Fates want Alice to come home to Rowangarth, they'll find a way of doing it. What we must concentrate on now is trying to keep Clemmy's spirits up. When Amelia and Albert go back to America, she is going to miss them. I'm worried about Clemmy and about Edward, too. Goodness only knows what he has to contend with, now.'

'You are right, mother. You usually are. As a matter of fact, I did hear – from Jinny Dobb, actually – that Aunt Clemmy has taken to shutting herself in her room; that little hideaway, she's got, in the tower. Sometimes, I believe, she locks the door and won't answer – even to Uncle Edward.'

'I know. When I called this morning she was in there. She didn't seem so bad, though. We talked about old times; about Albert breaking his arm climbing the tree for conkers and Elliot's first long trousers. She seems quite reasonable talking about the past. It's when the present catches up with her that the tears come. I think a holiday away from it all would do her good. I know how she is suffering.'

'Suffering? Aunt Clemmy has had everything her own way for as long as I can remember. She even fixed it so Elliot didn't go anywhere near the trenches – had you thought of that?'

'Julia – try to let the war rest? And be a dear and ask Cook for a fresh pot of tea? All this talking has made me thirsty. And remember, not a word about Williams – and especially to Alice.'

She watched her daughter cross the lawn and enter the house by the conservatory door. Perhaps, she frowned, she had been wrong to tell her so soon about Williams? Now, she would be full of schemes to bring Alice back home and it wouldn't do. It really wouldn't.

'Do we have to come back and spend Christmas at Pendenys, Mom?' Bas frowned.

He had stood on deck, watching Liverpool disappear in a shimmering haze, glad to be returning to Kentucky. Grandmother Sutton was bossy and sometimes quite awful to be with – at the best of times, that was. But since *that* had happened, he'd done his best to keep out of her way, counting the days to their return.

'Yes, dear, we do. I have as good as promised that we will. You mustn't be selfish, Bas. Poor grandmother has been through a terrible experience and it is our duty to help her.'

'But what about grandfather? No one seems to mind that he's lost a son, too. Kitty's right about grandmother. She *is* a drama queen. And I don't mind going back to Pendenys for Christmas if you'll remember to help grandfather, too,' he added hastily, knowing he had gone too far, expecting to be sent to his cabin in disgrace.

'Why is Pendenys Place so awful, Bas?' Albert, sensing a reprimand from Amelia and not altogether disagreeing with his son's remarks, intervened quietly. 'Your sister likes it, don't you, girlie?'

'Sure do! It's a great house. Wish I could have it, one day. It isn't fair Bas should get it, just because he's a boy!'

'But who says Bas will have Pendenys? Who told you that?'

'Oh – guess I heard it, somewhere or other . . .'

That was another good thing about Pendenys. So many passages and little ups and downs in the staircases; so many unexpected doors; dark corners to hide in. She had been hiding in one of those dark corners and heard everything they'd said – the butler, that was, and one of the footmen.

If Mr Nathan doesn't shape himself and get wed, that young Sebastian is going to get this place one day . . .

'Then you are quite, quite wrong, Kitty! Your Uncle Nathan stands to inherit, not your father. And who's to know your uncle hasn't got a young lady, some place? He'll probably think deep and hard, now, about getting married and having sons of his own; so don't you get any ideas about our branch of the family ever being saddled with *that* place, young lady!'

'Okay – don't get mad at me, Mom. And I guess I can always marry Drew. Rowangarth isn't as big as Pendenys, but it creaks a lot more. Wouldn't mind living at Rowangarth. Great-aunt Helen is heaps nicer than Grandmother Sutton,' she shrugged, totally unperturbed.

'Now just see here, Kathryn Sutton – don't get sassy with me!' Amelia flung. 'And don't get ideas about marrying your cousin Drew. Such talk, and you not yet seven!' Then she smiled, because no one could be angry with Kitty for long. She was such a charmer, so direct and honest. 'Now tell you what – it's first night on board and no one dresses for dinner, first night out. So how if you and Bas eat with your Pa and me, tonight?'

'In the grown-ups' dining-room?' Kitty breathed, eyes shining.

'If you try to act a little more grown-up and think, sometimes, of the feelings of others.'

'Sorry, Mom. Guess Grandmother Sutton isn't half bad,' she conceded, dropping her eyes, twisting her fingers as she had quickly learned to do when either of her parents called her Kathryn.

'What are we to do with your daughter, Bertie?' Amelia smiled when they were alone. 'She's so very *English*. And the sauce of her! Marry Drew, indeed!'

'She does have an English father.' Albert offered his arm.

'And as for marrying young Drew – well, she could do a whole lot worse. I suppose, though, that she'll break a lot of hearts before she marries some thoroughly acceptable all-American boy. Now how about a turn around the deck before dinner?'

Albert Sutton was well content. He was going home to Kentucky, for that, now, was where he belonged. Like his son, he had no liking for Pendenys Place and heaven forbid that either he or Bas should ever inherit it!

But Kitty – now there was a strange one! Amelia was right. Kitty was so very English it was uncanny – and frightening, at times. Kitty, he sighed inside him, carried the Pendennis streak. Mary Anne would have been proud of her American-born great-great-granddaughter.

'Did you know,' he asked, eager to rid his head of such thoughts, 'that this ship – the *Berengaria* – was once a German liner and we – the English, that is – took it as part of war reparations?'

'Now is that so? War reparations, uh? So forget that war, Bertie. It's over and done with and the only good thing ever to come out of it is that it made certain sure there'll never be another one! Neither Bas nor Drew will ever have to go to war – thank the good Lord.

'Now will you just look at that sunset, over the water, Bertie? If there's one thing I shall miss about England, it's the beautiful sunsets . . .

22

Alice sighed, laid down her pen, then read what she had written. Another link with her past gone. Poor Morgan.

My dear Julia,

This is to thank you for your birthday card and to say how sorry I am to have to send you sad news in return.

Morgan died, two days ago. Tom found him when he went to feed and water the dogs. He'd just slipped away in his sleep which is the kindest way to go, I suppose.

Even though it was a gentle passing, Daisy would not be consoled and in the end it was only Keth could comfort her.

'Dry your eyes, Daisy,' Keth had whispered. 'It's best you come with me to school. We can talk about him on the way. I liked Morgan, too. We'll give him a proper funeral – just like for real people.'

'Can we have a funeral, Dada?' Daisy had fixed Tom with red, tear-filled eyes.

'Of course we can, little lass. We'll find a nice place for him.'

'And we'll say a prayer for him, so he'll go to heaven? Dogs *do* go to heaven, Dada?'

'Heaven? Now that's one thing I can speak about with certain authority. Some humans won't ever get there, they're so wicked, but dogs are lovely, faithful creatures. I've never met up with a bad dog yet; only a bad owner.

So you can take it from me that God never turned a dog away – no, nor ever will,' Tom said gently. 'Now off you go to school with Keth. Morgan didn't suffer like some poor creatures do. We'll give him a good send-off; do the old lad proud.'

Alice smiled, remembering. 'Thank you, Tom,' she said when Daisy had turned to wave from the gate.

'Thank me? What for?'

'For being so nice about getting Morgan into heaven.' She had reached up to kiss his cheek. 'You old softie . . .'

We found Morgan a nice spot at the side of the lane between Willow End and Keeper's Cottage – beneath a young beech. We said 'Our Father' for him and sang 'All Things Bright and Beautiful'. Keth was there and Tom and Daisy and me. And I cried a little because Morgan was once Giles's dog and it was as if part of my life had gone with him.

Dear Giles. There would be three men in her life, Jinny Dobb said so very long ago. A wicked one, a weakly one and a straight and sound one. Elliot Sutton, Giles Sutton, and Tom.

Tom made a little wooden cross and put it over the grave and Daisy seemed happier. Keth said Morgan would be there, always, between the two cottages and not be lonely, ever. Keth is a good lad.

I'm glad that Mark Townsend took you out whilst you were in London, though why you make excuses every time you see him, I really don't know.

She did, Alice brooded; always went into great detail to explain how friendly and correct it had been. Yet why shouldn't they go out together? They were both free; Mark Townsend was a widower. But best be careful what she wrote. Julia was very touchy, still.

She took up her pen again, dipping it carefully into the ink bottle.

Give Drew a kiss and a hug from Lady and take good care of yourself.

She frowned as she blotted and folded the sheets of paper, wondering why she always felt a vague uneasiness whenever Mark Townsend took Julia out. Mind, nothing would come of it. It took two to make a couple and Julia simply wasn't available.

She propped the envelope on the mantelpiece. This afternoon she would go to the village to post it, then walk home with Daisy and Keth. This afternoon she would buy toffees to eat on the way home. Just this once, for a treat — because of Morgan.

There had never been any treats in Alice Hawthorn's young life; no toffees, no orange in her Christmas stocking. No Christmas stocking. Aunt Bella disliked Christmas, but Aunt Bella was a long time ago and two days past, Alice *Dwerryhouse* had reached her thirtieth birthday.

Now she could make her mark. Now she was considered old enough and wise enough to vote.

Women had died for that vote. It made her think of Emily Davison selling penny news-sheets in Hyde Park, and the fat policeman. And Julia and Andrew meeting.

She sighed deeply as she crossed the yard to fill a water bucket at the pump. Alice Dwerryhouse was a lucky woman. She had Tom and Daisy and a happy home. And at the next General Election, she could vote! What more, then, could she want, she demanded silently, vehemently.

What indeed? mocked the small voice of her conscience, and so annoyed was she that she could even think of wanting more that she set the potatoes to boil with such annoyance that water slopped out of the pan and made the hot coals hiss and spit.

'Dear Lord,' she whispered. 'I'm so selfish wanting to go home to Rowangarth, but I'll count my blessings. I *will*!'

Julia had replied to Alice's letter at once, sent sympathies about Morgan, and so angry was she this afternoon, that her pen flew across the paper furiously.

> Mother is in London, staying at Montpelier Mews and oh, how bitterly I regret promising her I would call in on Aunt Clemmy whilst she is away. But did I tell you that a verdict of accidental death was recorded at the inquest on Elliot?

She had thought at the time, Julia was forced to admit, that in all probability Elliot had been drinking. Stableyard talk had it he'd been seen earlier in the evening with a woman in the Coach and Horses, in Creesby, but there was always talk, trailing in Elliot's wake. Even during the war, talk of his womanizing with the wife of a serving officer had almost landed him in the trenches. Almost – because Aunt Clemmy's money had saved him.

> But about Aunt Clemmy – I found her in her little boudoir in the tower; the room Pendenys staff used to call her sulking room, though now I believe they are calling it the madhouse. And mad she will be if she doesn't make some effort to pull herself together. She looked dreadful and not a bit like she used to. Her hair needs waving and she smokes constantly. She is using Elliot's gold cigarette case and lighter, now, and has filled the room with his photographs. She is turning into a recluse . . .

'Come in – if you must,' Aunt Clemmy had snapped. 'I suppose your mother ordered you to visit, now that she's gone galavanting off to London!'

This morning, Julia had supposed, Aunt was in one of her vindictive moods. She alternated between sheer bitchiness and tearful self-pity. But bitchiness ran more true to form, and was better by far to deal with than tears and near hysteria, she acknowledged gratefully.

'How are you today, Aunt?'

'I am angry.' She had crushed her spent cigarette, then lighted another. 'It's that ungrateful Anna. Couldn't get away from Denniston House quickly enough; didn't know, poor thing, when she would be well enough to return to her husband, yet now – and Elliot not cold in his grave, yet – she's back, and acting as if she owns the place!'

'I think, Aunt, that maybe she does – or will. You did give it to them both as a wedding present.'

'So I did, and more fool me! And now, would you believe, she's setting the child against me. Teaching Tatiana Russian, so they can talk together behind my back and me not understanding a word of it!

'She's up to something, that Anna! They never spoke Russian in St Petersburg. Used English or French so their servants wouldn't understand what they were on about, I shouldn't wonder! So now, she and Tatiana and that great ugly Karl will be speaking in Russian so Denniston servants can't tell me what's going on, there!'

'Aunt Clemmy – be fair? It's right and proper that Tatiana should learn her mother tongue. Who knows but that one day they will be able to go back to Russia and claim what is theirs?'

'And would that you were right, Julia! I'd like nothing better than to see the back of Anna Petrovska and that mother of hers – that child, an' all!' She would never forgive Tatiana for being a girl! 'But they'll never go back to St Petersburg. Those Bolsheviks have got the upper hand. Those Petrovskys will never see their town house nor their Peterhof estate again. Anna and that child will be a liability, now. They came to visit yesterday, but I wouldn't see them! Tell me, why should Anna be alive, and my Elliot dead? And as for that old Countess Petrovska . . . !'

'Aunt – do please remember that the countess lost not only her homes but her husband and elder son, too. Surely you can understand, show some small pity?'

'Pity? You are getting like your mother, Julia! So saintly and reasonable and always ready to see the other's point of view, no matter how wrong they are! And what are you doing?' she demanded petulantly as Julia crossed the room.

'I'm opening a window, if you don't mind. This room is so hot, and full of cigarette smoke. It can't be good for you, Aunt Clemmy. It'll get on your chest and make you cough.'

'I'll cough if I want to! Leave the window shut. I like the smell of cigarette smoke. It reminds me of Elliot. He always smoked Turkish.' Her eyes filled with tears, her tight, angry mouth relaxed, then drooped pathetically. 'I want Elliot back, Julia. I miss him so. I can't go into any room that was his; can't bear to visit Denniston House. What is to become of me? How am I to live out each day?'

'You might try counting your blessings!' Julia's self-control snapped. 'You could have lost all your sons in that war. Jin Dobb's sister did.'

'But I don't care about Jinny Dobb's nephews. Why should I?'

'You should care because they died horribly in the trenches in a foreign country they'd scarce heard of. And my own husband died there too, helping the wounded, not sitting at a desk in Paris!'

She stopped, all at once red-cheeked. She had not meant to go that far but the words flung at her aunt had smouldered too long inside her and could no longer be checked.

'How *dare* you!' Clementina's mood reverted to one of anger. 'My, but while you live, Julia MacMalcolm, your Aunt Sutton will never be dead! You are just like she was – too direct for her own good. You are even getting to look like her, stupid old maid that she was!'

Old maid. The taunt hit Julia like a slap for she *was* an old maid. She was without a man, without love, without

360

the intimate closeness she had come to glory in. She and Andrew made love with such joy, such abandon. Just to think of his closeness had sent delirious want slicing through her.

Yet now she was untouched, unloved, unwanted. She didn't mind being compared to Aunt Sutton, but she did mind the cold celibacy that wrapped her round. She had tasted love – real love – and she missed it with an ache that never ceased to taunt her. Just as Aunt Clemmy was taunting her; cruelly, vindictively.

'I shall go now, Aunt, and perhaps come back when you are in a kinder mood.' Julia jumped to her feet, then turned abruptly. 'Is Uncle Edward in? Perhaps he might appreciate my company more.'

Her words were cold with anger, each one clipped and crystal clear. She waited in the doorway, but no reply came. Already the older woman was lighting yet another cigarette and doubtless wanting her to leave so she might fill a glass from the decanter standing on a side table.

And not only is Aunt becoming quite peculiar, but she is becoming ruder, if that is possible. My heart goes out to Uncle Edward. How he puts up with her, I really don't know. Aunt Clemmy deserves to be slapped. Hard.

Forgive me for sounding so discontented, but Aunt really got under my skin this morning. I really need to let off steam and there's no one here to talk to with mother away except Nathan, and he's always so busy. Be an absolute love and ring me, some time – reverse the charges. I do so need to talk to you, Alice.

I am coming to realize that where Aunt Clemmy is concerned, mother is a saint. Not a day passed without a visit to Pendenys. Why can't I be more like her?

Yet nothing could change how much she missed and wanted Andrew; missed him every bit as much as the day they had said their last goodbye that Paris afternoon in late March, nine years ago. All those long, lonely days without him. It hurt so much that sometimes she lay awake and wondered how it would be if she said yes, to Mark. He wanted her, she knew it. How would it be if she could close her eyes — and pretend . . .

No! No one but Andrew, even though there were days she could not recall his face; days when she had to run to her room and pick up the photograph that stood beside her bed. And even nine years on, she could still not hear his voice. His voice always eluded her. She could remember the sound of Robert's voice, and Giles's, could smile to hear in her memory the clipped tones of Sister Carbrooke or Ruth Love's gentle laugh. But Andrew's voice eluded her like a teasing spirit.

Oh, damn that war! Damn it, damn it, *damn it*!

23

'You look real smart,' Polly Purvis said. Just as he must have looked when he was a beat-keeper in Derbyshire, with high hopes of being a head keeper. But war came and Dickon had been billeted in Windrush Hall; the very same house Mr Hillier lived in, now. It was how they met, truth known; at a dance in Totten, not far from where she worked as head housemaid to gentry long since gone.

On her night off, that dance, and before the last waltz was called she was in love with a young soldier who could at any moment be sent to France.

'Smart? Then why the frown?'

'Sorry, love. Maybe I was remembering the night you and me met and how –'

'How I've changed – is that it?'

'No, it is *not*! I was thinking how like that young soldier you look. You pay for dressing, Dickon Purvis. Real posh.'

'Have to, haven't I? Going with Mr Hillier. Can't be looking like a tramp. And why isn't he taking Tom with him, I'd like to know.'

'You know why. Today is a reward, sort of. It's the first time Beth has really worked, and I reckon Mr Hillier wants you with him because she answers to you best of anybody.'

'You could be right, lass. Beth is *my* bitch; has been, right from the day she was weaned. And if she works like I think she will, Mr Hillier is going to be real pleased. Just wait till she has her first litter; her pups will be worth their weight in gold. And properly trained for the gun –'

'By you, of course,' Polly smiled.

'By *me*, if I've got anything to do with it. And if they shape up like Beth, Windrush retrievers will be famous.'

'Tom don't mind, do he?' Polly had no wish to offend Tom and Alice.

'No. 'Twas Tom suggested it — well, put the idea into Mr Hillier's mind, more like. Said it'd be better to take me with him as his loader so I could keep an eye on Beth, calm her down, if she needed it. And I appreciate it. Tom only did it so I would benefit, I shouldn't wonder. I could be ten bob better off at the end of the day.' Even more if Beth behaved, and carried well. A sovereign tip, maybe. More than a week's wages, and think what they could do with twenty shillings.

'Let me look at you.' Polly took the clothes brush from the dresser. 'Sure you'll be warm enough? It's still raw, underfoot.'

It had rained solidly for six days. Only now had the downpour ceased, leaving the clay-bound earth wet and squelchy and cold to stand on. She worried about his foot, which always pained him more in the cold of winter.

'I'll be fine.' Wasn't he wearing one of Tom's too-small tweed suits and a pair of highly polished brown leggings? 'And my foot will be all right.' It didn't hurt so much when he wore the hand-lasted boots Mr Hillier had seen fit to have made for him.

'Then away and enjoy yourself, Dickon love. And let's hope the master's going to give credit where credit is due.'

'He will. I was once a keeper, don't forget. I can load a shotgun quicker than most — with my eyes shut.'

And a loader needed to have his wits about him when the beaters put the birds up. Wasn't a lot of use holding a gun, if it wasn't loaded. Mr Hillier was taking his Purdeys; fine guns. Dickon had cleaned them last night, flannelled the inside of the barrels until they shone like glass.

'You'll not know when you'll be back? Will I keep your supper warm in the oven?'

'Best you do. Mr Hillier's likely to be asked in for a drink, when the shoot's over.' Mr Hillier, come to think of it, had been pleased to be asked to shoot at Shroveby Manor. Once, only the landed gentry attended such gatherings, but since the war a self-made man could be invited to take part – provided he conducted himself like a gentleman, that was, and had decent shooting of his own. Ralph Hillier, with his fine guns and the best retriever it had ever been Dickon Purvis's luck to handle, would be a contented man, tonight, all things considered.

Almost certainly he'd part with a sovereign.

'That's Dickon on his way, all smart,' Alice murmured from the window. 'Where are they going?'

'Shroveby, I believe, and the first shoot of the season. There'll be good sport. I shouldn't wonder. Hope Beth behaves herself. It's her first big shoot, an' all.'

'Mr Hillier's proud of that bitch.' Alice piled logs on the fire. 'Oh, I do so hate November.' In December there was Christmas to look forward to; January brought a new year and new hopes, whilst February's snowdrops and aconites and crocus that peeped from sheltered corners promised that spring was only just around the corner. But November was awful and tomorrow would be the anniversary of Andrew's death; tomorrow, she would telephone Julia and say, 'Hullo, love,' gently and softly. She had done it every year since it happened and she would be glad when that sad day was over.

'Then let's hope the master tips generous. Polly could do with a few shillings extra and where's that girl?' Irritably Tom drummed his fingers on the table top. 'Does she know her breakfast's ready?'

'She does, and she won't be long.' And you couldn't blame a bairn for not wanting to leave a warm bed on a cold, drab morning, though at least now the rain had stopped. Day after day, Keth and Daisy coming home from school drenched to the skin. Daisy had wellington boots, but Keth had none. It made Alice wonder how she could buy him a pair without offending Polly's pride. Christmas, happen?

'Good mornin', Daisy Dwerryhouse.' Tom took out his pocket watch, gazing at it meaningfully. 'Late down again. Tonight it's bed at seven sharp, and no listening to the wireless – is that understood?'

'Dada! That isn't fair! Keth stays up till nine!'

'Keth's older than you are and besides, he has to do homework, now, if he's to get his scholarship.'

'They say at school that he'll pass it easily,' Daisy hastened, eager to change the conversation. 'They only give five free places, but Keth'll get one, even his teacher says he will.'

'Of course he will.' Alice set porridge plates on the table. And everyone hoped he would, an' all; everyone except the lad's own mother who was worried out of her mind already.

'How am I to tell him he can't go?' she had confided. 'Because he can't, even if he passes. We can't afford the uniform and all the things he'll need, and that's final. Poor lad – and he's working so hard.'

'Keth *will* pass and he *shall* go,' Alice had countered hotly. 'We'll find a way, somehow. There'll be all sorts of things I can make for him – long socks, pullovers. And he'll be in short trousers 'til he's fourteen and shorts I can easy make from market remnants. We'll do it, between us . . .'

'Your breakfast's going cold.' Tom passed a hand in front of Alice's eyes. 'You were miles away, lass. Rowan-garth again, was it?'

'No. We're right enough here, at Windrush.' Alice picked up her spoon. 'As a matter of fact I was thinking about Keth and his scholarship.'

'He'll pass,' Daisy said confidently. 'He's top of the class, but he's stupid. He said even if he gets a place he doesn't want to go. But he does, Mam. He really wants to go to the Grammar School.'

'And he will, Daisy love.' Oh my word, yes! No matter what, they would get that dratted uniform together, between them. 'Keth shall have his chance, but best not say too much about it, lovey. It's all a matter of money you see, and Polly and Dickon don't have over much, at the moment.'

'Then let's hope Mr Hillier is going to show his appreciation – because if there's a better gun dog at that shoot than our Beth, then I'll eat my Sunday hat. And I think I'll have two fried eggs this morning, Alice – keep the cold out. And eat up, Miss Daisy, or there'll be Keth having to wait while you finish your breakfast.'

Which would please Alice and give her the excuse to provide the lad with a thick slice of dripping toast to eat whilst he waited, Tom reasoned comfortably. Hollow legs, that lad had. And fingers crossed for a good day's sport over at Shroveby – and that it didn't start to rain again.

The Shots, five of them, took up positions backs to the wood. With them, their loaders and retrievers behind them, sticks at the ready at the far end of the wood, stood the team of beaters, waiting for the signal to advance into the game covers beneath the trees; send the game birds, suddenly alarmed, into the air.

To the left of the Shots and a hundred yards away, the river flowed. On the surface it was brown and littered with branches and debris, but underneath it was a turbulent, heaving mass, swollen by the constant rain and reaching, almost, to the tops of its banks.

Beth sat at Dickon's feet, her body quivering with excitement, sometimes moving from him to be ordered, 'Heel Beth! Sit!'

'Just look at that head of hers, Purvis.' Ralph Hillier

fondled the bitch's ears, eager to show her off. 'Near perfect.'

Pleased, Dickon smiled, telling himself just for once that the war had never happened; that his foot was whole and he was head keeper to an earl; a duke, even, and Polly didn't have to go out scrubbing nor take in washing.

In the wood, the beaters began to walk forward, thrashing the undergrowth with their sticks, shouting and whooping to send the birds into the air. Startled pheasants took flight, wings flapping, trying to make height, and with them flew little fat partridge, whole coveys of them. For the first time in a week a watery sun broke through the clouds. The Shots raised their guns; the first bird fell.

Ralph Hillier smiled. This was going to be a good day; a good day all round.

Alice switched on the wireless for the six o'clock news bulletin; Tom took out his pipe and Daisy settled herself at his feet. He had been late finishing, realizing not for the first time how dependent he was becoming on Dickon, wondering how he could persuade Mr Hillier to raise him from dog boy to beat-keeper. Perhaps, he smiled, if the sport today had been good and Beth lived up to her promise, his employer might be in a mood to consider such a suggestion.

'Doing the night beat, are you, Tom?' Alice took up the sock she was knitting.

'Think I'd better. By the time Dickon gets back he'll not feel like walking the rounds; he'll have had enough, with that badly foot.'

There had been no shooting yet, at Windrush, and pheasants and partridge were thick on the ground; an invitation to poachers to take all they could.

'I'll give it till nine.' Tom settled his stockinged feet on the fender. 'No use going too early.' Nor did a keeper make his rounds at the same time each night. Best not advertise his movements, though in all fairness, no one minded the 'one-for-the-pot' man – some poor chap with bairns to feed and his dole and parish relief run out; aye – and most of what he owned taken by the bailiffs. Such a family was welcome to the odd bird, and all the rabbits he could snare. A man so desperate Tom turned a blind eye to; it was the greedy he must keep alert to and ahead of; those organized gangs who made a good living from poaching. 'Nine o'clock-ish, I'll go.'

He puffed on his pipe, his eyelids began to droop, then flew wide open at the sudden knocking, loud and urgent-sounding. He jumped to his feet.

'Who on earth can it be, at this time of night?' And whoever knocked on a front door, especially after dark? 'Stay where you are, love. I'll go.'

He pushed his feet into his slippers, then, taking the flash-light, made his way to the door.

'Who is it, then?' He shone the light into the stranger's face, for stranger it must be.

'I'm looking for Purvis's place – or for Tom Dwerry-house. Either will do.'

'I'm Dwerryhouse. What do you want with me?'

The man was a keeper, that much was obvious from his dress. At his feet, the thin beam of torchlight picked up the outline of a sack.

'Today – at the shoot – there's been trouble . . .'

'You'd best step inside.' Apprehension crawled the length of Tom's backbone. He struck a match and held it to the candle that stood on a shelf at the stair bottom. Then deliberately he closed the door on Alice and Daisy.

'I've brought the bitch back. We got her out,' the man said softly. 'Name of Hillier, Windrush, on the collar, and who in his right mind ever put a collar on a working dog, I'd like to know.' The stranger's voice rose angrily. 'Went into the river, after a bird. They shouldn't have let her. That river was running too strong, though I reckon she'd have made it out if it hadn't been for the willow . . .'

'Look – you're not making sense,' Tom hissed. 'Are you telling me you've got Beth outside, and if you are, why isn't Dickon Purvis here – or Mr Hillier? What's been going on?'

'Dada?' The door opened and a shaft of lampglow lit up the narrow passage.

'Go back in, little lass, and shut the door. I'm talking private to this gentleman.' Then Tom asked the question again.

'Going on? There's all hell let loose at Shroveby Manor. L' ɵ I'm trying to tell you, Mr Hillier's bitch got into trouble in the water and his loader tried to get her out. The outcome of it was that both men ended up in the river and that's all we know, for certain. There's men from the estate and police searching both riverbanks, but so far, neither's been found.'

'*Drowned*, you mean?' A fist of iron slammed into Tom's belly. 'They didn't get out?'

'Not as far as we know. They might have, farther down-river, but I know that stretch of water and it's treacherous, when it's in flood. They should have stopped the bitch going in after that bird. She was a game 'un, that's for sure. I got her out myself. But for all that, she didn't let go. She still had the bird in her mouth. Drowned, poor creature, her collar fast on a willow branch.'

'You're right. Shouldn't have had a collar on her. But Mr Hillier was right proud of Beth. Silver on leather, that collar was. Nothing but the best.'

He was talking nonsense; opening his mouth and words he didn't mean to say were slipping out. But maybe that was because he didn't want to hear any more, be told that more than likely Dickon and the master had been drowned, trying to help Beth. It made sense yet still he didn't want to believe it.

'Is there any chance at all?' he asked, eventually.

'None, in my opinion. It's a bad do. I was told either to see you or Purvis's wife. I don't suppose you could —'

'Tell Polly — prepare her, you mean?'

'I'd appreciate it, if you would. I ought to be getting back. The police'll be calling on Mrs Purvis before so very much longer, I shouldn't wonder. You couldn't, I suppose?'

'All right. But what am I to tell her, exactly?' You couldn't tell a woman her man wasn't coming home if there was the least chance he'd managed to get himself out of that river. *'Just tell me?'*

'I only know that Mr Hillier and Purvis went into the water after the bitch and got swept away. Neither of them got out nor had they, when I left Shroveby, been found. Dead or alive. And that's all I know. But if I was you, Mr Dwerryhouse, I'd not let that woman's hopes run too high.'

'And what of Mr Hillier? Have they been told, at Windrush?'

'Seems he had no near kin. I believe they telephoned through to the estate office there. They said they'd get in touch with his solicitors.'

'Aye.' Tom shook his head again. Whether he was trying to shake the bad news out or some small semblance of comprehension into it, he wasn't at all sure. 'All right, then. Leave it with me. Alice and me will go to Polly.'

'I'm obliged to you.' He held out his hand. 'Name's Ted Grimes — under-keeper at Shroveby. And I'm right sorry to have brought this news — as if there isn't enough misery in the world!'

He turned, fumbling with the door, letting himself out, mumbling a goodnight.

Tom stood, eyes closed, leaning against the wall of the passage, pulling gulps of air into his lungs, letting them go in little steadying puffs. How was he to tell Polly and Keth? How was he to tell Alice, even?

'Alice, love . . .' Reluctantly, he opened the kitchen door.

'What is it, Tom? Who was that? What has happened?'
She jumped to her feet, switching off the wireless, her face
all at once pale. '*Tell me!*'

'It's Dickon, and Mr Hillier.' There was no way round
it. Even in front of Daisy, it had to be said. 'An accident
over at Shroveby Manor, where the shoot was. Both of
them in the river. So far, they haven't been found. The
river was high, you see – all that rain. Both got into trouble
and they tried –'

'Polly? Does Polly know,' Alice demanded. 'Who's with
her?'

'She doesn't know. Keeper came over from Shroveby.
But there'll be the police calling on her before so very much
longer so it's best we tell her. They got Beth out – brought
her back.'

'Dear heaven!' Alice gathered a sobbing Daisy into
her arms. 'We must go to Polly. You stay here, Daisy. Stay
like a good girl and don't open the door if anyone
knocks.'

'No, Mam! Keth's my friend and I'm coming, too!'

'Then dry your eyes, like a brave little lass,' Alice whispered. 'And who's to know they aren't all right?' she said
with false brightness. 'Even now they might be out there,
trying to get back home in the dark.'

'They might, lass, but the man Grimes said he didn't
hold out much hope,' Tom said softly. 'We're just to tell
Polly that both tried to get Beth out and got pulled into
the river by the current. And we're to say that neither
of them has been found, yet. It's all we can tell her until
they're certain, but it's best it comes from us and not from
the constable. Just give me a minute to move Beth, then
we'll go to Willow End – all of us.'

They huddled round the hearth, numb and cold in spite of
a blazing fire; Daisy asleep in Alice's arms, Keth close to
his mother, thumb in mouth. He hadn't sucked his thumb,

Alice thought, since he was a small, hungry bairn, three years old.

'Another cup?' Polly whispered.

'No, thanks, love.' Alice shook her head, shifting her arm against Daisy's weight, wishing there was something she could do.

Through the uncurtained window a pale yellow sky told them another day had begun; the fifth day of November. Guy Fawkes day. The anniversary of Andrew's death and now, she was sure, the day on which Polly would be told that Dickon too was dead.

'I hate November,' she said. 'Always have.'

'Me, an' all.' Shivering, Polly hugged herself. 'It's the month of the dead, November is; the month, folks say, when spirits who die unchurched walk the earth looking for salvation.'

'Don't, Polly? Please *don't*,' Alice whispered. 'Pray, love. Pray with all your heart that –'

'That he'll come home? No, Alice – he's dead, I know it.' She nodded towards the window. Outside, silhouetted against the dawn light, a figure walked slowly, reluctantly almost, up the path. 'It's the Welby constable. He's come to tell me . . .'

That morning, Tom walked to school with a protesting Daisy.

'I don't want to go! I want Keth!'

'Keth is needed at Willow End. His Mam needs him more than ever, now. Polly doesn't want you under her feet. She's got more'n enough to contend with,' Alice had scolded. 'I'll meet you outside, when school is over; walk back with you.'

This was the day on which she always telephoned Julia – the anniversary of Andrew's death. Julia needed her sympathy, the comfort of her understanding, for hadn't Alice Hawthorn been there the night they met; hadn't she, Alice,

373

been the cause — in a roundabout way — of their meeting? Yet this morning, Polly's need of her was paramount; Polly who sat dry-eyed, in a stunned silence, hugging herself tightly, rocking back and forth.

'Why don't you try to sleep?' Alice had whispered. 'I'll fill a bed warmer and make you some hot milk and honey; help you drop off.' Lady Helen swore by milk and honey; Miss Clitherow, too.

Yet Polly had just sat there with Keth at her feet, staring into the fire as though she could see something in the shifting flames that no one else could.

A little before school ended, Alice asked for the Rowangarth number at the Post Office counter.

'Sit you down, Mrs Dwerryhouse,' the post mistress murmured. 'Won't take a minute, once I've got through to Trunks. And isn't the news terrible? Thought of nothing else since I heard. How is that poor woman going to manage, and Willow End a part of the job; wherever is she to go, and her with a growing boy to rear?'

Alice had nodded and murmured agreement, saying nothing, for a word exchanged in the post office was quickly added to and retailed with every three-ha'penny stamp.

'Julia,' she whispered into the receiver. 'It's Alice. Sorry I'm late ringing.'

'I thought you'd forgotten, but bless you, all the same. But tell me — what is the matter? Something is wrong. Is it Daisy?'

'No. Nothing wrong at Keeper's — but how did you know?'

'Because you usually ring early and you always say, "Hullo, love." And you are bothered. I can hear it in your voice. Tell me?'

'Oh, Julia love. I phone to give you comfort, help you through this day yet, oh dear . . .'

She stopped, close on tears, and bit hard into her bottom lip.

'Alice! *What is it?*'

'It's Dickon. He's dead. Him and Mr Hillier. Yesterday, it was. Tried to get a gun dog out of the river and both of them got pulled in. They came to tell Polly, last night. It's awful.'

'I'll come down. Drew will be all right, with mother. There must be something I can do?'

'No, Julia. Not yet, at least. Let's all of us catch our breath, first? And there'll have to be an inquest. Come next week? I'll be glad to see you and I know Polly will. It wouldn't have happened but for a fancy collar. Beth – that's the bitch – was wearing a collar, you see. Tom buried her this morning, with Morgan. Daisy is very upset about it all. Mr Hillier was fond of her and she's going to miss him. And as for Keth – but I'll write you a letter, tell you all about it.'

'Poor little Keth. Is he all right?'

'As right as may be, but what's to become of Polly I don't know.'

'Give Keth my love, won't you? And tell Polly I'll be thinking of her. Tell her I know just what she's going through.'

'I'll do that. And I'm sorry to pour my troubles out like this. It should be me comforting you today, shouldn't it? And when you come down, don't drive? Come by train? Don't want anything happening to you.'

'I won't drive. I'll change stations at London – come straight through. I won't stop over at Montpelier Mews. Monday, perhaps, or Tuesday?'

'I'll write you – and I'll ring again, when I know what's happening here. Take care, love? And I want to see you – I really do.'

She hung up the receiver, then left the little shop, eyes lowered. She didn't want to talk to anyone, however well-meaning. She wanted to go back to Keeper's Cottage with Daisy and make Tom's supper; draw the curtains on the night and pretend that none of this had happened.

But last night, Dickon had not come home to eat the supper Polly was keeping warm for him. Dickon was never coming home again.

Ralph Hillier's body was taken home, as he had wanted, to the village near Torvey Main colliery where once he had worked. His coffin was of finest oak, its fittings ornate. A service was read for him in West Welby church, attended by most of the village and all the staff from Windrush Hall.

He had, they were forced to admit, been a private man, for they knew little of him. He had been a fair employer, though, and in that fact lay their thoughts as they sang 'Abide with Me', a hymn he particularly liked. Ralph Hillier had given them work. He had no heir, no family truth known, to inherit. What was to happen now?

That same day, Dickon Purvis was laid to his rest without pomp and with little ceremony in a pauper's grave in West Welby churchyard. At the end of the service, which the Parish paid for, Tom drew Polly aside, handing her a brown envelope.

'I've been asked to give you this,' he said gently. 'Folk around these parts and Windrush staff, an' all, thought fit not to waste good money on flowers. They're offering it, instead, where they feel it'll do more good. No lack of respect, Polly. The fact that they're here shows their good intent. All they ask is that you accept it in the spirit they gave it in.'

'Beggars can't be choosers, Tom, and it's beggars me and Keth are, now. I'm grateful.'

At the church gates she stopped, and smiling gently at those who had waited until she left, she said, 'I thank you all. Me and Keth are grateful for your kindness.'

Then taking her son's hand she walked, head high, back to the cottage she knew they soon must leave.

'What's to become of her?' Alice fretted, that night. 'Where is she to go? Her mother can't help, that I do know. Polly's Mam gave up her home last year and went to live with her other daughter. There's no room there for two more. And Tom – how much was in that envelope?'

'Nigh on four pounds. At least they'll be able to eat, for a week or two. And Polly, being destitute, will qualify for a widow's pension.'

'Ten shillings? And how is she to manage on that? She'll have to leave Willow End. Half that pension will have to be paid out in rent!'

'Lass – happen we'll all have to leave,' Tom said softly. 'Mr Hillier had no kin. What's to become of Windrush is any man's guess. It'll go on the market, to my way of thinking, and them that buy it might have ideas of their own about who they employ.'

'I know that.' She had lain awake, turning it over and over in her mind since the night the keeper from Shroveby left Beth on their doorstep. 'But you and me will manage, somehow. You'll get another job and I can sew and scrub an' all, if I have to.'

'Aye, lass. But who's to give me a job and how soon? Aren't there decent men begging in the streets and tramping the length of the country, looking for work – *any* work? Mind, I know there's an empty cottage, at Rowan-garth, but Lady Helen has no use for a keeper, and I'm no woodman.'

'You could learn, Tom.'

'Happen I could. But I'm earning thirty shillings with a house and firewood and a suit of clothes thrown in. What is a woodman's wage? A pound a week, if he's lucky.'

'Twenty shillings,' Alice flashed, 'is better than nothing at all! It's twice what Polly will have. But don't think I'm going to start agitating to go home to Rowangarth, because I'm not.'

'No?' Tom reached out for her hand. 'I'd have thought it would've been the first thing you thought of.'

'It was, truth known.' Best not deny it. 'But I'm of a mind to stay on here just as long as they'll let us. It's Polly I worry about and there's Keth, too. Daisy loves him. He's the brother she never had and I know he cares for her. It'll break their young hearts when the time comes to part them, so I'm not for packing up and leaving till I have to – much as I long, sometimes, for Rowangarth. We'll just have to wait and see – all of us.'

'Then we won't have all that long to wait. Bailiff told me that all Windrush staff – indoors and out – are to be at the Hall tomorrow, at two sharp. We'll be told what's to do, then. Seems the solicitor has things to say.'

'Mr Hillier's Will? It's going to be read?'

'I don't think so. Wills are private things and only read to those that will benefit. But the solicitor will know what's to happen to Windrush – how long it'll be before it goes on the market. And how many staff are going to be kept on, because it's my belief they'll have to keep some on, for a time. I'm hoping I shall be one of them. The ground is thick with game birds – something will have to be done about them, for a start. Game birds are worth money.'

'Why didn't you tell me, Tom?'

'I meant to, in the morning. What you didn't know I reckoned you couldn't worry about and you're worrying already, aren't you?'

'N-no. But why is he sending for all the staff if there isn't something to tell them – something bad?'

'Then you'll have to tell yourself it's going to be something good. No use looking for trouble.' Tom lit a spill of wood at the fire, then held it to his pipe. 'We'll all of us know, this time tomorrow.'

'You'll have to cut down on tobacco.' It was all she could think of to say.

'Tomorrow I might have to, but tonight I'm enjoying a pipe.'

'I'm off to Willow End!' Alice reached for her shawl.

'You do that. Have a chat with Polly. Do you both good. And happen, when you've decided between you what's going to be said tomorrow at the big house, you'll let me know,' he grinned. 'Take the candle-lamp, and watch your step. It's slippy, underfoot.'

'*Men!*' Alice slammed the door behind her. Couldn't see further than the ends of their noses. Left the women to do the worrying. No use looking for trouble? They'd be jobless before so very much longer and all Tom Dwerryhouse could do was light a pipe! Mind, there was always Rowangarth . . .

She held up the lamp and its small, soft light touched the slender trunks of the beeches that lined Beck Lane. Briefly she paused beside the newly-turned earth. There were two of them, now. Company each for the other. Morgan and Beth. Beth of Winchester, who'd been the cause of it all.

She dashed away a tear, then walked, chin high, towards the light that shone from Willow End. She wondered what Polly would make of tomorrow. Not a lot, she supposed, and anyway, they would know soon enough.

Bad news always travelled fastest, didn't it?

24

'Just where have you been till now? Near on dark and me worrying about what's been happening at Windrush!'

'Sorry, Alice. Had to stay behind, after the meeting was over. Solicitor wanted to talk to me about the game — it's all to be culled.'

Which wasn't entirely true. The past hour, Tom had spent walking the game covers, though he'd told himself he was making sure nothing was amiss, as he always did. But truth known, he'd needed time alone; try to make sense of what had been said.

'Things won't be too bad, bonny lass. At least no one will be on the street, just yet. It takes time to wind up an estate, I was told. You and me and Polly could be here till spring. Polly is to stay in Willow End for the time being which is something to be thankful for.

'And all employees have been left a hundred pounds each; now what do you think to that? Dickon was included, so the solicitor said Polly is to have his money. And I've been left Mr Hillier's Purdeys.'

'But that's wonderful! All that money — well, I'll be grateful enough for it myself, but Polly won't be able to believe her good fortune. Does she know?'

'She wasn't at the meeting. The solicitor will be writing to her, he said.'

'And it's definite?'

'It was all set down in the Will . . .'

'Then keep an eye on the potatoes? I won't be a minute. Just want to tell Polly the good news. And Daisy's in the parlour. She's worrying about being parted from Keth so think on, and tell her we'll not be leaving just yet.'

She was gone in a flurry of excitement but Tom sat there, staring at the pan on the hob and the lid that lifted and fell in little puffs of steam.

But one thing was certain. Alice would get no more out of him till Daisy was safe in bed and out of earshot, because there were things to be told that Daisy mustn't know about – not for a long time.

Yet he should be glad, he supposed, for Alice's eagerness to carry the news to Polly. It gave him time to pull himself together, think on about which way would be best to tell her what else had been said this afternoon. At the best, it was news hardly to be believed; at the worst, it could make for trouble.

He raised his eyes to the mantelpiece where Beth's collar had been laid to dry, wondering what would have happened if she had not been wearing it.

Beth would've got out of that river, flooded or not. Dogs were natural swimmers and she would have gone along with the current until she was able to get out. Dogs didn't thrash and struggle, panic-stricken, as humans did. If only that willow branch had not been there, beneath the water; if only she hadn't been wearing that collar. She should not have been, but Mr Hillier hadn't known that.

Tom reached for his pipe. He didn't usually smoke until after supper but tonight he would allow himself the luxury of a fill. To puff on his pipe calmed him, helped him better to think. And think he must, tonight, and put things to Alice in such a way that she didn't fall in a faint at his feet.

And all because of a dog collar.

'So now you'd better tell me!' Alice stood, hands on hips, mouth tightly set. 'You hardly touched your supper; you haven't seemed the least bit interested in what Polly said when I told her about the money, and for a man that's

381

been left a pair of Purdey shotguns, you're acting in a strange way.

'Now the bairn's in bed, so you and me are going to talk, Tom Dwerryhouse. What you're holding back from me I don't know, but you've been in another world since you got back from the big house and I want to be told!'

'There's no keeping anything from you. I should have known.' He rubbed the back of his neck. He always rubbed it when he was bothered.

'No, Tom, there isn't. I know you too well. All right – so there's bad news to come – we'll manage. We've been through worse than this.'

'So where do I begin?' He cupped her face in his hands and kissed the tip of her nose, just as he'd done when they were courting.

'You begin at the beginning, and I want no soft-soaping,' she ordered. 'Tell me who was there and what was said – every word.'

She settled herself in the chair opposite, picking up her knitting, and he smiled across at her and said, 'I love you, Alice Hawthorn.'

'And I,' she said, severely, 'said no soft-soaping.'

'Right then! From the beginning. We-e-ll, we were all told to find a pew in the great hall . . .'

There had been eighteen staff there, inside and out. They had carried benches and chairs in and the estate manager and the solicitor from Winchester sat at a big table. No one had had much to say. They just sat there, eyes on the table.

'You could sense it, Alice; folk all uneasy, like. And then they told us. Apart from what the solicitor called bequests, everything is to go to the miners.'

'*Give* it, you mean?' The knitting dropped to her lap. 'How can you give Windrush to the miners?'

'They're to have it as a convalescent home, on account, I suppose, that Mr Hillier started work in the pits as a lad of twelve. And that's something I'll tell you about later.

'But the miners' union has already accepted – and gladly, too. Everything in the house is to be sold save Mr Hillier's portrait that was painted in oils. That's to stay and hang over the fireplace in the great hall.

'The auctioneers are coming next week. Everything is to be sorted and labelled, then sold at public auction. Farms are to be left alone – the tenants are safe – and there'll still be work for the three gardeners, though the solicitor hinted there'd have to be more vegetables grown, and less flowers. And they'll want a cook, when it's a home and starts taking men in, and a few housemaids to do the cleaning. But me – well, when I've cleared out the game birds, I'll be joining the rest of them, on the dole.'

'And Polly?' Alice sat unmoving, as if she couldn't cope with the enormity of it. It had been the same for him, Tom thought; had taken a bit of digesting.

'Polly is to stay until the estate has been wound up and formally handed over. Same as you and me. One thing they'll not want is to keep the shoot going and pay a keeper's wages for doing it. But I reckon we'll be all right until March, or April.'

'That'll be when we put our thinking caps on, Tom.'

'And that's when Willow End and Keeper's Cottage part company.'

'But Polly has nowhere to go. How can we leave her, Tom?'

'I don't know. You and her have become friends over the years and I know you'll miss her. But Keth and Daisy are closer, even. They're like brother and sister. It's going to be sad, parting those two.'

'And you wouldn't,' Alice hesitated, 'consider asking for the woodman's job? There's the cottage in Brattocks Wood empty, don't forget.'

'Wouldn't consider it? Lass, it hasn't been offered. And you know I'd take it. Keeper's jobs aren't all that thick on the ground. I could be a long time out of work.'

'The job doesn't have to be offered. You know we'd be welcome at Rowangarth, Tom. Julia wants us back.'

'And Polly and Keth?'

'I could ask Julia if she can find something,' Alice frowned. 'Polly will at least have a widow's pension — just a bit of a job would do.'

'We couldn't go yet.' Tom knocked out his pipe. 'Happen not until Lady Day.'

'I'm going to ring Julia — ask her.' Alice jumped to her feet. 'She said she wanted to come down. Why don't I ask her to come tomorrow?'

'Now steady on.' Tom took her hand, pulling her into his arms. 'You're as shocked as I was. Take a deep breath — and anyway, the post office is closed till morning. You can't knock 'em up.'

'No.' She sat down again, setting the chair rocking, just as Mrs Shaw had done in the old days when the war got too much for her. Mrs Shaw used to pull her long white apron over her face and weep into it just as she, Alice, longed to do now. 'But first thing in the morning I'm telephoning Rowangarth, asking Julia to come. She wants to, and I want her here, to talk things out.

'We're lucky, having something to fall back on. You'd live in Brattocks, wouldn't you, Tom? Daisy would like it. She loves staying at Rowangarth.'

'But Daisy wouldn't be staying at Rowangarth. She would be the gamekeeper's daughter — or the woodman's daughter — if we were to go back.'

'Daisy is Drew's sister,' Alice said softly. 'Or to put it plainer, she's still half-sister to young Sir Andrew whether she lives here or there. And I am still Drew's mother. There's nothing will change that. It's a complication that would have to be sorted, if we went home to Rowangarth. Could you live with it, Tom love?'

'I could live with it, because you've just put it tidily into a nutshell, haven't you? Home to Rowangarth, you said, and that's how it would be. And just think how pleased Reuben'd be, to hear we were going back.'

'So you'd consider it?'

'If her ladyship offers, you know I will.'

'And we'll ask Julia about Polly? Even if there's nothing for her at Rowangarth, I'm sure she could find a cottage, somewhere around Holdenby, for just a few shillings a week. Polly is a fighter. Surely there'd be something for her to do, up there?'

Her heart was thumping. Always, deep inside her, had been a longing to return to her youth, to the happiness she had known before the war began. And she wanted to turn back the clock, shut out everything bad that had happened betweentimes and start again. 'There'd be no more worrying about Elliot Sutton, either,' she whispered.

'No more worrying.' He reached up, taking the ornate dog collar. 'I think Polly should have this. I don't want her to know, but the solicitor told me that Mr Hillier left Beth to Dickon in his Will, but he wasn't to know, was he, that he'd –'

'That they'd die together,' Alice finished, gently. 'Ah, well, there's not a lot we can do, till tomorrow.' Now, it all depended on Rowangarth, and Julia.

'Not a lot, but lass – it's not quite all . . .'

'There's more?' Alice drew sharply on her breath.

'There is. It's the reason, really, I was late getting home. It's Daisy, you see. No!' He held up a hand as alarm widened Alice's eyes. 'Nothing wrong – just that she's in Mr Hillier's Will, an' all.'

'But that's wonderful!' Alice beamed. 'It just shows how fond of her he always was. And she's to have a hundred pounds, too?'

'No. I wasn't told till everyone had gone and I'm right glad I wasn't – knocked me sideways, I can tell you.'

'She's to have *more*?'

'Much, much more. And there's no other way to tell you, so best I say it straight out, as it was told to me – like the solicitor read it from the Will.

'*To Daisy Julia Dwerryhouse of Keeper's Cottage, Beck Lane, West Welby in the county of Hampshire – the sum of ten thousand pounds . . .*'

'What?' Alice jumped to her feet as if she'd been slapped. 'Ten thousand, you said – *Ten – thousand – pounds!*'

'That's right. Our Daisy's rich.'

The postman usually knocked – once, and gently – when he slipped a letter through the door, but this morning he brought the knocker down loudly and firmly, three times.

'Drat!' Alice fretted. They were late, this morning; had sat long into the night, talking about Daisy and Daisy's money and why Mr Hillier had done it. And of how Daisy must never know until she was older, and more able to live with the enormity of it.

'Mornin',' the postman said, offering the telegram. 'Came over the phone, just before I left, so I said I'd drop it in. No need to worry,' he added, seeing the question in Alice's eyes. Women still disliked those little yellow envelopes. A throwback from the war. 'Any reply?' he asked as Alice ripped open the envelope.

'No, thanks,' she beamed. 'Too late to reply. She'll be on her way, now. My friend is coming to stay,' she told him as if he didn't already know, him being married to the postmistress.

'There's a letter for Willow End,' he said, glad that Mrs Dwerryhouse was pleased with her news. It was worth a mention because he didn't often deliver letters to Willow End and this one was in a larger-than-average envelope, with the address done in typewriting.

'It'll be from Winchester,' Alice nodded. 'That one will be good news, too.' She rewarded him with a smile, then called, 'Daisy! It's your Aunt Julia — she'll be here by suppertime! And stop dawdling with your breakfast, *do*. There'll be Keth here and you not ready. And don't forget — you're not to go boasting at school about what Mr Hillier left you.'

They had told her, this morning, that it was a hundred pounds, on account, Tom said, that they couldn't keep the bequest entirely secret from Daisy. A hundred pounds, he insisted, would be sufficient to justify the visits to the solicitor's office and the signing she would have to do, even as a minor. There would be jealousy enough as it was amongst the estate children, none of whom had been mentioned in the Will. A hundred pounds, like everyone else had been left, didn't sound so sinfully enormous.

Alice drew her tongue round her lips. Just to think of all that money set the little pulses behind her nose beating dully. To *say* it made her want to bite on her tongue. She had not, when Tom told her, been able to visualize the vastness of Daisy's wealth until he'd said, 'Remember when we were in town not so long ago — those new houses?'

Someone was building a close of twenty and Alice had peered through the downstairs windows of the house almost completed. Two houses stuck together; semi-detached, the foreman builder said.

'Beautiful houses, madam.' He had raised his bowler hat, thinking Alice and Tom to be prospective buyers. 'Two rooms and a good-sized scullery downstairs and two bedrooms up, with a bathroom' — he had emphasized the bathroom — '*and* a flush closet. Five hundred pounds, sir, and it's yours.'

And Daisy could have bought all twenty, Tom said last night. That was how rich she was.

There was a knock on the back door, a lifting of the sneck and Keth stood there.

'Come you in, lad. We're a little bit late, this morning. You'll just have to run, part of the way. Eat that, while you're waiting.' Alice placed drippinged toast on a plate and motioned to him to sit down.

'There was a letter.' Keth gave one of his rare smiles. 'It was about the money you told us about, last night. It's true. When she gets it, Mam's going to open a bank account at the post office; then she can draw some out, when we need it.'

His eyes were bright and this morning, for the first time since it happened, Keth was not sucking his thumb. It was as if having money in the bank was a prop, a bulwark; something that would save them from the Workhouse.

'Then I'm very pleased, Keth. It'll be a relief to your Mam, knowing it's there.'

At the door, Alice kissed Daisy goodbye. 'And listen,' she whispered when Keth, eager to be on his way, had gone on ahead. 'Don't dare say one word about your own money, Daisy. Don't spoil it for Keth? That money his Mam's going to get means a lot to him, remember.'

'As if I would,' Daisy said scornfully, fixing her mother with a bright blue gaze.

'We-e-ll – happen you wouldn't.' Chastened, she hugged her daughter. 'Now off with you – don't dawdle.'

'Will Aunt Julia be here when we get back?'

'No. About five, it'll be – oh, *be off with you!*'

Sighing deeply, she began to clear the breakfast table. Soon, Polly would arrive, Alice knew it, eager to show her the letter from Winchester. Poor Polly. Not only must she learn to accept Dickon's death, but she had the worry, now, of finding work. A widow's pension would hardly provide a roof over their heads and a hundred pounds wasn't going to last for ever. A job for a widow with a child in tow would be hard to find. There were more jobless, now, than those in work, and if Julia didn't bring hope with her, Alice knew that she and Tom would join the unemployed, too. Only Julia – and Rowangarth – could help them now. Dear, safe, enduring Rowangarth; the little house on the edge of Brattocks Wood, the rooks in the far elms, Reuben in his tiny almshouse; all beckoning like a light in the darkness.

'It was Carver-the-young who came up with the solution, in the end,' Julia said when a protesting Daisy had been tucked up in bed and they were seated beside the hearth.

'I thought you didn't like young Carver.' Alice piled logs on the fire.

'Couldn't stand the man, but he's better for knowing,' Julia admitted. 'What he said made good sense. But I don't want either of you to think I'm rushing down here, organizing things, trying to get you back to Rowangarth, though I am, really, because that's what I always wanted.

'But I'm aware that two men have died and I'm very sad. I'd rather you never left here, and those men were still alive. But it has happened, and I want you to forgive me if I sound as if all I care about is what *I* want.'

'We don't think you're being selfish, Julia, and certainly not unfeeling. The truth of it is that Tom will soon be looking for work – Polly, too,' Alice sighed. 'I suppose there isn't hope for her? She's a good worker and it's going to break Daisy's heart if she and Keth are separated. Is there any hope?'

'There might well be. But first tell me, Tom, what do you know about leasing shooting rights?'

'Not a lot. Why – are you going to let a syndicate shoot over Rowangarth land?'

'Something like that. You've heard about the syndicates, then?'

'I have. They're starting up all over the place. During the war, a lot of men did well for themselves. There's money about, now – *new* money – and those men fancy themselves as Shots, only they haven't got shooting of their own. Some landowners are glad to accommodate them, I believe.'

'And so might Rowangarth be. We'd have to remain very firmly in charge, though, and there's no game at all, now, for anyone to aim at. But how long did it take you to get the shooting going here, Tom?'

'Two years – from scratch.'

'And could you do the same, at Rowangarth?'

'Reckon I could – if I was asked,' he said, cautiously.

'Then would you like to give it a try? Mother is in favour of it; Keeper's Cottage is empty – and it's like Carver said; you could pay your wages twice over, once you could organize the shoots. Each Shot would only be given a couple of brace of birds; the rest would belong to Rowangarth.'

'Pheasants and partridge always fetch a good price, in the towns.' Tom rubbed the back of his neck. 'And you'd expect any syndicate to pay well for a day's shooting?'

'Yes, indeed. And they'd pay. Like you said, Tom – new money.'

'It'd take a bit of thinking out.' Tom reached for his pipe. 'But I'd like to give it a try. And I'm grateful, Julia, you know that. Can it wait, though, for a while? There's things to be seen to here, first. I owe Mr Hillier that much.'

'Whenever you can make it – only don't waste any time. I want you both at Rowangarth so much. I'm not happy about the way it happened, though. Never think I am.'

'We won't, love.' Alice reached for her friend's hand, squeezing it tightly, blinking away tears of relief. 'And did you say there might be hope of something for Polly?'

'There might – there *is*. But will Polly approve?'

'Of what? She's pretty desperate.'

'Of taking over the bothy.'

'But the bothy job belongs to Jinny Dobb. Is Jin badly?'

'Jin is fine – and I've got to admit that it was I who brought the matter up,' Julia shrugged. 'But Jin and me – well, we understand each other.'

'Dear old Jin,' Alice smiled. 'What did you say to her?'

'I offered her retirement. It's hard work for an elderly lady, looking after the bothy and three apprentices. She said it couldn't have come at a better time. You remember her sister?'

'The one who had three lads and lost —'

'That's it. Lost them all in France. She never really got over it. Her husband died not long ago and Jin doesn't like her being alone, so she didn't mind at all being asked if she would like to go.

'I'll make it all right for her, and she'll qualify for an old-age pension in January — if she isn't working, that is. She'll be comfortable with her sister and, like she said, she can make quite a bit, telling fortunes and reading teacups. So if Polly is willing it might well be that things will turn out better than we had hoped.'

'She'll be willing, Julia. She can stay on at Willow End until the miners take over Windrush, but after that she didn't know where she was to go. All she has is a widow's pension between her and the Workhouse. Mind, she's to be given the hundred pounds that should have come to Dickon under Mr Hillier's Will, but that isn't going to last long.'

'So will you put it to her,' Julia asked, 'or will I?'

'You do it — in the morning. And I'm as sure as I can be that she'll accept, and gladly. And when she has, you can tell Daisy the good news because she'd have been broken-hearted having to be parted from Keth. You'll be the most favouritest aunt in the whole world.

'And now I'm going to make us all a hot drink and while I'm doing it, Tom will tell you something else — about our Daisy. And you'd best be sitting down when he tells you!'

She closed the parlour door quickly behind her, because not for anything could she talk about that money — not even to Julia — without feeling bothered.

Hot milky cocoa, that's what they would have, and Julia would need a drop or two of the medicinal brandy in it to help her over the shock. Because shock it would be – even to someone as rich as she was.

'I was right, then?' Alice remarked when she returned with the tray. 'Shocked, are you?'

'Goodness, *yes*! All that money! And Tom is right. Daisy mustn't be told – not how much – until she's older.'

'She won't be. I still can't visualize so much money. Tom says I'm to think of it as twenty newly-built houses. Daisy could live comfortable on the rents from twenty houses for the rest of her days.'

'Daisy could buy Rowangarth,' Julia said soberly. 'Not the farms, of course, but she could buy the house and the stable block and the parkland, *and* Brattocks Wood – and still have money left in the bank.'

'I'll never know why Mr Hillier did it,' Alice mused. 'Oh, I knew he was fond of Daisy – but not to the tune of ten thousand pounds. And imagine him leaving all of Windrush to the miners?'

'It was his to leave as he wanted,' Julia defended. 'I approve of what he did. Andrew's father was a miner, don't forget. You don't watch someone cough his lungs away with silicosis and not be upset by it. I'm glad about Windrush being a convalescent home.'

'Me too,' Tom said. 'And all Mr Hillier's money is to be invested to pay for the upkeep. It was a grand gesture. He was a fine gentleman, and I hope they put it on his gravestone!'

'Can I come in, Polly?' Julia knocked on the back door of Willow End Cottage, then lifted the sneck.

'Why, Mrs MacMalcolm, ma'am – come in do, and sit you down.'

'Thank you.' Julia gazed around the kitchen. What little there was in it had been lovingly cared for. 'I want to say first, Polly, how sad I am for you. I know how you are suffering. I lost my husband, too, so I do know the awful pain of it. But I'm here to tell you that Tom and Alice have agreed to come to Rowangarth to work, and I want you to come, too.'

'Me, Mrs MacMalcolm? But I'm a widow, with a boy to care for. I was once in gentleman's service, mind, but there'd be Keth to consider, you see.'

'I've considered you both,' Julia said gravely. 'How do you feel about taking charge of Rowangarth bothy? There would be plenty to do, but you would answer to no one but Miss Clitherow, our housekeeper.'

'I don't rightly know what a bothy is.'

'We've got one at Rowangarth. It's a house where the apprentices live. At the moment, we have three garden lads in it. Tom once lived there, when he was our under-keeper; before he and Alice were married.'

'And I'd have to look after the 'prentices?'

'You would cook for them, keep their beds clean and wash their working shirts. All other washing they would pay you for doing, or take it home for their mothers to see to – which they usually do.

'There are six bedrooms and a parlour and a large kitchen, where everyone eats. And there is a cellar and an attic and outside wash-house. The lads take their baths in there. They're all decent young men. Polly.'

'And would they pay for their own food, ma'am?'

'No. Rowangarth sees to that. You would have a vic-tualling allowance given to you each week, separately from your own wages. Coal and logs are provided and all the vegetables you need, from the gardens. Will you think about it? There'll be a home for you and Keth at Rowan-garth for as long as you want it. A roof, and heat and light, and the victualling money is good, and would allow for you and Keth.'

'You mean it, ma'am? Word of honour?'

'Word of a Sutton, Polly. Think about it, won't you?'

'There's no need to think.' Her eyes brimmed with tears

and she brushed them impatiently away. 'Had you thought, though? Young Drew who Keth thinks of as a friend is really Sir Andrew and it would be to him, really, that we're beholden. It's fine the three of them playing together when you come to Windrush, but at Rowangarth it wouldn't be right, now would it?'

'Once, Polly, some might have agreed with what you say, but we have had a dreadful war since then, and most of us have got our values right. It will be good for Drew to have Daisy and Keth near at hand. He has led a lonely life, with just two women to bring him up. Now that he goes to the vicarage for lessons he has the influence of Mr Sutton, of course, but he should mix more with children. I wouldn't like you to think that anything had to change.

'Alice will be living in the gamekeeper's cottage, but she'll still be Alice who was once my sister and is still my dearest friend. Please think about what I have said? I want you to come to Rowangarth.'

'Then I'll be glad to come and I'll do my best for you, and those lads. And I thank you, Mrs MacMalcolm, for I didn't know what was to become of us . . .'

'Good,' Julia said softly. 'I'll go and tell Alice. She'll be so pleased, and Daisy, too. And no one,' she smiled, 'is more pleased than I.'

She was still smiling when she walked into Alice's kitchen.

'Kettle's on,' Alice said. 'And I take it that Polly is willing?'

'She's willing. She's coming to look after the bothy. I've got what I wanted. I'm a selfish, spoiled woman to be so smug about it, but I don't care!'

'Spoiled? Selfish? Oh, no. Not you, Julia MacMalcolm. Never you . . .'

When spring came to the New Forest and beech leaves unfolded like wisps of pale green silk and bluebells opened in Beck Lane, came the time to leave, to pack up and go. Now that Windrush was a home in which sick miners could regain their strength and breathe sweet, clear air into dust-damaged lungs, it was time for Alice to say goodbye to the church in which she and Tom had been married, and Daisy christened; to the post mistress, the school mistress and the lady in the knitting wool shop.

Now the time had come, she wanted more than ever to leave; make the long, slow journey home. As the day grew nearer, she and Polly had packed boxes, made plans.

'If we use one van between us,' Alice had suggested, 'then that'll be money saved.'

The driver of the pantechnicon had agreed to take Tom, Keth and Tom's two dogs with him, provided the dogs were properly behaved – which they were. Tom and Keth would be company, he said, on the long drive north and help, too, with the unloading at the other end.

Alice and Polly with Daisy, on the other hand, were to stay behind when the cottages had been emptied, have a general sweep round and check that nothing, absolutely nothing, had been left behind. Then they would take the train to London, there to stay the night at Montpelier Mews.

'You'll like Julia's little white house,' Alice assured Polly. 'Sparrow looks after it. She's a good sort; worshipped Doctor Andrew. Then we'll catch the nine o'clock train from King's Cross and Julia will meet us at York, in her motor.'

'And Tom and Keth will have emptied the van and put up the beds,' Polly nodded. 'All planned like it was a military operation, isn't it?'

'But of course.' Alice hugged herself tightly. She was going home to start afresh where once she had been so happy. She was so lucky that sometimes she was afraid. 'I'm glad to be going, Polly.'

'Me, an' all. There's only one sadness. I'll be leaving

Dickon behind and only the Lord knows when I'll see his grave again. It isn't as if he's among his own. I'd have taken him back to Derbyshire, where he rightly belongs, if I could've afforded it. But I couldn't even bury him decent; had to get the Parish to do it.

'Well, I've made up my mind, Alice. Happen Dickon was buried a pauper, but I shall mark his grave, so folk will know who is there. That money Mr Hillier left us – I reckon half of it rightly belongs to Keth, and he shall have it. But with my share, I arranged for the stonemason to leave Dickon tidy and respectable, like.'

'A gravestone, Polly?'

'Only a simple one, but with his name on it and Rest in Peace. It'll be there, in place, before we leave. Do you think I'm a foolish, sentimental woman?'

Polly was weeping, now, and Alice gathered her close, laying a cheek on her hair, hushing her softly.

'Of course I don't. Sentimental, perhaps, but where's the woman who isn't? But foolish – no. I'd have done the same for Tom with my last penny. And before we leave, we'll all say goodbye to Dickon and we'll have a word with the Mothers Union. They won't let him go short of a flower or two.

'So dry your eyes, love. I'm glad you're coming home with us to Rowangarth. You and Keth will be happy there. And will I tell you what that soft old Tom has done? Only went to that same stonemason. It's a secret, because Daisy is so cut up about leaving Morgan behind.

'Would you believe it, those two dogs are to have their own gravestone – well, more like a marker. You won't say anything about it, will you, till Tom gets it set in place?'

'Not a word.' Polly smiled and mopped her eyes. 'And I'm thankful Dickon chanced through Windrush woods when he was tramping the roads, looking for work. I'm glad Tom caught him, snaring a rabbit. Where would we have been, but for that?'

'You might have all still been together,' Alice said soberly.

'And well we mightn't. Dickon wouldn't have lasted out another winter, sleeping rough. We had some little happiness, in the end, and for that I'm thankful . . .'

'Keep those bairns out of the way this afternoon, can you?' Tom asked of Alice. 'The stone is in the shed, and there's only this afternoon for it. Next couple of days we'll all be too busy, packing and flitting. Want to have a look at it?'

Carefully, Tom unwrapped the sacking in which the little stone lay. It was in granite, the face sanded and polished and bearing the initials B. and M. And beneath them, the date of the year, 1926.

'It's a lovely thought,' Alice smiled.

'And you think Daisy will like it?'

'She'll like it, you old softie. They both will.'

They liked the stone, they both said, very much. Indeed, it was the most beautiful gravestone, Daisy said tremulously, she had ever seen. She and Keth had stood there, in Beck Lane, half-way between Keeper's Cottage and Willow End, to say a proper goodbye to Morgan and Beth. Daisy squeezed her eyelids very hard, but it did nothing to stop the tears, and Keth reached for her hand and held it unashamedly.

'There now,' Tom said. 'That stone will let folks that pass here know there are two creatures resting there. And they'll stop, and wonder about them.'

'And they'll never disturb them, will they, Dada? I couldn't bear that,' Daisy sobbed dramatically.

'Of course they won't. That little stone makes the spot holy, sort of.'

'But we're leaving them. Do you think they'll know we've left them, Dada?'

'Of course they'll know. Those two were intelligent

creatures but they aren't going to bother about it, over much.'

'They're in heaven, you see,' Keth reminded.

'Of course they are! Didn't I tell you, little lass, that dogs alus get into heaven? Not all humans do, but dogs – yes. Now us grown-ups have a lot to do. The man with the van will be here tomorrow and me with all my traps and things to pack up and see to. You and Keth stay here a while. My, but it looks real bonny, that stone. *Real* bonny.'

'It does,' Keth said when they were alone and he'd let go of Daisy's hand, she having dried her tears, for the moment. 'And they are together, Morgan and Beth. They won't be lonely.'

'Not if they're in heaven, they won't. Do you believe in heaven, Keth?'

'For dogs – yes.'

'Dada is right. It looks pretty, with the beech trees and the bluebells all round it. I'm glad they've got the bluebells, Keth. When we live at Rowangarth and the bluebells are flowering there, we'll remember Beck Lane, won't we?'

'Mm. And that the bluebells will be chiming for Morgan and Beth.'

'Bluebells don't chime! Who ever heard of bluebells ringing, Keth Purvis!'

'Dogs. They can hear them. Does your dad have a dog whistle – a *proper* dog whistle?'

'Of course he does!'

'Well, my dad had one and Mam has given it to me, in case I want to go into keeping. But I don't. I want to sit the scholarship exam when I get to Yorkshire.'

All at once, he wanted to go to Grammar School because there was the money now, Mam said, for the uniform; fifty pounds put by in the bank for it.

'All right – so you want to go to Grammar School and be a clerk?'

'No. Something better than that. But about my dad's

whistle. It's one you blow and you don't hear it — not if you've got human ears. But it makes a sound a dog can hear. Dogs have better hearing than humans. They hear things that we can't.'

'So?' said Daisy huffily, because that was something she hadn't been told; something she would have to check with Dada.

'So bluebells *do* chime, but so softly that only a dog can hear the sound.'

'You're sure, Keth?' It would be awful if he was saying it and didn't mean it.

'I'm sure, and tomorrow afternoon before we go, we'll come and say another goodbye; then we won't worry about them, will we? We'll just remember them, without being sad.'

'Yes, Keth.' All at once, because she had never loved him so much, she wanted to hug him tightly and kiss his cheek. But she couldn't, because Keth was a boy and wouldn't like it. 'We'll come again, tomorrow.'

They would say goodbye to Keeper's Cottage and Willow End and Beck Lane. But mostly they would say goodbye to Morgan and Beth, then leave them together with the beech trees to shelter them and the bluebells to chime for them.

And tomorrow, she would not weep.

25

1927

'Dada! We came from York by Rolls-Royce!' An ecstatic Daisy threw herself into Tom's arms. 'You should have seen us!'

'I borrowed it, from Pendenys. Uncle Edward actually trusted me to drive it. We'd have been a bit cramped in my little car, you see,' Julia supplied. 'We dropped Polly off, at the bothy. I see you and Keth have been busy, Tom.'

'Keth's been a grand help. Willow End stuff didn't take long to see to — there won't be a lot left for Polly to do. We haven't long finished, here; the van has only just left. I've set things down where I think you'll want them, love,' Tom smiled, 'though you'll want to arrange it to your own liking, once you've got your breath.' He held out his arms and Alice went into them. 'Welcome home, lass.'

They stood, holding each other, not kissing nor speaking. Then Alice said, 'It's all very nice, love. Fire lit, kettle on the boil . . .'

'And cups and mugs unpacked,' Julia smiled. 'Tom, you are a jewel. Let's have a quick cup and wish good luck to Keeper's, then I'll pop off and bring Reuben over. He's been counting the days, and he might as well have a ride in the Rolls before I take it back.'

'I'm surprised Mrs Clementina allowed it.' Alice hung her coat on the door peg, unpinning her hat.

'Aunt Clemmy won't even know it's been out of the garage. She hardly sees anyone, these days. I think she's going a bit loopy. Poor Uncle Edward. She led him a dog's life before the accident and now he's more worried than ever by her carryings-on. Three staff have left already. I'm afraid she's come to rely on the bottle. She just sits in that room of hers in the tower – it's getting more like *Jane Eyre* every day!'

'Then I'm sorry for her.' Elliot Sutton was making trouble, Alice frowned, even from the grave. 'And where has Daisy got to?'

'Last time I looked out of the window,' Tom grinned, 'she was climbing the stile and making across the wild garden. She'll be off to find Drew.'

'Then let's have that cup of tea.' Alice hugged herself, eyes closed. 'I can't believe this, I really can't. We'll be all right, won't we, Julia? The Fates won't be jealous?'

'No, love, they won't. I guarantee it. And I'm truly glad you're back home – at last!'

'I'll be off, then,' said Jinny Dobb.

'It was kindly of you to stay behind and explain things,' Polly said gravely, holding out her hand. 'You make it all seem simple.'

'It is. Just treat them garden boys like you'd treat your own son. Be firm, though they're good lads and won't give back answers. And remember that the doors are locked at ten sharp, 'cept Saturday nights. And I'd be obliged, when you see Miss Clitherow, if you tell her you found all in good order.'

'I shall do that, and I hope you'll call – any time. You'll be welcome.'

'I'll call, missis. Happen one day you'll let me take a look at your hand?' Jin picked up her bag and the brown paper carrier containing her last-minute things, then walked to the door. Hand on knob, she turned. 'There's trouble in your face, etched deep, but it's trouble past. You'll find there'll be more to smile about, here. Good day to you both.'

'She's right. It's going to be all right, here,' Keth urged. 'Let's have another look round? This place is so *big*. When we put the beds up, Mr Dwerryhouse said I was getting the bedroom that he once slept in. It's the warmest in the house, he said, in winter. And there's a wireless, in the parlour. I'll be able to listen in.'

'Then make the most of it; it'll be school for you and Daisy, on Monday.'

'And I can sit the exam for the Grammar School?'

'Seems it means a lot to you, son – how come you changed your mind? Not so long ago, you weren't all that keen.'

'There wasn't the money, then, for all the things I'd need. Now, there is. The money was dad's, really, but he always wanted me to have a try. I'll pass it, for him.'

'Then do your best, for your dad.'

Polly gazed around her at the big, comfortable kitchen, thankful beyond belief. When they had told her that Dickon was dead it had been like the ending of her world, the ending of hope, yet things had turned out better than she dare imagine.

Dickon, my lovely. She sent her thoughts to a faraway churchyard. *We're going to be all right, Keth and me, so don't you worry none.*

Something to smile about, Miss Dobb had said. Perhaps, now, there would be . . .

'Thank you, Mary.' Helen Sutton smiled to the parlour-maid who set down the coffee tray.

'So, Julia MacMalcolm,' she said softly, when they were alone, 'are you pleased with this day?'

'Pleased to have Alice home – you know I am.'

'And so you should be, for you've schemed and fretted for long enough to get her back. And I'm happy for you, I truly am, though sad about the way it happened. Black, dear?' She always asked the question. 'And it is going to be so good for Drew, having young friends near. Tatiana is a nice child, but a little young for him.'

'And her nanny a little old! How that child is pampered, mother. Why isn't she allowed to run free, sometimes?'

'I'm sure it isn't for us to comment on how Anna rears her daughter. Perhaps that is the way Russian mothers do it. And Anna is a dear person — we mustn't criticize.'

'I suppose not, though one day that child will rebel, just see if she doesn't. She's half Elliot's, remember. One day, something is going to surface; it's bound to.'

'Don't speak unkindly of the dead,' Helen murmured, passing the cup. 'Would you like a little snifter?' A small brandy, really, but they always called it a snifter, as Aunt Sutton had done.

'No, thanks.' Julia rose to her feet. 'Shall I pour one for you?'

'A sherry for me, I think — I do find it helps me to sleep and besides, I want to raise a glass to Alice and Dwerryhouse, wish them well, at Keeper's.'

'We all do. And success to the shooting, once Tom gets it going again. That idea of young Carver's was splendid, and the syndicates will take care of his wages. It all turned out well, didn't it — the Williamses winning on the Irish Sweepstake, and Jin Dobb taking retirement.'

'It did, though I'm sure you'd have found a way, somehow,' Helen remarked wryly. When her daughter set her heart and mind on anything, even the Fates took notice. She had been just as single-minded over Andrew. 'So you have all you want, now?'

'No.' Julia stirred her cup noisily. 'I want Andrew, you know I do. I can never forgive that he was taken from me.'

'My dear — perhaps forgiveness comes hard to you,' Helen whispered, though *perhaps* didn't enter into it, really. Julia never trod the middle path. She loved with a burning intensity and hated with an equally frightening force. She was the most like Anne Lavinia of all the

Suttons; direct, uncompromising and brutally honest. 'But can't you try to accept that Andrew is gone? I accepted, a long time ago, that I would never see your Pa again in this life, but you, Julia – oh, *when* will you stop fighting the world?'

'Never! I want to love and be loved – *really* loved, do you understand, mother? And I wanted a clutter of children around me, but who am I to have them with?' She set down her cup with a ferocity that set it rattling in its saucer, then, folding her arms tightly, she began to pace the room. 'I wasn't given your serenity. I can't forget Andrew nor forgive his death – and cruelly, too, when I thought he'd survived that war.' She turned, eyes wild, then seeing the distress in her mother's eyes she hurried to where she sat, kneeling at her feet, laying her head on her lap as she had done as a child. 'I'm sorry, dearest. Forgive me?'

'Of course, of course,' Helen soothed. 'I understand, I truly do. But don't you think it would help if you were to go to France, see his grave? Don't you owe him that?'

'No. I can't.' She said it softly, sadly, now her anger was spent. 'I can't look at all those graves, row on row of them, and every one a young life. I've seen pictures of those cemeteries and I was there in France, don't forget. I saw more men die than I care to remember.

'And I won't read the cant on those gravestones. *RIP, In Death Triumphant. The Supreme Sacrifice.* Not one of those men wanted to die, mother, and I won't look at a cold, stone slab with Andrew's name on it, so never again ask me to?'

'I'm sorry, child, I truly am, though I shall pray with all my heart that one day you may be able to accept what it isn't in your power to change. And let's count our blessings. Alice is home again – surely that is something to be glad about in this sad world?'

'It is, mother.' Alice, the sister who understood, was home. 'And I will try, dearest. I truly will.'

* * *

That night she searched with her fingers along the door ledge, then slipped the key into the lock.

Nothing had changed. It could have been that same surgery picked up by a magic hand at the lodgings in Little Britain and gently, reverently placed in an upstairs room at Rowangarth.

Julia needed no visit to any cemetery; this room was Andrew and set out as he had left it, ready for him to pull out his chair, pick up his stethoscope.

From the narrow mantel above the black iron firegrate, his photograph smiled at her from a leather-bound frame. She had taken that picture to York when first she and Alice began their nursing training; carried it each day in the pocket of her uniform coat to Denniston House hospital; packed it in her trunk when she left for France.

It had stood beside her bed in the green-curtained cubicle in Celverte and each night she whispered, 'Goodnight, my love. God keep you,' as she blew out her candle. And he had smiled back and whispered, 'I love you, too.'

Yet now she could not hear his voice as once she had been able to; could not, as she had done on lonely days, close her eyes and abandon herself to remembered conversations, laughter between them or whispered love words in the intimate dark. They had killed Andrew's voice, too.

She walked to the window, staring through the trees to the glow from the cottage at the edge of Brattocks Wood, smiling a goodnight. Then she drew the curtains together.

'Alice is home, Andrew. They came today with Polly and Keth. There will be children, always, at Rowangarth, now. Things will get better for me, darling. Alice understands, you see.

'Mother said I should visit your grave, but I can't. This room is your memorial, your shrine . . .'

A gravestone was a cold thing. Here, in this room, she could sit in his chair, touch things he had touched, pretend that if she wished it and willed it with all her strength, his hand would open the door.

She looked once more around the room, then switched off the light.

'Goodnight, my love,' she whispered. 'God keep you.'

In the doorway she waited to hear him say, 'I love you, too,' hear it not with her ears but with her mind and her heart.

But she heard only the ticking of the mantel clock.

Alice closed the staircase door behind her. She was so tired she could sleep on her feet. But the curtains had been hung and she had had a moving around of furniture and her pots and pans were arranged on newly scrubbed shelves in the kitchen.

'Daisy's asleep. Just think, Tom, Reuben coming to Sunday dinner.'

'You're happy, aren't you, lass?'

'So happy, that if I let myself I'd be afraid. But I'll just set the kettle to boil, then pop out, for a breath of air.'

'Aye.' He knew where she was going, that tired as she was she would not sleep until she had told it to the rooks.

'I'll be all right, love. Just a walk to the end of the wood. It's light enough.'

Tonight, the moon was full and high and silver. She would be safe, in Brattocks. There was no one, now, she need fear; no poachers, for there was no game to take, and no man to harm her. Elliot Sutton was gone, and his evil with him. Now, Drew truly belonged to Giles.

'I might walk back by way of the bothy,' Alice murmured, reaching for her shawl. 'If Polly is showing a light, I'll call in. Won't be long, love.'

At the gate she closed her eyes, drawing on her memories, saying a goodbye to Windrush. Keeper's and Willow End would be silent, now, their unlit windows like sleeping eyes. But the same moon that lighted her way would shine, too, on the beeches and oaks and the deer in the forest, sleeping close. And on Morgan and Beth.

She gazed at that moon and the puff of silvered cloud beneath it. She was so happy she had to hold herself tightly, just to contain the ache of love inside her.

Nothing moved, save a hunting owl far to her left where the railway line ran alongside the wood for a short distance. Even the rooks had settled for the night, their lazy cawing stilled, though they would know already that she was home.

She let go a small sigh of contentment, gazing through a gap in the trees across to Rowangarth, dark against the sky, and the one light that shone palely yellow against the moonlight. Miss Clitherow, like as not, was still awake or Tilda, perhaps, reading one of her love books.

She shifted her gaze to the bothy. There were no lights. Polly was a-bed, and Keth. They would be all right. Rowangarth would be good to them. She smiled tremulously, then lifted her eyes to the sky.

'Thank you, Lord, with all my heart for prayers answered. And in this sad world, in all the sorrow and partings, I know I am lucky and so blessed. And I am grateful.'

She hugged her shawl around her. Now, she would tell it to the rooks.

'So this is your England – the country you would all die for?' Anna Sutton glanced around her, twirling the slender stem of her parasol, uncomfortable in the early August heat.

'Sorry?' Julia opened her eyes. It had been pleasant with the sun on her face, to listen to the far sounds of harvesting from the field at the end of the lime walk. 'This precious stone set in the silver sea, you mean? Don't know about dying, though I'd fight like a wild cat to keep this small part of it.'

'You love Rowangarth, don't you?' Anna moved her fan languidly, gracefully. 'The children love it, too. "Where shall we play today?" and the answer is always Rowangarth. You like children, don't you?'

'They're always welcome. I call them the Clan – especially when Albert's two are over here. I suppose,' she shrugged, 'they are the children Andrew and I never had. It's nice to see Tatiana enjoying herself – without her nanny,' she added, obliquely.

'There is no need for Nanny, when I am here,' Anna smiled, 'though the child begged to be allowed to come alone.'

'You should let her do it more often. She would come to no harm. Bas and Keth are very sensible – quite grown-up, too.'

'Yes. I must learn to loosen the ties. But Tatiana is all I have, you see; all I'm ever likely to have, though I started four babies . . .'

'Don't, Anna? You're happy enough now, aren't you?'

'I am more secure than most who had to leave Russia. What I have is better than being an aristocratic pauper. Denniston House is in trust for Tatiana and is mine to live in for as long as I want to. I have an allowance from Pendenys and Tatiana's education will be taken care of. I don't complain, though –'

She stopped abruptly, pink-cheeked, thinking about Natasha, which lately she often did. And about Natasha's child and where it was. And if it had been a son.

'Though?' Julia broke into her thoughts.

'Though the happiness I had hoped for was just – how do you say it – a daydream.'

'You loved Elliot? Yours wasn't an arranged marriage, then?'

'It was arranged – or more a manoeuvring on the part of Elliot's mother. But I loved him. He excited me. I thought we would be happy yet I was soon to know differently. I was to be the provider of an heir, you see, and when our son died what was left of our marriage died with him.

'I couldn't have endured, after that, for Elliot to have touched me. I didn't shed a tear, when he died,' she said with quiet candour. 'I am sorry for his mother, though. She loved him. She is a changed woman, now.

'She made an effort, though, when Albert and Amelia came — sent for the hairdresser and had her hair trimmed and waved. She even drank less, but only for a while. Amelia is worried about her.'

'Amelia is a good woman. She's happy in her marriage and shows concern for those of us who are — well — less fortunate,' Julia sighed. 'But even Amelia won't be able to do anything about Aunt Clemmy who is determined to be unhappy.'

'I realize that. Perhaps it is why I am so protective of Tatiana. Perhaps I fear the evil will touch her, too. The children don't like going to see Elliot's mother. Only Kitty can stand up to her. When Tatiana visits, the poor child is glared at as though it is she who should have been in that car, and not her father.'

'I can understand that,' Julia said. 'When Andrew was killed, you see, I would look at some of the men who came back from France and wonder why it hadn't been one of them. But I hope it didn't show on my face.'

'So here we are, then — you who cannot love again, and I who will not, exchanging confidences like schoolgirls.'

'It helps, sometimes,' Julia smiled. 'And I do hope you'll let Tatiana come to play, more often. She's one of the new generation of Suttons, though heaven only knows what lies ahead for any of them.'

'*Ahead*?' Alarm showed in Anna's eyes.

'Sorry. I'm not anticipating gloom and doom — just wondering what it will be like for them when they fall in love, and wondering who they will marry.'

'Tatiana will marry for love, of that I am determined. No one will arrange her life for her. She shall choose freely.'

'Don't worry, Anna. Marriages aren't arranged these days – well, hardly ever. Mine wasn't. My parents said I might marry where I chose, and I did, though I shall heave a sigh of relief if Drew marries happily. He's very close to Daisy, though it's in a brotherly way. I'd like it if he married someone like her.'

'Julia!' Anna laughed. 'No arranged marriages, we said, yet here we are –'

'Arranging them,' Julia supplied, 'and the children hardly out of the nursery! And Anna – it's good to hear you laugh.'

'It is good to laugh. Perhaps I can visit you more often? Oh it is bearable now that Amelia is here, but when they go back to Kentucky, I shall miss her. And you don't think me aloof?'

'Of course not. Who said you were?'

'Elliot's mother. I think she was talking to the maid who was cleaning her room – or maybe she was just grumbling to no one in particular. She does that, now. She wanted to know who I thought I was. "Aloof creature! Doesn't she realize that Russian countesses are two a penny?" So I slipped away, without them hearing.'

'That's Aunt Clemmy running true to form. Take no notice. Just be especially kind to Uncle Edward, poor soul. And say you'll stay to tea? The Clan is to have bread and jam and curranty cake – do share it with us?'

The children lay in the long grass of the wild garden, glad of the sheltering shadows thrown by Brattocks Wood. The sun shone from an almost cloudless August sky and butterflies fluttered amongst meadowsweet, tiny wild purple orchids and rosy willow herbs.

Kitty Sutton made a flapping motion with her hand, shooing away the bee that bumbled amongst the clover.

No one spoke. This was a special day; one to be stored in a memory corner and remembered in the cold of November.

'I wish the poppies weren't there,' Daisy broke the silence. 'They remind me of France.'

'You've never been to France,' Bas said without lifting his head.

'My Mam's seen them! She was there!'

'I don't think, Daiz, there were any poppies growing when Lady and mother were away at the war,' Drew reasoned. 'The poppies grew afterwards, all over No Man's Land, grandmother said, as if they knew it had to be covered up.'

'Who cares?' Bas yawned. 'It's over, now.'

'I care.' For the first time, Keth spoke. 'My father was wounded there and a lot of men were killed. You can't not care about all those men.'

'Guess I do.' Bas pulled at a piece of grass, then chewed on the soft white end. 'Anyway, there won't be any more wars. Mom said so, so why talk about it?'

'Daisy started it,' Tatiana muttered, her eyes all at once filling with tears. That War must not be talked about, Mama said, because That War had robbed them of everything they had, almost. Grandmother Petrovska was very poor, because of That War.

'She didn't so!' Kitty hastened to Daisy's defence. 'It was Bas, arguing about it! And for goodness sake, Tatty, don't boo-hoo, or your Mom won't let you out with us again.'

There had been a lot of persuading and pleading that Tatiana might be allowed to play without her nanny being there. She and Bas had promised, hand on heart, to take good care of her.

'I'm not boo-hooing.' Tatiana's lower lip jutted. 'I was thinking about the Bolsheviks and it made my eyes water. Lenin is wickeder than the Kaiser, Grandmother Petrovska says.'

'Mm. Guess I wouldn't like some hick to take over our

place,' Bas conceded. 'Would you like it, Drew, if someone had you thrown out of Rowangarth?'

'No, I wouldn't.' He loved Rowangarth and it was better than ever, now that Daisy and Keth lived close by. 'But I don't want to talk about sad things, today. We are all of us together; all the Sutton clan – well, that's what Mother calls us.'

'Is the Clan coming today?' he'd heard his mother ask. 'Better warn Cook, if they are.'

'I think,' Kitty said, 'that we six should always stick together, even though Bas and me only get to visit twice a year.'

Kitty would come more often were England not so far away, Bas brooded, though he disliked Pendenys Place, the more so since one day it might be his; if Uncle Nathan didn't get his skates on, he'd heard Pa say, and get himself a son. He was almost as good as Kitty, now, when it came to hearing things.

'Nothing can hurt us,' Kitty urged, 'if we stick up for each other. We should take an oath.'

'Like a secret society?' The thought pleased Drew. 'Shall we all be in it – the Sutton Six?'

'And meet secretly, and tell each other things,' Kitty said eagerly.

'What things?' Bas scowled.

'What the grown-ups say, for one thing.'

'Listening at keyholes?' Daisy breathed, wide-eyed.

'Not keyholes! My sister hides in closets and under beds. She's good at it. She ought to be a spy,' Bas said with relish. 'But we can't call ourselves the Sutton Six. Only four of us are Suttons. Daisy and Keth don't count.'

'Daisy does!' Pink-cheeked, Drew jumped to his feet. 'Daisy's mother was once called Sutton and Daisy's half my sister, so she's got to be in it.'

'Sorry, Keth. Guess it looks like you're the odd one out.' Bas raised an eyebrow, glad about it, really. Keth Purvis was too serious, treated them all like a bunch of kids. There had been too much fuss made about that scholarship and him passing it and getting to the High School for nothing. And Daisy stuck up for him all the time. If Keth said that black was white, Daisy would agree with him. What was more, Keth took it for granted that she would. It made Bas kind of mad, because he liked Daisy Dwerryhouse. Every time they came over she seemed prettier and more fun to hang about with. Keth should mind his own business.

'Think I care? I've better things to do than play kids' silly games. But I do qualify, in a roundabout way.' Keth rose to his feet, brushing grass seeds from his shirt. 'You see, Bas, you and Kitty aren't pure Sutton – not like Drew is. You've got some Pendennis in you.'

'So what? Mary Anne Pendennis was a character. We should be proud to have a fishwife as a great-grandmother – democratic, Mom said.'

'Well, for one thing,' Keth said softly, 'she was your great-*great*-grandmother and I'll tell you something else. She was *my* great-great-aunt. She was my great-great-grandfather's sister. My mother was a Pendennis before she married my dad, so what do you make of that, Bas Sutton?'

'Say – is that so? You wouldn't be kidding?' This was interesting.

'Why should I be? It doesn't matter at all who you are or what or who you came from. It's where you end up that matters and I shall end up good!' Like Mr Hillier, he would be, and people would say, 'That's Mr Keth Purvis, a self-made man. Won a scholarship to Creesby Grammar, then went to Cambridge – or maybe it would be Oxford. It would depend. But when he was rich he would marry Daisy – if he loved her as much as he loved her now. And he probably would.

'Well, that makes it all right,' Drew beamed, because he

liked Keth and didn't want him to be left out. 'But we can't call ourselves the Sutton Six.'

'No,' said Tatiana, who had been trying for ages to get a word in.

'And we can't be the Secret Six because that'd be too childish for words,' said Bas, who was almost as tall as Keth and only seven months younger.

'Then why can't we be the Clan, like mother calls us?' Drew hesitated.

'The Clan! That's it! And we'll not tell the grown-ups and we'll stick together and meet here, at Rowangarth, as often as we can. And it's gotta be a secret.' Kitty fixed the smallest Sutton with a warning glance. 'Okay, Tatty? No telling?'

'Oh, *no* . . .' This, thought Tatiana tremulously, was the very best day of her life, and if Mama ever again said that Nanny must come with her to Rowangarth to play, she would scream until she was sick on her new buckled shoes!

'And no talking in Russian, behind our backs?'

'No. I promise.' Of course not. They wouldn't understand what she was saying, anyway.

'Then that's fine, Tatty. Now I guess we'd better get back to Rowangarth for tea. Best not be late, or you'll not be allowed to play here again,' Bas warned.

'Then let's run,' Tatiana pleaded.

'Come on, Bas. You take one hand and I'll take the other,' Keth grinned. 'We'll go like the wind.'

They grasped Tatiana's hands, then ran whooping back, with Drew taking the lead and Kitty and Daisy giggling and skipping behind. And Tatiana, feet hardly touching the grass, eyes closed with delirious joy, laughed as she stumbled and slipped and was the centre of everyone's attention.

Now she belonged to the Clan, and what Grandmother Petrovska and Grandmother Sutton would say if they could see her now made her shiver with delight.

All at once it didn't matter that she didn't have a father or that Grandmother Sutton made her shake with fear. Nothing at all mattered but the Clan and Keth and Bas bearing her along with them.

And if Nanny sent her to bed without supper for coming home with her white socks grass-stained and her hair ribbons untied and her pretty starched frock creased and dirty – which it was – then she wouldn't care. Such was her sudden happiness that she wished that this day would never end and that Bas and Kitty could stay for ever and ever.

They couldn't, of course, but oh – wasn't it worth a wish?

26

June, 1931

'I don't suppose I could beg lunch, Helen.' Edward Sutton accepted the coffee cup, stirring it thoughtfully. 'I'd be so grateful.'

'But of course you could. Julia is in London and Drew is having lunch with Nathan whilst she is away. I do so dislike eating alone – but is something wrong, Edward?'

'It is. Clemmy!'

'But I thought she was making an effort. Yesterday, when I saw her, she seemed quite well.'

'That was yesterday. This morning, a letter came from Kentucky and goodness only knows I don't wish to sound disloyal, but –'

'But?' Helen prompted, gently.

'Albert and family intend coming – would like to stay five weeks. It's more than generous of Amelia – Albert isn't at all keen to spend so much time at Pendenys, and I can't say I blame him. Amelia has a strong sense of family, though. She feels that Bas and Kitty should be close to their English roots; she's the most fair-minded person I know – apart from yourself, of course.'

'Flatterer. But tell me about Clemmy?'

'She resents Albert. He's happily married, you see, and has a son. Elliot didn't. Albert is alive and to Clemmy's way of thinking, he has no right to be. No one has the right to life when Elliot is dead. Almost six years after, and she's still unbalanced about it. I tell you, Helen –' He gave a small, hopeless shrug.

'Hush, now. We must try to understand Clemmy's great affection for Elliot. She –'

'Affection!' Edward set down his cup with a clatter. 'It was – *is* – obsession. Clemmy could never see wrong in him, or if she did, she would never admit it. She ruined him. As soon as she read Amelia's letter she threw it down, said she wasn't feeling well and went to her room. No lunch, she said. She'll be shut in the tower, now, for God knows how long and just when I thought she was beginning to make headway.

'But she needs to be miserable, Helen. The letter from Kentucky was just the excuse she was looking for. I'm sorry, but it's got to be said!'

'Edward – don't get upset. Not on this beautiful day? I shall visit Clemmy as soon as Julia is back and I'm sure that by then she'll be over whatever is troubling her. Try to think that soon, Bas and Kitty will be with you.' Helen reached for photographs from the table at her side. 'Just look at our young ones, Edward. A new generation – ours, to watch growing up. The Clan, Julia calls them, and soon they'll all be together again.'

'I must say they're a handsome lot.' Edward's pleasure was genuine. Bas, his grandson, brown-eyed, serious; Kitty, Bas's sister, with her mother's violet eyes and black, curly hair – a throwback, that hair, from Mary Anne? And Drew, grey-eyed like his grandfather. 'Drew is very much like my brother,' Edward nodded. 'John would have been proud of him – proud of Giles, too.'

'True,' Helen smiled. 'Yet I have always thought that Drew is quite like you, Edward – but then, you and John were brothers.

'Hmm.' Edward studied Tatiana's likeness and a fierce proudness gazed back at him. 'Little Tatty isn't a bit like Elliot, you know.' Tatiana had inherited her mother's lustrous brown hair, her thick-lashed eyes. 'Pity that Clemmy can't take to the little girl. Not yet nine, yet she speaks

417

English, near-perfect French – from her governess, I suppose – and Russian. I'm glad Anna decided on a governess for Tatiana and got rid of that nanny. So possessive, she was . . .'

'You have three beautiful grandchildren, Edward. I have only Drew,' Helen admonished. 'But he is such a comfort. It was as if he was meant to be after all that happened to Rowangarth in the war.'

'There is Alice's child, don't forget. She is very close to you both.'

'Daisy is a delight.' Helen's finger picked out the elflike face, the impudent grin. 'What a pity photographs must be so dull. A colour painting would show them all so well. Daisy's hair, for instance – it's like pale gold and such blue eyes. She and Drew accept they are brother and sister, of course – well, half so – and are very protective, each of the other. Neither is what you would call an *only* child.'

'And the other one – the tall lad?' Edward pointed to Keth, standing a little aside of the group. 'A bright youngster, I believe?'

'Very brainy. He and Drew are close. They played together as small children when Alice lived in Hampshire. It's wonderful that they all seem to gather at Rowangarth. Julia says they're an unruly lot, but she's very possessive of them all. Her Clan, you know. It's so good for Drew to have someone close. Julia and I could have spoiled him between us.

'But give me a minute to let Mary know there'll be an extra place for lunch, then I want you to come with me to the orchid house. There's such a show, there – pity we can't snap them in colour. The ones John gave me when we were married are particularly beautiful. When my wedding orchids flower well, I always think Rowangarth will have a good year. Julia carried them at her wedding, too, if you remember, just as I did when I married John.'

'I remember. I was his best man and I envied him his

Helen. But let's take a turn in the garden? It is so peaceful, here. I'm feeling better already.

'I hope Drew's bride will carry John's orchids, too.' Helen opened the French door, stepping out onto the terrace. 'It would establish a tradition, wouldn't it?'

'Helen! Drew is only twelve!'

'I know, but he's growing up.' She linked her arm in Edward's. 'You'll have heard that Nathan thinks he should go to real school, now? It's almost certain we'll send him to Creesby Grammar, when the autumn term starts. He and Keth can go together – Daisy, too, perhaps. I believe Alice and Dwerryhouse are thinking of sending her there.'

'So you won't be sending Drew to Sedbergh? I'd have thought he would have followed Giles and Robert.'

'No. I lost too many of their young years. Drew won't be sent away. University, if he wants it, but not boarding school. And we aren't being possessive,' she hastened, 'but Drew is happy at Rowangarth and his happiness is all that counts.'

'Then Drew is lucky. I very much doubt if I could say that of any of my sons. Albert is happy, now, but he had to run away from home to find it. And Nathan, I suppose, is all right in his own way, though he ought to be thinking of getting married. Isn't natural to live as he's living. And as for Elliot – well, he was never happy. He was – well, he was *Elliot* . . .

'Mind, there must be a lot of men lying in French cemeteries willing to change lots with them. This country of ours, Helen – it's so unequal. The rich – *us* – manage to hang onto what we've got, but the poor are having a bad time of it. Such unemployment. Dole money cut and Public Assistance inspectors forcing their way into people's homes, making sure they have nothing more they can sell. It's monstrous! Just what did those soldiers of ours die for?'

'Truly awful, Edward, but there is nothing you and I can do about it except see to it that those who depend on us for a living are well cared for and make sure none of the elderly in Holdenby are without warmth and food. I try, you know. I visit all the time. But do look on the bright side, dear? All women have a vote, now. We'll change things! Now — let's look at the orchids?' To see something so beautiful gave her hope for the future; made her sure that somewhere — though where, she wasn't exactly sure — was a God who was merciful and kind and who would, in His own good time, sort out the terrible mess. 'And if we should see Catchpole, Edward, don't forget to admire them. He's more obsessed with those orchids than his father was. And tomorrow Julia will be home and I shall come to Pendenys and cheer Clemmy up, so do please smile?'

The waiter at the Ritz coughed discreetly, then bent to whisper softly. Mark Townsend pushed back his chair.

'Sorry, Julia. Please excuse me? Probably a client. Won't be long.'

Julia nodded, then looked around her at the diners. Mostly rich, of course; the clothes they wore, their jewellery, their aplomb proclaimed it. Exquisite, extravagant gowns in heavily beaded silk or startling creations in lamé.

The dress Julia wore was neither of those. Alice had made it ages ago from rose taffeta and a piece of gold lace. Against the glitter of short dresses and long cigarette holders, Julia could well have felt dowdy; would have, had it been important.

Money. The opulent dining room reeked of it, which was sad, Julia frowned, when a dividing line ran cruelly through the country. On the one hand, those who danced, dined and did without nothing; on the other, the have-nots. Andrew would have been so angry . . .

She took a sip of coffee, but it had gone cold. Sighing, she lit a cigarette. She smoked too much. Andrew would not have liked that, either, but Andrew was dead.

'Someone who thinks I'm available twenty-four hours a day.' Mark returned to smile an apology.

'Nothing serious?'

'I don't know. The minute I picked up the phone, the line went dead.'

'But how did they know you were here?'

'I haven't the faintest idea, though it can't have been important. I waited at the desk for a minute, but they didn't ring back.'

They didn't ring back, he frowned. *She* had said, 'Mark?', then hung up. She had known where he would be. The call, perhaps, had been to let him know.

'My coffee is cold, Mark. I don't suppose I could have another cup?'

You could. And we were talking about Drew . . . ?'

'Mm. He's going to Grammar School, and looking forward to it. A child who has been reared by two doting women and privately tutored, thinks a classroom full of boys and girls will be nothing less than wonderful. And he's talkie mad, now.' A small miracle, the talking pictures. No more reading words on a screen. Now, the actors actually spoke! 'He and Keth and Daisy go to the children's matinee every Saturday afternoon. They're all talkie mad, but that's the young ones for you,' she smiled indulgently.

'And you, Julia? How is your world?'

'I'm fine. Mother is amazingly well, Drew is a delight and Alice lives only a few hundred yards away. I'm contented, I suppose.'

Contented. All a widow could ever hope for. Sometimes she even felt vague pleasure, being with Mark. Mark wanted her with his eyes, but never touched her because he was still in love with his dead wife. That, Julia thought wryly, made her feel safe. Safe from ever falling in love again.

'Contented. That wasn't exactly what I meant, and I think you know it,' he admonished softly.

'Yes, I do,' she said flatly, 'and if I'm to be brutally honest, I suppose that nothing changes – except that I'm learning to accept what I can't change. But surely, Mark, you know what it's like? Don't you sometimes get lonely, too?'

She had asked him, long ago, if there was a woman in his life, and he had replied, briefly, that once there had been. In the war, he'd said, and there still were times when she coloured his thinking, which was a peculiar way, she remembered thinking, of putting it. 'Just when I think I am out of the woods, something happens,' was the way he'd put it.

That day she had apologized, red-cheeked, vowing never again to speak of his wife though sometimes she wondered what had parted them. An illness, had it been, or one of the air raids on London? But clearly he hadn't wanted to talk about it – apparently still didn't want to because he ignored her question, turning instead to call a waiter and ask for more coffee.

'There now,' he smiled. 'Another cup, then I must see you home, give you back to Sparrow. And I'm sorry if I was a little abrupt, but I'm only human, Julia. It's different for a man, you see.'

'Different? Women don't have feelings, then?' She drained her brandy glass at a gulp, then set it firmly on the table. 'And I really must go. Sorry, but I won't wait for the coffee. Sparrow will be waiting up for me and I'm catching an early train tomorrow.'

'Julia – don't go back?' He reached across the table, taking her hand. 'Stay another night?'

'No!' Too hastily, she pulled her hand away. Tonight, something had happened to their easy relationship. Tonight, Mark had abandoned caution, declared tacitly yet without any doubt, that the waiting game was coming to an end. Stay not another day, he'd said, but another *night*. 'Sorry, Mark. Must go back tomorrow. It's Daisy's birthday, you see – Alice's too. Nice, isn't it, both of them sharing a birthday?'

She was talking wildly, caught off balance, and they both knew it because he rose smiling to his feet and pulled back her chair.

'My dear – it's all right; it really is.' He picked up her wrap, draping it over her shoulders.

'Mark?' Pleading for his understanding, her eyes held his. 'I have enjoyed tonight. Thank you for being so very kind.'

And she *had* enjoyed being with him. The theatre, the supper afterwards had been a rare treat and quite perfect, but for one thing. The man she was with had not been Andrew.

'What I want to know,' Mary Strong grumbled, tight-lipped, 'is how much longer Will is going to shilly-shally. Nine years we've been walking out – four years since he gave me a ring – and still we're no further forward! He'll be getting his marching orders if he don't buck himself up!'

The parlourmaid tossed her head defiantly because the odds favoured Will. Women of her generation out-numbered men by two to one so it was no use her talking like that, though knowing it didn't help when all she wanted was to be Mrs William Stubbs and live in the rooms above the coach-house.

'I don't know why you're in such a rush to get wed.' Peevishly Tilda laid aside her newspaper. Tilda Tewk had long since accepted that her knight in shining armour had galloped past. Her beloved David's picture she had removed from the kitchen mantelpiece when public opinion decreed that, now the war was over, the Prince of Wales would surely be taking a wife.

Not that he'd been in all that much of a hurry. Talk had had it that he'd wanted the little duchess but she'd turned him down in favour of Prince Albert. It had been rumoured, too, that he'd then set his heart on a lady of breeding called Rosemary, and the King and Queen had been obliged to remind their reluctant son that nothing less than a princess would do.

After her prince, Tilda found all other men hard to love; even Rudolph Valentino came a poor second though women still wept to recall his sudden, sad death.

'I did hear it said,' Tilda set the kettle to boil, 'that the doctor was called to Denniston House today.' Tilda liked the new doctor. Young and fair and two years spent serving king and country in France. Doctor Ewart Pryce, said the brass plate outside the house where once Doctor James lived.

'And who's badly, then?' Cook asked. Not Countess Anna, that was certain. On Sunday, at church, she had looked nothing short of beautiful in a rose silk costume with matching shoes and the bonniest hat you ever did see. And the lass was devout, considering she hadn't been reared Church of England. Never missed a Sunday, nor a saint's day. If she had been given to uncharitable thoughts, Mrs Shaw could have been forgiven for thinking that Mr Elliot's widow was interested in the Reverend, though she was almost certain the law of the land didn't allow a man to covet his brother's widow.

'It's Miss Tatiana,' Mary supplied, much to Tilda's annoyance. 'She's got measles. Will had it from Deniston chauffeur that you can't put a pinhead between the spots. Poor little thing.'

'Then it's as well that young Drew had it when he was two, or it'd be him, next,' Tilda retorted. 'That Tatiana's never away from Rowangarth, these days. And that governess of hers is so hoity-toity she could take on Mrs Clementina!'

'Now, Tilda. Don't speak ill of the afflicted. Mrs Clementina hasn't been the same since her son was taken. The poor soul needs our pity.'

'It's Mr Edward I'm sorry for,' Mary frowned. 'I did hear he's just about at the end of his tether with her. Ought to have her certified, and put away!'

'Now that will *do*! I'll not have talk like that in my kitchen and there's Miss Julia back from London,' Cook pronounced as the drawing-room bell began to dance on its spring. 'Her'll be wanting a sup of tea so off you go, and see to it.'

'Kettle's just on the boil,' Tilda soothed when Mary had whisked, nose in air, up the kitchen stairs. 'I'll mash a pot for us, an' all. Sit you down – won't be a minute. And there was something I was meaning to ask you, Mrs Shaw.'

She picked up the morning paper, straightening it, folding it over, pointing to a man with a slanting fringe and a small, comic moustache, his arm extended in a wave to the camera. 'Who's this Herr Hitler, then?'

'Let's have a look. German, is he?' Cook hooked on her reading glasses, then gave a dismissive shrug. 'Funny-looking little feller. Now hurry up with that tea, Tilda. I'm fair parched . . .'

'Mam?'

'Mm?' Alice piped the final pink sugar daisy onto the centre of the cake, then stood back to admire her work. 'Now doesn't that look grand? Yours and mine to share. What was it you were saying?'

'I was trying to ask you – well, about the Grammar School. Isn't it going to cost you and Dada too much, if I don't pass my scholarship?'

'No, love. We'll manage.' Of course they could, though the lass wasn't to know it. The trustees who looked after her money could advance most things they asked for, provided they made sense, like money for education or to meet doctors' bills. All they had to do was ask, until Daisy came of age.

'But I know how much it costs, Mam. Twenty guineas

a year and my bus fares, too. And the uniform is expensive – I'd need so many things. It's going to cost more than fifty pounds, Keth said.'

'Oh, for goodness sake stop your nattering on, our Daisy. Had you forgotten about that hundred pounds Mr Hillier left you? And there's the money Sir Giles gave me and I put in the bank for you, when you were born – had you forgotten about that?'

'No, Mam. But is it going to keep me in Grammar School for five years?'

'It most certainly is. Me and Dada want you to get a bit of education and, scholarship or not, that's what you'll have. We can manage, so let's hear no more about it. And if you want to do something useful, get yourself upstairs with the mop! I saw dust under your bed, this morning!'

'The child will have to be told,' Alice said before Tom hardly had time to hang up his cap. 'She's going on about the money for Creesby Grammar and worrying about how we're going to get it.

'She's eleven tomorrow, Tom. Surely she's old enough to know about Mr Hillier's money? It bothers me, having to watch my tongue all the time. Can't we tell her? Tomorrow might be a good time. That ten thousand pounds is a weight on my conscience, though heaven knows I'm grateful she'll never want for anything.'

'It'll be nearer eleven thousand, now, with the interest it'll have earned,' Tom said, matter-of-factly. 'Nigh on two hundred a year she'll have been getting on that money, and it's five years come November, since Dickon and Mr Hillier were taken.'

'I know. I don't forget.' It still made Alice want to close her eyes, just to think of the awful way by which the money had come to Daisy. 'And there's something else, Tom. When we told Drew that I was his real mother, remember how Daisy took on about it? It wasn't only me being married to Giles – it was the deceit of it, too. Us not telling her – that's what got her most upset. And if we keep the money from her for very much longer, she'll get so she never trusts us again!'

'You're right. You usually are, love, though how the lass is going to cope with such a shock is beyond me. And she'll have to be warned not to go showing off about it.'

'She won't do that, Tom. She'll happen be nervous about it as I was – still am. There's a lot of sense in that young head.'

'Then we'll tell her tomorrow. There'll be Julia and Drew and Keth coming to tea – what if we tell her after they've gone home – give her time to sleep on it, sort of?'

'Sleep?' Alice clucked. 'I didn't sleep for a week when you told me about it! And there's something else to think on about. When the word gets round – and one day it will – that Daisy Dwerryhouse is an heiress, there could be all sorts of scroungers after her, courting her for her money. How long is it going to be before she starts wondering if young men like her for what she is or for what she's got coming to her?'

'Oh, Alice Dwerryhouse!' Tom gave a great shout of laughter. 'Our Daisy is only just eleven. There'll be no getting wed till she's of age. She'll have ten years to get used to it; learn to sort the wheat from the chaff. And fortune hunters will have *me* to contend with.'

'Aye. That's what worries me.' Visions of Tom with a shotgun ran through Alice's mind. 'But at least we're agreed. We tell her tomorrow night?'

'We'll tell her, you and me both. We'll manage, somehow.'

It occurred to him as he reached for his tobacco jar that they usually had – between them.

Keth pushed the *Evening Press* through Keeper's Cottage letterbox, then sighed relief that his paper round was finished until tomorrow. Not that it could be called a round; just the delivery of newspapers to Rowangarth and the cottages and houses dotted about the estate; papers left obligingly at the gate-lodge mornings, evenings and Sundays by the newsagent from Holdenby. And on Sunday mornings a florin lay on top of the neatly-bundled pile which, when added to the sixpenny-piece pocket money earned for carrying coal buckets at the bothy, gave Keth a feeling of great financial security. Two and sixpence; half a crown – thirty pennies.

His father, he often thought, had only earned ten shillings a week on account of his lameness, and it didn't seem right, when he thought about it. But Keth Purvis would earn much, much more. A place at University was his distant, golden dream. He and Mum wouldn't be poor when he was a man of means and letters.

He found Daisy sitting beneath the elms at the far end of Brattocks Wood, arms folded round her knees, so still she could have been one of the statues in the linden walk at Drew's house.

He loved Daisy very much, almost as much as he loved Mum; loved her when she giggled – even when she threw a tantrum. But most of all he loved the way she looked. She was the only girl he knew with such blue eyes and hair that shone on Sunday in church because she always had it washed Saturday nights, and rinsed in camomile, she said.

He ached, sometimes, to touch her; feel the softness and prettiness of her, stroke the pale gold hair. But Mam said you didn't touch girls – not even your own sister, if you had one – when they started to grow up because people might think the wrong things.

He didn't know what wrong things they could think, but Daisy *was* growing up, he supposed. This very minute, all faraway-looking, she seemed to be growing up quickly.

He wondered if she loved him as much as he loved her. She was always kind to him, except when she threw a tantrum, and she didn't snigger, all silly, when his voice went croaky – which it did a lot, these days. Sometimes it was like the voice he'd always had, but sometimes it went all low and wobbly and it was because he, too, was growing up, Mam said, and to think nothing of it at all, because big lads had to have big voices.

'Hullo,' he said, because he always knew to be careful when her mouth was set all obstinate. 'What are you doing?'

'Thinking. And I've been making a daisychain and don't dare say that only kids make daisychains!'

'I wasn't going to.' He wondered if she was poorly. They had eaten a lot, yesterday, at her birthday party; trifle, cherry buns and birthday cake decorated with pink daisies.

'Are you all right?' He picked up the daisychain she had made and put it on her head, like a little coronet. He did it to cheer her up, but she shook her head so angrily that it flew off and lay on the grass at her side, all sad-looking. 'I mean – well, you look serious.'

'That's because I was thinking, 'til you came. About my hair. Mam says now I'm eleven I can grow my fringe out.'

'Why?' He sat down beside her – not too near, because you could never be quite sure, with Daisy. 'I like your fringe.'

'Well I *don't*! It's my hair and I'll do what I want with it!'

He took a deep breath, staring at the little bruised flowers. Then he said, 'I think you'd better tell me – if it isn't a stomach ache, that is . . .'

'N-no.' For the first time she lifted her head. 'It's worse – and better – than a stomach ache, though last night, when they told me, I felt funny – like when you're going to be sick and trying not to.'

'Yes.' He knew the feeling. 'But what did they say to you, last night?'

'You won't tell? Promise you won't? It's so serious that I'm not even telling the Clan; only Drew.'

'Then hadn't it better wait till we get to Rowangarth? We said we'd go, this morning, to help clean out his rabbits. You'd forgotten, hadn't you?'

'No, I hadn't, but I don't feel like rabbits, today.' To a gamekeeper's daughter, rabbits were very ordinary. She would rather have Dada's ferrets, any day. 'And I want to tell you, before I tell Drew.'

'All right, then.' He was glad she wanted to tell him first. It made his cheeks feel warm. 'I promise I won't tell anyone.'

'And when you know, you won't be cross with me, no matter how awful you think it is?'

'No. Not with you, Daisy.'

'We-e-ll.' She took a deep breath, then the words tumbled out. 'I've got money. Mr Hillier left it to me.'

'I know. A hundred pounds.'

'No, Keth. More. A *terrible* lot more.'

'Two hundred? *Five* hundred?'

'No. It was like that when they told me last night. Quite a lot of money, they said. I think they were trying to break it to me gently. "What would you say," Dada said, "if it was a thousand pounds?" A *thousand* pounds!'

'That's a Rolls-Royce, Daisy.' His mouth had gone very dry.

'Yes. But when they told me – *really* told me – well, I know Mr Hillier was fond of me and I liked him, too. Mr Hillier was my grandpa, I suppose, next to Uncle Reuben . . .'

'And? How much, really, did he leave you?'

'Ten thousand pounds.' She took a deep breath, then let it go in little huffs. 'And if you're feeling funny about it, just think how I felt. I couldn't imagine ten thousand. I wrote ten down, then I put a comma and wrote three nothings after it. But I still couldn't imagine what ten thousand was.

'So Dada said I was to think of it in houses. D'you know, Keth, it would buy *twenty* little new houses. And worse than that, Mam said it would buy Rowangarth – or the best part of it.'

'It *is* serious, Daisy.' He looked at her, his eyes darker than ever. They'd been dark like that, she remembered, the day at West Welby churchyard at his Dada's funeral.

'Yes. But perhaps you'll be more used to it, by tomorrow. I felt ever so wobbly. Mam gave me something to help me drop off last night, but it didn't do any good. She came in to look at me and I pretended I was asleep, but I wasn't. I just lay there, thinking about it, and this morning it didn't seem quite such a shock.' She looked at him, wanting him to speak, but he did not.

'I can't have it till I'm ever so old, Keth – that's one good thing about it, but I can have some of it for important things. Someone called Sir Maxwell Briggs and the man who was Mr Hillier's solicitor and Dada are what they call my trustees. They are looking after the money 'til I'm old enough to have it all to myself. But they can let me have money for the Grammar School and for uniform and school books – for *sensible* things.'

She paused, searching with her eyes for his, but he was looking at the grass so there was no way of knowing if he was as shocked as she had been.

'You won't tell, Keth? I'd hate it if people knew about it – people who are poor wouldn't think it was fair.'

'People like me and Mum, you mean? Oh, it isn't fair but I'm not jealous and I'm sure Mum won't be.'

'But she mustn't know, Keth! No one must!'

'Sorry. I won't tell her, then.'

'No. Please don't? And I'm glad you aren't jealous.'

'Course not, Daisy. When I get used to it, I'll be ever so glad for you.'

But he wouldn't be glad. Not ever. He had thought, one day when he'd been to University and got a good job – a good *position* — that he would ask Daisy to marry him. Dad once said that a good wife was worth her weight in rubies and that no man got anywhere without a good woman behind him. That was when he'd thought it would be nice for Daisy to be his wife — one day, of course.

But now things were different. One day, Daisy would be rich and she would marry a rich man; not the son of someone who'd been a dog boy and walked lame and tipped his cap to his betters out of gratitude.

'What's the matter, Keth? You *are* cross about it, and I wish I hadn't told you. I wish *they* had never told *me*!'

'I'm not mad — honest. But I'm sad, Daisy. I'd thought that one day — when I got rich — you and me would be married. I wanted to buy you things, but now you'll always be richer than me and —'

'But that wouldn't matter, Keth — *if* I said I'd marry you, that is . . .'

'Well, I haven't asked you, so it really doesn't matter, does it?'

'No.' Her eyes filled with tears. They spilled down her cheeks and she sniffed very loudly, but he still wouldn't look at her.

Daisy was crying. He didn't like it when she cried. It made him feel panicky inside but there wasn't anything he could do about it — not even lend her his handkerchief — because he felt like crying, too. He felt like — like the daisychain in the grass, all limp and thrown away, so he said instead, 'If we don't go and help Drew see to his rabbits his mother won't let him go to the matinee this afternoon, and it's cartoons and cowboys . . .'

'*Ooooh!*' Daisy pulled her sleeve across her eyes, all at once angry. 'You care more about Popeye than you do about me! Well, you can marry Maisie Smith when you get rich!' Maisie Smith had a snotty nose and bit her nails. 'And see if I care, Keth Purvis!' She stumbled to her feet, then ran, sobbing, to the shed in which she knew she would find her father. 'Dada!' she choked, flinging herself into his arms.

'Now whatever is the trouble, little lass?' He sat down on an upturned box, lifting her onto his knee, mopping her eyes with a large, red-spotted handkerchief.

'Nothing's the trouble,' she choked, gasping for breath between sobs that were really hurting inside her. 'But I hate grown-ups and I hate Mr Hillier and –

'Now, now, *now*! Hate is a bitter-strong word for a little lass to use and you don't hate anybody, Daisy Dwerry-house, is that clear?'

'All right. I don't hate Mr Hillier, but I don't like Keth Purvis and I never want to talk to him again!'

'So you won't want your pocket money for the pictures this afternoon, then?'

'No! Oh yes, I suppose so but oh, Dada, isn't ten thousand pounds a lot of money?'

'It is, Daisy. Just to think of it gives your Mam the shivers even yet – and she's known about it for nigh on five years. But we reckoned you were old enough to be sensible about it – and let's face it, you can't have it for ten more years, and in ten years' time I reckon you'll be able to cope with being a rich young lady. Now tell me – did you and Keth have words about it?'

'Yes, and now Keth says he won't be able to marry me because I'll be too rich. So I told him to marry Maisie Smith and I ran away. He'll have gone to Rowangarth. We said we'd help Drew clean out his rabbits . . .'

'Then I think you should go after him and tell him you're sorry if you upset him. I know that temper of yours, our lass.'

'But he upset me too, Dada!'

'Then you've both got some apologizing to do, I reckon. And lass – about marrying Keth or anybody else for that matter – that's something else you've got ten years in front of you to consider, don't forget. So off you go and give a hand with those rabbits like you promised. And be back home sharp for your dinner or you'll miss the bus into Creesby.'

'And what was all that about?' asked Alice from the back door.

'Nothing, love. Just Daisy being – well – being Daisy. She's off to Rowangarth. She'll be as right as rain afore you can say Jack Robinson.'

She wouldn't, of course. What they had told her last night would take a bit of digesting. But in ten more years sh · just might have got the hang of it and learned to live witi. it. He hoped so, because if she didn't there'd be nothing but trouble ahead. Nothing was more certain.

Daisy caught up with Keth as he was crossing the wild garden and she called, 'Keth! Wait?'

So he turned and stood there, because he'd wanted her to come so he could tell her that Maisie Smith wouldn't do.

She stood, breathing deeply because she had run very quickly. And when she lifted her eyes to his he was smiling and it gave her the courage to say, 'I'm sorry, Keth. I don't want us to fall out over that money. And I don't want you to give me things, anyway – not things you buy with money.'

'Then what kind of things?'

'O-oh, things like taking me to school when I was little and being with me when Morgan died. And do you remember the butterfly, Keth?'

'N-no . . .'

'You do!' His cheeks had gone red, so she knew he remembered. 'I still have it, in the matchbox. I shall keep it for always because it was the first thing you ever gave me.'

She had been reminded of it only yesterday. Mam had

brought out her box of precious things because she wanted to wear her pearl eardrops on her birthday.

'Mam! The butterfly!' It was then that she saw the matchbox, and remembered.

'Aye. Keth brought it to you, ever so gentle,' Mum had smiled, 'when he was a little lad of three – maybe four.'

'I really am sorry, Keth.' Things like butterflies were more important than money.

'Me, too. I suppose I'll have to work a bit harder if I'm to be as rich as you.'

'Keth, it *doesn't* matter!' She reached for his hand.

'No. It doesn't. Not when you think about it. So are we going to Drew's?'

'I suppose so. But I'm not helping clean out those rabbits. And Keth – I've decided I'm not going to tell Drew about the money. Not just yet. I want just you and me to know.'

'All right,' he smiled.

'And I didn't mean it about Maisie Smith – honest.'

'Daft ha'porth,' he said softly, squeezing her hand so tightly she felt happy inside and forgot about the ten thousand pounds, because like Dada said, ten years was a long time.

Hands still clasped, they walked slowly to the stableyard where Drew's rabbit hutch stood against the coach-house wall. And she knew that something strange and nice and comforting had happened and that she would always love Keth, no matter what.

Not like Mam loved Dada – she couldn't imagine how that would be. But when she was a woman, when she was twenty-one, she would know. And it would be wonderful.

27

'Y'know, whenever I think of England it's your Rowangarth that comes first to my mind.'

'But it's a very ordinary old house.' Helen blushed with pleasure. 'The Sutton who built it was a yeoman, newly knighted by Elizabeth Tudor; it isn't grand, like Pendenys.'

'Exactly!' Amelia Sutton laughed. 'that's why I like it so much. It's so protective, so enduring. Guess that's why the youngsters always gather here. Hope they're not bothersome?'

'Not a bit. We both like having them. Julia calls them the Clan and says they're an unruly lot, but she adores them. I suppose they're the children she and Andrew never had. They planned to have several, you know.' Sadness briefly dulled her eyes, then she smiled. 'Instead, she has Drew, and the Clan.'

'I never knew Andrew. I wish I had,' Amelia said softly. 'He was a self-made man, I believe; the son of a miner who made good. Now that I admire. We Americans don't hold with people who have titles and inherit their wealth. And that, if you please, is a bit of a contradiction, because I like *you*, Helen, and I sure as heck will take good care that Bas and Kitty inherit all that my parents left to *me*! But you know what I mean – I'm talking about the superaristocrats and your royalty. Don't hold with them.'

'Why not, pray?' Helen was genuinely surprised.

'I do believe you really don't know what I mean, Helen. I'm talking about those who think they are the Lord's anointed. They wouldn't do at all, in Kentucky. And as for your royals – if they don't get their skates on they'll be extinct before so very much longer. Tell me now, who is there to take over?'

'The crown will pass to the Prince of Wales. And the Duke of York has two little girls,' Helen reminded.

'I know. And delightful creatures they are, too. That little Elizabeth is real cute. But it's *sons* your royalty needs, Helen; sons to carry on, I mean. Your Prince of Wales should be finding himself a wife – now wouldn't that be romantic?'

'He will, I suppose, in time. The heir to the throne usually marries the daughter of foreign royalty.'

'Then why is he setting his cap at a married woman – an *American* married woman. Well, that's what I hear.'

All at once a cloud covered the sun and a long, dark shadow fell across where they sat. It made Helen shiver and she said,

'I think Catchpole was right; it is going to be dull, today. Let's go into the conservatory? You take the tray, dear, and I'll fold the chairs.' And although she had intended to ignore Amelia's amazing statement, Helen found herself asking, 'What did you hear – about the American lady, I mean.' Asked it as soon as they were settled.

'We-e-ll.' Amelia held out her cup to be refilled. 'I had this from my cousin Aimee who is not given to idle gossip. She only thought it worth a mention because it's well known that in England, divorce is a nasty word. Indeed, I would not myself include a divorced person on my dinner-party lists. And *she* is divorced!'

'But *who*? And how do you know about this?'

'From my cousin, like I said. She lives in Baltimore and got it from a Mrs Merryman – the lady's aunt. 'Wallis and Ernest,' she said, 'are regular visitors to Fort Belvedere.' You know the place, Helen?'

'I've heard of it – a grace and favour residence. The

Prince of Wales sometimes stays there. But who is Ernest and who is Wallis?'

'*She* is Bessie Wallis Simpson – wife of Ernest.'

'A married lady? Then surely the Prince can have a man and wife on his guest list?'

'Not if the wife has been married before – and divorced. Ernest is her second husband, so if a divorced person can't go in the royal enclosure at Ascot, how come one of them can be buddy-buddies with the heir to your throne?'

'But isn't divorce thought of in more liberal terms, in America?'

'I assure you, Helen, it is not! Indeed, middle-Americans will not so much as *say* the word. And if by liberal you mean film stars and actresses and high flyers who seem to make a habit of it – well, I assure you they are not exactly approved of in my country, either!'

'But there has been no mention in England – not so much as a whisper – about the Simpsons. Nothing in the society columns. The King and Queen would be aghast,' Helen frowned. Divorce was a word to be avoided if at all possible. A divorcee – and there were some, even here – could never be accepted in polite society. Not ever. 'Do you think it is one small incident that has been blown up out of all proportion? I'm sure that the Prince of Wales will marry soon – and what a day that will be!'

'Oh my word, yes! And when he does, Helen, you must cable me at once. I must come over and see the wedding – get a hotel booked in London – make a holiday of it.'

'But you don't approve of our royalty,' Helen teased.

'No more do I – but they sure know how to put on a parade. All those gilded coaches, I mean, and bands and uniforms. And oh, the horses! I'd swim here, just to see the horses. If they've got a saving grace in my eyes, then it's the fact that your royalty does know good horseflesh when they see it. Anyway, be sure to let me know at once – either way.' A scandal or a wedding and Amelia would be on the next liner over. 'And meantime, I shall tell Aimee that there just isn't any truth in it; that no one in England has even so much as heard of the lady, and they surely would've, now wouldn't they?'

'One would imagine so, Amelia — but what is far more important is poor Clemmy. Edward is very concerned about her. Sometimes, she seems to be doing so well, then something happens and she's upset again.'

'What you're really saying is that she's up and down like an elevator and making no effort at all to come to terms with Elliot's death. It's five years, since it happened. I'd say you'd be better to be concerned about father-in-law. If he weren't such a gentleman, he'd have given her the slap she needs long before this. And I'm sorry for Anna. It's my belief that if her family weren't so short of money, she'd pack her bags and take herself back to her mother. But she has Tatiana's future to think of, you see.

'And Tatiana's afraid of mother-in-law,' Amelia rushed on. 'Can't say I blame the child. Bas is always uneasy about being at Pendenys, too. He's real bothered, you know, that one day it might just pass to him. If it did, I guess he'd give it away!'

'To his sister?' Helen quirked an eyebrow. 'Kitty loves the place.'

'Only because she thinks it's spooky — and you know what a little drama-puss my daughter is?' Amelia smiled indulgently.

'So what are we to do about Clemmy?' Helen frowned. 'I really am concerned for her. She took Elliot's death so badly. If only for Edward's sake, we must help her.'

'Helen! You lost both your sons so tragically and a much-loved husband, yet you don't act up like Bertie's mother. He's fast losing patience with her. Says we come over here far too often and I don't want him to forbid our visits. I like being here, especially at Rowangarth. Give me your house and my horses, and I'd be content. But Bertie is different. He's getting very American in his outlook. Says there's nothing for him at Pendenys, though one day we might be saddled with it.'

'If Nathan doesn't marry, you mean? I wish he would.'

'Couldn't agree more. But maybe there was someone in his life, and he lost her? Bertie says he used often to think that Julia and Nathan would tie the knot, but there you are. It wasn't to be . . .'

'No, Amelia. Julia is devoted to Nathan, but not in *that* way. I think she, too, would be glad to see him married. It must be very lonely in that vicarage, though he seems contented there. Oh, dear. We're a couple of matchmakers, aren't we? First the Prince, then Nathan!'

'And add Julia to the list. Poor, poor girl. Cut out for marriage and motherhood, yet look what happened. Why has no one come along for her, Helen?'

'Because there can't ever be another. I wish they'd had a child. At least there'd have been something of Andrew to hold on to. But she's clinging to memories, now. I love her so much. If only it were possible to put back the clock.

'But talking about clocks – I suppose you know that very soon I shall be seventy? And because I have lived out my three score years and ten, I intend to throw a party. Catchpole says there is a long spell of good weather ahead, so we could have it outdoors. Will you help me with my party, Amelia? It'll be such fun – a buffet supper, and dancing . . .'

'Throw in some fireworks, and you can count me in!'

Helen laughed with sheer delight. They would have such a fine time. A party would cheer people up, so everyone must be asked. Not just Rowangarth and Pendenys, but the new young doctor and the butcher, the grocer, the fishmonger! And children. There must be children! Clemmy must come, too.

'You'll tell Clemmy and Edward? A party might be just the thing to take her out of herself; meet people, instead of shutting herself away from them. If only she could bring herself to do it, it might well start her back on the road if not to recovery, then perhaps to acceptance. You'll try to persuade her to come, Amelia?'

'I'll do my best.' But she wouldn't come. Her mother-in-law was determined to be miserable, Amelia thought; would put a damper on any party. But she would try to persuade her – though not too hard! The road to recovery, indeed. My, but if there was ever a cock-eyed optimist, it was Helen Sutton, bless her. 'Let's start right now, making lists? About fifty invitations, would you say?'

'Oh, at *least* fifty!' Helen laughed.

Bas tapped timidly on the door in the tower. 'She's not in,' he whispered.

'Yes she is. She's always in.' Kitty knocked more loudly, opened the door with a flourish, then said, 'Good morning, grandma. Might we come in?'

'I suppose so. What do you want? You know I'm busy!'

'Doing what, grandma?' Kitty seated herself opposite; Bas moved to stand behind her chair. He felt safer with his sister between him and Grandma Sutton.

'I didn't say you could sit, girl.'

'No. But it's more comfortable.'

Bas shuddered. His sister was too much. They'd been told not to upset grandma, but Kitty didn't care one bit what she said.

He didn't like this room in the tower. It was small and hot and smelled of cigarette smoke. And grandma never opened the window, so it smelled of people, too. And it sure wasn't fair that just because they were children they had to be polite to grown-ups and considerate of their feelings – especially when they were grown-ups like Grandma Sutton.

'Well – what is it?' Clementina snapped. She disliked the way the boy cringed. Elliot had never cringed. And she disliked intensely the girl's aplomb. Dark-haired she was, like Elliot. Mary Anne's hair, though those eyes were her mother's. Could stare anyone out, with that dark blue gaze. She'd be a madam, when she grew up. Had the makings of one already. 'Hurry up! Say what you came to say, then go!'

'We came to wish you good morning, grandma, and to ask how you are,' Kitty replied with disturbing candour. 'And we hope you'll be going to Aunt Helen's party. Has Mom told you about it?'

'She has, and neither myself nor your grandfather will be there! And why your great-aunt Helen wants the world and his wife to know that she's seventy, I really don't know!'

'I suppose that's because she doesn't look seventy,' Kitty beamed. 'She doesn't, you know. I think she's really beautiful. I wish I were fair, like she is.'

'Well, you've got black hair – Pendennis hair – so there's nothing you can do about it! Pass me my cigarette case, boy – and the lighter!'

'Yes, ma'am.' In his eagerness to oblige, Bas tripped and almost fell. He didn't know why he was so uneasy when he came into this room. He wasn't afraid when he took his pony at a jump, nor anything like that. Why, then, should he feel such fear in grandma's company? It was as if there was evil, here. He could almost smell it. He'd said so to Kitty, but she said she didn't feel or smell anything and she would've, if there'd been anything spooky about it.

Clementina took an oval-shaped cigarette from the gold case that once had been Elliot's and flicked the matching gold lighter. She inhaled deeply, then blew out smoke that drifted, pale blue, to the ceiling. Bas offered an ashtray.

'You're sure you won't come to Rowangarth party, grandma? There'll be fireworks and Aunt Helen is to hire a marquee and a floor, for dancing,' Kitty urged. 'Absolutely everybody is going to be there. It would be awful if you were to miss it. I heard Mom say this morning that the fish man and his wife had accepted, and –'

'And you think a Pendenys Sutton would mix socially with a fishmonger, child?'

'I sure don't see why not. Aunt Helen doesn't mind, and it's her party. And the Clan will be there.'

'Who on earth . . . ?'

'Oh, you know the Clan, grandma – we four Suttons and Daisy and Keth.'

'*Keth*? What sort of a name is that?'

'It's an old Scottish name, his Mom said. Keth's in the Clan because he's a Pendennis. His Mom runs the bothy, at Rowangarth.'

'His mother a servant and he's a *Pendennis*? Stuff and nonsense, child!'

'He is so, grandma.' Bas felt obliged to support his sister, because if Keth said it was true, then it *was* true. 'His great-great-grandfather was brother to our Mary Anne. Keth's Mom's maiden name was Pendennis and she's dark, like Kitty is and Keth. Unnatural dark . . .'

'*Pah*!' Clementina had heard enough. Impudent, those Kentucky children. Mind, she had seen that boy. The first time, the six of them were running across the grass below the window. She had looked down and felt quite faint. So dark, the strange boy was; could have been Elliot in his early teens. There was no mistaking the hair, the warm apricot of his skin. It had been as if time had turned round on itself and Robert and Giles and Elliot and Albert and Nathan were boys again, with Julia striving to keep up with them.

It had been uncanny, yet when she summoned up enough courage to look again, they had passed out of sight.

'We-e-ll, if you're all right, grandma, and you don't want us to do anything for you, I guess we'll be going.' Kitty got to her feet. 'Shall I pass you the brandy, before we go?'

Bas sucked in his breath and closed his eyes, waiting for

443

the explosion. But it did not come. Instead, his grandmother said quietly – much, much too quietly –

'No, thank you. I am not an invalid. I am well able to pick up a decanter, should I wish to drink from it.'

She waved a dismissive hand and Bas opened the door with all haste, waiting impatiently as a smiling Kitty placed a pretty kiss on her grandmother's cheek, then bobbed the smallest curtsey.

She was play-acting again, he fretted. His stupid little sister just couldn't help it. It was like Pa said. There was mischief inside her which was all very well most times. Kitty was fun, but she sure didn't have to mock Grandmother Sutton because that's what she was doing. And getting away with it, too.

'Thank goodness that's over,' Bas sighed, when the door was closed behind them and they had negotiated the winding stone staircase. 'You sure do look for trouble, Kitty Sutton,' he grinned, able to smile again with the ordeal behind him. 'Now let's get out of here quick, before Mom decides there's something else she wants us to do. Shall we call at Denniston House and ask if Tatty can come with us to Rowangarth?'

Tatty was improving with every visit, Bas conceded. Since her nanny left, she had been allowed to grow up.

'Mam'selle mightn't let her come, Bas.'

'It's nothing to do with Mam'selle – not when it's school holidays. Let's ask Aunt Anna.' The aunt who had claims to being a countess, though only a Russian one, Mom said, was the prettiest lady Bas had ever seen. He wondered if Tatty would grow up to look like her. If she did, he considered, there'd be a whole lot of guys falling for her – himself included. 'C'mon,' he said. 'Race you to Denniston!'

Kitty would win, of course. She always did.

Helen sat comfortably, contentedly watching from the conservatory as young Catchpole, the apprentices and Will

Stubbs carried off trestle tables, took down lanterns lit for the dancing, carted away benches and chairs.

Through the wide-open door came the night scent of bruised grass mingling with honeysuckle, tea roses and sweet-scented stock and she closed her eyes and breathed in not only the scent of it but the mood of it, too.

It had been such a party. Old friends, new friends, children – so many lovely people. Different people, of course, because her long-ago friends were gone. Once, there had been large, formal dinner parties which took days and days to prepare. Now, on her seventieth birthday, she had asked everyone – tradesmen, relations, tenant farmers, because the war had been a great leveller. Few had escaped it in one way or another. Women had proved themselves, earned the right to vote, to walk unaccompanied wherever they chose.

She, Helen, had adapted to that change, even welcomed it. Clementina had not and therein lay her inability to adjust to Elliot's death. Clemmy was unable to acknowledge change or to accept sympathy, and she would never alter.

Helen shook her head clear of all sad thoughts and looked out to the end of the avenue of linden trees where a moon rose, a half-round of palest gold. It was all so beautiful, so precious. Memories of such a night she must store inside her in small, secret places; hide them in a corner of her consciousness until she had need of them some lonely winter evening.

Edward, she was glad to recall, had come to her party, bringing Anna with him, and Albert and Amelia and their children. Clemmy had pleaded indisposition. She could not yet face people. Helen would understand, she said.

Poor Clemmy. All her love and hopes and dreams squandered on Elliot. With his death it was as if there was nothing left for her to strive for, and poor Edward trapped in a loveless marriage with a wife growing more and more strange every day.

Granted, Edward was born a second son and second sons shifted for themselves and married where they could, but he had not deserved Clementina's indifference nor a son like Elliot.

Julia had enjoyed the evening, Helen mused; had danced with Nathan and Albert and waltzed with her Uncle Edward. Julia, so beautiful yet so apart for all that, as though in the middle of the noise and music and laughter she waited for someone to call her name, kiss her lips. Poor Julia, who had loved too well, too passionately.

Children! Think of the young ones, of Julia's Clan. They had been allowed to stay up late on so important a birthday. Tatiana, watched from a distance by Anna, had been the liveliest of them all until she was sick, though whether from over eating or over excitement or a mixing of both, Helen had not been sure.

A small, silvered cloud briefly covered the moon and shapes faded into silhouettes. She closed her eyes and let the peace wash over her. It was sad, she thought, that mankind could not choose the moment on which it should die. On so perfect a night what better, more gentle a time to close her eyes and drift away down the linden walk, on and up towards the moon and out into eternity, where John waited . . .

'There you are!' Julia, carrying a tray. 'You were so still I thought you'd dozed off.'

"No. Just thinking about how wonderful everything has been. Such a lovely evening. People were so kind.'

'And you really enjoyed telling them you were seventy and no one believing it. Drew is in bed. He'll sleep late, tomorrow – they all will. Just thought you'd like a cup.'

'I'd love one. Do you know, Julia, when I was sixty I thought I should be grateful to see seventy, but now that I have, I don't feel a day older. Would you think me selfish if I hoped for eighty?'

'Eighty at least, then you can be around when Drew marries. Have you anyone in mind for him, by the way?'

'Strangely, no. I often think that Drew and Daisy are so lovely together, but it can't be, of course. So I shall wish that he loves as I did and as you did, my dear. No matter who she is, I hope he marries for love.'

'With just one proviso,' Julia whispered softly, sadly. 'That whoever she is, they be allowed to grow old together.'

'Wasn't it strange, tonight?'

Kitty Sutton sat cross-legged on her brother's bed. They still used the nursery wing, each time they visited Pendenys Place. It was one of the better things about it, Bas was forced to admit. It was fun to share the night nursery with his sister; sleeping in white-painted iron beds piled with soft blankets and fat ciderdowns at Christmas and linen sheets and blue-checked bedspreads in summer. And by far the best thing about their small, private domain high beneath the eaves, were the two staircases leading to it; one that ran from the kitchen and was wooden and narrow and bare; the other that started in the vast, echoing hall and went up and up, softly carpeted.

'Strange, Kit? It was a swell party – till Tatty was sick, that was.'

'Tatty's always sick. You know when she's going to throw up,' Kitty said disparagingly. 'She gets two red blobs, on her cheeks. It's because she's half Russian, I suppose. But wasn't it strange when the lady who was serving at the buffet called Drew *Sir* Andrew?'

'That was Ellen. Once, she was parlourmaid at Rowangarth – before Mary, I believe. She's married, now, though she always comes back when there's a party, to help out. Drew told me about her.

'And she only called him that because he really is Sir Andrew, though I don't think the aunts at Rowangarth bother with it — not yet, at least. Perhaps, when he's older . . .'

'That's all right, then, because titles are silly — especially when you're only twelve.' Kitty waved a dismissive hand.

'You won't be so off-hand about it if you marry Drew, will you? You'd have to be Lady Sutton, then!'

'*Marry Drew?*' She tilted her chin dismissively and her long, dark curls swung like a horse's mane, Bas thought, suddenly missing his horses.

'Why not, Sis? You like England, don't you? And you like Rowangarth, as well.'

'Of course I do. But you don't marry a guy just 'cos you like the house he lives in, now do you?'

'Guess some folks might.'

'Well, I'm not going to get married for ages and ages. There's so much I want to do. I love Kentucky and I love England, too, but there's a lot of world in between and I want to see all of it! And I don't know what I want to do or to be, yet, but whatever it is, I want to do it real well. I want that people say, "Hey! That's Kathryn Sutton, the famous surgeon." Or maybe I'll be a crooner or a show-jumper. I don't know, yet.'

'Dad wouldn't want you to be a crooner, Kitty, though I think right now that people should call you the famous greedy guts. You sure ate a lot, tonight!'

'Yes, I know. I had two lots of trifle, but I wasn't sick, like Tatty. Do you think it's kind of awful, being half Russian?'

'I don't think so. You and me are half English, but it's all right.'

'Mm.' Kitty Sutton liked being half English. It made her kind of different at school and it meant she could come to England twice a year. She liked England very much and Pendenys and Rowangarth especially. She didn't know why, because she thought like an American child and talked like one, too.

Perhaps, she frowned, it was her half-English blood that accounted for it. She wasn't quite sure. All she knew for certain was that if, suddenly, ships ceased to sail or flying boats ceased to fly, she would be very hurt and upset and would miss England dreadfully.

All at once, she could no longer fight sleep and she stretched her long legs and pulled back her bedcovers.

''Night, Bas,' she said, drowsily. 'And you got it in one. It sure was a swell party . . .'

'Oh my word, but I'm tired.' Polly Purvis eased off her shoes.

'Then why did you go, Mum? How do you think I felt? Me enjoying the party with the Clan whilst you slaved in Rowangarth kitchen.'

'I wasn't slaving, Keth! Miss Clitherow said they'd be grateful for help, so I went. Nothing wrong in that. Ellen from Home Farm was there, an' all. She always helps out and she enjoyed it, like I did. She was telling me about the way it used to be at Rowangarth, before the war. Oh, those dinner parties must have been something to see . . .'

'Well, I think you should go to bed. I'll bring you up a drink, and leave the fire safe.' Keth was not convinced. It always bothered him that his mother was employed by Rowangarth, yet he was treated as a friend by Drew, who was really a baronet.

'Goodness, no. The 'prentices aren't in, yet. Helping clear away, up at the house. Can't go to bed till I've seen to things. And Keth – I really enjoyed being at Rowangarth – and there'll be ten shillings extra in my wages, next week.'

'But do you have to work so hard, now? Haven't things got better, since we came to live here?'

'They have.' No denying that things were easier. Now she had bed, board and food as well as a wage and a weekly widow's pension. 'But a few shillings extra never comes amiss, now does it?'

'Sorry, Mam. But I worry about you and I worry because I'll be fourteen in a week and most lads of fourteen leave school. I could be out working for you.'

'Oh, aye? You'd rather take a five-shillings-a-week job – if you can get one, that is. Precious few jobs for lads without an education these days, and you know it or why were you so set on getting to the Grammar School? And now that you've got there, why all this nonsense about wanting to work? I want you to make something of yourself!'

'Are you saying that dad didn't?'

'That I'm not! He came back from that war lamed, and there was precious little work about, even for the able-bodied. If his foot hadn't got shot he'd have been a head keeper. Mind, if he hadn't gone to the war, then him and me wouldn't have met, and though it was hard going, sometimes, I wouldn't have had it any different. We were happy enough, at Willow End.'

'Yes.' Keth supposed they were, but happy enough wasn't good enough. It was why, somehow, he must get to University and forget all thoughts of leaving school.

Not that Daisy would ever have to worry, now that she was rich. It had been a shock, when she told him. He had even wondered why Mr Hillier and his father had had to die, so she might have that money.

But it wasn't Daisy's fault. His father had fallen in the river trying to pull Beth out and Mr Hillier had been sucked in, too, trying to help them both.

Some people got rich because of a flooded river but he, Keth Purvis, would have to do it the hard way or he'd never be able to marry Daisy and he wanted to. Even though he was only fourteen next week he knew he loved her. He always had, even when she'd been a baby, tucked up in that great big pram.

He wished he could tell his mother about Daisy's money, but he had promised not to. It was just that things weren't going to be easy for him for a long time; not until he was twenty-three, at least. Nine more years. Nineteen-forty. It was a lifetime away.

'What are you brooding about, son?'

'Not brooding. Just thinking about Willow End – and Beck Lane and Windrush.' Which wasn't a lie, really, because he often thought about Beth and Morgan and the little grave marker. The beech trees would be in full leaf, now, and the bluebells beneath them faded. He wondered if anyone lived in Willow End and Keeper's Cottage or if they were empty, and lonely. 'And I don't want to leave school at term end, Mum. I shall keep on and one day I'll buy you a fur coat – and that's a promise.'

'What – *me*? Polly Purvis in a fur coat!' She gave a great shout of laughter as if she really thought it funny. Then all at once her face gentled and she cupped her son's face in her hands and kissed his forehead, though she hadn't kissed him since he was ten. 'Thanks for your thought, Keth, but if ever you've got that kind of money, then I think you should buy yourself a little motor with it and take me back to West Welby, just once. I'd like to visit Willow End again and go to see your dad – let him know that you and me managed all right, between us.'

'I'll do that, I promise. We'll tell dad . . .' And in that moment he loved her so much that he gathered her to him, and hugged her tightly. 'And we'll take Daisy with us, won't we?'

'Yes, Keth. We'll take Daisy.'

28

The Summer of 'Thirty-Four

It was, said Amelia to Edward Sutton, just about the only course left open to him.

'It's sad,' she said firmly, 'but mother-in-law is getting worse.'

On each of their twice-yearly visits, it became more obvious that Clementina not only spurned help, but was quickly becoming past it.

'There was nothing else I could do,' Edward said wearily. 'Sometimes, you see, I worry that she'll harm herself. Clemmy doesn't know Miss Hannah is a nurse – I especially asked she did not wear her uniform – but engaging her was all I could do, except –'

'Except getting mother-in-law committed and looked after by professionals,' Amelia finished, though whether for diminished responsibility or an increasing dependence on alcohol, would be hard to decide.

'I'm grateful that you and Albert still visit so regularly. It must be a great trial to you both and it can't be good for Kitty and Bas.' Because no matter how they tried, Clemmy's state of health could not be hidden from them.

'Kitty and Bas are growing up. Kitty is going on fourteen and Bas will be seventeen next February. They must learn that the world can be hard, sometimes. I can't stop the wind from blowing on them, you know.'

'You're a good woman, Amelia. I don't suppose,' Edward smiled wanly, 'you have a sister tucked away, somewhere, for Nathan?'

'I haven't. When I met Bertie, I was alone in the world,

except for two cousins. But if I had ten sisters and all of them charming and beautiful and I paraded them in front of his church porch, Nathan wouldn't notice them. He's in love with Julia – didn't you know?'

'*Julia*? But –' He shook his head in disbelief. 'Are you sure?'

'Sure as I can be. I've thought so for a long time, though don't ask me why.'

It was just the little things, really. The way his mouth formed the smallest smile when Julia came into a room; his eyes following her, waiting for her to come to his side – the way he said, 'Hullo, Julia,' so softly it was almost a blessing.

'Then poor Nathan. Julia loved just as Helen loved. Once, and for ever. It's a sad world, Amelia.'

'It can be, and that is why I can't for ever shield my children. They must learn, you know.' Bas, her adored firstborn. Tall, now, and straight; no longer a boy. And Kitty, more and more beautiful with every year. Kathryn Norma Clementina Sutton who fearlessly embraced the world and shook it by the shoulders until it noticed her. 'But tell me – where is mother-in-law getting her drinks from? Surely you don't –'

'Make it easy for her? Of course not. The key to the wine cellar is in my possession, now, and though I've never given orders that drinks are not to be left about, the servants are very tactful about it. Only the minimal amounts in decanters and small measures of wine poured at meals. It's as if they understand, but –' He stopped as the door opened and a footman placed a tray beside Amelia. 'Here's tea.'

'Mm. This is one of the things I cross the Atlantic so regularly for!' Amelia lifted the pot. 'Let's have a cup in peace – before my two get back from Rowangarth . . .'

'"Get back from Rowangarth," she said!' Kitty raised her eyes dramatically, waiting until she had the complete attention of her audience. 'But I hadn't gone to Rowan-garth. I was there, behind the sofa – the big one, you know, in the window – and scared stiff they'd find me!'

'Scared stiff?' Bas demanded scornfully. 'Nothing scares you, Kitty Sutton. You were listening – eavesdropping. You're always doing it and it isn't funny. One day you'll get caught and Mom's going to hit the roof!'

'I shan't get caught. Whenever I listen I have my hand-kerchief in my hand in case I want to sneeze. And besides, the big window was wide open. I crept out when the talk got boring. They didn't even know I'd been there. And if you don't want to hear what they were talking about – well, see if I care! But it was – oooooh – *awful* . . .'

'Was it about Herr Hitler or the Prince of Wales?' Daisy demanded.

Mam always threw the paper down when there was any-thing about Herr Hitler in it though she was ever so inter-ested in the Prince of Wales and when he was going to find a princess.

'No. More awful than Hitler. Mom said she wouldn't trust Mullins – that he's flat-footed and shifty-eyed.'

'Mullins?' Keth frowned.

'Pendenys butler,' Drew supplied. 'But he can't help being flat-footed, Kitty. It's all those stairs he has to walk up.'

'Guess not. But he's shifty-eyed. Mom said to Grand-father Sutton she reckons it's him getting booze to grandma and –'

'Mom wouldn't say *booze*,' Bas snapped. 'You're making it up. You didn't hear them talking about anything. You just want to be the centre of attention!'

'I did so hear it and okay – Mom didn't say booze; she said brandy. She *did*!'

'Do tell?' Drew urged. He liked it when Kitty did her impersonations.

'No! Not if you don't believe me!'

'But we do believe you, don't we, Daiz? And I think Aunt Amelia probably did say brandy, because I heard Will Stubbs and Young Catchpole talking about Aunt Clemmy being on the brandy. A dipso-something, they said.'

'Dipsomaniac,' Keth supplied. 'And it's sad. Dipso-maniacs drink themselves to death.'

'Good,' said Tatiana – they had forgotten Tatty. 'How long does it take?'

'Not long.' Kitty slid her eyes dramatically from right to left. 'They've got a nurse in, at Pendenys, called Miss Hannah. Grandma thinks she's a new servant. She's there, just in case. And grandpa says that if Mullins is bringing booze – *brandy* into the house, he'll be out on his ear! We-e-ll, dismissed without a reference, actually.'

'I still think it's very sad.' Keth pulled on his jacket. 'You should feel sorry for people like her, even if she is a bit of a martinet.' Martinet was the word his mother had used. 'And you aren't telling us anything new, Kitty. All Holdenby is talking about Mrs Sutton – and half the tradesmen in Creesby, too.

'And I'm not staying here to listen to you doing your party piece, Kitty. I've got papers to deliver and homework to do!'

'I'll come with you, then,' Bas said. 'You coming too, Drew?'

'*Well!*' said Kitty when she and Tatiana and Daisy had been deserted for a paper round. 'It serves them right, 'cos they've missed the best bit – though I couldn't have told – not when Drew was there. It's Uncle Nathan, you see. Mom said he's in love with Aunt Julia!'

'Oooh! I wish she was in love with him, but Mam says there'll never be another Andrew. Mam was there the night Aunt Julia and the doctor met,' Daisy hastened, determined that Kitty should not have all the limelight. 'In those days, young ladies like Aunt Julia couldn't go anywhere alone –

not even to the shops — and Mam went to London with her as a chaperon. Mam did the sewing at Rowangarth, then; before she married Sir Giles, that was.'

She could talk, now, about Mam being married before, because she'd had time to get used to it. And she mentioned it because Tatty and Kitty ought to be reminded from time to time that Mam had once been Lady Sutton and that she, Daisy, had every right to be one of the Clan.

'Don't you mind about it?' Tatiana asked, wide-eyed. 'Your mother, I mean . . .'

'Not really.' Now that she was fourteen and understood that Mam and Dada still loved each other and had secret little kisses when they thought she wasn't looking, it didn't hurt any more. It just made her sad about Sir Giles who had been dreadfully injured crawling into No Man's Land, Mam said, trying to bring back wounded soldiers. 'Mam looked after Sir Giles, you know. They had to special-nurse him. He was so ill they sent for the priest — an army padre. It was your Uncle Nathan, you know, and it was him married Mam and Sir Giles in France.'

'Aah.' Tatiana's eyes brimmed with tears. 'It's as sad as the Bolsheviks killing Grandfather Petrovsky and Uncle Basil. I hate wars and I hate Lenin!'

The words came, bitter and voluble, then, in keeping with her suddenly red cheeks; strange words, foreign words.

'Well, heck — what was all that about?' Kitty demanded.

'I was swearing and cursing, in mother's language. I always do it when I'm angry or upset. That way, not many people know what I'm saying.'

'Your mother taught you Russian swear words?' Daisy gasped.

'Of course not! Karl taught me — you know — Karl the Cossack. He's mother's major-domo, sort of. Karl teaches me swear words and I teach Karl English. He speaks it quite well, now. Only he says it's best only between me and him so people don't know that he understands quite a bit of what they are saying. That way he gets to hear a lot more.'

'That's sneaky!' Kitty exploded.

'Like hiding behind sofas, listening,' said Tatiana.

'Guess you're right.' Kitty was always gracious in defeat. 'You couldn't teach me a few so I can swear at Bas?' Tatty was coming on apace, she was forced to admit; a whole lot better than the spoiled brat who couldn't go anywhere without her nanny. Maybe it was because of Mam'selle.

'All right – but just a few of the not so bad ones, to start off with. The bad ones – the really wicked ones – I might teach you later.'

'Gee, thanks, Tatty. And isn't it nearly teatime? Let's not wait for those guys?'

'We could go to Keeper's, if you like,' Daisy offered. 'Mam is baking, today. There'll be bread and honey – linden blossom honey – and cut-and-come-again cake.'

'Let's!' said Tatiana, who loved bread and honey.

So they linked arms and made off, completely contented. There were times, Daisy thought, that life was very nice. Times like today; sunny, and the air buzzy with bees and the far meadow shimmering with buttercups. And almost like in the poem – honey still for tea; sort of contented, and safe.

Now she was fourteen and she and Mam had had a woman-to-woman talk about her periods and about her blushing a lot when Keth smiled at her, she felt a dizzy happiness she couldn't explain but which was warm and lovely and precious.

She loved Keth very much; knew she would always love him and that when he went away to University he would ask her to be his serious girl.

'I think,' she said gravely, breaking the easy silence, 'that when I'm ever so old – older than twenty-one, I mean – I shall always remember this summer.'

The summer of 'thirty-four. Even in spite of Mrs Clementina's brandy, she would remember it.

'Do I have to, Mam?' Piano practice took up far too much time and what good did it do? 'I said I'd go to Drew's. He'll be wondering where I am.' Daisy gazed at the sheet of music before her. Piano practice was a nuisance and it was only because Mam thought it tasteful to have a piano in the front parlour.

'Why on earth do you want a piano?' Dada had asked, and Mam said, 'So Daisy can learn, of course.'

Daisy didn't mind one bit her Mam going up in the world, but she resented five-finger exercises and all that went with them; resented the daily half-hour her piano teacher in Creesby insisted upon.

'Fifteen minutes more, if you please, and Drew isn't waiting on you. Drew is with your Dada, walking the covers.'

Drew was learning to handle a shotgun. His tuition under Tom began with an air rifle, shooting at tin cans, and now he had progressed to a single-barrelled gun which he handled with skill; as Dada had known he would, of course.

Dada had been strict, mind, allowing no backsliding, insisting on all the rules of safety; never to point a gun – even unloaded – at anyone nor climb a fence or a gate, whilst holding one. And Drew knew by now the importance of pulling the barrel through; of keeping it clean and shining and that any carelessness or sloppiness would be frowned upon, maybe even reported to her ladyship.

Drew admired Tom. Not only had he known him all his life, but Tom was kind like Uncle Nathan, though of course he and Uncle Nathan were very different. His uncle knew about books and verbs and paintings and about the Bible. Uncle Nathan even made the Bible interesting.

Daisy's father knew about the weather and the tracks of birds and animals, and there wasn't a bird's egg he couldn't instantly put a name to nor birdsong he didn't recognize at once.

Tom could walk without making a sound; never snapped a twig underfoot and could steal up on a creature without its knowing. And Tom was Daisy's Dada, which meant, in a roundabout way, that he could share him with Daisy, just as he and Daisy shared Lady. In the summer of 'thirty-four, Drew Sutton was a contented young man, and almost six feet tall.

'I'm bored.' Daisy ignored the Strauss waltz and began, impudently, to play a few bars of 'Red Sails in the Sunset'. She liked the popular tunes – those Henry Hall played on the wireless; was in a state of bliss when they took a day trip to Scarborough. Not for Daisy Dwerryhouse the sea and the sand, but the music shops along the sea front, where she could listen to the pianists who played the song of the day, then sold sheets of music for sixpence.

She wished Mam would let her have dancing lessons. Now she was fourteen she was allowed to go to the parties at school and it was awful that she couldn't dance at all when there were girls in her class who could do the Tango!

'Then bored you must be, Miss, 'til Tatiana and Bas and Kitty get back from London. But if you're so fed up, then take a mop and duster up to your room and give it a good clean – and a tidy out, too!'

Daisy returned to the Blue Danube waltz with renewed concentration. You couldn't win, with Mam. She wouldn't mind betting that Mam had been the terror of the wards when she was nursing.

Daisy sighed, and surrendered. And anyway, soon now she would hear the snap of the letterbox as Keth pushed the evening paper through it. That would be her cue to run after him, calling for him to wait, and she would walk the remainder of the round with him, content just to be at his side.

She really did love Keth, but Keth had to study hard so

459

he could sit the County Major examination that would give him not just a place at University but would pay, too, for his residence and books, he said.

Keth *had* to pass because jobs were even worse to get, now, with those who had one living in fear of losing it. It had been so awful, Daisy brooded, that there had been a hunger march from the north, all the way down to London.

'Poor souls,' Mam had said. 'I don't blame them one bit, taking a petition to Parliament.' Someone had to do it, she said, to let those in the south know how desperate for work the north of England was.

Daisy had wept when those men got to Hyde Park. It seemed so wrong they should be charged by the police and the march broken up. Their long, weary walk had come to nothing and the million signatures they collected along the way never reached Downing Street. She wept because Dada might have been one of those men and because the guilty feeling about her money was never far from her mind.

And then Mam had gone all faraway looking and told her about a Hyde Park of long ago when she and Aunt Julia had gone to a Suffragette meeting and been charged themselves by policemen waving truncheons, led by a sergeant on horseback. And Aunt Julia pulled her skirt above her knees, which was a most unladylike thing to do in those days, and kicked out like a hoyden.

'Oh, *Mam*,' Daisy breathed. 'What did you do, then?'

'Do? I joined in, an' all! Couldn't have your Aunt Julia taking all the bother, now could I? Besides, I was supposed to be looking after her . . .'

She had felt quite peculiar, Daisy remembered, and found it hard to believe that Mam, let alone Aunt Julia, could have brawled with the London police and had resolved to remember it next time Mam gave her a ticking-off for being pert. Answering back wasn't anywhere near so bad as fighting in Hyde Park.

Mam had smiled softly, then, and said, 'That was when Julia met the young doctor – and fell in love . . .'

Grown-ups could be very inconsistent, Daisy frowned.

Keth laid down his pen, closed his book and sighed relief. Physics, mathematics and general science he was confident he had conquered, yet now there was aerodynamics, a subject that had only excited his attention when the faceless men from the Air Ministry came to offer a great deal of money to farmers willing to give up their acres.

Mr Edward and her ladyship had been quite worried, Keth remembered, until they learned that the new aerodrome was to be built three miles on the other side of Holdenby, nearer, really, to Creesby.

Then Lady Helen began to worry again. Why, she wanted to know, did the government need to build aerodromes if it wasn't for bombing planes to take off from and who did we want to bomb, anyway? And when no one came up with an answer, Daisy had told him, Lady Helen presumed it was because Herr Hitler had decided that Germany needed an air force, and now that he was Chancellor and almost as important as General Hindenburg and was seen on the newsreels at the picture houses, ranting about the Jews who had burned down the Reichstag, people were listening to him in Germany and saying yes, of course they needed an air force – a *Luftwaffe* – and an army and a navy, too. Germany defeated, humiliated and never again to be allowed to transgress, was rising defiantly.

Not that they would fight, everyone said. How could they when they had lost just as many of their young men as the British and French?

But for all that, aeroplanes and all things concerned in lifting them off the ground became Keth's new interest, or would be, when the aerodrome was finally finished. Its construction had been delayed because some farmers had refused to give up their fields and farmhouses in the hope, some said, of getting more compensation than was offered. But now that all were satisfied and the building of an aerodrome more fact than fantasy, it might be interesting, Keth considered, to have bombers – or would it be fighter planes – flying overhead.

But first must come the exams. They were always there at the back of his mind, sometimes a worry, sometimes a challenge. But soon they would be behind him and waiting would take over from worry; waiting for the letter that would tell him he had been given a place at Manchester, perhaps, or Leeds. He had never aspired to Oxford or Cambridge. His feet were firmly planted on red bricks, and besides, Leeds and Manchester were nearer to home and to his mother about whom he constantly worried.

It was neither right nor decent at seventeen, when most boys had been working for three years, that he should still be at school and kept there by his mother. Sometimes he felt like a pansy, living off her, though one day it would all be worth it; it *would*.

But in the summer of 'thirty-four, Keth's dreams held substance and were mostly golden. That summer he could look forward with the confidence of the young to the day when the waiting was over and the business of getting on in the world could begin. He stuffed his books into his satchel, then called, 'Won't be long, Mum. Just going to see to the papers!'

'Well, now!' Amelia stirred her coffee, then settled herself comfortably for a chat. It had been announced on the early news bulletin on the wireless, read with pleased surprise in the morning papers and was now being talked about by delighted women throughout the entire country. 'A royal wedding! That'll be the second of your princes down the aisle.'

Prince George to the Princess Marina of Greece. Such a

beautiful bride she would be, women sighed, gazing at her picture.

'Everyone here is very pleased,' Helen smiled. 'Women do so like a wedding.'

'Pity about the date, though.' Amelia preferred June weddings. 'November seems a bit drear. Ah, well. Guess I'll have to ring round and book a London hotel before we go back – just to be on the safe side.'

'Amelia Sutton! You really do take the plate of biscuits!' Helen laughed. 'Coming over for the wedding? I thought you didn't hold with royalty.'

'No more do I, but I do like a good show, a parade with horses, and I'm not going to miss this one. The papers say it's going to be quite something.'

'Will you all be coming?'

'No. Bertie said not on your life – twice a year is more'n enough for him. And the kids can't miss school, so I've almost decided to fly over alone, then sail back. That way I'll only be gone about twelve days. And I could pick up some Christmas goodies in London, whilst I'm over.'

'You're very brave, Amelia – flying, I mean. I wouldn't dare.'

'But there's nothing to it, Helen – or so my friends who have flown the Atlantic tell me. It's all the rage, now. They say its quite luxurious, especially by flying boat, and so quick. I've almost made up my mind to try it – one way, that is.'

'Then if there'll only be yourself, I'm sure Julia would want you to stay at Montpelier Mews. There's only one guest bedroom, but it's very comfortable and quaint and you should feel quite at home there, Amelia. The house was once a stable!'

'Then I just might take you up on your offer – but won't you be going down to watch the wedding?'

'Myself – no. Quiet honestly, to see so lavish a wedding might make me feel a little guilty when there is such poverty about. I'll make do with the newsreels . . .'

'Ha! Now who's criticizing the royals! But there's poverty in America, too.' The Wall Street crash had seen to that. Amelia had good reason to be grateful she had suffered little, so carefully was her fortune invested. Land and livestock — and gold, of course. 'But I won't miss that wedding procession. Those horses and postilions and marching bands will surely be something to see. We don't have anything like it, back home.'

'You'll want to see the bride?' Helen teased.

'I will, too. And a celebration will do good — cheer people up. Everybody loves a wedding and they'll surely broadcast it on the wireless. It might even provide a few jobs.

'I shall not apologize for my enthusiasm, Helen — especially when a big wedding is justified, once in a while — though what your heir to the throne is doing is not! Not justified, I mean!'

'But what, exactly, is the Prince of Wales doing that he shouldn't be?' Helen frowned.

'Surely you know? Those two often get themselves in the American gossip columns. And your prince shouldn't be going to the Welsh valleys giving sympathy to out-of-work miners, then presenting his Bessie Wallis with jewels; fifty thousand pounds-worth at a time, so the newspapers have it! Sympathy comes cheap, to my mind!'

'Amelia! It *can't* be true. We'd know about it here, if it were. I'll admit that on occasion a Mr and Mrs Simpson are in the Court Circulars, but only as dinner guests. And always together. Are you sure about all this?'

Helen was worried. Of course princes had affairs; lots of young men did, then settled down into marriage, wild oats sown. But no scandal concerning the heir to the throne had appeared in British newspapers and surely if there were any truth in it . . . ?

'I only know what I've read. Pity I didn't remember to bring the cuttings over with me. Guess all I can say is that the English Press is far more discreet than ours. Perhaps out of respect for your king and queen they are being – well – *diplomatic* in the hope it'll blow over.

'But talk has it back home that he's real smitten, though how your church will countenance him marrying a divorcee I don't know – especially as she's still hitched to the second husband. Still, I'll be over for the big parade. Hope the weather holds good. You can't trust it, in November.'

'We'll keep our fingers crossed.' Helen was relieved to talk about the weather. 'The November fogs in London are simply terrible. Pea-soupers, we call them. A mixing of damp and fog and chimney smoke. It's one of the things I like least about London. Let's hope the sun shines on the bride.'

Julia and Andrew had been married in November on a cold, crisp day. A wartime wedding. Julia in blue, carrying John's orchids and, as they left the church, the sun shining briefly through the cloud. A good omen, she had thought.

'Let's hope so. And I must leave you, Helen. Got packing still to see to. And thanks for the offer of a bed, at Mont-pelier Mews. If Julia doesn't want to go down for the wedding, I'd like to stay there. Check it out with her, then let me know?' She kissed Helen warmly. 'See you before we leave.'

Helen was smiling, long after Amelia had departed on a gust of high spirits. She could not help but like Albert's wife; so honest and fair and frank; so genuinely grateful for her happiness.

She drained her half-empty cup. Gone cold, of course, which was only to be expected since Amelia had dropped if not her bombshell, then an extremely splashy pebble, into the pond of British respectability.

Surely the prince could not, would not, be so foolish as to get himself into the American papers? He couldn't be *that* indiscreet; not with a divorcee?

Yet Amelia did not lie. She was, truth known, not a little

worried herself about the gossip the articles were causing in Kentucky. And surely newspapers did not print things which were not true – or had at least a modicum of truth in them?

But the American lady was only a fling, surely? And soon, just as suddenly as the beautiful Marina had entered the life of Prince George, then so would some suitable foreign princess be found for the Prince of Wales. And there would be yet another bride and another wedding to gossip about!

29

The summer of 'thirty-four had seemed golden with hope, yet by the year end Helen Sutton had reason to look back on it with unease. What left her vaguely agitated was the murder of Herr Dollfuss – for murder it was and the Austrian Nazi party implicated in it – and the assassination of the King of Jugoslavia, a killing which awakened long-ago memories of a Sarajevo twenty years past. And Europe thrown into madness because of it.

There had, though, been the marriage of the beautiful Marina to the newly-created Duke of Kent, then that of his brother Prince Henry to the daughter of a Scottish duke. The weddings gladdened women's hearts including that of Amelia – she whose frank warnings of a royal scandal to come were already taking substance.

Now, newspaper editors had flung discretion aside; now Fleet Street confirmed what was already common knowledge in America and whispered asides amongst London society. The Prince of Wales and his American friend had indeed holidayed together at Biarritz and *without a chaperon*!

Then blatantly following Biarritz, the Prince and his companion embarked upon a cruise with the Press of the world waiting at every port of call like hounds scenting blood. Gossip had it that Queen Mary despaired of her son's behaviour and would not have That Lady's name mentioned, and the King said his son's goings-on would be the death of him!

Only gossip, mind, but the world and his wife were

talking about it. How soon, Cook asked of Miss Clitherow, before King George put his foot down? Such carryings-on were not acceptable, with That One a married woman and her husband being made a fool of because, mark Cook's words, there was no smoke without fire!

'Strange that none of it seems to have reached the Prime Minister's ears,' Miss Clitherow's mouth rounded into a moue of disapproval. 'But Mr Baldwin won't be able to ignore the gossip, once it's in the newspapers. We can only hope their majesties have some suitable lady in mind for the Prince and meantime they're letting him have his fling. Frankly, Cook, I'm just as worried about that Mr Hitler.

'And is Hitler his real name, I ask myself. I did read it is really Schicklgrüber. Talk has it he's illegitimate!'

'Wouldn't surprise me one bit,' Mrs Shaw sighed. 'With that funny moustache, what else can you expect? He's the image of Charlie Chaplin and nowhere near as funny!'

'Then more's the pity. The Germans are getting arrogant again and Hitler is encouraging them. Lady Helen is worried about it too, if you ask me!'

'Then what say I pop down to the kitchen and bring us up a pot of tea?' Cook enjoyed a cup of tea in the privacy of the housekeeper's sitting room. A cup of Sutton Premier tea was a soother and, when all else failed, the answer to unanswerable problems and the most enduring thing in a rapidly unenduring world.

Yet still there was Rowangarth. Rowangarth would always be there and a Sutton in it to take care of them all. No matter what, Cook decided firmly as she pushed the kettle further into the hot coals, Rowangarth would endure.

'Mother! You are not to upset yourself! And you *are* upset. Whose worries have you taken on board, now?'

'Sorry, Julia. Can't help it, though. Spain on the brink of civil war; that fat Mussolini threatening Abyssinia and

Hitler encouraging him; Germany re-arming, though they were forbidden at the Armistice to do so!

'And now they are sending soldiers to the Rhineland – right on the border with France. I tell you, Hitler will be wanting Alsace and Lorraine back, before so very much longer. And now that dreadful Zeppelin!'

'But dearest – so many good things have happened, too. The King well again, and the Silver Jubilee next year.' Holdenby planned to celebrate the Jubilee in great style. 'And – and –'

'Tell me – what else?'

'We-e-ll – there were the royal weddings, don't forget.'

'But I have – forgotten them, I mean. Long ago. I'm more concerned with the Prince of Wales and *his* wedding. Imagine! Holding hands in public with that woman! What is Mr Simpson thinking of to allow it? And as for that newspaper photograph of the two of them on holiday – she in a bathing costume and the Prince in a pair of shorts, *and nothing else*!'

'Got skinny legs, hasn't he?' Julia grinned.

'His legs have nothing to do with it. Frolicking half over Europe *has*! And all the time Amelia was right. There *is* something going on between the Prince and that woman and we *are* being spied upon by Germany! Why else would that Zeppelin of theirs fly over us? Checking up on the new aerodrome, I shouldn't wonder!'

'Probably just flying, mother – showing the flag, sort of. Germany has been on its knees since the Armistice. It's understandable they might want to sabre-rattle a little.'

'That airship was spying. Will Stubbs saw a swastika on its tail!'

'Will was probably romancing, as usual.'

'No. He saw it and he saw the number on its side, too.' Helen refused to be comforted or sidetracked. 'LZ 129, he said it was. That monstrous thing was so low that he could see it. He couldn't have made that up, now could he?

'Sinister, he said it was. Made him feel quite queer.'

'Dearest.' Julia cupped her mother's face in gentle hands, whispering a kiss on her forehead. 'You're afraid there'll be another war, aren't you? You worry for Drew and the rest of the Clan. But think – peculiar little man that Hitler is, he isn't so stupid as to start another fight with France and England, and risk America coming in again, too.

'Russia, now that's quite another thing altogether. Hitler hates the Bolsheviks – Communists, you know – so let him take on Russia if he wants something for his soldiers to do. They're a worse threat to him than we are. Germany won't tangle with us again! Drew won't go to war.'

'You think not?'

'I do, so stop frowning, dearest. It will give you wrinkles.'

'I'm entitled to wrinkles, at seventy-two! But perhaps you are right, Julia. I do so want you to be right. I'm worrying too much, aren't I?'

'You are. That Zeppelin was nowhere near the RAF station and what the Prince of Wales gets up to – and Herr Hitler as well, for that matter – is no concern of ours.'

'I suppose not. But the Prince *is* making a laughing stock of himself and of this country, too. And I can't help worrying, just a little, about Germany.' Anna was of same opinion, too, and truth known, Helen pondered, so was Julia if she would admit it. *Oh, please God, no more wars . . . ?*

'That photo, Tom, is disgraceful!' Alice flung down the newspaper. 'I don't know what's got into the Prince of Wales. Have you seen it – half naked, the pair of them!'

'Course I have. Thin as a rake, that Simpson woman is,' Tom grinned. 'Flat-chested as a lad. I wouldn't look twice at her.'

'An' you'd better not! She's common,' Alice fumed, because that was not all she was bothered about, though

470

the Prince's behaviour had all at once become news and people could talk about little else. 'And there's something else — on the newsreel at the pictures. German soldiers, *thousands* of them, strutting and cheering and arrogant as they come. It made my blood run cold.' Spoiled their evening out, her and Polly.

'Don't worry yourself, lass. Of course Hitler is re-arming Germany. Got to, hasn't he? Promised them work, didn't he, and their dignity back?'

'We-e-ll . . .' What Tom said made sense. There seemed to be no out-of-works in Germany — only here, in England. The Germans were all at once busy building warships and aeroplanes and guns. 'Maybe he's only doing what he thinks best.'

'Aye. And setting men to work again, building good, straight roads all over Germany. Can't blame him for providing jobs. Could do with a few less unemployed in this country, an' all.'

'So you don't think it'll come to fighting, Tom?'

'I don't, and anyway, I'm getting too old for the Army. There'd be a lot called up before me. And had you forgotten — I'm dead. They don't conscript dead men.'

'But you're missing the point, Tom! If — just *if* — it happened again, it wouldn't only be Drew and Keth who'd have to go. They'd take Daisy, too. They could conscript women, an' all.'

'Now you *are* talking nonsense! There'll be no more galavanting to Creesby pictures if that's the mood you're going to come home in. Now say after me — *There isn't going to be any more war.* Go on — say it!'

'There won't be a war,' Alice whispered, eyes on her shoes. 'There won't be — will there?'

'No love. *No.* And I'd go as far as to say you'd be better employed saving your worrying for Keth, and his exams. Now that *is* something worth bothering yourself about!'

*   *   *

The dining table at Pendenys Place was always set for two, even though it was many weeks since Clementina and Edward had shared a meal at it. Indeed, it had become the habit of the parlourmaid to fill a plate and carry it up the spiralling stairs to the tower room in which the mistress spent most of her time. This evening, however, no tray left the dining room.

'Have you forgotten Mrs Sutton?' Edward asked of the butler.

'Sir.' Mullins bent nearer, lowering his voice to a whisper. 'Mrs Sutton sent a message she was not to be disturbed – not even for a tray. I understand that it's a little stomach upset. I think madam intended going early to bed.'

'Thank you.' Edward covered his glass as more wine was offered. He drank little; lately, he drank even less. It was his conscience, he supposed. The more Clemmy drank the less he felt he ought to. Now she was unwell again though he knew it had more to do with brandy than an upset stomach.

He wondered who was bringing it into the house for her. He had thought, more than once, of trying to trace its source, but there was no retailer in Holdenby and it would be near impossible to cover all the wine and spirit shops in Creesby, or even the public houses.

Today was Thursday. Since Monday, Clemmy had not noticeably been unwell. Now she was indisposed, which meant that yesterday, when half the staff had an evening off, someone had brought a bottle – or bottles – back from Creesby.

There were sixteen indoor servants in all, which meant it could have been any one of eight; any one of the staff, really, since time off was taken on alternate Wednesdays and Thursdays.

But tonight, his suspicion must fall on one of those who had been into Creesby yesterday evening, though in whom to confide posed a problem since any of the eight could be the one to blame.

There was only one thing to do. He pushed aside the plate that all at once held no interest for him. First, he would find the bottle and then he would ask – nay, *demand* of Clemmy – who had brought it into the house.

He pushed back his chair, nodded his thanks as he left the room, then made for his wife's bedroom.

'Clemmy?' he whispered.

The light from the passage fell on the bed on which she lay, partly clothed, still, in a heavy sleep. Quietly, Edward pulled the door shut, then made for the almost hidden door that opened onto the staircase winding upwards for four floors.

The tower, built by Clementina's father to look like one he once saw in a Welsh castle, had been his worst vulgarity. Its stairs were of stone and would have been downright dangerous, had it not been for the sturdy rail, held to the wall by iron brackets. At each curve in the stairs, small narrow windows posed as arrow slits; it was all too theatrical, too dramatic to merit even indulgent amusement.

At an iron-hinged door on the second floor Edward paused, pulling in his breath, despising himself. What he was doing smacked of listening at keyholes or steaming open letters. It was an ungentlemanly act, yet do it he must. Tonight, he had come to a crossroads and if his wife was ever to be helped back to health and sanity, it was now.

The half-empty bottle he soon found, clumsily hidden. It bore no clue as to its origin, save that it was his wife's favourite brandy and one which could be bought from any decent-class merchant in any town in any county.

Sighing deeply, despairingly, he closed the door behind him, then placed the bottle on a side table in the library. The library would be the last place Clemmy would think of to look for it, tomorrow. Then he picked up the telephone.

'Holdenby 102, if you please,' he asked of the operator.

* * *

Helen had just finished eating when Mary called her to the phone.

'It's Mr Edward, milady. And shall you take coffee in the small parlour?'

'No. I think that since it is such a beautiful evening, I'll have it in the conservatory, Mary. Hullo, Edward?'

'Are you alone?'

'I am. Julia is eating with Nathan, tonight. Do come over,' she said gently, anticipating his request. 'I was just about to have coffee. Don't ring the doorbell – I'll be in the conservatory. Come round the side.'

'Bless you. Five minutes?'

'I shall look forward to it.' Frowning, she hung up the receiver, then called, 'Mary?'

'Milady?' The parlourmaid turned.

'Mary – could you hold coffee for about five minutes? I'll ring when I want it. Mr Edward is coming over and –'

'And an extra cup on the tray?'

'Yes, please, and I don't have to tell you, do I?'

'No, milady. And sugar lumps.' Mr Edward liked sugar lumps in his coffee.

'Mary, what would I do without you?' she smiled, though what Edward wanted to talk about that gave such an edge to his voice, such abruptness to his words, she hadn't the least idea.

Or had she? Was it Clemmy, whose behaviour was below-stairs talk not only in Pendenys and Rowangarth, but in many other places, public houses included, if second-hand gossip was to be given credit.

She switched on the small, pink-shaded lamp, then settled to await her visitor. Today, this first day of April, promised that winter was gone. The sky had been high and wide and blue; primroses, violets and wild anemones – windflowers, they were called, hereabouts – peeped through on bank and hedgerow. Only yesterday she thought she had seen the flashing dart of a first swallow and wished on it, just in case. Now, the sudden chill of the evening reminded them all, and Young Catchpole in particular, to beware of a sudden rogue frost.

Helen pulled her wrap around her and then, as she heard the crunch of footsteps on the gravel path outside, rang the bell, for coffee.

'Not long to go, now,' Daisy whispered.

'Four weeks and two days.' Keth linked his little finger with hers. 'I'll be glad when it's all over.'

The examination for University couldn't come soon enough, for what lad of near eighteen was still kept by his mother?

'Me, too. Not that I want you to go, but –'

'But the sooner I get there, the better I'll be pleased.' He would be twenty-two before it was all over and done with and he could begin to earn real money. At twenty-two, he brooded, most men had been earning for eight years – those who had jobs, that was. And at twenty-two, Dad had married Mum. 'Will you get tired of waiting, Daisy?'

'Waiting for what?' She said it all hoity-toity, though she knew what he meant. But meaning something and saying it were very different and she wanted Keth to tell her he loved her. She had loved him ever since she could remember with a kind of happy love, though now she blushed whenever they met or, like now, when he twined her fingers in his.

She was growing up; she had known it even before she and Mam had had their talk about *things*. She loved him differently, now, and she wanted him to kiss her. A lot of girls in her class had been kissed. It was quite nice, they said, if you liked the boy who kissed you. And she liked – *loved* – Keth, and one day they would be married, she was sure of it. She looked up, startled, as he touched her cheek.

'You were miles away. What were you thinking about?'

'Shall I tell you – *really* tell you?' All at once her tongue ran away with her and she couldn't stop it.

'Okay – if you want.'

'No!' She felt her cheeks flame.

'Tell me, sweetheart?' He asked it softly, as if he had been able to read her thoughts and wanted her to say them out loud. And he had called her sweetheart, which made her blush more than ever because he had never called her sweetheart before.

'I can't tell you,' she whispered, stopping in her tracks because they were almost at Keeper's, and if he was going to kiss her, she didn't want it to be spoiled because Dada might be standing at the window, waiting for her to get home.

'Please?' His voice was still low, yet different, somehow. 'I want you to.'

'If I do, you won't laugh? And you won't tell the boys, at school?'

'No. It'll be our secret. It'll have to be, won't it?'

'Yes.' He knew. He had probably loved her too, ever since he could remember. All at once, she felt warm inside. 'I was thinking about being kissed. Some of the girls I know have been kissed – by a boy, I mean . . .'

'And you haven't, Daisy?'

'Only by Drew on my birthday, and brothers don't count.'

'So if I kissed you, would you tell the girls at school?'

'No, Keth – our secret.'

'Then I'll tell you something – I haven't kissed a girl, either, though I suppose I could have, if I'd wanted.'

Gently he took her face in his hands, then bent to lay his mouth on hers, and it was a sweet kissing; a gentle awakening to love and it made silly little tears prick her eyes so she had to try very hard not to sniff them away, and spoil everything.

'Will you be my girl, Daisy – for always?'

'Yes, please.' She began to walk away from him because she didn't want him to kiss her again tonight in case the

476

next one wasn't as precious and perfect as their first. She reached for his hand and they walked slowly, not speaking, towards Keeper's Cottage. At the gate they stopped and she said, 'Thank you for bringing me home, Keth, and thanks for helping me with my homework. I'm awful at maths.'

'I know.' It was almost dark and because he stood in the shadow of a tree, she could not see his face, though she knew he was smiling. 'Goodnight, sweetheart,' he said softly. 'See you tomorrow.'

And tomorrow and tomorrow, she exulted as she walked up the path. Keth and Daisy. For ever!

'Where is it?' The morning-room door crashed open. 'Where have you put it? How dare you go into my room? And why is the dining-room door locked? Who gave orders to lock it?'

Clementina stood there, hair uncombed, her dressing-gown stained.

'The dining-room door is locked because –' Edward lay down his knife and fork, slowly, to give himself time to adjust to the tirade of anger – 'because I gave orders that it was to be.' Because, truth known, there were decanters and bottles in the dining room and he had known it was the first place she would search. 'And I went in your room to take away the brandy bottle.' He pushed back his chair, then crossed the room to close the door. 'Now please sit down and have a cup of coffee – and some toast, perhaps?'

She hardly ate, now. She was too thin and her complexion was sallow. Clemmy had been buxom and bonny; now she looked old and raddled.

'I want a drink.' She shook her head violently. 'You have no right to interfere. This is *my* house and never forget it!'

'And you are *my* wife and never forget you are a Sutton,' he flung. 'You are making yourself ill. If every mother who had lost a son acted as you are acting, this country would be ungovernable!'

'How dare you speak to me like that!' Noisily, clumsily, she pulled out a chair to sit down heavily. 'Don't forget who is mistress of Pendenys!' She reached for the coffee pot, filling a cup with hands that shook.

'Clemmy – *please* . . . ?' The sight of her sickened him. She had become a danger not only to herself, but to them all. 'I ask you one last time to see a doctor, *any* doctor? Go to London if you wish, but do something about your health before it is too late?'

'Doctor? I don't need a doctor! And if I did, I wouldn't want that whippersnapper from the village! Who does he think he is? Last time he came he told me that the remedy lay in my own hands, that there was nothing the matter with me that I couldn't cure for myself! Still wet around the ears, that one. Richard James would never have spoken to me like that.'

'When Richard was our family physician you were a different woman, Clemmy. You had pride and self-respect, yet look at you now? What Albert will think when he sees you, I don't know.'

'Then tell him not to come. I don't want him! It's Elliot I want, not Albert and his brat. And who is that boy who comes with him – the dark boy?'

'No one comes with him except Kitty, our grand-daughter.'

'There *is* a boy. He's dark, like Elliot.' She had seen him from the tower window, running with half a dozen of them, across the grass, taking Tatiana with them – off to Helen's, no doubt. 'And don't tell me I imagined him. I've seen him often enough, though I suppose you'll tell me he was never there. You'd like me to be mad, wouldn't you, Edward?'

'No. I just want you to get well. I want some order in our lives again. Is that too much to ask? It's as if there is a blight on this house. Even the servants –'

'Ha! The servants! You've noticed, then? The po-faced one — Hannah! She's always there, snooping and spying! But she isn't a servant, is she, Edward? You think I don't know you've hired a minder for me, a *keeper*. She's a nurse. I heard one of the housemaids saying she was taking clean towels to Nurse Hannah's room.

'Well, you can throw her out, or I will! You're having me watched, aren't you, so you can get me put away and get your hands on my money! But it won't work. This is *my* house and you live off *my* money, Edward. And if I refused to sign cheques or decided to stop your allowance, where would you be? Where, eh?

'And I want a drink, I tell you. I paid for it and if I want to drink myself to death, it's damn-all to do with you or anyone else!' She subsided, exhausted, head on her hands, moaning softly.

'Very well. I'll give you one, though to see you drinking at breakfast time makes me very sad, Clemmy. But first you must tell me where you get your brandy from.'

'Go to hell!'

'No drink, then. Which of the servants brings it in for you?'

'None of them! I ring up the wine merchant in Creesby and tell him to put a bottle on Pendenys' account.'

'Not our regular supplier, Clemmy?'

'N-no. The little shop in Fishergate, as a matter of fact.'

'And Mullins collects it?' It was a shot in the dark but the jerking up of her head, the sudden tightening of her mouth told him he had guessed right.

'I want a drink, Edward. Either open the dining-room or I'll ask for the spare set of keys!'

'Sit down, Clemmy, and please don't shout? I'll get you a drink. Just finish your coffee . . . ?'

He rose to his feet. His breakfast had gone cold but he had no stomach for it, now. And if one drink would quieten Clemmy, then so be it.

'What's this? What is it?' She grasped the glass he offered. 'I asked you for a brandy.'

'A brandy it is — with soda in it.'

'Then damn you, Edward Sutton and damn your drink!' White with rage she hurled the glass into the hearth, then swept her arm across the table, knocking over the coffee pot and all else in her way. They fell with a crash and a clatter and she threw back her head and laughed. 'Don't think to patronize me in my own house! Don't tell me what I may and may not drink!' She picked up a serving dish and hurled it to the floor.

'Stop it, Clemmy! Stop it!' Edward grasped her wrists but she freed herself with a strength born of rage. 'Please, *no*!'

'Mrs Sutton! Calm yourself *at once*!' Nurse Hannah ordered from the doorway.

'Why you — you —' Lost for words, Clementina reached for another dish.

'Oh, *no*!' The nurse was too agile, had dealt before with too many such rages. Grasping Clementina's hand she pulled it into the crook of her arm, holding it vice-like.

'Let me *go*!'

'Then be still, Mrs Sutton; be very still. Breathe deeply, now. Big breaths. Go-o-o-od. That's good,' she said softly. 'Just do as I ask and everything will be all right.' She slid her eyes to the door and Edward hurried to close it.

'The doctor?' he murmured.

'On his way, sir. I took the liberty . . .'

'I don't want a doctor. I don't want *him*!' Clemmy made to protest but her arm was still firmly held and she knew it was useless to try to free herself. 'And you'll be sorry for this! You'll both be sorry! You, nurse, are dismissed, so you can pack your bags and leave! *Now*!'

'Of course, madam. Just as you say. But first I'll wait for the doctor. Now — are you going to walk slowly and calmly to your room, or will we wait here until Doctor Pryce arrives?'

'I would like to go to my room.' Best he shouldn't see the mess when he arrived. 'And if you will let go of my arm, I am perfectly able to take the stairs alone.'

Her voice was calm again and level with reason. Gone was her anger and with it her violence, but the nurse was not deceived. Together they walked up the wide staircase, Clementina with her arm still captive; Nurse Hannah holding her hand in a grip of iron.

From the foot of the stairs Edward watched their progress, breath indrawn. Unobtrusively, a housemaid appeared with a cloth and dustpan and brush. Inside the morning room, the parlourmaid was already clearing what was left on the tables.

All was quiet; the blessed quiet, after a storm. A storm in a teacup and all over a glass of brandy. Clemmy was beyond all reason. Soon, she would be beyond all aid. With the help of the young doctor he must face her, Edward knew it; offer an ultimatum. Either she must try to help herself or she must be committed for treatment.

He walked dejectedly to the library. He had no wish to face the doctor; not just yet, until he was calmer, more able to think and speak and act with reason.

He opened the door, closing it quietly, thinking about what Helen had said, last night. 'Be kind to her, Edward? Her world ended the night Elliot died . . .'

He walked to his desk, pulling out the chair, leaning his chin on his fists on the desktop, wondering what his wife would do next.

The brandy bottle was the first thing his eyes lit upon. It stood there mocking him and he wanted to take it and hurl it against the wall with the same violence Clemmy had used only minutes before.

Instead, he opened the window and poured the contents onto the grass outside.

'God help me,' he whispered, his cheeks flushing with shame; shame that only moments before, he had come near to killing Clemmy; had wanted to close his fingers round her throat and still that harsh, sickening voice.

Only Nurse Hannah's entry into the room had prevented it.

30

'Well, that's it!' Keth threw down his bulging satchel. No more Creesby. Grammar School had ruled his life since ever he could remember; now, all he could do was wait for that letter. 'I called at Home Farm. There'll be work next week, when they start haymaking.' And there was still the paper round, though it had become an embarrassment. Pushing papers through letterboxes was for kids, not for a young man almost six feet tall.

'You'll be done with all that, soon.' Polly understood her son's frustration. The mind, the body, the hopes of a man hidden in a school uniform.

But all that would change. Soon skimping and making do and all the worrying and waiting would be over when Keth was given a county major scholarship.

Ten pupils had taken the examination; if only two were successful, the school at Creesby would count itself fortunate – and extremely proud. And one of those would be Keth.

Soon, at the end of the month, the letters would be sent – pass, or fail. That waiting was cruel, even more so when almost certainly most of the young hopefuls would be faced with disappointment.

Keth had said little about the examination itself – not that Polly could blame him for that. His entire young life had moved slowly towards that one day; small wonder now that day was past, that he was drained of all feeling.

'I'm taking Daisy to the pictures tonight – is that all right? A celebration, sort of, now it's over . . .

'Of course it is. You deserve a bit of a treat.' She dipped into her pinafore pocket and brought out a shilling. 'Buy yourselves some chocolate, in the interval.'

'No, Mum. Thanks, but no.'

'Take it, Keth? Let your mother celebrate, too? And mind you take good care of Daisy and don't miss the last bus home.'

Take good care. He knew exactly what she meant. At Windrush he had stood beside Daisy's pram, he and Morgan guarding her. And later, he had walked with her to school each day, holding her hand, taking care of her as if she were his little sister. But now he loved her, Polly was sure. To do well for Daisy had been a part of the force that drove him. When he got his scholarship he would lay it at Daisy's feet, which was right and proper, because she, his mother, would like nothing better than for them to marry. One day, that was, when Keth had a good position and could support a wife; one day, if three years of separation did not come between them or if some other young man hadn't caught Daisy's eye.

'I'll take care. I'll get out of this uniform, now, then I'll fill the coal buckets and bring in the logs.'

'Thanks, son. I'll put the kettle on. And don't look so worried!' He *did* look worried, which was only to be expected since his future had already been decided during that three-hour examination. And his quietness, really, was a reaction, like as not, to all the years of studying that all at once were over, as far as grammar school was concerned. 'I'll cut us a piece of cake.'

'Not for me, ta,' he called over his shoulder.

'It's chocolate. I baked it special.'

'No, Mum. Honestly – I'm not hungry.'

'Please yourself, then.'

But for all that, she cut two slices and placed them on two blue and white plates.

Worn out, that's what. She was glad they were going

into Creesby, tonight. Take the lad out of himself for an hour or two; do him good.

'My dear Clemmy! How good it is to see you looking so much better!' Helen settled herself in Pendenys morning room. So good that she had abandoned her retreat in the tower and was presiding over morning coffee, at home to callers, though only she herself, Helen frowned, ever called.

'The hairdresser came – trimmed my hair, put on an auburn tint. Hasn't gone too far, has she?'

Clementina turned her head to the light, eager for Helen's approval. Only in her sister-in-law's company did she feel remotely at ease and her hand cease to shake when she poured. Though she resented Helen's aplomb, her breeding and beauty – for she was still beautiful – Clementina Sutton knew that in a world turned hostile by her own stupidity, Helen was her only true woman friend.

'Your hair looks beautiful – quite a change for the better. I mean it.' She really did.

'You think so?' Clementina was pleased. 'Got to make an effort, I suppose, for Amelia. She's so pernickety, that one. No sooner see the back of them than they're here again! Can't understand how they can take so much time away from those mares of theirs.'

'They have a good stable staff. The Stud manager is entirely reliable. And Amelia looks forward to her visits to England. I hear they'll be flying over, this time.'

'And rather them than me! Don't like aeroplanes. How they get them off the ground is a mystery to me – all that weight!'

'I fear we shall have to get used to them, Clemmy. Stubbs heard that a squadron of bombers has arrived at the new aerodrome. Surely you have seen them, flying around?'

Clementina had, and flying in dangerously low to land. Frightening horses and livestock – and why pick the wilds of the North Riding for an aerodrome? Why should she have to put up with the noise?

'Do you think this dress a little unfashionable?' Clementina could still change the subject as abruptly as before.

'Indeed I do not. Those of us who kept our longer dresses are to be congratulated. Thank goodness those awful flapper frocks are out of style.' Too short, they had been. Legs all over the place. So embarrassing.

'Ah!' Helen could always be relied upon to say the right thing. It gave Clementina the confidence to say, 'You know that young doctor we got when Richard James retired? He had the audacity, would you believe, to tell me that unless I was willing to pull myself together, I had better not expect him to call again. Obviously, he didn't know about Elliot and my terrible grief.' He had gone on to ask her if she were determined to kill herself, though no need to tell Helen that!

'Killing yourself! That's just what you are doing, Mrs Sutton.' He had been rude, and angry. 'Carry on like this for very much longer and you'll be dead!'

'I'd got myself upset you see, Helen. I'll admit it. I'd had a few small brandies the night before because it was Elliot's birthday. No one remembered, but me. Edward and I had an argument over breakfast and I accidentally knocked over a coffee pot and broke a dish.

'Then that dreadful woman Hannah rushed into the room and marched me upstairs – *up my own stairs* – as if I were a naughty child being sent in disgrace to bed!

'Then she took it upon herself to send for that doctor and he was most aggressive – sided with her, though they always stick together, those medical people. She left, of course. I told her to pack up and go!'

'There now,' Helen murmured, because it wasn't quite the version Anna had brought to Rowangarth, next day.

Nurse Hannah had refused to stay one more night at Pendenys and was driven to Holdenby station in the Rolls-

Royce. And Mullins had been obliged to hand in his notice, too. Poor Mullins. Fond of his Madeira, but he had been with Edward and Clemmy since Pendenys was built. A sad old man. Nowhere to go, Anna had said.

'But I suppose I shall have to forgive that doctor –'

'Doctor Pryce,' Helen corrected softly.

'Yes. Better ask him to dinner to even the seating up. Amelia likes to act hostess when she's over and I must admit she does it quite well.'

'A dinner party would be splendid!' This was indeed an improvement, Helen thought gratefully. Perhaps the breakfast upset had finally jerked Clemmy to her senses. 'Whom shall you ask?'

'I'm not at all sure. There'll be Edward and I and Albert and Amelia, but then I have a surplus of ladies. So I thought if we asked the doctor he would do to take Anna in to table, and Nathan, of course, can escort Julia. And as for you, Helen – well, we really should ask the Bishop.' Nathan, she had decided, had too much on his hands now that two minor clerics had retired, not to be replaced. Now Nathan had to say Eucharist in three parishes each Sunday and the services of a curate were called for, to Clementina's way of thinking. 'Would you mind the Bishop, Helen? He's quite human, really.'

'Of course not! I like him.' The Bishop grew orchids almost as well as the Catchpoles grew them at Rowangarth. Their conversation over dinner would be pleasant.

'Then that's all seen to, though I shall leave it all to Amelia, when they arrive. Don't know how I shall endure five weeks of them. Flying over gives them extra days, sadly.'

An impudent granddaughter and a tongue-tied grandson, both of whom annoyed her, she frowned; always made her want to demand of the Almighty why her youngest son had a wife and two children yet Nathan wasn't even wed! And Elliot – poor, poor Elliot, had never given an heir to Pendenys.

'Sadly?' Helen demanded. 'You know you like having them — now be honest!'

'No, I don't.' This morning Clementina was in a confiding mood. 'Oh, you will understand, Helen — will know how I feel when I see Albert's son. It always reminds me that Elliot's boy was stillborn. It hurts dreadfully.'

'I'm sure it does, my dear. But Bas cannot be held responsible for that. He's growing up into a fine young Sutton, Clemmy — show him a little kindness?' Helen urged.

'Ah, well.' Clementina sighed dramatically and drained her cup. She longed for a brandy but the doctor had not only been extremely rude, but had demanded that she stop her drinking. Her drinking! As if she were a raddled old tart swilling cheap gin! No more than three small brandies a day with plenty of soda, he'd said. It hurt, sometimes, just to think of a big, fat brandy balloon and the comfort that sipping from it had always given.

And to make matters worse, Edward watched her like a wayward child. Edward thought he'd got the upper hand, but she could wait until the dinner party. Let him try counting her drinks, then!

It wasn't as if she particularly liked brandy, but she had come to need the feeling of release it gave her, the freedom from sleepless nights. Elliot had liked his brandy, and now she understood why.

'Why so sad? A penny for your thoughts,' Helen said gently.

I was thinking about Elliot,' came the trembling retort. 'A penny wouldn't buy them.'

A genuine tear ran down her cheek, though whether it was for her son or for herself, she did not know. Delicately, dramatically, she dabbed it away.

From his bedroom window Keth saw the postman pushing his cycle along the lane that led to the bothy and a sudden churning inside told him that this was the day for the letter.

He was at the back door long before the postman lifted the knocker.

There were two letters; one for his mother and –

He recognized the headmaster's writing on the envelope; big and bold and black, and a shiver sliced through him.

'Was that the post?' Polly called from the kitchen.

'Yes.' He stuffed the letter into his pocket. The apprentices were seated at the table; he couldn't open it, read it out, whilst they were there. Just in case. 'One for you, Mum, that's all.'

'And nothing from?' She had no need to say more.

'No. Maybe it'll come by the second post. Or tomorrow.'

'Aye. Well – no news is good news.' She passed him a plate of porridge. 'And don't say you aren't hungry,' she warned.

He picked up his spoon, even though he wasn't hungry. He really wasn't. Not now the letter had come. And he didn't know why his hand was shaking.

'Are you doing anything special this morning?'

'Course not.' Not now he was finished with school. 'Anything you want doing?'

'There is. Alice wrote out her shortbread recipe and I left it behind. Be a good lad, and pick it up for me.'

He said he would, then asked who was writing to her, from Creesby. He didn't really care who it was, but at least Mum's letter was the safer bet. His own, now ... He swallowed loudly, and it hurt his throat.

'Only the butcher. I forgot to pick up the meat bills – got to give them to Miss Clitherow at the month end. One boiled egg or two, lads?'

'No eggs for me; just bread and jam, thanks.' He would open the letter on the way to Keeper's Cottage. Daisy would be the first to know, which wasn't fair, really, when it ought to be Mum.

'No jam this morning. Only marmalade. And wipe that

look of gloom off your face, son. The letter'll be here by second post, I know it will!'

'Any news, Keth?' Daisy had seen him, through the kitchen window, and ran to meet him. He didn't usually come this early, so there had to be a reason. 'The letter . . . ?'

'It came.'

'Oh, my Lor'! *And*?'

'And I'm too scared to open it. Mum doesn't know I've got it.'

'Idiot! Give it to me – I'll open it for you. Tell you what – let's walk to the end of the wood, Keth? Let's tell it to the rooks.'

'If you like.' He didn't know why he should feel like this. Since ever he could remember it had been *when* he went to University, not *if*. He'd done his best, he really had, though it had all been a bit of a nightmare. Everybody in that room had said so, afterwards.

'I hope you get Leeds.' Daisy had set her heart on Leeds, which was only twenty-five miles away.

'Sweetheart, I don't care where it is. I just want to get there.'

They leaned against the fence below the elm trees because the grass was still too wet to sit on and Daisy opened the envelope. Smiling, she drew out the folded sheet of paper and passed it to him.

The paper crackled as he unfolded it, the black words seemed to squirm on the paper and were difficult to read. He had to blink them into focus.

'*Daisy!*'

He made himself read on; something about getting in touch with the school – with luck, another chance next year.

'Let me see!' She snatched the letter from his hand, reading it with ever widening eyes. 'I don't believe it. You've got someone else's letter! No University places for Creesby this year? But they always get one; some years it's *two*. Keth, you've got to get on to the school this minute. The Head is bound to be there, this morning. Let's go and ring him up?'

'No. I've failed.' His stomach hurt as if someone had aimed a terrible blow at it. He wanted to be sick. He wanted to be dead. 'Stay on at school another year and have Mum taking on more work because I've grown out of my shoes again? Oh, no! And I couldn't do any better, even if they let me sit it again. I'm just not good enough!'

'Keth – *listen*! You don't have to sit it again. There's my money. You can have that!'

'The hell I can! Oh, I didn't mean it like that, you know I didn't. I'm sorry. But they wouldn't let you have any of your money for me – even if I was willing to take it, and I'm not. I've lived off Mum for long enough – I'll not sponge off you, as well!'

'Then what are we to do? I just can't take it in. We were so sure. What will you do, Keth?'

'Try to get a job, I suppose. Line up at the Labour Exchange, cap in hand with the rest of them. And there won't be any dole for me, you realize that, don't you? Oh . . . *God*!'

He began an anxious pacing, staring at the ground, kicking at the grass. Above them the rooks cawed and the sun rose higher in the sky, making dapples through the leaves. Across the cow pasture a dog barked.

People were living their lives as if nothing had happened, he thought. The world hadn't stopped spinning, just because Keth Purvis had made a mess of everything. And why should it? He wasn't all that important; the son of a lame dog boy and a mother who had to work and take in washing, as well. People like him didn't get favours from life. He should have known it.

A bomber flew over them and the noise of it beat inside his head.

'I suppose I could join the Air Force. Surely I'm not all that dim?'

'No, Keth. No, no, *no*! You're not joining *anything*. And will you stand still, and look at me! It's a shock, I'll grant you that, but we'll get used to it. Something will turn up.'

'It's worse than a shock, Daisy.' He was shaking so much he had to force the words out because now the shock had turned to anger; anger against himself and his stupidity in thinking that he, Keth Purvis, could get a place at University. 'It's the end of everything, because nothing will turn up!'

'Don't say that?' The tears she had been fighting ran unchecked, now, down her cheeks. 'I'm still your girl, aren't I?'

'Are you? You're sure you still want to be? Take a good look! A failure, that's me! Don't you see – it's over, for us. I didn't care about your money too much because I thought that one day I'd end up good.

'But things have changed. Oh, it's all right now, because people don't know about that ten thousand pounds, but wait 'til they do! They're going to think I married you for your money!'

'I don't care what they think! It's none of *their* business!' Angrily she dashed away her tears because all at once she *was* angry. Keth was acting like a fool, hurling her love in her face and all because of his stupid pride. 'And if it hurts you so much, then I'll give the money back to Windrush and the miners. I'll give it to a dogs' home if it'll make you feel better about it!

'But don't say it's over; don't shut me out of your life? I couldn't bear it. You and me have been together since I can remember – it just isn't possible to send me away. And what's more, I won't let you!' She stood there, eyes blazing blue, her fingers clenched into fists as if any moment she would pummel him with them. 'Did you hear what I said, Keth Purvis! Did you?'

'Oh, Daisy love.' For the first time that morning he felt a relaxing of the tension inside him and his body went limp because he could no longer fight. 'I'm sorry. Forgive me?'

'What am I to forgive you for, will you tell me?' Gently she took his hand, lingering her lips over it, leaving a kiss in the upturned palm.

'For failing the exam. For letting you down and letting Mum down and being so big-headed as to think I was just that bit better than the others, that bit brainier.'

'But you *are* better and brainier, and please, Keth don't stop loving me? It'll be all right, I promise you. And you are *not* a failure. You'll get to University, I know it.'

'I won't, but what the heck?' He pushed the letter into his pocket, then reached for her hand, tucking her arm in his, standing close because he needed the comfort of her nearness. 'Come with me to tell Mum? Be with me when I thank her for all she's done for me. I don't know what I'll do if she breaks down. Help me?'

'I'll come,' she said softly. 'And Keth – promise you'll never ever again say it's over between us, because I couldn't bear to lose you.'

'I won't, because I couldn't let you go. Just give me time, will you, to think things out – get used to it.'

'All the time you want, Keth.'

For the rest of her life, if that was how long it took.

'Now tell me,' Helen asked, 'how was the flight over? That's twice you've done it – weren't you the least bit afraid, Amelia?'

'A few butterflies, taking off and landing, but between you and me there is nothing to beat a sea voyage. We have passages home booked on the *Queen Mary*. I'm determined to be pampered all the way across. I'm told that the *Queen* is the absolute end in luxury. Oh, but this is so nice,' she beamed, her smile taking in her mother-in-law and Julia.

'I'm coming to think of the North Riding as my second home. Such peace, here . . .'

'*Peace*?' Clementina winced as a plane hurtled low over Pendenys. 'One day, those irresponsible fools will take the tower with them!'

'What on earth was it?' Amelia gasped.

'They do come in a bit low,' Julia grinned, 'the lads from the aerodrome, I mean. It's got its bombers since last you were here, Amelia, and is officially known as RAF Holdenby Moor. Drew is fascinated by it all. That noisy monster, according to him, was a Hampden bomber, I believe that another RAF station is being built about ten miles away, quite near York.'

'But why do they want all these aerodromes?' Helen fretted. 'And what do those bombers intend to drop their bombs on?'

'I suppose that if Germany can build bombers,' Amelia said, 'then so can we – I mean *you*. Better safe, than sorry.'

'Perhaps if we'd had a little more to throw at the Kaiser in 1914, he'd have thought twice about starting that war,' Julia said soberly.

'Oh, but I remember the old Flying Corps,' Clemmy gushed. 'Such glamorous young men, they were. So brave and dashing. And that Red Baron – did you ever see anyone so handsome?'

'He, Aunt, was a German who shot down our planes!' Julia glared. He could well have been responsible for the death of Ruth Love's husband!

'Really? I often wondered why Elliot didn't go in for flying, in the war,' Clemmy mused.

'You can't fly a desk, Aunt Clemmy!'

'What was that? What did you say?'

'I said that the Flying Corps lads got killed. A lot of them. I know!'

'Clementina – is it possible for me to have another of these little biscuits?' Helen hastily interrupted, flinging a

494

warning glance in her daughter's direction. 'And Amelia – do tell us all the news from America? What have your newspapers been printing that we don't know about?'

'The Prince of Wales, you mean? Well, it seems your prince – sorry! I mean your *king* . . .' How could she have forgotten the death of old King George? With his wife and children at his bedside, it had been, on the very day they left Southampton for New York, in January. So beautiful, so regal, the way Queen Mary had at once kissed the hand of her eldest son in a gesture of homage. It had brought quite a lump to her throat, just to hear of it. '. . . seems *your* king is all set to marry *our* Bessie Wallis – leastways, that's what the *New York Mirror* thinks. King to marry Wally, the headlines said. And, would you believe –' dramatically she lowered her voice 'it said that Ernest Simpson – you know, *her* husband – has spent the night in a hotel at Bray with a Mrs Simpson *who was not his wife*. Must be true. They even got the room number. Four, it was. A put-up job that divorce is going to be! Simpson is giving her grounds, I believe, but why does she want free of him if it isn't to marry your king? Our papers seem to think the wedding will be next June.'

'Oh, dear.' Helen had heard rumours of the so-called divorce, but had loyally ignored them. 'So it's true, then?'

'Seems it is. That woman's got her claws in. She wants to be queen!'

'Marry the King in June?' Julia frowned. 'That's a month after the Coronation.' Their new king was being crowned in May.

'I don't believe a word of it.' Clementina, though eager to hear the views of the American Press, resented her son's wife telling her what clearly everyone in England ought to know – and didn't. 'Now, I think I shall ring for a fresh pot of tea, and then we will discuss the dinner party.

'Amelia has kindly agreed to organize it for me, haven't you dear, and I have come up with the idea that it should have a typically American flavour to it, in honour of my American daughter and her American children.'

'Your grandchildren from America are half English, mother-in-law,' Amelia corrected. 'And where are they, by the way, and where on earth has Bertie got to? He promised faithfully to have tea with us!'

'Your husband was last seen,' Julia gleefully supplied, 'heading in the direction of Rowangarth with Bas, Kitty and Tatiana. There'll be a meeting of the Clan, I shouldn't wonder. I saw Albert just as we arrived. He was dropping the children off then going to the village to see Nathan, he told me.'

Solemnly she winked in the direction of her cousin's wife, and Amelia, lips twitching, winked solemnly back.

'The *Clan*?' Clementina frowned. 'Tell me, pray – have I met them . . . ?'

31

He had hated telling Drew and Bas. For the first few days after the letter came, Keth lived through a nightmare, believing he would find it was all a terrible mistake and he was waiting for the second letter that would put it right. But no letter came, so he told them, forcing the words out as if each one were stuck in his throat and hurt, just to say it.

'So that's it. I made a mess of things,' he finished, tight-lipped. 'My own fault. Can't put the blame on anything but my own stupidity.'

No use saying the exam was getting harder; no use pretending, now it was over, that the invigilator who sat unblinking behind pebble-thick spectacles had put the fear of the devil into him nor that the fly that buzzed incessantly nor the wall clock's too-loud ticking had distracted him.

The fault was his alone. He had given too much attention to the English paper. He should have left it until the end instead of attacking it head on. Precious time wasted on it and the other papers – the important ones – suffered.

'It's rotten luck,' Drew sympathized. 'I'm not going to University. My father wanted to, but didn't; I can go if I want, grandmother says, but I'd rather look after Rowan-garth. I don't think a degree is all that important – well, not for me.'

'Maybe not, but for Keth it is,' Bas defended. 'It's all right for you and me, Drew. If we aren't all that bright – and I guess neither of us is – we can be paid for through college. Keth can't, which is pretty rotten, because he's got more brains than you and me both!'

'They talk about putting back the clock,' Keth said bitterly. 'I'd give a lot to be able to do differently. Getting a degree was all I ever wanted; now I'll be lucky even to get a job. Everyone who sat it said it was harder than they thought, but I should still have passed. Mum did without a lot to keep me in school and look at the way I repaid her.'

'Was your Mom mad at you?' Bas shifted uneasily.

'No. It was as if – well, if she'd been a candle it'd have b ˑ n as if I'd blown her out. At first she didn't say anything – stunned, sort of – then she smiled and said it wasn't the end of the world.'

'And it isn't, Keth . . .'

'It's the end of *my* world. I used to think one day I'd be Mister Keth Purvis and have a car and a decent house, but that's – that's –'

'That's the way the cookie crumbles, old chum,' Bas said, eyes on his shoes, feeling guilty because to read veterinary science was all he'd ever wanted – and helping run the Stud, back home. 'Sure wish there was something I could do to help.'

'Thanks for the thought, but there isn't. There'll be a couple of weeks' work for me at Home Farm, then I'll join the unemployed. It's Mum I'm sorry for. I told Daisy. She was upset for me, but things are different for her. Daisy has –' He stopped, remembering they didn't know about the money. 'I mean, Daisy only wants to have her own home and children in it. It's different, for girls.'

'Wonder who Daisy will marry – one day, that is. She sure is pretty,' Bas said.

'She's very pretty. Most of the boys at school think so, too.' Drew was very proud of his sister. 'Daiz could marry anyone she wanted.'

'Don't be stupid! Daisy'll have to stay in school for

another year, yet,' Keth glared, all at once remembering how much things could change in just a few days. 'She's still a kid!'

Even as he said it, Keth knew he was degrading something precious and wonderful. Kid, he'd called her, yet he loved her till it hurt.

'I think Daisy likes you, Keth, better'n anyone – better than me, even.' Drew pointed in the direction of the wild garden and the stile the three girls were climbing. 'They're coming and they've got Tatty with them. I didn't think Aunt Anna would've let her come out today. She's in disgrace, mother said.'

'Good old Tatty. She's improving. What did she do?' Bas grinned.

'Swearing. She can swear in Russian, you see, and she often does. But she forgot that Aunt Anna was there to hear her and she got early-to-bed for a week. Suppose it was Kitty who persuaded Aunt Anna to let Tatty out. She's ever so good at saying the right things, isn't she?'

'She is, so.' Bas was well acquainted with his sister's ways. 'Kitty's an actress. She's always doing it. She can weep her way out of trouble like no one I've ever known. Pa falls for it all the time, though she doesn't fool Mom. Still, it must've worked.' He waved a welcoming hand. 'Hurry up, you lot, or it'll be too late to do anything before teatime.'

Bas was all at once glad for the strange English custom of afternoon tea and that they always seemed to eat it – or did you *take* it? – at Aunt Julia's place. Plates of sandwiches, cherry scones and chocolate cake. And lemonade like only Rowangarth cook could make it.

'Hi Keth, Drew.' Kitty was always first; could outrun any of the Clan. 'Say, Keth – I sure am sorry about your exam. Daisy told me. Bloody awful luck, that was.'

'Watch your tongue, Sis!' Bas warned. He slid his eyes in Tatiana's direction. 'Or at least learn to swear in Russian!'

'I'll say what I like!' Kitty stuck her nose in the air. 'The stable boys back home say bloody all the time!'

'Okay. But don't say I didn't warn you! Now – where are we going?'

England wasn't half bad, Bas was forced to admit and it was good to be with the Clan. If only Pendenys could vanish in a puff of smoke, England would be a real nice place.

He was sorry for Keth, though. Real sorry. It made him wonder what it was like to be poor like Keth was and he felt suddenly guilty, because he knew he would never know.

'They were all right about it when you told them, weren't they?' Daisy leaned her bicycle against the fence, waiting as Keth delivered the last of the evening papers. 'They all felt sorry for you.'

'I suppose they did, but it's all right for them. They don't have to prove themselves – it's known as having money. Oh, let's get off home!'

'But you don't have to prove yourself.' Stubbornly, Daisy stood her ground. 'Not to me, you don't.'

'But I *do*. I thought if I got a degree I could get rich. Mr Hillier got rich.'

'He didn't go to University, though. Mr Hillier started with a stall in the Saturday market. Dada told me so.'

'All right, then. But I wanted to give you things, and now I can't.'

'Then I'll settle for a daisychain, Keth – and you. Did you know that Dada gives buttercups to Mam? I think buttercups must be special between them, 'cos he always brings home the first ones he finds. Mam puts them in a glass on the windowsill and she goes all pink. I've seen her.'

'Any fool can give you a daisychain. I'm really mad with that exam, and I'm madder with myself!'

'With me, too? With the world? And I don't want *any fool*, I want you.' The bitterness in him shocked her. 'Don't talk any more about University? Like your Mum said, it isn't the end of the world. Don't spoil things between us?'

'I'm trying, honest I am. And I know I'll have to go to the Labour Exchange, soon. But they'll be starting haymaking next week at Home Farm. The grass looks just about ready for cutting. I'll think about a job, when the hay is all stacked – but not until then.'

To stand in a queue outside the doors of that gaunt, no-hope building would be to finally say goodbye to University.

'Keth – I *do* understand.' She glanced around her then took a step nearer so they stood close. She wanted him to kiss her, to hold her so she could show him how much she loved him. But most of all she wanted him to come back to her because since the letter came, a frightening barrier had grown between them, and it made her afraid.

'Let's go home?' he shrugged, oblivious to the pleading in her eyes, pedalling off, leaving her standing there.

'Keth – *please*?' she called after him, but he did not wait for her, nor turn at her call.

Ten at dinner, Amelia said, was neither too big nor too small. She walked round the table, checking it yet again, briefly envying Pendenys' Georgian silver and exquisite antique glasses and cutlery, trying to imagine what they must have cost Bertie's grandfather to buy, for nothing but the rarest and best had been used in the furbishing of the house he built for his daughter.

Amelia smiled briefly. She had tentatively suggested an American menu to Cook who had at once declared that most of the ingredients she had never heard of, much less be able to buy in Creesby, and anything, anything at all save English cooking was likely to bring on an attack of her unmentionables and then where would they be?

Amelia had not pressed the matter. Pendenys staff was not what it had once been. Staff knew that nowadays the mistress of Pendenys Place cared little for what went on beyond the door of the tower staircase, and since the butler's departure, discipline had deteriorated still further.

'Very well, Cook.' Amelia conceded defeat, though all the time wishing she could stay longer and lick the place into shape again. 'A simple meal it shall be. And in Mullins' absence, I shall choose the wines.'

Pendenys, she brooded, shifting a salt cellar half an inch to the right. Such a strange house. Albert's father was clearly ill at ease here; Albert and Bas disliked it and Nathan was happy to be in his vicarage.

Would this echoing place really come to her son, one day, and if it did, what on earth would he do with it? Give it to Kitty, perhaps?

Taking into account that Pendenys' cook had almost forgotten what a dinner party was like, the meal had been without fault. Amelia relaxed visibly as cold cucumber soup was followed by a haddock soufflé that was nothing short of amazing, for it had reached its point of perfection at exactly the right time.

Ribs of beef were followed by summer pudding, served with individual silver dishes of thickly-whipped cream, and after that – and only the gentlemen had been able to partake of them – came savouries, the recipe for which was known only to Cook herself and jealously guarded, though the Bishop, happy in Helen's company, detected the faintest hint of Stilton therein.

The evening was warm. The scent of a summer night drifted in through open windows. The footmen who served were efficient and unobtrusive. Amelia should have been pleased with the success of her efforts; could have been, had not her mother-in-law, oozing charm at the start of the evening, been quickly and obviously becoming more and more relaxed as each course progressed. Vainly Amelia tried to catch the eye of the footman so she might offer the smallest of frowns in the direction of the decanters, but Clementina sat at the foot of the table and she, Amelia, sat on Edward's right at its head.

It was a little worrying. Clementina, she knew, had had her brandy severely rationed and was the better for it, but tonight, when all others drank sparingly of the wines, the mistress of Pendenys took glass after glass with no one able to prevent her. And there really was, all things considered, nothing she could do about it save hope that when port and cigars came to the table and the ladies withdrew, Clementina would be able to leave the room without mishap.

As soon as the last plate was cleared, Amelia rose to her feet, smiling round the table, indicating that coffee would be served to the ladies in the drawing room. Her eyes did not leave her mother-in-law and the footman who pulled back her chair.

Carefully, as if troubled by an aching back, Clementina rose to her feet, lifting her head, straightening her shoulders, steadying herself, hand on table. Then, as she passed the sideboard she reached for the brandy decanter with splendid aplomb, carrying it like a trophy to the room next door, placing it on the table to the right of her chair.

Coffee awaited the ladies on a silver tray; a parlourmaid stood beside it to hand out cups; a second maid carried a cream jug and sugar bowl.

'Be kind enough to pour, Amelia.' Clementina's words were slurred though her smile was gracious; the sly smile of a cat who had lapped deeply at forbidden cream and intended taking more. Tonight, after a month of near abstinence, Clementina intended to drink her fill and it were better she should not do it here. Draining her coffee cup she rose to her feet, hand on the mantelshelf.

'I am tired, my dears. If you will excuse me I think I will

go to bed before my headache comes on. Amelia, will you take care of our guests?' She grasped the decanter, then walked carefully towards the door.

You had, Amelia grudgingly conceded, to admire her nerve, and since she was in her own house and would remind them, should any one of them dare to protest, that it was her own brandy and she could drink the lot if she felt so inclined, they watched without speaking as she left the room.

'Well,' Julia gasped as the door slammed, 'the leopard doesn't change its —'

She was silenced by a glance from her mother, who smiled in the direction of the wide-eyed maids, saying, 'Thank you, both. We can manage nicely. You may go, now.'

'Oh dear, I had so hoped . . .' Amelia whispered, clearly distressed.

'That mother-in-law had mended her ways?' Anna demanded tartly. 'I fear not. She depends too much on the drinking. Since Elliot died, it is worse and worse. But you all know that. I only hope such things will not be inherited by Tatiana.'

'Don't worry. Aunt Clemmy will sleep it off and be her usual self in the morning,' Julia grinned. 'And didn't she carry it off well? The way she sneaked the decanter was —'

'Please, Julia!' There was an unfamiliar edge to Helen's voice that silenced her daughter at once. 'I think that tomorrow I must have a word with Edward. Unless Clemmy gets help, she will make herself ill. The young doctor seems very efficient; perhaps he and Edward can urge Clemmy to seek a cure before it is too late. Now please — not another word,' she whispered as sounds from the dining room indicated that the men were about to join them. 'Clemmy pleaded indisposition — a headache, don't forget!'

Had the Bishop not been here, Helen fretted, they could

have discussed the matter with Doctor Pryce, here and now, as a family. But it must wait until tomorrow. She lifted her chin and smiled, as the door opened.

'You should have seen the old cat,' said the head parlourmaid when they were seated in the servants' sitting room and eager and willing to give a detailed and dramatic account of the mistress's latest fall from grace. 'Downing wine at table as if tomorrow was the start of prohibition, then crafty as you please she lifts the brandy and takes it with her to the drawing room.

'They say drinkers are like that – sly, I mean. She knew nobody'd say a word in front of His Grace. Poor Mrs Amelia didn't know where to look, she was that embarrassed. I used to wonder where Mr Elliot got his drinking habits from, and now I know.'

'And then what happened?' Pendenys cook demanded testily. She could have done without an upset above stairs to take away her glory after all the effort she had put into the dinner party.

'Don't ask me, Cook. All I can say is thank goodness I don't have to answer upstairs bells for she'll be as drunk as a lord afore so very much longer. I wouldn't go into her bedroom if there was a five-pound note at the end of it and that's a fact!'

'Then you'll not need to. I know where she is,' a housemaid supplied. 'Never saw me, she didn't. Slunk across the hall and up those tower stairs with her bottle. She'll be in her sulking room now, and there she'll stay, 'til morning if you want my opinion. A drunk she may be but stupid she ain't. She's never been known to risk coming down them twisting stairs when she's had a few. Don't worry. She'll not be bothering us tonight.'

And in the end, they all knew it would be left to the master to make sure she was all right; to wait until she was asleep before returning the decanter to the dining room. Or maybe Lady Helen would have a word with her, beg her not to over indulge. Her ladyship had a soothing way with the mistress. Happen she would be able to do something?

But they all knew one thing was certain. In the morning there'd be no living with Mrs Clementina who, once her headache had worn off, would rant and rage like a fishwife.

But then, fishwife she was – or almost so. Breeding would out. It always did.

'Good morning, mother.' Nathan peered round the door. All was in darkness and he crossed the room carefully to draw back the curtains and open a window. 'How are you?'

'Close that damn door!' Clementina hissed from the chair, angry that her son should find her still wearing last night's clothes. 'And I'm all right, since you ask, though two calls in two days is a bit unusual!'

'I came to see father. I couldn't leave without seeing you, now could I?'

'I suppose not. And what did you talk about? Me, was it?'

'No,' Nathan said softly, though they had discussed his mother at great length. 'I wanted to ask father if there is an empty cottage, at Pendenys. I have need of one for a parishioner – that's all.'

'Then you should've asked me. This is my house, Nathan, and estate cottages are mine to grant, not your father's. And if you had a ha'porth of sense you'd have got yourself married years ago and had a son or two!'

'Mother – what has my marrying got to do with a cottage?'

'You may well ask! Has it never occurred to you that Pendenys will come to you one day, yet here you are, gone fifty, and still unwed. You'll have folk thinking you're a nancy boy.'

'I'm forty-eight next birthday, mother.'

'Albert's younger'n you and he's got two children. That Sebastian of his will get this place one day – had you realized that?'

'No, but I can't say I've given it all that much thought.'

'Then you should!' The light was hurting her eyes and her mouth felt as if it were stuffed with cotton-wool. She reached for a cigarette, then flicked the lighter. 'Damn!' She threw it down as it sparked, but refused to light.

Nathan dipped into his pocket for a match. He did not smoke, but always carried matches and a packet of cigarettes. It was a throwback to his army days, he supposed, and the many cigarettes he had lit and placed between the lips of wounded men. Now, he offered them to men tramping the roads.

'Thanks.' She inhaled deeply, then lay back in the chair, her head thumping. 'Did you never want to marry?' She asked it so suddenly that he was caught off guard.

'Marry? I – I suppose I would – if the right woman came along. The war, you know. It unsettled many of us.'

'That war has been over almost twenty years. There'll be another one before so very much longer. Don't you ever lift your nose out of your Bible, lad, and read what the papers say?'

'Spain, you mean? The fighting there?'

'Spain wasn't what I meant. I'm talking about Hitler and all the tanks and soldiers and planes they've got in Germany. And this government can't see beyond the end of its nose!'

A bomber flew low over the house and she flinched at its noise.

'And those noisy things! I swear they take Pendenys as a bearing when they're coming in to land! Why couldn't they build their aerodrome somewhere else?'

'If as you say, Germany has too many planes, then perhaps you should be glad we have a few of our own,' Nathan countered mildly. 'But I must go.'

'Yes, of course. Your flock.' She offered a cheek for his kiss. 'And before you leave, tell Mullins I want a tray of coffee and get someone to run me a bath.'

'I'll do that.' He raised a hand in goodbye, but she had already turned her back. 'Goodbye, mother. God bless . . .'

He wished last night's lapse had not happened. What Albert had said this morning made sense. They must somehow get her into a nursing home; wean her from her dependence on brandy.

But she was full of guile. Cures came only to those who wanted to be cured, and his mother did not wish to be. She drank, he was sure, to escape a world without love, for she had loved no one but her father, and Elliot.

Sadly, quietly, he closed the door. Carefully he negotiated the curving stone staircase. Mullins was gone, of course, but he had not contradicted his mother. Her memory was never good after a bout of drinking.

He closed the staircase door behind him, then crossed the hall to the table on which he had left his hat and gloves. His footsteps echoed loudly and it made him remember his childhood when he had stood in the exact centre of the tessellated floor and called his name loudly. And his name had echoed above and all around him, as if he were shouting in a church, except that the great hall at Pendenys was loftier than All Souls, in the village. And it wasn't right, he'd thought all those years ago, to shout in church.

Now that church had become his and Pendenys Place was a mockery of a house, without a scrap of happiness in it. And one day, as he had just been reminded, it would pass to him. It made him wonder about the entail, and if it would be possible to get rid of it.

'Good morning,' he smiled to a passing housemaid. 'I wonder if you could tell the kitchen that Mrs Sutton would like some coffee – she's in the tower room. And would someone be so kind as to run her a bath, afterwards?'

'Yes, sir.' The girl returned the smile because she liked

the reverend. Decent, like his father. And he didn't need to tell her where *she* was. The whole house knew it and about what happened last night, too. 'Mornin', sir.' She bobbed a curtsey as he left because she was sorry for him. Sad that he didn't have a wife, especially as there were plenty in the parish would be more than glad of the chance to live in that vicarage.

Ah, well, she thought. It took all sorts to make a world – including madam in the tower!

'Good morning, mother.' Albert Sutton's smile was stiff with apprehension.

'Morning? It's nearly noon! What kept you? Your brother was here hours ago. Waiting for me to sober up, were you?'

'No, I was *not*. I was told you were in your bath and –'

'Well, you've been, now, so close the door behind you when you go. Anyway, it isn't you I want to see, it's Sebastian, so tell him to come up. I'd like to talk to him.'

'Talk?' His mother could still make him uneasy; still had a tongue as sharp as a razor. Albert's nose twitched. She had been drinking again. They should have searched for the decanter when she was in the bathroom. But his mother was cunning, had probably taken it with her. It wasn't going to be easy to persuade her to get treatment, yet stop her drinking she must, even if they had to get two doctors to certify her!

Yet could they do that? Maybe only if she were insane could she be forced to go. And his mother was far from insane.

'Well, off you go! Don't stand there staring out of the window!'

He left without further comment. His mother was nobody's fool. Tipsy or sober, she never lost her shrewdness. It came from her father; from Grandfather Elliot whom he could scarcely remember, and so astute was his mother that she had more than doubled the fortune he'd left her, in spite of her extravagant spending.

But what immediately concerned him — concerned them all — was to have her properly looked after and, if possible, cured of her need to drink. And the sooner it happened, the better for them all!

'Where is Bas?' Daisy asked of Kitty when she joined them in Rowangarth conservatory.

'He'll be along.' Kitty sat down beside Drew and Daisy. 'Where's Keth?'

'Chopping wood for his mother, this afternoon. And he's mending a puncture for Bas. He can't always be with us, I suppose. Not now. You'll have to put up with me and Daiz till Tatty arrives. Aunt Anna is coming to tea. There's a lot of talking going on — I think it's about the dinner party, last night,' Drew said guardedly.

'Dinner party my foot! It's about Grandma Sutton, because she did it at the dinner party. And by the way, Bas has been summoned to *The Presence*,' Kitty giggled, 'so he mightn't get here.'

'What has Bas done?'

'Nothing, as far as I know. Grandma just wants to talk to him. But don't you want to hear about last night, and what they're all talking about?'

'You know we do!' Daisy loved Kitty's performances. She always made them laugh and Daisy needed to laugh. Keth was so moody, so angry with the world. She could imagine him wielding the axe with great heavy blows and the logs splintering and scattering at the force of it. 'Have you been listening again?'

'No. I just happened to be sitting beneath the morning-room window which just happened to be open. Pa was there, and Uncle Nathan and grandfather. They were talking about grandma going into hospital because of the brandy.

'Last night, at the dinner party, she had too much to drink and made a fool of herself, though Pa said rather she'd made a fool of *them* in front of the Bishop and the doctor.

'I think they're going to have to lock up all the bottles, or she'll do herself a mischief – at least that's what Pa said. I think he thinks grandmother is a bad example to us and he's afraid that one day Bas and me will start drinking, too – inherited, sort of.'

'Does drinking run in families?' Daisy frowned.

'I don't know. I believe Aunt Anna thinks it does. I expect she'll talk about it when she comes here for tea. She was there, last night, so she must've seen it all. Wish I'd known grandma was going to make a scene. I'd have stayed awake and –'

'And hidden in the sideboard cupboard?' Drew teased.

'Say – that's not a bad idea! Just might try it, one night. Y'know, you'd be surprised the things grown-ups say when they think there aren't any little ears around. It beats listening to the wireless, any day.'

'And aren't you ashamed of listening?' Daisy asked.

'No.' Kitty's blue eyes opened wide. 'And anyway, I always tell you guys, now don't I? Does your grandma drink, Drew?'

'I'm afraid she does.' His cheeks flushed red. 'I haven't seen her, mind, but she does say that a glass of sherry helps her to sleep. I don't think she ever makes a fool of herself, though.'

'Of course she doesn't! By drinking I don't mean the odd glass of sherry – Mom likes one, too. I'm talking about the way Grandma Sutton does it – all the time, I mean. Tippling, the servants call it. I heard Mom say that if the servants are talking about it, then all Holdenby will know, too. It's exciting, isn't it – being notorious . . .'

'I don't know about that. Would you like to be notorious, Daiz?' Drew wasn't at all sure he would like it if Cook and Tilda and Mary sniggered about grandmother's glass of sherry.

'Don't know, really. What I do know is that I can't stop thinking about Keth. I didn't really want him to go away to University, but now that he can't go, I wouldn't care how far away he went. I think it was rotten of them, not giving him a pass.'

'Mm. I don't want to go to University – leastways not unless I can study speech and drama. I want to be an actress, you know, though I wouldn't mind being a crooner with one of the big dance bands. I told Pa and he went berserk. "You'll stay at home, Kathryn Sutton," he said, "and learn from your mother how to run a house!" That's because he thinks that all girls are fit for is getting married and having babies.

'I started to weep. It usually works, but that time it didn't, so I went and asked Mom and she said I was to leave Pa to her and that if I still wanted to act when I'd finished High School, then she'd be on my side. Mom's an absolute love. And here's Tatty.' Kitty nodded in the direction of the car pulling up at the front door. 'Go and tell her we're here, Drew.'

'You're very bossy with him, aren't you?' Daisy challenged as Drew ran across the lawn.

'Am I?'

'Yes, you are. And don't open your eyes all wide and innocent, Kitty Sutton. Drew's my brother and I don't like you giving him orders!'

'Sorry. I don't mean to be bossy with him. It's just the way I am. When I get uppity with Bas he just pulls my hair and neither of us thinks any more about it. But I'll try to be kinder to Drew.'

'You'd better, an' all, because Drew really likes you, I know he does.'

'Does he so?' Kitty let go a giggle of excitement. 'Like Keth likes you, you mean?'

'Ssssh!' Red-cheeked, Daisy tossed her head. 'They're coming back. Do you like Tatty, by the way?'

'Sure do, though she was a pain, once.' Tatiana had changed and much for the better. She was fourteen, now, and spoke fluent Russian which wasn't half bad, Kitty was forced to admit. 'Hi, Tatty. What's news?'

'News is,' Tatty threw herself into a basket chair with such gusto that it creaked and cracked all over, 'that the families are talking. About *things*.'

'No. Not about *things*. It'll be about Grandma Sutton. She had too much to drink, last night.' The subject had begun to bore Kitty.

'Oh. Is that all?'

'It's enough when you consider that Bas is with her now in that room of hers. Said she wanted to see him. I wanted to go, too, but Mom said I wasn't to,' Kitty shrugged, 'because I provoke her.'

'Poor Bas,' Tatiana sighed. 'Well, since he's not here, nor Keth, there'll be more for each of us.' She pulled out a bar of chocolate, handing it to Kitty. 'Share it out. It's a half-pound bar and we've got to eat it before I go home because Mama doesn't know I've got it. Karl gave it to me.'

Carefully Kitty snapped the bar into four. She really envied Tatty having someone like Karl.

'Where shall we go?' Daisy demanded of Drew.

'To the garden – to the hot house. Catchpole is picking peaches. There are quite a few ripe and he likes to pick them with the sun on them. Cook wants them to preserve in brandy, for special. He'll give us some, if I ask him.'

'Peaches and chocolate. We'll be sick.'

'Who cares?' Tatiana grinned. She was really happy when the Clan was together. It was too bad that Mama said they were to visit Grandmother Petrovska, next week. It was awful, at Cheyne Walk. Perhaps, if she made herself really sick, Mama would leave her behind, at Denniston House.

She thought about Bas. Poor Bas – having to spend this lovely afternoon with Grandmother Sutton. She wondered what they were talking about, then sent her love winging to him – just for luck.

'Hey! Wait for me!' she yelled.

32

'Do I have to go, Mom?' Grandma Sutton unnerved him, made him feel all tongue-tied and awkward. 'She glares so.'

'She has asked especially that you visit her, Bas. You are her only grandson, and important to her. She won't keep you long. She usually has a little doze after her lunch.'

'Okay — if I must, though I don't see why she didn't want Kitty to go, too.'

'Bas, dear,' Amelia smiled indulgently. 'Kitty is far too precocious for grandma's liking. Your sister isn't afraid of her and neither must you be. Remember she is an elderly lady, and try to be kind to her.'

'How old, Mom?'

'It isn't polite to ask a lady's age, Bas. I don't even know myself, though I guess she's about seventy.'

'Aunt Helen is older than that and she's twice as pretty!'

'Then don't let grandma hear you say that!' She gave a smiling twitch to the tie she had insisted her son should wear. 'Just be polite and ask her if there is anything she wants — any errands running.'

'All right. But I hope she doesn't keep me long. I told Keth I'd be over to the bothy to collect my bike.'

'She won't. Now off you go, and don't be afraid of her.'

She watched him go, loving him dearly. She was so contented with her lot; she who had everything she had ever dreamed of and could ask for no more. Soon, Bas would be eighteen; another year and he'd be leaving home for University, though which one they hadn't yet decided.

She stopped her dreaming as she heard the closing of the staircase door and the clicking of the latch. She wished Albert's mother had eaten more, at lunchtime. She had seen the tray being carried away, the food on it hardly touched, which meant only one thing.

She wondered if she should wait a few minutes, then go to the tower room. Not that she was fighting her son's battles, but because Bertie's mother could be sharp-tongued when the mood was on her and Bas did not have his sister's self-confidence.

Resolutely she turned on her heel, reminding herself that her son was no longer a child and that she had promised Helen she would go to Rowangarth for tea.

She liked Rowangarth – no, *loved* it; loved the oldness of it and the kindliness and the sense of permanence about it. It made her wonder if houses affected people and whether, if her mother-in-law had lived there, perhaps Rowangarth would have made her a nicer person. A little more like Helen, perhaps?

She shrugged, then went to collect her hat and gloves and tell Bertie she was going to Rowangarth. And to suggest that he keep an eye on the tower room . . .

'Come in then, boy! Don't stand there gawping. Your father gawped, did you know?'

'I'm not sure what gawp means, grandma.' He *wouldn't* be afraid of her!

'You don't? Well, in Yorkshire, people who gawp are usually gormless, but then you won't know what gormless is, either!'

'It isn't a word we use back home.'

'Oh, for pity's sake sit yourself down. And close that window! I don't know who keeps opening it. Now, tell me what you want?'

'But I thought it was you wanted to see *me*.'

'Well, if I did I've changed my mind.' She felt very sleepy.

She had emptied the coffee pot on her tray but it had done nothing to keep her alert.

'Is there anything I can do for you?' Hope surged high. She wasn't going to keep him. 'Any errands I can run?' he added, remembering his mother's words.

'Do? Yes, you can put more coal on the fire, then you can fill this for me.' She reached for the slim gold lighter that once was Elliot's. Elliot always lit a cigarette so elegantly. Elliot had done everything perfectly, had even given her a grandson, though Anna had killed it.

'It needs fuel, I think. Do you have some, grandma?'

'I *know* it needs fuel. There's a bottle in the cupboard.'

'Can't find it,' Bas called.

'Then try the drawer! What a fuss over so small a task.'

'It's okay. It's here.' He spied the bottle on the mantelpiece, which was a pretty stupid place for it to be. 'I'll see to the fire, then if you like I'll bring you up more coal.'

Mom was right. Grandma was old and old people got tetchy from time to time. Pity for her washed over him.

'Bring up coal! Indeed you won't! Coal-carrying is servant's work and you are not a servant. One day you will be master of Pendenys Place – had you thought of that; had you, eh?'

'No, grandma.' He had thought of little else since Uncle Elliot died. He didn't want Pendenys.

'Then you should! You'll never get on in this world if you don't use your brain, think ahead.'

'Yes, grandma.' He dropped to his knees, poking out the ashes, adding more coal. His face burned from the heat. This was not a day for a fire, but perhaps the old felt the cold more.

He rose to his feet, picking up the lighter, examining it. 'This screw at the bottom needs to come off, first. Have you a small coin I could use?'

'Of course I haven't. For goodness sake what a fuss you're making!'

Bas fished into his pocket, laying the strange coins on his hand. Half-crowns, florins; a silver threepenny piece would have done just fine, if he'd had one.

'I'll try to unscrew it with my thumbnail . . .'

'Oh, give it to me. I'll do it myself!' So ungainly the boy was; so coltish! All at once she didn't want him even to touch something that once was Elliot's. Roughly she snatched the lighter, then reached up for the bottle. The suddenness of her movement made her dizzy and she swayed on her feet, grabbing for the mantelpiece, missing it, dropping the bottle on the hearth.

'Grandma!' Bas cried as it shattered, ignited. 'Oh, God, *no*!'

With a dull thud a wall of flame burst high and wide, licking at her skirt. She was on fire! The hearthrug was on fire!

'Grandma!' He tried to pull her away but she stood there, beating at the flames, making them worse with her frenzied flapping. 'On the floor! Get down!'

He knew what to do. Roll her in a rug! But the rug was burning. The room was burning!

Her screams filled his head and he didn't know how to stop her. He took off his coat, wrapping her in it, trying to put out the flames.

'Get out! The door, grandma!' He grasped her arm. 'Try to make it to the door!'

A screen barred their way. It was old and painted in oils. Even as he pushed it aside it burst into flames to fall, blazing furiously, across the doorway.

No way out, and grandma screaming so. Her hair was alight. He could smell the burning. His heart thudded. He tried to think but there was no way out.

He staggered coughing, retching, to the window, flinging it open, taking in gulps of air. So far to the ground. He daren't jump. He couldn't jump. Not without grandma.

She lay still, now, on the floor, eyes wide in a blackened

face, her lips moving and no sound coming. She was going to die. He was going to die.

'*Up here! Help us!*' he screamed. 'For God's sake, *help us*!' There were people down there. A gardener, who didn't even look up; someone riding a bicycle. Normal things, in a safe world yet they were trapped up here. Soon they'd be dead!

Keth pulled hard on the bicycle brakes when he saw the smoke. It billowed black from a tower window, near the top. Someone was in there! Someone waving, calling!

He threw down the cycle and made for the house, flinging open the first door he came to, running up a passage to where a maid was sweeping the floor.

'The tower! It's on fire!'

The girl let go a gasp. The young man's eyes were wild as he shook her arm roughly.

'*Tell me!* Where's the tower?'

'Up there.' She pointed along the passageway. 'Across the hall . . .' Then she ran after him, because she wasn't sure she should have told him. 'That's the tower door, but you shouldn't —'

'Fire!' Keth yelled. 'Get help! Tell someone!'

His feet slammed down hard on the stone steps. Stupid things, all twisting. Up and up until he could smell burning, see smoke coming from beneath a door.

He lifted the iron door sneck, and it was hot in his hands. He pushed hard on the door, but it wouldn't open.

'Is anyone in there?' He hammered on it with his fists. He had seen someone at the window, but how to get in?

He pushed open the next door along. The room was empty and he flung open the window. It opened inwards, thank God! He leaned out. There was a ledge beneath him, in ornamental stone, a good foot wide. Without thinking, he lowered himself onto it, steadying himself against the stonework, taking deep breaths, getting his balance.

Don't look down. Just take it easy. Not far to go. No more than ten feet.

The smoke was thicker, now, belching from the window to his left. Arms spread wide against the wall, he inched along the ledge. No more than ten feet? Ten *miles*!

Smoke, making him cough. He mustn't cough. If he did, he'd fall. Inch by inch by inch. His groping left hand felt the metal of the window frame and it was hot, like the doorknob.

He could see into the room, now. Flames shooting, roaring. Someone kneeling at the window.

'Bas! It's Keth!' Don't let him be dead? '*Bas!*'

'Keth! Grandma's in there!'

'Get out, Bas. Onto the ledge. Careful. Slowly, now.'

'My hands, Keth . . .'

'Get *out*, Bas. Hurry! Just get out, then I can help you!'

Slowly, clumsily, crying out every time his hands touched the stonework, Bas lowered his feet to the ledge.

'Good. That's good. Face the wall, now. Take it easy. Hold on.'

'Can't, Keth. My hands. All burned. Grandma's on the floor!'

'We can't go in there!' The flames were getting worse, now, shooting through the window in vicious probing tongues. The heat was acrid against the back of his throat. 'Lean in against the wall. I'll hold on to you. Just go careful and don't look down!'

God, Keth prayed, don't let him fall? If he goes, I go too. God – did you hear me . . . ?

'Can't, Keth. My hands!'

'You can! You *will*! Just along to the window. Not far.' Only ten miles. He pressed his arm against Bas's back. 'Now – when I say move, you move your right foot – the same time as I do. Just slide it along. Okay – *move*. That's it. And again! Gently. Don't look down. And again . . .'

Someone was there. From the corner of his eye, someone

was leaning from the window to their right. Hands. Helping hands.

'It's all right, Bas. We're nearly there. Slowly, now.' His mouth was dry, his heart thudded in his ears. Then someone took his hand, gently, firmly. A voice said, 'I've got you.' Hands, clinging on to his jacket, pulling him inward into the safe room. Hands, reaching out for Bas.

He fell in a sprawl of arms and legs. They'd got Bas, too – Mr Albert and with him the gardener and a footman. It was all right!

'*Out*! Everybody out, before the whole lot goes up!'

'No, Pa! Grandma's in there. I couldn't lift her! Somebody, please try . . . ?'

'Out, I said!' Mr Albert, pushing them through the door. Down, down. Damn the stupid stairs! Someone was going to fall! Then out, into the high, echoing hall and the tower door slammed shut behind them. Safe, where the air was clean and cool. Safe, and God – thank you!

'You all right, Keth?'

'Yes, sir. Just give me time. Shaking a bit . . .'

'Bas?' Wiping his forehead, Albert Sutton turned to his son.

'I'm going to be sick.' His face was deathly pale. 'My hands, Pa . . .' He held them awkwardly and they were dreadful to look at. Burned, soot-blackened, fingers bent like claws.

'It's all right, Bas. I know what to do. Where's the nearest tap, Mr Sutton?'

'Tap?'

'Yes. Or a pump. Anything with cold water,' Keth jerked.

'There's a pump in the stableyard.'

'Show me where it is, Bas.'

Together they stumbled to the old lead pump, Albert following behind, red-faced, agitated.

'Now, Bas – your hands. Hold them out. No! Don't even

try to take your coat off. Just do as I say!' He began to pump the handle and ice-cold water gushed out to fill the trough. 'Cold water. It'll take the pain out. Just put your hands in it, Bas, and keep them there.'

'You're sure?' Albert Sutton frowned. 'Shouldn't we put something on them?'

'No, sir! Just cold water till the doctor gets here. How's that, Bas?'

'Better. Much better. They still hurt like hell, though. But grandma. I couldn't open the door to get her out. I tried. Sorry, Pa.'

'There was nothing we could have done.' Keth shook his head, gravely. 'When I got to the window the whole room was blazing.'

'She was on fire, Pa – all her clothes. I just couldn't put it out!'

'It's all right, Bas. Of course you tried. Only thank God you are all right. Nobody's going to blame you.'

They heard a distant clanging bell, and another, farther away. The fire brigade would soon be here.

'Is all the staff out?' Albert Sutton asked of the footman. 'Are they all right – everyone accounted for?'

'All safe, Mr Albert. Cook's agitated, though. She left the pans on, in the panic. Says the bottoms'll be burned out.'

'Tcha! A few pans?' He thought about his mother and knew he would never see her again. 'Where is my father?'

'He went early to York. An appointment with the tailor, if you remember. You could try him at the Station Hotel; he said he'd be lunching there.'

'No. He'll have left, by now. Best leave it a while. My wife is at Rowangarth. Could you send someone to bring her back here. And reassure her. Don't mention my mother, though, or that Bas has been burned. Did you phone for an ambulance?'

'I did, Mr Albert. It's coming with the engines. And I

phoned the doctor in Holdenby. If you'll excuse me, I'll go to the front, to meet them – show them where the hydrants are. And the ornamental lake could be used . . .'

'Good idea. And everyone is to stay outside. Fires are funny things.' Could burst out anywhere or run along joists, or beams. 'No heroics, now. No one is to take any risks, going back into the house trying to get things out. We're all safe – well, almost all – let's be grateful at least for that.'

'My, but that water's good.' Bas took a shuddering breath, his face still drained of colour, his mouth set tightly against pain that seemed to shoot to the very tops of his arms. 'Keep pumping, Keth? How did you know what to do?'

'Daisy's Mam told me. She was a nurse, once. I burned myself when we used to live in Hampshire. A coal fell out of the fire at Daisy's house and stupid, I grabbed it.

'Mrs Dwerryhouse hustled me into the yard and put my hands under the pump, just like now. "Cold water for a scald or a burn," she said. "Never forget that, Keth."'

'And you didn't . . .'

'No. Next day, my fingers were red, but they hadn't blistered. They healed fine. Yours will take a bit longer, but I think they'll do.'

'I can move my fingers, now. I want to sit here for ever with my hands in the water.'

'Then don't get too comfortable. The ambulance has just arrived. You'll have to go to hospital. Those burns aren't small ones like mine were. And you'll have breathed smoke in, too . . .'

'Whatever you say. And I haven't said thank you yet, have I?' Bas whispered. 'I'd given up, you know. I thought grandma was dead and I thought I was going to die, too. We couldn't get out of the door. The screen fell across it. And then you were there, at the window . . .'

'I was bringing your bike back.'

'Then thank the Lord for a puncture.' Bas tried hard to smile.

'Aye. It was a thorn. If I'd known, I'd have kept it for you,' Keth grinned. 'And thank *you*, Bas. I was pretty low – feeling sorry for myself. But after this afternoon, I'm glad just to be alive. And I'm sorry about the old lady, but we couldn't have got her out.'

'I suppose not. Uncle Elliot died that way, too. She *was* dead? She wouldn't know we were leaving her?'

'Dead? I don't know. I didn't see her. But I'd say she would have to be, in that inferno. It was lucky you had the sense to get to the window. If you hadn't, you'd have suffocated on the smoke, like the old lady probably did. Just don't think about it, Bas.'

'Nobody's asked, yet, how it happened.'

'Well, you can tell them later. They'll want to know, I suppose, but not now. Over here!' he called, waving his arm. 'Here's the nurse. She'll be looking for you. And the fire engines are here, too. It's going to be all right.'

'Which one of you is Sebastian Sutton?' the nurse asked.

'That's me, I guess.' Bas forced a smile, even though his grandmother's screams still filled his head. He'd be glad to go to the hospital; anywhere away from here. He hoped they would give him something to help the pain; something to help him forget those awful cries.

'Right, young man. Your hands, they said. Let's get them covered up, keep the air away from them. Soon have you comfortable.'

There was nothing more he could do at Rowangarth, Keth had decided, now that the fire engines were there and Bas away to hospital in the ambulance. Best not get in the way. He recalled the agonized inching along the ledge and thanked God again that neither had fallen.

He hadn't thought about anything at the time but hanging on to Bas, getting him to that safe, open window. Now, just to imagine what could have happened made him shake all over. And there was a churning inside him that reached up to his throat as if any minute he could be sick.

'Keth!' It was Daisy, running after him, calling to him to wait. 'They said there was a fire, at Pendenys. You're all dirty and you smell of smoke. Were you there? Are you all right?'

'A fire in the tower, but it's fine, now.' Best not tell her, just yet, about Mrs Clementina. 'I'd been mending a puncture for Keth – that's why I was there.'

'Pendenys car took Mrs Amelia back there and Mrs Anna, too. Tatty and Kitty are still with Aunt Julia. I came to find you. I had a feeling that – well, I knew somehow you were there. Must be getting like old Jinny. You *are* all right? Tell me, Keth?'

'There's nothing to tell. The fire was in the tower. It burned upwards, like a flue, so it didn't spread to the rest of the house. And I'm fine – really I am.' For the first time since the letter came he smiled, then pulling her close to him, tilting her chin, he kissed her gently. 'And I love you, Daisy Dwerryhouse.'

'Keth!' He had come back to her! She laid her head on his chest, holding him tightly. 'You were so bitter, so far away. I couldn't seem to get near you. And I still want to help, if you'll let me. Don't let that money come between us? Let me talk to Dada – see what he thinks about it?'

'No, sweetheart. I wasn't going to tell you this, but they've taken Bas to hospital. He was in the tower, you see, and his hands got burned. And Mrs Clementina's dead, Daisy.

'So all at once I feel glad to be alive and not to have to worry about my hands. And I know I shall make it. I don't care about the scholarship.'

'But *why* must you make it? Why drive yourself so?'

'Have you ever been poor, Daisy? Even before you got all that money – have you? Have you known what it's like

525

to see your father crippled and bitter and your mother working herself to a standstill?'

'N-no, but —'

'Well, I have! I don't want Mum to end her days in the Workhouse. I want to be able to provide for her, see she doesn't go short when she's old. And that's only one of the things that's driving me. But it'll be all right, love. I've calmed down and come to my senses. You've got five years to go before you come of age; you might fall in love with someone else, though I'll do my best to see you don't. By the time you've got your fortune, I plan to have a bit of brass of my own, an' all. And don't ask me how, because I don't know myself. I just feel it, though.'

'There won't be anyone else, Keth. You know there won't. And I don't want you to be rich. I've got enough for us both and your Mum, too, and if you really love me, you'll let me share it with you.'

'We'll see,' he smiled, 'but at this moment, the great tycoon has to deliver his evening papers!'

She smiled into his eyes because all at once, even in spite of Mrs Clementina and Bas's hands, she was happy again.

'My dear, you mustn't blame yourself. Nothing you could have done would have made any difference. It was a sad, tragic accident.' Helen held Edward's hands tightly. 'Clemmy had not been well for some time . . .'

'I know. But I didn't look in on her before I went to York. I never said goodbye. I thought she would be asleep, still, you see — well, after last night . . .'

'She probably was.'

'Yes, but we were talking about making her take treatment. Get her into a nursing home, we said, for her own good. But she outwitted us. She was Clemmy, right up until the end. And I still don't know how it happened. No one does.'

'When Amelia and Albert get back from the hospital,

they'll be able to tell us. Bas may well know. He was with her, I believe?'

'Yes. And it's young Keth we have to thank for getting him out, by what I've been told. And at least Bas is all right. I phoned the hospital. As far as they can tell, he's not in any danger. Shocked, and his hands, of course. You know, Helen, there were times when Clemmy drove me to distraction but for all that, I'd have wanted a kinder end for her. Strange that both she and Elliot died the way they did.'

'She's at peace, now. She'll be with Elliot. She never got over his death.'

'You believe all that, Helen? You believe in heaven?'

'Oh, yes! Sometimes I long to be with John and with Robert and Giles, too. But then I think of Drew. You've got to believe in God, Edward, when you think of the way Drew came to us. Drew was a miracle. When everything seemed hopeless, Alice gave us another chance.'

'Strange, but I never liked that tower.' Edward did not want to talk about miracles. 'I used to think it was arrogant – pushy, almost – though now I suppose I must have instinctively known there was trouble in it and around it. It's gutted, now. It will be better to have it pulled down, rather than restore it.'

'Ssssh. You can think about that later, Edward – when you aren't so upset. It must have been terrible for you to come home to it all without warning.'

'It was, though the worst was over by the time I got back. The fire was out and they'd found Clemmy and – and taken her away. The young doctor came – decent of him. He said there'll have to be an inquest. But we must think about Bas, and hope it hasn't harmed him too much. Bas could have died, you know, but for young Purvis. But Albert will tell me all about it, later. We must be thankful, I suppose, that the firemen stopped the blaze from spreading and none of the staff suffered, though I believe Cook is in a state over her best pans. They were burned dry by the time the firemen would let anyone back in the house.

'A few pans, Helen. As if they matter when Bas could have been trapped there, too, and the Purvis lad hurt – or even worse – going in like he did.'

'Keth is a fine young man. It was just the sort of thing he'd do. Now – are you sure there isn't anything I can do for you? I shall stay until Amelia and Albert get back – see how Bas is. Drew is very anxious.'

'No, my dear. You get off home. It was kind of you to come – and they'll be back before so very much longer. Amelia will ring you, I've no doubt. Let me send for a car for you – save calling Julia?'

'If you are sure? Tatiana has gone home, now, but Kitty is still at Rowangarth with Drew and Julia. It would be a help if someone could drive me back.'

'Then I'll ring for a car, now. And you'll call tomorrow – or let me call on you? You're a comfortable soul to be with, Helen. Thank you for being kind to Clemmy when most of us had despaired of her. She liked you and trusted you. Bless you for that.'

'I'll call again tomorrow,' she said, gently touching his cheek. 'And I'll remember Clemmy in my prayers tonight, and you too, Edward.'

'Amelia – you're crying. Please don't cry,' Albert murmured. 'Bas is all right. They said so. They gave him something for the pain and he was sleeping when we left. He's in good hands.'

'I know. It's such a relief, that's all. Your mother insisted on seeing him. How could she have been so thoughtless – keeping lighter fuel on the mantelpiece?

'Bas didn't want to go, you know, but I said he had to be kind to her. Kind! And I might never have seen him again. Keth not only saved his life, Bertie, but what he did afterwards probably saved Bas's hands, too. I've got to

528

thank him — now — before I go to bed. I couldn't rest, if I didn't. Drive back by way of Rowangarth, will you, and drop me off?'

'Shall I come with you?'

'No, dear. You get back to Pendenys. Your father will be in need of comfort. I'll collect Kitty from Helen's — they'll want to know how Bas is making out. But I *must* see Keth — you do understand?'

'I do. Bas is mine, too. Tell young Purvis I'm grateful. I'll see him myself tomorrow — thank him personally. Now dry your tears, Amelia — we've been very lucky.'

'Do you think I don't know it? Bas never liked Pendenys, you know. Probably it was a foreboding.'

'I know how he feels. I never liked it, either. It has never been a happy house.'

'Well, maybe things will get better after today. Now take the next road to your right — drop me off at the back of Helen's place. I know where the bothy is.'

'There'll be no peace for any of us, unless I do.' He smiled fondly, understanding her, loving her. 'And you'll tell his mother, too, how grateful we are?'

'I'll tell her.' Amelia put away her handkerchief, tears dried. Oh my word, yes, she would tell her!

'And will you stay, Mrs Purvis, to hear what I have to say to your son?' Amelia asked, when she was seated in the rocking chair in the bothy kitchen.

'If you like, ma'am, though I hope the lad didn't do anything wrong, at Pendenys. I know he was there this afternoon, but he said it was only to take back a cycle.'

'Then I thank God he was, for whatever reason. And nothing is wrong — far from it.' She rose, smiling, to her feet as Keth came into the room, holding out her hand to him. 'Keth — you know what I am here for?'

'I hope it's to tell me that Bas is all right.' He looked down at the floor.

'Bas will be fine. They'll keep him for about a week, they said — mainly because of his hands — and to keep an eye on his chest. But that isn't what I came to say. It seems you didn't tell your mother, Keth, that this afternoon you saved my boy's life.'

'No more did he!' Polly's face flushed bright red. 'Said he came away and left it to the firemen. Said it was him raised the alarm, but that was all I was told!'

'He raised the alarm and more besides, Mrs Purvis. He went into the tower and, because he couldn't get into the room, he climbed along a ledge to get there.

'And he brought Bas out, supporting him because his hands were useless, all the way along to the next window. My husband was waiting there to help and he saw it all. It was your son who risked his life getting to Bas and risked it again, bringing him safely out.'

'Why, you daft young varmint! You could both of you been killed,' Polly cried. 'Oh, I didn't mean that! It's just that you don't know what they're getting up to when they're out of your sight!'

'You are right. Keth did act like a daft young varmint, and because he did, my son is alive tonight. Keth might even say that he didn't think before he went in; perhaps he didn't. But for all that, I owe him Bas's life. How will I ever repay him?'

'He don't want repaying, do you, lad?'

'Course I don't. And I wasn't frightened, Mrs Sutton, until we were both safe out of that tower. I was shaking all over, once we were down. But at the time all I could think was that I'd never live with myself if I didn't try to help Bas. He's my friend . . .'

'Oh, I think I'm going to weep again.' Amelia pulled an already damp handkerchief from her sleeve and dabbed hastily at her eyes. Then she took a deep breath and said, 'Forgive me, Keth, for saying this, but Kitty tells me you weren't able to get a place at University.'

'That's right. I made a mess of it. I've accepted it, now. As a matter of fact, I realized how lucky I am to be alive after what happened today at Pendenys. I'll survive, Mrs Sutton. It's my mother you should be sorry for, her keeping me for so long when I could have been, *should* have been, working.'

'I see. Then if I told you I would like to see you through University, pay your fees, you'd tell me you had changed your mind – that you no longer want to go?'

'I didn't say that!' Keth's eyes jerked upward to meet those of Amelia Sutton. 'What I meant was that if I'd won a scholarship, it would have taken care of everything. I'd not have had to worry about books or lodgings. All that would have been paid for me.

'But fees cost a lot – education isn't cheap – and there'd be so many extras. No! I couldn't let you do it, though I'm grateful for your thought.'

'Not even when I tell you that the hospital doctor told me that what you did for Bas's hands means that there's a good chance he'll be able to use them normally again? Think, Keth – Bas wants to take up animal husbandry. He couldn't do it with crippled hands any more than he could sit a horse, hold the reins. His life would have been very different had you not known what to do.'

'Mrs Dwerryhouse told me about burns a long time ago.'

'Keth – please look at me? Look me in the eyes and tell me there is nothing on earth you'd like more than to go to University? But if your stiff-necked British pride won't permit you to accept my gratitude, then why don't you come over to Kentucky? Bas will be going to University next year – the two of you could go together. And in America a young man can work his way through college. There's no shame in that, in my country. You could stay with us, during vacations, be a part of our family. And there's always a job, at the Stud. We often give work to students.

'Think about it, won't you? Don't prevent a mother showing her gratitude? Don't you see — I might tonight be mourning my son's death. Not every penny I nor his father possesses would have given him back to us. Can't you be as glad as we are that Bas is alive and will soon be well, thanks to you? He couldn't have got out of that room without you; he told us so. Please, Keth — at least don't dismiss it out of hand? Think about it?'

'He'll think on about it,' Polly whispered at the bothy door. 'I'll shake some sense into that head of his — after I've given him a good talking to about acting like a young fool!'

'Then remember that every time I look at my son, I shall thank heaven for your young fool, Mrs Purvis. I meant what I said. I have always believed that if in life you receive a great favour, then you should do all in your power to pass on some of it. All I ask is that Keth won't think of my offer as charity, and refuse it.

'Speak very firmly to him, won't you? And tell him my husband intends seeing him tomorrow to thank him, too. If only you knew how grateful we both are . . .'

'I'll speak to the lad, never fear. Now can you find your way to Rowangarth, Mrs Sutton? It's getting dark. Shall I come with you? I know the path better'n you do.'

'Thank you, no. I can manage. They'll be waiting for news of Bas and Kitty is still there. I can telephone from there for a car to take us home.

'Goodnight, Mrs Purvis.' She held out her hand. 'We'd be glad to have Keth come to Kentucky. We'd take good care of him — if you can spare him, that is.'

Polly stood in the doorway, listening to the receding footsteps, wondering why all at once she felt so churned up inside.

'You daft young beggar!' she gasped as she closed the kitchen door behind her. 'Didn't you think on before you went rushing in?'

'No, I didn't. And you're right. I *was* a daft young beggar. But no more heroics, I promise.'

'I should think not! And lad — you'll take Mrs Amelia up on her offer?'

'I don't know, Mum. It's charity, whichever way you look at it, and I've got my pride.'

'Idiot! It isn't charity; more a thanksgiving on her part. And you can throw your precious pride down the drain! Pride is a cold companion and it never yet filled empty bellies!

'Mr Albert'll be coming tomorrow to see you, so like as not he'll tell you that the offer still stands. And you'll tell him you'll accept, and thank him kindly.'

'I'd like to go to America — I've got to admit it. They aren't so stuck up, there, so class conscious. Bas said that in the United States a man gets credit for what he does and not for what his father is, like in England. Nobody is expected to tip his cap in Kentucky, he said.'

'Then think on about what Mrs Amelia said? I want you to.'

'Even though you mightn't see me for two, maybe three years? You wouldn't miss me?'

'Of course I'd miss you, but you can put pen to paper, can't you? They have postage stamps in America, don't they? Now get yourself off to bed. I'll bring you a drink up. And son —'

'Yes, Mum?' He paused in the doorway.

'Your dad would have been proud of you this day. Real proud!'

33

'Of course, it would all start to happen, just as we're leaving for home,' Amelia complained.

It. The King's great affair, some called it, though others were not so polite. But happening it was, with the Press so long gagged having their day, together with the entire population.

'Surely not a divorcee? Not for the King of England,' said some. 'The ruler of the Empire and Commonwealth must abide by the rules!'

On the other hand, there were those who said that if the King had got some of the muck of the trenches on his boots, then happen he'd have earned the right to wed where he pleased!

Rumours were two a penny. *She* had not only stayed at Balmoral with the King, but had had the cheek to sleep in Queen Victoria's bed!

But *She* hadn't had it all her own way, by all accounts, having been thoroughly snubbed at a dinner party by the Duchess of York. Looked right through her, the little duchess had, as if the woman weren't there at all!

'One in the eye for Wallis,' Amelia had sighed with delight, she being totally opposed to divorce and not best pleased when one of her fellow countrymen was making a laughing stock of America by acting like a gold-digger. Marry the English King, indeed, and That One on her second divorce!

'She thinks she can be Queen of England, you know, and he's so bewitched by her he'll have a darn good try at getting her crowned! He won't be able to marry the woman, will he?'

'I doubt it, Amelia. She'll never be accepted as queen. It would have to be a morganatic marriage, with no title nor claim to the throne, and that's not what she wants, it seems, nor the King, either!'

'So what'll he do? Give her up?'

'I don't know. He ought to.' Helen stirred her tea thoughtfully. 'I believe – and I had this from the sister of one who works in the Foreign Office – that the Dominions are completely opposed to the King marrying her. I heard they'd all made it quite plain to Mr Baldwin.'

'Hmm. It's come to something when even the book-makers are offering odds – will she, won't she? Might be worth a small bet . . .'

'Amelia! You *wouldn't*!'

'Too darn right I wouldn't. But it's going to make interesting reading now your newspapers are finally on to it. One thing *is* certain. Your king is going to have to make up his mind before the Coronation – next May, isn't it? – whether he wants the lady or the crown. Guess he can't have both.'

'I think,' said Helen carefully, 'that he will choose duty. He'll give her up. Or he'll probably have it announced that she has given *him* up. It would be the gentlemanly thing to do, of course.'

'I hope you're right.' Divorce was a dirty word. Rather have a gambler in the family, a gaol bird, even, than a divorcee. 'My, but it's been quite a visit. Albert'll be glad to get back to Kentucky.'

Clementina laid to her rest beside Elliot; the gutted tower demolished, Bas out of hospital and day by day his hands healing, growing more supple.

The Kentucky Suttons were returning on the liner *Normandie*, which promised great excitement for its passengers since the French were all set to break the *Queen Mary*'s record for the fastest crossing of the Atlantic and claim the Blue Ribband.

'It'll be quite something,' Amelia smiled. 'They'll really be steaming. I do wish you'd visit us in Kentucky, Helen. You'd surely be welcome. Just telegraph that you're coming and we'll roll out the red carpet.'

'I've never visited America . . .' Helen mused.

'Then there's no time like the present. Come for Thanksgiving – that's the fourth Thursday in November – and stay over. You could return home with us when we come for Christmas.'

'You still intend coming as usual?'

'We must. Father-in-law is on his own, now. He'll be lonely in that great house when he gets over the shock. Nathan is near of course, and Rowangarth, but I've told Bertie he mustn't neglect his father.'

'You're a good soul, Amelia.'

'I'm a contented woman, and when I think we could well have been going back to Kentucky without Bas – well, I've been counting my blessings a lot, these last few weeks. Bas is so lucky to be alive and well. Guess I'll have to watch myself and not spoil him too much.

'Ah, well, I'll telephone you tomorrow before we leave. Say goodbye to Julia for me?'

'I will.' Helen laid a cheek on Amelia's, making a little moue with her mouth. 'Godspeed, my dear, and a safe landfall.'

'Thanks. And you'll let me know if anything happens – you know what I mean – anything in the newspapers or magazines. They'll want to know back in Kentucky how Wallis is doing, now she's made her bid to grab your king. Send them airmail, Helen? They'll take no time at all, that way!'

When Amelia had left, Helen thought long and hard about the King's problem, with the Dominions and Empire – nay, the entire world – waiting impatiently for the next act in the drama. She hoped His Majesty would make the right decision, but sometimes she doubted that he would. It was all very upsetting.

'You're sure you don't mind, Polly? Sure you can spare the time?'

'My time, Mrs MacMalcolm, is paid for by Rowangarth and you are providing the ingredients, so if I can't bake a few apple pies for a good cause, then it's a poor look on.'

At last, however briefly, the people of Holdenby had something other than the King's indiscretion to talk about. The Marchers were coming; men from Jarrow, tramping the length of the country to beg Parliament for work.

'It *is* a good cause, Polly. Andrew would have wanted me to help.'

Andrew's father had been a miner and a sick one at that. Andrew, had he lived, would have considered it his duty to help those men on their way.

'Alice is baking bread and making soup and Rowangarth is providing sandwiches and more soup – we should do pretty well for food, though it's a pity they'll have to sleep on the floor.'

'Pity they ever had to make the march in the first place! Going all that way just to ask for work! And most of those men saw service in the trenches! Not much of a deal for them, was it? Makes me glad, sometimes, that Dickon didn't live to see what he fought for!'

'Don't say that, Polly? Never say that? You know you don't mean it?'

'No, ma'am, I don't. There's times, even though he wasn't a well man, I'd give all I own to have him back. Sometimes I miss him so it hurts something cruel. Just to know he'd be coming through that door tonight would be right grand, even though he wasn't always in the best of moods because of the pain.'

'I know. I'm a widow, too. It's why I want to help the Marchers – because they are Andrew's kind of people. He would want me to.'

'Then I'll bake the pies, and gladly. When will you want them?'

'Day after tomorrow. That's when they're expected. And thanks, Polly. Mother is going round with a collection tin. She's trying to get fifty pounds.'

'That's a terrible lot of money! Who's she going to give it to?'

'It's for the Marchers' fund. They're all men on the dole, but they forfeited their dole money by going on the march, you see. The authorities at Jarrow said that men who draw unemployment money most always be available and ready to be employed, and by being on a march, they've made themselves unavailable.'

'That's downright wicked!' Polly dipped into her pinafore pocket and offered a florin. 'Here – give this to her ladyship. Only wish it could be more.'

'Thank you, Polly. Mother will raise the money, I'm sure of it. She's already bullied forty pounds out of the family though she says she hates asking in the village. But Holdenby people will give willingly, I know. There isn't so much unemployment hereabouts, you see. Not like on Tyneside.'

'It's a queer carry-on, isn't it, Mrs MacMalcolm? Germany rearming, war in Spain and the King disgracing us with a married woman. It's a sad world for our young ones to be growing up in.'

'It is. And talking about the young ones – Daisy told me about Keth going to America. He *will* go to Kentucky next year?'

'I don't know.' Polly pushed back her chair as Julia rose to leave. 'He wants to go to University; it's all he's ever thought about, but it's his pride, you see.'

'Then tell him from me that pride will get him nowhere.

538

Amelia really wants to help Keth through college. Can't you knock some sense into his head?'

'He's a mite too big for that. I'd have to stand on a stool, now, to box his ears!' Polly laughed, opening the bothy door. 'But when Mrs Sutton comes over for Christmas, I think he'll ask her if he can take her up on her offer. Keth can be a bit stubborn at times, but he's not so stupid as to throw away a second chance. And I'll get him to bring the pies round on Wednesday. About noon, shall us say?'

'About noon, Polly . . .'

'Here you are, mother. Two shillings from Polly, ten shillings from Alice and Daisy, and Tom has given money for cigarettes for the men. How is your collection coming along?'

'I've made it, Julia – and more! About fifty-three pounds. People are so good. Perhaps we could use the surplus for a few comforts for the men – cigarettes, matches, mints . . . ?

'They'd like that. All along the march, people have helped them, you know. Even if the government won't listen to them when they get to London, at least those men will know they have the sympathy of the people.'

'It makes me very proud of my fellow men,' Helen smiled. 'And it makes me aware of how very comfortable we are at Rowangarth, compared to most. It makes me feel guilty, almost, spending so much money on a passage to New York.'

'You've decided to visit Amelia and Albert, then?'

'We-e-ll, almost. I have never seen the New World and Amelia is keen for me to go.'

'You wouldn't consider flying?'

'Goodness, no! It could be very dangerous, flying in November and December – the fogs, you know. Thanksgiving day goes back more than three hundred years, I believe, to when the early settlers gave thanks for their first harvest. Rather nice, I think.'

'Then you must go, dearest. You'd have a wonderful time. Amelia would make you so welcome and you know you're fond of her.'

'She's a dear, kind person. Albert was lucky, finding her. I only wish Nathan could be as fortunate. Why do you suppose he has never married?'

'Haven't the faintest idea. Shall I tell him you're worried about him?' Julia teased.

'You'll do no such thing!' Helen clucked. 'Whatever would he think of me? Now – about your Marchers from Jarrow? They're making a stop the other side of Harrogate, I believe, so why are twenty of them coming to Holdenby? They can't be expected to walk another nine miles.'

'There isn't enough room for them at the scheduled stop so someone is driving them over in a chara. And they'll want washing bowls and the use of towels. Doc Pryce says he'll have a look at their feet. They're mostly marching in shabby boots, you see, and their feet are suffering dreadfully, I believe.'

'You're enjoying it, aren't you – helping, I mean?'

'I am, mother. Oh, I find no joy that men have to beg for work, but I'll be good with the washing bowls and serving meals. It'll be just like it was in France when Alice and I were –' When she and Alice were young and in love and everyone pulling together because there was a war on, and the next mail might bring a letter from Andrew. 'Yes, I shall enjoy it . . .'

Even though Andrew had been dead for almost eighteen years; even though she still loved him every bit as much and wanted him, still. Even though the Fascists were fighting in Spain, whilst in Germany –

But not to think of Germany and what might be, or Andrew's life would have been taken in vain.

'Will you need your furs when you go to Kentucky? What do you plan to take?' Julia asked brightly. 'And when you next write to Amelia tell her, will you, that Mrs

540

Simpson's divorce is being heard in Ipswich, on the twenty-seventh. I read it in the morning paper. Did you see it?'

'Afraid I missed it.'

'You were probably meant to! Just a small piece.'

'But why Ipswich?' Helen frowned.

'Why not? Anywhere but London, I would say, when that divorce is obviously a put-up job. But you know the way Amelia laps up everything the King and Mrs Simpson get up to, so don't forget to send her the cutting.'

'Amelia will probably know already. The whole world knows and is laughing at us. Poor Queen Mary. Has the King never thought about the way he's upsetting his mother?'

'I doubt it. He's a fool in love. If he gave to the unemployed the money he spends on jewels for his Wallis, then people might respect him more. I hope he does give up the throne for her. We'd be better off without him – and her!'

Julia! The King to *abdicate*? But that would be awful! Give up the throne for a divorcee? He couldn't. He *wouldn't*!'

But he could, Helen thought, and he well might. What was yet in doubt, was *when*!

The Marchers from Jarrow alighted from the charabanc, arranged themselves into lines of four, then marched, straight-backed, across the school playground to Holdenby village hall. Their faces were pinched and pale and some of them walked badly in boots with paper-thin soles, but they walked with dignity of purpose and with heads held high.

Julia blinked back tears. No rabble, this. Gentlemen in cloth caps, more like. It made her wish there was more she could do.

'Are you ready, Hawthorn?' she said in her best Sister Carbrooke voice as she fastened on her apron.

'Ready,' Alice whispered tremulously, and all the time knowing that if there really was a heaven, then Andrew and Giles and all those men who hadn't come home would be looking down and wondering what had happened to that country fit for heroes to live in. And being glad, perhaps, that someone cared.

When Alice got home at nearly midnight, Tom was waiting beside the kitchen fire.

'You look tired, love. Kettle's on.'

'I'm not so bad. It is nothing like it was, in France.'

'In France you and Julia were bits of lasses. Sit you down, and take off your shoes. What was it like, then?'

'Awful, Tom. Those Marchers were wonderful. Not a grumble between them. Just gratitude. That's what got me – that they should be grateful that people are trying to help them along their way; yet if you had been amongst them, I'd have been bitter and angry. We've let them down, you know.'

'No. Not us, Alice. Not the likes of you and me. Ordinary folk are doing what they can to help. It's the system that's to blame. They wanted us when they needed soldiers, then threw us on the scrap heap. Them and Us. It'll never be any different. Not for you and me, love, though Daisy'll be all right. But I'll tell you what, bonny lass. If there's ever another war, they'll not get me!'

'There *won't* be another war. But forget Hitler, *please*? Let me tell you about tonight? They were such a grand bunch of men. They didn't mind sleeping rough – said they'd be grateful for washing water, so they could shave, in the morning.

'Doctor Pryce was there, seeing if any of them needed medicine, though it was mostly sore feet. Julia gave them the money Lady Helen collected. They said they'd never expected such kindness, all along the way, though to my way of thinking it might be different when they get farther south.'

'Don't judge them, Alice, just because there aren't as

many folk out of work down there. The southerners will be just as generous,' Tom reasoned. 'Leastways, I hope they will. But did the marchers have a good feed?'

'That they did! Plenty of soup and sandwiches and pies and buttered teacakes and in the morning, the Mothers Union is going to see to the breakfasts. Porridge and eggs and bread and jam. We've done our bit for them, around Holdenby.'

Gratefully she accepted the tea Tom poured, wrapping her fingers around the mug, rocking gently as she sipped. Then she said softly, 'Are you ready for a shock, Tom?'

'Why, love? What's happened?'

'Something you'll hardly believe.'

Never believe the man who'd looked at her strangely. At every turn he'd been looking and she had frowned, because she knew him, didn't she? Someone from France. One of the soldiers she had nursed, maybe?

It hadn't been until the men were seated at the trestle tables and she walked round with a jug of soup, topping up plates, that she said to him without any preamble at all, 'Should we know each other, you and me?'

'I don't know. Have I been gawping?'

'You have,' she smiled. 'I was a nurse, in the war, perhaps that was it. Were you wounded?'

'No. I was one of the lucky ones – if you can call this lucky.' Then he'd coloured, as if he knew he shouldn't have said that; not to someone who'd been decent enough to show sympathy.

'Which regiment?'

'The West Yorkshires. I was a marksman.'

'Then that narrows it down a lot. Did you ever come across Tom Dwerryhouse?

'He knew you, Tom. And then he remembered me. He was the soldier who called at Celverte, at the convent – gave me the letters I'd written to you and your Testament, with the buttercups pressed inside it.'

'Geordie! Geordie Marshall, by the heck! So the old son of a gun made it!'

'He did. He was sorry, when I told him you and me were married, that once he'd told me not to hope, over much, that you were alive. He'd heard, you see, you were in the lorry that got a direct hit from a shell. It was kind of him to find me, in Celverte, but that was when I gave up hoping – accepted that you really were dead.'

'And so did everyone else. What did you tell him – about me, I mean?'

'That you'd been taken prisoner; same story we told everybody – and the Red Cross never told about it. I told him you'd likely go over to see him in the morning, and if you do, it'll be up to you what you tell him, Tom.'

'I'll go. Just imagine Geordie turning up like that! I'll tell you something, Alice. He was the only man I've ever met who was a better shot than I am. We'd go out into No Man's Land – sometimes sniping, but mostly keeping watch over the stretcher bearers and doctors who were trying to get the wounded back to our lines.

'I used to feel bad; my stomach would churn something awful, but not Geordie. Cool as a cucumber, that one. He'd smile as he pulled the trigger. He hated Germans . . .'

'Then you'll have to get there before nine o'clock. The chara will be there at quarter-past. The march leaves Harrogate at ten. It was him remembered me. I'd never have known him, though Lord knows I should have, after Celverte.'

Hope died, that day. Tom, she had accepted, was never coming back to her.

She put down her cup, going to stand behind his chair, wrapping her arms around him, laying a cheek on his head.

'We are so lucky, you and me, Tom. And when I saw those men, desperate for work and their dole stopped just because they were on the march, it made me shudder to think about Daisy's money.'

'It makes me shudder an' all, lass, but it was given to her and there's nowt we can do about it. And fair play, it hasn't caused the bother I thought it might. She's been sensible about it, never said so much as a word to anybody.'

'She told Keth . . .'

'Well, happen she would. Keth's always been close. But Geordie! Imagine him turning up like that!' He shook his head, bemused. 'Who'd have thought it?'

Alice lay awake that night, too tired to sleep, her mind too active. And she thought of that young nurse, carrying a rape child and, with Tom's death, all hope gone.

She closed her eyes, counting her blessings, wishing for a miracle that those brave, proud men from Jarrow – every single one of them – might find work.

Then she thanked God yet again for her happiness and begged, as she always did, that she might be allowed to keep it.

34

The trees in Brattocks Wood stood black and gaunt and wet with mist; the air was cold and damp and the torch Keth carried made little impact on the drifting fog.

November. Month of the dead when lost souls roamed the earth in search of absolution – or so Jinny Dobb said.

He pushed open the gate of Keeper's Cottage, seeing lamplight dimly ahead. He was not able to meet Daisy so often now he was working, lucky to find work as odd-job man in a Creesby hotel. There he wore a dung-coloured, long-sleeved coat and fetched and carried and swept from eight in the morning until seven at night. Thirty-two men had applied for the job, which was given to him because he was young and strong and could be hired for a pound a week, he thought bitterly, crunching his feet into the gravel of the path.

The tips he earned he kept for himself; half of the wages he gave to his mother and what remained was hoarded in the Penny Bank against the time when he went – when he *might* go – to America. And he wanted to go there even more, now he knew the demeaning grind of cheap labour. Indeed, the only good thing about it was that he had ceased to be a burden on his mother's purse. All else about the job only made him surer than ever that it was not for him.

The door opened. A finger of lamplight illuminated the passage and he sniffed in the sweet warm scent of burning apple logs.

'Keth, love! Come in and shut the door. What a night!' Daisy offered her mouth for his kiss, twining her arms around his neck, whispering, 'It's all right. Dada's walking the game covers, though he'll not be out long – there'll be no poachers out tonight. And Mam's at Rowangarth, sewing for Lady Helen for America.'

Her lips gentled his cheek searching for his mouth and he pulled her close, loving her, wanting her.

'Sit you down. Mam didn't light the parlour fire, tonight. Tell me about today?'

She sat, arms round knees, on the brass stool that stood at the side of the fire, smiling her pleasure at seeing him.

'Today, sweetheart, was exactly like yesterday and exactly as tomorrow will be. Boring and soul-destroying. I hate it.'

'So you'll go to Kentucky?' Not that she wanted him to leave her but she knew that if he did not he would regret it every day for the rest of his life.

'If the offer's still open when they come over in December, then I'll ask Mrs Sutton to help me. I was talking to Bas before they went back to Kentucky and it seems that in America, going to University isn't just for rich people but for anyone willing to work hard. Girls, too.

'He said some Universities give free places for special talents – like being good at sport, or music. Getting a degree is easier over there than it is here – for people like me, I mean. A lot of the students have a job – it's the accepted thing. It makes me mad to think that here, the well-off take education for granted. But even in America, it's going to cost money. It goes against the grain, you know, to accept charity.'

'But it *isn't* charity, can't you get that into your head, Keth Purvis? And as for the cost – Mrs Amelia wants to do it. Bas's life is priceless. It's her way of saying thank you for what you did. Don't deny her?'

'I won't. Pride is something I can't afford, but had you thought I might be away for three years? It's the one thing that takes the shine off it – not seeing you. You'll forget what I'm like.'

'I won't! I'll write every day and don't forget that by the time you're back I'll be nearly twenty-one and we can be married.'

'Three years, though. It's a lifetime.'

'Then I'll have to keep myself busy, won't I? I'll be leaving school at Christmas and Mam wants me to go to the Technical School to learn shorthand and typing.'

'But I always thought you'd be a nurse, Daisy.'

'Mm. I've thought about it, but –' She shrugged expressively. 'Mam says you've got to have a vocation for it. For Mam, it was the only way to get to France to be near Dada, but she said it wouldn't be easy for someone like me.'

'Someone who's had a sheltered life, you mean?' Keth asked without rancour.

'No. What I think she meant was that I couldn't take the discipline. She says I've got Dada's temper and it wouldn't do. I suppose,' she sighed, 'that I'd be better working in an office, 'til you get back.'

'I haven't gone yet, sweetheart.'

'You will, though. You know you will.'

'I want to. But you won't need to work, Daisy – had you forgotten that?'

'No, and Mam's not likely to let me, either.' She rose to set the kettle to boil as she heard the barking of the dogs outside. 'But I've never had that money, don't you see? It's as if it doesn't exist, except to pay school fees. Mam says I must plan my life as if Mr Hillier never left it to me. If I don't, she says, I'll get idle and spoiled. You'll stay for a cup, Keth?'

She bent quickly to brush his lips with her own as her father's footsteps crunched on the gravel outside.

'By the heck, but it isn't fit to send a dog out tonight.' Tom nodded to Keth, then held his hands to the fire. 'Your Mam not back yet?'

'No, though she won't be long. And she likes doing it for Lady Helen. Said it's like old times, being back in Rowangarth sewing-room.'

'Aye.' Tom smiled fondly, reaching for his tobacco jar, taking his pipe from the rack that hung beside the fire. 'When is her ladyship sailing – from Liverpool, will it be?'

'From Tilbury, on the twelfth. Aunt Julia's going to London to see her off. Drew, too. They're leaving the day before, and staying the night at Montpelier Mews.'

'And how come young Drew can get time off school to go galavanting to London?'

'He's in the sixth form, now,' Keth supplied, 'seeing if he wants to go to University. Not that he will, but he doesn't have classes every day.'

'And you, Keth? Shall you be going to University?'

'I want to . . .'

'Then take Mrs Sutton up on her offer. You'd please her, if you did. And if you can't bear to take charity – and there's times when I think that's the only thing holding you back – then tell yourself, and her, too, that you'll pay it all back, once you're settled in a profession. But she was a mighty thankful woman that day of the fire, and she really wants you to go to college with Bas. Mrs Mac-Malcolm told me so.'

'Keth'll go. I'll never speak to him again, if he doesn't.' Daisy slipped the cosy over the teapot. 'Want a teacake, either of you?'

'Not for me – just a pipe.' Tom reached for his slippers. 'Keth'll have one, though. Reckon I ought to go over to Rowangarth, mind – walk your Mam home.'

'Dada – she'll be all right! It's only a step, and she isn't afraid of the dark! Leave her be. She's enjoying herself.'

'Aye. They'll be gossiping away, the three of them.' And Alice would be all right. There was no Elliot Sutton, now, for her to worry about. What happened out there in Brattocks was a long time ago, though he'd never regret blacking young Sutton's eye. He should, he considered calmly, have killed him like he'd wanted to, though it wouldn't have done a lot of good, him dangling at the end of a rope in Wakefield Gaol, because of it.

But a lot of water had flowed under a lot of bridges since then and Tom Dwerryhouse was no longer twenty-two, no longer so hot-headed. Alice had seen to that; rubbed the edge off his temper over the years, only to see it surface in Daisy. My, but the lass could get herself into a paddy, given half a chance!

'What's so amusing, Dada – or can't you tell us?'

'Happen not yet,' Tom grinned. 'Maybe I'll tell you when you're twenty-one, though.'

'When I'm twenty-one, Keth will be back from Kentucky,' she said softly, avoiding her father's eyes, gazing into the fire, 'and me and Keth will likely have something to tell you!'

'Tell me? What about?' Shocked, Tom sat bolt upright in his chair. 'If you're meaning what I think you are, then I'll be hoping that before Keth – or any young man – gets ideas into his head, he'll have the good manners to talk to your Mam and me about them first!'

'And I will, sir.' Keth's cheeks coloured hotly. '*When* there is something – when the time is right – I will.'

'Ar, well . . .' Tom was lost for words. It wasn't five minutes since Daisy had been sitting in that big, shiny pram at another Keeper's Cottage, with Morgan lying there and a three-year-old Keth never more than a stride away.

But it had to be admitted that Daisy would be seventeen, next birthday, and the same age as her Mam had been when they'd met in Brattocks Wood and fallen deep in love.

Daisy was no longer a child and more fool him for not seeing it 'til now. Daisy, he realized half amazed, was in love and the time was fast approaching when Alice and she would have to have a woman-to-woman talk about –

well, *things*. And the sooner the better, if Keth loved Daisy as he'd loved Alice!

'I'd best be off home.' Keth rose to his feet, still uncomfortable about what had been said though glad, for all that, for its saying. 'Goodnight, Mr Dwerryhouse.'

'Goodnight, lad. And you'd better walk Keth to the gate, Daisy, though don't take all night about it.'

'I won't, Dada.' Mischievously, she planted a kiss on the top of her father's head. 'It's much too cold to stand necking.'

'*Necking*? What ever kind of a word is that!' Tom exploded, then rubbed the back of his neck, biting on his lips to stop the smile that threatened. 'Is that what they teach you at Grammar School, then?'

The kitchen door slammed and from behind it he heard his daughter's laugh. Something to tell him, indeed! He should have expected it, though. Daisy was a little beauty and a good catch for any man if you took that money of hers into account. Thank the Lord she'd had the sense to learn to live with it and not blab it to all and sundry. There'd be half the scroungers in the Riding at the door, otherwise.

He gazed frowning at the glass-fronted, double-locked cabinet and the pair of Purdey shotguns it held.

Did you have to leave her all that brass, Mr Hillier, he demanded silently. Wouldn't it have been better if it hadn't been *quite* so much . . . ?

Yet come to think of it, wasn't it providential that it seemed it was Keth she had set her heart on and not some smooth-talking opportunist, or the penniless second son of a peer? He closed his eyes, setting his chair rocking, thinking all at once about Geordie Marshall and the Marchers who must be half-way to London, now.

He had gone early to see him at the village hall to find he hadn't changed. Geordie still carried himself arrogantly, was thin as ever, his wit as sharp, his grin as roguish. Only his eyes were different – without hope.

When they parted, Tom had pressed two pound notes into his friend's hand, begging him to take them. 'For all the fags you offered me, Geordie lad . . .'

'All the fags you didn't take, Tom. You didn't smoke.'

'Yet you offered them, just the same. Take it?' It was part of the rabbit-skin money he kept in a tin in the shed. 'For old time's sake?'

But Geordie had refused, asking instead that it should be sent to his mother. 'Ma needs it more'n I do . . .'

So Tom had written the address on the back of a feed bill fished out of his pocket and promised he would do that, and tell her that her son was all right. That letter was on the mantelpiece, now, ready to be posted. It stood there, an accusation from his past, and tears rose in his throat for all those who lay in long, straight rows in cemeteries in France – aye, and in Germany, too. He had not wept since a morning when he and eleven others had snuffed out the life of a young frightened boy.

Angrily, he dashed the tear away. The past was over and done with. Alice and Daisy were the only ones he'd be prepared to fight for and die for, now. It was just that last week the past had walked into his life, then walked out of it, straight-backed and proud. Near on twenty years, gone in a flash. It was a sobering thought.

'I nearly stowed away, Sparrow. I didn't half want to sail with that liner,' Drew sighed. 'I think if I didn't know what I was going to do, I might have considered going to sea when I'm old enough.'

'Now why a sailor, all of a sudden?' Sparrow demanded. 'You know you'll have your work cut out seeing to Rowangarth. Rowangarth ain't just any old house; it's what you was born into – your inheritance. You have to look after it and the land and the farms, and suchlike. And the people who work there depend on you, and the tenants and the pensioners. Then you'll hand it down, when you're dead and gorn, to your own son.

'That's what they mean by landed gentry. You're a gent and you've got land and you've got to see to it that nobody nicks it orf you and yours. So no more talk about going to sea, if you please!'

'Just a thought, Sparrow, but the *Queen Mary* is such an unbelievable thing. You can't call it a ship. It's like a whole town! A purser came to grandmother's cabin to see if she had all her wanted-on-voyage luggage and she asked him if I could go with him and have a look at things.

'And he said, "Certainly, milady. A pleasure. I'll have the young man back in good time for all-ashore." They come round before they sail shouting, 'All ashore that's going ashore!" – for the visitors, you know. He showed me quite a lot of the ship but he said it would take a week to see it all.

'Grandmother said she was going to feel guilty, living in such luxury for almost a week, but mother said she deserved it and that she was to enjoy it.'

'Your mother is quite right, young sir. Your grand-mother's a dear, good lady. Imagine, though – her going all the way to America . . .'

'Would you like to go to America, Sparrow?' Drew turned the bread on the fork he held to the fire.

'To America, to France – anywhere would suit me. I sometimes stand on Chelsea Bridge and look at that old river and wish I could be a leaf on it, and where I'd end up, if I was.'

'Very wet, somewhere in the Channel, I shouldn't wonder.'

'Maybe so – and here's where I'm happiest, looking after this little house for Mrs MacMalcolm. Haven't been so content. Only wish Smith could see me, and Roland, my boy. But Smith got took with his stomach and my boy gave his all for king and country.'

'Like mother's husband did, and both her brothers,'

Drew said softly. 'I wish I'd known my father – but who is Smith?'

'Smith was Roland's father, bless your life! Smith's my name, see? Emily Smith I am though the doctor always called me Sparrow. Your mother inherited me, so to speak, when the doctor was took. Ar, but they were a lovely couple. I used to do for Doctor MacMalcolm when he lived in Little Britain, and one day he told me he'd just met the lady he intended marrying, and that lady was your mother.'

'They met in Hyde Park, didn't they? Mother tripped, and hit her head?'

'Tripped! That wasn't what the doctor told me! Said he'd been walking in the park and there at his feet all of a sudden, was this vision, laid all pale-faced and unconscious to the world.

'Your mother, it was. She and Hawthorn – Mrs Dwerryhouse as now is – had been to a Suffragette meeting and the coppers came and started a fight. Tripped, indeed!'

'You mean mother was fighting in the Park?' Drew grinned, not able to believe it, and all the time wishing he had been there, to cheer her on, or pitch in beside her.

'Well, more like they was defendin' themselves against them truncheons,' Sparrow conceded. 'But I did hear that your mother was kicking out like a mad thing. And if what I was told is to be believed, young Hawthorn threw herself at a great copper ten times her size and sent him flying.

'But it was love at first sight, make no mistake about it. Mrs MacMalcolm's grief was terrible to see when the doctor was killed. That old Kaiser had a lot to answer for, starting that fighting, but there's no cause for you to worry,' she hastened, seeing the sadness that all at once showed in his eyes. 'There'll be no more wars.'

'Won't there, Sparrow? Will Stubbs said the Germans are getting above themselves again. Will reads all the newspapers.'

'Then take no notice of him! You can't believe all you

read in the papers. They prints 'em lurid, so they'll sell. Best you listen to what the man on the wireless says when he reads out the News.

'Now what if I butter that toast for you and, since your mother isn't in, I don't see why you shouldn't stay up late. There's a good play on the wireless, tonight. *Doctor Fu Manchu* — ever so creepy, I shouldn't wonder.

'And I think I must be getting old. Stay up late, indeed, and you seventeen, now, and almost a man. To think it's all them years since you was born. Saved your mother's reason, you coming like you did. There were times I'd fear for her state of mind, she took on so about the doctor.

'But she's survived and I reckon it was you, needing to be brought up, that helped pull her through. That house must've been a terrible sad place, at one time.'

'It must. I've often thought about how it was. That's why I don't want there to be any more wars, Sparrow. And I've often wished mother wasn't so alone. I wish there could be someone for her. People do marry again. My mother — my *first* mother — did, and she's very happy. Well, you know she is, don't you? But would you think Mr Townsend is sweet on mother?'

'I'm sure I don't know, young Drew!' Sparrow bristled. 'But if he is, then he's wasting his time. It's just that he was once your great-aunt Anne Lavinia's solicitor and your mother took him on. But mark my words, she ain't sweet on him!'

No, indeed! Sparrow brooded. But every time Mrs Mac-Malcolm came to the mews house, that Townsend chappie was on the phone for her, though how he managed it with such uncanny accuracy, she couldn't for the life of her tell. On the phone or on the doorstep before she'd hardly had time to hang her coat behind the door! Sparrow did not hold with Mark Townsend. Dotty about Mrs MacMalcolm he was, though the girl could never see it.

'Come to think of it, I don't know why your mother

should want to go out on a night like this. Fog coming off the river when him and her went orf, and cold with it, too. Far better if she'd stayed at home like you and me, keeping the fire warm.

'Now – do you want more toast or would you like a slice of chocolate cake? I made one special when I knew you'd be coming,' she smiled, conspiratorily.

And let them as had no more sense, she brooded darkly, silently, go out on a night like this, for much good would it do them if they got that fog on their chests and turned bronchial with it!

'Now build up that fire for me if you've finished toasting and I'll cut some cake. Then we'll switch on the wireless, eh?'

Sweet on Mrs MacMalcolm, indeed. Cheeky fellow!

It had come to something, Cook sighed mournfully, when the royal family was being made a laughing stock of by a divorced woman. And a foreigner, at that!

'But our royalty always marries foreigners,' Mary Strong reasoned. Leastways, they had done until the old king thought it politic to get some new blood into the family – good Scottish blood, as it happened.

'We-e-ll, not foreign, exactly – more commoners, I was meaning.'

'But the Duchess of York and the Duchess of Gloucester were both commoners,' Tilda protested.

'You know what I'm trying to say, girl!' Cook clucked tetchily. Tilda Tewk had the knack, still, of saying the wrong thing at the wrong time, even if there was almost always a grain of truth in it. 'Them two are ladies, through and through. I was talking about common commoners – and *she's* one of them, all right!' Cook refused to have Mrs Simpson's name spoken, now, in Rowangarth kitchen. 'Miss Clitherow says we can't have a divorced woman as queen – not even as consort. I'll tell you this for nothing – you wouldn't find me curtseying to her!'

'She's a *twice* divorced woman, now,' Tilda, who had once loved a younger King Edward with all her romantic heart, said with relish. 'She's got her divorce, remember. Only got to wait six months, now, then it'll be proper.'

'*Absolute*,' Mary corrected, stabbing her needle into the tablecloth she was embroidering for her bulging bottom drawer. 'Three husbands she'll have had if she manages to land the King!'

It wasn't right, not *three* men, when she, Mary brooded, hadn't been able to land one, in spite of the many last chances and verbal warnings she had given to Will Stubbs!

'Well, she'll not get him! Mr Baldwin won't stand for it, nor Parliament.' Nor any God-fearing woman, neither!

'He could marry her – morganatic.' Mary knew all about it. Will had told her. Morganatic meant the King could marry her but she could never be crowned queen, nor considered royal. That would be one in the eye for her!

'He can't even marry her – not divorced, he can't. The Archbishop would never allow it. They couldn't marry in church, much less Westminster Abbey – has she thought of that, eh?'

'She's given up her Ipswich house, now she's got that divorce. She's back in London, again. It said in the paper that a man in the street tried to throw vitriol in her face and there's been ever so many bricks thrown through her front windows. I believe she's going to Fort Belvedere. They won't be able to get at her there, will they?'

'Well, the King is going to have to make up his mind before he's crowned. It's going to be a choice of the throne or *her*! It's so shaming, us that's always been looked up to in the world!'

The chair in which Cook sat began to rock furiously and Tilda was quick to recognize the signs. Any minute now, Cook's apron would go over her face and she'd start boo-hooing.

'Never you mind, Mrs Shaw. Don't take on, so,' she soothed. 'I'll make us a sup of tea.'

God bless tea, Tilda sighed inside her, and drat that Simpson woman for making a fool of the man Tilda Tewk had loved with a pure heart ever since he'd been a dashing young prince. The mess the King had got himself into didn't bear thinking about. It really didn't.

As soon as they left the brightly-lit foyer of the theatre in Drury Lane, Julia knew they had been foolish ever to set out from Montpelier Mews.

'We-e-ll!' she gasped. The fog outside was thick and yellow and dense, wrapping them in a strange, silent blanket. 'I've never seen anything like it, Mark!'

'What we call a pea-souper. Everything stops . . .'

He didn't seem at all dismayed, she thought, irritated. But then he rarely showed emotion of any kind.

'What are we to do?' The silence was uncanny.

'Try to get a taxi, I suppose. Thank goodness we didn't drive in.'

'You'll not get a cab,' offered a man in the same predicament as themselves. 'Not a taxi on the streets – well, stands to reason, doesn't it?'

'I think it's disgraceful,' the woman beside him said petulantly. 'How could they even think of clearing off when people most need them?'

'Because they wouldn't be a lot of use to anybody if they'd stayed. Can't see their hand in front of their face. Be reasonable, old dear . . .'

There were many stranded theatregoers. A taxi driver, had one magically appeared, could have named his own price.

'Could we try the Underground?' Julia hesitated. 'If we could make it part of the way, perhaps we could sort of feel our way back to Montpelier. The fog mightn't be so dense, farther out.'

'No chance. The Tube will be disrupted, I shouldn't wonder. It usually is when there's sudden fog like this. Not all of it runs underground, Julia. There could be trains at a standstill all over the place.'

'Then what are we to do?' She had never seen such fog, such thick, acrid, frightening fog. 'If only we could get somewhere near Hyde Park, it mightn't be so bad, there.' After all, she reasoned, shivering, it was probably the concentration of coal smoke that made London fogs so chokingly thick.

'No. There's only one thing we can do.' Mark dropped his voice almost to a whisper. 'We can surely find our way to the Waldorf from here? They're sure to have rooms, there. We're going to have to stay put, I'm afraid, 'til this lot lifts, and in my experience it can last all night.'

'But what will Sparrow think? She'll be worried half out of her mind – Drew, too!'

'Fog doesn't affect telephones, Julia. We can let them know you're all right.'

'We-e-ll – if you're sure, then?' It wasn't right, Julia fretted. Not stopping out all night. But then, whispered the voice of reason, Mark lived here, knew all about London fogs. Perhaps he really did know best.

'I'm sure,' he said firmly, taking her arm. 'Now, take it easy. I think we can make the hotel, if we're careful. Best get a move on.'

The hotel, when eventually they reached it, had no rooms available, the desk clerk said. Unusual circumstances, he sympathized politely. Suddenly everyone was looking for a room for the night.

'So what now?' Julia sighed. She was very cold, Her sandals were thin and not intended for walking London streets; her hair clung damply to her head and she would have given anything for a mug of Sparrow's scalding tea to wrap her fingers around.

It took them almost an hour to find refuge in a small

hotel in a side street, though neither of them knew where exactly it was, nor how far they had come from the theatre.

'Is there a telephone I can use?' Julia asked the receptionist who wasn't used to late rushes. One more room, then she could put up the No Vacancies sign and get off to her bed. But it was always the same, when the fog came down.

'I'll get you the number if you'll write it down for me. You can take it on the extension in the lounge. If you'd like to go there and wait, I'll get it as soon as I can,' she grumbled. 'I'm just about run off my feet!'

'I could take it in my room?' Julia smiled.

'No telephones in rooms, Mrs Townsend.' Did the woman think this was the Ritz, then?

'*Mrs Townsend?*' Julia hissed when they were out of earshot of the desk. 'Why did you do that?'

'Because we got the last room they had. Don't be so stuffy, Julia. Nobody asks questions in places like this.'

'Asks questions? Just what are you playing at, Mark? Why didn't you ask for separate rooms? I'm going, now, to ask her for another!'

'Too late, I'm afraid.' He nodded in the direction of the desk and the No Vacancies notice newly placed there.

'I'll get that number now, Mrs Townsend,' the girl called. 'Won't be a tick.'

'Now!' Julia flung when at last she could shut the bedroom door behind them. 'I want to know why you have done this! Did you really think you could get away with it? Mrs Townsend, indeed! What do you think I am, then – a tart?'

'Julia love, I'm sorry. If you only knew how much –'

'Don't *love* me! You surprise me, Mark. If it's a woman you want there are plenty available and better at it than I am, I shouldn't wonder! And I'm not in the habit of having cheap little affairs in back street hotels, though full marks for trying! A widow, desperate for a man – is that how you see me?'

'Julia! I've said I'm sorry! But I've loved you for a long time, you see. Tonight seemed the opportunity I've been hoping for. I thought you cared for me, too.'

'I do care for you, Mark, but caring is as far as it goes. I do *not* love you. I haven't even wondered what it would be like to share a bed with you, and if you've got hold of the wrong end of the stick, then I'm sorry. I've never encouraged you – now have I?'

'You've been happy enough in my company. We've had good times together. Am I so repulsive, Julia?'

'No. You are not repulsive and I have enjoyed your company. But I – I – well, to put it simply you are not Andrew, so now I suggest you find yourself somewhere else to sleep.'

'But where? Everywhere will be full.' Her anger had shaken him. He had not thought it could be so cuttingly fierce. And he had not realized, he thought sadly and too late, that she loved Andrew MacMalcolm so; that any woman was capable of loving so deeply, so enduringly.

'I don't care. Just *go*!'

'Very well.' He picked up his coat. It was wet, she noticed, as were his shoes and the bottoms of his trousers. 'But please believe me, Julia, I'm sorry.'

'It's a bit late for that, isn't it?' She was wavering, she knew it. Not about letting him share the bed, but about flinging him out into the night. She felt sorry for him, even, for all her seething anger. And perhaps she was half to blame for not making it plain enough there was no chance of anything other than friendship between them.

'Mark!' Sighing deeply, she pulled back the bedcover, giving him a pillow and the eiderdown. 'You can stay. Over there!' She pointed to the farthest corner of the room. 'But first I'd like you to give me time to get undressed and into bed. Wait outside, please. I'd like ten minutes, if you don't mind!'

'Thank you, Julia. I should have known better than –'

'Oh, *do* shut up!' She walked to the door, holding it open. '*Ten minutes*!'

Then she closed the door, covering her face with her hands, wanting to weep until there were no more tears in her. But instead she whispered, 'Andrew, I'm sorry. So very sorry . . .'

35

Cook had no stomach for Christmas. True, mincemeat and puddings and peaches in brandy had long since been made and labelled and stored in the keeping pantry and the Christmas cake, baked five months ago, sealed in a tin with Bramley apples to keep it moist. Soon, she supposed, she would have to take it out and cover it with almond paste, but not yet. Tomorrow, maybe. Or the next day . . .

But the Christmas of 1936 would not be a good one, Cook felt it in her ageing bones. She had said as much to Miss Clitherow only that afternoon in the housekeeper's sitting room when invited to take tea there.

The importance of the occasion, and the seriousness, had been marked by the use of Miss Clitherow's best rosebud china and silver teapot, for important and serious it was when any day now Britain, the Empire and the Commonwealth, could be called upon to face the most shaming scandal ever.

And scandal it was, Miss Clitherow agreed and shaming without doubt when a man born to be king, a man who'd had years enough to get used to the idea that duty came before all else, was prevaricating with all and sundry and trying his level best to make That Woman queen whilst keeping the crown and all the trappings that went with it. Having his cake and eating it, except that the cake wasn't to everybody's liking. Stale, secondhand cake never was.

'You'll take a little brandy in your tea?' Miss Clitherow reached for a bottle marked *Linctus. Adult use only*, and trickled a capful into each dainty cup. 'I fear we may need fortifying, before this matter comes to a head. I cannot for the life of me see why the King should act so strangely. Why doesn't he get the crown safely on his head, first?' He'd have been in a far better bargaining position if only he'd thought on and played it careful-like, instead of rushing in, chancing all for love. 'Kings right through history have always had their – their *lady friends*.' The housekeeper baulked at 'mistresses'. 'Why couldn't the King keep her as his *friend*? You'd think she'd be content with that.'

'Nay, not her! It's queen or nothing for That One. She's got delusions of grandeur and she isn't acceptable, Miss Clitherow, oh, dearie me, *no*! For one thing, her's not Church of England, for another her's far too old to give the King a son – and sons are what it's all about, let's face it – and for another, her's . . .' She left the word hanging on the air, her lips forming it silently.

'*Divorced*.' Emboldened by the brandy, the housekeeper forced the word from her button-round mouth, though she, too, disliked it every bit as much as Cook did. Divorce was for actresses and film stars and chorus girls and not for decent, law-abiding, God-fearing folk and certainly *not* for the King of England! 'And you know and I know, Cook, that such persons are not acceptable in society. Lady Helen – and I can say this without fear of contradiction – has never received a divorced person, nor called upon one, nor sat one at her table. Not even an innocent party, and That One is *not* innocent!'

'It's so degrading.' Cook shook her head, closing her eyes, because for two pins she'd have burst into tears, so mortifying was it.

'Degrading.' Agnes Clitherow took another almond biscuit from the Silver Jubilee tin. 'And supposing he gives up duty for desire? What then? Abdication, that's all that's left to him!' As though he were some Eastern-European head of state few of whom, in the housekeeper's opinion, could be commended for their stability. 'To see our king slinking out of the country, for he couldn't for shame stay, Cook, would be the worst thing that has happened to this country since – since . . .'

'Oliver Cromwell?' Mrs Shaw sighed. 'Mind, there's no shortage of younger brothers.'

'To take the throne, you mean? True, there's the Duke of Kent and Princess Marina – such a beautiful queen she would make, and there's the Duke of Gloucester and that bonny wife of his, I suppose, but when all is said and done, I think that the sooner we get Prince Albert onto the throne, the better!'

'But he's a happily married man, a family man. Wouldn't be fair to wish the crown on the Duke of York. Folks say he don't want it, you know.'

'It isn't always what a man *wants*, especially when he's born royal. And he's got two pretty princesses and the little duchess. The little duchess, now, would make a lovely queen. Always smiling . . .'

'Ah, yes – our own little duchess. Do you know, the more I think about it, the more I'm sure the little duchess would suit us very nicely.'

'Very nicely indeed.' Miss Clitherow reached for the linctus bottle, dividing the contents equally between the two empty cups. Then, little finger extended genteelly, she murmured, 'To the Duke of York and his lovely Elizabeth, God bless them.'

'Amen to that,' Cook had murmured, cup held high in salute. She had, she supposed, felt somewhat comforted having discussed the King's great problem in the privacy of the housekeeper's sitting room, but now, the effects of the fortifying brandy fast wearing off and her head thumping most uncomfortably, Cook thought about Christmas, which was almost upon them and very little done, and felt that this year she had no stomach for festivities. None at all . . .

*   *   *

Events, now that the King's private business was private no longer, came to a head with alarming speed. No more was it will he, won't he? but *when*?

Already, the newly-divorced Mrs Simpson had fled England for the greater safety of France and now a lonely, careworn king had received the Prime Minister and informed him of his intention to relinquish the throne, yet all the while refusing to see the bewildered brother on whom the throne would be thrust.

On the afternoon of the next day, King Edward's act of abdication was accepted by Parliament and George VI was, within a minute, the new King of England. Prince Albert had assumed his father's name and his smiling little duchess was now Queen Elizabeth.

His Royal Highness the Duke of Windsor, said the announcer, who had interrupted a programme to break the momentous news in a measured, funereal voice, would broadcast to the nation this evening.

It would be listened to with sadness by many; with disbelief and shame by others and by a militant minority with delight that the selfish man was getting his come-uppance and his foolish, jewel-grabbing woman with him. Only publicans who had had the foresight to place a wireless set in their bar parlours would sell any ale tonight. Most people would hug their firesides this bleak December night and listen, unspeaking, to the making of history.

That evening, Julia and Drew went down to the kitchen, pulling up chairs to the table around which Miss Clitherow, Cook, Tilda and Mary already sat.

Tilda wept silently for her long-ago love, remembering him as he had been in the war years, so young, so handsome in his soldier's uniform, his smile so boyish and beguiling.

She had loved him devotedly and given him up without thought of self. His framed photograph lay now in the top, left-hand drawer in which she kept her bloomers and woolly vests. Something more intimate than that, Tilda could not imagine.

Miss Clitherow sat straight-backed and black-clad; Cook, apron at the ready in case it all got too much for her, fidgeted with the plum-coloured chenille table cover.

Mary's needle stabbed into a tray cloth she was embroidering to match the tablecloth newly folded into her bottom drawer. Mary Strong had no sympathy for a king who couldn't find himself a decent, unwed woman when the country was full of decent, unwed women like herself.

And when the sad, selfish broadcast was over, Cook sighed deeply, switched on the new-fangled electric kettle and enquired of Julia and Drew if they would care to stay for a sup of tea.

'Thanks, Cook, but no. I've a call booked to America to mother. She'll want to know all about it, I shouldn't wonder. About ten o'clock, they said. Better be within earshot . . .'

'A call to America,' Cook breathed when they had left. 'Whatever next?'

'It runs under the Atlantic, I believe, along a cable – a submarine cable I think they call it,' Mary supplied.

'Wonders will never cease.' Cook opened the cupboard door, reaching up for the bottle of brandy with a hand that still shook from the effort of holding back her tears.

'A little drop in our tea to steady our nerves, wouldn't you say, Miss Clitherow?' Cook sought the housekeeper's approval for the misappropriation of the cooking brandy and received a sanctioning nod of approval.

Julia propped open the door of the little winter parlour the better to hear the telephone in the hall.

'Can I speak to grandmother, too?'

'All right – but just a quick hullo. Calls to America cost a lot of money, don't forget.' It was the first one she had ever made, truth known.

'Will we be able to hear her properly?'

'I should hope so!' She had discussed the call with the operator at the tiny telephone exchange in Holdenby.

'You'll want to wait until after the broadcast, Mrs Mac-Malcolm?' The operator hoped that not one of the subscribers connected to her switchboard would want to make a call when the King was speaking on the wireless.

Afterwards, of course, there would be a rash of little lights flashing and dials dropping with a click and everyone ringing everyone else with a '*Well*, and what do you think to that, then!' when all the time they'd known the King – the Duke of Windsor, beg pardon – would take the easy way out because people had known all along he'd never really wanted to be king.

Julia's call to Kentucky came through at ten minutes past ten which, Julia had been assured, would be late afternoon over there.

'Your call to Kentucky is on the line, Mrs MacMalcolm. Go ahead, caller,' the operator said in her best GPO voice. 'You're thrrrrrrrough, now.'

'Amelia?' Julia didn't know why she was shouting and dropped her voice to a more normal tone. 'Can you hear me?'

'Clear as a bell, honey. Everything okay? What goes on, in England? Oh, and your mother's in the bath, by the way. Will I send for her?'

'No! Best you shouldn't!' Julia had a fearful mental vision of a clock ticking away the seconds – and the pounds.

'Okay. I'll get her to call you from here tomorrow night, then? How's your king?' It could be the only reason for the call, Amelia reasoned.

'Which one are you talking about? We've got a new one, now!'

'So he did it! She finally got him! When was it?'

'He was on the wireless, not so long ago. Said he was

giving up the throne for the woman he loved. Said his brother – the new king, you know – had a blessing denied to him – a happy home life with a wife and children . . .'

'Ha! Whingeing right till the end! My heart bleeds for him.' Amelia's sarcasm came over clearly. 'So now what? A new start with a new king?'

'Looks like it . . .'

'And everywhere is calm? There's been no trouble?'

'There's no fighting in the streets, if that's what you mean. I think everybody's glad it's over and done with.'

'Sure. They would be. Thanks for calling, Julia. I'll tell your Mom everything is fine at Rowangarth and I'll get her to call you tomorrow night – okay?'

'She's fine, by the way. Having a great time. 'Bye, honey. See you in ten days, God willing . . .'

'You heard?' said Julia, laying down the phone. 'That was Aunt Amelia. Grandmother was in the bath – it would've cost the earth to have got her out of it. Sorry, Drew, but she's ringing tomorrow night – Amelia said she would – and you can take the call – all right?'

'Fine. So what do we do now, mother? Bit of an anti-climax, isn't it?'

'Do? We get on with our lives, I suppose.'

'We could drink the new king's health. Grandmother would want to, if she were here.'

'But of course! Be a dear, and ask Miss Clitherow to bring up a bottle – champagne, of course. She's got the wine cellar key. Tell her we'll be down to the kitchen for a toast.'

'Me, too?'

'We-e-ll, maybe just half a glass . . .'

'Mother! In two weeks and two days I shall be eighteen – remember? And next week, I'm leaving school – for good! And I think that tonight I shall pull rank and be Sir

Andrew. I shall not only propose the loyal toast – I shall pop the cork, too! So what have you to say to that,' he grinned.

'I'd say,' she said with mock severity, 'that you'll be getting sent to bed without supper for your cheek – big as you are! Now off you go and see to that champagne. And tell Mary the best glasses,' she called after him.

Then a sudden trembling took her and tears filled her eyes and ran down her cheeks. Her son – Giles's and Alice's son – was almost a man. Eighteen at Christmas and Andrew killed just eighteen years ago; all the years slipping past like eighteen minutes.

So what did they do now, Drew had asked.

'Do?' she whispered to the empty room. 'Like I just said, I get on with my life, I suppose.'

More lonely, bleak, unloved and unloving years; more years of trying to bring back the sound of Andrew's voice and the love in it. And lying wide-eyed in the darkness, wanting him until her body ached from it.

Dear, sweet Jesus in heaven – how was she to live through the emptiness ahead?

The next day – and the date would always stay in Julia's memory, had she but known it – HRH the Duke of Windsor was driven to Portsmouth huddled in the back of a limousine, trilby hat pulled low over his eyes. There, he was to board HMS *Fury* and be borne away to France. Not to his love, because the laws of divorce insisted they must not meet for six months, until a divorce *absolute* was granted to Mrs Bessie Wallis Simpson.

Six months apart, with only letters and phone calls to hold them together. Julia glared at the telephone on the oak table in the hall, willing it to ring and for Andrew to be there, on the other end of it.

So a king had given up his throne for love? She, Julia, would give up life itself to be with Andrew, but she could not because there were times when she did not believe in heaven nor in God, either.

Saturday, the twelfth day of December. Tomorrow, on the thirteenth, Nathan and the congregation of All Souls would offer prayers for King George and his smiling queen.

Those dates she would always remember, because on the fourteenth, the letter had come. In an expensively thick envelope it had been and the postmark a London one.

Dear Madam, it began, and when she had read it, then read it through again, the breath left her body in a gasp.

'God, *no*!' she choked. 'Alice!' She must tell Alice! *Now*! Alice would know what to do – oh, *please* she would know what to do?

Blindly, panic-stricken, choking on her sobs, she made for the door.

36

'Thank God you're in!' Julia thrust the envelope into Alice's hand. 'Look at that! Go on – *read it!*'

'For goodness sake . . .'

'Read it! You'll never believe it! I can't!' Hugging herself tightly, Julia paced the floor. 'Where is Daisy – Tom?'

'Daisy's at school – you know she is – and Tom's out all day. Tomorrow is the first shoot of the season . . .'

'So there's no one here?' No one to hear what they would say. 'So what do you think of it? I can't make head or tail of it. And who is Beulah Townsend? I've never heard of the woman!'

'Julia – calm down! You want me to read the letter – all right, let me read it? If you want to do something useful, put the kettle on. Seems you could do with a cup of tea.'

'Laced with hemlock!'

'The kettle!' Alice hissed, frowning as she arranged the words and sentences into some awful kind of order. Then taking a deep, shuddering breath she said, 'I don't believe this. Just let me get it straight? This woman, Beulah Townsend is divorcing her husband for adultery and naming *you*?'

'That's it. Mark's wife . . .'

'But you said he was a widower.'

'I thought he was. I mentioned it on the odd occasion, but he always clammed up. So I left it alone. I thought she'd died in the war and he didn't want to talk about her.'

'Look, Julia – I don't want to ask this, but I've got to. I know you've been out with him quite a bit over the years, but have you ever – just once, even . . . ?'

'Committed adultery with him? The answer is no, no, no! Word of a Sutton. On Drew's life, I swear it!'

'That's all I wanted to know. So how has this Beulah woman got you involved? When *might* it have happened? And you know you've got to tell Nathan about this.'

'I tried to. I rang him before I came here. But he's got a funeral, somewhere. He's got three parishes, now, don't forget.'

'Did you leave a message?'

'Yes. Told his housekeeper that if I wasn't at Rowangarth, I'd be here. Maybe he'll come over.'

'Of course he will, if you said it was urgent. Anyway, when might this adultery have happened?'

'When mother went to Amelia's, I think. We saw her off at Tilbury, remember? It was the night of the fog. I told you about it.'

'The night you stayed at some hotel?' Alice set cups on a tray, her mouth all at once dry.

'The Flowers Hotel. All we wanted was somewhere to sleep. London was dead. There was no chance of getting back to Montpelier Mews.'

'Someone must have been following you – had you considered that?'

'It's the only explanation I can think of. But how did his wife know we'd be at the theatre?'

'You tell *me*, love. She must have been having him followed, but how she knew when you'd be in London and likely to go out with him, I don't know. I've heard they have private detectives who do that. They follow people, then get witnesses to make statements in court about –'

'Alice! Do you have to?'

'Sorry. But a lot of divorces are put-up jobs like Mrs Simpson's was. Collusion, I think they call it. And maybe it isn't you in particular she's got it in for. Perhaps she's been having Mark Townsend followed for ages and you were the one that happened to be in the wrong place at the wrong time.'

'And do you think that's any consolation to me? *Do you*? Can't you see – the shame of it? I'm a Sutton, Alice, and Suttons don't get mixed up in sleazy divorces – not even innocently. Just think how people went to town on the King and Mrs Simpson. A divorcee – a social leper, that made her. And now *I'm* going to be named co-respondent in a divorce case. God! It'll kill mother when she finds out!'

'Then you must defend yourself.' Alice spooned sugar into Julia's cup. 'You can't let that woman get away with it. And come to think of it – do you think Mark Townsend might have something to do with this? You said he admitted he was keen on you.'

'I know. And I told him it wasn't on – you know I did. But I didn't know about Beulah, I honestly didn't.' Julia winced as the scalding liquid burned her tongue. 'I'll ring Mark. I should have phoned him right away, told him.'

'Oh, no, you don't! From now on, you don't get in touch with him and don't take any calls from him, either! Her solicitors will have been in touch with him, too. He'll know what's going on.'

'Then why hasn't he phoned me?' Julia paced the floor again, incapable of sitting still.

'Maybe he has and thank goodness you're here. But I think you should get in touch with Carvers.'

'How can I? Carver-the-old wouldn't touch divorce with a very long stick and Middle Carver is more for money matters. That only leaves Carver-the-young, and I don't think –'

'All right! You don't like him, I know that, but you've got to tell him.' Young Mr Carver had been instrumental in getting them all back to Rowangarth. If Julia wasn't in such a state, Alice would have reminded her of that. 'At least ask him to recommend you to a good lawyer; one who specializes in – in –'

'In nasty little cases like this one? Oh, you're right!' She held up her hand as Alice made to protest. 'But how am I to get out of this mess? No one is going to believe me. Would you, I mean? Mark slept on the floor all night, but a chambermaid came in with morning tea, and saw us.'

'And jumped to the wrong conclusions. Pity you ordered that tea.'

'But we *didn't*, Alice.'

'Then that proves it. That chambermaid is going to be paid to swear in court that you and him were in that room together when she brought the tray in.'

'Then what am I to do?' Julia's face drained of all colour. 'And mother'll be home in a week! What am I to tell her?'

'Do? You drink up your tea, then we go over to Rowangarth and phone young Mr Carver. And when Lady Helen comes home, you tell her the truth. I believe you and she'll believe you, too. So get that tea down you. We've been in worse corners than this, you and me. We'll manage.'

Carver-the-young agreed to see Julia at once. For one thing she had sounded so distraught and anyway, he had no appointments that morning. He smiled, offered coffee, then read the letter she laid on his desk.

'There is no doubt about it, Mrs MacMalcolm.' He cleared his throat noisily. 'You are indeed being cited as co-respondent in a Mrs Townsend's petition for divorce. On the grounds of adultery,' he added, almost with satisfaction. 'Now, that's the worst of it, so let's think of a way out. You deny the allegation, of course?'

'Absolutely,' Julia whispered. 'Word of a Sutton. What I do not deny is that Mark Townsend and I shared a room when we weren't able to get home from the theatre – fog, it was.'

'Ah, yes. Those London fogs. And you categorically deny that any intimacy took place?'

'I've said so. I'll see a doctor, if it would help.'

'I very much doubt it. But we have agreed the most important thing — that you have been wrongly implicated — so we mustn't make things easy for Mrs Townsend.'

'Easy? She's holding all the aces it seems to me, but what I want to know is why should Mark Townsend never have told me about her? I asked him and he gave me to understand there was no woman in his life.'

'There wasn't, Mrs MacMalcolm. When Townsend was serving at the Front, Beulah had an affair. He found out about it, though. Such things always surface, in the end. He and Beulah tried a reconciliation, but it didn't work. They parted, in the end, and she's been trying to get free of him ever since.'

'So why didn't he divorce her? And how come you know so much about it?' Julia demanded, hot-cheeked.

'He couldn't divorce her for the wartime affair once they'd become reconciled and had — er — co-habited. The fact that they got together again wiped out — legally, anyway — her fall from grace, as it were.

'Pity they ever tried again to make a go of it. It would've been all plain sailing for Townsend, otherwise. And I think that in the end he just held out stubbornly — trying to punish her. Then came the Flowers Hotel incident and she had what she wanted. You were obviously being watched. Devious, Beulah is — always was.'

'You know her?' Julia gasped.

'I knew her — once,' he said, tight-lipped. 'And half London society knew about the wartime affair. I suppose I was more privy to it than most. Townsend and I were at law school together, you see, and when war came, we joined the same regiment — I thought you knew.'

'No, I didn't.' How could she have known? 'But what are my chances of getting out of this without the world and his wife knowing about it?' And *especially* without her mother knowing.

'Now there we must proceed with caution. But I think

there might be hope. All I need is a little time. I'll be in touch tomorrow, maybe, or the next day, and meantime, don't have any dealings with Townsend. If he phones, refuse the call.' He rose to his feet, holding out a hand, his face slablike. 'I'll see you to the door. Try not to worry too much.'

Not to worry! Julia fumed silently. Oh, but he was enjoying seeing her squirm. She had never liked Carver-the-young; she liked him still less, now! Head down against the driving rain, she hurried to the car park.

'"Don't worry," he said – but what do you make of it?' Julia demanded of Alice who had come at once to hear the outcome of the visit. 'I could wring Mark Townsend's neck. I should have realized he was smitten long before I did. He really must have thought he was sharing that bed with me! Talk about seizing the moment! But do you think there is any hope? Do you think I'll be able to get out of it?'

'I don't know,' Alice brooded. 'But by all accounts that solicitor knows something he isn't telling you.'

'Then I wish he would – good *or* bad. God! What is Drew going to make of it all? And as for mother – well, you know what her generation think about divorce. She'd never get –' She stopped, as Mary opened the door.

'The Reverend is here, Miss Julia. I said you had someone with you so he said he'd wait in the library.'

'Then do you think Cook could rustle up something to eat – sandwiches, perhaps, and a pot of tea? Are you staying, Alice?'

'No. I'll get back home.' She waited until the parlourmaid had closed the door then said softly, 'You know where I am if you need me. An' it's best you and Nathan have a talk about things. He'll know what to do. Say hullo to him, from me,' she smiled, kissing Julia's cheek. 'And tell him *all* about it? He's not only your friend, he's your parish priest, too. Nathan will help.'

Nathan always had. He always would, Alice thought as she made her way back to Keeper's Cottage. But what a mess it all was! And how was Lady Helen to take it, when she got home?

My, but this had been a nasty old year, she thought, pulling up her collar, sinking her hands into the pockets of her coat. She would be glad when it was over and done with.

1936? A good riddance to it! And surely, she thought as she stepped thankfully into the warmth of her kitchen, things could only get better?

Julia opened the library door with a flourish, then closed it with a bang, leaning against it dramatically, eyes screwed tightly against tears.

'My dear!' Nathan rose to his feet. 'What is it? Urgent, you said on the phone and I've been trying to get you ever since.'

'Nathan!' She ran to him, arms outstretched, and he gathered her to him, hushing her gently, holding her close.

'Tell me?' He offered a handkerchief, guiding her to a chair. 'Aunt Helen – is she all right?'

'Fine,' Julia choked. 'Drew, too . . .'

'Then what is it? This morning, it seemed important. Are *you* all right?'

'Yes – oh, *no*,' she sniffed, dipping into her pocket, pulling out the envelope. 'A fine mess I've got myself into. Go on – see what it says. It doesn't make pretty reading.'

'I don't believe this,' Nathan said eventually, carefully folding the letter.

'Then I'm glad, because it isn't true. Oh, we spent the night together, but nothing happened. Circumstantial evidence, but who's going to believe it? And what is mother going to say when she hears?' Her voice trailed into a whisper as fresh tears rose in her throat and she covered her face with her hands, shaking her head from side to side. 'Nathan – who will believe me?'

'I do.' He sat down on the arm of her chair, laying a protective arm across her shoulders. 'But don't you think you'd better start at the beginning? You're being cited in a Mrs Townsend's petition for divorce – and you are denying it?'

'Absolutely!'

She drew in a long, deep breath, fighting to control the emotion that seethed inside her, gazing round the room that smelled of wood smoke in winter and gillyflowers in summer and of old, musty books; the room where once, in another life it seemed, Giles had worked at his books with Morgan sprawling on the hearthrug.

She jumped to her feet, walked over to the window and dabbing her eyes dry she lifted her chin. Then, as Nathan had asked, she began at the beginning, leaving nothing out.

'Young Carver says there's hope, but I don't think he'll be able to do anything,' she finished, eyes fixed on the bare branches of the linden trees. 'It's all too awful even to think about. Since that letter came, it's suddenly hit me that Drew is growing up and soon he'll fall in love, then who will I have?'

'Me, Julia.' Nathan said it softly, simply.

'*You*, Nathan? But you're always here. What I'm trying to say is how am I going to cope with the loneliness when Drew goes – because one day he will, you know.'

'Drew won't leave Rowangarth. He'll never be far away. And I didn't make myself clear. What I am trying to say is that I'll always be here for you, with you. I'm asking you to marry me, Julia.'

'*Me*? Marry *you*? Why?' She sounded ungrateful and brusque but it was all she could think of to say.

'Is it so very funny?'

'Of course it is! You haven't grasped one word of what I've been saying, have you? I've got myself tangled up in a divorce. Innocently, but no one is going to believe that. From now on, I won't be nice to know. Me and Mrs Simpson, both – scarlet women!

'And you, Nathan, are a man of the cloth, a priest, and priests don't get involved with co-respondents in divorce cases – that's what I meant. I didn't mean you aren't a nice person, because you are. What I *am* trying to say is that your goodness makes me want to weep, and –'

'Julia, dearest girl, don't start crying again? You never could weep prettily, even as a child. And as for not getting involved with you, I don't think there was ever a time when I wasn't – involved, I mean. Trouble was, I didn't realize it until you told me you'd fallen in love with Andrew.'

'And you still – *care* . . . ?' She stared at him blankly.

'I still love you.'

'But when Andrew and I were married, it was you who blessed us. Did you mean it?'

'With all my heart. I loved you; I wanted you to be happy.'

'But all these years, Nathan?' She took a step away from him because all at once they were standing too close and it unnerved her. 'All the years between – hasn't there been anyone else for you?'

'No. All those years I've been trying to fall out of love with you, and I can't. So will you marry me, Julia MacMalcolm?' His smile was gentle, his eyes tender, but for all that she cried,

'No, Nathan! No, *no*! You don't love me – not really. You're doing this because I'm Julia, Giles's sister. You're trying to shield me, to defy convention to protect me from all the sneers and gossip, because sneers and gossip there'll be before so very much longer.

'Soon, they'll all be talking about me, sniggering over their teacups. It'll start in Holdenby and end up only God knows where, and at each telling it'll be added to and titillated and people are going to say that's how women like me get our cheap little thrills.

'Widows, Nathan. Women alone. No one is going to believe that nothing happened between me and Mark Townsend so there's no use rushing to my defence by announcing our engagement. It's too late! I'm going to have to stand up in court and deny it, or plead guilty so I don't have to appear.'

'And who told you that?'

'No one told me. I just know it. An undefended petition, I think they call it, and all because the so-called guilty parties are too ashamed to appear in public and swear on oath they are innocent.'

She paused to draw breath, will herself to be calm.

'Anyway, Nathan, your bishop wouldn't stand for it for one thing, and for another, I – well, I don't think I love you. Not the way you would want me to love you,' she finished softly, sadly.

'Then I'd wait until you did want me. God knows I've waited long enough already.'

They spun round, startled, as the door opened and Mary came in. Julia had forgotten the sandwiches.

'There you are, Reverend. Cook says she's sorry it took so long. Cold beef – your favourite, she says.'

'Thank you. Tell Cook she spoils me.'

'I'll pour, Mary.' Julia lifted the teapot, forcing her lips into a smile. 'D'you think she heard anything?' she asked when they were alone again.

'I don't think so – but would it have mattered if she had?' He accepted the plate Julia offered, then laid it aside. 'I was saying I wouldn't ask anything of you that you weren't willing to give. I know how much you loved Andrew, but it was a long time ago, Julia. Why can't you visit his grave, weep over it, say a decent goodbye as a lot of other women have done?'

'Because I will not look at a slab of stone with Andrew's

name on it. Andrew was a living, breathing person and to me he still is. Can't you see that, Nathan?'

'I can only see that you are punishing yourself and punishing the whole world. Do you think Andrew would want you to be like this? He gave his own life but he didn't expect you to give yours.'

'He didn't give his life. It was taken from him!' Julia flung, tight-lipped. 'My husband was *killed*. Don't be so mealy-mouthed, Nathan. It's me, Julia, you are talking to! And for heaven's sake eat your sandwiches!'

'Sorry, but suddenly I'm not hungry. I've made a fool of myself – rushed in without thinking. But I wasn't taking advantage of your situation, Julia; wasn't asking you to marry me whilst you were down on your luck and in need of someone to cling to. I asked you because I love you and I always will. But like I said, forget it ever happened. I'll call again later when we've both calmed down and talk about that letter. Do you think young Carver can handle it? Would it be better if you got a London solicitor?'

'I don't know – I honestly don't. Alice thinks young Carver has something up his sleeve. He was at law school with Mark Townsend and served in the same regiment. He knew Beulah Townsend, too, so let's see what he comes up with, first?

'And Nathan, I'm sorry – about the way I said no to what you asked me, I mean. It's time I grew up. God knows, I'll be forty-four, next birthday. I didn't mean to sound ungrateful, though. It's just that I can't think straight at the moment. Say you aren't too hurt? You're the nicest, kindest person and if I ever – well, if ever I *did* . . .'

'Yes. I know. I should have realized you are still in love with Andrew.'

He gathered her to him and she went willingly into the strong, safe shelter of his arms. Then he kissed her cheek gently and walked to the door.

'I'll see myself out,' he smiled. 'And try not to worry too

much? Things have a way of sorting themselves out. I'll come back tonight, if you'd like me to?'

'Come to dinner? Drew's staying the night with a school friend and there'll be no one. I can't bear to be alone tonight, Nathan . . .'

'Then I'll be with you about seven.'

She had held his heart and his love for as long as he could remember. And his was the love that couldn't be turned off, just like her love for Andrew. It was the way things were. He knew where he stood with her now, and he must accept it.

'There's something going on,' said Mary sniffily, 'and it's something to do with London, if you ask me. Miss Julia's got herself into a fine old tizzy. All I said was wasn't it lovely that her ladyship would be home in three days and just in nice time for Christmas and she said, "*Christmas*", all snappy as if she hated Christmas, and we all know she doesn't.'

'I think,' Tilda dropped her voice to a whisper, 'she might be coming up to *that* age . . .'

'The change? Not her,' Mary snorted. 'She's a young woman!'

'Not all that young, though she carries her age well, same as her ladyship. You wouldn't think she was over –'

'Tilda Tewk! How often must I tell you that a lady's age is her own business,' Cook interrupted irritably because she knew it wasn't Miss Julia's time of life that was the cause of all the upset. It was that letter; the one Mary had signed for off the postman. *That* morning had been the start of it.

'Well, she's away again and that'll make twice in three days,' Mary offered primly. "If the Reverend phones, Mary, tell him I'm at Carvers and that I'll ring him back." It's something legal, if you ask me!'

'Legal about what?' Tilda didn't trust lawyers. 'Surely Rowangarth isn't short of money?'

'No. It isn't money,' Mary protested. 'It's something to do with London, though. I'm sure of it.'

'Then we'd better ask Jin Dobb to tea,' Tilda suggested hopefully. 'Jin'll soon get to the bottom of it for you.' Though Jin, try as she may, had never found a man in Tilda Tewk's tea leaves.

'Us'll do no such thing!' Cook huffed. 'And see to the kettle. Miss Julia'll want coffee the minute she gets back.'

Miss Julia always wanted coffee, lately, was drinking far too much of it. Someone should tell her that too much coffee could give her a bad back, and then where would she be?

All the same, Cook pondered, she'd give a lot to find out what was bothering the poor lass. Not a bit like herself Miss Julia wasn't. Oh, my word, no!

Young Carver, Julia thought angrily as she parked her car behind the solicitors' offices, had hemmed and hawed each time she phoned him and this morning, no matter what, they would have to come to an understanding. Either he got a move on, or she must find herself another solicitor.

'It's early days, yet,' or stupid platitudes about how long it had taken to build Rome was all she had managed to get out of him. Didn't he realize her mother would soon be home?

'Now see here, Mr Carver,' she flung the minute the office door was closed on them, 'we are simply no further forward. Leave it with you, you said. A little time, you said, but time is fast running out – or hadn't you realized?'

'I have indeed.' Carver-the-young rested his hands on the pristine sheet of blotting paper on his desktop, then entwined his fingers as if he were about to start praying. His face was inscrutable as ever; his eyes narrowed almost to slits. 'I might even say,' he shrugged, 'that it *has*. Run out, I mean. But do have a cup of coffee – or a sherry, perhaps?'

'No!' Julia hissed. 'No, *thank* you.' She wasn't here to drink coffee and be told she was in a worse mess than ever. And how he dare look so pleased with himself, so *smug*, almost, she really didn't know. 'Mr Carver, I am just about at the end of my tether! Can't you imagine what this scandal will do to my mother when she hears about it? She is totally against divorce. She'll be devastated – and as for Drew . . .'

'Mrs MacMalcolm – calm down, *please*. As I said, time has run out – but not for you. Mrs Townsend, you see, is in no position to divorce her husband for adultery. She cannot petition on those grounds because she has had lovers herself – several, in fact. She is guilty of the same misdemeanour as her husband and, in my book, two wrongs don't make a right.'

'But I thought Mark Townsend had condoned her lapse by taking her back to – to –'

'To the marital bed? Yes, that was so. But it was after their reconciliation broke down and they parted by mutual consent that her affairs took place; three, that I know of, so she cannot petition on the grounds of her husband's adultery.'

'Adultery with *me*, Mr Carver.'

'With any woman, Mrs MacMalcolm.'

'Then forgive me, but isn't it a little unlikely that any of those men are going to come forward and admit it?'

'Now there you have a point. But we are lucky, because one of them will – *has* . . .'

'Then God bless the man, who ever he is!' Julia gasped.

'Thank you. That man is myself.'

'*You*? You and her – you've . . . ?' How could he admit it so – so *blatantly*? 'I – I'm sorry, Mr Carver, but doesn't it all seem a little improbable? I mean – just when we need a small miracle, you happen to have one, up your sleeve!'

'Believe me, it's true. For a time I was very attracted to Beulah Townsend. Then my legal training surfaced, so to speak, and I realized the foolishness of getting entangled with a married woman.

'Anyway, she dropped me for some other fellow, so I was well out of it, I suppose. Beulah was an attractive woman, though, and very available. Are you shocked, Mrs MacMalcolm?'

'No. Not really.' She looked down to fidget with her wedding ring. 'And it's different for men, I suppose. But how are you, a partner in a firm of respected solicitors, going to stand up in court and admit to *that*? How can you, when you are acting for me? And it's such a coincidence that I still don't know if I believe you.'

'You may please yourself. I'm not worried either way because I have already phoned both Townsend and Beulah's solicitors and given them the facts, told them to sort it out as best they can.'

'And?' Mark would take no notice, Julia frowned. He wanted rid of his wife because truth known he wanted her, Julia, though she had been too stupid over the years to see it and too trusting ever to think he would stoop so low. And to her shame, though thumbscrews wouldn't drag it out of her, she had sometimes wondered – just *wondered* – what it would be like to be made love to again. 'Did what you told him do any good, or wasn't he interested?'

'Not at first, but he's thought it all out and I can't say I blame him for getting the best deal he can. Beulah is still going ahead with her petition and Townsend has agreed to let her divorce him, provided she doesn't demand alimony, which she won't. I hear that as soon as she is free of him, she plans to marry an elderly millionaire. She's been looking for one for some time, it seems.'

'So nothing has changed,' Julia whispered, dully. 'I'd have thought he'd have done the decent thing by me, especially as he knows nothing happened that night.'

'But of course he knows and I'm trying to tell you that you are out of it. Oh, the divorce will go ahead, but an unknown woman is to be cited, not you.'

'You mean they are going to use one of those women who make a living out of spending nights in hotel bedrooms, supposedly committing adultery?'

'Not even that, Mrs MacMalcolm. The fact is that I was able to persuade Beulah's solicitors to advise her that adultery with an unknown and therefore unnamed woman at the Flowers Hotel would make more sense – especially as I could make it known that she is in no position to petition for divorce, herself being not exactly lily white, as it were . . .

'When the case gets into court, the divorce judge will assume the woman was a prostitute. The petition will go through undefended by Townsend, so there'll hardly be a ripple – won't even merit a mention in the papers.'

'Y-yes . . .' The truth was only now beginning to manifest itself. 'But Mr Carver – hadn't you thought? Mark Townsend could have used what you told him and counterpetitioned, naming *you*! Where would your good name have been then – not to mention your practice?'

'Believe me, I'd thought. But it was a calculated risk and the bluff paid off. In the end, it was worth the gamble.'

'Then I'm grateful for what you have done – and it *is* all right?' Julia grasped the chair arms tightly because all at once she felt very dizzy. 'I'm finding it all just a little hard to believe – I really am.'

'Then believe this.' He handed her a sheet of thick, expensively-headed notepaper. 'Confirmation from Beulah Townsend's solicitors. All in black and white, just as I told you.

'And a word to the wise? I think Townsend will try to get in touch with you. I have the feeling he still has designs on you — might even try to persuade you he agreed to let his wife divorce him without fuss in order to save your reputation.

'Now to my way of thinking, that just isn't so. I believe he was willing to let that divorce go to court, naming you, so he could do the honourable thing afterwards and marry you — which would have been expected of him as a gentleman. I may be wrong, of course . . .'

'No.' Julia shook her head vehemently. 'You are right. I think he did want to marry me. I didn't think he'd go to such lengths, though. And Mr Carver,' she forced her eyes to meet his. 'You really didn't have to do it — put your reputation on the line, I mean.'

'You're right. I didn't,' he said flatly. 'But there is a tide in the affairs of men, as they say . . .'

'Well, no one will ever hear about it from me,' she whispered. 'And if there is ever anything I can do in return, please ask?'

'Thank you. I will. Indeed, I think that some time within the next few days you should sign an authorization for one of my clerks to go to Townsend's offices and collect all documents relating to any dealings you or your aunt may have had with him. Best you shouldn't have any more contact with the man.'

'So what does it all mean?' Not for a long time had she felt so drained, so near to tears.

'It means that as soon as maybe, you will sever all connections with Townsend and that Carver, Carver and Carver will be your sole legal advisers. Is that acceptable, Mrs MacMalcolm?'

Weak with relief, unable to trust herself to speak, Julia nodded.

'Good. And I am pleased to say again that you are no longer implicated in the divorce petition Townsend versus Townsend. Let them get on with their shabby little fight, though why they are each so eager to untie the knot is beyond me. They deserve each other so well it's a crying shame to break up such an alliance.

'Now, do have a coffee, Mrs MacMalcolm; better still, why not a small sherry?' He walked to a table to return with a circular silver tray on which stood glasses and two decanters. 'Medium, or dry?'

'It's over?' Julia whispered.

'It's over. Forget it. And if I may say so, it was most unprofessional of Townsend to place you in such a position in the first place.'

'Ah, yes. But in all fairness, Mr Carver, how was he to know there'd be a little man in a raincoat and trilby watching us, because there must have been.'

'Now there, I'm afraid, it was the fault – the unwitting fault – of your housekeeper.'

'Sparrow? Oh, surely not! She was devoted to Andrew. I'm very fond of her.'

'Unwittingly, I said. Mark Townsend lives not far away in Montpelier Gardens – but you'd know that?'

'Y-yes . . .'

'Your Sparrow, I'm afraid, is friendly with Townsend's cook, so it wouldn't be unusual for them to talk about the comings and goings of their respective employers. Below-stairs do it all the time, I believe. But I discovered that the cook's son-in-law works as a clerk for Beulah Townsend's solicitors.'

'So as far as I was concerned, the man in the raincoat almost always knew when to be on the alert – even in a pea-souper fog,' Julia gasped.

'*Especially* in a pea-souper. No blame attached to your housekeeper, of course, though you might ask her in future not to talk about your comings and goings.'

'I'll do that.' Julia gazed into the eyes of the hitherto disliked solicitor. 'And I'd like medium, please – and could you possibly make it a large one?'

Alice would never believe this, she really wouldn't, and

how could she, Julia reasoned hazily, when she didn't quite believe it herself?

All at once she felt light-headed and lighthearted. She gazed through the window to find that in the cold, bleak, December street outside, the sun was shining brilliantly.

Or so it seemed.

37

'This will be the most marvellous Hogmanay,' Helen enthused. 'To have Albert and Amelia will give me the chance to pay back a little of their hospitality. Such kindness, in Kentucky – I'm glad I made the trip. America is so *vast*!'

'And Nathan?' Julia asked.

'He'll be along after the Watch-night service. And Edward is looking forward to being at Rowangarth. But so he would – he was born here. It will be quite like old times, he said, if he manages to remember that far back! This will be Drew's last birthday party, until he's twenty-one, of course. Clever of Alice to have him on new year's eve – well, give or take a day. Eighteen, now. Had you realized it, Julia? The years have slipped by so quickly.'

'I'm not likely to forget, mother. Andrew was killed just before Drew was born . . .'

'I'm sorry, dear – truly I am. And it's so tragic that for you it doesn't seem to get any easier. Can't you try to accept?'

'That was what Nathan said, not so long ago. He wants me to go to Étaples, to the grave.'

She thought a lot about the afternoon Nathan asked her to marry him; shuddered to remember how she had thrown his love back without thought in his face. And he did love her. The pity of it was that she could not love him as he deserved.

Oh, she wanted to be loved again; she'd be inhuman if she didn't, but Andrew prevented it and what made it so awful was that even eighteen years after, she could not bring the sound of his voice into her mind, her heart, nor remember his face without a photograph to remind her.

All a part of her grief, she had been told. Alice had been the same way, too, when she thought Tom dead. But her own torment, Julia sighed, had lasted and, desperately as she longed to recall things they had said – husky, intimate whisperings or shared laughter – they eluded her. That April afternoon at the Gare du Nord and the old lady, selling violets. More than two years since they met and touched and she had flown to his arms. '*My darling love*,' he whispered, '*it is you, really you . . . ?*' She knew the words – they were safely stored in her heart – but she could not *hear* him saying them.

'And so you should.' Her mother, interrupting her thoughts. 'Andrew would want it. You owe it to him – a last goodbye.'

'Yes, we-e-ell . . .' Not to talk about it today; not just yet when everyone was trying to be happy. 'By the way, I told Catchpole the apprentices were to have new year's eve and new year's day off. They're all going home, so Polly and Keth will see the new year in at Keeper's – Reuben, too. Now that it's all settled about Keth going to Kentucky it might be the last time they are all together for three years. Keth won't be able to afford to come home, Alice says. He'll need all the money he can earn just to help him through college. Amelia is taking care of the bulk of the expenses, of course, and Keth will stay with her and Albert during vacations, but I'm afraid Daisy and Keth will be quite a long time apart.'

You mean . . . ?' Helen frowned.

'That they're in love? Of course they are! You've only to look at them when they're together to know it.'

'But Daisy is so young.'

'The same age as Alice was, when she met Tom. And you, dearest, if I remember were –'

'Seventeen and a bit the night I met your Pa.' Helen's smile was gentle.

'And I wasn't all that much older when I met Andrew. The Garth Suttons fall in love early.'

'And for ever, it would seem,' Helen finished. 'But about new year – I think it will be good for Edward to be with us – Clemmy, I mean . . .'

'Mother! Aunt Clemmy gave him a dog's life, and you know it!'

'All the same, he's bound to miss having her there. But oh, there won't have been such a family gathering at Rowangarth since – since –'

'Since Pa left us; since my wedding, you mean?'

'Something like that. But I am – well, I'm nearer eighty than seventy, you know, and I intend to make the most of what is left to me, starting at once!'

'Dearest – *please*? You don't look your age – not by ten years – and you are active and disgracefully healthy. Let's not think about you getting old? *Sixty*-six is no age at all!'

'Flatterer! But we *will* have a good party. We'll forget about all the things the warmongers are saying and we'll make sure no one in Holdenby goes hungry, nor is alone.'

'But we always have done . . .' Besides, there weren't so many hungry, now; not so many men out of work because suddenly coal was needed for factories, factories which, though people tried not to think about it, were all at once turning out trucks and lorries and guns for the Army and bombers for the Air Force. And wasn't the new aerodrome near York giving jobs to building workers who had been years on the poverty line? The shipyards, too; busy again with orders from the Admiralty though Julia insisted it was only to let Hitler know he'd better not get ideas about starting another war. That, really, was all it amounted to – wasn't it . . . ?

'Mam – can I ask you something?' Daisy said softly, hesitantly. 'Before Dada gets back?'

'Women's talk, is it?' Alice dampened a tea towel and draped it over the bowl of royal icing. 'Won't have to be long about it, love, or that icing'll go stiff.'

'I won't be. In fact, you might not like what I'm going to say . . .'

'Oh?' Serious, was it then? 'Try me, and see.'

'It's just that – well, did you? You and Dada, I mean?'

'Did we what?' Alice drew sharply on her breath because she knew what was to come.

'Did you – before you were married – ever . . .'

Her voice trailed out and she turned her back to fidget with an ornament on the mantelpiece.

'Were we ever lovers, are you trying to say? And Daisy – look at me, love?'

Reluctantly she turned, biting nervously on her lip, eyes bluer and wider than ever.

'Is that what you're asking, lass?'

'Yes, Mam.'

'Why? Have you and Keth –?' Alice's insides began to churn though why, she didn't know. She had known this moment would come, sooner or later.

'No. Honestly we haven't. But it would be easy to, especially now that Keth is going to America.'

'Not yet he isn't going. Not 'til next summer.'

'Yes, but we'll be a long time apart and there have been times when Keth has wanted to or I've wanted to . . .'

'Then thank the good Lord neither of you has wanted to both at the same time!' Alice breathed.

'I suppose you *could* say that. But did you ever – you and Dada?'

'While we were courting?'

Daisy nodded, eyes on hands.

'Well, if you want the truth, we did. And fools we were, though I can't rightly blame your Dada. It was me that wanted to, more'n him. It was only the once and Tom said we must never risk it again. And he was right, Daisy. He

594

was going to war, you see, and I was too young to get wed. Your Uncle Reuben was my nearest of kin and he wouldn't give him permission.

'So it happened, and a right old pickle I'd have been in if I'd fallen for a bairn. A shotgun wedding, happen, and all Holdenby knowing we'd had to get married. That isn't the way it should be, and you know it, or we wouldn't be talking like this, now would we?'

'But there are ways and means, aren't there – of not having babies, I mean.'

'There are, but I wouldn't know about such things. Me and your Dada always hoped for two or three little ones, though they weren't granted to us. But those ways and means, as you call them, aren't always to hand when things happen, so think on.

'But thank you for telling me. I hope you and me will always be able to talk things over. I'm not condemning you, either, for feeling the way you do. It happens to us all, truth known. Only safe way is to wait 'til you're wed, as far as I know.

'Y'see it's wrong, so folks say, to do things like that out of wedlock, but once the Church gives its blessing, then all of a sudden it's not only right, but it's expected! It's a funny old world, you know – but meantime, try counting to ten? And if that doesn't work, count to ten again and think of me and your Dada and of Polly, eh? And think on that we'd all of us be more hurt than angry at the shame of a hasty wedding because folk can count, you know.'

'I'll think on, Mam. We both will.' On an impulse, she flung her arms around Alice and hugged her tightly. 'And thanks for listening and for not being shocked.'

'Shocked? How could I be? 'Twould be the kettle calling the pot black, wouldn't it? But it isn't worth the risk, Daisy. Far better you wait 'til you've got a wedding ring on your finger for there's no joy in fumbling in dark corners. When you're wed it's – it's . . .'

'It's what, Mam?' Impishly, Daisy challenged her mother.

'It – it's – well, to put it in a nutshell, it's *lovely*! So now, if you've nothing better to do than get in my way when I'm up to my eyes icing Drew's cake, you'd do better to take that loaf of bread to your Uncle Reuben. And stay a while – have a chat with him and don't forget to remind him he'll be having new year at Keeper's and stopping the night with us, an' all.'

When her daughter had gone, Alice took up the bowl and began to beat the icing, but such a task was near useless, when her hands shook so.

Daisy – that bonny little bairn who not so long ago had sat in her pram at Windrush and gurgled and flirted with Mr Hillier.

Daisy – going to school, her hand in Keth's; Keth always there to look after her. Like a big brother, he'd been, but not any longer. Now they were in love and there was no use tut-tutting about it because it was the way of things and had happened to her and Tom. Falling in love began at the beginning of time and would last until Judgement Day.

And could you blame the child, Alice brooded, so like she had been at that age. And could you blame Keth who had always loved her, it seemed; could you blame him when Daisy was so beautiful, so fair and slim and tall? Daisy Dwerryhouse could turn the head of any young man she met, yet she wanted only Keth.

But it was a dear, funny old world and her own world was good because Tom had been given back to her and they'd had Daisy and were as happy, now, as the day they were wed, nearly eighteen years ago.

So did it matter that in three days, another year would be upon them, and the icing would hardly be set on the cake when the time came to cut it if she didn't get a move on. Yet she paused to smile, to count her blessings.

Tom and Daisy and Reuben, her wonderful family. And mother-in-law and Julia – and Drew, half hers; Drew who was growing up so like Giles.

'Lord.' She closed her eyes tightly. 'Let the warmongers be wrong. Don't let Keth and Drew have to go to war, and maybe Bas. And may Daisy and Tatiana and Kitty never know the heartache of parting from their sweethearts.' Because it *was* warmongering and scaremongering to think that Hitler could be so stupid as to start another war when people had hardly got over the last one.

She picked up the bowl again, beating furiously as the dogs outside began to bark. Tom was back from his rounds of the game covers and Brattocks Wood.

Tom. As long as she had Tom, nothing could harm her. And she would stop her fretting about Daisy and they would have the best new year's eve ever.

'In here, love,' she called, all at once needing to feel his lips, cold from the December night, on hers. 'Kettle's on,' she said softly as he came in from the cold, rubbing his hands, holding them to the fire. 'And love – kiss me, please?'

'With pleasure,' he smiled, laying his mouth on hers.

His lips were cold as she knew they would be and they told her, silently, what she needed to know. Tom loved her, still, and all else was of little consequence.

'I love you,' she whispered. 'And thank you.'

'What for, lass?'

'Oh, nothing in particular – and everything,' she smiled. 'Now mash us both a sup of tea whilst I get this icing on the cake.'

Then she offered her mouth to be kissed again.

Julia was close to tears by the time Nathan arrived. The party was over and Rowangarth strangely silent; everyone save herself in bed, or gone home. But for the fact that Nathan had promised to come immediately the church service was over, she too would be in bed and weeping into her pillow, she shouldn't wonder.

She should not be feeling like this. Everything had gone so well – Drew's birthday party and the Clan together again and having a wonderful time. Then later, the letting-in of another year; some dark-haired estate worker – Catchpole, these last few years – bringing in coal and salt and bread on the first stroke of midnight, wishing a good new year to one and all and receiving a glass of whisky in return.

And she wasn't depressed and fighting tears because all at once everything seemed to go flat and the party abruptly ended. There had been more to it than that. Her strange feelings began, she supposed, when she took the photographs; a feeling that today, *now*, she must have all the young ones on record; capture their youth and their beauty so that nothing and no one, could take it away from her.

They had started with luncheon in the conservatory which normally was closed for the winter, the plants removed to the safety of Catchpole's greenhouses; but this year, because the young ones wanted dancing, Mary had lit paraffin stoves and placed them in corners with the nursery fireguards to protect them.

This morning, the sky was a bright, winter blue and a slant of brief December sunlight glanced through the glass of the conservatory roof, whitening last night's thin covering of snow outside into blinding brilliance. This was the time, she knew, as she went in search of her camera.

'Quickly, all of you!' she had called. 'I want a snap of you together.' The light would never be so good. 'Now whilst you are all looking so smart – come on! Hurry!'

She arranged them in a group with the open glass doors framing the Christmas tree in the drawing room a little to their left. The Clan. Her six young Suttons almost grown up and each one a delight.

So they had smiled for the camera because today they

were especially happy, then returned to their dancing.

They *were* beautiful, she insisted. Bas and Keth tall and straight and Drew so like Giles it was uncanny. And Kitty, such an imp, so attractive that eyes were drawn to her the minute she came into a room. Even Tatiana. The Clan still called her Tatty, though her coltishness was fast disappearing and she grew more like Anna every day.

But of them all, Daisy was the brightest star. She with her pale blonde hair and eyes so blue you had to notice them. Dressed today in rose pink with her blue daisy pinned to the collar of her frock.

Julia recalled the giving of that daisy-shaped sapphire brooch at Daisy's christening more than sixteen years ago. Drew had been two, then; that little boy who had saved her sanity.

Irritably she tried to close down her thoughts, poking ash from the fire, placing more logs to burn. She poured whisky into a glass, not because she wanted it but because there was nothing else to do, but think. And she did not want to think about Nathan because she had been doing just that on and off all day, though why, she did not know.

Lately, she had thought about him differently; wanted, sometimes, to feel his closeness in the night. Yet there her imaginings always ended because she could never envisage Nathan as a lover nor could she want him the way she had shamelessly wanted – *needed* – Andrew.

Yet for all that it might have been good to have a closeness with him; one that did not demand what could only ever belong to Andrew. That closeness might well have been had not Nathan loved and wanted her as any normal man might.

She accepted, now, that he must always have loved her and if sometimes lately she felt guilt at the loneliness she had forced upon him, she could always find mitigation – absolution, even – for what she had done to his life.

Nathan should not have loved her when he knew she

was Andrew's; should have found someone else – heaven only knew, he'd had time enough. Twenty years, almost.

But Nathan loved as she loved – once, and for all time – though he had said he would never ask anything of her she was not prepared to give him and would wait for as long as it took. Twice since he asked her she had almost broached the subject again. Almost, because it hadn't happened. Things, on the surface, had reverted to what they had always been between them and not by so much as a look, a touch or a whisper had Nathan indicated that he might ask her again.

Why, then, did she sometimes want him to ask her again to marry him and why, perversely, did she hope he never would? Was it the talk of war? Surely there wouldn't, couldn't be another one so soon after? It was, it really was, only people like Winston Churchill growling out warnings about German military might that made people worry. Warmonger, they were calling him and people like him. And there *wasn't* going to be a war even though, since summer, fighting had intensified in Spain, with German-built planes bombing Spanish civilians.

Yet Jewish people were being forced to leave Germany and Austria, she frowned. Could it really be true they were the cause of everything that went wrong in Germany – even the burning of the Reichstag building?

No! The warmongers were wrong! She had talked to Alice about it and Alice too said they were. Dear, precious Alice. She had come early, today, carefully carrying Drew's birthday cake and bearing her brightly-wrapped present. A Fair Isle pullover she had knitted herself and Drew had loved it and hugged her and said, 'Thank you, Lady.' He still called her Lady.

Julia tilted her glass, trickling whisky down her throat. If Nathan kissed her – if he came, that was – her breath would smell of it and she wouldn't care. And where was he when he'd said he would come?

Five more minutes. Just five minutes she would give him, then she would do the rounds of the house, switch off the lights and go to bed, and weep.

He came ten minutes later. She heard his car wheels on the gravel of the drive and went at once to the front door.

'Sorry I'm late. It was the old ones, you know. They like to talk about the way things used to be. New year's eve seems to bring it on.' He placed a hand on each of her shoulders, bending to kiss each cheek. 'Happy new year, Julia . . .'

She closed her eyes as he did so, making a little moue with her mouth, breathing deeply so she wouldn't chide him for his lateness.

'Come in, Nathan. Suppose you could do with a drink?'

'Just a small one – if you'll join me.'

'I've already had one.' Oh, what the heck? She was too miserable, too apprehensive, ever to get tipsy tonight.

She handed him a glass, then raised her own, wishing him a happy new year, trying hard to smile. Then suddenly she said, 'I'm glad you came. I thought you weren't going to. I'd already given you up – decided to go to bed and have a good weep.'

'But why? Is something the matter? Tell me, Julia?'

'Oh, it's anything or nothing.' She sat on the hearthrug at his feet, kicking off her shoes, leaning her back against the sofa. 'It's a feeling I've had most of the day – like something's going to happen to my world. All at once, I just had to take a photo of the Clan,' she rushed on. 'Without any warning, I knew I had to have them all as they were this afternoon; my six younglings. I hope the light was good enough. I desperately need them to come out all right.'

'Why the feeling, Julia?'

'I don't know. A goose walked over my grave, I suppose. I love them all so. I've watched them grow up. They're so young, so — so *innocent*, almost. I'd kill to defend them, Nathan.'

'Defend them from what, from whom?'

'That's it — I don't know. It's just a feeling. After the last one, we said Germany mustn't ever re-arm, yet the first thing Baldwin did as Prime Minister was to agree that Germany could have a navy, and now they've got an army and an air force.

'Then the Italians marched into Abyssinia. Why? And who tried to stop them or tried to stop Hitler sending troops into the Rhineland? And now they're fighting in Spain. The only good thing about last year is that we got a decent king and queen out of it.'

'Julia, be a love and pour me another — a small one? And whilst you're doing it, try to listen to what I'm going to say? I don't think we are heading for war with Germany. Hitler is a Fascist; what he fears, I'm almost sure, is Communism. I think if he's ever foolish enough to fight anyone, it'll be the Russians.'

'You're sure?' She grasped at the small straw of comfort.

'Who can be sure of anything? But you asked me, Julia, and I've told you what I believe. So what else is bothering you, because something is.'

'You know me too well, Nathan Sutton.'

'I do. In all your moods. So out with it?'

'It's Drew — something he said; said innocently, I'm sure of it, but he was talking about Tatty. They had the gramophone in the conservatory for dancing and Drew said Tatty was going to teach him how to Tango — the way they do it in France.

'Then he remarked that she was growing up, now, and she wasn't half bad, he said. "Tatty's getting nicer, isn't she, mother, and she's getting prettier, too, just like Aunt Anna."

'I tell you, Nathan, my stomach hit the floor. What if Drew was to fall in love with her? He can't — *mustn't* —

love her and we can't ever tell him why. Oh, he realizes that Daisy is his half-sister, and that's all above board, but we can't tell him that Tatty is, too. He'd have to know, then, about Elliot and Alice and he'd be broken-hearted – mother, too. All the lies we told, Nathan . . .

'White lies, to protect the innocent.'

'And to cheat Pendenys? Rowangarth would have passed to your father when Giles died, but for Drew – and the title, too.'

'No, Julia. No cheating. Alice and Giles married whilst she was pregnant, *before* Drew was born. Giles was entitled to suppose that Drew was his, claim him as his own – which he gladly did. Giles knew the score, when he married Alice. It was his idea. So no more worrying about Drew and Tatiana because it just won't happen. I'd be prepared to promise you that.'

'But cousins can marry – just what if it *did*?'

'Then you'd pick up the phone, and tell me. That's what I'm here for. So no more thoughts of going to bed and weeping. Anyway, I'd half expected the party to still be going on when I got here.'

'So did I. Everything was going great, then it sort of fizzled out. Keth and Daisy left before midnight. Keth wanted to let in the new year at Keeper's, he being dark. Then, when Catchpole had done his stuff here, mother and your Pa suddenly got tired. Then Tatiana fell asleep on the sofa so Anna rang for Karl to come over. He just picked Tatty up in his arms and put her in the back of the car. Amelia said then that they'd better all go, too – with your Pa getting drowsy, I mean.

'Anna was sorry to break things up – she doesn't get a lot of fun – but all at once everything went dead and I had to wait up for you on my own.'

'And worried, and brooded? Julia MacMalcolm, what am I to do with you?'

'I don't know. I'm getting old, I suppose. It keeps hitting

me, you see, that before long Drew *will* marry and leave me. Not that he'll ever leave Rowangarth, but he'll love someone else more than he loves me. I'll be alone again. So what *can* you do with me – except marry me, of course.'

The words came out without thought, without warning, yet she had known they were there, waiting to be spoken. Waiting, because all at once she needed someone to be with her, always; because she was weary of being alone and because, truth known, no one else but Nathan knew her so well – and would agree to her terms.

'Marry you?' His voice was little more than a whisper.

'Either that, or refuse me and buy me a silken gown. That's the way it goes. A lady can propose in leap year. The man accepts – or pays a forfeit – a silken gown.'

'I see. And you're joking, of course. Another whisky and you'll do a striptease?'

'No, Nathan.' She was staring, now, into the fire, wondering why she had said it, yet unwilling to recant.

'Julia – please look at me?'

Slowly she turned, placing her glass on the hearth, kneeling back on her heels, looking up at him.

'Why now? Tell me?'

His eyes were dark with pleading; with unhappiness, too. And his mouth was set traplike, as though he were hurt by her teasing. Only she wasn't teasing.

'Why not now?'

'Because this is no longer 1936. Your proposal is two hours late. Sorry about the silken gown . . .'

'You don't want to marry me? You've changed your mind?'

'No. It's you who have changed yours. I still want you, still love you, but I've realized I can't marry you, Julia.'

'Why?' Her mouth had gone dry and she rose to her feet, then walked over to the decanter, pouring more whisky into her glass.

'Put that down! You don't need it.' Gently he took the

glass from her hand, placing it on a table. 'I can't marry another man's wife, you see, and that's what you still are. Andrew's *wife*, not his widow. You'll never accept that he's dead and, until you do, there'd be no chance of any happiness for you and me.'

'So that's it, then.' She gave a hopeless little shrug. She looked so bewildered, so vulnerable, that he wanted to gather her to him, to shelter her, care for her so the world should never hurt her again. But he didn't touch her.

'No. That isn't it. I want you to go to Andrew's grave, though. Only when you've been will you know what to do. And when you have, it will be *me*, asking *you* . . .'

'Still on my terms, though. You'd have to give me time, Nathan. And I might never – well – love you. Not *that* way.'

'Then that's a risk I would have to take. But go to bed, now. You look all-in. And drink that whisky, if you must. At least it might help you to sleep.' He tilted her chin with his forefinger, then laid his lips gently on hers. 'I'm going home, now. Lock the door behind me. I'll probably call in tomorrow – wish Aunt Helen and Drew a happy new year. Goodnight, Julia . . .'

He thought about her on the drive back to the vicarage. Poor lonely, tormented Julia. He had almost capitulated, yet he knew he could never share her with a memory.

'My dearest girl,' he whispered into the darkness. 'What on earth am I to do with you?'

What indeed, but love her to the end of his days.

38

Julia filled the trug with roses and lilies for the vases in the house; poppies, too, though once cut they would soon drop their petals. Poppies she loved for all that; had come to associate them with her other life, when once she was young.

Soon she was going back to that other life. On Thursday she would leave for France and a cemetery at Étaples. Six months ago she had promised Nathan she would and it could no longer be put off.

There had been excuses and evasions; Drew leaving school and the need to settle him at the Estate Manager's offices, in York. For only a few months, of course, so he might grasp the essentials of running an estate like Rowangarth. Just four days a week, travelling by train, back and forth, but it had taken up her time.

There had been the Coronation, too, last month in May. Weeks of planning parties for the young, the old, for almost everyone. And services of thanksgiving at All Souls because at last we had a good king and a smiling queen. One who didn't have two husbands still alive, said spinsters acidly; who because of the war had been denied the chance of one, even.

Such an event the Coronation, and the newspapers full of pictures of the little princesses and London putting on its decorations, getting ready to celebrate.

Amelia had come over by flying boat and stayed at Montpelier Mews, finding herself a prime position near Buckingham Palace to see the processions – the horses, of course. Then quickly back to Kentucky to tell her family and friends about it all and how the British were just about the best there was, when it came to putting on a parade – with horses, that was.

Strange, Julia frowned, that one so fiercely American should be taken up with the crowning of a British king, and Amelia, in her turn, thought it equally strange that Julia had not availed herself of free accommodation in London when half the world seemed intent upon grabbing every room to be had there. But Julia was too busy. She had been elected to organize the celebrations in Holdenby and was too taken up to go anywhere. Especially to Étaples.

Sharply, she turned her thoughts away from Thursday, recalling good things because now there were good things to think about. Unemployment had fallen – how pleased Andrew would have been about that even if, she thought soberly, it was only because so very much money was being spent on the defence of Britain. *Defence*, the government stressed, and she agreed with them, but only because she needed to. And at the Coronation Thanksgiving services in Holdenby church she had prayed not only for the new king and his queen but fiercely and imploringly for continued peace that her beloved Clan should never know the like of a conflict people now called the Great War.

'Please, *please*,' she had entreated, 'not again?' Not when she had yet to erase the last one from her mind, her heart.

'When,' asked Daisy who had been waiting at the bus stop, 'are you giving that job up?'

'Not yet.' Keth linked her little finger with his own, needing to touch her, wanting to kiss her, knowing he must wait until they were out of the village. 'I'll keep it until just before I leave. I've got to give Mum all the money I can, you know that.' And save as much as he could in case jobs for students weren't easy to come by in America for there was unemployment there, too. Foreigners – and he would be a foreigner even though Mrs Amelia was sponsoring him – had little chance of getting work when so many Americans were without it.

But with luck he would find something, and if he didn't, he knew he could work for his keep at the Kentucky stables. It wouldn't be an easy three years for all that, yet he accepted with gratitude the second chance he had been given. Nothing else really mattered.

As they left the last cottage behind them and turned into the lane that led to Rowangarth bothy, he took her in his arms.

'When I'm away,' he whispered, lips on hers, 'you won't forget me, find someone else?'

'You keep asking that. Will *you* find someone else, Keth?'

'You know I won't!'

'There's your answer, then,' she chided softly.

'I'm lucky, Daisy. Mrs Amelia's so generous. She didn't have to do it, but I'll pay her back, one day. Every penny.'

'No, you won't. Mrs Sutton wants to help you through college. It's part of getting over almost losing Bas. It's the way a woman reasons. Bas is alive and well and his hands are healed.' Only slight scarring on his right one which didn't matter at all, he'd said. 'She doesn't want you to pay her back. Don't spoil it for her?

'And don't forget my money, Keth. It'll be ours – yours and mine. We'll be able to have a house and a telephone and a car. And I can buy things for Mam and Dada. Don't spoil it for me, too?'

'But it's me who should provide for *you*. Can't you see that, Daisy? Soon, you'll be able to have anything that takes your fancy and I want to buy you things with money I've earned myself.'

'And like I've said before, if Mr Hillier's money is going to make trouble between us, I shall give it back to

Windrush and tell them the miners can have it. And I'll tell you something else! There aren't two people happier than Mam and Dada, and do you know the most precious thing Mam has? It's a buttercup, pressed in her Bible. She's got an engagement ring and a gold locket and real pearl earrings from Aunt Julia, but the buttercup is what she loves best.'

'So what are you trying to say?' He shook his head because the way women thought, sometimes, defied all reason.

'I'm trying to tell you that I'd rather have a flower from you, my stubborn darling, than anything else at all. Just give me a daisychain and it'll be more precious than possessions. And kiss me, please, and promise never to love anyone else.'

'I love you.' Gently he cupped her face in his hands, laying his mouth on hers. 'Only you, ever. It's the way it's always been, ever since I can remember. You shall have your daisychain, sweetheart,' he smiled indulgently, 'if that's what you want.'

'It's all I want,' she smiled, suddenly very sure of their love, 'and for us to be married, one day. Nothing else is important, Keth. I'll wait for you for as long as it takes. A daisychain might be a foolish, fragile thing, but it will hold us together.'

And he said he supposed it would, and kissed her again.

Julia gazed through the window of her Calais hotel room, trying to think that in this country, only last week, the man who had once been King of England at last married the woman he had given up his throne for. Julia hoped they would be happy, even though not one member of the royal family had been there, which was very sad, really.

She thought, too, of Rowangarth and the gentle June evening in which, perhaps, her mother and Drew were walking now, wondering where she, Julia, was and how she was – and sending her their love. But to think sanely and sensibly of anything when long-ago memories crowded into her mind to torment her was impossible.

Had the Gare du Nord changed in twenty years? She had thought to go on to Paris, later, but the mood had left her. No khaki uniforms at that railway station, now; no old lady selling violets and, at the main entrance, no young nurse waiting for the husband she had not seen for two years.

She swallowed hard on the choke of tears in her throat. Would Andrew be near her when she found him at Étaples or did the wraith of a young doctor still wait at a Paris railway station for the girl he loved, to smile tenderly, tell her to take off her ridiculous uniform hat? Would that nurse hear him say it if she listened with her heart?

'*You haven't had your hair cut, Julia?*'

'*No. I just pin it up tightly.*'

'*Never have it cut . . .*'

Two long-ago hours together at the Gare du Nord, holding hands, sitting closely at one of the tables outside, making plans for the future. They were in love and dared to tilt at Fate, then, because Andrew had been promoted to major and was to be moved from the front line to a hospital at Cotterets. He'd be safer, there; might even be given leave. Yet though now she listened with her heart, still she could not bring back his voice, not even here in Calais, so near to where he lay.

She took off her shoes and lay on the bed, calling back a day twenty years ago when she and Alice, Ruth Love and Sister Carbrooke were on their way to Celverte. The day had been almost unbearably hot and their stiffly-starched collars and thick woollen stockings were cruelly uncomfortable.

That afternoon, on the train, they ate sandwiches spread with margarine and filled with fish paste and the French family who shared their compartment wished them luck.

'Merci, madame.' Julia had smiled brilliantly back because every second, every metallic clack of the wheels took her nearer to Andrew. The heat, the stockings that made her legs itch, the collar that rubbed her neck until it was sore mattered nothing when soon, perhaps around the next corner, even, she might see her love walking towards her. Life was good that day and golden with hope, yet tonight, a middle-aged, loveless woman had come reluctantly to say goodbye to a memory.

She reached for her cigarettes, lighting one, inhaling deeply. She wished now that she had hired a car. She had intended driving herself from Calais to Étaples but her mother had begged her not to. Cars still worried her and to think of her daughter driving on the wrong side of the road filled her with dread. So, Julia sighed, she would take a taxi there because that was what she had promised to do, and ask the driver to return for her later.

She stubbed out the cigarette. She hadn't really wanted it, had only lit it because it would help ease the ache of an empty stomach. She really ought to eat something. If she did not, her insides would protest all night and she would lie awake, dreading the morning to come and almost certainly weeping.

She swung her legs to the floor, then walked to the dressing table to comb her hair. She gazed into the mirror, wanting to see a young nurse eager for love, seeing instead a woman whose life centred on a young man and an old house; a woman almost too old to bear children. Twenty years had passed so quickly she had not noticed it. She had thrown those years away the night of the telegram; flung them furiously into the night because all around her were the sounds of joy and happiness that the war had ended.

Was she then to throw away the next twenty years? Did she want to? Did she have the right, when Andrew and those who lay with him had not been given that choice?

She picked up her handbag and room key and made

for the dining-room. She wasn't hungry but she would go through the motions of eating and perhaps a bottle of red wine, if she drank it all, would make her sleep.

She wished Nathan were here to help and comfort her, but she must go alone to Andrew's grave. It was not right that another man, however good and kind and gentle, should be with her.

Tomorrow, she would go to Étaples, tell Andrew she was sorry she had not come before this and, if she could find the strength, say goodbye to him.

The taxi driver set her down at the cemetery gates and she stood bewildered, trying to take in the vastness of it, how far ahead and to each side of her it reached.

A gardener walked towards her pushing a wheelbarrow and she showed him the piece of paper on which she had written the location of the grave she sought, asking him in which direction it lay.

He told her gently, speaking slowly because although she spoke his language better than most who came here from England he was trying, she knew, to be kind.

Smiling, she thanked him. Outside the hotel had been a flower-seller and she bought a bunch of violets. Andrew had given her a posy of violets that afternoon in Paris. He would be glad she remembered the violets.

She walked slowly, reluctantly, to the section of the cemetery in which he lay, cold in spite of the warmth of the sun because it was awful to see such a stretch of gravestones, each one a life. Some woman's husband, father, brother, sweetheart, son. How was she to find Andrew amongst so many?

Her camera case hung on her arm. She wanted to take photographs of the place, of his grave, but panic sliced through her as she feared she might not even find it.

Row eight. At least she had found that, but there must be many row eights, here. She stood, looking down the meticulous straightness of the stones, realizing that at least someone cared. The grass was short cut, shrubs flowered and, at intervals, small clumps of trees — trees only a few years old — grew bravely to gentle the starkness.

Somewhere, a bird sang. It sounded like the blackbird that sang each summer evening on the farthest linden tree, at Rowangarth, and it gave back the courage she thought had failed her, because she knew she would find him. She had only feared she might not because even now, so near to him, she doubted she could stand so close without breaking down and crying out her torment and anger and grief to the skies.

Private James Jennings, Army Medical Corps, she read on a stone. Private William Smith, Army Medical Corps and beside him, Driver John Cunliffe of the Army Service Corps — names she had never forgotten. They had been killed with Andrew on a day when the war had only a week to run. Killed because of an aching tooth. At least they were still together.

Andrew's gravestone would be the same as all the rest, but that was as it should be because there were no officers or privates in heaven — if there was a heaven, that was. *If* there was a God, she thought bitterly, because if God was all that clever, then why had He let all this happen?

She ranged her eyes around, taking in the sea of stones and they came to rest on Andrew's.

Major Andrew MacMalcolm — RAMC
31.8.1887–5.11.1918

Above his name was carved the insignia of the Medical Corps, but that was all. They had written to ask her, when at last the Army was able to tell her to which War Graves Cemetery he had been taken, what she would wish to be placed on his stone. And she had written brusquely back that only his name and rank and the dates of his birth and death should be chiselled there. She wanted no message between them for other people to read. They had loved with passion and delight, whispering words special only to them. There was nothing, she decided at the time, that could be placed on his memorial but the stark, simple facts of his existence. All else belonged to them alone and to the ten nights they spent together; fleeting, precious, wonderful nights.

She stood there, looking at the stone, wanting to touch it, fearing it might be cold and forbidding. She laid her camera and handbag on the ground, then placed the violets beneath his name.

'Andrew?' she whispered. 'It's Julia . . .'

She reached out to touch the stone. It was not cold as she feared and she was able to gentle her fingertips across the letters of his name as once she had gentled them across his face, his body.

The blackbird had stopped its singing and all around her was a hush, a gentle quietness as though those who lay there were at peace, almost.

And then she heard his voice; the voice her heart had wanted to hear for so long. She heard it as clearly as the day on which he first said those words to her.

'My dear, I hoped you would come . . .'

'Andrew!' She closed her eyes, pleading silently with him not to leave her or take away his love, and as she did so she heard his laugh, soft and throaty because he too remembered the first time she had set out to find him.

The morning after their first meeting, it was, when he had been correct and professional in caring for her poor bruised face. And she was so sure he must be married but, after he left Aunt Sutton's house, Alice had said he was not.

'With two buttons missing on his shirt? Not a chance he's married.'

So next morning, without a chaperon, she set out alone,

insisting that this was 1913 and the time would soon come when any young lady could walk anywhere she pleased, and alone!

She had taken the motor bus to King Edward Street, then quickly found the street called Little Britain in which he lived. Number 53A was a mean lodging, above a stationer's shop with the gates of St Bartholomew's church close by, but she was in love and could only stand there and wonder how she would bear it if he did not answer her knock.

And when his door opened and he stood smiling at her, she knew it was the same for him, too.

'Miss Sutton.' His voice was low, indulgent, and he laid gentle fingers to the bruising beneath her eye. 'My dear,' he had said. 'I hoped you would come . . .'

'Andrew – remember what a hussy I was, in those days? And you and I walked in Hyde Park – *without* Alice – and I brought you back to Montpelier Mews to tea and we ate cucumber sandwiches and cherry cake and wondered what mother or Aunt Sutton would say if they found us together, unchaperoned. And neither of us cared!'

How long she knelt there she had no means of knowing. All she cared was that she had found him again, could recall the sound of his voice again, hear his laugh. And as she remembered glad things and sad things, she knew that no more would she feel Andrew's lips gently on hers, nor the hard passion of a lover's kiss. And never again would they lie in warm, intimate closeness nor reach heights of loving she had never known to exist.

Andrew was gone. One November day a land mine had snuffed out his life like a raging wind blowing out a candle flame and no matter how she yearned for him or fumed against the bleakness of a life alone, nothing would ever change it.

She looked at the watch on her wrist. Soon the taxi would come to the gates and she knew she must go. She was glad she had asked the driver to return or she might never have been able to walk away from this small space that was Andrew's.

She had knelt there for so long, telling him that Giles was dead and that Tom and Alice were married, and about Drew being hers.

'Tom and Alice had Daisy and there's a new young clutch of Suttons growing up, Andrew.

'Elliot died,' she whispered. 'He married Anna from St Petersburg – Leningrad, it is now – and they had a daughter. Elliot was burned to death in his car; Aunt Clemmy is dead, too . . .

'Cecilia is a nun in India, now, and we have sold the tea gardens at Shillong and there was a fire at Pendenys and Uncle Edward had the tower pulled down . . .

'And Nathan has asked me to marry him.' She got to her feet, her hand on his stone because her legs were cramped after so long kneeling, 'and I don't know what to say to him. Tell me, Andrew?'

But she knew he never could, never would tell her. What had been between them had passed into time far away. She and Andrew had been young together; now she was middle-aged – Nathan, too.

Andrew was once an army doctor and he lay with other soldiers. His gravestone said that he was thirty-one; he would always be thirty-one and she, Julia, must grow old without him into loneliness – or marry Nathan and share a different, comfortable love. Standing beside Andrew's grave she was all at once wise and she knew he could read her thoughts because once he had been a part of them.

The camera still lay with her handbag and she picked it up and hung it on her arm. No photographs of a name chiselled out of stone nor of a cemetery where so many lay. No reminders of death. She must say goodbye, now, and never come back. Andrew was with his friends, his comrades. In a hundred years from now, he would still be young, still a part of that first, passionate life. From first to last they had shared so few nights that they could be counted on the fingers of her hands.

'I have to go, now. I won't ever forget our love. Goodbye, my darling.'

She laid her fingertips to her lips; just once more she gentled his name, then smiling softly she walked away.

At an archway where roses climbed she turned, but he was gone from her, lost already in a sea of stones.

An awful sadness took her and she wanted to run back to him but in that instant the blackbird began to sing again and all at once it was singing in the far linden tree and Rowangarth was calling her back.

'Goodbye, Doctor MacMalcolm,' she whispered; then she turned and straightening her shoulder, tilting her chin, walked with Sutton pride to where the taxi waited.

Tomorrow, at this time, she would be in London at the little white house in Montpelier Mews. Their love had started there and tomorrow it would end there. She would tell Sparrow about the cemetery at Étaples and about all the flowers and the birdsong; tell her that it was well kept and cared for with respect and that soldiers who died together one November day now lay together in safe, sad closeness.

What she would not tell Sparrow when she returned, was that Nathan might ask her again to marry him and if he did . . .

39

Julia had been home for some days before Nathan phoned. His call was brief.

'Hullo! You're back, then. How was it?'

'I've been back almost a week, Nathan.' She tried not to sound piqued. 'As for how it was – well, I didn't go on an outing to Blackpool, you know.'

'I do know.' There was no reproof in his voice. 'I was giving you a little time, that's all.'

'Time?' He mustn't ask her. Not yet. 'What do you mean – *time*?'

'Time to settle down, sort of. I figured you were bound to be upset. Look – do you want to tell me how it was – get it off your chest, I mean? Parsons are good listeners.'

'Nothing – well – *personal*, Nathan?'

'Absolutely nothing personal. Will you be at Eucharist, tomorrow?'

'No!' Her reply uncompromising. She didn't want to take Communion. She didn't know why except that perhaps she was still angry with God about those rows and rows of graves. 'Mother and Drew will be there, though.'

'Then come to Evensong – stay to supper at the vicarage? I'd like to know how it went.'

'All right. Thanks . . .'

Her doubts must have shown in her voice because he said, 'Julia – it's *me*, Nathan. Supper and a chat over a glass of wine. I'm not going to ask you to marry me!'

'You're not.' She said it flatly and he couldn't be sure whether she was relieved or disappointed.

'Positively not. Just you and me, like it used to be, before —' Before he'd blundered in and spoiled whatever chance he might have had. 'What I'm trying to say is I'd like to see you — no strings attached.'

'Then I'd like that, too.'

She replaced the receiver, frowning, wondering if she'd expected him to ask her and if she was disappointed or glad that he would not. She made a face at Julia in the mirror. Neither, really. Just glad that perhaps he wasn't going to hustle her so soon after, give her time to sort out the muddle inside her, to accept that she was no longer Andrew's wife, but his widow. When she could say, 'My husband was killed in the war,' without screaming inside her; then she would know she had finally let him go.

She smiled sadly. Dear Nathan. He deserved better than second best.

Sunday was Keth's only day off and Daisy resented spending even an hour of it in church. Being apart from Keth when she was storing up memories against the time he would leave her, she resented bitterly. She wanted Keth to go to America; wanted him to do well because that was what *he* wanted. Rich people, he said, had nothing to worry about; poor people like himself had to get there the hard way and a good degree, to his way of thinking, was the *only* way.

He still resented failing his scholarship, but because he was Keth and too honest for his own good, he was always ready to admit that he alone had failed it; was angry with himself for being so stupid.

Now, because of being worse than stupid, he was being given another chance, because stupid he had been, going into that blazing tower without thought. And brave and wonderful too, she blushed with pride.

'I'm going to early church tomorrow, Mam — get it over

with. Keth and I are going out on the bikes all day. I don't suppose I could have sandwiches to take with me?'

'What do you mean – get it over with?' Tom lowered his evening paper. 'Church on Sunday is a must, and so is Sunday dinner. Your Mam spends a lot of time cooking it an' you'll have the manners to be at home to eat it!'

'But Dada . . .' She walked to his chair, leaning over the back of it and he knew her eyes would be wide with pleading and that soon she would run her fingers through his hair, or maybe kiss him. He knew all her wiles.

'But *nothing*, Daisy Dwerryhouse. Church with your Mam and me tomorrow, and if you can't bear to be parted from Keth he can come to Sunday dinner – is that all right?' he smiled in Alice's direction.

'Course it is. Keth doesn't have to be asked but Tom – couldn't she – just this once? They've been planning this outing all week.'

'Oh, all right . . .' Tom shook the paper so it crackled, then retreated, defeated, behind it. No use trying to be master in your own house when the womenfolk ganged up on you. 'But only this once, Miss. Sundays are kept proper, at Keeper's. And mind you call on your Uncle Reuben afore you leave.'

'That was good of you, love,' Alice smiled when Daisy had left. 'They have so little time left together. The Kentucky Suttons will be here, soon, then there'll only be four weeks before Keth goes back with them. Don't say you've forgotten what saying goodbye is like – for three years, an' all.'

'I haven't forgotten, but I was going off to fight. Keth isn't. He'll be coming back. You and me, bonny lass, didn't know if –'

'If we'd ever see each other again. I know. But that doesn't make it any easier for Daisy and Keth.'

'Aye, but three years'll give her time to make up her mind if it's Keth she wants. She's a bairn, still.'

'She's seventeen, Tom – the same age as I was when I met you.'

'Seventeen . . .' He folded his paper, dropping it to the floor at his side, smiling, loving her every bit as much as the afternoon, more than twenty years ago, he had met her in Brattocks Wood. Her, and that daft dog, Morgan. And now Morgan lay with Beth beneath the beech trees at the side of Beck Lane, a long way away, a long time away. 'Old Morgan needed a bit of licking into shape, if I remember rightly.'

'So he did. You bellowed at me something awful – said he'd frighten the hen pheasants off the nests.'

'I remember. But our Daisy – seventeen.' He pulled his fingers through his hair in the old, familiar gesture. 'I hope you've had a talk to the lass about – well – *things*.'

'I have. Things, as you call them, don't change. Daisy and me understand each other. You've just got to bring them up right, then hope for the best. Mother Natures's a cunning old lady.'

'And Keth's a decent lad, isn't he?' Tom clearly sought comfort.

'He's the one Daisy wants, decent or not. But I trust him. I've always trusted Daisy to him, Tom. He took her to school, remember, and watched over her like he was her big brother.'

'But he isn't her brother, now!'

'He isn't. They'll be wed, those two, mark my words. And Keth'll think on about Daisy – you know what I'm talking about.'

'He'd better!' Tom jerked. 'By the heck, but he'd better!'

Julia stood at the church gates, waiting until Nathan had locked away the altar silver and checked the vestry. Nathan was overworked, she frowned, especially now when there was no need for him to work at all. Since Elliot's death there was no denying that one day Nathan would inherit Pendenys Place and much, much more besides.

'Sorry to keep you.' Smiling, Nathan took her arm. 'Did you drive over?'

'No. It's too lovely a night.'

'So shall we go back through the churchyard or by way of the village and in through the orchard gate?'

'The orchard.' Julia did not want to see gravestones tonight and besides, she liked to walk through the village. 'I'm not very hungry, Nathan, so don't expect –'

'Me neither. What I most want is your company. I've been thinking about you a lot since you got back, wondering how things went.'

'You'd only to pick up the phone,' she said peevishly, then regretted it at once. 'Sorry! France was a bit traumatic, for all that, but I'll tell you about it when we get to your place – if you want to listen, that is.'

'You know I do. I'd like to have been with you for old time's sake, but it wouldn't have been right.'

'No.' They walked in silence, past the ornamental village pump placed there by her Grandfather Sutton almost a hundred years ago, past the almshouses where Reuben and Old Catchpole lived; where doubtless Miss Clitherow would end her days.

Over to her left lay Home Farm and beyond Brattocks Wood, its cupola and weathercock visible above the tree-tops, was Rowangarth stable block. And all around her, all she could see from left to right would one day belong to Drew. The public house, the tiny shop, three farms, three almshouses and, to be exact, thirty-two cottages. Even the vicarage belonged to Rowangarth.

Young Drew, the villagers called him, but at his coming-of-age, two and a bit years from now, he would be known by common consent as Sir Andrew. Alice had borne a rape child, and the line had been saved. Andrew Robert Giles Sutton – the son she and Andrew had never made together.

At the cemetery at Étaples she had doubted the existence of God yet there was something beyond their seeing and knowing and touching, or why had Drew been conceived that night and why, when Giles died, had Tom come back from the dead to marry Alice?

'Penny for them?' Nathan lifted the latch of the orchard gate, pushing it open, holding it for her.

'I was thinking about – oh, just about everybody. Drew, Miss Clitherow, even . . .'

'In short – none of my business!'

'No – truly!' She felt her cheeks redden. 'I was probably, though I didn't know it, thinking how lucky I am to be walking home on such a night as this. Really lucky.'

'One of the benefits of being in a state of grace,' he grinned.

'No, Nathan. Nothing to do with having just been to church. I'm off God. There wasn't much sign of Him at Étaples – all those young lives . . .'

'Yes, love. I was in that war, too.'

'So you were. I'm feeling a bit Bolshie tonight, I suppose.'

'Be my guest.' Nathan lifted the large cobble beside the back doorstep, taking the key hidden beneath it, opening the door. 'It's pot luck, tonight.' His cook and housemaid always had Sunday afternoon and evening off.

Cake in blue tin. She read the pencilled note left beside the tray, then peeped beneath the damp tea towel and the layer of greaseproof paper to where daintily-cut sandwiches lay garnished with parsley. 'Bet it's walnut cake. Your cook spoils you.'

'She's an absolute love.' He took Julia's jacket, hanging it on a brass peg. 'But come into the sitting room, and have a drink. Preaching is thirsty work. What did you think of my sermon, by the way?'

'Since the gist of it was about counting blessings, I take it that it was aimed at me.'

'Not a bit of it. When I wrote it I hadn't the faintest idea you'd be at Evensong. But did it ring any bells?'

'Not really.' She pulled off her shoes, settling herself on the floor, leaning her back against a leather fireside chair. On a side table stood an uncorked bottle of red wine; beside it, two glasses. He filled one, passing it to her, then poured his own, sitting in the chair on which she leaned. She was grateful he had not chosen the chair opposite. She needed, tonight, to be close to someone.

'Sure you're comfortable? A cushion, perhaps?'

'I like sitting on the floor. I'm fine.' More than he knew. Here, if he asked her again to marry him, she would not have to meet his eyes head on; could gaze instead at the empty chair opposite.

'So you got there, Julia . . . ?'

'Yes. No problem at all. I'd thought, afterwards, to go on to Paris for a couple of nights, then I thought, "What the heck?" I wanted to get back to Rowangarth, you see.'

'Yes, I do see. When I was in France, Blighty was always Rowangarth on a summer evening such as this. Never Pendenys. I'd think of us all when young – Giles and me, especially – and you, of course, always tagging along behind us. You were a terrible nuisance, in those days.'

'Mm.' She smiled, relaxing a little. 'I forget, sometimes, how close you and Giles were. Always together. It must have been awful for you to – to'

'Conduct his burial service? Yes, it was. He was closer to me than either of my brothers. I still can't remember a time when he wasn't there, which is just as it should be, considering we were born only weeks apart. But about Étaples . . .'

'*What* about Étaples? You know what a war cemetery is like. You've visited.'

'Only the once to Ypres, ten years ago. I suppose, though, that one is much the same as the other.'

'I wouldn't know about that. The one at Étaples was

one too many for me. Row after row. It made me angry, at first. My heart started banging, then I took a deep breath and tried to take stock.

'At least he isn't alone, Nathan, but I wished I could really have tuned-in to that place, asked them all how it was for them. I had the right, you know. I was one of them, once. I cared about them, even though my motives were selfish at first – getting nearer to Andrew, I mean. But I *did* care, Nathan, just as Andrew did. Nursing got to me. In the end, I'd hurt inside when we lost a patient. I couldn't bear it, when one died . . .'

'You saved Giles,' he prompted.

'No. That was Alice and Ruth Love. Sister made me distance myself from him till he started to pull round. Alice hardly left him – asked if she could special him. Strange, wasn't it, that he should be brought to our ward.'

'Yes – but wonderful.'

'I know, yet we saved him for nothing. Imagine after all he went through, him dying of 'flu.'

'He died of 'flu because his war wounds left him too weak to fight it. You were meant to save him, at Celverte. Perhaps you doubt your faith, sometimes, but Someone up there knew an unborn child was in need of a father and Someone knew that a young woman, soon to be mad with grief, would need something to live for . . .'

'Drew,' she whispered fondly. 'Alice didn't want anything to do with him when he was born, you know, but I'm glad she called him for Andrew.'

Andrew. She gazed into her glass. Such a beautiful colour, the wine . . .

'It was better at the cemetery than I thought, Nathan. I'd intended taking photographs, but I didn't. I heard his voice again, you see. I'd never been able, before, to remember it – that soft, Scottish lilt, the *sound* of it. Then all at once I heard it again – in my mind, I mean. I even heard him laughing, the way he used to.

'That was when I really saw that place. It wasn't like cemeteries, here; not all sombre, sagging gravestones and yew trees. It was really well kept. Someone cares, thank God, and they were all together, in straight rows, just as if they'd been on parade. They weren't lonely, Nathan, or forgotten.

'There were flowers and shrubs and trees, but it was the bird that finally did it. I don't know if they have blackbirds in France, but it sounded like the Rowangarth blackbird – the one that always sings at twilight at the end of the linden walk. There was one at Étaples, singing Sunset for those men. I vanted to weep, with relief. Andrew is all right, Nathan.'

'.nd you, Julia?'

The clock ticked gently, the curtains moved a little in the breeze that brought summer evening scents into the room. The peace of it was such that she wanted to hold her breath, lest she disturb it.

'Me? I realized I am Andrew's widow, not his wife. It took me nineteen years to face up to it. I didn't come to that decision all by myself, either. Andrew did it. He told me. I even knew he didn't want me to photograph him as a name on a gravestone.

'It was Andrew, you see, who caused that blackbird to be singing there. He isn't in France, Nathan; he's as near as I want him to be. He absolved my bitterness. Can you understand?'

'I think I can. Love is stronger than anything I know. It's powerful stuff . . .'

'Yes. You should know. It helped you bless me and Andrew when we were married, even though –'

'Even though I too loved you,' he finished for her.

'Mm. Can I have some more wine, please?' She turned to smile up at him.

'Only if you eat some of the sandwiches Cook left. Can't have you weaving home through the village under the influence.'

He was walking into the kitchen as he said it, so she couldn't read his face. It would be all right, though. Andrew had set her free to love again and one day she would love Nathan – not as she had loved Andrew; not wildly and without reason, but gently and safely and for what remained of the rest of her life. Nathan would know when the time was right.

He returned with a tray, then half filled their glasses.

'To all those we have loved and lost,' he smiled gently and she raised her own glass and said, 'God keep them.'

For just a moment he held her gaze steadfastly, as if he were putting his mark on her, claiming her. Then he said, 'Now for heaven's sake, will you eat some of these sandwiches, woman?'

September

'I wanted us to talk, just you and I, before we leave,' Amelia had said, sitting at the bothy kitchen table, drinking tea from Polly's best china cups. 'You know we'll take real good care of Keth; he's important to us, and we all like him.'

'I know that, ma'am. I'm grateful, though it's hard to tell you how much. You didn't have to do it.'

'But I did! Your son risked his life for Bas. My husband watched, helpless, knowing that any minute they could both crash down. Thank heaven I was at Rowangarth . . .'

She stopped, shuddering visibly, eyes closed.

'There now – don't take on, Mrs Sutton.' Polly placed a hesitant arm across the shaking shoulders. ''Twas all right, in the end.'

'But you weren't there, Mrs Purvis. It was the longest five minutes of my husband's life, he said, watching them on that ledge.'

'Good job I wasn't there,' Polly smiled cheerfully. 'Mind, when I saw the state of him when he got home and found out what he'd been up to, I could've cuffed his ear for being such a darned young fool.'

'But such a brave young fool. He's one of us, now, so don't say I mustn't help with his education, will you? I want to – *need* to. It'll be like paying God back – saying thank you to Him.

'We leave in two days; sail from Liverpool this time, on the *Berengaria* – and there's just one thing. We are having Christmas at home in Kentucky, this year. Albert wants it, you see. We've come over here since Kitty was a baby; he says he's getting too old for the twice-yearly migration, as he calls it.

'I worry about father-in-law, but there it is – family comes first. Keth will have his vacations with us. He'll be away three years – you realize that, don't you?'

'Aye. But it isn't likely he could afford to keep popping home. It wouldn't be like taking the bus from Holdenby to Leeds, would it now? Three years will soon pass. It'll be an adventure for him, starting with the crossing. I'm sorry he doesn't have a fancy suit to wear at table . . .'

'People aren't obliged to dress for meals on board. Keth's Sunday suit will do nicely. Bas's dinner jacket suddenly doesn't fit him, so he won't be dressed up, either. Don't worry so, Mrs Purvis.'

'It's a fine University he'll be going to. One of the very best, Mrs MacMalcolm told me.'

'A very good one. Pennsylvania University, at Philadelphia. My father and his brother both went there. Every bit as good, Albert says, as your Oxford and Cambridge.'

'There now!' Polly was impressed.

'He and Bas will be in different faculties, but together, for all that – and perhaps we'll all get over in 'thirty-nine. We'll have to see how things go.'

'You mean with Mr Albert's father being – well – elderly?'

'On all sorts of things. There's Europe, too. I think that's what my husband is most apprehensive about, truth known.'

'About that Hitler and his ranting and goose-stepping, you mean? Aye, he bothers me, an' all. He bothers any woman who's got a son.'

'Oh, I don't think anything will happen – not really – yet it's always there, at the back of my mind. But America would keep out of it this time, if war broke out in Europe, I'm pretty sure of it. So if the worst happened, Keth would be better off with us, you know.'

'There are all ways of looking at it,' said Polly, soberly. 'I'd wish him in Timbuktu – anywhere – if the balloon went up again. I haven't forgotten, yet, the state they sent my Dickon back home in. But you don't think . . . ?'

'No. Not really. It's just that – well, it's men who start wars, but it's we women who bear the sons they take for their armies, so we worry more. I just wish Hitler would stop his demanding bits of *this* country and bits of *that* country. And there are things going on in Germany, I believe, that we can only guess at.

'But let's not talk about Hitler. An upstart, that's what Albert calls him. A guy with a chip on his shoulder. Let's talk about Keth? He's got everything packed?'

'That he has. Tom and Alice and Daisy bought him a cabin trunk as a going-away present – real smart, it looks. And talking about Daisy, she's going to miss him cruel. They're very close, she and Keth.'

'Mm. I'd noticed.'

'Aye – well, it's like Alice says. Three years apart will give them both time to see if they want each other at the end of it. Alice reckons it's all for the best, Keth going. She and Tom'll give them their blessing if they still want to wed when Keth comes home – and so will I, an' all.'

'Daisy is a lovely girl. She's going to grow up into a beauty. She and Kitty are close, you know. It's going to be strange for the Clan at Christmas, Kitty says, them not being together. Oh, and Keth's passport! He's got it okay?'

'He has. Keeps looking at it. Says he can't imagine him ever having one. Makes him feel important, I think.'

'Well, there'll be no trouble at Immigration when we get to New York. Albert has everything seen to. It'll all go smoothly.'

'It's beyond thinking about,' Polly said, bemused just to imagine how it would be. 'And I've told Keth he's to answer to you and Mr Sutton. Don't take any back-answers, though I don't think he'll give any. You chastise him, though, if he steps out of line. Don't spoil him, will you?'

'I'll tell him off good, don't worry. And I'll stand on a chair,' Amelia laughed, 'and box his ears if he gets sassy!'

'You do that, Mrs Sutton – with my blessing. And I can't thank you enough for what you are doing for my boy. I'm not good at words, but I'm grateful.'

'It works both ways.' Amelia rose to her feet, wrapping Polly warmly in her arms. 'We'll take good care of your son, never fear, and I'll see he writes home regularly. We'll send a cable, the minute we're home. The car will call, day after tomorrow, at six. We're taking Pendenys' little pick-up, too, for all the luggage.

'Getting the milk train from Holdenby and the eight-fifteen from York to Liverpool. Don't know exactly what time we sail. On the afternoon tide, it'll be.

'Now would you like to come to York, to wave us off – or you could come to Liverpool, if you'd like? You'd be welcome. I should've thought of it before this.'

'No, thank you. I'd have asked, if I'd wanted to. Truth known, I'd rather wave him off from here. Happen when he comes home, though, I could be there to meet him. Would be something to look forward to.'

'Just as you say. Well – see you on Wednesday morning then, bright and early.'

'Bright and early,' Polly said gravely.

*　　*　　*

'You've got my photograph?' Daisy whispered.

'You know I have. I've got two of you – and the big one Mrs MacMalcolm took last Christmas. Remember – all the Clan together? It'll remind me of Rowangarth, and home.'

'And of me?'

This was their last night together. She had known it would come, but not for a minute had she thought it would come so quickly or feel so final, when it did.

There was so much to say but she couldn't remember a word of it. Now, she just wanted to stay here in his arms, feel his closeness, store up kisses.

Last night had shocked and surprised and delighted her all at the same time when things became bewilderingly passionate between them; out of hand, almost.

'Darling,' Keth had pleaded. 'I want you.'

Yet from the giddy heights of her need of him she had whispered, 'No, Keth. We can't. It isn't allowed, you know it isn't . . .'

'Hell, of course I know, but I'd be careful.'

'I know you would.' They had talked about it. Going to Creesby, but getting off at Holdenby, it would be like, and fingers crossed that they both got off in time. And there were other ways, she had heard, yet still they had held back. 'You see, Keth, I've never – *we've* never . . .'

'I know, sweetheart. Neither of us have, but that's the way I want it to be – don't you?'

'Y-yes.' She wouldn't want to think there had ever been anyone else. 'But if we did – if we tried – I'd spoil it, I'm sure I would. I don't know what to do, you see. Fumbling in dark corners, Mam said it would be like.'

'You've told your Mam about us!' It came as a shock that she could do such a thing.

'Of course. Ages ago. And Mam understood, Keth. Her and Dada did it once and she was sorry, afterwards. She said it's best to wait. It's lovely, she said – heaps better – when you're married.'

'Daisy! What if she told your dad . . . ?'

'She didn't tell him. Women's talk, she said. There are things we don't tell the menfolk.' She felt the tension and the need leave him, then, and she smiled and whispered, 'Mam understands, Keth.'

'Sorry, Daisy. I shouldn't have said what I did. It's just that I love you so. Three years – it's a lifetime.' He knew how beautiful she was. She would grow even more beautiful and other men would want her and he wouldn't be there to stop them. 'You'll never stop loving me? Say you won't?'

'Never, Keth Purvis. It's always been you. I won't change, I promise. I want you just as much as you want me; it's just that deep down, I want us to wait.'

'But I do worry. That money of yours, for one thing.'

'Then don't let it bother you, Keth. I've got used to it. I wish you would try to.'

'I will, though sometimes I don't know why you bother with me and my moods.'

'I don't like it when you're jealous, I'll admit it. People say jealousy is a part of loving, but it isn't. Look at me, darling?' In the fading light of Brattocks Wood she cupped his face in her hands, forcing his eyes to meet hers. 'I love you,' she said softly, insistently. 'There won't ever be anyone else for me. Not ever. I want you to go to America and get your degree and we'll be married when you get back. I love you, *love you*, and I want you, I really do, but thank you for not making me . . .'

That had been last evening. Tonight was different. Tonight, Keth had promised not to say goodbye to her, not actually say it. 'See you,' perhaps, or 'So long,' but not goodbye. They had tried never to say it in the war, Mam said. 'Never say goodbye,' she smiled sadly.

Tonight, there were few words between them. Just a

throbbing sadness, a longing for it to be over so the pain would go, yet a need to stay locked together for all time so there would be no need for parting.

'You ought to have a ring,' Keth whispered, lips against hers.

'I don't want one. *I* know we're engaged. Rings are to let other people know.'

She had the daisychain he gave her on her birthday. He'd fastened it around her wrist. Gold, he'd said it was really made of, and sapphires and pearls. And she had taken it off carefully when she got home and laid it in her Bible, just as Mam had done with Dada's buttercups. She had his butterfly, too. He had forgotten about the butterfly in the matchbox.

'It's time to go.' She was shaking. Was it the sudden chill of a September evening or was it because she knew that soon, when they had kissed, he would walk away from her and they would not meet nor touch nor kiss for three years?

July, he'd said it would be. In the summer of nineteen-forty he would be home. There would only be a year to wait until she came of age. They could be engaged officially, he said, and she'd replied that that would be marvellous; a year for Keth to find a job and for her and Mam to plan the wedding, make her dress.

The summer of 'forty. It would be her watchword, hers to wear like a talisman, words to say over and over when she missed him and wanted him unbearably.

'Kiss me just once more?' she whispered, offering her lips.

Their kiss was without passion. Gentle, despairing maybe, sad without doubt. Their lips lingered, putting off the moment, yet it was Keth who broke free, Keth who whispered, 'I love you, Daisy Dwerryhouse,' breaking the lock of the fingers clenched behind his neck, stepping back from her. 'I'll love you always.'

He left her, then, walking quickly, his heels slamming

angrily against the grass of the wood, and she stood there waiting with breath indrawn in case he should call one last goodbye.

But there was nothing. He had gone. For three years they would never laugh together nor touch nor kiss. They would want each other but it would be a want diluted by the vastness of the ocean between them.

'Take care,' she whispered into the twilight. 'See you . . .'

Keth had awakened at four and could not go back to sleep again. Beside him, the alarm clock ticked loudly and he had swung his feet to the floor, then pressed the fat button to cancel the ring.

Best he should get up and light the kitchen fire for Mam. Then he would wash and shave and take her a cup of tea to bed at five, before her own alarm sounded.

He had wanted to leave; wanted not to leave. Inside him, just where his heart should be, sadness lay like a cold, heavy stone; yet his stomach churned with excitement. This was the first day of the great adventure, yet it was the first day without Daisy.

Things passed quickly, then. Mam hearing him lighting the fire because she, too, had been awake; Mam coming downstairs. He and Mam eating bread and jam and drinking tea and checking that his passport was in his coat pocket and checking the mantel clock with his wristwatch because the minutes were ticking off much, much too quickly.

Then the cars coming and Mam, white-faced, holding him tightly, taking his face in gentle hands, saying, 'God bless you, son. Look after yourself . . .'

And he, trying not to look back because Mam said he mustn't, even though he knew she was still there, watching him out of sight; then peering through the trees towards Keeper's Cottage, wondering if Daisy were awake, knowing she was not because there was no light in her room.

And now, at Holdenby station, the five of them surrounded by luggage and the porter waiting importantly with a trolley, asking them to stand back if they pleased, as the signal fell with a clunk.

'It's coming,' Kitty sighed. 'Oh goodbye, dear old Holdenby and goodbye everybody.' She had looked dramatically at her father, her glance telling him he was real mean not wanting to come over at Christmas as they had always done. 'Can you hear it yet?'

'No.' Keth whispered, wanting her not to talk to him because Daisy would surely be sending him her love and he wanted to hear her voice in his mind, his heart.

'Say, Keth,' Bas smiled. 'Got a message for you. Tell me – which side of the compartment will Brattocks Wood be?'

'The side farthest from the door – why?'

'Then guess you'd better sit there. Daisy said you were to look out. She said you'd know where.'

'But of course!' The train ran alongside Brattocks Wood for a little way, about half a mile out of the station. The far end of the wood, it was, not far from the elm trees in a little clearing. 'What did she say, Bas? When did she tell you?'

'Yesterday, when the Clan was at Rowangarth, saying goodbye. Said I wasn't to forget.'

Daisy. He would see her again. Last night they had been sad and he'd walked away from her in despair. But Daisy understood, loved him. Now it would all come right.

The little local train clanked and hissed importantly, then came to a squealing stop at the platform. Keth and Bas supervised the loading of the large luggage into the guard's van; Albert helped his wife and daughter into the compartment. Then Kitty said, 'Here y'are, Keth. This end. Now all of us – get ready to wave!'

The stationmaster blew his whistle, waved his green flag.

The train jerked, juddered, took up a slow, slipping rhythm, then pulled and strained, gained speed slowly.

Holdenby behind them and ahead of them, trees. Brattocks Wood where Daisy would be, at the very end of Rowangarth lane.

And there she was; Daisy, with the labradors, smiling, waving a handkerchief.

Keth leaned out calling, 'Love you, Daisy!' He knew she hadn't heard him over the noise of the train, but he'd said it and she had seen him say it and his going-away memory would be of Daisy, there when he had so needed her to be; Daisy, smiling. All over in a few seconds, but *she had been there*!

'Gee,' Bas smiled, 'that was real nice.'

'Romantic . . .' Kitty sighed.

Mr and Mrs Sutton were smiling; the whole world was smiling. Keth Purvis was going to America and when he came home in the summer of 'forty, Daisy would be waiting for him and loving him and wanting him, still.

'Nice,' Keth grinned, then leaned back in his seat, eyes closed, remembering Daisy. And life was all at once good.

40

'Come in, do.' Alice returned Julia's kiss. 'Where on earth have you been? Seen neither hide nor hair of you all week.' She pushed the kettle further into the coals, reaching for the teapot. 'You'll surely have time to stay for a cup?'

'I've been busy planning a party – mother's seventy-eighth, by the way; I've just been to Nathan's and yes please, I'd love a cuppa.'

'Nathan's?' She was spending quite a bit of time at the vicarage, these days. Lucky they were cousins so the village couldn't read too much into her comings and goings. 'Again?'

'Nathan's. Again,' Julia smiled mysteriously. 'You'll be coming to mother's do? I'd thought to have a tea party, this year. Don't want anything that's going to go on too long. She gets a bit tired, these days.'

'She's all right?' Alice looked up sharply.

'Course she is. Just a little slower, that's all. How's your lot?'

'Tom's fine.' Julia wasn't going to volunteer anything, then, about Nathan. 'He's at the rearing field, checking up. It's a busy time for him, with all the young chicks.'

'And Daisy?'

'Missing Keth – but then, she would be. Keth's always been there, ever since she can remember. She's taking her shorthand and typing exams, soon, but you'll know that. Sorry she isn't in; took it into her head to call on Reuben.

'And Keth's fine. Letters coming regularly. Don't mind the kitchen, do you? I haven't lit the parlour fire, yet.'

'The kitchen's fine.' Julia pulled out a chair, leaning her elbows on the table. She looked so much more relaxed these days, Alice considered. Better by far since she'd been to Andrew's grave and started to face facts a bit.

'By the way, I've got a bit of news from you, hot from the vicarage.' Julia poured milk into the cups, spooning in sugar. 'Thought you should be the first to know – after mother, of course. Nathan's –'

'*Mam*!' The kitchen door burst open and Daisy stood there, gasping for breath as if she had run all the way from the almshouses. 'Did you hear it on the wireless? It's Hitler! He's marched into Austria!'

'Oh, my Lord!'

'You're sure?' Julia's voice was sharp.

'Of course I'm sure. I wouldn't make up a thing like that. Turn the wireless on, Mam?'

'Too late.' Alice glanced at the mantel clock. 'News'll be over, now. So tell me – what exactly did it say?'

'Said the German armies had marched into Austria and that half the population had turned out to greet them. Said the Viennese were jubilant.'

'Well, they would be. There's a strong German element, there. Austria was on the Kaiser's side, in the war,' Julia nodded, lips pursed.

'So is there going to be trouble?' Alice whispered.

'I doubt it. Hitler's been going on lately about more living space for Germany. Maybe now he'll be satisfied.'

'So you don't think it's serious, Aunt Julia?' Daisy's eyes were wide with concern.

'No, dear. I don't think it's so much an invasion as an annexing, really.'

'And we'll not interfere? We'll let them get on with it?'

'No reason why not, Daisy. They weren't firing shots or anything, were they?'

'N-no. Seemed by what I heard that Hitler wasn't exactly unwelcome.'

'There you are, then. Now just settle down, lovey, and get your homework finished,' Alice soothed. 'When your Dada gets back, we'll ask him about it. Like your Aunt Julia says, it mightn't be all that serious. Off you go upstairs. I've lit the oil stove in your bedroom.' Alice closed the staircase door. 'What do you think, Julia? *Really* think, I mean,' she asked when they were alone.

'I don't know. Didn't want to upset the child, but it looks as if Anthony Eden was right – Churchill, too.'

'Mr Eden resigning from the government, you mean, because he thinks we're letting Hitler get away with too much? You think taking over Austria is too much, then?'

'As long as he stops there and doesn't get any more ideas, I suppose we can learn to live with it. What do you want us to do, Alice – tell him to stop it, or else?'

'You know I don't!'

'Sorry, love. And can you blame us for getting a bit jittery when Germany really *is* throwing its weight about a bit?'

'Wouldn't you, if you were Hitler and you'd got all those tanks and planes and soldiers?'

'And what about the Duke of Windsor and his woman?' Julia flung. 'Remember, they went to Germany in October, to Berchtesgaden. If that isn't kow-towing, I don't know what is! Remember that picture in the papers and Mrs Simpson smiling all over her face, shaking Hitler's hand?'

'She's the Duchess of Windsor now . . .'

'I don't care if she's the Queen of Hearts, neither of them should have gone! He doesn't represent Britain, now. He should keep his nose out of things and especially out of Germany!'

'All right – they shouldn't have gone, but it's all water under the bridge, now. Tom reckons if Hitler really intends making trouble, he'll go for Russia.'

'Then I hope Tom is right. Just as long as this country keeps out of it, that's all. Last time, we went in because

Belgium wanted to stay neutral. *If* it happens again, surely we'll have learned our lesson? And anyway, the French are building those defences. The Germans won't be able to march into France, like they did last time. The Maginot Line, isn't it called? They say it's really strong – guns, tank traps. You name it . . .'

'Hitler has built one an' all.' The Siegfried Line, they were calling it. No need for trenches, if it happened again, Alice sighed. French and German fortifications each facing the other and a ready-made No Man's Land between them. 'This tea has gone cold. Better make another pot. Tom'll be in, soon, and he'll want a sup. And Julia – you were going to tell me something when Daisy came in – something about Nathan?'

'Oh, yes! Don't say anything just yet, but it'll be common knowledge, soon. Not before time, mother said when I told her, but she's very pleased, for all that. Nathan has got a curate, at last.'

'A *curate*!' A curate, and she had thought – she'd been *sure* – that Nathan had proposed to Julia. 'I'll put the kettle on . . .' There really wasn't anything else to say.

'That's enough!' Cook glared at the wireless. 'Turn it off, Tilda. Life's depressing enough without having Hitler morning, noon and night. That man is worse'n the Kaiser!' At least the Kaiser had been a gentleman.

'All right, Mrs Shaw. Don't get yourself upset. There's nothing you and me can do about it if the Germans want to take over Austria. We should mind our own business, not get entangled with that lot in Europe. Look where it landed us, in 1914!' Mary sniffed.

'Mind our own business, eh? And who says so?'

'Will says so. There's no need to stick our nose in, he said. What happens over there needn't concern us. We've got the Channel between us and them and we should be glad of it!'

'That Will Stubbs of yours ought to be in Parliament, he's got so much to say!'

'Will is a well-read man,' Mary countered, nose in the air. 'There's things going on in Germany if folk but knew it, he said, that would make your hair curl! You've only got to read the newspapers.'

'Newspapers!' Cook still harboured a sneaking mistrust of Fleet Street.

'Yes, Mrs Shaw. Will was only talking about them the other night – the Duke and Duchess of Windsor, I mean. Said if the newspapers hadn't got hold of it, none of us would've been any the wiser about him and her hob-nobbing with Hitler.'

'He has a perfect right,' Tilda said mutinously, 'to go where he pleases.' Tilda Tewk still loved her Prince of Wales, was ready to clasp him to her bosom the minute his skinny wife divorced him.

'Not to Germany. Not when they were our enemies. Will was there, in the trenches. He knows what the Kaiser's lot got up to. And serving king and country entitles him to an opinion if you'll pardon me, Mrs Shaw!'

'I see.' Cook's cheeks flushed deep crimson. 'Then might we have the benefit of that opinion, Miss?'

'Oh, you might! Will says the Duke of Windsor only went to see Hitler so he could stake his claim, like. Will reckons that if there's another war and Hitler wins it, the Duke hopes he'll make him King of England again, and her the Queen!'

'*Another* war!' Cook's fingers strayed to her apron corners, a sign Mary should have noted. 'The *next* war you're on about, and some of us still not over the last one yet!'

'Will says –'

'Will, Will, *Will*!' Not only Hitler to torment her but Will Stubbs, an' all! 'All right – so your man's entitled to his opinion – it's a free country, I'll grant you. But I don't want his opinions in my kitchen, is that understood, Mary Strong?'

'Ha! Sorry I spoke, I'm sure. But there are others here who did their bit for king and country and went very yellow doing it. And they have the right to an opinion, too!' Last word flung, Mary opened the kitchen door with a flourish, stormed up the back stairs and out, in search of Will.

Will would know what it all meant – those Germans marching into Austria without so much as a by-your-leave. Will Stubbs was nobody's fool and she should know! He'd managed to remain a bachelor all these years, and that took some doing!

'There now, Mrs Shaw, don't get yourself upset,' Tilda hushed, filling the kettle, placing it to boil. 'And if those Austrians want to cheer Hitler, then let them! None of our business.'

'No, but are we going to make it our business? See where our interference landed us in 'fourteen and all because somebody shot an Archduke in Sarajevo. Us hadn't even heard of Sarajevo, 'til then.' She still plucked at her apron corners, ready to lift it, bury her face in it, and weep. It was either that, or the tea. 'Make us a good strong cup, Tilda lass,' she sighed.

And happen Tilda was right. Austria had nowt to do with us.

There were times, Julia thought as she strolled the walled vicarage garden at Nathan's side, when she almost knew contentment. She breathed in deeply of the scents around her; of second-flowering honeysuckle and lilac and, edging the path, beds of old-fashioned pinks to add their sweetness to her pleasure.

'I like your garden,' she said softly, tucking an arm in his. 'Not too big, and sheltered, too.'

'My sentiments, exactly. I like the house, as well. What

was it, before Rowangarth let the parish have it?'

'The Dower House. Mother should be living here now, all things being equal. But they aren't equal, are they, though I might tell the Bishop that Rowangarth wants it back, once Drew is married,' she teased.

'You'd live here, then?'

'If I had to – quite happily. I suppose, though, that when Drew marries, I'll stay at Rowangarth. The south wing could be made into a nice little apartment. I've often thought it.'

'So you wouldn't move in here – if I left, I mean?'

'No.' Her reply was without compromise.

'Good. That's one problem solved. It's the new curate, you see. I was so relieved to get him I practically guaranteed him somewhere to live. And he'll need a decent place because he's got two sets of twins and a widowed mother to house. Would you object to him having the vicarage, Julia?'

'Not at all. But if you left here, where would you go?'

'Father's getting old, and he's lonely in that great place. I could go to Pendenys.'

'But would uncle like being involved in parish affairs – people calling, and all that sort of thing? And people dying.' People, Nathan once said, always sent for the priest in the small hours of the morning. It was a strange fact that that was when most people died. 'Pendenys is a bit out of the way, isn't it, for parishioners?'

'I suppose it is, but parish business could still be taken care of at the vicarage by the curate and it's as father says – who is going to take over Pendenys Place, when he goes? Kentucky won't want it. Albert never liked it and Bas hates to think he might inherit it. Only that madcap Kitty has a good word to say for it.'

'Then leave it to Kitty. And somehow, it isn't so – so *theatrical*-looking since Uncle Edward had the tower demolished. It was that tower made it look so odd.'

'Of course, it might be more bearable to live in if I were married, Julia – had children.'

'True. But there were three of you there, once. As children, did you like it?'

'I didn't. I always thought it was like living in a Town Hall.'

'Then why wish it on your children? And should you even be thinking about a family – now, I mean, when everybody's got the jitters about Germany and Italy?' All at once, her near contentment vanished.

'Czechoslovakia, you mean?' Hitler, now that he had expanded his *living space* into Austria, was making scarcely-veiled hints that parts of Czechoslovakia rightly belonged to the Third Reich, too. 'Is he going to march in there, as well? And if he does, will that be the end of it? The man's a lunatic – power mad.'

'So it isn't just me getting goose pimples whenever I think of him – see him on the newsreels? You worry about him, too, Nathan?'

'Yes, though I think I'd be a bit too old to go to war again. But that's a selfish attitude when there's the young generation to think about. It's them we should worry over.' He stopped, biting on his words, knowing he had said entirely the wrong thing. 'Sorry, Julia.'

'Then don't be. You're right, anyway. But I love the young Suttons so much, you see. My Clan. I've watched them grow up. I don't want them to have to face what we faced, Nathan.'

All at once, the beauty of the soft July evening was as nothing because she had voiced the fears that until now she had managed to push behind her. Because no one, she had thought, not even arrogant, goose-stepping Germany, could want another war.

'It's the newspapers. They blow things up out of all proportion.'

'No!' Julia shook her head. 'They're only trying to wake people up to the truth.'

'But people don't want facing with the truth.'

'Then they are fools! Even Parliament is divided, now. A lot of MPs are beginning to think that Winston Churchill wasn't scaremongering when he warned about Hitler – nor Mr Eden.'

'I read, somewhere, that some members of Parliament are going to try and get it debated in the Commons.'

'Debated? What that man wants is *telling*! No farther – *or else*!' Julia gasped, red-cheeked.

'And what if we did, and he called our bluff – because bluff it would be. We aren't armed, like Germany is. But why did we get onto this subject, Julia, on a glorious night like this?'

'Because everyone is worried, if they'll admit it. I was at Denniston House yesterday, and Anna feels as I do. She was going to give Tatiana a year in Switzerland at a finishing school, but now she says she wouldn't dream of letting her go to Europe. Poor little Tatty.'

'Little Tatty, as you call her, is sixteen now, and quite the young lady. Soon she'll be every bit as beautiful as Anna. Do you remember Elliot's wedding, Julia? Anna was so in love.'

'I remember it. I wanted to yell, "Run, Anna Petrovska! Don't be such a fool. I know things about him that'd make your hair curl!" And Nathan – do you ever think about Tatty and Drew – getting fonder of each other, I mean.'

'Often. But I think Tatiana will have half the young men in the Riding at her feet before so very much longer. I doubt she'll fall in love on her own doorstep.'

'What could we do to stop it, Nathan, if they did?'

'I don't know. It would hurt so many people if the truth had to come out. But this started out being such a promising evening and now we've had the lot – Hitler to Elliot.

Anyway, the gnats will start biting, soon – I think we should go inside and have a drink.'

Gnat bites. If that were all they need worry about, Julia fretted.

'I'd like that,' she sighed. 'A *large* one!'

'I see,' said Tom, passing the evening paper to Alice, 'that Mr Chamberlain's been in touch with the French Prime Minister, trying to arrange talks with that Fascist lot. Appeasement, that's what.'

'And isn't that better than war, or had you forgotten what it's like – what it would be like for Daisy and Drew, for all the youngsters?' Alice snapped. 'Your memory is short, Tom, and it wouldn't be just the young men they'd take, next time. It'd be the young women, an' all.'

'Conscript women? Oh, Alice! Who ever told you that? They couldn't do such a thing! I'd be waiting with a shotgun if they came for our Daisy!'

'No one told me. I read it, somewhere.'

'Then forget it. They'll print anything, these days. Frightening folk to death. The dratted newspapers have got everybody in a tizzy. And happen if France and us go and see Hitler – warn him he's gone far enough – he'll have another think about taking a piece of Czechoslovakia and turn his attention to Russia, like I've always thought. Those Bolshies'd give him what for! Soon put paid to his goosestepping and sieg-heiling!'

'So you don't think, Tom, that –

'That he'd start a war in Europe? Not a chance, love.'

'Honestly? I couldn't bear it to happen again; not to see Daisy and Drew have to go. You're not just saying it . . . ?'

'Listen to me, lass – there *isn't* going to be a war! Adolf Hitler will get his bluff called afore so very much longer, and that's my opinion for what it's worth. Hitler doesn't worry me!'

And there were times, he thought, that if someone called

him the best and biggest liar in the entire Riding, they wouldn't be far wrong.

'That's it, then. No more school!'

Examinations behind her, Daisy was restless for the results. Without a piece of paper to say you'd passed this or that, decent jobs were still not easy to find around Creesby.

The trouble was, she frowned, that everybody was on edge and sick to death of war talk and reading about war talk. And there hadn't been a letter from Keth for two weeks, now. Busy with his own exams, of course, but surely he could write two lines on the back of a postcard. *I'm okay. I love you.* It was all she needed to know.

But he couldn't, she supposed, write that he loved her on something as public as a postcard. Not around Holdenby.

She missed Keth. It hurt inside her just to think that he had only been away ten months. Ten *years*. And it hurt to think that she was rich, really, yet Keeper's didn't have a telephone. Not that many people did, mind.

But these days, you could ring up all the way to America, yet imagine what the men who looked after her trust fund would say if she asked them for money to have a phone put in so she could make expensive calls to America.

'Mam – I do miss Keth. If I could see him for just a minute, talk to him . . .'

'I know, lovey. Your Mam does know what it's like. There were times I'd have given all I had, just to hold your Dada, touch him.'

'I'd forgotten – sorry. Selfish of me when you didn't even know if Dada was coming back.'

'For a time I was sure he wasn't, truth known. So cheer up, lass. It'll soon be a year. One down – only two to go!'

'But Mam – what if there's a war? Not just two years to wait, then. Goodness only knows when he'd get back. You said that in your war, civilians weren't allowed berths on ships.'

'We-e-ll, don't know how it would be for men, but Cecilia – she was Sir Robert's young lady, back in Shillong – couldn't get a sailing to England. Men were allowed a passage home from India if they intended to enlist, like Sir Robert did. But wives and children had to stay behind, sit out the war in India. Government said it was too risky for womenfolk on ships. Look what happened to the *Lusitania*.'

'Mam?' Daisy gazed at her with eyes so blue it made her marvel. Her child was so good to look at, Alice brooded, that sometimes her beauty made her wonder how folk as ordinary as she and Tom had done it!

'Aye, lass?'

'There won't be a war, will there?'

'No, please God.'

'That's good, then. But if there is, I shall go.'

'Be a nurse? That you will *not*!'

'But you did. And you did it sneaky, too. You told them you were a year older so you could go to France, so what's so special about me that I can't?'

'I wanted to get nearer your Dada and your Aunt Julia was missing the doctor, too, so we went together. Life could be uncertain, when I was your age. We lived from day to day and letter to letter.'

'And I would want to get to Keth.'

'Now don't talk such nonsense! Keth would be in America, wouldn't he – safe out of it. And America wouldn't come in on our side – not another time. There's too many pacifists there, and I don't blame them. If I had the Atlantic Ocean between me and Hitler, I'd thank the good Lord for it, I can tell you, and let Europe get on with it.

'So let's have no more war talk. We've got to keep hoping that it won't happen. And Daisy love, I do understand about you and Keth.'

Oh, drat that Hitler! Alice fumed. If he walked up

Keeper's path this very minute, she'd take down Tom's shotgun and let him have both barrels, right in his backside!

'Put the kettle on, lass?' All at once she felt tired and drained and helpless. 'Let's have a sup of tea, shall us?'

Had Daisy known something so wonderful, so completely unbelievable, so madly, marvelously magic would happen, she would have been very afraid because she would have been insane, loopy, daft as a brush. Or delirious with fever, perhaps, and a temperature of 104°.

But what, with hindsight, she would remember about this day was that it had started out to be a very ordinary one; that she had nearly missed the eight o'clock bus from the lane end, that she had worn her blue dress with the white collar and cuffs and her black court shoes – very sensible and correct for the office, of course. And at half-past five, just as she was putting the cover over her typewriter, the counting house manager had given her her first pay packet.

Fifteen shillings a week, she earned now, less five pence deductions, and Mam said she might keep it all for herself – this week, at least. After that, though, so she might know that money didn't grow on trees and to learn the value of it, she must contribute five shillings each week to the housekeeping, pay the Yorkshire Road Car Company another five for her weekly bus ticket, and have the remainder to fritter as she pleased.

And on this madly marvellous day she had learned that four shillings and sevenpence would not take a lot of frittering because she laddered a silk stocking getting off the bus and there, at a ping, went one shilling and elevenpence!

She was actually brooding about stockings when she heard the whistle that made her blood tingle cold. She stopped at the laneside, drawing in her breath because all at once her breathing was loud and harsh and there was a noise in her ears.

Then she heard the whistle again and she shouted, '*Keth*!' and began to run, even though she knew Keth was in America and she was probably sickening for that fever.

He was standing where Rowangarth lane branched off into Brattocks Wood and the footpath that ran through the trees to Keeper's Cottage; standing there in grey flannel trousers and a white shirt and looking exactly like Keth Purvis who was really in America and she knew that if she spoke the figure would vanish.

So she said nothing. She just stood there, looking at him – at *it* – because this was an hallucination, a vision, the first symptom of fever even though he was so dearly, heart-breakingly like Keth that she wanted to weep. Then he moved, tossing something flimsy and white into the air, and ran laughing, arms wide, to where she stood.

'Daisy! Darling! Where have you been? I've been waiting hours!'

That was when she began to weep; great tearing sobs that started in the pit of her stomach and hurt, really hurt as they jerked from her throat.

'Ssssh, it's all right. It's me – it *is* . . .'

So she buried her face deeper into his chest, not caring about his clean shirt, and let her fingertips touch his arms, his neck, his mouth. And when they touched his lips he kissed them and whispered, 'I love you, darling. Don't cry? I can't kiss you, if you're crying . . .'

She knew, then, that it really was him and she stepped back, blowing her nose loudly, inelegantly.

'Keth – *why* . . . ?' she choked.

He kissed her then, hard and long, and her head began to spin and the delicious tingles she always felt when they were close were back again. And she felt so dizzy and weak that she had to cling even more tightly to him so that for a little while it didn't matter why he had come home.

"Tell me?' he whispered, urgently.

'I love you, love you, love you.'

'And I love you, my darling, and you're even more beautiful than ever I remembered.'

'I'm not! I've been crying. My eyes are red!'

'They aren't, and your eyelashes are all long and wet and spiky. Beautiful . . .'

'Why didn't you tell me you'd be home? It's a wonder I didn't faint!'

'Not you,' he laughed, entwining his fingers in hers.

'Have you seen Mam?'

'I have. She told me you were usually on the twenty-past six bus.'

'I was, but I went to Reuben's, first. I'm working now, at Morris and Page, and I bought him some tobacco out of my first pay packet. Mam says I can keep all my wages, this week. Nearly fifteen shillings! All mine!'

'Oh, Daisy Dwerryhouse! You're rich – rich beyond most men's dreams, yet –' He shook his head, smiling, looking at her with that special look. Loving her with his eyes she supposed it was. 'Don't ever change, darling girl.'

'Have you had your supper?' She didn't want him to start talking about Mr Hillier's money. Not tonight.

'I have. At the bothy. And your Mam is keeping yours hot between two plates.'

'I couldn't eat it. I'd be sick. Are Kitty and Bas here – the family?'

'Nope. Just me.'

'Then why? Keth – you haven't flopped your exams?'

'No. Did rather well, as a matter of fact.'

That was when she looked up and saw them, caught on a thorn of bramble; daisies, made into a chain, swinging there fragile and helpless.

'Oh, Keth, you remembered. You made me a daisychain.' The tears came again. 'Why did you throw it away?'

'Oh – suppose I was just standing there, getting bored – so I made it. I was going to hang it round your neck and smile and kiss you – romantic, sort of, like they do it in the movies, but then I saw you and –'

'Then give them to me now?' She picked them carefully from the thorn, handing them to him. 'It isn't broken. Hang it round my neck and kiss me – please?'

So he did as she asked and they walked without speaking to Keeper's Cottage because all at once it didn't matter why he was home; only that he was there, beside her, walking close, thighs touching.

She had never loved him or wanted him so much.

It wasn't until Daisy had eaten almost all the supper Alice had kept warm on the bottom shelf of the fire oven and they were half-way up Holdenby Pike that Daisy said, 'When are you going to tell me, Keth, how you managed to get home? And why didn't you tell me you were coming?'

'Because I didn't know, love, until a couple of weeks ago.'

'So that's why your letters stopped. Keth – who paid your passage over? Have you won a bursary?'

'No such luck. Mrs Sutton wanted to buy me a sailing ticket, but I said no. I talked to her first, and to Mr Sutton, and they agreed with what I intended doing. And it's all right. My place is there for me at college, if I go back. But I might not. It's why, really, Bas and Kitty aren't here, this year. I don't think they'll come over again until things settle down. Kitty wanted to come with me, but Mr Sutton wouldn't hear of it.'

'So *why*, Keth?'

'I've come home to look after Mum. The way things are, it wouldn't have been right, her being alone; not after what she's been through, all her life. And I wanted to be with you, too.'

'But I don't understand, I really don't.' They had stopped walking now, and stood opposite, cheeks flushed, eyes not meeting.

'I'm home, Daisy, because there's going to be a war. I wanted to stay at college but there's no one but me to look after Mum. I worked my passage over. It's easy to pick up a ship. As long as you have a passport, there's no bother.

'I was lucky. Got a tanker sailing into the Mersey. I worked in the galley – peeled and scrubbed the whole way across. I never want to clean another pan or peel another carrot, ever.'

'But why are you so sure, Keth? Who said there'd be a war? Oh, I know people here keep thinking there could be, but there's going to be talks, we think. They're trying to get a meeting with Hitler to talk sense into him. You didn't have to do it, Keth. You went there to read physics and maths and all the time it seems you've been debating the political situation in Europe, is that it?' Her eyes flashed anger; Tom's temper surfaced in her, then burst out in a torrent of abuse. 'You fool! You *idiot*! If there *is* going to be a war, then that's where I want you – in America, well away from it all! *If* war comes, they'll have you in the Army soon as look at you and it'll be goodbye to all we've ever hoped for and dreamed about! Stupid! Stupid! *Stupid*!'

Her fists pummelled his chest. She closed her eyes, hitting out blindly, weeping in sharp, angry sobs.

'Daisy! *Stop it!*' He grasped her wrists, holding them tightly, and she struggled against his grip, even though he was hurting her.

'Let me go, Keth Purvis. Don't dare to – to *assault* me!'

'I'll slap you.' His voice was low and slow as if he were fighting for control of his temper. 'I will, Daisy. I mean it!'

'Oh, Keth . . .' She let go a shuddering sigh and he felt her body grow limp. 'I'm sorry, but it's all been such a shock. And I'm as afraid as you are that there'll be a war and I know it was good of you to think about your Mum – but *please* go back to Kentucky? Don't throw everything away – your life, even.'

'I'll go back when – *if* – they get things sorted out here. Everybody in America thinks it'll come to war. Mr Sutton does, and so do I. But if a small miracle happens, then I'll go back. I want to, Daisy. I want that degree more than anything.'

'More than me?'

'More than you, right now, because without it I can't have you, don't you see?'

'Of course you can. I'd marry you tomorrow!'

'Listen! When we get married, it'll be me who provides for you. I mean it.'

He loosened his grip on her wrists, then, and gathered her to him, kissing her, caressing her, holding her so close that she felt his need of her. And she pressed closer, glorying in her power over him and his over her.

'My money. What are we to do with it, then,' she murmured.

'Oh, I reckon our kids should have it. They'll want bikes and toys –'

'And ponies, perhaps.'

'And a fancy school, I shouldn't wonder.'

'How many shall we have, Keth?'

'Lord knows. Dozens . . .'

'We'll need a big house.'

'*I'll* give you a big house. Daisy Dwerryhouse.'

'When you get your degree, uh?'

'*If* I get my degree. Or maybe I'll have to do it the hard way. Mr Hillier started with a market stall and a coal round, don't forget.'

'So he did!'

They began to laugh, and all the tension left them and the accusations. They even forgot, for a little while, about Austria and Czechoslovakia and Germany.

'Keth?' She stirred in his arms. 'When you go back, how are you to get there?'

'I'll manage. I can work my passage again.'

'Peel your way back?'

'There are worse ways, but not many. I might get taken on as a stoker on a coal-burning ship. Lord! Imagine *shovelling* my way across!'

'We'll think about it later. Promise you'll go back?'

'I want to, Daisy. If I can, I will. I promise.'

'Then let's not say that man's name any more. Let's enjoy each day as it comes?'

'And make this a wonderful summer, what's left of it.'

'Our *daisychain* summer, Keth. One we'll always have, no matter what happens?'

'No matter what.' He bent to kiss her again. 'I want you Daisy, so much.'

'I want you, too. Have you ever, Keth – since you left?'

'No. And I know you haven't. That's why it's best to wait, I suppose.'

'Mam says so, too . . .'

'So we'll not do anything stupid? We'll wait?'

'If we can,' she smiled, suddenly wise. 'If we can, my darling . . .'

Peace for our Time

'There! That's the parish magazines seen to.' Julia fished in her pocket, emptying its contents into the toffee tin on Nathan's desk. 'Everybody paid. What a job! Everyone wanted a chat – mostly about Mr Chamberlain and what he's going to do about Hitler. Your new curate's wife is welcome to the job. When are they arriving, by the way?'

'Soon. One set of twins has measles and they're expecting the other two to go down with it. She was most apologetic and looking forward to being here – eventually.

'She liked the house the day she came to see it, though I could almost hear her mind boggling at the size of the windows. I'll leave as much as I can for them, and your mother has offered to help out with curtains and rugs and odd pieces of furniture. Luckily, she said, Miss Clitherow always keeps the seven-year rule.'

'Does she? And what is that?'

'Never throw anything away. Keep a thing for seven years, Miss Clitherow says, and you'll always find a use for it.'

'So you've made up your mind to move out to Pendenys?'

'I have, even though I was thankful, I remember, to leave it to come here. Father says I'm a fool, but it seems wrong, my living alone here. This house needs a family in it. Your mother said she had no objection to the curate having it. I did ask her. After all, it's Rowangarth's house, though the church doesn't pay rent for it.'

'I know that. But it's sad you're going back to the Place.

No one should have to live there. I wish your father liked London a bit more, then he could use the Cheyne Walk house and close Pendenys Place down — or give it to the Riding to use as a museum.'

'Or as a Town Hall! Are you going to stay to tea? It's nearly time. I'll pop downstairs and ask Cook to put another cup on the tray.'

Julia took off her jacket, draped it across a chairback, then walked to the window. Soon, Mr Chamberlain and Monsieur Daladier were to meet Mussolini and Hitler, make a last-minute appeal for sanity; or a warning, would they give, that he was to go no farther?

And what would they achieve? Promises, soon to be broken, or a genuine desire on the part of the dictators for peace? Germany had been badly treated at the end of the war, Julia admitted reluctantly, had been subjugated and belittled and perhaps they wanted not revenge but a place, once more, amongst the nations of Europe.

Yet Hitler was a madman. Jinny Dobb said he listened to fortune-tellers and occultists and a man – a head of state – who would do that was to be feared. Germany was riding high, and cock-a-hoop that it should be feared again. Could an old, frail man halt its march to power?

Anna thought there would be a war, Julia frowned; Albert thought so, too; even Keth had come home because of it.

Poor Keth, poor Daisy, poor Clan. All of them young and good to look at and loved. Not another war, oh, *please*, no more killing? Not Drew? Not her beloved young ones?

'Here we are.' Nathan set down the tray. 'Thought I'd bring it with me – save their legs. Shall I pour?'

'Please,' Julia murmured, without turning, still gazing out of the window, seeing nothing, returning to her thoughts.

Nathan didn't summon servants, but carried trays to

save their aching feet. Nathan was prepared to give up a house he was happy in because a curate with a small stipend and a large family needed it more. Dear Nathan, who once said he loved her. But that was a long time ago, when she had said goodbye to Andrew, and he had not mentioned marriage since.

Perhaps he wasn't content with her terms? Maybe he wanted a wife who loved him – *really* loved him – and not one who clung to memories.

She knew now that she was no longer Andrew's wife, but his widow. The fact had come to her in a flash of recognition at the cemetery at Étaples. It had not been a road-to-Damascus, blinding revelation; more something she had gathered to her out of the atmosphere and recognized and accepted. And then the blackbird began to sing again and it was as if Andrew was telling her from so many years away, that she was free.

'Nathan,' she said softly, turning to take the cup he offered. 'Once, I asked you to marry me. It was new year, remember, only I'd left it too late . . .'

'I do remember. And I thanked you and told you that when the time was right, *I* would ask *you*. Is the time right, Julia? If I asked you again, what would you say to me?'

His eyes sought hers anxiously, as if he should not ask because he feared her answer.

'I would say,' she said so softly that when she turned to face the window again, he could scarcely hear her words, 'that once there was a girl, crazily besotted with her man, and hot for loving. It was her first love and it was wild and frightening and too wonderful to last.

'And the woman I am now, realized that when I stood beside a grave at Étaples and all at once heard Andrew's voice again that I could bring back everything we had said, all those years ago.

'But it was a young nurse Andrew was talking to and I am middle-aged and dried up because I have shut out love, and if you were to ask me, I would want you to take me as I am.

'The wildness has gone from me, Nathan. I need someone by my side; someone to lean on. And I want comfort and a shared fireside and if love – a different love – grows out of that, then I shall accept it gratefully. That is what I would say to you, my dear.'

'Then knowing that the Julia I first fell in love with has passed the first flush of her youth and that I, too, have grown older with her and am willing to wait until that different, gentler loving happens, will you marry me?'

'There's a condition.' She placed her cup and saucer on the windowsill and turned, chin high, to face him. 'I won't be mistress of Pendenys Place. I couldn't live in a Town Hall, Nathan!'

'Oh, my lovely Julia – stubborn to the end! Don't change, will you? And since you will not have Pendenys, then I shall have to live with you, at Rowangarth. How does that suit you?'

'Seems I'd be getting the best of both worlds . . .'

There was a tap on the door and Cook stood there, a jug in her hand.

'You forgot the hot water, sir.'

'Oh, dear. My head won't ever save your feet, will it? And I'm sorry, but we've let this tea go cold. Mrs MacMalcolm has just said she will marry me, you see, and . . .'

'Oh, sir! Oh, madam! Oh, just wait till I tell them!' She was gone in a flurry of excitement, the hot water jug still in her hand.

'Well, that's done it,' Julia laughed shakily. 'It'll be half round the village already and I've hardly had time to say yes. Think we'd better phone mother before it reaches Rowangarth.'

'I love you, Julia. We'll be happy, I know it. And I'll wait . . .'

'Thank you for understanding.'

She took a step nearer, needing his kiss, and he cupped her face in his hands and took her mouth gently, warmly. Then picking up the phone he said to the operator, 'Good afternoon. Will you put me through to Rowangarth, please . . .'

The last day of September, and so warm they sat on the grass beside the stile that separated Brattocks Wood from the wild garden.

'Can you believe it, Keth? Can you?'

It was going to be all right. Mr Chamberlain and Monsieur Daladier had done what no one even wildly dreamed they would do. There was to be peace. Germany, Hitler said, had made its last territorial demand in Europe.

The Italian dictator, Benito Mussolini, had been there, though he had come away from the meeting empty-handed. But not so Hitler. Germany was to be allowed the area of Czechoslovakia that was morally theirs, with no opposition to the occupation voiced by England and France.

Yet, as Mam pointed out only that morning, it seemed that Russia, which minded very much about having Fascists so near to its frontier, was not asked to that meeting, and what was even more strange, Czechoslovakia wasn't consulted at all!

Mind, the remaining boundaries of that depleted country had been guaranteed. It had all been written down and signed by the four men. No more aggression. Mr Chamberlain had his piece of paper to prove it. What can't speak can't lie, Alice supposed, and sighed with relief along with the rest of the world.

That precious piece of paper had been clutched in Mr Chamberlain's old, frail hand. He waved it as he stepped from his plane at Croydon airport and waved it again from a first-floor window at Downing Street and called to the anxious crowds waiting below that it was peace for our time.

It was all they wanted to hear. Four small, precious words that meant there would be no war; no killings nor partings; no more young, precious lives thrown to waste.

'Believe it, sweetheart? It was sudden, wasn't it – Hitler giving in like that?'

'Yes, but Dada said – he's *always* said – that Germany wouldn't dare to go to war with us and France, again. Hitler's more afraid of Russia, Dada says.'

'Then I'm glad that someone can put the wind up him.' Keth chewed reflectively on a stem of grass. 'I'll have to be leaving – you realize that?' He said it without looking at her because he couldn't bear to see the pain in her eyes. 'I cabled Kentucky this morning. I'll have to get back for the start of the new term. It's been wonderful being with you, Daisy. Now I almost wish I hadn't come home because we've got to say goodbye all over again.'

'But it's only for two years, this time.' She tried to make light of it, that two years would pass quickly. 'I've been thinking, Keth. It might take you ages to find a ship. It isn't so easy, here. In England you've got to have a seaman's card, or something, to get taken on as crew. You could be ever so late, getting back to college.'

'I'll manage. I got here, I'll get back. Liverpool is nearest. I'll go there.'

'Yes, an' you'd get back quicker if you got yourself a proper sailing ticket – and it needn't cost the earth,' she hastened. 'I've got money, Keth. Let me give some to you? A one-way ticket doesn't cost a lot. Let me, please?'

'Daisy! I thought we'd agreed –'

'Not Mr Hillier's money! I've got some of my own. Mam gave me the bank book when I left school. It's money she put away for me when I was born. I've had bikes out of it, and one or two more things, but it was Mam's money when she was Lady Alice.

'Sir Giles used to give her a clothing allowance, only she didn't spend much of it, her being able to sew better than most. And when she married Dada, she didn't think it right she should use another man's money, sort of, to help furnish the house she and Dada would live in — so she put it all in the bank, for me!'

'So you've got *two* fortunes, Daisy?'

'No,' she laughed. 'There isn't a lot — well, nothing at all if you compare it to what I'll get, one day. But there's enough to get you back to America and I want you to have it.'

'No, love. Thank you, but *no*. I've got some money of my own. I worked in that hotel for a year, remember, and saved a few pounds. And I worked in Kentucky during vacation — I can get back under my own steam. Most merchant ships have a few cabins set aside for passengers and they're cheap, too. I love you for offering, but I can't take your money.'

'Then let me come to Liverpool with you — see you off?'

'No! For one thing, your dad would hit the roof and for another, I might be a couple of days getting a cabin fixed up. I'd have to go round the shipping offices, see what is sailing and from which dock. It wouldn't be right — even if they'd let you come.'

'You're sure you'll have enough money?'

'I'm sure. Merchant ships' cabins are very basic. They aren't de luxe, like on the liners. I'll make it all right.'

'Then hurry up and get back to college. We are all right, now. There isn't going to be a war and two years will soon pass. I don't want you to go, but we've had a lovely bonus, haven't we? That day you stood there, I couldn't believe it. I hadn't expected it for two more years.

'But everything is going to be all right, now. Peace for our time, Keth. We'll be married on my twenty-first, and oh, isn't it lovely about Aunt Julia getting married? Mam's thrilled to bits. Mind, it's only going to be a quiet wedding. They're getting married in York, and not at All Souls. Mam is making her dress. She's going to have a long one and a big hat with roses on it . . .'

'And you, my darling — what will you wear to our wedding?'

'Silk, Mam says. People with my colouring look awful in stark white. Oh, Keth, there's so much to look forward to. I couldn't have borne it if you'd had to go to fight. That's why it doesn't seem so bad that you're going to America.'

'At least I'll know I'll be coming back alive!' He rose to his feet, dusting himself down, reaching for her hand. 'The grass is getting damp — you'll catch a cold. Let's walk.'

'All right. Where to?'

'Into Brattocks. I want to kiss you.'

'And run into Dada, doing his rounds? Tell you what — let's go to the far end, to the elms? Let's tell it to the rooks, tell them about peace.'

'And what else will you tell them?' He pulled her arm into his because he couldn't bear for them not to be touching; not when he was so soon to leave her.

'I shall tell them that you are going away and that you'll be back in no time at all with a degree in your pocket. And I'll tell them that I love you and that we'll be married on my birthday. That's all I know — all that matters, anyway.'

'Do you thank them for things?'

'You should do — why?'

'Then thank them for these weeks together.'

'For our daisychain summer?' Oh, yes, she would thank them for that; thank them she and Keth had been lovers and that it had been wonderful and that she hadn't felt guilty about it — not even after the first time when she had gone home and Dada had been sitting there. He'd frowned, she remembered, and looked at his watch pointedly, as if to remind her she was late getting in. And still she hadn't felt guilty.

'Kiss me, Keth?'

He took her in his arms, then, and it was a kiss she would remember always; one to sustain her through two lonely years until he came home to her.

'I love you,' he whispered throatily. 'You're mine.'

'Yours . . .'

'Come on,' he said softly. 'Let's tell it to the rooks, tell them it's peace.'

'Peace *in* our time; peace *for* our time.'

They were young. All at once, time was on their side. Nothing else mattered.